ROYAL FLUSH

OTHER BOOKS BY REX STOUT

Novels

HOW LIKE A GOD · GOLDEN REMEDY · SEED ON THE WIND
O CARELESS LOVE! · MR. CINDERELLA · FOREST FIRE
THE PRESIDENT VANISHES

Nero Wolfe Mysteries

FER-DE-LANCE · THE LEAGUE OF FRIGHTENED MEN
THE RUBBER BAND · THE RED BOX · SOME BURIED CAESAR
OVER MY DEAD BODY · BLACK ORCHIDS
WHERE THERE'S A WILL · NOT QUITE DEAD ENOUGH
TOO MANY COOKS · THE SILENT SPEAKER
TOO MANY WOMEN · AND BE A VILLAIN
TROUBLE IN TRIPLICATE · THE SECOND CONFESSION
THREE DOORS TO DEATH · IN THE BEST FAMILIES
CURTAINS FOR THREE · MURDER BY THE BOOK
TRIPLE JEOPARDY · PRISONER'S BASE · THE GOLDEN SPIDERS
THREE MEN OUT · THE BLACK MOUNTAIN
FULL HOUSE: A NERO WOLFE OMNIBUS · BEFORE MIDNIGHT
THREE WITNESSES · MIGHT AS WELL BE DEAD
THREE FOR THE CHAIR · IF DEATH EVER SLEPT
AND FOUR TO GO · ALL ACES: A NERO WOLFE OMNIBUS
CHAMPAGNE FOR ONE · PLOT IT YOURSELF
THREE AT WOLFE'S DOOR · TOO MANY CLIENTS
FIVE OF A KIND: THE THIRD NERO WOLFE OMNIBUS
HOMICIDE TRINITY: A NERO WOLFE THREESOME
THE FINAL DEDUCTION · GAMBIT · THE MOTHER HUNT
TRIO FOR BLUNT INSTRUMENTS · A RIGHT TO DIE
THE DOORBELL RANG

Tecumseh Fox Mysteries

DOUBLE FOR DEATH · THE BROKEN VASE · BAD FOR BUSINESS

Mysteries

THE HAND IN THE GLOVE · MOUNTAIN CAT
ALPHABET HICKS · RED THREADS

ROYAL FLUSH

THE FOURTH NERO WOLFE OMNIBUS

REX STOUT

NEW YORK · THE VIKING PRESS

PUBLISHED IN 1965 BY THE VIKING PRESS, INC.
625 MADISON AVENUE, NEW YORK, N.Y. 10022

PUBLISHED SIMULTANEOUSLY IN CANADA BY
THE MACMILLAN COMPANY OF CANADA LIMITED

LIBRARY OF CONGRESS CATALOG CARD NUMBER: 65-19269

PRINTED IN U.S.A.

CONTENTS

FER-DE-LANCE

I

THERE was no reason why I shouldn't have been sent for the beer that day, for the last ends of the Fairmont National Bank case had been gathered in the week before and there was nothing for me to do but errands, and Wolfe never hesitated about running me down to Murray Street for a can of shoe-polish if he happened to need one. But it was Fritz who was sent for the beer. Right after lunch his bell called him up from the kitchen before he could have got the dishes washed, and after getting his orders he went out and took the roadster which we always left parked in front. An hour later he was back, with the rumble seat piled high with baskets filled with bottles. Wolfe was in the office—as he and I called it, Fritz called it the library—and I was in the front room reading a book on gunshot wounds which I couldn't make head or tail of, when I glanced through the window and saw Fritz pull up at the curb. It was a good excuse to stretch my legs, so I went out and helped him unload and carry the baskets into the kitchen, where we were starting to stow the bottles away in a cupboard when the bell rang. I followed Fritz into the office.

Wolfe lifted his head. I mention that, because his head was so big that lifting it struck you as being quite a job. It was probably really bigger than it looked, for the rest of him was so huge that any head on top of it but his own would have escaped your notice entirely.

"Where's the beer?"

"In the kitchen, sir. The lower cupboard on the right, I thought."

"I want it in here. Is it cold? And an opener and two glasses."

"Mostly cold, yes, sir. Very well."

I grinned and sat down on a chair to wonder what Wolfe was doing with some pieces of paper he had cut into little discs and was pushing around into different positions on the desk blotter. Fritz began bringing in the beer, six at a time on a tray. After the third trip I had another grin when I saw Wolfe glance up at the array on the table and then around at Fritz's back going through the door. Two more trays full; whereupon Wolfe halted the parade.

"Fritz. Would you inform me when this is likely to end?"

"Very soon, sir. There are nineteen more. Forty-nine in all."

"Nonsense. Excuse me, Fritz, but obviously it's nonsense."

"Yes, sir. You said one of every kind procurable. I went to a dozen shops, at least that."

"All right. Bring them in. And some plain salt crackers. None shall lack opportunity, Fritz, it wouldn't be fair."

It turned out that the idea was, as Wolfe explained to me after he had invited me to draw my chair up to the desk and begin opening the bottles, that he had decided to give up the bootleg beer, which for years he had bought in barrels and kept in a cooler in the basement, if he could find a brand of the legal 3.2 that was potable. He had also decided, he said, that six quarts a day was unnecessary and took too much time and thereafter he would limit himself to five. I grinned at that, for I didn't believe it, and I grinned again when I thought how the place would be cluttered up with empty bottles unless Fritz ran his legs off all day long. I said to him something I had said before more than once, that beer slowed up a man's head and with him running like a brook, six quarts a day, I never would understand how he could make his brain work so fast and deep that no other man in the country could touch him. He replied, also as he had before, that it wasn't his brain that worked, it was his lower nerve centers; and as I opened the fifth bottle for him to sample he went on to say—not the first time for that either —that he would not insult me by acknowledging my flattery, since if it was sincere I was a fool and if it was calculated I was a knave.

He smacked his lips, tasting the fifth brand, and holding up the glass looked through the amber at the light. "This is a pleasant surprise, Archie. I would not have believed it. That of course is the advantage of being a pessimist; a pessimist gets nothing but pleasant surprises, an optimist nothing but unpleasant. So far, none of this is sewage. As you see, Fritz has marked the prices on the labels, and I've started with the cheap ones. No, here, take this next."

It was at that moment that I heard the faint buzz from the kitchen that meant the front door, and it was that buzz that started the ball rolling. Though at the time it appeared to be nothing interesting, just Durkin asking a favor.

Durkin was all right up to the neck. When I consider how thick he was in most respects I am surprised how he could tail. I know bull terriers are dumb, but good tailing means a lot more than just hanging on, and Fred Durkin was good. I asked him once how he did it, and he said, "I just go up to the subject and ask him where he's headed for, and then if I lose him I know where to look." I suppose he knew how funny that was; I don't know, I suspect him. When things got so Wolfe had to cut down expenses like everybody else from bankers to bums, Saul Panzer and I got our weekly envelopes sliced, but Durkin's was stopped altogether. Wolfe called him in when he was needed and paid him by the day, so I still saw him off and on and knew he was having hard sledding. Things had been slow and I hadn't run across him for a month or more when the buzzer sounded that day and Fritz brought him to the door of the office.

Wolfe looked up and nodded. "Hello, Fred. Do I owe you something?"

Durkin, approaching the desk with his hat in his hand, shook his head. "How are you, Mr. Wolfe. I wish to God you did. If there was anybody owed me anything I'd be with him like a saddle on a horse."

"Sit down. Will you sample some beer?"

"No, thanks." Fred stayed on his feet. "I've come to ask a favor."

Wolfe looked up again, and his big thick lips pushed out a little, tight together, just a small movement, and back again, and then out and back again. How I loved to watch him doing that! That was about the only time I ever got excited, when Wolfe's lips were moving like that. It didn't matter whether it was some little thing like this with Durkin or when he was on the track of something big and dangerous. I knew what was going on, something was happening so fast inside of him and so much ground was being covered, the whole world in a flash, that no one else could ever really understand it even if he had tried his best to explain, which he never did. Sometimes, when he felt patient, he explained to me and it seemed to make sense, but I realized afterward that that was only because the proof had come and so I could accept it. I said to Saul Panzer once that it was like being with him in a dark room which neither of you has ever seen before, and he describes all of its contents to you, and then when the light is turned on his explanation of how he did it seems sensible because you see everything there before you just as he described it.

Wolfe said to Durkin, "You know my failing on the financial side. But since you haven't come to borrow money, your favor is likely granted. What is it?"

Durkin scowled. Wolfe always upset him. "Nobody needs to borrow money worse than I do. How do you know it's not that?"

"No matter. Archie will explain. You're not embarrassed enough, and you wouldn't have brought a woman with you. What is it?"

I leaned forward and broke in, "Damn it, he's alone! My ears are good anyhow!"

A little ripple, imperceptible except to eyes like mine that had caught it before, ran over Wolfe's enormous bulk. "Of course, Archie, splendid ears. But there was nothing to hear; the lady made no sound audible at this distance. And Fritz did not speak to her; but in greeting Fred there was a courtesy in his tone which he saves for softer flesh. If I should hear Fritz using that tone to a lone man I'd send him to a psychoanalyst at once."

Durkin said, "It's a friend of my wife's. Her best friend. You know my wife's Italian. Maybe you don't know, but she is. Anyway, this friend of hers is in trouble, or thinks she is. It sounds to me like a washout. Maria keeps after Fanny and Fanny keeps after me and they both keep after me together, all because I told Fanny once that you've got a devil in you that can find out anything in the world. A boob thing to say, Mr. Wolfe, but you know how a man's tongue will get started."

Wolfe only said, "Bring her in."

Durkin went out to the hall and came right back with a woman in front of him. She was little but not skinny, with black hair and eyes, and Italian all over though not the shawl kind. She was somewhere around middle age and looked neat and clean in a pink cotton dress and a black rayon jacket. I pulled over a chair and she sat down facing Wolfe and the light.

Durkin said, "Maria Maffei, Mr. Wolfe."

She tossed Fred a smile, showing little white teeth, and then said to Wolfe, "Maria Maffei," pronouncing it quite different.

Wolfe said, "Not Mrs. Maffei."

She shook her head. "No, sir. I'm not married."

"But in trouble anyhow."

"Yes, sir. Mr. Durkin thought you might be good enough—"

"Tell us about it."

"Yes, sir. It's my brother Carlo. He has gone."

"Gone where?"

"I don't know, sir. That's why I am afraid. He has been gone two days."

"Where did he—no, no. These are not phenomena, merely facts." Wolfe turned to me. "Go on, Archie."

By the time he had finished his "no, no" I had my notebook out. I enjoyed this sort of business in front of Wolfe more than at any other time because I knew damn well I was good at it. But this wasn't much of a job; this woman knew what to get down as well as I did. She told her tale quick and straight. She was housekeeper at a swell apartment on Park Avenue and lived there. Her brother Carlo, two years older than her, lived in a rooming-house on Sullivan Street. He was a metal-worker, first-class she said; for years he had made big money working on jewelry for Rathbun & Cross, but because he drank a little and occasionally didn't turn up at the shop he had been one of the first to go when the depression came. For a while after that he had got odd jobs here and there, then he had used up his small savings, and for the past winter and spring he had been kept going by his sister. Around the middle of April, completely discouraged, he had decided to return to Italy and Maria had agreed to furnish the necessary funds; she had, in fact, advanced the money for the steamship ticket. But a week later he had suddenly announced that the trip was postponed; he wouldn't say why, but he had declared that he would need no more money, he would soon be able to return all she had lent him, and he might stay in this country after all. He had never been very communicative, but regarding the change in plans he had been stubbornly mysterious. Now he was gone. He had telephoned her on Saturday that he would meet her Monday evening, her evening off, at the Italian restaurant on Prince Street where they often dined together, and had added gaily that he would have enough money with him to pay back everything and lend her some into the bargain if she needed it. Monday evening she had waited for him until ten o'clock, then had gone to his rooming-house and been told that he had left a little after seven and had not returned.

"Day before yesterday," I observed.

Durkin, I saw, had his notebook open too, and now he nodded. "Monday, June fourth."

Wolfe shook his head. He had been sitting as still and unobservant as a mountain with his chin lodged on his chest, and now without moving otherwise his head shook faintly as he murmured, "Durkin. Today is Wednesday, June seventh."

"Well?" Fred stared. "Okay with me, Mr. Wolfe."

Wolfe wiggled a finger at Maria. "Was it Monday?"

"Yes, sir. Of course. That's my evening off."

"You should know that evening. Durkin, annotate your notebook, or, better perhaps, throw it away. You are a full twelvemonth ahead of your times; next year Monday will be June fourth." He turned to the woman. "Maria Maffei, I am sorry to have to give you a counsel of desperation. Consult the police."

"I have, sir." A gleam of resentment shot from her eyes. "They say he has gone to Italy with my money."

"Perhaps he has."

"Oh no, Mr. Wolfe. You know better. You have looked at me. You can see I would not know so little of a brother as that."

"Do the police tell you what boat your brother sailed on?"

"How could they? There has been no boat. They do not investigate or even consider. They merely say he has gone to Italy."

"I see, they do it by inspiration. Well. I'm sorry I can't help you. I can only guess. Robbery. Where is his body then? Again consult the police. Sooner or later someone will find it for them and your puzzle will be solved."

Maria Maffei shook her head. "I don't believe it, Mr. Wolfe. I just don't believe it. And there was the phone call."

I broke in. "You mentioned no phone call."

She smiled at me with her teeth. "I would have. There was a phone call for him at the rooming-house a little before seven. The phone there is in the downstairs hall and the girl heard him talking. He was excited and he agreed to meet someone at half past seven." She turned to Wolfe. "You can help me, sir. You can help me find Carlo. I have learned to look cool like the grass in the morning because I have been so long among these Americans, but I am Italian and I must find my brother and I must see anyone who has hurt him."

Wolfe only shook his head. She paid no attention.

"You must, sir. Mr. Durkin says you are very tight about money. I still have something left and I could pay all expenses and maybe a little more. And you are Mr. Durkin's friend and I am Mrs. Durkin's friend, my friend Fanny."

Wolfe said, "I am nobody's friend. How much can you pay?"

She hesitated.

"How much have you got?"

"I have—well—more than a thousand dollars."

"How much of it would you pay?"

"I would pay—all of it. If you find my brother alive, all of it. If you find him not alive and show him to me and show me the one who hurt him, I would still pay a good deal. I would pay first for the funeral."

Wolfe's eyelids lowered slowly and raised slowly. That, as I knew, meant his approval; I had often looked for that sign, and frequently in vain, when I was reporting to him. He said, "You're a practical woman, Maria Maffei. Moreover, possibly, a woman of honor. You are right, there is something in me that can help you; it is genius; but you have not furnished the stimulant to arouse it and whether it will be awakened in search of your brother is problematical. In any event, routine comes first, and the expense of that will be small."

He turned to me.

"Archie, go to Carlo Maffei's rooming-house; his sister will accompany you as authority. See the girl who heard the phone call; see others; examine his room; if any trail is indicated phone here for Saul Panzer any time after five; returning here bring with you any articles that seem to you unimportant."

I thought it was unnecessary for him to take that dig at me before a stranger, but I had long since learned that there was no point in resenting his pleasantries. Maria Maffei got up from her chair and thanked him.

Durkin took a step forward. "About that being tight with money, Mr. Wolfe, you know how a man's tongue will get started—"

I rescued him. "Come on, Fred, we'll take the roadster and I might as well drop you on the way."

II

WHEN I parked the big shiny black roadster in front of the number on Sullivan Street Maria Maffei had given me I felt that I might never see it alive and happy again—the roadster I mean—for the street was littered with rubbish and full of wild Italian kids yelling and dashing around like black-eyed demons. But I had had the roadster in worse places than that, as for instance the night I chased young Graves, who was in a Pierce coupé with a satchel of emeralds between his knees, from New Milford all over Pike County, up and down a dozen mountains in a foot of mud and the worst rain I ever saw. It was Wolfe's orders that after every little rub the roadster should be fixed up as good as new, and of course that pleased me just as well.

It was just another rooming-house. For some reason or other they're all alike, whether it's a high-hat affair in the Fifties or a brownstone west of Central Park full of honest artist girls or an Italian hangout like this one on Sullivan Street. With, of course, a difference in details like garlic. Maria Maffei took me first to the landlady, a nice fat woman with wet hands and a pushed-in nose and rings on her fingers, and then upstairs to her brother's room. I looked around a little while Maria Maffei went to get the girl who had heard the phone call. It was a good-sized room on the third floor with two windows. The rug was worn and the furniture old and sort of broken, but it was clean and really not a bad room except for the noise from the hoodlums below when I opened the window to see if the roadster was still on its feet. Two large traveling bags were stacked in a corner, one flimsy and old and done for, the other one old too but sturdy and good. Neither was locked. The flimsy one was empty; the good one contained a lot of small tools of different shapes and sizes, some of which had pawnshop tags hanging on them, and some pieces of wood and metal and odds and ends like coil springs. The closet contained an old suit of clothes, two overalls, an overcoat, two pairs of shoes, and a felt hat. In the drawers of the bureau which stood between the windows was an assortment, not scanty for a man who had been living on his sister for a year, of shirts, ties, handkerchiefs, socks, and a lot of miscellaneous junk like shoestrings, lead pencils, snapshots, and empty pipe-tobacco cans. In an upper drawer was a bundle of seventeen letters in envelopes all with Italian postage stamps, fastened with a rubber band. Scattered around in the same drawer were receipts and paid bills, a tablet of writing-paper, a few clippings from newspapers and magazines, and a dog collar. On top of the bureau, along with comb and brush and similar impedimenta, as Wolfe would say, were half a dozen books, all in Italian except one that was full of pictures and designs, and a big stack of magazines, different monthly issues for three years back, all with the same name, *Metal Crafts*. In the corner by the right window was a plain rough wood table with its top scarred and cut all over, and on it was a small vise, a grinder and buffer with an electric cord long enough to reach the lamp socket, and some more tools like those in the traveling bag. I was looking over the grinder to see how recently it had been used when Maria Maffei came in with the girl.

"This is Anna Fiore," the woman said.

I went over and shook hands with her. She was a homely kid about twenty with skin like stale dough, and she looked like she'd been scared in the cradle and never got over it. I told her my name and said that I had learned from Miss Maffei that she had heard Mr. Maffei answering the phone call before he went out Monday evening. She nodded.

I turned to the woman. "I expect you'd like to get along back uptown, Miss Maffei. Anna and I will get along."

She shook her head. "If I'm back by dinner it will be all right."

I got a little gruff. The truth was that I agreed with Durkin that it was a washout and that there was nothing to be expected from it but fanning the air. So I told Maria Maffei that I could easily do without her and she'd better trot along and she'd hear from Wolfe if there was anything to hear. She shot a glance at the girl and showed her teeth to me, and left us.

I pulled a couple of chairs face to face and got the girl deposited on one in front of me, and pulled out my notebook.

"You've got nothing to be scared of," I told her. "The worst that can happen to you is that you'll do a favor to Miss Maffei and her brother and she might give you some money. Do you like Miss Maffei?"

She seemed startled, as if surprised that anyone should think it worth the trouble to learn her likes and dislikes, but the answer was ready behind the surprise. "Yes, I like her. She is nice."

"Do you like Mr. Maffei?"

"Yes, of course, everybody does. Except when he drinks, then a girl should stay away from him."

"How did you happen to hear the phone call Monday evening? Were you expecting it?"

"How could I be expecting it?"

"I don't know. Did you answer the phone?"

"No, sir. Mrs. Ricci answered it. She told me to call Mr. Maffei and I called upstairs. Then I was clearing the table in the dining room and the door was open and I could hear him talking."

"Could you hear what he said?"

"Of course." She looked a little scornful. "We always hear everything anyone says on the telephone. Mrs. Ricci heard him too, she heard the same as I did."

"What did he say?"

"First he said, 'Hello.' Then he said, 'Well this is Carlo Maffei what do you want.' Then he said, 'That's my business I'll tell you when I see you.' Then he said, 'Why not here in my room.' Then he said, 'No I'm not scared I'm not the one to be scared.' Mrs. Ricci says it was 'It's not me that's scared,' but she don't remember right. Then he said, 'Sure I want the money and a lot more.' Then he said, 'All right seven-thirty at the corner of.' Then he said, 'Shut up yourself what do I care.' Then he said, 'All right seven-thirty I know that car.'"

She stopped. I said, "Who was he talking to?"

I supposed of course that the answer would be that she didn't know, since Maria Maffei had not known, but she said at once, "The man that called him up before."

"Before? When?"

"Quite a few times. In May. One day twice. Mrs. Ricci says nine times before Monday altogether."

"Did you ever hear his voice?"

"No, sir. Mrs. Ricci always answers."

"Did you ever hear this man's name?"

"No, sir. After Mrs. Ricci got curious she asked it, but he always just said 'Never mind tell him he's wanted on the phone.'"

I began to think there might be some fun in this somewhere, possibly even some money. Not that the money interested me; that was for Wolfe; it was the fun I was after. Anyway it might not be just a stick-up and a stiff in the East River. I decided to see what I could get, and I went after that girl. I had heard Wolfe do it many a time, and while I knew most of his results came from a kind of feeling that wasn't in me, still a lot of it was just patience and hit-or-miss. So I went after her. I kept at it two hours, and collected a lot of facts, but not one that meant anything to me. Once I thought I might be getting warm when I learned that Carlo Maffei had two different women with whom he appeared publicly on different occasions, and one of them was married; but when I saw that wouldn't tie up with the phone call I threw it out. Maffei had mentioned going to Italy but had given no details. He had pretty well kept his business in his own bosom. He had never had callers except his sister and a friend from his old prosperous days with whom he had occasionally gone to dine. I pumped her for two hours and couldn't see a gleam anywhere, but something about that phone call kept me from calling it a dull day and putting on my hat. Finally I said to her, "You stay here a minute, Anna, while I go down and see Mrs. Ricci."

The landlady confirmed the girl's version of the phone call and said she had no idea who the caller was though she had tried on several occasions to find out. I asked her a few questions here and there, and then requested permission to take Anna with me uptown. She said no, she couldn't be left alone with the dinner to get, so I produced a dollar bill, and she asked what time she might expect the girl back, saying that it must not be later than nine o'clock.

After taking my dollar! I told her, "I can make no promises, Mrs. Ricci. When my boss gets started asking questions nights and days are nothing. But she'll be back safe and sound as soon as possible."

I went upstairs and got Anna and some of the stuff from the bureau drawer and when we got to the street was relieved to find that the roadster hadn't lost a fender or a spare tire.

I moseyed along uptown taking it easy, not wanting to reach Thirty-fifth Street too soon, since Wolfe was always upstairs with the plants from four to six and it wasn't a good idea to disturb him during those two hours unless you had to. Anna was overwhelmed by the roadster; she kept her feet pulled back against the seat and her hands folded tight in her lap. That tickled me and I felt kindly toward her, so I told her that I might give her a dollar if she told my boss anything that would help him out. It was a minute or two after six when I pulled up in front of the old brownstone less than a block from the Hudson River where Wolfe had lived for twenty years and where I had been with him a third of that.

Anna didn't get home that night by nine o'clock. It was after eleven when Wolfe sent me to the *Times* office for the papers, and it was well past midnight when we finally hit on the spot that Anna recognized. By that time Mrs. Ricci had telephoned three times, and when I got to Sullivan Street with the girl a little before one the landlady was waiting out in front, maybe with a knife in her sock. But she didn't say a word, only glared at me. I had given Anna her dollar, for something had happened.

I had reported to Wolfe up in the front plant room, the sun-room, leaving Anna down in the office. He sat there in the big chair with a red and tan orchid eight inches wide tickling the back of his neck, looking not interested. He really wasn't interested. He barely glanced at the papers and things I had brought with me from Maffei's room. He admitted that the phone call had a dash of possibility in it, but couldn't see that there was anything to bother about. I tried to persuade him that since the girl was already downstairs he might as well take it up and see what he could get; and I added with malice, "Anyway, she cost a dollar. I had to give the landlady a dollar."

"That was your dollar, Archie."

"No, sir, it was an expense dollar. It's down in the book."

I went with him to the elevator. If he had had to do his own lifting and lowering I don't think he would ever have gone upstairs, even for the plants.

He began on Anna at once. It was beautiful. Five years earlier I wouldn't have appreciated it. It was beautiful because it was absolutely comprehensive. If there was anything in that girl, any bit of knowledge, any apparently forgotten shred of feeling or reaction, that could show us a direction or give us a hint, it simply could not have kept away from him. He questioned her for five hours. He asked her about Carlo Maffei's voice, his habits, his clothing, his meals, his temper, his table manners, his relations with his sister, with Mrs. Ricci, with Anna herself, with everyone Anna had ever seen him with. He asked her about Mrs. Ricci, about all the residents of the rooming-house for two years, about the neighbors, and about the tradesmen who delivered things to the house. All this he did easily and leisurely, careful not to tire her—quite different from the time I watched him with Lon Graves; him he wore down and drove halfway crazy in an afternoon. It seemed to me he got only one thing out of the girl, and that wasn't much, only an admission that she had removed something from Maffei's room that very morning, Wednesday. Little pieces of paper from his bureau drawer with mucilage on the back, and printed on the front S. S. *LUCIA* and S. S. *FIORENZA*. Of course they were steamship luggage stickers. From the newspaper file I learned that the *Lucia* had sailed on the 18th of May and the *Fiorenza* on the 3rd of June. Evidently Maffei had decided on Italy not once, but twice, and had given it up both times. Anna had taken them, she said, because they were pretty colors and she wanted to paste them on the box she kept her clothes in. During dinner, which the three of us ate together in the dining room, he let Anna alone entirely and talked to me, mostly about beer; but with the coffee he moved us back to the office and went at it again. He doubled back and re-covered the ground, he darted around at random on things so irrelevant and inconsequential that anyone who had never seen him pull a rabbit out of that hat before would have been sure he was merely a nut. By eleven o'clock I was through, yawning and ready to give up, and I was exasperated that he showed not the slightest sign of impatience or discouragement.

Then all at once he hit it.

"So Mr. Maffei never gave you any presents?"

"No, sir. Except the box of chalk I told you about. And the newspapers, if you call that a present."

"Yes. You said he always gave you his morning paper. The *Times*."

"Yes, sir. He told me once he took the *Times* for the classified ads. You know, the job ads."

"Did he give you his paper Monday morning?"

"He always gave it to me in the afternoon. Monday afternoon, yes, sir."

"There was nothing peculiar about it that morning, I suppose."

"No, sir."

Apparently Wolfe caught some faint flicker in her eye, some faint movement that I missed. Anyway he insisted.

"Nothing peculiar about it?"

"No, sir. Except—of course, the cut-out."

"The cut-out?"

"A piece cut out. A big piece."

"Did he often cut out pieces?"

"Yes, sir. Mostly the ads. Maybe always the ads. I used the papers to take the dirt up in and I had to watch for the holes."

"But this was a big piece."

"Yes, sir."

"Not an advertisement then. You will pardon me, Miss Fiore, if I do not say *ad*. I prefer not to. Then it wasn't an advertisement he cut out of Monday's paper."

"Oh no, it was on the front page."

"Indeed. Had there ever been a piece cut out on the front page before?"

"No, sir. I'm sure not."

"Never anything but advertisements before?"

"Well, I'm not sure of that. Maybe only ads, I think it was."

Wolfe sat for a minute with his chin on his chest. Then he turned to me. "Archie, run up to Forty-second Street and get twenty copies of Monday's *Times*."

I was glad for something to wake me up. Not that it was anything to get excited about, for I could see that Wolfe was just taking a wink at the only crack that had shown any chance of light; I wasn't expecting anything and I didn't think he was. But it was a fine June night, cool but soft and pleasant, and I filled my lungs with good air snatched from the breeze I made as I rolled crosstown to Broadway and turned north. At Times Square I saw a cop I knew, Marve Doyle who used to pound the cement down on Fourteenth Street, and he let me leave the car against the Broadway curb while I ran across the street to the *Times* office. The theater and movie mob was slopping off the sidewalks into the street, deciding between two dollars at a speak and two nickels at a Nedick's.

When I got back to the office Wolfe was giving the girl a rest. He had had Fritz bring in some beer and she was sipping at a glass like it was hot tea, with a stripe of dried foam across her upper lip. He had finished three bottles, though I couldn't have been gone more than twenty minutes at the outside. As I came in he said, "I should have told you city edition."

"Sure, that's what I got."

"Good." He turned to the girl. "If you don't mind, Miss Fiore, it would be better if you did not overlook our preparations. Turn her chair around, Archie; there, the little table for her beer. Now the papers. No, don't rip it off; better intact I think; that's the way she first saw it. Remove the second sections, they'll be a find for Miss Fiore, think of all the dirt they'll hold. Here."

I spread open a first section on the desk before him and he pulled himself up in his chair to hunch over it. It was like seeing a hippopotamus in the zoo get up for a feed. I took out all the second sections and stacked them on a chair and then took a front page for myself and went over it. At the first glance it certainly looked hopeless; miners were striking in Pennsylvania, the NRA was saving the country under three different headings, two boys had crossed the Atlantic in a thirty-foot boat, a university president had had heart failure on a golf course, a gangster had been tear-gassed out of a Brooklyn flat, a Negro had been lynched in Alabama, and someone had found an old painting somewhere in Europe. I glanced at Wolfe; he was drinking the whole page. The only thing that looked to me worth trying at all was the painting which had been found in Switzerland and was supposed to have been stolen from Italy. But when Wolfe finally reached for the scissors out of the drawer it wasn't that one he clipped, it was the gangster piece. Then he laid the paper aside and called for another one. I handed it to him, and this time I grinned as I saw him go after the article about the painting; I came in second anyhow. When he called for a third paper I was curious, and as he ran the scissors around the edges of the story about the university president I stared at him. He saw me. He said without looking up, "Pray for this side, Archie. If it's this one we shall have an *Angræcum sesquipedale* for Christmas." I could spell that because I kept his accounts for him on orchids as on everything else, but I could no more have pronounced it than I could have imagined any connection between the university president and Carlo Maffei.

Wolfe said, "Show her one."

The last one he had clipped was on top, but I reached under it and got the next one; the painting piece had been in a large box in the lower right quarter of the page. As I held it out, spread open, to Anna, Wolfe said, "Look at that, Miss Fiore. Is that the way the piece was cut out Monday morning?"

She gave it only a glance. "No, sir. It was a big piece out of the top, here, let me show you—"

I snatched it out of the way before she could get hold of it, tossed it back to the table, and picked up another. I spread it in front of her. This time she took two glances, then she said, "Yes, sir."

"You mean that's it?"

"It was cut out like that, yes, sir."

For a moment Wolfe was silent, then I heard him breathe and he said, "Turn her around, Archie." I took the arm of her chair and whirled it around with her in it. Wolfe looked at her and said, "How sure are you, Miss Fiore, that the paper was cut out like that?"

"I know it was, sir. I'm sure."

"Did you see the piece he had cut out? In his room, in the wastebasket perhaps, or in his hand?"

"No, I never saw it. It couldn't have been in the wastebasket because there isn't any."

"Good. If only all reasons were as good as that. You may go home now, Miss Fiore. You have been a good girl, good and patient and forbearing, and unlike most of the persons I avoid meeting by staying inside my house, you are willing to confine your tongue to its proper functions. But will you answer just one more question? I ask it as a favor."

The girl was completely tired out, but there was enough life left in her to let the bewilderment show in her eyes. She stared at him. Wolfe said, "Just one more question. Have you ever at any time seen a golf club in Carlo Maffei's room?"

If he was looking for a climax he got it, because for the first time in all these hours the girl shut up on him. It was funny how plain you could see it happen. For an instant she just looked, then when the question had clicked what little color she had left her till she was dead white and her mouth dropped half open; she looked absolutely like an idiot, and she began to tremble all over.

Wolfe bored at her, quiet. "When did you see it?"

All of a sudden she shut her lips tight, and her hands in her lap closed into fists. "No, sir." It was just a mumble. "No, sir, I never did."

Wolfe looked at her a second, then he said, "All right. It's quite all right, Miss Fiore." He turned to me. "Take her home."

She didn't try to stand up till I went over and touched her shoulder. Then she put her hands on the arms of the chair and got to her feet. He had certainly got her somehow, but she didn't seem exactly scared, just caved in. I got her jacket from the back of a chair and helped her put it on. As she started for the door I turned to say something to Wolfe, and couldn't believe my eyes. He was raising himself out of his chair to stand up! Actually. I had at one time seen him refuse to take that trouble for the departure from that room of a woman worth twenty million American dollars who had married an English duke. But anyway I said what I had started to say, "I told her I'd give her a dollar."

"Then you'll have to do it, I'm afraid." He raised his voice a little to reach the door. "Good night, Miss Fiore."

She didn't reply. I followed her to the hall and took her out to the roadster. When we got to Sullivan Street Mrs. Ricci was waiting in front with a glare in her eye that made me decide not to stop for any amenities.

III

By THE time I had garaged the car and walked the two blocks back to Thirty-fifth Street the office was dark and when I went up a flight I saw a ribbon of light under the door of Wolfe's bedroom. I often wondered how he ever got his clothes off, but I know Fritz never helped him. Fritz slept up above, across the hall from the plant rooms; my room was on the second floor, the same floor as Wolfe's, a fair-sized room in front with its own bath and a pair of windows. I had lived there seven years, and it certainly was home; and seemed likely to remain so for another seven, or even twenty-seven, for the only girl I had ever been really soft on had found another bargain she liked better. That was how I happened to meet Wolfe—but that story isn't for me to tell, at least not yet. There are one or two little points about it that will need clearing up some day. But that room was certainly home. The bed was big and good, there was a desk with plenty of drawer-space and three chairs all roomy and comfortable, and a real carpet all over, no damn little rugs to slide you around like a piece of butter on a hot cake. The pictures on the walls were my own, and I think they were a good selection; one of Mount Vernon, the home of George Washington, a colored one of a lion's head, another colored one of woods with grass and flowers, and a big framed photograph of my mother and father, who both died when I was just a kid. Also there was a colored one called September Morn, of a young woman apparently with no clothes on and her hair hanging down in front, but that was in the bathroom. There was nothing unusual about the room, it was just a good room to live in, except the big gong on the wall under the bed, and that was out of sight. It was connected up so that when Wolfe turned on a switch in his room, which he did every night, the gong would sound if anyone stepped in the hall within five feet of his door or if any of his windows was disturbed, and also it was connected with all entrances to the plant rooms. Wolfe told me once, not as if it mattered much, that he really had no cowardice in him, he only had an intense distaste for being touched by anyone or for being compelled without warning to make any quick movements; and when I considered the quantity he had to move I was willing to believe him. For some reason questions like that of cowardice have never interested me as regards Wolfe, though ordinarily if I have cause to suspect that a man is yellow as far as I'm concerned he can eat at another table.

I took one of the newspapers from the office upstairs with me, and after I had undressed and got into pajamas and slippers, I made myself comfortable in a chair with cigarettes and ashtray handy and read that university president article three times. It was headed like this:

PETER OLIVER BARSTOW
DEAD FROM STROKE
PRESIDENT OF HOLLAND
SUCCUMBS ON LINKS

Friends Reach His Side
With His Last Breath

It was quite a piece, with a full column on the front page, another column and a half on the inside and in another article a long obituary with comments from a lot of prominent people. The story itself didn't amount to much and there was really nothing to it except another man gone. I read the paper every day and this one was only two days old, but I couldn't remember noticing this. Barstow, fifty-eight-year-old president of Holland University, had been playing golf Sunday afternoon on the links of the Green Meadow Club near Pleasantville, thirty miles north of New York, a foursome, with his son Lawrence and two friends named E. D. Kimball and Manuel Kimball. On the fairway of the fourth hole he had suddenly pitched forward and landed on his face, flopped around on the ground a few seconds, and then lay still. His caddy had jumped to him and grabbed his arm, but by the time the others got to him he was dead. Among the crowd that collected from the clubhouse and other players was a doctor who was an old friend of Barstow's, and he and the son had taken the body in Barstow's own car to the Barstow home six miles away. The doctor had pronounced it heart disease.

The rest was trimmings, all about Barstow's career and achievements and a picture of him and this and that, and how his wife had collapsed when they brought him home and his son and daughter bore up well. After the third reading I just yawned and threw up the sponge. The only connection that I could see between Barstow's death and Carlo Maffei was the fact that Wolfe had asked Anna Fiore if she had seen a golf club, so I tossed the paper away and got up saying to myself aloud, "Mr. Goodwin, I guess you haven't got this case ready for the closed business file." Then I took a drink of water and went to bed.

It was nearly ten o'clock when I got downstairs the next morning, for I need eight hours' sleep when I can get it, and of course Wolfe wouldn't be down till eleven. He arose always at eight, no matter what time he went to bed, had breakfast in his room with a couple of newspapers, and spent the two hours from nine to eleven in the plant rooms. Sometimes I could hear old Horstmann, who tended the plants, yelling at him, while I was dressing or taking a bath. Wolfe seemed to have the same effect on Horstmann that an umpire had on John J. McGraw. Not that the old man really disliked Wolfe, I'm sure he didn't; I wouldn't wonder if he was worried for fear Wolfe's poundage, having at least reached the limit of equilibrium, would topple over and make hash of the orchids. Horstmann didn't think any more of those plants than I do of my right eye. He slept in a little room partitioned off of a corner, and I wouldn't have been surprised if he had walked the floor with them at night.

After I got through in the kitchen with a dish of kidneys and waffles and a couple of glasses of milk—for I absolutely refused to let Fritz dress up the dining table for my breakfast, which I always had alone—I went out for ten minutes' worth of air, hoofing it down around the piers and back again, and then settled down at my corner desk in the office with the books, after dusting around a little and opening the safe and filling Wolfe's fountain pen. His mail I left on his desk unopened, that was the custom; there wasn't any for me. I made out two or three checks and balanced my expense book, not much to that, things had been so quiet, and then began going over the plant records to be sure Horstmann had his reports up to date. I was in the middle of that when I heard the buzzer in the kitchen, and a minute later Fritz came to the door and said a man named O'Grady wanted to see Mr. Wolfe. I took the card and looked at it and saw it was a new one on me; I knew a lot of the dicks on the Homicide Squad, but I had never seen this O'Grady. I told Fritz to usher him in.

O'Grady was young, and very athletic judging from his make-up and the way he walked. He had a bad eye, conscientious and truculent; from the way he looked at me you might have thought I had the Lindbergh baby in my pocket.

He said, "Mr. Nero Wolfe?"

I waved at a chair. "Have a seat." I glanced at my wrist. "Mr. Wolfe will be down in nineteen minutes."

He scowled. "This is important. Couldn't you call him? I sent in my card, I'm from the Homicide Squad."

"Sure, I know, that's all right. Just have a seat. If I called him he'd throw something at me."

He took the chair and I went back to the plant records. Once or twice during the wait I thought I might try pumping him just for the fun of it, but a glance at his face was enough; he was too young and trustworthy to bother with. For nineteen minutes he sat as if he was in church, not saying a word.

He got up from the chair as Wolfe entered the office. Wolfe, as he made steady progress from the door to the desk, bade me good morning, asked me to open another window, and shot a glance at the visitor. Seated at the desk he saw the card I had laid there, then he took a look at the mail, flipping the corners of the envelopes with his quick fingers the way a bank teller does the checks when he is going over a deposit. He shoved the mail aside and turned to the dick.

"Mr. O'Grady?"

O'Grady stepped forward. "Mr. Nero Wolfe?"

Wolfe nodded.

"Well, Mr. Wolfe, I want the papers and other articles you took yesterday from Carlo Maffei's room."

"No!" Wolfe lifted his head to see him better. "Really? That's interesting, Mr. O'Grady. Have a chair. Pull him up a chair, Archie."

"No, thanks, I've got a job on. I'll just take those papers and—things."

"What things?"

"The things you took."

"Enumerate them."

The dick stuck his chin out. "Don't try to get funny. Come on, I'm in a hurry."

Wolfe wiggled a finger at him. "Easy, Mr. O'Grady." Wolfe's voice was clear and low, with a tone he didn't use very often; he had used it on me only once, the first time I had ever seen him, and I had never forgotten how it sounded; it had made me feel that if he had wanted to he could have cut my head off without lifting a hand. He went on with it. "Easy now. Sit down. I mean it, really, sit down."

I had a chair shoved behind the dick's knees, and he came down onto it slowly.

"What you are getting is a free but valuable lesson," Wolfe said. "You are young and can use it. Since I entered this room you have made nothing but mistakes. You were without courtesy, which was offensive. You made a statement contrary to fact, which was stupid. You confused conjecture with knowledge, which was disingenuous. Would you like me to explain what you should have done? My motives are entirely friendly."

O'Grady was blinking. "I don't charge you with motives—"

"Good. Of course you had no way of knowing how ill-advised it was to imply that I made a journey to Carlo Maffei's room; unfamiliar with my habits, you were not aware that I would not undertake that enterprise though a *Cattleya Dowiana aurea* were to be the reward. Certainly not for some papers and—as you say—things. Archie Goodwin"— a finger circled in my direction—"doesn't mind that sort of thing, so he went. What you should have done was this. First, answered me when I wished you good morning. Second, made your request courteous, complete, and correct as to fact. Third—though this was less essential —you might as a matter of professional civility have briefly informed me that the body of the murdered Carlo Maffei has been found and identified and that the assistance of these papers is required in the attempt to discover the assassin. Don't you agree with me that that would have been better, Mr. O'Grady?"

The dick stared at him. "How the hell—" he started, and stopped, and then went on, "So it's already in the papers. I didn't see it, and his name couldn't have been for it's only two hours since I learned it myself. You're quite a guesser, Mr. Wolfe."

"Thank you. Neither did I see it in the papers. But since Maria Maffei's report of her brother's disappearance did not arouse the police beyond a generous effort at conjecture, it seemed to me probable that nothing less than murder would stir them to the frenzy of discovering that Archie had visited his room and removed papers. So. Would you mind telling me where the body was found?"

O'Grady stood up. "You can read it tonight. You're a lulu, Mr. Wolfe. Now those papers."

"Of course." Wolfe didn't move. "But I offer a point for your consideration. All I ask of you is three minutes of your time and information which will be available from public sources within a few hours. Whereas—who knows?—today, or tomorrow, or next year, in connection with this case or another, I might happen upon some curious little fact which conveyed to you would mean promotion, glory, a raise in pay; and, I repeat, you make a mistake if you ignore the demands of professional civility. Was the body by any chance found in Westchester County?"

"What the hell," O'Grady said. "If I hadn't already looked you up, and if it wasn't so plain you'd need a boxcar to get around in, I'd guess you did it yourself. All right. Yes, Westchester County. In a thicket a hundred feet from a dirt road three miles out of Scarsdale, yesterday at eight p.m. by two boys hunting birds' nests."

"Shot perhaps?"

"Stabbed. The doctor says that the knife must have been left in him for a while, an hour or more, but it wasn't there and wasn't found. His pockets were empty. The label on his clothes showed a Grand Street store, and that and his laundry mark were turned over to me at seven o'clock this morning. By nine I had his name, and since then I've searched his room and seen the landlady and the girl."

"Excellent," Wolfe said. "Really exceptional."

The dick frowned. "That girl," he said. "Either she knows something or the inside of her head is so unfurnished that she can't remember what she ate for breakfast. You had her up here. What did you think when she couldn't remember a thing about the phone call that the landlady said she heard every word of?"

I shot a glance at Wolfe, but he didn't blink an eyelash. He just said, "Miss Anna Fiore is not perfectly equipped, Mr. O'Grady. You found her memory faulty then?"

"Faulty? She had forgot Maffei's first name!"

"Yes. A pity." Wolfe pushed his chair back by putting his hands on the edge of the desk and shoving; I saw he meant to get up. "And now those papers. The only other articles are an empty tobacco can and four snapshots. I must ask a favor of you. Will you let Mr. Goodwin escort you from the room? A personal idiosyncrasy; I have a strong disinclination for opening my safe in the presence of any other person. No offense of course. It would be the same, even perhaps a little accentuated, if you were my banker."

I had been with Wolfe so long that I could usually almost keep up with him, but that time I barely caught myself. I had my mouth open to say that the stuff was in a drawer of his desk, where I had put it the evening before in his presence, and his look was all that stopped me. The dick hesitated, and Wolfe assured him, "Come, Mr. O'Grady. Or go, rather. There is no point in surmising that I am creating an opportunity to withhold something, because even if I were there would be nothing you could do to prevent it. Suspicions of that sort between professional men are futile."

I led the dick into the front room, closing the door behind us. I supposed Wolfe would monkey with the safe door so we could hear the noise, but just in case he didn't take the trouble I made some sort of conversation so O'Grady's ears wouldn't be disappointed. Pretty soon we were called back in, and Wolfe was standing on the near side of the desk with the tobacco can and the envelope I had filed the papers and snapshots in. He held them out to the dick.

"Good luck, Mr. O'Grady. I give you this assurance, and you may take my words for what they are worth: if at any time we should discover anything that we believe would be of significance or help to you, we shall communicate with you at once."

"Much obliged. Maybe you mean that."

"Yes, I do. Just as I say it."

The dick went. When I heard the outer door close I went to the front room and through a window saw him walking away. Then I returned to the office and approached Wolfe's desk, and grinned at him and said, "You're a damn scoundrel."

The folds of his cheeks pulled away a little from the corners of his mouth; when he did that he thought he was smiling. I said, "What did you keep?"

Out of his vest pocket he pulled a piece of paper about two inches long and half an inch wide and handed it to me. It was one of the clippings from Maffei's top bureau drawer, and it was hard to believe that Wolfe could have known of its existence, for he had barely glanced through that stuff the evening before. But he had taken the trouble to get O'Grady out of the room in order to keep it.

METAL-WORKER, *must be expert both design and mechanism, who intends returning to Europe for permanent residence, can get lucrative commission. Times L467 Downtown.*

I ran through it twice, but saw no more in it than when I had first read it the afternoon before in Maffei's room. "Well," I said, "if you're trying to clinch it that he meant to go for a sail I can run down to Sullivan Street and pry those luggage stickers off of Anna's wardrobe. And anyway, granting even that it means something, when did you ever see it before? Don't tell me you can read things without looking at them. I'll swear you didn't—" I stopped. Sure, of course he had. I grinned at him. "You went through that stuff while I was taking Anna home last night."

He waited till he was back around the desk and in his chair again before he murmured sarcastically, "Bravo, Archie."

"All right," I said. I sat down across from him. "Do I get to ask questions? There's three things I want to know. Or am I supposed to go up front and do my homework?" I was a little sore, of course; I always was when I knew that he had tied up a nice neat bundle right in front of me without my even being able to see what was going in it.

"No homework," he said. "You are about to go for the car and drive with reasonable speed to White Plains. If the questions are brief—"

"They're brief enough, but if I've got work to do they can wait. Since it's White Plains, I suppose I'm to take a look at the hole in Carlo Maffei and any other details that seem to me unimportant."

"No. Confound it, Archie, stop supposing aloud in my presence; if it is inevitable that in the end you are to be classed with—for instance— Mr. O'Grady, let us at least postpone it as long as possible."

"O'Grady did a good job this morning, two hours from a coat label and a laundry mark to that phone call."

Wolfe shook his head. "Cerebrally an oaf. But your questions?"

"They can wait. What is it at White Plains if it's not Maffei?"

Wolfe gave me his substitute for a smile, an unusually prolonged one for him. Finally he said, "A chance to make some money. Does the name Fletcher M. Anderson mean anything to you without referring to your files?"

"I hope so." I snorted. "No thanks for a bravo either. Nineteen-twenty-eight. Assistant District Attorney on the Goldsmith case. A year later moved to the country and is now District Attorney for Westchester County. He would admit that he owes you something only if the door were closed and he whispered in your ear. Married money."

Wolfe nodded. "Correct. The bravo is yours, Archie, and I shall manage without the thanks. At White Plains you will see Mr. Anderson and deliver a provocative and possibly lucrative message. At least that is contemplated; I am awaiting information from a caller who is expected at any moment." He reached across his rotundity to remove the large platinum watch from his vest pocket and glance at it. "I note that a dealer in sporting goods is no more punctual than a skeptic would expect. I telephoned at nine; the delivery would be made at eleven without fail; it is now eleven-forty. It really would be well at this point to eliminate all avoidable delay. It would have been better to send you— Ah!"

It was the buzzer. Fritz passed the door down the hall; there was the sound of the front door opening and another voice and Fritz's in question and answer. Then heavy footsteps drowning out Fritz's, and there appeared on the threshold a young man who looked like a football player bearing on his shoulder an enormous bundle about three feet long and as big around as Wolfe himself. Breathing, he said, "From Corliss Holmes."

At Wolfe's nod I went to help. We got the bundle onto the floor and the young man knelt and began untying the cord, but he fumbled so long that I got impatient and reached in my pocket for my knife. Wolfe's murmur sounded from his chair, "No, Archie, few knots deserve that," and I put my knife back. Finally he got it loose and the cord pulled off, and I helped him unroll the paper and burlap, and then stood up and stared. I looked at Wolfe and back again at the pile on the floor. It was nothing but golf clubs, there must have been a hundred of them, enough, I thought, to kill a million snakes, for it had never seemed to me that they were much good for anything else.

I said to Wolfe, "The exercise will do you good."

Still in his chair, Wolfe told us to put them on the desk, and the young man and I each grabbed an armload. I began spreading them in an even row on the desk; there were long and short, heavy and light, iron, wood, steel, chromium, anything you might think of. Wolfe was looking at them, each one as I put it down, and after about a dozen he said, "Not these with iron ends. Remove them. Only those with wooden ends." To the young man: "You do not call this the end?"

The young man looked amazed and superior. "That's the head."

"Accept my apologies—your name?"

"My name? Townsend."

"Accept my apologies, Mr. Townsend. I once saw golf clubs through a shop window while my car was having a flat tire, but the ends were not labeled. And these are in fact all varieties of a single species?"

"Huh? They're all different."

"Indeed. Indeed, indeed. Plain wooden faces, inset faces, bone, composition, ivory— Since this is the head I presume that is the face?"

"Sure, that's the face."

"Of course. And the purpose of the inset? Since everything in life must have a purpose except the culture of Orchidaceæ."

"Purpose?"

"Exactly. Purpose."

"Well—" The young man hesitated. "Of course it's for the impact. That means hitting the ball, it's the inset that hits the ball, and that's the impact."

"I see. Go no further. That will do nicely. And the handles, some wood, really fine and sensitive, and steel— I presume the steel handles are hollow."

"Hollow steel shaft, yes, sir. It's a matter of taste. That one's a driver. This is a brassie. See the brass on the bottom? Brassie."

"Faultless sequitur," Wolfe murmured. "That, I think, will be all, the lesson is complete. You know, Mr. Townsend, it is our good fortune that the exigencies of birth and training furnish all of us with opportunities for snobbery. My ignorance of this special nomenclature provided yours; your innocence of the elementary mental processes provides mine. As to the object of your visit, you can sell me nothing; these things will forever remain completely useless to me. You can reassemble your bundle and take it with you, but let us assume that I should purchase three of these clubs and that the profit on each should be one dollar. Three dollars? If I give you that amount will it be satisfactory?"

The young man had, if not his own dignity, at least that of Corliss Holmes. "There is no obligation to purchase, sir."

"No, but I haven't finished. I have to ask a favor of you. Will you take one of these clubs—here, this one—and stand there, beyond that chair, and whirl it about you in the orthodox manner?"

"Whirl it?"

"Yes; club, strike, hit, whatever you call it. Pretend that you are impacting a ball."

Beyond snobbery, the young man was now having difficulty to conceal his contempt. He took the driver from Wolfe, backed away from the desk, shoved a chair aside, glanced around, behind, and up, then brought the driver up over his shoulder and down and through with a terrific swish.

Wolfe shuddered. "Ungovernable fury," he murmured. "Again, more slowly?"

The young man complied.

"If possible, Mr. Townsend, more slowly yet?"

This time he made it slow motion, a cartoon, derisive, but Wolfe watched it keenly and soberly. Then he said, "Excellent. A thousand thanks, Mr. Townsend. Archie, since we have no account at Corliss

Holmes, will you please give Mr. Townsend three dollars? A little speed now, if you don't mind. The trip I mentioned is imminent and even urgent."

After the quiet weeks that had passed it made my heart jump to hear Wolfe ask for speed. The young man and I had the package together again in no time; I went to let him out the front door, and then back to the office. Wolfe was sitting there with his lips fixed to whistle, but with no sound that could be heard six feet away; you only knew the air was going in and out by his chest rising and falling. Sometimes, when close enough to him, I had tried to hear if he really thought he was doing a tune, but without success.

He stopped as I came in and said, "This will only take a minute, Archie. Sit down. You won't need your notebook."

IV

WHEN I'm driving I don't see much of anything except the road, for I have the type of mind that gets on a job and stays there until it's time for another one. That day I hit a good clip, too; on account of the traffic it took a long while to get to Woodlawn, but from there to White Plains my clock covered just twenty-one minutes. But in spite of my type of mind and the hurry I was in I enjoyed the Parkway out of the corner of my eye. Lots of the bushes were covered with flowers, the new crop of leaves on the trees was waving easy in the breeze like a slow dance, and the grass was thick and green. I thought to myself that they couldn't make a carpet if it cost ten thousand dollars that would be as nice to walk on as that grass.

The hurry didn't help any. When I got to the courthouse there was nothing but bad luck. Anderson was away and wouldn't be back until Monday, four days. In the Adirondacks, they said, but wouldn't give me his address; it wouldn't have been a bit unpleasant to head the roadster for Lake Placid and step on it. His chief assistant, whose name, Derwin, I had never heard before, was still out to lunch and wouldn't be back for half an hour. No one around seemed to care about being helpful.

I went down the street to a phone and got Wolfe in New York. He said to wait for Derwin and try it on him; and I didn't mind having time for a couple of sandwiches and a glass of milk before he was expected back. When I returned Derwin was in his office, but I had to wait for him twenty minutes, I suppose for him to finish picking his teeth. The place was certainly dead.

When I consider the different kinds I've seen it seems silly to say it, but somehow to me all lawyers look alike. It's a sort of mixture of a scared look and a satisfied look, as if they were crossing a traffic-filled street where they expect to get run over any minute but they know exactly the kind of paper to hand the driver if they get killed and they've got one right in their pocket. This Derwin looked like that; otherwise he seemed very respectable, well dressed and well fed, somewhere around forty, under rather than over, with his dark hair brushed back slick and his face happy and pleased-looking.

I laid my panama on a corner of his desk and took a chair before I said, "I'm sorry to have missed Mr. Anderson. I don't know if you'll be interested in my message, but I'm pretty sure he would."

Derwin was leaning back in his chair with a politician's smile. "If it is connected with the duties of my office, I certainly will, Mr. Goodwin."

"It's connected all right. But I'm at a disadvantage since you don't know my employer, Nero Wolfe. Mr. Anderson knows him."

"Nero Wolfe?" Derwin wrinkled his forehead. "I've heard of him. The private detective, you mean, of course. This is only White Plains, you see, the provinces begin a little farther north."

"Yes, sir. Not that I would call Nero Wolfe a private detective. As a description—well, for one thing it's a little too active. But that's the man I work for."

"You have a message from him?"

"Yes, sir. As I say, the message was for Mr. Anderson, but I telephoned him half an hour ago and he said to give it to you. It may not work out the same, for I happen to know that Mr. Anderson is a rich man, and I don't know that much about you. Maybe you're like me, maybe your salary is the only rope that holds Saturday and Sunday together for you."

Derwin laughed, just a trick laugh, for in a second his face was solemn and businesslike. "Maybe I am. But although I am not particularly rushed this afternoon, I am still waiting for the message."

"Yes, sir. It's like this. Last Sunday afternoon, four days ago, Peter Oliver Barstow, president of Holland University, died suddenly while playing golf on the links of the Green Meadow Club over toward Pleasantville. You know about that?"

"Of course. It was a loss to the community, to the whole country in fact. Of course."

I nodded. "His funeral was Tuesday and he was buried at Agawalk Cemetery. Mr. Nero Wolfe wants to bet you—he would rather bet Mr. Anderson but he says you'll do—that if you'll have the body lifted and an autopsy made you'll find proof of poison. He will bet ten thousand dollars and will deposit a certified check for that amount with any responsible person you name."

I just grinned as Derwin stared at me. He stared a long time, then he said, "Mr. Nero Wolfe is crazy."

"Oh no," I said. "Whatever you bet on, don't bet on *that*. I haven't finished yet with Nero Wolfe's bet. The rest of it is that somewhere in Barstow's belly, probably just below the stomach, somewhere between one and three inches in from the skin, will be found a short, sharp, thin needle, probably of steel but possibly of very hard wood. It will be pointing upward, approximately at an angle of forty-five degrees if not deflected by a bone."

Derwin kept staring at me. When I stopped he tried his trick laugh again, but it didn't work so well. "This is about as big a bunch of nonsense as I've ever heard," he said. "I suppose there is a point to it somewhere, if you're not crazy too."

"There's a point all right." I reached in my pocket for the check Wolfe had given me. "There are very few people in the world who would risk ten thousand on a bunch of nonsense, and you can take it from me that Nero Wolfe isn't one of them. Peter Oliver Barstow was murdered, and he's got that needle in him. I say it, Nero Wolfe says it, and this ten grand says it. That's a lot of testimony, Mr. Derwin."

The lawyer was beginning to look not nearly as happy and pleased as he had when I went in. He got up from his chair and then sat down again. I waited. He said, "It's preposterous. Absolutely preposterous."

"Wolfe isn't betting on that." I grinned. "He's just betting that it's true."

"But it can't be. It's merely preposterous and—and monstrous. Whatever the stunt may be you're trying to pull, you've hit the wrong man; I happen to be acquainted with the Barstow family and therefore know the facts. I won't recite them to you; such idiotic nonsense. Do you know who signed the death certificate? I don't suppose—"

"Sure," I put in, "Dr. Nathaniel Bradford. Coronary thrombosis. But if all the doctors in the world were as good as him, and if they all said coronary thrombosis, Nero Wolfe's money is still right here ready to talk."

I had seen the change come over Derwin's face; he had got over his shock and was now ready to be clever. His voice was sharp. "See here, what's your game?"

"No game at all. None. Except to win ten grand."

"Let me see that check."

I handed it to him. He looked it over thoroughly and then pulled his desk telephone over, took off the receiver, and in a moment spoke to someone. "Miss Ritter, please get me the Thirty-fourth Street branch of the Metropolitan Trust Company." He sat and looked at the check and I folded my arms and got patient. When the bell rang he took the phone again and began asking questions, plenty of them; he certainly made sure there could be no mistake.

When he hung up I said pleasantly, "Anyway we're getting started, now that you know it's real dollars."

He paid no attention, but just sat frowning at the check. Finally he said in a shrewd voice, "Do you mean that you are actually empowered to wager this money on that proposition as you stated it?"

"Yes, sir. That check is made out to me, and certified. I can endorse it just like that. If you want to phone Wolfe, the number is Bryant nine, two-eight-two-eight. In order to avoid any misunderstanding, I would suggest that you have your stenographer type a memorandum of the details for us to sign. I should tell you that Wolfe undertakes to furnish no reasons or suggestions or clues and will not discuss the matter. It's a bet, that's all."

"Bet, hell. You're not expecting any bet. Who do you expect to bet with you, Westchester County?"

I grinned. "We hoped for Mr. Anderson, but lacking him we're not particular. Anyone with ten thousand dollars; Wolfe wouldn't care; a chief of police or a newspaper editor or maybe some prominent Democrat with a strong sense of civic duty."

"Indeed!"

"Yes, sir, indeed. My instructions are to do my best to get the money covered before dark."

Derwin got up, kicking his chair back. "Hah! Bet? Bluff."

"You think so, sir? Try me. Try covering it."

Evidently he had decided something, for with my words he was crossing the room. At the door he turned to say, "Will you wait here for me ten minutes? I imagine you will, since I have your check in my pocket."

It wasn't endorsed. He was gone before I could toss a nod at him. I settled down to wait. How was it going? I wondered. Had I passed up any advantages? Would it have been better to postpone my last threat for more stubbornness if he had it in him? How could I force him to act quick? And after all, did this third-rater have the authority or the guts to undertake a thing like this with his boss gone? What Wolfe wanted was quick action; of course I knew he no more expected a bet than I expected him to give me the ten grand for my birthday; he was after an autopsy and that needle. I could see now how he had guessed the needle, but how he had ever connected it with Carlo Maffei in the first place—I stopped myself to switch back to the immediate job. If this Derwin laid down and played dead on me, where would I go next? Between four and six I would have to use my own judgment; I wouldn't dare to interrupt Wolfe with a phone call while he was upstairs with the damn plants. It was now two-fifty. Derwin had been gone ten minutes. I began to feel silly. What if he left me sitting there holding my fingers all afternoon, and him with the check? If I let a third-rate brief-shark do that to me I'd never be able to look Wolfe in his big fat face again. I should never have let him out of my sight, certainly not without getting the check back. I jumped out of my chair and crossed the room, but at the door I calmed down and took it easy; softly I turned the knob and pulled and stuck my head out. There was a dinky hall leading to the outer office, and I could hear the girl on the telephone.

"No, operator, person-to-person. No one but Mr. Anderson will do."

I waited till she had hung up, then I went on out and over to her desk. "Would it be much bother to tell me where Mr. Derwin has gone to?"

She seemed interested in me; she took a good look. But she answered straight enough. "He's in Mr. Anderson's room telephoning."

"You wouldn't lie to me just for practice?"

"I don't need any practice, thanks."

"All right. If you don't mind, I'll try one of these chairs. It was awful in there all alone."

I sat down within three feet of the entrance door, and I had no sooner got disposed than the door opened and a man came in, a husky, busy-looking man in a blue suit and black shoes, with a stiff straw hat. From where I sat, as he went toward the girl with his back to me, it was easy to see that he had a gun on his hip. The girl said, "Howdedo, Mr. Cook, Mr. Derwin's in Mr. Anderson's room." When the man had gone on through another door I said to the girl, "Ben Cook maybe?" She nodded without looking at me, and I grinned, and sat and waited.

It was all of fifteen minutes more before the door of Anderson's room opened again and Derwin appeared and called to me, "Come in here, Goodwin."

I went. When I got inside and saw that they had actually staged me it was too funny not to laugh. Ben Cook was in a chair that had been drawn alongside the one by the desk—that one of course for Derwin—and one had been placed just right for me, quite close and facing them and the light.

"Amused, huh," the husky man grunted. Derwin waited till he was back in his chair to inform me, "This is the chief of police."

I was pretending to blink at the light. "Don't tell me," I said. "Do you think Ben Cook's reputation stops at Bronx Park?"

Derwin went stern on me. Lord, it was funny. He even went so far as to shake a finger at me. "Goodwin, I've been pretty busy for half an hour, and now I'm ready to tell you what comes next. You'll tell us what you know, if anything, while we're waiting for Wolfe. What reason have you—"

I hated to interrupt the show, but I couldn't help it. It was involuntary. "Waiting for Wolfe? Here?"

"Certainly, here. If he knows what's good for him, and I think I made that plain on the telephone."

I didn't laugh. I just said, "Listen, Mr. Derwin. This is one of your bad days. You never had a chance at so many rotten bets in your life. Nero Wolfe is about as apt to come here as I am to tell you who killed Barstow."

"Yeah?" It was Ben Cook. "You'll tell us plenty. Plenty."

"Maybe. But I won't tell you who killed Barstow, because I don't know. Now if you want to ask about roads, for instance—"

"Cut it out." Derwin got sterner. "Goodwin, you have made a most startling accusation in a most sensational manner. I won't pretend that I have a lot of questions ready for you, because I obviously have nothing to base them on. I have just one question, and I want a prompt and complete answer. For what reason and for what purpose did your employer send you here today?"

I sighed and looked solemn. "I've told you, Mr. Derwin, to get a bet down."

"Come on, act as if you had some sense. You can't get away with that, you know damn well you can't. Come on. Let's hear it."

Ben Cook said, "Don't try to be bright. You'd be surprised how we treat bright boys up here sometimes."

I could have kept it going all night, I suppose, if I had wanted to, but time was passing and they gave me a pain. I said, "Listen a minute, gentlemen. Of course you're peeved and that's too bad, but I can't help it. Let's say I tell you to go to hell and get up and walk out, what are you going to do—? Yes, Chief, I know it's only a short distance to the station, but I'm not going that way. Honest, you're acting like a pair of dumb flatfeet. I'm surprised at you, Mr. Derwin. Nero Wolfe offers to let you in right at the beginning of a big thing, and the first thing you do is spill it to Ben Cook and the next is to drive me to take it away from both of you and toss it to the wolves. You can't touch me, don't be silly. Nero Wolfe would love a suit for false arrest, and I never go to police stations except to visit friends unless you can show me a warrant, and think how funny it would be after the reporters got my story and then the proof followed of Barstow's murder. As a matter of fact, I'm beginning to get a little bit sore and I've got half a mind to demand that check back and walk out on you. Get this: I'll tell you exactly nothing. You understand that maybe? Now you can give me that check or talk sense yourself."

Derwin sat with his arms folded and looked at me without making any effort to open his mouth. Ben Cook said, "So you've come out to the country to show the hayseeds how it's done. Sonny, I'm plenty big enough to take you to the station with nothing at all but the inclination. That's all I need."

"You can afford to be breezy," I told him. "Derwin has handed you a firecracker that he might have to set off himself, and you know it." I turned to Derwin. "Who did you telephone to in New York? Headquarters?"

"No. The District Attorney."

"Did you get him?"

Derwin unfolded his arms, pulled himself back in his chair, and looked at me helplessly. "I got Morley."

I nodded. "Dick Morley. What did he tell you?"

"He told me that if Nero Wolfe was offering to bet ten thousand dollars on anything whatever he would appreciate it if I'd take him on for another thousand, only he would give me ten to one."

I was too sore to grin. I said, "And still you invite me in here to tea instead of getting a spade and beating it to Agawalk Cemetery. I repeat that I'll tell you nothing and Wolfe will tell you nothing, but if ever you had a sure thing to go on it's right now. The next thing to do is to give me back that check, and then what?"

Derwin let out a sigh and cleared his throat, but he had to clear it again. "Goodwin," he said, "I'll be frank with you. I'm out of my depth. That's not for publication, Ben, but it's a fact anyhow. I'm clear out of my depth. Good Lord, don't you know what it would mean—an exhumation and autopsy on Peter Oliver Barstow?"

I put in, "Rot. Any of a dozen excuses is enough."

"Well, maybe I'm not good at excuses. Anyway, I know that family. I can't do it. I've telephoned Anderson at Lake Placid and couldn't get him. I'll have him before six o'clock, before seven sure. He can take a sleeper and be here tomorrow morning. He can decide it then."

"That lets today out," I said.

"Yes. Not a chance. I won't do it."

"All right." I got up. "I'll go down to the corner and phone Wolfe

and see if he'll wait that long, and if he says okay I'll head south away
from the hayseeds. I might as well have that check."

Derwin took it from his pocket and handed it to me.

I grinned at Ben Cook. "Shall I give you a lift as far as the station,
Chief?"

"Run along, sonny, run along."

V

WOLFE was as nice as pie that evening. I got home in time to eat dinner
with him. He wouldn't let me say anything about White Plains until
the meal was over; in fact, there wasn't any conversation to speak of
about anything, for he had the radio going. He was accustomed to say
that this was the perfect era for the sedentary man; formerly such a man
could satisfy any amount of curiosity regarding bygone times by sitting
down with Gibbon or Ranke or Tacitus or Greene but if he wanted to
meet his contemporaries he had to take to the highways, whereas the
man of today, tiring for the moment of Galba or Vitellius, had only to
turn on the radio and resume his chair. One program Wolfe rarely
missed was the Joy Boys. I never knew why. He would sit with his fingers interlaced on his belly, his eyes half closed, and his mouth screwed
up as if there was something in it he would spit out any minute. Frequently I went for a walk at that time, but of course when dinner was a
little early so that it came then I was caught. I have my radio favorites
all right, but the Joy Boys seem to me pretty damn vulgar.

In the office after dinner it didn't take me long to report. I hated
apologizing to Wolfe because he was so invariably nice about it; he always took it for granted that I had done everything possible and that
there was nothing to criticize but the contrariety of the environment, as
he put it. He made no comments and didn't seem much interested in the
report or the apology either. I tried to get him started, tried for instance
to find out if he had really had some sort of wild idea that I might kid a
District Attorney into covering a bet of ten thousand dollars just like
that, but he only stayed nice and quiet. I asked him if he thought it
likely that I could have taken any line at all that would have persuaded
Derwin to start the digging that afternoon. He said probably not.

"Frogs don't fly." He was sitting at his desk examining with a magnifying glass the rostellum from a *Cymbidium Alexanderi* that Horstmann had brought down wilty on the stem. "He would have needed a
touch of imagination, just a touch, but I would judge from your description that he lacks it. I beg you not to reproach yourself. This affair

may prove unprofitable in the end. With Fletcher M. Anderson it might have been different. He is a rich man with professional ambitions, and no fool. He might easily have reflected that if a quiet and unadvertised autopsy proved me wrong he would win ten thousand dollars; if it proved me right he would have to pay me, but he would get a remarkable and sensational case in return, and he might also infer that having pocketed his money I would have further information to be placed at his disposal. Your errand at White Plains was in essence a primitive business enterprise: an offer to exchange something for something else. If Mr. Anderson had only been there he would probably have seen it so. It may yet materialize; it is still worth some small effort. I believe, though, it is getting ready to rain."

"What are you doing now, changing the subject?" I stuck to the chair near his desk, though I saw that I was being regarded as a mild nuisance, for I had some questions to ask. "It was clouding up as I came in. Is it going to rain all over your clues?"

He was placid, still bent over the magnifying glass. "Some day, Archie, when I decide you are no longer worth tolerating, you will have to marry a woman of very modest mental capacity to get an appropriate audience for your wretched sarcasms. When I mentioned the rain I had your own convenience and comfort in mind. This afternoon it struck me as desirable that you should visit Sullivan Street, but tomorrow will do as well."

It was hard to believe unless you were as well acquainted with him as I was; I knew that he was really serious, he thought that leaving the house at any time was an unpleasant venture, but to go out in the rain was next to foolhardy. I said, "What do you think I am, the Chinese army? Of course I'll go. That was one of my questions. Why do you suppose Anna Fiore closed up so hard on O'Grady? Because he wasn't all grace and charm like you and me?"

"Likely. Excellent conjecture, Archie. The more so because when I sent Panzer for her today she confessed only reluctantly to her name and she would not budge. So your grace and charm will be needed. If it would be convenient have her here in the morning at eleven. It's not of great importance but can do no harm for passing the time, and such stubbornness deserves a siege."

"I'll go get her now."

"No. Really. Tomorrow. Sit down. I would prefer to have you here, idle and useless, while I purposelessly inspect this futile flower. Futile and sterile apparently. As I have remarked before, to have you with me like this is always refreshing because it constantly reminds me how distressing it would be to have someone present—a wife, for instance—whom I could not dismiss at will."

"Yes, sir." I grinned. "Go on with the rest of it."

"Not just now. Not with the rain falling. I dislike it."

"All right, then tell me a few things. How did you know Carlo Maffei had been murdered? How do you know Barstow was poisoned? How do you know he's got a needle in him? Of course I see how it got there since you had the boy from Corliss Holmes show us, but how did you get that far?"

Wolfe laid down his magnifying glass and sighed. I knew I was making him uncomfortable, but aside from curiosity it was a matter of business. He never seemed to realize that while it was all very well for me to feel in my bones that he would never get us committed to a mistake, I could do my part with a little more intelligence if I knew what was making the wheels go round. I don't believe he ever would have opened up once, on any case, big or little, if I hadn't kept nudging him.

He sighed. "Must I again remind you, Archie, of the reaction you would have got if you had asked Velasquez to explain why Aesop's hand was resting inside his robe instead of hanging by his side? Must I again demonstrate that while it is permissible to request the scientist to lead you back over his footprints, a similar request of the artist is nonsense, since he, like the lark or the eagle, has made none? Do you need to be told again that I am an artist?"

"No, sir. All I need to be told is how you knew Barstow was poisoned."

He took up the magnifying glass. I sat and waited, lighting another cigarette. I had finished it, and had about decided to go to the front room for a book or magazine, when he spoke.

"Carlo Maffei is gone. Common enough, beaten and robbed probably, until the telephone call and the advertisement. The telephone call as a whole does not lack interest, but it is the threat, 'I'm not the one to be scared,' that has significance. The advertisement adds a specification; to that point Maffei has been this and that, he now becomes also a man who may have made something intricate and difficult that would *work*. The word *mechanism* made that a good advertisement, but it also offered magnificent suggestions to an inquiring mind. Then, quite by accident just as the creation of life was an accident, Maffei becomes something else: a man who clipped the Barstow news from the paper on the morning of his disappearance. So, read the Barstow news again and find the aspect of it that closely concerned Carlo Maffei. An obscure Italian metal-worker immigrant; a famous learned wealthy university president. Still there must be a connection, and the incongruity of the elements would make it only the more plain if it was visible at all. There is the article; find the link if it is there; stop every word and give it passage only if its innocence is sure. But little effort is required; the link is so obvious that it is at once apparent. At the moment of, and for some time immediately preceding, his collapse, Barstow had in his hands and was using not one, but an entire assortment, of instruments which if they were not intricate and difficult mechanisms were admirably adapted to such a use. It was a perfectly composed picture. But while it needed no justification, nothing indeed but contemplation, as a work of art, if it were to be put to practical uses a little fixative would help. So I merely asked Miss Fiore if she had ever seen a golf club in Maffei's room. The result was gratifying."

"All right," I said. "But what if the girl had just looked and said no, she never saw one anywhere?"

"I have told you before, Archie, that even for your amusement I shall not advise replies to hypothetical questions."

"Sure, that's an easy out."

Wolfe shook his head regretfully. "To reply is to admit the validity of your jargon, but I have learned not to expect better of you. How the devil do I know what I would have done *if* anything? Probably bade her good night. Would I have found varnish for my picture elsewhere? Maybe; maybe not. Shall I ask you how you would have seen to eat if your head had been put on backwards?"

I grinned. "I wouldn't have starved. Neither will you; if I know anything I know that. But how did you know that Maffei had been murdered?"

"I didn't, until O'Grady came. You heard what I said to him. The police had searched his room. That could only be if he had been taken in a criminal act, or been murdered. The first was unlikely in the light of other facts."

"All right. But I've saved the best till the last. Who killed Barstow?"

"Ah." Wolfe murmured it softly. "That would be another picture, Archie, and I hope an expensive one. Expensive for the purchaser and profitable for the artist. Also, one of its characters would be a worthy subject. To continue my threadbare metaphor, we shan't set up our easel until we are sure of the commission. Yet in point of fact that isn't strictly true. We shall get in a spot of the background tomorrow morning if you can bring Miss Fiore here."

"Let me get her now. It's only a little after nine."

"No—hear the rain? Tomorrow will do."

I knew there was no use insisting, so after a try at a couple of magazines had got me good and bored I got a raincoat from upstairs and

went out for an hour at a movie. I wouldn't have admitted to anyone
else, but I did to myself, that I wasn't any too easy in my mind. I had
had the same kind of experience often before, but that didn't make me
like it any better. I did absolutely feel in my bones that Wolfe would
never let us tumble into a hole without having a ladder we could climb
out with, but in spite of that I had awful doubts sometimes. As long as
I live I'll never forget the time he had a bank president pinched, or
rather I did, on no evidence whatever except that the fountain pen on
his desk was dry. I was never so relieved in my life as I was when the
guy shot himself an hour later. But there was no use trying to get Wolfe
to pull up a little; I hardly ever wasted time on that any more. If I undertook to explain how easily he might be wrong he would just say, "You
know a fact when you see it, Archie, but you have no feeling for phenomena." After I had looked up the word phenomena in the dictionary
I couldn't see that he had anything, but there was no use arguing with
him.

So here I was uneasy again. I wanted to think it over, so I got my
raincoat and went to a movie where I could sit in the dark with something to keep my eyes on and let my mind work. It wasn't hard to see
how Wolfe had doped it out. Someone wanted to kill Barstow, call him
X. He put an ad in the paper for an expert to make him something,
fixing it to get someone intending to leave the country for good so if he
had any curiosity later on it wouldn't hurt him any. Maffei answered the
ad and got the job, namely to make an arrangement inside a golf club
so that when the inset on the face hit a ball it would release a trigger
and shoot a needle out of the handle at the other end. Probably X presented it as a trial of skill for the European commission to follow; but he
gave the Italian so much money for doing it that Maffei decided not to
go back home after all. That started an argument, and perhaps Maffei
agreed to go on the next boat; anyhow X proceeded to use the club for
its calculated purpose, putting it in Barstow's bag (it had of course been
made identical in appearance with Barstow's own driver). Then Maffei
happened to read Monday's *Times* and put two and two together,
which wasn't strange considering the odd affair he had been paid to
construct. X had telephoned; Maffei had met him, made him a present
of his suspicions, and tried blackmail. X didn't wait this time for an
expert design and mechanism, he just used a knife, leaving it in Maffei's
back to keep from soiling the upholstery of the car. He then drove
around the Westchester hills until he found a secluded spot, put the
body in a thicket and pulled out the knife and later tossed it into a
handy stream or reservoir. Arriving home at a decent hour, he had a
drink or two before going to bed, and when he got up in the morning

put on a cutaway instead of a business suit because he was going to his
friend Barstow's funeral.

Of course that was Wolfe's picture, and it was a lulu, but what I
figured as I sat in the movie was this, that though it used all the facts
without any stretching, anyone could have said that much a thousand
years ago when they thought the sun went around the earth. That
didn't stretch any of the facts they knew, but what about the ones they
didn't know? And here was Wolfe risking ten grand and his reputation
to get Barstow dug up. Once one of Wolfe's clients had told him he was
insufferably blithe. I liked that; Wolfe had liked it too. But that didn't
keep me from reflecting that if they cut Barstow open and found only
coronary thrombosis in his veins and no oddments at all in his belly,
within a week everybody from the D. A. down to a Bath Beach flatfoot
would be saving twenty cents by staying home and laughing at us instead of going to a movie to see Mickey Mouse. I wasn't so dumb, I
knew anyone may make a mistake, but I also knew that when a man
sets himself up as cocksure as Wolfe did, he has *always* got to be right.

I was dumb in a way though. All the time I was stewing I knew
damn well Wolfe *was* right. It was that note I went to sleep on when I
got home from the movie and found that Wolfe had already gone up to
his room.

The next morning I was awake a little after seven, but I dawdled in
bed, knowing that if I got up and dressed I would have to dawdle anyway, since there was no use bringing Anna Fiore until time for Wolfe
to be down from the plant rooms. I lay, yawning, looking at the picture
of the woods with grass and flowers, and at the photograph of my father
and mother, and then closed my eyes, not to nap, for I was all slept out,
but to see how many different noises from the street I could recognize.
I was doing that when there was a knock on the door and in answer to
my call Fritz came in.

"Good morning," I said. "I'll have grapefruit juice and just a tiny cup
of chocolate."

Fritz smiled. He had a sweet sort of faraway smile. He could catch a
joke but never tried to return it. "Good morning. There's a gentleman
downstairs to see Mr. Wolfe."

I sat up. "What's his name?"

"He said Anderson. He had no card."

"What!" I swung myself to the edge of the bed. "Well well well well.
He's not a gentleman, Fritz, he's a noovoh reesh. Mr. Wolfe is hoping
that soon he'll be less reesh. Tell him—no, don't bother. I'll be right
down."

I doused some cold water over my face, got on enough clothes for an emergency, and gave my hair a few swipes with a brush. Then I went down.

Anderson didn't get up from his chair when I entered the office. He was so sunburned that on the street it would have taken me a second glance to recognize him. He looked sleepy and sore and his hair hadn't been brushed any better than mine.

I said, "My name's Archie Goodwin. I don't suppose you remember me."

He kept his chair. "I suppose not, I'm sorry. I came to see Wolfe."

"Yes, sir. I'm afraid you'll have to wait a little. Mr. Wolfe isn't up yet."

"Not long, I hope."

"I couldn't say. I'll see. If you'll excuse me."

I beat it to the hall and stood there at the foot of the stairs. I had to decide whether this was a case when Wolfe would want to break a rule. It was a quarter to eight. Finally I went on upstairs and down the hall to a point about ten feet from his door where there was a push-button in the wall. I pushed it, and right away heard his voice faintly.

"Well?"

"Turn off the switch. I'm coming in."

I heard the little click and then: "Come."

You would never believe there was such a thing in the world as Wolfe in bed if you didn't see it. I had seen it often, but it was still a treat. On top was a black silk puffy cover which he always used, winter and summer. From the mound in the middle it sloped precipitously on all sides, so that if you wanted to see his face you had to stand well up front, and then you had to stoop to look under the canopy arrangement that he had sticking out from the head of the bed. It was also of black silk, and extended a foot beyond his chin and hung quite low on all three sides. Inside it on the white pillow his big fat face reposed like an image in a temple.

His hand came from beneath the cover to pull a cord that hung at his right, and the canopy folded back against the headboard. He blinked. I told him that Fletcher M. Anderson was downstairs and wanted to see him.

He cursed. I hated to hear him curse. It got on my nerves. The reason for that, he told me once, was that whereas in most cases cursing was merely a vocal explosion, with him it was a considered expression of a profound desire. He did it seldom. That morning he cursed completely. At the end he said, "Leave, get out, go."

I hated to stammer, too. "But—but—Anderson—"

"If Mr. Anderson wishes to see me he may do so at eleven o'clock. But that is unnecessary. What do I pay you for?"

"Very well, sir. Of course you're right. I break a rule and I get bawled out. But now that that's done with may I suggest that it would be a good idea to see Anderson—"

"You may not."

"Ten thousand dollars?"

"No."

"In the name of heaven, sir, why not?"

"Confound it, you badger me!" Wolfe's head turned on the pillow, and he got a hand around to wiggle a finger. "Yes, you badger me. But it is a valuable quality at times and I won't cavil at it. Instead I'll answer your question. I shall not see Mr. Anderson for three reasons: first, being still in bed I am undressed and in an ugly temper. Second, you can do our business with him just as well. Third, I understand the technique of eccentricity; it would be futile for a man to labor at establishing a reputation for oddity if he were ready at the slightest provocation to revert to normal action. Go. At once."

I left the room and went downstairs to the office and told Anderson that if he wanted to wait he could see Mr. Wolfe at eleven o'clock.

Of course he couldn't believe his ears. As soon as he became able to credit the fact that the message was like that and that it was meant for him, he blew up. He seemed especially indignant that he had come straight to Wolfe's place from a sleeper at Grand Central Station, though I couldn't see why. I explained to him several times how it was, I told him it was eccentricity and there was no help for it. I also told him that I had been to White Plains the day before and was acquainted with the situation. That seemed to calm him a little and he began asking me questions. I fed it to him in little pieces, and had the fun of seeing the look on his face when I told him about Derwin calling Ben Cook in. When he had the whole story he sat back and rubbed his nose and looked over my head.

Finally he brought his look down to me. "This is a startling conclusion Wolfe has made. Isn't it?"

"Yes, sir. It is indeed."

"Then he must have some startling information."

I grinned. "Mr. Anderson, it is a pleasure to talk with you, but there's no use wasting time. As far as startling information is concerned, Wolfe and I are the same as two mummies in a museum until that grave is opened and Barstow is cut up. Not a chance."

"Well. That's too bad. I might offer Wolfe a fee as a special investigator—a sort of inquiry and report."

"A fee? That's like saying as long as a piece of string."

"Say, five hundred dollars."

I shook my head. "I'm afraid he's too busy. I'm busy too, I may have to run up to White Plains this morning."

"Oh." Anderson bit his lip and looked at me. "You know, Goodwin, I rarely go out of my way to be offensive, but doesn't it occur to you that this whole thing is fairly nasty? It might be better to say unethical."

I got sore at that. I looked back at him and said, "Look here, Mr. Anderson. You said you didn't remember me. I remember you. You haven't forgotten the Goldsmith case five years ago. It wouldn't have hurt you a bit to let people know what Wolfe handed you on that. But let that go, let's say you needed to keep it for yourself. We wouldn't have minded that so much. But how ethical was it for you to turn it around so that Wolfe got a nice black eye instead of what was really coming to him? You tend to your own ethics maybe."

"I don't know what you're talking about."

"All right. But if I go to White Plains today somebody will know what I'm talking about. And whatever you get this time you'll pay for."

Anderson smiled and got up. "Don't bother, Goodwin. You won't be needed at White Plains today. On information that I have received I have decided definitely on the exhumation of Barstow's body. You will be here throughout the day, or Wolfe? I may wish to get in touch with him later."

"Wolfe is always here, but you can't get him between nine and eleven or four and six."

"Well. Such an eccentric!"

"Yes, sir. Your hat's in the hall."

I went to the front-room window and watched his taxi roll off. Then I turned to the office, to the telephone. I hesitated; but I knew Wolfe was right, and if he wasn't, a little publicity wouldn't make it any harder for us. So I called the *Gazette* office for Harry Foster, and by luck he was in.

"Harry? Archie Goodwin. Here's something for you, but keep it so quiet you can hear a pin drop. This morning at White Plains, Anderson, the District Attorney, is going to get a court order for an exhumation and autopsy on Peter Oliver Barstow. He'll probably try to keep it mum, but I thought you might like to help him out. And listen. Some day, when the time comes, I'd be glad to tell you what it was that made Anderson so curious. Don't mention it."

I went upstairs and shaved and did my dressing over. By the time I had finished with that, and with breakfast and a little chat in the kitchen with Fritz about fish, it was nine-thirty. I went to the garage for the roadster and filled up with gas and oil, and headed south for Sullivan Street.

Since it was school hours it wasn't as noisy and dirty around there as it had been before, and it was different otherwise. I might have expected the decorations, but it hadn't occurred to me. There was a big black rosette with long black ribbons hanging on the door and above it was a large wreath of leaves and flowers. A few people were standing around, mostly across the street. A little distance off a cop stood on the sidewalk looking uninterested; but when my roadster pulled up some yards short of the door with the wreath on it I saw him cock an eye at me. I got out and went over to him to say hello.

I handed him a card. "I'm Archie Goodwin of Nero Wolfe's office. We were engaged by Maffei's sister to look for him the day before his body was found. I've come to see the landlady and check up a little."

"Yeah?" The cop stuck my card in a pocket. "I don't know a thing except that I'm standing here. Archie Goodwin? Pleased to meet you."

We shook hands and as I moved off I asked him to keep an eye on my car.

Mrs. Ricci didn't seem very glad to see me, but I could understand that easy enough. That dick O'Grady had probably raked her over for letting me take stuff from Maffei's room, of course without any right or reason, but that wouldn't deter O'Grady. I grinned when I saw the landlady's lips go shut, getting ready for the questions she thought I had come to ask. It's never any fun having a murdered man lying upstairs, even when he was only a roomer. So I sympathized with her a little before I mentioned that I'd like to see Anna Fiore.

"She's busy."

"Sure. But this is important; my boss would like to see her. It would only take an hour or so, here, a couple of dollars—"

"No! For the love of God can't you let us alone in our house? Can't you let the poor woman bury her brother without cackling in her ears to drive her crazy? Who are you that—"

Of course she would have to pick me to blow up on. I saw it was hopeless to get any cooperation out of her, she wouldn't even listen to me, so I removed myself and went back to the front hall. The door to the dining room was open, but the room was empty. After I had slipped in there I heard footsteps in the hall, and, looking through the crack between the door and the jamb, I saw Mrs. Ricci start upstairs. She went on up, and I could hear her continue on the second flight. I stuck behind the door and waited, and luck came my way. Not more than ten minutes had passed before there were steps on the stairs, and using the crack again I saw Anna. I called her name, softly. She stopped and looked around. I called, still softly, "In the dining room." She came to the threshold and I moved around where she could see me.

"Hello, Anna. Mrs. Ricci told me to wait here till you came down."

"Oh. Mr. Archie."

"Sure. I came to take you for a ride. Mrs. Ricci was angry that I came for you, but you remember on Wednesday I gave her a dollar? Today I gave her two dollars, so she said all right. But hurry up; I told her we'd be back before noon."

I grabbed Anna's hand, but she held back. "In that car like the other day?"

"Sure. Come on."

"My jacket is upstairs and look at my dress."

"It's too warm for a jacket. Hurry; what if Mrs. Ricci changed her mind? We can buy you one—come on."

With my hand on her arm I worked her out of the dining room and down the short hall to the entrance door, but I didn't want to look anxious outside; there was no telling how important that cop might think he was and any interruption might queer it. So I threw the door open and said, "Go on and get in, I'll tell Mrs. Ricci good-by." I waited only a few seconds before I followed her; she was at the roadster opening the door. I went around to my side and climbed in, stepped on the starter, waved to the flatfoot, and shot off down Sullivan Street in second with the engine roaring so that no yelling from an upstairs window could hurt Anna's ears.

She certainly was a scarecrow. Her dress was a sight. But I wasn't ashamed to have her beside me as, headed uptown again, I circled through Washington Square and rolled into Fifth Avenue. Not a bit. The clock on the dash said twenty after ten.

Anna said, "Where are we going, Mr. Archie?"

I said, "You see how it is about your dress in this low seat? Nobody can see you anyway except your face and there's nothing wrong with that. What do you say we drive around Central Park? It's a beautiful morning."

"Oh yes."

I didn't say anything and she didn't either for about ten blocks and then she said again, "Oh yes."

She was certainly having a swell time. I went on up the Avenue and into the park at Sixtieth. Up the west side to 110th, across to Riverside Drive, up to Grant's Tomb, where I circled around and turned downtown. I don't think she glanced at the trees or the grass or the river once; she kept looking at people in other cars. It was five minutes to eleven when I drew up in front of Wolfe's house.

Mrs. Ricci had already telephoned twice. Fritz had a funny look when he told me about it. I settled that at once by calling her up and giving her a piece about obstructing justice. I didn't know how much of it she heard with her yelling, but it seemed to work; we didn't hear another peep out of her before noon, when I left to take Anna home.

Wolfe came in while I was phoning Mrs. Ricci. I watched him stopping to tell the girl good morning on his way to the desk. He was elegant with women. He had some sort of a perverted idea about them that I've never caught the hang of but every time I had ever seen him with one he was elegant. I couldn't describe how he did it because I couldn't make it out myself; it was hard to see how that enormous lump of flesh and folds could ever be called elegant, but he certainly was. Even when he was bullying one of them, like the time he sweated the Diplomacy Club business out of Nyura Pronn. That was the best exhibition of squeezing a sponge dry I've ever seen.

He started softly with Anna Fiore. After he had flipped through the mail, he turned and looked at her a minute before he said, "We no longer need to indulge in any conjectures as to the whereabouts of your friend Carlo Maffei. Accept my condolences. You have viewed the body?"

"Yes, sir."

"It is a pity, a real pity, for he did not seek violence; he got in its path by misadventure. It is curious on how slender a thread the destiny of a man may hang; for example, that of the murderer of Carlo Maffei may hang on this, Miss Fiore: when and under what circumstances did you see a golf club in Maffei's room?"

"Yes, sir."

"Yes. It will be easy to tell us now. Probably my question the other day recalled the occasion to your mind."

"Yes, sir."

"It did?"

She opened her mouth but said nothing. I was watching her, and she looked odd to me. Wolfe asked her again, "It did?"

She was silent. I couldn't see that she was a bit nervous or frightened, she was just silent.

"When I asked you about this the other day, Miss Fiore, you seemed a little upset. I was sorry for that. Would you tell me why you were upset?"

"Yes, sir."

"Was it perhaps your memory of something unpleasant that happened the day you saw the golf club?"

Silence again. I saw that something was wrong. Wolfe hadn't asked the last question as if it meant anything. I knew the shades of the tones of his voice, and I knew he wasn't interested; at least, not in that question. Something had him off on another trail. All at once he shot another question at her in another tone.

"When did you decide to say 'Yes, sir,' to anything I might ask you?"

No answer; but without waiting Wolfe went on: "Miss Fiore, I would like to make you understand this. My last question had nothing whatever to do with a golf club or with Carlo Maffei. Don't you see that? So if you have decided to reply nothing but 'Yes, sir,' to anything I may ask about Carlo Maffei that will be all right. You have an absolute right to do that because that is what you decided to do. But if I ask you about other things you have no right to say 'Yes, sir,' then, because that is not what you decided to do. About other things you should talk just as anyone would. So, when you decided to say nothing but 'Yes, sir,' to me, was it on account of anything that Carlo Maffei had done?"

Anna was looking hard at him, right at his eye. It was clear that she wasn't suspecting him or fighting against him, she was merely trying to understand him. She looked and he looked back. After a minute of that she said, "No, sir."

"Ah! Good. It was not on account of anything he had done. Then it had nothing to do with him, so it is all right for you to tell me anything about it that I may ask. You see that, of course. If you have decided to tell me nothing of Carlo Maffei I won't ask you. But this other business. Did you decide to say 'Yes, sir,' to Mr. O'Grady, the man that came and asked you questions yesterday morning?"

"Yes, sir."

"Why did you do that?"

She frowned, but said, "Because something happened."

"Good. What happened?"

She shook her head.

"Come, Miss Fiore." Wolfe was quiet. "There is no reason on earth why you shouldn't tell me."

She turned her head to look at me, and then back at him again. After a moment she said, "I'll tell Mr. Archie."

"Good. Tell Mr. Archie."

She spoke to me. "I got a letter."

Wolfe shot a glance at me and I took it up. "You got a letter yesterday?"

She nodded. "Yesterday morning."

"Who was it from?"

"I don't know. There was no name, it was on a typewriter, and on the envelope it said only Anna and the address, not the rest of my name. Mrs. Ricci gets the mail from the box and she brought it to me but I didn't want to open it where she was because I never get a letter. I went downstairs where I sleep and opened it."

"What did it say?"

She looked at me a moment without replying, and then suddenly she smiled, a funny smile that made me feel queer so that it wasn't easy to look at her. But I kept my eyes on hers. Then she said, "I'll show you what was in it, Mr. Archie," and reached down and pulled her skirt up above her knee, shoved her hand down inside of her stocking, and brought it out again with something in it. I stared as she unrolled five twenty-dollar bills and spread them out for me to see.

"You mean that was in the letter?"

She nodded. "One hundred dollars."

"So I see. But there was something typewritten."

"Yes. It said that if I would never tell anyone anything about Mr. Maffei or anything he ever did I could keep the money. But if I would not do that, if I told about him, I would have to burn it. I burned the letter, but I will not burn the money. I will keep it."

"You burned the letter?"

"Yes."

"And the envelope?"

"Yes."

"And you think you won't tell anyone about Mr. Maffei or about that golf club?"

"I never will."

I looked at her. Wolfe's chin was on his chest, but he was looking at her too. I got up from my chair. "Well, of all the damn fairy stories—"

"Archie! Apologize."

"But good heavens—"

"Apologize."

I turned to the girl. "I apologize, but when I think of all the gas I burned up riding you around the park—" I sat down.

Wolfe said, "Miss Fiore, did you happen to notice the postmark? The little round thing on the envelope that tells where it was mailed?"

"No, sir."

"Of course not. By the way, that money did not belong to the man who sent it to you. He took it from Carlo Maffei's pocket."

"I will keep it, sir."

"No doubt you will. You may not be aware that if the police knew of this they would take it from you ruthlessly. But do not be alarmed; your confidence in Mr. Archie is not misplaced." He turned to me. "Grace and charm are always admirable qualities and sometimes useful. Take Miss Fiore home."

I protested. "But why not—"

"No. Get her to burn those bills by replacing them from your expense book? No. She would not do it; but even if she would, I would not see money burned to save beauty herself from any grave that might be dug for her. The destruction of money is the only authentic sacrilege left us to abhor. Possibly you don't realize what that hundred dollars means to Miss Fiore; to her it represents the unimaginable reward for a desperate and heroic act. Now that she has it safely back in its crypt, take her home." He started to get himself out of his chair. "Good day, Miss Fiore. I have paid you a rare compliment; I have assumed that you mean what you say. Good morning."

I was at the door telling her to come on.

Going back downtown I let her alone. I was plenty sore, after kidnaping her and driving her around in style for nearly an hour, to have her go moron on us, but there was no use wasting breath on her. At Sullivan Street I just dumped her out on the sidewalk with a good deal of satisfaction, thinking that Wolfe had been elegant enough for both of us.

She stood there. As I pulled the gearshift lever to go on she said, "Thank you, Mr. Archie."

She was being elegant! She had caught it from Wolfe. I said, "You're not welcome, Anna, but good-by and no hard feelings," and rolled off.

VI

IT WAS during the half-hour that I was gone taking Anna Fiore home that Wolfe had a relapse. It was a bad one, and it lasted three days. When I got back to Thirty-fifth Street he was sitting in the kitchen, by the little table where I always ate breakfast, drinking beer with three bottles already gone, arguing with Fritz whether chives should be used in tomato tarts. I stood and listened a few minutes without saying anything, then I went upstairs to my room and got a bottle of rye from the closet and took a drink.

I had never really understood Wolfe's relapses. Sometimes it seemed plain that it was just ordinary discouragement and funk, like the time the taxi-driver ran out on us in the Pine Street case, but other times there was no accounting for it at all. Everything would be sailing along and it would look to me as if we were about ready to wrap up the package and deliver it C.O.D., when for no reason at all he would lose interest. He was out and that was all there was to it. Nothing that I could say made the slightest dent on him. It might last anywhere from one afternoon up to a couple of weeks, or it was even possible that he was out for good and wouldn't come back until something new turned up. While it lasted he acted one of two different ways: either he went to bed and stayed there, living on bread and onion soup, refusing to see anyone but me and forbidding me to mention anything I had on my mind; or he sat in the kitchen telling Fritz how to cook things and then eating them on my little table. He ate a whole half a sheep that way in two days once, different parts of it cooked in twenty different ways. At such times I usually had my tongue out from running all over town from the Battery to Bronx Park, trying to find some herb or root or maybe cordial that they needed in the dish they were going to do next. The only time I ever quit Wolfe was when he sent me to a Brooklyn dock where a tramp steamer from China was tied up, to try to buy some baddenroot from the captain. The captain must have had a cargo of opium or something to make him suspicious; anyway he took it for granted that I was looking for trouble and filled my order by having half a dozen skinny savages wrap things around my skull. I quit the next afternoon, phoning from the hospital, but a day later Wolfe came and took me home, and I was so astonished that he actually came himself that I forgot I had quit. That finished that relapse, too.

This day I knew it was a relapse as soon as I saw him sitting in the kitchen arguing with Fritz, and I was so disgusted that after I had gone upstairs and had a couple of drinks I came down again and went out. I started walking, but after a few blocks the appetite from the drinks was quite active and I stopped at a restaurant for a meal. No restaurant meal was much after seven years of Fritz's everyday cooking, but I wouldn't go home to eat; in the first place I was disgusted and in the second place those relapse menus couldn't be depended on—sometimes it was a feast for an epicure, sometimes it was a dainty little taste good for eighty cents in Schrafft's, and sometimes it was just a mess.

But after the meal I felt better, and I walked back to Thirty-fifth Street and told Wolfe what Anderson had said that morning and added that it looked to me as if there would be something doing before the full moon came.

Wolfe was still sitting at the little table, watching Fritz stir something in a pan. He looked at me as if he was trying to remember where he had seen me before. He said, "Don't ever mention that shyster's name to me again."

I said, hoping to get him sore, "This morning I phoned Harry Foster at the *Gazette* and told him what was up. I knew you'd want plenty of publicity."

He didn't hear me. He said to Fritz, "Have boiling water ready in case it should disunite."

I went upstairs to tell Horstmann he'd have to nurse his babies alone that afternoon and maybe for a week. He would be miserable. It was always funny how he pretended to be annoyed when Wolfe was around but if anything happened to keep Wolfe from showing up on the dot at nine or four he was so worried and anxious you might have thought mealy bugs were after him. So I went upstairs to make him miserable.

That was two o'clock Friday afternoon, and the first sane look I got from Wolfe was eleven Monday morning, sixty-nine hours later.

In between things happened a little. First was the telephone call from Harry Foster Friday around four. I'd been expecting it. He said they had dug Barstow up and done the autopsy but wouldn't make any announcement. It wasn't his story any more; others had got wind of it and were hanging around the coroner's office.

A little after six the second phone call came. This time it was Anderson. I grinned when I heard his voice and glanced at my wrist; I could see him fuming around waiting for six o'clock. He said he wanted to talk to Wolfe.

"I'm sorry, Mr. Wolfe is busy. This is Goodwin."

He said he wanted Wolfe to come to White Plains. I laughed at him. He rang off. I didn't like it; he struck me as a bad guy. After thinking it over a little I called up Henry H. Barber at his apartment and got all the dope on things like accessories and arrests of material witnesses. Then I went to the kitchen and told Wolfe about the two phone calls. He wiggled a spoon at me.

"Archie. This Anderson is a disease. Cleanse the telephone. Did I forbid mention of his name?"

I said, "I'm sorry, I should have known better. You know what I think, sir. A nut is always a nut even when it's you. I want to talk to Fritz."

Wolfe wasn't listening. I told Fritz that for dinner I would come and get sandwiches and take them to the office, and then I told him that when the buzzer rang, until further notice, he was not to go to the door, I would attend to it. Under no circumstances was he to open the door.

I knew it was probably uncalled-for precaution, but I was taking no chances on anyone busting in there with Wolfe in one of his Bloomingdale moods. I was glad he hadn't tried to send me for anything and I hoped he wouldn't, for I wouldn't have gone. If it was a washout, all right, but I wasn't going to let them make ninnies of us if I could help it. Nothing happened that night. The next morning I stayed out of Wolfe's way, mostly in the front room, opening the door to a gas man and an expressman, and once to a slick youth that wanted to get helped through college. I helped him as far as the bottom of the stoop. It was around eleven when I obeyed the buzzer by opening the door again and found a big husky standing against it, coming in with it, his foot sliding along. I gave him a good solid stiff-arm and pushed him back, and went on out, shutting the door behind me.

I said, "Good morning. Who invited you?"

He said, "It wasn't you anyhow. I want to see Nero Wolfe."

"You can't. He's sick. What do you want?"

He smiled, being smooth, and handed me a card. I looked at it.

"Sure. From Anderson's office. His right-hand man? What do you want?"

"You know what I want." He smiled. "Let's go in and talk it over."

I didn't see any sense in trying to be coy. Anyway I had no idea when Wolfe might kick out of it, and that made me sick. So I covered it all in as few words as possible. I told him that Wolfe didn't know one thing that they didn't know, at least nothing that applied to Barstow, and that what he did know came to him in a dream. I told him that if they wanted Wolfe on the case at a price to say so and name the price and he would take it or leave it. I told him that if they wanted to try any funny warrants they would be surprised how funny they'd turn out to be before Wolfe got through with them. Then I told him that I could see that he weighed twenty pounds more than I did and that therefore I wouldn't attempt to go back in the house until he had departed, and that I would appreciate it if he would get a move on because I was reading an interesting book.

He inserted a few remarks as I went along, but when I finished all he said was, "Tell Wolfe he can't get away with it."

"Sure. Any other message?"

"Just go to hell for you."

I grinned, and stood on the stoop watching him as he walked off, headed east. I had never heard of him before, but I didn't know Westchester very well. The name on the card was H. R. Corbett. I went back to the front room and sat and smoked cigarettes.

After lunch, some time around four, I heard a newsy out in the street calling an extra. I went out and called him and bought one. There it was taking up half of the front page: BARSTOW POISONED—DART FOUND IN BODY. I read it through. If ever I had a pain in the neck it was then. Of course Wolfe and I weren't mentioned; I hadn't expected that; but to think of what that piece might have meant to us! I kicked myself for bungling with Derwin, and again with Anderson, for I was sure it could have been handled somehow to let us in, though it was hard to see how. And I kicked Wolfe for his damn relapse. At least I wanted to. I read it again. It wasn't a dart at all, it was a short steel needle, just as Wolfe had said, and it had been found below the stomach. Sore as I was at Wolfe, I handed it to him. There was his picture.

I went to the kitchen and laid the paper on the table in front of Wolfe without a word, and went out again. He called after me, "Archie! Get the car, here's a list for you."

I pretended I didn't hear. Later Fritz went.

Next day the Sunday papers were full of it. They had sent their packs running around sniffing all over Westchester County, but they hadn't found a thing. I read all the articles through, and I learned a lot of details about the Green Meadow Club, the Barstow family, the Kimballs who had been in the foursome, the doctor who had pulled a boner, and a lot besides, but nobody really knew any more than Wolfe had known Wednesday evening when he had asked Anna Fiore if she had ever seen a golf club in Carlo Maffei's room. Not as much, for there was no accepted theory as to how the needle got in Barstow's belly. All the papers had pieces by experts on poisons and what they do to you.

Sunday evening I went to a movie, telling Fritz to open the door to no one. Not that I expected anything; it looked as if Anderson was playing his own hand. Possibly, through motive or discoveries he had made, he was really lining it up. I would have got drunk that evening if it hadn't been Sunday. When I got back from the movie Wolfe had gone up to his room, but Fritz was still in the kitchen washing up. I fried a piece of ham to make myself a sandwich and poured a glass of milk, for I hadn't had much dinner. I noticed that the *Times* I had put there in the morning for Wolfe was still on top of the refrigerator just as I had left it. It was ten to one he hadn't looked at it.

I read in my room until after midnight and then had trouble going to sleep on account of my mind working. But apparently there was no trouble about it after I once got started, for when I pried my eyes open in the morning enough to glance at the clock on the stand it was after nine. I was sitting on the edge of the bed yawning when I heard a noise overhead that woke me up good. Either that was two pairs of footsteps and I knew both of them or I was still dreaming. I went out in the hall and listened a minute and then ran downstairs. Fritz was in the kitchen drinking coffee. "Is that Mr. Wolfe up with Horstmann?"

"And how." That was the only slang Fritz ever used and he always welcomed a chance to get it in. He smiled at me, glad to see me excited and happy. "Now I will just get a leg of lamb and rub garlic on it."

"Rub poison ivy on it if you want to." I went back up to dress.

The relapse was over! I was excited all right. I shaved extra clean and whistled in the bathtub. With Wolfe normal again anything might happen. When I got back down to the kitchen a dish of figs and a fat omelet were ready for me, and the newspaper was propped up against the coffeepot. I started on the headlines and the figs at the same time, but halfway through a fig I stopped chewing. I raced down the paragraphs, swallowing the mouthful whole to get it out of the way. It was plain, the paper stated it as a fact. Although no confirmation was needed, I turned the pages over, running my eyes up and down and across. It was on page eight toward the bottom, a neat little ad in a neat little box:

I WILL PAY FIFTY THOUSAND DOLLARS REWARD TO ANY PERSON OR PERSONS WHO WILL FURNISH INFORMATION RESULTING IN THE DISCOVERY AND RIGHTEOUS PUNISHMENT OF THE MURDERER OF MY HUSBAND PETER OLIVER BARSTOW

ELLEN BARSTOW

I read it through three times and then tossed the paper away and got calm. I finished the fruit and omelet, with three pieces of toast and three cups of coffee. Fifty grand, with the Wolfe bank balance sagging like a clothesline under a wet horse blanket; and not only that, but a chance of keeping our places on the platform in the biggest show of the season. I was calm and cool, but it was only twenty minutes after ten. I went to the office and opened the safe and dusted around and waited.

When Wolfe came down at eleven he looked fresh but not noticeably good-humored. He only nodded for good morning and didn't seem to care much whether I was there or not as he got himself into his chair and started looking through the mail. I just waited, thinking I would show him that other people could be as hard-boiled as he was, but when he began checking off the monthly bill from Harvey's I popped at him.

"I hope you had a nice week end, sir."

He didn't look at me, but I saw his cheeks folding. "Thank you, Archie. It was delightful; but on awakening this morning I felt so completely water-logged that with only myself to consider I would have remained in bed to await disintegration. Names battered at me: Archie Goodwin, Fritz Brenner, Theodore Horstmann; responsibilities; and I arose to resume my burden. Not that I complain; the responsibilities are mutual; but my share can be done only by me."

"Excuse me, sir, but you're a damn liar, what you did was look at the paper."

He checked off items on the bill. "You can't rile me, Archie, not today. Paper? I have looked at nothing this morning except life, and that not through a newspaper."

"Then you don't know that Mrs. Barstow has offered fifty thousand dollars for her husband's murderer?"

The pencil stopped checking; he didn't look at me, but the pencil was motionless in his fingers for seconds. Then he placed the bill under a paperweight, laid the pencil beside it, and lifted his head.

"Show it to me."

I exhibited first the ad and then the first-page article. Of the ad he read each word; the article he glanced through.

"Indeed," he said. "Indeed. Mr. Anderson does not need the money, even granting the possibility of his earning it, and only a moment ago I was speaking of responsibilities. Archie, do you know what I thought in bed this morning? I thought how horrible and how amusing it would be to send Theodore away and let all those living and breathing plants, all that arrogant and pampered loveliness, thirst and gasp and wither away."

"Good God!"

"Yes. Just an early morning fantasy; I haven't the will for such a gesture. I would be more likely to offer them at auction—should I decide to withdraw from responsibilities—and take passage for Egypt. You know of course that I own a house in Egypt which I have never seen. The man who gave it to me, a little more than ten years ago—yes, Fritz, what is it?"

Fritz was a little awry, having put on his jacket hurriedly to go to the door.

"A lady to see you, sir."

"Her name?"

"She had no card, sir."

Wolfe nodded, and Fritz went out. In a moment he was back on the threshold, bowing in a young woman. I was on my feet. She started toward me, and I inclined my head in Wolfe's direction. She looked at him, stopped, and said, "Mr. Nero Wolfe? My name is Sarah Barstow."

"Be seated," Wolfe said. "You must pardon me; for engineering reasons I arise only for emergencies."

"This is an emergency," she said.

VII

FROM the newspapers I was pretty well up on Sarah Barstow. She was twenty-five, popular, a graduate of Smith, and prominent both in university society at Holland and in various groups in summer Westchester. Of course beautiful, according to the papers. I thought to myself that this time that detail was accurate, as she arranged herself in a chair in front of Wolfe and sat with her eyes on him. She wore a tan linen dress with a coat to match and a little black hat on sideways. Her gloves showed that she was driving. Her face was a little small but everything on it was in place and well arranged; her eyes were too bright in the pupils and too heavy around the edges from tiredness, and from crying perhaps, and her skin was pale, but health and pleasantness showed through that. Her voice was low and had sense in it. I liked her.

She started to explain herself, but Wolfe wiggled a finger at her. "It is unnecessary, and possibly painful to you, Miss Barstow, I know. You are the only daughter of Peter Oliver Barstow. All you need tell is why you have come to me."

"Yes." She hesitated. "Of course you would know, Mr. Wolfe. It is a little difficult—perhaps I wanted a preamble." She had a try at a smile. "I am going to ask you a favor, I don't know how much of a favor it will be."

"I can tell you that."

"Of course. First I must ask you, do you know that my mother had an advertisement in the paper this morning?"

Wolfe nodded. "I have read it."

"Well, Mr. Wolfe, I—that is, we, the family—must ask you to disregard that advertisement."

Wolfe breathed and let his chin down. "An extraordinary request, Miss Barstow. Am I supposed to be as extraordinary in granting it, or do I get reasons?"

"There are reasons of course." She hesitated. "It is not a family secret, it is known that my mother is—in some degree and on various occasions

—irresponsible." Her eyes were earnest on him. "You must not think there is anything ugly about this or that it has anything to do with money. There is plenty of money and my brother and I are not niggardly. Nor must you think that my mother is not a competent person —certainly not in the legal sense. But for years there have been times when she needed our attention and love, and this—this terrible thing has come in the middle of one of them. She is not normally vengeful, but that advertisement—my brother calls it a demand for blood. Our close friends will of course understand, but there is the world, and my father—my father's world was a wide one—we are glad if they help us mourn for him but we would not want them—Father would not want them—to watch us urging on the bloodhounds—"

She gave a little gasp and stopped, and glanced at me and back at Wolfe. He said, "Yes, Miss Barstow, you are calling me a bloodhound. I am not offended. Go on."

"I'm sorry. I'm a tactless fool. It would have been better if Dr. Bradford had come."

"Was Dr. Bradford considering the enterprise?"

"Yes. That is, he thought it should be done."

"And your brother?"

"Well—yes. My brother greatly regrets it, the advertisement I mean. He did not fully approve of my coming to see you. He thought it would be—fruitless."

"On the theory that it is difficult to call off a bloodhound. Probably he understands dogs. Have you finished, Miss Barstow? I mean, have you any further reasons to advance?"

She shook her head. "Surely, Mr. Wolfe, those are sufficient."

"Then as I understand it, your desire is that no effort be made to discover and punish the persons who murdered your father?"

She stared at him. "Why—no. I didn't say that."

"The favor you ask of me is that I refrain from such an effort?"

Her lips closed. She opened them enough to say, "I see. You are putting it as badly as possible."

"Not at all. Clearly, not badly. Understandably, your mind is confused; mine is lucid. Your position as you have so far expressed it is simply not intelligent. You may make any one of several requests of me, but you may not ask them all at once, for they are mutually exclusive. You may, for instance, tell me that while you are willing that I should discover the murderer, you request me not to expect to be paid for it as your mother has offered. Is that your request?"

"It is not. You know it is not."

"Or you may tell me that I may find the murderer if I can, and collect the reward if I choose to take advantage of the legal obligation, but that the family disapproves of the offer of reward on moral grounds. Is that it?"

"Yes." Her lip trembled a little, but in a moment she pulled it up firm. Then suddenly she stood up and shot at him, "No! I'm sorry I came here. Professor Gottlieb was wrong; you may be clever—good day, Mr. Wolfe."

"Good day, Miss Barstow." Wolfe was motionless. "The engineering considerations keep me in my chair."

She was going. But halfway to the door she faltered, stood a moment, and turned. "You *are* a bloodhound. You are. You are heartless."

"Quite likely." Wolfe crooked a finger. "Come back to your chair. Come, do; your errand is too important to let a momentary resentment ruin it. That's better; self-control is an admirable quality. Now, Miss Barstow, we can do one of two things: either I can flatly but gracefully refuse your original request as you made it and we can part on fairly bad terms; or you can answer a few questions I would like to ask and we can then decide what's to be done. Which shall it be?"

She was groggy, but game. She was back in her chair and had a wary eye on him. She said, "I have answered many questions in the past two days."

"I don't doubt it. I can imagine their tenor and their stupidity. I shall not waste your time or insult your intelligence. How did you learn that I knew anything of this business?"

She seemed surprised. "How did I learn it? Why, you are responsible for it. That is, you discovered it. Everyone knows it. It was in the paper—not New York, the White Plains paper."

I had a grin at that. Derwin would phone Ben Cook to come and assist me to the station, would he?

Wolfe nodded. "Have you asked the favor of Mr. Anderson that you have asked of me?"

"No."

"Why not?"

She hesitated. "Well—it didn't seem necessary. It didn't seem— I don't know how to express it."

"Use your wits, Miss Barstow. Was it because it appeared unlikely that he would do any discovering worthy the name?"

She was holding herself tight. Her hands—damn good hands with strong fingers and honest knuckles—were little fists in her lap. "No!" she said.

"Very well. But what made you think it likely, at least possible, that my discovering might be more to the point?"

She began, "I didn't think—" But he stopped her.

"Come, control yourself. It is an honest plain question. You did think me more competent at discovery than Mr. Anderson, did you not? Was it because I had made the original discovery?"

"Yes."

"That is, because I had somehow known that your father was killed by a poisoned needle propelled from the handle of a golf club?"

"I—don't—know. I don't know, Mr. Wolfe."

"Courage. This will soon be over. Curiosity alone prompts the next question. What gave you the strange idea that I was so rare a person as to respond favorably to the idiotic request you meant to make of me?"

"I didn't know. I didn't have that idea really. But I was ready to try, and I had heard a professor at the university, Gottlieb, the psychologist, mention your name—he had written a book called *Modern Crime Detection*—"

"Yes. A book that an intelligent criminal should send as a gift to every detective he knows."

"Perhaps. His opinion of you is more complimentary. When I telephoned Professor Gottlieb he said that you were not susceptible of analysis because you had intuition from the devil, and that you were a sensitive artist as well as a man of probity. That sounded—well, I decided to come to see you. Mr. Wolfe, I beg you—I beg of you—"

I was sure she was going to cry and I didn't want her to. But Wolfe brusquely brought her up.

"That's all, Miss Barstow. That is all I need to know. Now I shall ask a favor of you: will you permit Mr. Goodwin to take you upstairs and show you my plants?"

She stared; he went on, "No subterfuge is intended. I merely wish to be alone with the devil. Half an hour perhaps; and to make a telephone call. When you return I shall have a proposal for you." He turned to me. "Fritz will call you."

She got up and came with me without a word. I thought that was pretty good, for she was shaky and suspicious all over. Instead of asking her to walk up two flights of stairs I took her down the hall and used Wolfe's elevator. As we got out on the top floor she stopped me by catching my arm.

"Mr. Goodwin. Why did Mr. Wolfe send me up here?"

I shook my head. "No good, Miss Barstow. Even if I knew I wouldn't tell you, and since I don't know we might as well look at the flowers."

As I opened the door to the passage Horstmann appeared from the potting room. "All right, Horstmann. May we look around a little?" He nodded and trotted back.

As many times as I had been there, I never went in the plant rooms without catching my breath. It was like other things I've noticed; for instance, no matter how often you may have seen Snider leap in the air and one-handed spear a hot liner like one streak of lightning stopping another one, when you see it again your heart stops. It was that way in the plant rooms.

Wolfe used concrete benches and angle-iron staging, with a spraying system Horstmann had invented for humidity. There were three main rooms, one for Cattleyas, Laelias, and hybrids, one for Odontoglossums, Oncidiums, and Miltonia hybrids, and the tropical room. Then there was the potting room, Horstmann's den, and a little corner room for propagation. Supplies—pots, sand, sphagnum, leafmold, loam, osmundine, charcoal, crocks—were kept in an unheated and unglazed room in the rear alongside the shaft where the outside elevator came up.

Since it was June the lath screens were on, and the slices of shade and sunshine made patterns everywhere—on the broad leaves, the blossoms, the narrow walks, the ten thousand pots. I liked it that way, it seemed gay.

It was a lesson to watch the flowers get Miss Barstow. Of course when she went in she felt about as much like looking at flowers as I did like disregarding her mother's ad, and down the first rows of Cattleyas she tried to be polite enough to pretend there was something there to see. The first one that really brought her up was a small side-bench, only twenty or so, of *Laeliocattleya Lustre*. I was pleased because it was one of my favorites. I stopped behind her.

"Astonishing," she said. "I've never seen one like that. The colors —amazing."

"Yes. It's a bi-generic hybrid, they don't come in nature like that."

She got interested. In the next walk were some *Brassocattlaelias Truffautianas* and I cut off a couple and handed them to her. I told her a little about hybridization and seedlings and so on, but maybe she didn't hear me. Then, in the next room, I had a disappointment. She liked the Odontoglossums better than the Cattleyas and hybrids! I suspected it was because they were more expensive and difficult, but it turned out that she hadn't known that. No accounting for tastes, I thought. And best of all, even after we had been through the tropical room, she liked a little thing I had never looked at twice, a *Miltonia blueanaeximina*. She talked about its delicacy and form. I nodded and began to lose interest, and anyway I was wondering what Wolfe was up to. Then at last Fritz appeared. He came down the walk clear up to us and bent himself at the middle and said that Mr. Wolfe expected us. I grinned and would have liked to dig him in the ribs as I went by, but I knew he'd never forgive me.

Wolfe was still in his chair, and there was no indication that he had been out of it. He nodded at Miss Barstow's chair and at mine, and waited till we were arranged to say, "You liked the flowers?"

"They are wonderful." She had a new eye on him, I could see that. "They are too much beauty."

Wolfe nodded, "At first, yes. But a long intimacy frees you of that illusion, and it also acquaints you with their scantiness of character. The effect they have produced on you is only their bluff. There is not such a thing as too much beauty."

"Perhaps." She had lost interest in the orchids. "Yes, perhaps."

"Anyway they passed your time. And of course you would like to know how I passed mine. First I telephoned my bank and asked them to procure immediately a report on the financial standing of Ellen Barstow, your mother, and the details of the will of Peter Oliver Barstow, your father. I then telephoned Dr. Bradford and endeavored to persuade him to call on me this afternoon or evening, but he will be otherwise engaged. I then sat and waited. Five minutes ago my bank telephoned me the report I had requested. I sent Fritz for you. Those were my activities."

She was getting worked up again. Her lips were getting tight. Apparently she didn't intend to open them.

He went on. "I said I would have a proposal for you. Here it is. Your notebook, Archie. Verbatim, please. I shall use my best efforts to find the murderer of Peter Oliver Barstow. I shall disclose the result of my efforts to you, Sarah Barstow, and if you interpose no objection I shall also disclose them to the proper public authorities, and at the proper time shall expect a check for the sum your mother has offered as a reward. But if my inquiries lead to the conclusion that the murderer is actually the person you fear it is, whom you are now endeavoring to shield from justice, there will be no further disclosure. Mr. Goodwin and I will know; no one else ever will. Just a moment! This is a speech, Miss Barstow; please hear all of it. Two more points. You must understand that I can make this proposal with propriety. I am not a public servant, I am not even a member of the bar, and I have sworn to uphold no law. The dangerous position of an accessory after the fact does not impress me. Then: if your fears prove to be justified, and I withhold disclosure, what of the reward? I find I am too sentimental and romantic to make it part of this proposal that under those circumstances the reward shall be paid. The word blackmail actually strikes me as unpleasant. But though I am handicapped by romance and sentiment, at least I have not pride further to hamper me, and if you should choose to present a gift it would be accepted. Read it aloud, Archie, to make sure it is understood."

Miss Barstow's voice was first. "But this—it's absurd! It—"

Wolfe wiggled a finger at her. "Don't. Please. You would deny that you came here with that nonsense to shield someone? Miss Barstow! Really now. Let us keep this on a decent level of intelligence. Read it, Archie."

I read it through from my notes. When I had finished Wolfe said, "I advise you to take it, Miss Barstow. I shall proceed with my inquiry in any event, and if the result is what you fear it would be convenient for you to have the protection I offer. The offer, by the way, is purely selfish. With this agreement I shall expect your interest and cooperation, since it would be well for you, no matter what the outcome, to get it over with as speedily as possible; without it I shall expect considerable obstruction. I am no altruist or *bon enfant,* I am merely a man who would like to make some money. You said there was too much beauty upstairs; no, but there is too much expense. Have you any idea what it costs to grow orchids like that?"

Sarah Barstow only stared at him.

"Come," Wolfe said. "There will of course be no signing. This is what is humorously called a gentlemen's agreement. The first step in fulfilling it will be for Mr. Goodwin to call at your home tomorrow morning—it can wait till then—to talk, with your permission, with yourself and your brother and mother and whosoever—"

"No!" she exploded. Then she shut up.

"But yes. I'm sorry, but it is essential. Mr. Goodwin is a man of discretion, common decency, and immeasurable valor. It really is essential. I'll tell you what, Miss Barstow." He put his hands on the edge of the desk and shoved his chair back, moved his hands to the arms of the chair and got himself to his feet, and stood in front of her. "You go on home, or about your errands, whatever they may be. People often find it difficult to think in my presence, I do not leave enough space. I know you are suffering, your emotions are tormenting you with their unbearable clamor, but you must free your mind to do its work. Go. Buy hats, or keep a rendezvous, or attend to your mother, whatever you may have in mind. Telephone me this evening between six and seven and tell me what time Mr. Goodwin may arrive in the morning, or tell me that he is not to come and we are enemies. Go."

She stood up. "Well—I don't know—my God, I don't know—"

"Please! That is not your mind speaking, it's the foam of churned feelings and has no meaning. I do not wish to be your enemy."

She was right in front of him, facing him, with her chin tilted up so that her eyes could be on his. "I believe you," she said. "I really believe you don't."

"Indeed, I do not. Good day, Miss Barstow."

"Good day, Mr. Wolfe."

I took her to the front door and let her out. I thought she might have handed me a good day too, but she didn't. She didn't say anything. As she went out I saw her car at the curb, a dark blue coupé.

Back in the office, Wolfe was in his chair again. I stood on the other side of the desk looking at him.

"Well," I said, "what do you know about that?"

His cheeks folded. "I know I'm hungry, Archie. It is pleasant to have an appetite again. I've had none for weeks."

Naturally I was indignant; I stared at him. "You can say that, after Friday and Saturday and Sunday—"

"But no appetite. A desperate search for one. Now I'm hungry. Lunch will be in twenty minutes. Meantime: I have learned that there is a person attached to a golf club called a professional. Find out who fills that post at the Green Meadow Club; see if we have any grateful client who might introduce us on the telephone; invite the professional, urgently, to dine with us this evening. There is a goose left from Saturday. After lunch you will pay a visit to the office of Dr. Nathaniel Bradford, and stop at the library for some books I need."

"Yes, sir. Who do you think Miss Barstow—"

"Not now, Archie. I would prefer just to sit here quietly and be hungry. After lunch."

VIII

AT TEN o'clock Tuesday morning, June 13, I drove the roadster through the entrance gate of the Barstow place, after it had been opened for me by a state trooper who was there on guard. Another husky was with him, a private watchman of the Barstows', and I had to furnish plenty of proof that I was the Archie Goodwin Sarah Barstow was expecting. It looked likely that many a newspaper man had been sent to climb a tree around there in the past three days.

The house was at the low point of a saddle between two hills about seven miles northeast of Pleasantville. It was built of stone, quite large, well over twenty rooms I should say, and there were a lot of outbuildings. After going through about three hundred yards of trees and shrubbery the drive circled around the edge of an immense sloping lawn and entered under the shelter of a roof with two steps up to a flagged terrace. This was really the side of the house; the front was around the corner looking over the lawn down the hill. There were gardens ahead as you entered, and more gardens at the other edge of the lawn, with boulders and a pool. As I eased the roadster along taking it in I thought to myself that fifty grand was nothing. I had on a dark blue suit, with a blue shirt and a tan tie, and of course my panama which I had had cleaned right after Decoration Day. I've found it's a good idea to consider what kind of a place you're going to, and dress accordingly.

Sarah Barstow was expecting me at ten, and I was right on the dot. I parked the roadster in a graveled space the other side of the entrance, and pushed the button at the door on the terrace. It was standing open, but double screen doors kept me from seeing much inside. Soon there were footsteps and one of the screens came out at me and with it a tall skinny guy in a black suit.

He was polite. "If you will excuse me, sir. Mr. Goodwin?"

I nodded. "Miss Barstow expects me."

"I know. If you will come this way. Miss Barstow would like you to join her in the garden."

I followed him across the terrace and along a walk to the other side of the house, then down an arbor and among a lot of shrubbery till we came to an acre of flowers. Miss Barstow was on a shady bench over in a corner.

"All right," I said. "I see her."

He stopped, inclined his head, and turned and went back.

She looked bad, worse than she had the day before. She probably hadn't slept much. Forgetting or disregarding Wolfe's instructions on that detail, she had telephoned before six o'clock. I had taken the call, and her voice had sounded as if she was having a hard time of it. She had been short and businesslike, just said she would expect me at ten in the morning and hung up.

She invited me to sit beside her on the bench.

At bedtime the evening before Wolfe had given me no instructions whatever. Saying that he preferred to leave me fancy free, he had merely repeated his favorite saying, any spoke will lead an ant to the hub, and had reminded me that our great advantage lay in the fact that no one was aware how much or how little we knew and that on account of our original coup we were suspected of omniscience. He had finished, after a yawn that would have held a tennis ball, "Return here with that advantage unimpaired."

I said to Miss Barstow, "You may not have any orchids here, but you certainly have a flower or two."

She said, "Yes, I suppose so. I asked Small to bring you out here because I thought we should not be interrupted. You will not mind."

"No, indeed. It's nice out here. I'm sorry to have to pester you, but there's no other way to get the facts. Wolfe says that he feels phenomena and I collect facts. I don't think that means anything, having looked up the word phenomena in the dictionary, but I repeat it for what it's worth." I took out my notebook. "First just tell me things. You know, the family, how old are you, who you're going to marry, and so on."

She sat with her hands together in her lap and told me. Some of it I had read in the papers or got out of *Who's Who*, but I didn't interrupt. There was only her mother, her brother, and herself. Lawrence, her brother, was twenty-seven, two years older than her; he had graduated from Holland at twenty-one and had then proceeded to waste five years (and, I gathered between the lines, a good portion of his father's time and patience also). A year ago he had suddenly discovered a talent for mechanical design and was now devoted to that, especially as applied to airplanes. Her mother and father had been mutually devoted for thirty years. She could not remember the beginning of her mother's difficulty, for that had been years before, when Sarah was a child; the family had never considered it a thing to be ashamed of or to attempt to conceal, merely a misfortune of a loved one to sympathize with and as far as possible to ameliorate. Dr. Bradford and two specialists described it in neurological terms, but they had never meant anything to Sarah; to her the terms had been dead and cold and her mother was alive and warm.

The place in Westchester was the old Barstow family estate, but the family was able to be there less than three months of the year since it was necessary to live at the university from September to June. They came each summer with the servants for ten or eleven weeks, and closed the place up each fall on leaving. They knew many people in the surrounding countryside; her father's circle of acquaintance had of course been wide not only in Westchester, and some of his best and oldest friends lived within easy driving distance from the estate. She gave the names of these and I took them down. I also listed the names of the servants and details regarding them. I was doing that when Miss Bar-

stow suddenly got up from the bench and moved away to the path in
the sunshine, from under the shelter of the trees that shaded us. There
was the sound of an airplane overhead, so close that it had forced us
to raise our voices. I went on writing, "—Finnish, 6 yrs, N Y agcy, sgl,"
and then looked at her. Her head was way back showing all her throat,
with her gaze straight above, and one arm was up waving a handkerchief back and forth. I jumped out from under the trees and cocked an
eye at the airplane. It was right over us, down low, and two arms could
be seen extended, one from one side and one from the other, waving
back at her. The plane dipped a little, then swung around and headed
back, and soon was out of sight behind the trees.

She went back to the bench and I joined her; she was saying, "That
was my brother. This is the first time he has been up since my father—"

"He must be pretty reckless, and he certainly has long arms."

"He doesn't fly; at least, not solo. That was Manuel Kimball with
him, it's Mr. Kimball's plane."

"Oh. One of the foursome."

"Yes."

I nodded and went back to facts. I was ready for golf. Peter Oliver
Barstow had not been a zealot, she said. He had rarely played at the
university, and not oftener than once a week, occasionally twice, during the summer. He had nearly always gone to Green Meadow, where
he was a member; he of course had had a locker and kept his parapher-
nalia there. He had been quite good, considering the infrequency of his
play, averaging from ninety-five to a hundred. He had played usually
with friends his own age, but sometimes with his son and daughter. His
wife had never tried it. The foursome of that fatal Sunday, E. D.
Kimball and his son Manuel and Barstow and his son Lawrence, had
never before played together, she thought. Probably it had been an
accident of propinquity; her brother had not mentioned whether it had
been prearranged, but she knew that he did sometimes have a game
with Manuel. She especially doubted that the foursome had been arranged beforehand because it had been her father's first appearance at
Green Meadow that summer; the Barstows had come to Westchester
three weeks earlier than their custom on account of Mrs. Barstow's
condition, and Barstow had expected to return to the university that
Sunday night.

When she had said that Sarah Barstow stopped. I glanced up from
my notebook. Her fingers were twisted together and she was staring off
at the path, at nothing. She said, not to me, "Now he will not return
there at all. All the things he wanted to do—all he would have done—
not at all—"

I waited a little and then shook her out of it by asking, "Did your father leave his golf bag at Green Meadow all year?"

She turned back to me. "No. Why—of course not, because he sometimes used them at the university."

"He had only the one bag of clubs?"

"Yes!" She seemed emphatic.

"Then he brought them with him? You only got here Saturday noon. You drove down from the university and the luggage followed in a truck. Was the bag in the car or in the truck?"

It was easy to see that I was touching something raw. Her throat showed muscles and her arms pressed ever so little against her sides; she was tightening up. I pretended I didn't notice it, just waited with my pencil. She said, "I don't know. Really I don't remember."

"Probably in the truck," I said. "Since he wasn't much of a fan he probably wouldn't bother with it in the car. Where is it now?"

I expected that would tighten her up some more, but it didn't. She was calm but a little determined. "I don't know that either. I supposed you knew it can't be found."

"Oh," I said. "The golf bag can't be found?"

"No. The men from White Plains and Pleasantville have searched everywhere, this whole house, the club, even all over the links; they can't find it."

Yes, I thought to myself, and you, young lady, you're damn well pleased they can't! I said, "Do you mean to say that no one remembers anything about it?"

"No. That is, yes." She hesitated. "I understand that the boy who was caddying for Father says that he put the bag in the car, by the driver's seat, when they—when Larry and Dr. Bradford brought Father home. Larry and Dr. Bradford do not remember seeing it."

"Strange. I know I am not here to collect opinions, only facts, Miss Barstow, but if you will permit me, doesn't that strike you as strange?"

"Not at all. They were not likely to notice a golf bag at such a time."

"But after they got here—it must have been removed sometime—some servant, the chauffeur—"

"No one remembers it."

"I may speak with them?"

"Certainly." She was scornful. I didn't know what kind of a career she had mapped out, but I could have warned her not to try the stage.

That was that. It looked to me as if the kernel was gone, leaving practically no nut at all. I switched on her.

"What kind of a driver did your father use? Steel shaft or wooden?"

"Wood. He didn't like steel."

"Face plain or inset?"

"Plain, I think. I think so. I'm not sure I remember. Larry's has an inset, so has mine."

"You seem to remember your brother's all right."

"Yes." Her eyes were level at me. "This is not an inquisition, I believe, Mr. Goodwin."

"Pardon." I grinned at her. "Excuse it please, I'm upset. Maybe I'm even sore. There's nothing in Westchester County I'd rather look at than that golf bag, especially the driver."

"I'm sorry."

"Oh no, you're not. It raises a lot of questions. Who took the bag out of the car? If it was a servant, which one, and how loyal and incorruptible is he? Five days later, when it became known that one of the clubs had performed the murder it had been designed for, who got the bag and hid it or destroyed it? You or your brother or Dr. Bradford? You see the questions I'm up against. And where is it hidden or how was it destroyed? It isn't easy to get rid of a thing as big as that."

She had got up while I was talking and stood very composed and dignified. Her voice was composed too. "That will do. It wasn't in the agreement that I was to listen to idiotic insinuations."

"Bravo, Miss Barstow." I stood up too. "You're absolutely right, but I meant no offense, I'm just upset. Now, if I could see your mother for a moment. I'll not get upset any more."

"No. You can't see her."

"That *was* in the agreement."

"You have broken it."

"Rubbish." I grinned. "It's the agreement that makes it safe for you to let me take liberties with it. I'll take no liberties with your mother. While I may be a roughneck, I know when to keep my gloves on."

She looked at me. "Will five minutes be enough?"

"I don't know. I'll make it as short as possible."

She turned and started for the path that led toward the house, and I followed her. On the way I saw a lot of pebbles I wanted to kick. The missing golf bag was a hot one. Of course I hadn't expected to have the satisfaction of taking that driver back to Wolfe that evening, since Anderson would certainly have copped it. I gave him credit for being able to put two and two together after they have been set down for him ready to add; and I had counted on a request from Sarah Barstow to persuade him to let me give it the once-over. But now—the whole damn bag was gone! Whoever had done it, it not only gave me a pain, it struck me as pretty dumb. If it had been just the driver it would have made sense, but why the whole bag?

The house inside was swell. I mean, it was the kind of a house most people never see except in the movies. While there were plenty of windows, the light didn't glare anywhere, it came in soft, and the rugs and furniture looked very clean and careful and expensive. There were flowers around and it smelled good and seemed cool and pleasant, for outdoors the sun was getting hot. Sarah Barstow took me through a big hall and a big room, through to another hall, and on the other side of that through a door. Then we were in a sort of sun room, with one side all glazed, though most of the blinds were pulled down nearly to the floor so there wasn't much sunshine coming in. There were some plants, and a lot of wicker chairs and lounges. In one chair a woman sat by a table sorting out the pieces of a jig-saw puzzle. Miss Barstow went over to her.

"Mother. This is Mr. Goodwin. I told you he was coming." She turned to me and indicated a chair. I took it. Mrs. Barstow let the jig-saw pieces drop from her fingers and turned to look at me.

She was very handsome. She was fifty-six, her daughter had told me, but she looked over sixty. Her eyes were gray, deep-set and far apart, her hair was nearly white, and while her face with its fine features was quite composed, I got the impression that there was nothing easy or natural about that, it came from the force of a strong personal will. She kept looking at me without saying anything until I was guessing that I didn't look very composed myself. Sarah Barstow had taken a chair some distance away. I was about ready to open up from my end when Mrs. Barstow suddenly spoke.

"I know your business, Mr. Goodwin."

I nodded. "It really isn't my business, it is that of my employer, Mr. Nero Wolfe. He asked me to thank you for permitting me to come."

"He is welcome." The deep-set gray eyes never left me. "Indeed, I am grateful that someone—even a stranger whom I shall never see—should acknowledge my authority over the doors of my house."

"Mother!"

"Yes, Sarah. Don't be offended, dear; I know—and it is of no importance whether this Mr. Goodwin does or not—that the authority has not been usurped. It was not you who forced me to resign, it was not even your father. According to Than, it was God; probably His hands were idle and Satan furnished the mischief."

"Mother, please." Sarah Barstow had got up and approached us. "If you have anything to ask, Mr. Goodwin—"

I said, "I have two questions. May I ask you two questions, Mrs. Barstow?"

"Certainly. That is your business."

"Good. The first one is easy to ask, but may be hard to answer. That is, it may require thought and a long memory. Of all people, you are the one probably in the best position to answer. Who wanted, or might have wanted, to kill Peter Oliver Barstow? Who had a grievance against him, a new one or maybe a very old one? What enemies did he have? Who hated him?"

"That isn't a question. It is four questions."

"Well—maybe I can hitch them together."

"It isn't necessary." The composure did not escape from the will. "They can all be answered at once. Myself."

I stared at her. Her daughter was beside her with a hand on her shoulder.

"Mother! You promised me—"

"There, Sarah." Mrs. Barstow reached up and patted her daughter's hand. "You have not permitted those other men to see me, for which I have been thankful. But if Mr. Goodwin is to ask me questions he must have the answers. You remember what your father used to say? 'Never lay an ambush for truth.'"

Miss Barstow was at me. "Mr. Goodwin! Please!"

"Nonsense." The gray eyes were flashing. "I have my own security, daughter, as good as any you might provide for me. Mr. Goodwin, I have answered your first question. The second?"

"Don't rush me, Mrs. Barstow." I saw that if I just pretended Sarah Barstow wasn't there, Old Gray Eyes would be right with me. "I'm not done with the first one. There may have been others, maybe you weren't the only one."

"Others who might have wanted to kill my husband?" For the first time the will relaxed enough to let the twitch of a smile show on the lips. "No. That is impossible. My husband was a good, just, merciful and well-loved man. I see what you would have me do, Mr. Goodwin: look back over all the years, the happy ones and the miserable ones, and pick out of memory for you a remorseless wrong or a sinister threat. I assure you it isn't there. There is no man living my husband wronged, and none his enemy. Nor woman either. He did not wrong me. My answer to your question was direct and honest and was a relief to me, but since you are so young, not much more than a boy, it probably shocked you as it did my daughter. I would explain the answer if I could. I do not wish to mislead you. I do not wish to give pain to my daughter. When God compelled me to resign my authority He did not stop there. If by any chance you understand Him, you understand my answer too."

"All right, Mrs. Barstow. Then the second question: why did you offer a reward?"

"No!" Sarah Barstow stood between us. "No! No more of this—"

"Sarah!" The voice was sharp; then it softened a little. "Sarah dear. I *will* answer. This is my share. Will you stand between us? Sarah!"

Sarah Barstow went to her mother's side, placed her arm across her mother's shoulders, and lowered her forehead onto the gray hair.

The will re-created the composure. "Yes, Mr. Goodwin, the reward. I am not insane, I am only fantastic. I now greatly regret that the reward was offered, for I see its sordidness. It was in a fantastic moment that I conceived the idea of a unique vengeance. No one could have murdered my husband since no one could have wanted to. I am certain that his death has never seemed desirable to any person except myself, and to me only during torments which God should never impose even on the guiltiest. It came to me that there might be somewhere a man clever enough to bring God Himself to justice. I doubt if it is you, Mr. Goodwin; I do not know your employer. I now regret that I offered the reward, but if it is earned it will be paid."

"Thank you, Mrs. Barstow. Who is Than?"

"Sir?"

"Than. You said that Than told you God forced you to resign your authority."

"Oh. Of course. Dr. Nathaniel Bradford."

"Thank you." I closed my notebook and got up. "Mr. Wolfe asked me to thank you for your forbearance; I guess he knew there would be some if I got started filling up my notebook."

"Tell Mr. Wolfe he is welcome."

I turned and went on out, figuring that Miss Barstow could use my room for a while.

IX

MISS BARSTOW invited me to lunch.

I liked her better than ever. For ten minutes or more I waited for her in the hall which connected the sun room with other apartments. When she joined me there she wasn't sore, and I could see why: I hadn't pulled Mrs. Barstow's leg for any of that stuff, she had just handed it to me on a platter, and that wasn't my fault. But how many people in Sarah Barstow's place would have stopped to consider that? Not one in a thousand. They would have been sore anyhow, even if they had realized I didn't deserve it and tried not to show it; but she just wasn't sore. She had made a bargain and she was going through with it, no matter how many sleepless nights it brought her and no matter how many kinds of bad luck she had. She certainly had just had some. I could see that ten minutes earlier or ten minutes later Mrs. Barstow might have had different ideas in her head and all I would have got out of it would have been to exchange the time of day with a polite clam. I had no idea what it was that had happened to make her feel like opening up, but if it was my blue shirt and tan tie I hadn't wasted the money I had spent on them.

As Saul Panzer would have said, lovin' babe!

She invited me to lunch. She said her brother would be present, and since I would want to see him anyway that would be convenient. I thanked her. I said, "You're a good sport, Miss Barstow. A real one. Thank the Lord Nero Wolfe is the cleverest man on earth and thought up that agreement with you, because if you're in for trouble that's the only thing that will help you out of it."

"If I'm in for trouble," she said.

I nodded. "Sure, I know you've got plenty, but the one that bothers you most is your fear that there's worse ahead. I just wanted to say that you're a good sport."

As it turned out, I not only met her brother at lunch, I met Manuel Kimball too. I was glad of that, for it seemed to me that what I had learned that morning made the members of that foursome more important than they had been before. The preceding afternoon, after about two hours of telephoning, I had finally found a hook-up with the professional of the Green Meadow Club and he had accepted Wolfe's invitation to dinner. He had never had any dealings with Barstow, had only known him by sight, but Wolfe had got out of him twenty bushels of facts regarding the general set-up at the club and around the links. By the time the professional left to go home around midnight he had a bottle of Wolfe's best port inside of him, and Wolfe knew as much about a golf club as if he had been a professional himself. Among other things he learned that the members kept their bags in their lockers, that some of them left their lockers unlocked, and that even with the locked ones an ingenious and determined man could have got a duplicate key without any great difficulty. With such a key, of course, it would have been simple to await a propitious moment to open the locker, take the driver from the bag, and substitute another one. So Barstow's companions in the foursome that Sunday were of no more importance than any of the members or attendants or visitors who had access to the locker-rooms.

But now that was out, since Barstow's bag had not been in his locker since the September before. He had brought it down with him from the university. That changed the picture and made the members of the foursome a little more interesting than lots of other people.

Where we ate surely wasn't the dining room because it wasn't big enough, but it had a table and chairs and windows that you couldn't see much through on account of a lot of shrubbery just outside. The tall skinny guy in the black suit—otherwise Small, the butler, as an established guest like myself was aware—waited on us, and while the meal seemed to me a little light it was nothing that Fritz would have been ashamed of. There was some stuff in tambour shells that was first class. The table was small. I sat across from Miss Barstow, with her brother on my right and Manuel Kimball on my left.

Lawrence Barstow didn't resemble his sister any, but I could see traces of his mother. He was well put together and had the assurance that goes with his kind of life; his features were good and regular without anything noticeable about them. I've seen hundreds of him in the lunch restaurants in the Wall Street section and in the Forties. He had a trick of squinting when he decided to look at you, but I thought that was perhaps due to the blowing his eyes had got in the airplane breeze. The eyes were gray, like his mother's, but they didn't have the discipline behind them that hers had.

Manuel Kimball was quite different. He was dark and very neat and compact, with black hair brushed straight back and black restless eyes that kept darting around at us and seemed to find any degree of satisfaction or repose only when they were looking at Sarah Barstow. He made me nervous, and it seemed to me that he set Sarah Barstow a little on edge too, though that may have been only because he didn't know where I came in on the family crisis and wasn't supposed to know. That morning she had informed me that there had been no intimacy between the Kimballs and Barstows; the only points of contact had been propinquity in their summer residences and the fact that Manuel was a skilled amateur pilot and his offers to take Larry Barstow up and teach him to fly had been most convenient since Larry had developed an interest in airplane design. She herself had been up with Manuel Kimball two or three times the summer before, but aside from those occasions she had scarcely ever seen him except as the companion of her brother. The Kimballs were newcomers, having bought their place, two miles south, only three years previously. E. D. Kimball, Manuel's father, was known to the Barstows only slightly, through chance and infrequent meetings at large social or public gatherings. Manuel's mother was dead, long since, she had vaguely gathered. She could not remember that there had ever been more than a few casual words exchanged between her father and Manuel Kimball except one afternoon the preceding summer when Larry had brought Manuel to the Barstow place to settle a wager at tennis, and she and her father had acted as umpire and linesman.

In spite of which, I was interested in Manuel Kimball. He had at any rate been one of the foursome; and he looked like a foreigner and had a funny combination for a name, and he made me nervous.

At lunch the conversation was mostly about airplanes. Sarah Barstow kept it on that, when there was any sign of lagging, and once or twice when her brother started questions on affairs closer to her bosom she abruptly headed him off. I just ate. When Miss Barstow finally pushed her chair back, punching Small in the belly with it, we all stood up. Larry Barstow addressed me directly almost for the first time; I had seen indications of his idea that I might as well have been eating out back somewhere.

"You want to see me?"

I nodded. "If you can spare a quarter of an hour."

He turned to Manuel Kimball. "If you don't mind waiting, Manny. I promised Sis I'd have a talk with this man."

"Of course." The other's eyes darted to rest on Sarah Barstow. "Perhaps Miss Barstow would be kind enough to help me wait."

She said yes, without enthusiasm. But I got a word in. "I'm sorry." To Miss Barstow, "May I remind you that you agreed to be present with your brother?" It hadn't been mentioned, but I had taken it for granted, and I wanted her there.

"Oh." I thought she looked relieved. "Yes. I'm sorry, Mr. Kimball; shall we leave you here with the coffee?"

"No, thanks." He bowed to her and turned to Larry. "I'll trot along and have a look at that gas line. If one of your cars can run me over? Thanks. I'll be expecting you at the hangar any time— Thank you for a pleasant luncheon, Miss Barstow."

One thing that had surprised me about him was his voice. I had expected him, on sight, to sound like a tenor, but the effect he produced was more like that of a murmuring bull. The voice was deep and had a rumble in it, but he kept it low and quite pleasant. Larry Barstow went out with him to tell someone to take him home. His sister and I waited for Larry to come back, and then all three of us went out to the garden, to the bench where I had been taken on my arrival. Larry sat at one side on the grass, and Miss Barstow and I on the bench.

I explained that I wanted Miss Barstow present because she had made the agreement with Nero Wolfe and I wanted her to be satisfied that nothing was said or done that went beyond the agreement. I had certain things I wanted to ask Lawrence Barstow and if there was any question about my being entitled to answers she was the one to question it.

She said, "Very well, I'm here." She looked about played out. In the morning she had sat with her shoulders straight, but now she let them sag down.

Her brother said, "As far as I'm concerned—your name's Goodwin, isn't it?"

"That's it."

"Well, as far as I'm concerned, your agreement, as you call it, is nothing more than a piece of cheap insolence."

"Anything else, Mr. Barstow?"

"Yes. If you want it. Blackmail."

His sister had a flash left. "Larry! What did I tell you?"

"Wait a minute, Miss Barstow." I was flipping back the pages of my notebook. "Maybe your brother ought to hear it. I'll find it in a minute." I found the page. "Here it is." I read it just as Wolfe had said it, not too fast. Then I closed the notebook. "That's the agreement, Mr. Barstow. I might as well say that my employer, Mr. Nero Wolfe, keeps his temper pretty well under control, but every once in a while I blow up. If you call him a blackmailer once more the result will probably be bad all around. If you don't know a favor when you see it handed to you I suppose you'd think a sock on the jaw was a compliment."

He said, "Sis, you'd better go in the house."

"She can go in a minute," I said. "If the agreement is to go overboard she ought to see it sink. If you don't like it, why did you let her come to Wolfe's office alone to make it? He would have been glad to see you. He said to your sister, we shall proceed with the inquiry in any event. That's our business, not such a rotten one either, a few people think who have dealt with us. I say the same to you: agreement or no agreement, we're going to find out who murdered Peter Oliver Barstow. If you ask me, I think your sister made a swell bargain. If you don't think so there must be some reason, and that's one of the things we'll find out on the way."

"Larry," Miss Barstow said. Her voice was full of things. She repeated it. "Larry." She was telling him and asking him and reminding him all at the same time.

"Come on," I said. "You're all worked up and looking at me all through lunch didn't help you any, but if something goes wrong with your airplane you don't just kick and scream, do you? You pull your coat off and help fix it."

He sat looking not at me but his sister, with his lower lip stuck up and pushed out so that he looked half like a baby about ready to cry and half like a man set to tell the world to go to hell.

"All right, sis," he said finally. He showed no signs of apologizing to me, but I thought that could wait for a rainy day.

When I began feeding him questions he snapped out of it. He answered prompt and straight and, as far as I could see, without any figuring or hesitation anywhere. Even about the golf bag, where his sister had flopped around like a fish on a bank, it was all clear and ready with him. The bag had been brought down from the university on the truck; there had been no luggage with them in the car except one suitcase, his mother's. When the truck had arrived at the house about three o'clock in the afternoon its load had been removed and distributed at once; presumably the golf bag had been taken straight to his father's room, though he had no knowledge of that. At Sunday breakfast he and his father had arranged to play golf that afternoon. . . .

"Who suggested it? You or your father?"

He couldn't remember. When his father had come downstairs after lunch he had had the bag under his arm. They had driven to the Green Meadow Club in the sedan, parked, and his father had gone straight to the first tee, carrying his bag, while Larry had gone around by the hut for caddies. Larry wasn't particular about his caddy, but there had been one the preceding summer that his father had taken a fancy to, and by chance that boy was there and Larry had taken him with another. On his way to the first tee Larry had fallen in with the Kimballs, also ready to tee off, and since he hadn't seen Manuel for some months and was eager to discuss plans for the summer he had asked them to make it a foursome, feeling sure his father wouldn't mind. When they had reached the tee his father had been off to one side, practicing with a mashie. Peter Oliver Barstow had been cordial with the Kimballs and had greeted his caddy with delight and sent him off to chase balls.

They had waited for two or three other matches to get started and had then teed off. Manuel Kimball had driven first, then Larry, then Barstow, and last the elder Kimball. Larry couldn't remember seeing his father take the driver from the bag or from his caddy; while they were waiting he had been busy talking with Manuel, and during the moments immediately preceding his father's drive Larry had been driving himself. But he remembered well his father's actual swing at the ball, on account of an unusual circumstance. At the end of the swing there had been a peculiar jerk of the club, and as the ball sailed away with a bad slice Barstow had made an exclamation, with a startled look on his face, and begun rubbing his belly. Larry had never seen his father so suddenly and completely abandon his accustomed dignity in public. They had asked him what was wrong, and he had said something about a wasp or a hornet and started to open his shirt. Larry had been impressed by his father's agitation and had looked inside his shirt at the skin. There had been a tiny puncture, almost invisible, and his father had regained his composure and insisted that it would be nothing. The elder Kimball had made his drive and they had proceeded down the fairway.

The rest had been detailed in the newspapers many times. Thirty minutes later, on the fairway of the fourth hole, Barstow had suddenly collapsed on the ground, kicking and clutching the grass. He had been still alive when his caddy seized his arm, but by the time the others reached him he was dead. A crowd had collected, among them Dr. Nathaniel Bradford, an old Barstow family friend. Manuel Kimball had gone for the sedan and driven it along the edge of the fairway to the scene. The body had been lifted into the back of the sedan, Dr. Bradford had sat on the seat holding the head of his old friend on his lap, and Larry had taken the wheel.

Larry could remember nothing of the golf bag. Absolutely nothing. He knew the caddy's story, that the bag had been placed in front leaning against the seat, but he could not remember seeing it there while driving or at any other time. He said that he had driven the six miles slowly and carefully, and that later, after getting home, he had found blood all along his lower lip where he had bitten it. He was a better liar than his sister. If it had not been for her give-away I might have been fooled by his tale as he told it. I went after him from every angle I could think of, but he didn't leak once.

I passed that up and asked him about the Kimballs. His story was the same as his sister's. There had been no contact to speak of between the families; the only connection had been himself and Manuel, and the basis of that was Manuel's convenience as owner and pilot of an airplane; Larry had intended to get one for himself as soon as he secured a license.

Then I asked the question that had started the fireworks with Mrs. Barstow before lunch. I asked both Larry and his sister, but not only was there no fireworks, there was nothing at all. They declared that they knew of no one who had a serious grievance against their father, or hatred or enmity for him, and that it was unthinkable that there ever should have been such a person. In his remarkable career—he had achieved the presidency of Holland University at forty-eight, ten years before—he had many times faced opposition, but he had always known the trick of melting it instead of crushing it. His private life had been confined to his own home. His son, I gathered, had had deep respect for him and a certain affection; his daughter had loved him. They agreed that no one could have hated him; and as his daughter told me that, knowing what I had heard from her mother's lips only three hours previously, her eyes challenged me and appealed to me at once.

Next Dr. Bradford. I turned to Miss Barstow on that instead of her brother. The way the thing seemed to be shaping up I expected some hesitation and covering, but there certainly was no sign of it. She told me, simply, that Bradford had been a schoolmate at college with her father, that they had always been close friends, and that Bradford, who was a widower, had been almost like one of the family, especially during the summer since he was then also a neighbor. He had been the family physician, and it was on him they had chiefly relied to remove Mrs. Barstow's difficulty, though he had called in specialists to assist.

I asked Sarah Barstow, "Do you like him?"

"Like him?"

"Yes. Do you like Dr. Bradford?"

"Certainly. He is one of the best and finest men I know."

I turned to her brother. "Do you like him, Mr. Barstow?"

Larry frowned. He was tired; he had been pretty patient; I had been after him for two hours. "I like him well enough. He's what my sister says all right, but he likes to preach. Not that he ever bothers me now, but when I was a kid I used to hide from him."

"You arrived here from the university Saturday noon. Was Dr. Bradford here between that hour and Sunday at two?"

"I don't know. Oh yes, sure. He was here Saturday for dinner."

"Do you think there is any chance that he killed your father?"

Larry stared. "Oh, for God's sake. Is that supposed to shock me into something?"

"Do you, Miss Barstow?"

"Nonsense."

"All right, nonsense. Anyhow, who suggested first that Bradford should certify it as a heart stroke? Which one of you? Him?"

Larry glared at me. His sister said quietly, "You said you wanted me here to see the agreement was observed. Well, Mr. Goodwin, I've been —patient enough."

"Okay. I'll lay off of that." I turned to her brother. "You're sore again, Mr. Barstow. Forget it. People like you aren't used to impertinence, but you'd be surprised how easy it is to let it slide and no harm done. There's only a couple of things left. Where were you between seven o'clock and midnight on Monday evening, June fifth?"

He still glared. "I don't know. How do I know?"

"You can remember. This isn't another impertinence; I seriously request you to tell me. Monday, June fifth. Your father's funeral was on Tuesday. I'm asking about the evening before the funeral."

Miss Barstow said, "I can tell you."

"I'd rather he would, as a favor."

He did. "There's no reason I shouldn't. Or should either. I was here, at home."

"All evening?"

"Yes."

"Who else was here?"

"My mother and sister, the servants, and the Robertsons."

"The Robertsons?"

"I said so."

His sister spoke. "The Robertsons are old friends. Mr. and Mrs. Blair Robertson and two daughters."

"What time did they come?"

"Right after dinner. We hadn't finished. Around seven-thirty."

"Was Dr. Bradford here?"

"No."

"Wasn't that peculiar?"

"Peculiar? Why? But yes, of course it was. He had to address a meeting in New York, some professional meeting."

"I see. Thank you, Miss Barstow." I turned back to her brother. "I have one more question. A request rather. Does Manuel Kimball have a telephone at his hangar?"

"Yes."

"Will you telephone him that I am coming to see him and that you would like him to give me an interview?"

"No. Why should I?"

Miss Barstow told me, "You have no right to ask it. If you wish to see Mr. Kimball that is your business."

"Correct." I closed my notebook and got up. "Positively correct. But I have no official standing in this affair. If I call on Manuel Kimball on my own he'll just kick me out on my own. He's a friend of the family, anyway he thinks so. I need an introduction."

"Sure you need it." Larry had got up too and was brushing grass from the seat of his trousers. "But you won't get it. Where's your hat, in the house?"

I nodded. "We can get it when you go in to telephone. Look here, it's like this. I've got to ask you to phone Manuel Kimball, and the Robertsons, and the Green Meadow Club. That's all I have on my mind at present but there may be more later. I've got to go around and see people and find out things, and the easier you make it for me the easier it will be for you. Nero Wolfe knew enough, and told the police enough, to make them dig up your father's body. That was a good deal, but he didn't tell them everything. Do you want to force me to go to the District Attorney and spill enough more beans so that he will give me a ticket that will let me in wherever I want to go? He's sore at us now because he knows we're holding out on him. I'd just as soon go and make a friend of him, I don't mind, I like to make friends. You folks certainly don't. If this strikes you as some more blackmail, Mr. Barstow, I'll just get my hat and call it a day as far as you're concerned."

It was a crime, but I had to do it. The trouble with those two, especially the brother, was that they were so used to being safe and independent and dignified all their lives that they kept forgetting how scared they were and had to be reminded. But they were plenty scared when it came to the point, and if I had cared to make them a present of all my ideas that afternoon I would have had to admit that it looked to me as if they had reason to be scared.

They gave in, of course. We went into the house together, and Sarah Barstow telephoned the Robertsons and her brother phoned the club and Manuel Kimball. I had decided that there wasn't a chance in a million that I would get anything out of any of the servants, particularly if they had been trained by that tall skinny butler, so as soon as the telephoning was over I got my panama from the hall and beat it. Larry Barstow went with me out to the side terrace, I suppose to make sure that I didn't sneak back in and listen at keyholes, and just as we came to the steps a car rolled along the drive and stopped in front of us. A man got out, and I had the pleasure of a good grin as I saw it was H. R. Corbett, the dick from Anderson's office who had tried to crash the gate at Wolfe's house the morning I was acting as doorman. I passed him a cheerful salute and was going on, but he called to me.

"Hey, you!"

I stopped and turned. Larry Barstow stood on the terrace watching us. I said, "Did you address me, sir?"

Corbett was moving into my neighborhood. He paid no attention to my fast one. "What the hell are you doing here?"

I stood and grinned at him a second and then turned to Larry Barstow on the terrace. "Since this is your home, Mr. Barstow, maybe it would be better if you would tell him what the hell I'm doing here."

It was plain from the look on Larry's face that although he might never send me a Christmas card, I would get one long before Corbett would. He said to the dick, "Mr. Goodwin has been here at my sister's invitation, to consult with us. He will probably be here again. Would you like to investigate that?"

Corbett grunted and glared at me. "Maybe you'd like a trip to White Plains."

"Not at all." I shook my head. "I don't like the town, it's so slow you can't get a bet down." I started to move off. "So long, Corbett. I don't wish you any bad luck, because even with good luck you won't have much of a tombstone."

Without bothering to think up an answer to the threats and warnings he tossed at my back, I went over to the roadster where it was parked, got in and turned around, and rolled off.

X

I WENT to the Robertsons' first, because I knew it wouldn't take long and I might as well get it done. Mrs. Robertson and both of the daughters were at home, and expecting me after Sarah Barstow's phone call. They said they had been at the Barstows' the evening of June fifth, the day before the funeral, arriving well before eight o'clock and leaving after midnight. They were certain that Larry and Sarah and Mrs. Barstow had been present the entire evening. I made sure there was no possibility of a mistake about the date, and then tried a few casual questions about the Barstow family but soon gave it up. The Robertsons weren't discussing their old friends that afternoon with a stranger; they wouldn't even let on that Mrs. Barstow was otherwise than completely all right, not aware how much I knew.

I got to the Kimball place a little after five o'clock. It wasn't as dressed up as the Barstow estate, but was much larger; I drove over half a mile after I entered their private road. It was mostly on low ground, with some of the old stone fences still running through the meadows and a couple of brooks wandering around. Some woods were at the left. The house was on a knoll in a park of evergreens, with a well-kept lawn, not very large and no sign of flowers that I could see as I drove up. Not as big as the Barstows', the house was brand-new, wood with panels and a high steep slate roof, one of the styles that I lumped all together and called Queen William.

Back of the house, over the knoll, was an immense flat meadow. I was sent in that direction, along a narrow graveled drive, by a fat man in a butler's uniform who came out of the house as I drove up. In the large meadow were no stone fences; it was level and clean and recently mowed and was certainly perfect for a private landing field. On the edge about halfway down its length was a low concrete building with a flat roof, and the graveled drive took me there. There was a wide and long concrete runway in front, and two cars were parked on it.

I found Manuel Kimball inside, washing his hands at a sink. The place was mostly full of airplane, a big one with black wings and a red body, sitting on its tail. In it tinkering with something was a man in overalls. Everything was neat and clean, with tools and oil cans and a lot of junk arranged on steel shelves that ran along one side. Besides the sink there was even a rack with three or four clean towels on it.

"My name's Goodwin," I said.

Kimball nodded. "Yes, I was expecting you. I'm through here for the day; we might as well go to the house and be comfortable." He spoke to the man in overalls. "Let that wait till tomorrow if you want to, Skinner, I won't be going up till afternoon." When he had finished wiping his hands he led me out and took his car, and I got in the roadster and drove back to the house.

He was decent and polite, no doubt about that, even if he did look like a foreigner and had made me nervous at lunch. He took me into a large room in front and steered me to a big comfortable leather chair and told the fat butler to bring us some highballs. When he saw me looking around he said that the house had been furnished by his father and himself after their personal tastes, since there had been no women to consider and they both disliked decorators.

I nodded. "Miss Barstow told me your mother died a long time ago."

I said it casually, without thinking, but I always have my eye on whoever I'm talking to, and I was surprised at what went over his face. It was a spasm, you couldn't call it anything else. It only lasted a fraction of a second, but for that moment something was certainly hurting him inside. I didn't know whether it was just because I had mentioned his mother or he really had a pain; anyhow, I didn't try it again.

He said, "I understand that you are investigating the death of Miss Barstow's father."

"Yes. At her request, in a way. Larry Barstow's father too, and Mrs. Barstow's husband, at the same time."

He smiled and his black eyes swerved to me. "If that is your first question, Mr. Goodwin, it is neatly put. Bravo. The answer is no, I have no right to distinguish the dead man in that fashion. No right, that is, but my own inclination. I admire Miss Barstow—very much."

"Good. So do I. It wasn't a question, just a remark. What I really want to ask you about is what took place on the first tee that Sunday afternoon. I suppose you've told the story before."

"Yes. Twice to a detective whose name is Corbett, I believe, and once to Mr. Anderson."

"Then you ought to have it by heart. Would you mind telling it again?"

I sat back with my highball and listened without interrupting. I didn't use my notebook because I already had Larry's tale to check with and I could record any differences later. Manuel Kimball was precise and thorough. When he got through there was little left to ask, but there were one or two points I wasn't satisfied on, particularly one on which he differed from Larry. Manuel said that after Barstow thought a wasp had stung him he had dropped his driver on the ground and his caddy had picked it up; Larry had said that his father had hung onto the driver with one hand when he was opening his shirt to see what had happened to him. Manuel said he felt sure he was right but didn't insist on it if Larry remembered otherwise. It didn't seem of great importance, since the driver had in any event got back into the bag, and in all other respects Manuel's story tallied with Larry's.

Encouraged by his sending for more highballs, I spread the conversation out a little. He didn't seem to object. I learned that his father was a grain broker and went every day to his office in New York, on Pearl Street, and that he, Manuel, was considering the establishment of an airplane factory. He was, he said, a thoroughly skilled pilot, and he had spent a year at the Fackler works in Buffalo. His father had engaged to furnish the necessary capital, though he doubted the soundness of the venture and was entirely skeptical about airplanes. Manuel thought Larry Barstow showed promise of a real talent in structural design and hoped to be able to persuade him to take a share in the enterprise.

He said, "Naturally Larry is not himself just at present, and I'm not trying to rush him. No wonder, first his father's sudden death, and then the autopsy with its astonishing results. By the way, Mr. Goodwin, of course everybody around here is wondering how Nero Wolfe—that's it, isn't it?—how he was able to predict those results in such remarkable detail. Anderson, the District Attorney, hints at his own sources of information—he did so to me the other day, sitting in the chair you're in now—but the truth of the matter is pretty generally known. At Green Meadow day before yesterday there were only two topics: who killed Barstow, and how Nero Wolfe found out. What are you going to do, disclose the answers to both riddles at the same dramatic moment?"

"Maybe. I hope so, Mr. Kimball. Anyway we won't answer that last one first. No, thanks, none for me. With another of your elegant highballs I might answer almost anything. They won't come any better than that even after repeal."

"Then by all means have one. Naturally, like everybody else, I'm curious. Nero Wolfe must be an extraordinary man."

"Well, I'll tell you." I threw my head back to get the end of the high-ball, and with the slick ice-lumps sliding across my upper lip let the last rare drops trickle in, then suddenly came down with the glass and my chin at the same time. It was just one of my little tricks. All I saw was Manuel Kimball looking curious, and he had just said he was curious, so it couldn't be said that I had made any subtle discovery. I said, "If Nero Wolfe isn't extraordinary Napoleon never got higher than top-sergeant. I'm sorry I can't tell you his secrets, but I've got to earn what he pays me somehow, even if it's only by keeping my mouth shut. Which reminds me." I glanced at my wrist. "It must be about your din-ner time. You've been very hospitable, Mr. Kimball. I appreciate it, and so will Nero Wolfe."

"You're quite welcome. Don't hurry on my account. My father won't be home and I dislike eating alone. I'll run over to the club for dinner later."

"Oh," I said. "Your father won't be home? That throws me out a little. I had figured on finding a bite to eat in Pleasantville or White Plains and coming back for a little talk with him. In fact, I was just about to ask you for a favor: to tell him I was coming."

"I'm sorry."

"He won't be back tonight?"

"No. He went to Chicago on business last week. Your disappointment isn't the first one. Anderson and that detective have been wiring him every day, I don't exactly see why. After all, he barely knew Barstow. I imagine their telegrams won't start him back till he's through with his business. My father is like that. He finishes things."

"When do you expect him?"

"I hardly know. Around the fifteenth, he thought when he left."

"Well. That's too bad. It's just routine, of course, but any detective would want to complete the foursome, and since you can't do me the favor with your father that I wanted to ask, maybe you will do me an-other one. More routine. Tell me where you were between seven o'clock and midnight Monday evening, June fifth. That was the eve-ning before the Barstow funeral. Did you go to the funeral? This was the evening before."

Manuel Kimball's black eyes were straight at me, concentrated, like a man trying to remember. "I went to the funeral," he said. "Yes, that was Tuesday. A week ago today. Oh yes. I think it was; yes, I'm sure. Skinner would know. I was in the clouds."

"In the clouds?"

He nodded. "I've been trying flying and landing at night. A couple of times in May, and again that Monday. Skinner would know; he helped me off and I had him wait till I got back to make sure the lights would be in order. It's quite a trick, very different from the daytime."

"What time did you go up?"

"Around six o'clock. Of course it wasn't dark until nearly nine, but I wanted to be ahead of the twilight."

"You got well ahead of it all right. When did you get back?"

"Ten or a little after. Skinner would know that too; we fooled around with the timer till midnight."

"Did you go up alone?"

"Completely." Manuel Kimball smiled at me with his lips, but it appeared to me that his eyes weren't cooperating. "You must admit, Mr. Goodwin, that I'm being pretty tolerant. What the devil has my flying Monday night or any other night got to do with you? If I wasn't so curious I might have reason to be a little irritated. Don't you think?"

"Sure." I grinned. "I'd be irritated if I was you. But anyway I'm much obliged. Routine, Mr. Kimball, just the damn routine." I got up and shook a leg to get the cuff of my trousers down. "And I am much obliged and I appreciate it. I should think it would be more fun flying at night than in the daytime."

He was on his feet too, polite. "It is. But do not feel obliged. It is going to distinguish me around here to have talked to Nero Wolfe's man."

He called the fat butler to bring my hat.

Half an hour later, headed south around the curves of the Bronx River Parkway, I was still rolling him over on my mind's tongue. Since there was no connection at all between him and Barstow or the driver or anything else, it could have been for no other reason than because he made me nervous. And yet Wolfe said that I had no feeling for phenomena! The next time he threw that at me I would remind him of my mysterious misgivings about Manuel Kimball, I decided. Granted, of course, that it turned out that Manuel had murdered Barstow, which I had to confess didn't seem very likely at that moment.

When I got home, around half past eight, Wolfe had finished dinner. I had phoned from the drugstore on the Grand Concourse, and Fritz had a dish of flounder with his best cheese sauce hot in the oven, with a platter of lettuce and tomatoes and plenty of good cold milk. Considering my thin lunch at the Barstows' and the hour I was getting my knees under the table, it wasn't any too much. I cleaned it up. Fritz said it seemed good to have me busy and out working again.

I said, "You're darned right it does. This dump would be about ready for the sheriff if it wasn't for me."

Fritz giggled. He's the only man I've ever known who could giggle without giving you doubts about his fundamentals.

Wolfe was in his chair in the office, playing with flies. He hated flies and very few ever got in there, but two had somehow made it and were fooling around on his desk. Much as he hated them, he couldn't kill them; he said that while a live fly irritated him to the point of hatred, a killed one outraged his respect for the dignity of death, which was worse. My opinion was it just made him sick. Anyway, he was in his chair with the swatter in his hand, seeing how close to the fly he could lower it without the fly taking off. When I went in he handed me the swatter and I let them have it and raked them into the wastebasket.

"Thank you," Wolfe said. "Those confounded insects were trying to make me forget that one of the *Dendrobiums chlorostele* is showing two buds."

"No! Really?"

He nodded. "That one in half sunlight. The others have been moved over."

"One for Horstmann."

"Yes. Who killed Barstow?"

I grinned. "Give me a chance. The name just escapes me—I'll remember it in a minute."

"You should have written it down. No, just your light. That's better. Did you get enough to eat? Proceed."

That report was an in-between; I wasn't proud of it or ashamed of it either. Wolfe scarcely interrupted once throughout; he sat as he always did when I had a long story: leaning back, his chin on his chest, his elbows on the arms of the chair with his fingers interlaced on his belly, his eyes half closed but always on my face. Halfway through he stopped me to have Fritz bring some beer, then with two bottles and a glass within reach at the edge of the table he resumed his position. I went on to the end. It was midnight.

He sighed. I went to the kitchen for a glass of milk. When I got back he was pinching the top of his ear and looking sleepy.

"Perhaps you had an impression," he said.

I sat down again. "Vague. Pretty watery. Mrs. Barstow is just some kind of a nut. She might have killed her husband or she might not, but of course she didn't kill Carlo Maffei. For Miss Barstow you can use your own impression. Out. Her brother is out too, I mean on Maffei, his alibi for the fifth is so tight you could use it for a vacuum. Dr. Bradford must be a very interesting person, I would like to meet him some time. As for Manuel Kimball, I suppose there's no chance he killed Barstow, but I'll bet he runs over angels with his airplane."

"Why? Is he cruel? Does he sneer? Do his eyes focus badly?"

"No. But look at his name. He made me nervous. He looks like a Spaniard. What's he doing with the name Kimball?"

"You haven't seen his father."

"I know. Of course the bad news about the golf bag never being in his locker threw me off my stride and I was looking for something to kick."

"Bad news? Why bad?"

"Well, good Lord. We thought we had the membership of the Green Meadow Club to run through the sifter, and now we've got everybody that's been in Barstow's home at the university for the past nine months."

"Oh no. By no means. No known poison, exposed to the air, by being smeared on a needle for instance, will retain an efficacy sufficient to kill a man as Barstow was killed for more than a day or two. Probably only a few hours. It depends on the poison."

I grinned at him. "That's a help. What else did you read?"

"A few interesting things. Many tiresome ones. So the golf bag's itinerary is not bad news at all. Its later disappearance interests us only indirectly, for we never could have expected to come upon the driver. But who caused it to disappear and why?"

"Sure. But as far as that's concerned, who came to ask you to return the reward unopened and why? We already knew there's someone in that family with funny ideas."

Wolfe wiggled a finger at me. "It is easier to recognize a style from a sentence than from a single word. But as for that, the removal of the golf bag from the scene was direct, bold, and forthright, while the visit to our office, though direct enough, was merely desperate."

I said, "Doctors know all about poisons."

"Yes. This one—this Dr. Bradford—is satisfactorily forthright. Three times today I was told that he was too busy to come to the telephone, and the indication was that that condition could be expected to continue. You are intending to resume in the morning?"

I nodded. "The club first, I thought, then the coroner, then back to town for Doc Bradford's office. I'm sorry old Kimball's gone; I'd like to clean up that foursome. You don't think Saul Panzer would enjoy a trip to Chicago?"

"It would cost a hundred dollars."

"That's not much of a chunk out of fifty grand."

Wolfe shook his head. "You're a spendthrift, Archie. And unnecessarily thorough. Let us first make sure no murderer can be found within the commuting area."

"Okay." I got up and stretched. "Good night, sir."
"Good night, Archie."

XI

THERE was a point on the public road from which the Green Meadow clubhouse could be seen, but at a considerable distance; to reach it you turned off the highway into a grove, and when you left that you were winding around a hollow. The clubhouse had a grove of its own, on top of a moderate hill; on one side were a bunch of tennis courts and an outdoor pool; everywhere else, in all directions, were smooth rolling fairways dotted with little tee plateaus, sand traps of various shapes and sizes, and the vivid velvet carpets of the putting greens. There were two courses of eighteen holes each; the Barstow foursome had started on the north course, the long one.

The club professional, who had dined with us at Wolfe's place Monday evening, wasn't there yet when I arrived and wasn't expected until eleven o'clock, so the only introduction I had to offer was Larry Barstow's phone call the preceding afternoon, which had been received by the chief steward. He was nice enough and went with me out to the caddy master. Two of the caddies I wanted to see didn't come on weekdays, since the schools they attended weren't out yet, and the other two were out on the links somewhere with early morning matches. I monkeyed around for an hour trying to find someone for a page in the notebook, but as far as real information was concerned they were about as helpful as a bunch of Eskimos. I hopped in the roadster and beat it for White Plains.

The coroner's office was in the same building as Anderson's, where I had been six days previously trying to get Wolfe's money covered, and as I passed the door with DISTRICT ATTORNEY painted on the glass panel I stuck out my tongue at it. The coroner wasn't in, but by luck there was a doctor there signing papers and he was the one who had done the Barstow autopsy. Before leaving home in the morning I had telephoned Sarah Barstow, and now this doctor told me that he had had a phone call from Lawrence Barstow and had been told that I would visit the coroner's office as a representative of the Barstow family. I thought to myself, I'll have that Barstow brat fixing my flat tires before I get through with this.

But I came away as good as empty. Everything that the doctor could tell me I had read three days earlier in the newspapers except for a bunch of medical terms which the papers hadn't tried to print for fear of a typesetters' strike. I don't high-hat technical words, because I know there are a lot of things that can't be said any other way, but the doctor's lengthy explanation simply boiled down to this, that nothing conclusive could be said regarding the poison that had killed Barstow, because no one had been able to analyze it. Additional tissues had been sent to a New York laboratory but no report had been received. The needle had been taken by the District Attorney and was presumably being tested elsewhere.

"Anyway," I said, "there's no chance he died of old age or something? He was actually poisoned? He died a violent death?"

The doctor nodded. "Absolutely. Something remarkably virulent. Hæmolysis—"

"Sure. Just between you and me, what is your opinion of a doctor who would go up to a man who had just died like that and would say coronary thrombosis?"

He stiffened as if he had just got rigor mortis himself, only much quicker. "That is not a question for me to decide, Mr. Goodwin."

"I didn't ask you to decide anything, I just asked your opinion."

"I haven't got any."

"You mean you have, only you're going to keep it to remember me by. All right. Much obliged."

On my way out of the building I would have liked to stop in and ask Derwin for Ben Cook's telephone number or some such pleasantry, but I had too much on my mind. By the time I got back to the Green Meadow Club it was nearly noon and I had pretty well decided that life would be nothing but a dreary round until I had had the pleasure of meeting Dr. Bradford.

The two caddies were there. Their boss rounded them up for me, and I made a deal with them: I would get sandwiches, two apiece, bananas, ice cream, and root beer, and we would go over under a tree and eat, drink, and be merry, provided they wouldn't expect me to pay for their lost time. They signed up and we collected the provisions from the lunch counter and found the tree.

One of them, a skinny pale kid with brown hair, had been Manuel Kimball's caddy and the other had been Peter Oliver Barstow's. This other was a chunky lad with snappy brown eyes and a lot of freckles; his name was Mike Allen. After we got arranged under the tree, before he took his first bite he said, "You know, mister, we don't get paid."

"What do you mean, you work for fun?"

"We don't get paid all the time, only when we're out on a round. We're not losing any time. We couldn't get another match till after lunch anyhow."

"Oh. You don't say so. You're too darned honest. If you don't watch out you'll get a job in a bank. Go on and eat your sandwich."

While we chewed I got them onto the Barstow foursome. The way they rattled it off it was easy to see they hadn't gone over it more than a thousand times, with Anderson and Corbett of course, the other caddies, families and friends at home. They were glib and ready with an answer on every little detail, and that made it pretty hopeless to try to get anything fresh out of them, for they had drawn the picture so many times that they were now doing it with their eyes shut. Not that I really expected a damn thing, but I had long since learned from Wolfe that the corner the light doesn't reach is the one the dime rolled to. There was no variation worth mentioning from the versions I had got from Larry Barstow and Manuel Kimball. By the time the sandwiches and stuff were down I saw that the pale skinny kid was milked dry, so I sent him back to his boss. Chunky Mike I kept a while, sitting with him under the tree. He had some sense in him and he might have noticed something: for instance, how Dr. Bradford had acted when he arrived at the scene on the fourth fairway. But I didn't get a bite there. He only remembered that the doctor had been out of breath when he had run up with everyone waiting for him, and when he stood up after examining Barstow he had been white and calm.

I checked up on the golf bag. There was no uncertainty in him about that; he had positively put it in the front of Barstow's car, leaning against the driver's seat.

I said, "Of course, Mike, you were pretty excited. At a time like that everybody is. Isn't there a chance you put it in some other car?"

"No, sir. I couldn't. There was no other car there."

"Maybe it was someone else's bag you put in."

"No, sir. I'm not a dummy. When you're a caddy you get so you glance at the heads to make sure all the clubs are in, and after I leaned the bag against the seat I did that, and I remember seeing all the new heads."

"New heads?"

"Sure, they were all new."

"What made them new? Do you mean Barstow had had new heads put on?"

"No, sir, they were new clubs. The new bag of clubs his wife gave him."

"What!"

"Sure."

I didn't want to startle him; I picked a blade of grass and chewed on it. "How do you know his wife gave them to him?"

"He told me."

"How did he happen to tell you?"

"Well, when I went up to him he shook hands and said he was glad to see me again, of course he was one of my babies last year—"

"For God's sake, Mike, wait a minute. What do you mean he was one of your babies?"

The kid grinned. "That's what us fellows call it. When a man likes us for a caddy and won't take another one he's our baby."

"I see. Go on."

"He said he was glad to see me again, and when I took his bag I saw they were all new Hendersons, genuine, and he said he was glad to see I admired the new clubs his wife had given him for his birthday."

There were a couple of bananas left and I handed him one and he began peeling it. I watched him. After a minute I said, "Do you know that Barstow was killed by a poison needle shot out of the handle of a golf driver?"

His mouth was full. He waited till most of it was down before he answered. "I know that's what they say."

"Why, don't you believe it?"

He shook his head. "They've got to show me."

"Why?"

"Well—" He took another bite and swallowed it. "I don't believe you could do it. I've handled a lot of golf clubs. I just don't believe it."

I grinned at him. "You're a skeptic, Mike. You know what my boss says? He says that skepticism is a good watchdog if you know when to take the leash off. I don't suppose you happen to know when Barstow had a birthday?"

He didn't know that. I started to fish around a little more, here and there, but there didn't seem to be any more nibbles in that pool. Besides, the lunch hour was over, afternoon players were beginning to stroll up, and I saw Mike had his eyes on the caddy benches and was beginning to lose interest in me. I was about ready to scramble up and tell him the picnic was over, but he beat me to it. He was on his feet with a sudden spring, the kind young legs can make, and he tossed at me, "Excuse me, mister, that guy's my baby," and was off.

I gathered up the papers and banana skins and went to the clubhouse. There were a good many more people around than when I had arrived in the morning, and finally I had to send an attendant for the chief steward because I couldn't find him. He was busy, but he took time to show me where the library was and tell me to help myself. I looked around the shelves and in a minute had it spotted, the fat red *Who's Who in America*. I turned to the entry I had already read in Wolfe's office: BARSTOW, Peter Oliver, author, educator, physicist; *b*. Chatham, Ill., Apr. 9, 1875 . . .

I put the book back and went out to the lobby, where I had seen some telephone booths, and called Sarah Barstow at her home and asked if I could drop in to see her for a minute. It was only a couple of miles out of my way returning to New York, and I thought I might as well clean this detail up. As I was going along the veranda to where I had parked the roadster I met Manuel Kimball. He was with some people, but when he saw me he nodded and I returned it, and I could guess what he was saying to the people with him because after I got past they turned to look at me.

Ten minutes later I was on the Barstow drive.

Small took me to a room in front that I hadn't been in the day before. In a little while Sarah Barstow came in. She looked pale and determined, and I realized that with my phone call I must have scared her some more without wanting to. I should have been a little more explanatory; I don't believe in pulling a dog's tail if there's anything else to do.

I got up. She didn't sit down.

"I'll only keep you a minute," I said. "I wouldn't have bothered you, only I ran across something that made me curious. Please tell me, was your father's birthday April ninth?"

She looked as if she was trying to breathe. She nodded.

"Did your mother give him a bag of golf clubs his last birthday?"

"Oh!" she said, and put her hand on the back of a chair.

"Listen, Miss Barstow. Buck up. I think you know Nero Wolfe wouldn't lie to you, and while he's paying me you can regard me as Nero Wolfe. We might try tricky questions on you, but we wouldn't tell you an honest lie. If you've been nursing the idea that the driver your father killed himself with was in the bag when your mother gave it to him on his birthday, forget it. We have reason to know it couldn't have been. Impossible."

She just looked at me with her lips working but not opening. I don't believe she would have been able to stand without her hand on the chair. She had a good hold on it.

I said, "Maybe I'm telling you something and maybe I'm not. But I've brought this right to you as soon as I found it out, and I'm giving it to you straight. If it's any help to you, you're welcome, and how about making it fifty-fifty? I could use a little help too. Was that what was eating you, that birthday present? Was that the reason for all the fol-de-rol?"

She got her tongue working at last but all she said was, "I don't believe you would lie to me. It would be too cruel."

"I wouldn't. But even if I would, I know about the birthday present anyhow, so you can answer my simple question without running a temperature. Was that what was eating you?"

"Yes," she said. "That—and—yes, it was that."

"What else was it?"

"Nothing. My mother—"

"Sure." I nodded. "Your mother got goofy sometimes and got ideas about your father, and she gave him a golf bag on his birthday. What else?"

"Nothing." She took her hand off the chair, but put it back again. "Mr. Goodwin. I think—I'll sit down."

I went and took her arm and shoved the chair back a little with my foot, and held on to her until she got seated. She shut her eyes and I stood and waited till she opened them again.

"You're right," she said. "I ought to buck up. I'm no good. It has been a strain. Not only this, a long while. I always thought my mother was a wonderful woman, I still think so, I know she is. But it is so ugly! Dr. Bradford says he believes that now, since father is dead, Mother will be completely cured and will never again have any—difficulties. But much as I love my mother, that is too high a price. I think we would be better off without modern psychology, everything it tells us is so ugly. It was at my father's suggestion that I studied it."

"Anyway, this is one thing off your mind."

"Yes. I can't appreciate it yet, but I will. I ought to thank you, Mr. Goodwin, I'm sorry. You say that my mother had nothing—that she couldn't—"

"I say that the driver that killed your father wasn't anywhere on April ninth. It didn't exist until at least a month later."

"How sure are you?"

"Just damn sure."

"Well. That's a good deal." She tried to smile at me, and I admired her nerve, for it was easy to see that she was so near gone from worry and grief and loss of sleep that you might as well have expected a guffaw from Job. Anyone with an ounce of decency in him would have got up and left her alone with the good news I'd brought her; but business is business, and it wouldn't have been right to pass up the chance that she was unstrung enough to loosen up at a vital point.

I said, "Don't you think you might tell me who took the golf bag from the car and where it is now? Now that we know that the driver is not the one that was in it when your mother gave it to him?"

She said without hesitation, "Small took it from the car."

My heart jumped the way it did when I saw Wolfe's lips push out. She was going to spill it! I went right on without giving her time to consider, "Where did he take it to?"

"Upstairs. To Father's room."

"Who took it away from there?"

"I did. Saturday evening, after Mr. Anderson came. It was Sunday that the men searched the house for it."

"Where did you put it?"

"I drove to Tarrytown and got on the ferry and dropped it in the middle of the river. I filled it full of stones."

"You're lucky they weren't tailing you. Of course you examined the driver. Did you take it apart?"

"I didn't examine it. I—was in a hurry."

"You didn't examine it? You mean you didn't even take it out and look at it?"

"No."

I stared at her. "I've got a better opinion of you. I don't believe you're such an awful fool. You're stringing me."

"No. No, I'm not, Mr. Goodwin."

I still stared. "You mean you actually did all that? Without even looking at the driver? Leave it to a woman! What were your brother and Bradford doing, playing billiards?"

She shook her head. "They had nothing to do with it."

"But Bradford says that your mother will be all right now that your father's dead."

"Well? If that is his opinion—" She stopped; the mention of her mother had been a mistake, it had her down again. After a minute she looked up at me, and for the first time I saw tears in her eyes. Two hung there. "You wanted me to go fifty-fifty, Mr. Goodwin. That's my share."

Something about her, the tears maybe, made her look like nothing but a kid, trying to be brave. I reached down and patted her on the shoulder and said, "You're a good sport, Miss Barstow. I'll let you alone."

I went to the hall and got my hat and left.

BUT, I thought, in the roadster again headed south down the highway. Plenty of BUT. Part of it was that as much as I respected filial devotion and as much as I liked Sarah Barstow, it would have been a real satisfaction to put her across my knees and pull up her skirts and give her a swell fanning for not taking a look at that driver. I had to believe her and I did believe her. She hadn't made that up. Now the driver was gone for good. With a lot of luck and patience it might have been grappled out of the river, but it would have cost more money than Nero Wolfe was apt to let go of. It was just simply good-by driver. As I went through White Plains it was a temptation to leave the Parkway and run over to the District Attorney's office and say to Anderson, "I'll bet you ten dollars that the golf bag containing the driver that killed Barstow is at the bottom of the Hudson River halfway between Tarrytown and Nyack." It wouldn't have been a bad idea at that, for he might have sent a couple of boats out and found it. But as things turned out it was just as well I didn't.

I had had it in mind to go back to New York by another route, Blueberry Road, and just for curiosity take a look at the spot where Carlo Maffei's body had been found; not that I expected to discover that the murderer had left his scarfpin or automobile license lying around, just thinking that it never hurts a spot to look at it. But dropping in on Sarah Barstow had used up some time, and I wanted to make a call in the city. So I took the quickest way in.

On upper Park Avenue I stopped at a drugstore and phoned Wolfe. He had called Bradford's office once more, around eleven-thirty, but it had been the same story, too busy to come to the phone. He told me to go to it. I thought to myself, If he's busy now he's going to be positively rushed before we get through with him. It took me less than ten minutes to get to Sixty-ninth Street, and I parked around the corner.

Dr. Nathaniel Bradford certainly had an office. The entrance hall was wide enough to have a row of Brazilian ferns along each side, and the anteroom was big and grand. The lights and rugs and pictures and chairs made it plain, but not noisy, that everything done in that place was on a high level, including making out the patients' bills. But the chairs were all empty. The girl in starched white at a desk over in a corner told me that Dr. Bradford was not in. She seemed surprised that I didn't know that, just as I would know that Central Park begins at Fifty-ninth Street, and asked if I was a former patient. Then she said that the doctor was never in his office in the afternoon before four-thirty, and that he never saw anyone except by appointment. When I said that that was what I wanted to see him for, to make an appointment, she raised her eyebrows. I went back to the street.

At first I thought I would wait around for him, but it was only a little after three, so I went and sat in the roadster and let my mind out for a stroll to see if it would run across an idea for passing the time. In a few minutes it did, a pretty one. I went to a restaurant on Park Avenue to look at a telephone book, and then went back to the car and stepped on the starter and started along Sixty-ninth Street, and at Fifth Avenue turned downtown. At Forty-first Street I headed east.

As usual every car along the curb was laying its head on the next one's tail, and I had to go nearly to Third Avenue to find a space where I could edge the roadster in. I walked back almost two crosstown blocks, and found that the number I was looking for was one of the new office buildings a mile high. The directory said that my meat was on the twentieth floor. The elevator shot me up and I found it on a door down the corridor: METROPOLITAN MEDICAL RECORD.

It was a young man, not a girl, at the desk in the outside room; that was nice for a change. I said to him, "I'd like to ask a favor, if you're not too busy to help me out a little. Would you have any record showing the meetings of medical associations and so on held in New York on June fifth?"

He grinned. "The Lord knows I'm not busy. Yes, sir, we have. Of course. Just a minute. June fifth?"

He went to a stack of magazines on a shelf and took off the top one. "This is our last issue, it would have it." He began flipping the pages and stopped around the middle and looked at it. I waited. "Nothing on the fifth, I'm afraid— Oh yes, here it is. Most of the big meetings come later. On the fifth the New York Neurological Society was at the Knickerbocker Hotel."

I asked if I could look at it and he handed it to me. I ran through the paragraph. "I see. This is a notice of the meeting. Of course it was printed before the meeting took place. You wouldn't have anything later? A report, a write-up?"

He shook his head. "There'll be one in our next issue, I suppose. Was it something particular you wanted? The daily papers may have run it."

"Maybe. I haven't tried them. What I'm looking for is a report of Dr. Bradford's paper. As a matter of fact, all I want is to make sure he was there. You wouldn't know?"

He shook his head. "But if all you want to know is whether he was there or not, why don't you ask him?"

I grinned. "I hate to bother him. But of course it's quite simple; I happened to be in the neighborhood and thought that by dropping in here I could save time."

He said, "Wait a minute," and disappeared through a door to an inner office. He didn't take much more than the minute he mentioned. When he came back he told me, "Mr. Elliot says that Dr. Bradford was at the meeting and delivered his paper."

Elliot, he said, was the editor of the *Record*. I asked if I could speak to him. The young man disappeared through the door again, and after a moment it opened once more and a big red-faced man in his shirt sleeves came through. One of the brusque breezy kind. "What's all this? What's this about?"

I explained. He wiped his forehead with his handkerchief and said that he had attended the meeting and that Dr. Bradford had delivered his most interesting paper to applause. He was writing it up for the August *Record*. I questioned him, and he took it very nicely. Yes, he meant Dr. Nathaniel Bradford whose office was on Sixty-ninth Street. He had known him for years. He couldn't say at what hour Bradford had arrived at the hotel, but it had been a dinner meeting and he had seen Bradford at his table as early as seven and on the speaking platform as late as ten-thirty.

I guess I went out without thanking him. Driving back uptown I was sore as a pup. Of course it was Bradford I was sore at. What the devil did he mean by fooling around at a meeting reading a paper on neurology when I had him all set up in Westchester County sticking a knife into Carlo Maffei?

I supposed it would have taken me about a year to get introduced to Dr. Nathaniel Bradford if I hadn't been so sore when I got back to his office. There were two patients waiting this time. The doctor was in. I asked the girl at the desk for a piece of paper and sat down and held it on a magazine and wrote on it:

Dr. Bradford: For the last few days I've been sure you were a murderer but now I know you are just an old fool. The same goes for Mrs. Barstow and her son and daughter. It will take me about three minutes to tell you how I know.

Archie Goodwin
For Nero Wolfe

By the time the two patients had been taken care of some more had come in, and I went over to the girl and told her I was next. She got impatient and began explaining to me what an appointment was. I said, "It wouldn't break any furniture if you just handed him this note. Honest, I'm in a hurry. Be human. I've got a sister at home. Don't read it yourself because there's a swear-word in it."

She looked disgusted, but she took the note and went away with it through the door where the patients had gone. After a while she came back and stood on the threshold and said my name. I took my hat along with me because there had been time enough to call a cop.

One look at Dr. Bradford was enough to show me that I had been wasting a lot of pleasant suspicions which might have been avoided if

I had happened to catch sight of him somewhere. He was tall and grave and correct, the distinguished old gentleman type, and he had whiskers! There may have been a historical period when it was possible for a guy with whiskers to pull a knife and plunge it into somebody's back, but that was a long time ago. Nowadays it couldn't be done. Bradford's were gray, so was his hair. To tell the truth, as tight as his alibi for June fifth had been made by my trip to Forty-first Street, I had been prepared to try to find a leak in it until I got a look at him.

I went over to where he sat at his desk, and stood there. He just looked at me until the door had closed behind the girl; then he said, "Your name is Goodwin. Are you a genius too?"

"Yes, sir." I grinned. "I caught it from Nero Wolfe. Sure, I remember he told Miss Barstow he was a genius, and of course she told you. Maybe you thought it was only a joke."

"No. I kept an open mind. But whether you are a genius or merely an impertinent ass, I can't keep my patients waiting for you. What is this note you sent me, bait? I'll give you three minutes to justify it."

"That's plenty. I'll put it this way: Nero Wolfe discovered certain facts. From those facts he reached a certain conclusion as to the cause and manner of Barstow's death. When the autopsy verified his conclusion it also verified his facts; that is, it made them an inseparable part of the picture, and whoever killed Barstow has got to fit those facts. Well, the Barstows don't fit, none of them. You don't either. You're a wash-out."

"Go on."

"Go on?"

"That's a good general statement. Specify."

"Oh no." I shook my head. "That's not the way us geniuses work, you can't shake us empty like a bag of peanuts. For one thing, it would take a lot longer than three minutes. For another, what do you expect for nothing? You've got a nerve. Something happens to get you into such a state that you can't tell coronary thrombosis from an epileptic fit, and to keep you on such an edge for days that you're afraid to go to the telephone, and it's all right for Nero Wolfe to spend his time and money chasing the clouds away for you and turning on the sunshine, but he mustn't make a nuisance of himself. I've got to send you in a trick note just to have the honor of looking at your whiskers. You've got a nerve."

"Dear me." Dr. Bradford was sweating. "Your indignation is eloquent and picturesque, but it demonstrates nothing but indignation." He looked at his watch. "I don't need to tell you, Mr. Goodwin, that I'm tremendously interested. And while I shall continue to regard the vocation of raking scandal out of graveyards as an especially vile method of

making a living, I shall certainly be vastly grateful to you and Nero
Wolfe if the general statement you have made can be substantiated.
Can you return here at half past six?"

I shook my head. "I'm just a messenger. Nero Wolfe dines at seven
o'clock. He lives on West Thirty-fifth Street. He invites you to dine with
him this evening. Will you?"

"No. Certainly not."

"All right. That's all." I was fed up with the old pillar, moss and all.
"If you get a rash from your curiosity itching don't blame us. We don't
really need anything you're likely to have, we just like to clean up as we
go along. My three minutes are up."

I turned to go. I didn't hurry, but I got to the door with my hand on
the knob.

"Mr. Goodwin."

I kept my hand on the knob and looked around at him.

"I accept Mr. Wolfe's invitation. I shall be there at seven."

I said, "Okay, I'll give the girl the address," and went on out.

XII

I'VE sometimes wondered how many people there were in New York
from whom Nero Wolfe could have borrowed money. I suppose more
than a thousand. I made it a severe test to narrow it down. Of course
there were more than that who felt grateful to him, and as many more
who had reason to hate him, but there's a special kind of attitude a man
has to have toward you before you can bump him for a loan and get
something more substantial than a frown and a stammer for your trouble; a mixture of trust and goodwill, and gratitude without any feeling
of obligation to make it unpleasant. At least a thousand. Not that Wolfe
ever took advantage of it. I remember a couple of years ago we were
really hard up for cash for a while, and I made a suggestion regarding
a multimillionaire who didn't owe Wolfe much more than his life.
Wolfe wouldn't consider it. "No, Archie, nature has arranged that
when you overcome a given inertia the resulting momentum is pro-
portionate. If I were to begin borrowing money I would end by devising
means of persuading the Secretary of the Treasury to lend me the gold
reserve." I told him that as things stood we could use it and more too,
but he wasn't listening.

After that Wednesday evening dinner I could have added Dr. Nathaniel Bradford to the thousand. Wolfe got him completely, as he always got everyone when he cared to take the trouble. Between six and

seven, before Bradford arrived, I had made a condensed report of the
events of the day, and at the dinner table I had seen at once that Wolfe
agreed with me in erasing Bradford right off the slate. He was easy
and informal, and to my practiced eye he always kept on a formal basis
with a man as long as there was a chance in his mind that the man was
headed for the frying-pan at Sing Sing or a cell at Auburn, with Wolfe
furnishing the ticket.

At dinner they discussed rock gardens and economics and Tammany
Hall. Wolfe drank three bottles of beer and Bradford a bottle of wine;
I stuck to milk, but I had had a shot of rye upstairs. I had told Wolfe
of Bradford's observation about a vile vocation and threw in my opinion
of him. Wolfe had said, "Detach yourself, Archie, personal resentment
of a general statement is a barbarous remnant of fetish superstition."
I had said, "That's just another of your flossy remarks that don't mean
anything." He had said, "No. I abhor meaningless remarks. If a man
constructs a dummy, clothes and paints it in exact outward resemblance
to yourself, and proceeds to strike it in the face, does your nose bleed?" I
had said, "No, but his will before I get through with him." Wolfe had
sighed into my grin. "At least you see that my remark was not meaningless."

In the office after dinner Wolfe said to Bradford that there were
things he wanted to ask him but that he would begin by telling him.
He gave him the whole story: Maffei, the clipped newspaper, the question about the golf club that stopped Anna Fiore, the game with Anderson, the letter Anna got with a hundred bucks. He told it straight
and complete, and then said, "There, Doctor. I asked you for no pledge
beforehand, but I now request you to keep everything I have said in
confidence. I ask this in my own interest. I wish to earn fifty thousand
dollars."

Bradford had got mellow. He was still trying to make Wolfe out, but
he was no longer nursing any hurtful notions, and the wine was making
him suspect Wolfe of being an old friend. He said, "It's a remarkable
story. Remarkable. I shall mention it to no one of course, and I appreciate your confidence. I can't say that I have digested all the impli-
cations, but I can see that your disclosure of the truth regarding Barstow was a necessary part of the effort to find the murderer of the man
Maffei. And I can see that you have relieved Sarah and Larry Barstow
of an intolerable burden of fear, and myself of a responsibility that was
becoming more than I had bargained for. I am grateful, believe me."

Wolfe nodded. "There are subtleties, certainly. Naturally some of
them escape you. All that we have actually proven is that of you four—
Mrs. Barstow, her son and daughter, and yourself—none of you killed

Carlo Maffei, and that the fatal driver was not in the golf bag on April ninth. It is still possible that any one of you, or all of you in conspiracy, killed Barstow. That theory would only require a colleague to dispose of Maffei."

Bradford, suddenly a little less mellow, stared. But the stare soon disappeared and he was easy again. "Rot. You don't believe that." Then he stared again. "But as a matter of fact, why don't you?"

"We'll come to that. First let me ask, do you think my frankness has earned a similar frankness from you?"

"I do."

"Then tell me, for example, when and how Mrs. Barstow previously made an attempt on her husband's life."

It was funny to watch Bradford. He was startled, then he went stiff and quiet, then he realized he was giving it away and tried to dress up his face in natural astonishment. After all that he said, "What do you mean? That's ridiculous!"

Wolfe wiggled a finger at him. "Easy, Doctor. I beg you, do not suspect me of low cunning. I am merely seeking facts to fit my conclusions. I see I had better first tell you why I have dismissed from my mind the possibility of your guilt or that of the Barstows. I cannot feel such a guilt. That is all. Of course I can rationalize my feeling, or lack of it. Consider the requirements: a wife or son or daughter who plans the murder of the father with great deliberation, shrewdness, and patience. The lengthy and intricate preparation of the tool. If the wife or daughter, a fellow conspirator who killed Maffei. If the son, the same requirement, since he did not do it himself. Archie Goodwin went there, and he could not spend hours in such a household without smelling the foul odor that it would generate and without bringing the smell to me. You also would have required an accomplice for Maffei. I have spent an evening with you. Though you might murder, you would not murder like that, and you would trust no accomplice whatever. That is the rationalization; it is the feeling that is important."

"Then why—"

"No, let me. You, a qualified and competent observer, certified a heart attack when the contrary evidence must have been unmistakable. That is adventurous conduct for a reputable physician. Of course you were shielding someone. The statement of Miss Barstow indicated whom. Then on finding Barstow dead you must have immediately conjectured that his wife had killed him, and you would not reach so shocking a conclusion without good reason, surely not merely because Mrs. Barstow had in her neurotic moments wished her husband dead. If that constituted murder, what kitchen in this country could shut its door to the hangman? You had better reason, knowledge either of her preparations for this crime or of a previous attempt on her husband's life. Since our facts make the former untenable, I assume the latter, and I ask you simply, when and how did she make the attempt? I ask you only to complete the record, so that we may consign these aspects of the case to the obscurity of history."

Bradford was considering. His mellowness was gone and he was leaning forward in his chair as he followed Wolfe's exposition. He said, "Have you sent someone to the university?"

"No."

"They know about it there. You really guessed it then. Last November Mrs. Barstow shot a revolver at her husband. The bullet went wide. Afterward she had a breakdown."

Wolfe nodded. "In a fit, of course. Oh, don't object to the word; whatever you may call it, was it not a fit? But I am still surprised, Doctor. From a temporary fit of murderous violence, is it permissible to infer a long-premeditated diabolical plot?"

"I made no such inference." Bradford was exasperated. "Good God, there I was with my best and oldest friend lying dead before me, obviously poisoned. How did I know with what he was poisoned, or when or how? I did know what Ellen—Mrs. Barstow—had said only the evening before. I went by my feelings too, as you say you do, only mine were wrong. I got him safely and quietly buried, and I had no regrets. Then when the autopsy came with its amazing results I was too bewildered, and too far in, to act with any intelligence. When Mrs. Barstow proposed to offer the reward I opposed it unsuccessfully. In one word, I was in a funk."

I hadn't noticed Wolfe pushing the button, but as Bradford finished Fritz was on the threshold. "Some port for Dr. Bradford. A bottle of the Remmers for me. Archie?"

"Nothing, thanks."

Bradford said, "I'm afraid none for me, I should be going. It's nearly eleven and I'm driving to the country."

"But, Doctor," Wolfe protested, "you haven't told me the one thing I want to know. Another fifteen minutes? So far you have merely verified a few unimportant little surmises. Don't you see how shrewdly I have labored to gain your confidence and esteem? To this end only, that I might ask you, and expect a full and candid reply: who killed your friend Barstow?"

Bradford stared, discrediting his ears.

"I'm not drunk, merely dramatic," Wolfe went on. "I am a born actor, I suppose; anyway, I think a good question deserves a good set-

ting. My question is a good one. You see, Doctor, you will have to shake
the dust from your mind before you can answer me adequately—the
dust remaining from your hasty and unkind inference regarding your
friend Mrs. Barstow. From that and your funk. Understand that it really
is true, despite the anxieties you have harbored for many months, that
Mrs. Barstow did not kill her husband. Then who did? Who, with the
patience of a devil and the humor of a fiend, prepared that lethal toy
for his hand? I believe you were Barstow's oldest and closest friend?"

Bradford nodded. "Pete Barstow and I were boys together."

"A mutual confidence was sustained? Though superficial interests
separated you intermittently, you presented a common front to life?"

"You put it well." Bradford was moved, it showed in his voice. "A
confidence undisturbed for fifty years."

"Good. Then who killed him? I'm really expecting something from
you, Doctor. What had he ever said or done that he should die? You
may never have heard the story whole, but surely you must have caught
a chapter of it, a paragraph, a sentence. Let the past whisper to you; it
may be the distant past. And you must discard reluctance; I am not asking you for an indictment; the danger here is not that the innocent will
be harassed but that the guilty will go free."

Fritz had brought the beer and the port, and the doctor was leaning
back in his chair again, glass in hand, with his eyes on the red rich
juice. He jerked his head up and nodded at Wolfe and then resumed
his contemplation. Wolfe poured himself some beer, waited for the foam
to subside, and gulped it down. He always thought he had a handkerchief in the breast pocket of his coat but rarely did, so I went to a drawer
where I kept a stack for him and got one and handed it to him.

"I'm not listening to whispers from the past," Bradford finally said.
"I'm being astonished, and impressed, that there are none, of the kind
you mean. Also I'm seeing another reason why I so readily concluded
that Mrs. Barstow—was responsible. Or rather, irresponsible. It was because I knew, or felt, unconsciously, that no one else could have done it.
I see now more clearly than I ever did what an extraordinary person
Pete Barstow was. As a boy he was scrappy, as a man he fought for
every right he believed in, but I'll swear there wasn't a man or woman
alive who could have wished him serious harm. Not one."

"Except his wife."

"Not even she. She shot at him from ten feet and missed him."

"Well." Wolfe sighed, and gulped another glass of beer. "I'm afraid
I have nothing to thank you for, Doctor."

"I'm afraid not. Believe me, Mr. Wolfe, I'd help you if I could. It
is curious, what is happening inside of me at this moment; I would

never have suspected it. Now that I know Ellen is out of it, I am not sure I disapprove of the reward she offered. I might even increase it. Am I vindictive, too, then? For Pete, maybe; I think he might have been for me."

It was altogether a bum evening, as far as I was concerned. For the last ten minutes I was half asleep and didn't hear much. It was beginning to look to me as if Wolfe was going to have to develop a feeling for a new kind of phenomenon: murder by eeny-meeny-miny-mo. That was the only way that needle could have got into Barstow, since everybody was agreed that no one had wanted it there.

It was a bum evening, but I got a grin out of it at the end. Bradford had got up to go and walked toward Wolfe's chair to tell him good night. I saw him hesitating. He said, "There's a little thing on my mind, Mr. Wolfe. I—I owe you an apology. In my office this afternoon I made a remark to your man, a quite unnecessary remark, something about raking scandal out of graveyards—"

"But I don't understand. Apology?" Wolfe's quiet bewilderment was grand. "What had your remark to do with me?"

Of course Bradford's only out was the door.

After seeing the distinguished old gentleman to the entrance and sliding the night bolt in, I went to the kitchen for a glass of milk on my way back to the office. Fritz was there and I told him he had wasted enough good port for one evening, he might as well shut up shop. In the office Wolfe was leaning back in his chair with his eyes shut. I sat down and sipped away at the milk. When it was all gone I was pretty well bored and began talking just for practice.

"It's like this, ladies and gentlemen. The problem is to discover what the devil good it does you to use up a million dollars' worth of genius feeling the phenomenon of a poison needle in a man's belly if it turns out that nobody put it there. Put it this way: if a thing gets where no one wants it, what happened? Or this way: since the golf bag was in the Barstow home for the twenty-four hours preceding the killing, how about finding out if one of the servants has got funnier ideas even than Mrs. Barstow? Of course, according to Sarah's information there's no chance of it, and another objection is that it doesn't appeal to me. Lord, how I hate tackling a bunch of servants. So I guess I'll drop in on the Barstows in the morning and go to it. It looks like it's either that or quit and kiss the fifty grand good-by. This case is a lulu all right. We're right where we started. I wouldn't mind so much if there was anyone to help me out on it, if only I didn't have to do all the thinking and planning for myself, in addition to running around day after day and getting nowhere—"

"Continue, Archie." But Wolfe didn't open his eyes.

"I can't, I'm too disgusted. Do you know something? We're licked. This poison-needle person is a better man than we are. Oh, we'll go on for a few days fooling around with servants and trying to find out who put the ad in the paper for the metal-worker and so on, but we're licked as sure as you're full of beer."

His eyes opened. "I'm going to cut down to five quarts a day. Twelve bottles. A bottle doesn't hold a pint. I am now going to bed." He began the accustomed preparations for rising from his chair. He got up. "By the way, Archie, could you get out fairly early in the morning? You might reach the Green Meadow Club before the caddies depart with their babies. That is the only slang epithet you have brought me recently which seems to me entirely apt. Perhaps you could also kidnap the two who are attending school. It would be convenient if all four of them were here at eleven. Tell Fritz there will be guests at lunch. What do boys of that age eat?"

"They eat everything."

"Tell Fritz to have that."

As soon as I had made sure that he could still get into the elevator, I went on upstairs and set my alarm for six o'clock and hit the hay.

In the morning, rolling north along the Parkway again, I wasn't singing at the sunshine. I was always glad to be doing something, but I was not so liable to burst from joy when I suspected that my activity was going to turn out to be nothing but discarding from a bum hand. I didn't need anybody to tell me that Nero Wolfe was a wonder, but I knew this gathering in the caddies was just a wild stab, and I wasn't hopeful. As a matter of fact, it seemed to me more likely than ever that we were licked, because if this was the best Wolfe could do—

It was a motor cop. With the northbound half of the Parkway empty at that hour of the morning I had been going something above fifty without noticing, and this bicycle Cossack waved me over. I pulled alongside the curb and stopped. He asked for my license and I handed it to him, and he got out his book of tickets.

I said, "Sure I was going too fast. It may not interest you, I don't know, but I'm headed for Anderson's office in White Plains—the District Attorney—with some dope on the Barstow case. He's in a hurry for it."

The cop just had his pencil ready. "Got a badge?"

I handed him one of my cards. "I'm private. It was my boss, Nero Wolfe, that started the party."

He handed the card and the license back. "All right, but don't begin jumping over fences."

I felt better after that. Maybe luck was headed our way after all.

I got the two caddies at the club without any trouble, but it took over an hour to round up the other two. They went to different schools, and while one of them didn't need any persuading to go for a ride to New York, the other one must have been trying to qualify for teacher's pet or a Rhodes scholarship. At first I kidded him, and when that didn't work I switched to the ends of justice and the duties of a good citizen. That got him, and the woman in charge of the school, too. I suspected I wouldn't care an awful lot for his companionship, so I put him and another one in the rumble seat, and with the other two in with me I found the trail back to the Parkway and turned south. I kept the speedometer down to forty thenceforth, for I knew I couldn't expect Anderson to do me nothing but favors.

We arrived at a quarter to eleven, and I took the boys to the kitchen and fed them sandwiches, for the lunch hour was one. I wanted to take them up and show them the orchids, thinking it wouldn't hurt them any to get impressed, but there wasn't time. I got their names and addresses down. One of them, the pale skinny kid who had caddied for Manuel Kimball, had a dirty face and I took him to the bathroom for a wash. By the time Wolfe appeared I was beginning to feel like a Boy Scout leader.

I had them arranged on chairs in a row for him. He came in with a bunch of Cymbidiums in his hand which he put into a vase on his desk, then he got into his chair and flipped the mail. He had told the boys good morning as he entered; now he turned and settled himself comfortably and looked them over one by one. They were embarrassed and shifted around.

"Excuse me, Archie. Bad staging." He turned to the boy at the end, one with red hair and blue eyes. "Your name, sir?"

"William A. Riley."

"Thank you. If you will move your chair over there, near the wall— much better. And your name?" When he had got all their names and scattered them around he said, "Which one of you expressed doubt that Peter Oliver Barstow was killed by a needle shot from the handle of a golf driver? Come, I'm only trying to get acquainted; which one?"

Chunky Mike spoke up. "That was me."

"Ah. Michael Allen. Michael, you are young. You have learned to accept the commonplace, you must yet learn not to exclude the bizarre. Now, boys, I'm going to tell you a story. Please listen, because I want you to understand it. This happens to be a true story. There was a meeting in a public hall of a hundred psychologists. A psychologist is—by courtesy—a man trained to observe. It had been arranged, without their knowledge, that a man should run into the hall and down the aisle, followed by another man waving a pistol. A third man ran in by another door. The second man shot at the first man. The third man knocked the second man down and took the pistol from him. They all ran out by different doors. One of the psychologists then arose and stilled the clamor, and announced that the events had been prearranged, and asked each of his colleagues to write down immediately a complete detailed report of the whole affair. They did so, and the reports were examined and compared. Not one was entirely correct. No two agreed throughout. One even had the third man shooting at the first man."

Wolfe stopped and looked around at them. "That's all. I'm not a good story-teller, but you may have caught the point. Do you see what I'm getting at?"

They nodded.

"You do. Then I shall not insult your intelligence with an exposition. Let us go on to our own story. We shall sit here and discuss the death of Peter Oliver Barstow, more particularly the events on the first tee which led up to it. At one o'clock we shall have lunch, then we shall return here and resume. We shall discuss all afternoon, many hours. You will get tired, but not hungry. If you get sleepy you may take a nap. I state the program thus in full so that you may know how elaborate and difficult an undertaking confronts us. Mr. Goodwin has heard two of your stereotypes; I fancy the other two are practically identical. A stereotype is something fixed, something that harbors no intention of changing. I don't expect you boys to change your stories of what happened on that first tee; what I ask is that you forget all your arguments and discussions, all your recitals to families and friends, all the pictures that words have printed on your brains, and return to the scene itself. That is vitally important. I would have left my house and journeyed to the scene myself to be with you there, but for the fact that interruptions would have ruined our efforts. By our imaginations we must transfer the scene here. Here we are, boys, at the first tee.

"Here we are. It is Sunday afternoon. Larry Barstow has engaged two of you; two of you are with the Kimballs, carrying their bags. You are on familiar ground, as familiar to you as the rooms of your own homes. You are occupied with activities so accustomed as to have become almost automatic. The straps of the bags are on your shoulders. You, Michael Allen, when you see Mr. Barstow, your last season's baby, at a distance from the tee practicing with a mashie, you do not need to be told what to do; you join him, pick up his bag, hand him a club perhaps—"

Mike was shaking his head.

"No? What do you do?"

"I begin chasing balls."

"Ah. The balls he was hitting with the mashie."

"Yes, sir."

"Good. What were you doing, William Riley, while Michael was chasing balls?"

"I was chewing gum."

"Exclusively? I mean, was that the utmost of your efforts?"

"Well, I was standing holding old Kimball's bag."

Listening to him start, I was thinking that Wolfe's long words would get the kids so tied up that pretty soon they would just go dead on him, but it worked the other way. Without telling them so he had given them the feeling that he was counting on them to help him show how dumb the hundred psychologists had been, and they weren't going to get licked at it because it took long words to do it.

He went along inch by inch, now with this boy, now with that, sometimes with all of them talking at once. He let them get into a long discussion of the relative merits of various brands of clubs, and sat with his eyes half closed pretending he enjoyed it. He questioned them for half an hour regarding the identities and characteristics of the other caddies and golfers present, those belonging to the matches which immediately preceded the Barstow foursome at the tee. Every time one of the boys bolted ahead to the actual teeing off Wolfe called him back. Among all the irrelevancies I could see one thing, perhaps the main thing, he was doing: he wasn't losing sight for a single instant of each and every club in each and every bag.

For lunch Fritz gave us two enormous chicken pies and four watermelons. I did the serving, as usual when there was company, and by speeding up with my knife and fork I barely managed to get my own meal in by the time the casseroles were empty. The watermelons were simple; I gave a half to each of the boys and the same for Wolfe and myself, and that left one for Fritz. I suspected he wouldn't touch it but thought there might be use for it later on.

After lunch we resumed where we had left off. It was wonderful the way Wolfe had long since opened those boys' minds up and let the air in. They went right ahead. They had forgotten entirely that someone was trying to get something out of them or that they were supposed to be using their memories; they were just like a bunch of kids talking over the ball game they had played the day before, only Wolfe was on top of them every minute, not letting them skip a thing and all the time making them go back, and back again. Even so they were making progress. Larry Barstow had made his drive, and Manuel Kimball had made his.

When the break came it was so simple and natural, and went along so easy with all the rest of it, that for a minute I didn't realize what was happening. Wolfe was saying to Chunky Mike, "Then you handed Barstow his driver. Did you tee up his ball?"

"Yes, sir. No—I couldn't, because I was over hunting a ball he had put in the rough with his mashie."

"Exactly, Michael, you told us before you were hunting a ball. I wondered then how you could have teed up for Barstow."

William Riley spoke. "He teed up himself. The ball rolled off and I fixed it for him."

"Thank you, William. So you see, Michael, you did not tee up for him. Wasn't the heavy golf bag a nuisance while you were hunting the lost ball?"

"Naw, we get used to it."

"Did you find the ball?"

"Yes, sir."

"What did you do with it?"

"Put it in the ball pocket."

"Do you state that as a fact or an assumption?"

"I put it in. I remember."

"Right away?"

"Yes, sir."

"Then you must have had the bag with you while you were hunting the ball. In that case, you could not have handed Barstow his driver when he teed off, because you weren't there. He could not have removed it from the bag himself, because the bag wasn't there. Had you perhaps handed him the driver previously?"

"Sure. I must have."

"Michael! We need something much better than 'must have.' You did or you didn't. Remember that you are supposed to have told us—"

William Riley butted in. "Hey! Mike, that's why he borrowed old Kimball's driver, because you were off looking for the ball."

"Ah." Wolfe shut his eyes for a tenth of a second and then opened them again. "William, it is unnecessary to shout. Who borrowed Mr. Kimball's driver?"

"Barstow did."

"What makes you think so?"

"I don't think so, I know. I had it out ready to hand to old Kimball, and Barstow's ball rolled off his tee and I fixed it for him, and when I stood up old Kimball was saying to Barstow, 'Use mine,' and Barstow reached out and I handed old Kimball's driver to him."

"And he used it?"

"Sure. He drove right away. Mike didn't come back with the bag until after old Kimball had drove too."

I was having all I could do to stay in my chair. I wanted to do a dance like "Spring on the Mountaintop" that I'd seen in the movies, and pin a bunch of orchids on William Riley, and throw my arms halfway around Wolfe which was as far as they would go. I was afraid to look at Wolfe for fear I would grin so hard and wide I'd bust my jaw.

He was after the pale skinny kid and the one that wanted to be a good citizen, but neither of them remembered anything about Barstow borrowing the driver. The skinny one said he had his eyes glued far out on the fairway, spotting the place where Manuel Kimball had pulled his drive into the bushes, and the good citizen just didn't remember. Wolfe turned to Chunky Mike. Mike could not say positively that Barstow's driver had been in the bag when he had had it with him hunting the ball, but he could not remember handing it to Barstow, and he could not remember receiving it back and returning it to the bag. During all this William Riley was straining his politeness to keep still. Finally Wolfe got back to him.

"Excuse me, William. Do not think I doubt your memory or your fidelity to truth. Corroboration is always helpful. And it might be thought a little curious that you had forgotten so informing a detail."

The boy protested, "I hadn't forgotten it, I just didn't happen to think of it."

"You mean that you have not included that incident in any of your recitals to your friends?"

"Yes, sir."

"Good, William. I put my question badly, but I see that you have the intelligence to stick to the main clause. Possibly you mentioned the incident to Mr. Anderson?"

The boy shook his head. "I haven't seen Mr. Anderson. The detective came and asked me a few questions, not much."

"I see." Wolfe sighed, deep and long, and pushed the button. "It is tea time, messieurs."

Of course for Wolfe that meant beer. I got up and collected the boys and herded them into the kitchen; sure enough, the watermelon was intact. I cut it into four quarters and passed it around. Fritz, having been to answer Wolfe's bell, was arranging a glass and two bottles on a tray; but as he went down the hall I noticed that he turned toward the stairs instead of the office. I glanced at my wrist. It was two minutes to four. The son-of-a-gun had saved his schedule!

I left the boys with the melon and hurried out and caught him on his way to the elevator. He said, "Give the boys my thanks, pay them adequately but not generously, for I am not a generous man, and take them home. Before you leave, telephone the office of E. D. Kimball and learn when he is expected to return from Chicago. He is probably still alive, since he had either the shrewdness or the luck to remove himself a thousand miles from his destiny. If by any chance he has returned get him here at once; on that there must be no delay."

"Yes, sir. And don't you think that if this news got to Mr. Anderson it would only confuse and upset him? Hadn't I better try to persuade the boys to keep it in the family?"

"No, Archie. It is always wiser, where there is a choice, to trust to inertia. It is the greatest force in the world."

When I got back to the kitchen Fritz was cutting an apple pie.

XIII

AFTER I had finished delivering the caddies here and there all over Westchester, I certainly would have loved to run over to Kimball's place and say to Manuel, "Would you mind telling me whether your father keeps his golf bag in his locker at the club and whether you have a key to it?" I had an idea he would recognize that as a question that couldn't be answered just by lifting his eyebrows. I already had him down for two thousand volts. But I realized that if it was him we had a big advantage in his ignorance of what we had found out, and I also realized that if I expected Manuel Kimball to be arrested and convicted of murder there would have to be a little more evidence than the fact that he made me nervous.

I had another temptation, to stop in at Anderson's office and offer to bet him ten thousand dollars that nobody had murdered Peter Oliver Barstow. Wolfe had certainly started a game of hide-and-seek. For two days he and I had been the only two people alive, except the man that did it, who knew that Barstow had been murdered; now we were the only two, with the same exception and the caddies, who knew that he had been killed by accident.

I did go to the Green Meadow Club, after getting the last caddy delivered; it was close by. I went intending to go into the locker question a little, but after I arrived I got cold feet. It might ruin everything if it became known that we had the faintest interest in lockers, since it was common knowledge that Barstow's bag had never been in his. So I just had a little talk with the caddy master and said hello to the chief steward. Maybe I was hoping to get another eyeful of Manuel Kimball, but I didn't see him anywhere.

E. D. Kimball, as his son had told me, had a grain brokerage office on Pearl Street. When I had telephoned there a little after four o'clock I had been told that Kimball was expected back from Chicago the next day, Friday, on the Century. If it hadn't been for that I think I would have tried to start something there in Westchester that evening, if it had been nothing more than to wait till dark and sneak over to the Kimball place and peek in at the windows; but with Kimball on the way there was nothing to do but wait. I went on home.

After dinner that evening Wolfe had me take my notebook and read to him again about my visit to Manuel Kimball, also everything that Sarah and Larry Barstow had said about him, though that wasn't much. We had a general discussion and got our minds to fit; we even considered the possibility that the lending of the driver had been planned and that old Kimball had murdered Barstow, but of course that was out, that was nothing but drivel. I took a few cracks at Manuel, but when Wolfe put it up to me seriously I had to say that not only was there no evidence against Manuel, there wasn't even any reason to suspect him. As far as I knew, it was no more likely to be him than any other member of the Green Meadow Club who had had opportunity to get at the Kimball locker.

"All the same," I insisted, "if he was my son I'd send him on a trip around the world and build a fence across the Pacific Ocean so he couldn't get through."

Before we went to bed Wolfe outlined again my program for the following day. I didn't care much for the first number on it, but of course he was right; the caddies were sure to talk, and the talk would get to Anderson, and it wouldn't hurt us any to get there first since the information was certain to reach him anyhow. I could perform that errand of mercy and still get to Kimball's office almost as soon as he arrived from Grand Central.

So early the next morning found me in the roadster bound for White Plains again. I was hoping the same motor cop would trip me up, it would have been so neat, since I could have handed him the same yarn as the day before and maybe this time have had the pleasure of an escort to the courthouse. But I made it from Woodlawn to the Main Street bridge without seeing anything more exciting than a squirrel running up a tree.

I was creeping along Main Street behind three lumbering buses like a pony following the elephants in a circus parade, when an idea struck me. I liked it. Wolfe seemed to have the notion that all he needed to do to have anybody call at his office, from the Dalai Lama to Al Capone, was to tell me to go and get him, but I knew from long experience that you never knew when you were going to run up against someone with as many feet as a centipede and all of them reluctant. And here was I, not only supposed to haul a prominent grain broker out of his office immediately upon his return from a week's absence, but also headed for a revelation to the District Attorney that would probably result in my having the pleasure of meeting H. R. Corbett or some other flatfooted myrmidon in the anteroom of E. D. Kimball's office—and wouldn't that have been nice? So I parked the roadster in the first available spot and went to a telephone, and called up Wolfe and told him we were putting the soup before the cocktail. He was a little stubborn and gave me an argument, because he was full of the idea that it would pay us to hand Anderson something before he inevitably got hold of it himself, but when he saw that I intended to go on talking right up to a dollar's worth he said all right, I could return to New York and proceed to Pearl Street and wait for my victim.

On the way back I reflected that it was just as well the motor cop hadn't favored me with his attention after all.

When I got to the number on Pearl Street and left the elevator at the tenth floor, I discovered that E. D. Kimball & Company wasn't only selling chicken feed to backyard poultry kings. It had a suite that took up half the floor, with its name on doors everywhere and a double one covered with the names of exchanges all over the country for an entrance. The clock on the wall said a quarter to ten; if the Century was on time it was already at Grand Central, and Kimball might be expected in fifteen or twenty minutes.

I spoke to a girl at a desk, and after using the telephone she took me to an inside room and left me with a square-jawed guy who had his feet on the window sill looking at the morning paper. He said, "Just a minute," and I sat down. After a little he threw the paper on his desk and turned around.

"Mr. E. D. Kimball will be here pretty soon," I said. "I know he'll be busy catching up with the week he's been away. But before he gets started on that I need ten minutes with him on an urgent personal matter. I'm a private detective; here's my card. He never heard of me; I work for Nero Wolfe. Can you fix it for me?"

"What do you want? Tell me what you want."

I shook my head. "It really is personal, and it's damn urgent. You'll just have to trust my honest young face. If you think it's a racket phone the Metropolitan Trust Company at Thirty-fourth Street. They'll tell you that I make a little change in my spare time tending baby carriages."

Square-Jaws grinned. "I don't know. Mr. Kimball has a dozen appointments, the first one is ten-thirty. I'm his secretary, I know more about his business than he does. You'd better tell me."

"I'm sorry, it has to be him."

"All right, I'll see what I can do. Go on out front—no, wait here. Want to look at the paper?"

He tossed me the paper and got up and gathered some mail and stuff together and left the room with them. At a quick early breakfast I had taken a glance at the front page but hadn't had time for more. Turning through, I saw that the Barstow case was already back to page seven, and not much of it there. Anderson was saying that "progress was being made in the investigation." Dear old progress, I thought, you haven't changed a bit since I saw you last except you're covered with wrinkles and your teeth are falling out. The coroner had nothing definite on the poison, but soon would have. There had never been, in any paper that I had seen, any hint of a suspicion that it was a family job; and now, I thought, there never would be. But this piece took another little crack at Dr. Bradford, and I knew it would be a long time before he would be able to look coronary thrombosis in the face without swallowing hard. I turned to the sports page.

The door opened, and the secretary was there.

"Mr. Goodwin. This way."

In the next room but one, a big room with windows on two sides, a lot of old furniture, and a ticker going in a corner, a man sat at a desk. He was smooth-shaven, his hair was turning gray, and while he wasn't fat there was size to him. He looked worried but amused, as if someone had just told him a funny story but he had a toothache. I wondered whether it was the worry or the amusement that came from what the secretary had told him about me, but found out on acquaintance that it was neither one, he always looked that way.

The secretary said, "This is the man, Mr. Kimball."

Kimball grunted and asked me what I wanted. I said that my business was strictly personal. Kimball said, "In that case you'd better take it up with my secretary so I won't have the bother of turning it over to him." He laughed and the secretary smiled and I grinned.

I said, "I only asked for ten minutes, so if you don't mind I'll get started. Nero Wolfe would like to have you call at his office this morning at eleven o'clock."

"Goodness gracious!" The amusement was on top. "Is Nero Wolfe the King of England or something?"

I nodded. "Something. I'll tell you, Mr. Kimball, you'll get this quicker and easier if you let me do it my own way. Just humor me. On

Sunday, June fourth, Peter Oliver Barstow died suddenly while he was playing golf with his son and you and your son. On Thursday the eighth you left for Chicago. On Sunday the eleventh the results of an autopsy were announced. I suppose it was in the Chicago papers?"

"Oh, that's it." The worry had ascended. "I knew that would be a nuisance when I got back. I read a lot of poppycock about poison and a needle and whatnot." He turned to his secretary. "Blaine, didn't I write you this would be a nuisance when I returned?"

The secretary nodded. "Yes, sir. You have an appointment at eleven-thirty with a representative of the Westchester District Attorney. I hadn't had time to mention it."

I kept my grin inside. "It's not poppycock, Mr. Kimball. Barstow was killed by a poisoned needle shot out of the handle of a golf driver. That's wrapped up. Now come with me a minute. Here you are at the first tee, ready to shoot. All four of you with your caddies. No, don't wander off somewhere, stay with me, this is serious. Here you are. Larry Barstow drives. Your son Manuel drives. Peter Oliver Barstow is ready to drive; you are standing near him; remember? His ball rolls off its tee and your caddy fixes it because his caddy is off hunting a ball. Remember? He is ready to drive but hasn't got his driver because his caddy is off with his bag. You say, 'Use mine,' and your caddy straightens up from fixing his ball and hands him your driver. Remember? He drives with your driver, and then jumps and begins rubbing his belly because a wasp stung him. It was that wasp that came out of your driver that killed him. Twenty minutes later he was dead."

Kimball was listening to me with a frown, with the worry and amusement both gone. He went on frowning. When he finally spoke all he said was, "Poppycock."

"No," I said. "You can't make it poppycock just by pronouncing it. Anyway, poppycock or not, it was your driver Barstow used on the first tee. You remember that?"

He nodded. "I do. I hadn't thought of it, but now that you remind me I recall the scene perfectly. It was just as you—"

"Mister Kimball!" The secretary was secretarying. "It would be better perhaps if you—that is, upon reflection—"

"Better if I what? Oh. No, Blaine. I knew this would be a nuisance, I knew it very well. Certainly Barstow used my driver. Why shouldn't I say so? I barely knew Barstow. Of course the poisoned needle story is a lot of poppycock, but that won't keep it from being a nuisance."

"It'll be worse than a nuisance, Mr. Kimball." I hitched my chair toward him. "Look here. The police don't know yet that Barstow used your driver. The District Attorney doesn't know it. I'm not suggesting that you hide anything from them, they'll find it out anyway. But whether you think the poisoned needle is poppycock or not, they don't. They know that Barstow was killed by a needle that came out of his driver on the first tee, and when they find out that it was your driver he used, what are they going to do? They won't arrest you for murder just like that, but they'll have you looking in the dictionary for a better word than nuisance. My advice is, see Nero Wolfe. Take your lawyer along if you want to, but see him quick."

Kimball was pulling at his lip. He let his hand fall. At length he said, "Goodness gracious."

"Yes, sir, all of that."

He looked at his secretary. "You know, Blaine, I have no respect for lawyers."

"No, sir."

Kimball got up. "This is a fine to-do. I have told you before, Blaine, that there is just one thing in the world I am good at. Trading. I am a good trader, and that is surprising when you consider how soft I am really. Soft-hearted. With the more personal aspects of life I do not know how to deal." He was moving back and forth behind his desk. "Yes, this appears to be more than a nuisance. Goodness gracious. What would you do, Blaine?"

I glared at the secretary. He hesitated. "If you care to go to see this Nero Wolfe, I could go with you. If I were you I would take a lawyer."

"What appointments have I?"

"The usual sort of thing, nothing important. At eleven-thirty the man from the Westchester District Attorney."

"Oh, I would miss him. Well, tell him anything. How's the ticker?"

"Firm at the opening. Cotton easing off."

Kimball turned to me. "Where is this Nero Wolfe? Bring him here."

"Impossible, Mr. Kimball. He is—" But Wolfe had once found out that I had told a man he was infirm, and I didn't want that to happen again. "He is an eccentric genius. It's only up on Thirty-fifth Street. I've got my car down below and I'd be glad to run you up."

Kimball said, "I've only met one genius in my life; he was an Argentine cowboy. A *gaucho*. All right. Wait for me in the front office."

Back in the front room I had first entered, I sat on the edge of a chair. Meeting E. D. Kimball and looking at him and talking with him had somehow cleared my mind. I saw plainly what I should have realized the night before, that the minute it came out that it was Kimball's driver that had been turned into what Wolfe called a lethal toy, and the minute Kimball himself arrived on the scene, we were probably turning into the home-stretch. It was the same as if you found a man murdered and by some kind of hocus-pocus were able to bring him back to life long enough to ask him who killed him, and get his answer. That's what E. D. Kimball was, a man who had been murdered and was still living. I had to get him up to Wolfe's place and lock the door, and get him there quick, before Corbett got a chance at him—or, as far as that was concerned, anyone else. Anyone at all. How did I know but what it was the secretary, Square-Jaw Blaine, who had had that driver made and found opportunity to get it into Kimball's bag? At that moment, as I sat there on the edge of the chair, Blaine might be sticking a knife into Kimball as he had into Carlo Maffei. . . .

It was ten-fifty. I got up and began walking up and down the linoleum. Anderson's man—I was sure it would be Corbett—was due at half past eleven, and he might take it into his thick head to come early and wait. I had just decided to ask the girl at the desk to phone in to Blaine for me, when the inner door opened and Kimball appeared with his hat on. I was pretty glad to see him. He nodded at me and I jumped to the entrance door to open it for him.

As we got into the elevator I observed, "Mr. Blaine isn't coming."

Kimball shook his head. "He's needed here more than I need him. I like your face. I find I usually do like a man's face, and it pays every time. Trust is one of the finest things in the world, trust in your fellow man."

Yes, I thought to myself, I'll bet a successful trader like you can use up lots of trust.

It was only half a block to where I had parked the roadster. I cut across as far west as I could get to avoid the traffic, and it was still short of eleven-fifteen when I was ushering Kimball in ahead of me at Wolfe's door.

I took Kimball to the front room and asked him to wait there a minute, then returned to the entrance and made sure the latch was caught. Then I went to the kitchen. Fritz was making cherry tarts; a pan was just out of the oven and I nabbed one and stuffed it in and darned near burned my tongue off. I told Fritz, "One guest for lunch and don't put any poison in it. And be careful who you let in; if there's any doubt, call me."

In the office, Wolfe was at his desk. As soon as I saw him I stopped, exasperated, for he was cleaning house. He had only one drawer in his desk, a wide shallow one in the middle, and since he had begun having his beer in bottles instead of brought up from the basement in a pitcher, he had formed the habit, every time he opened a bottle, of pulling the drawer out and dropping the bottle cap in there. Fritz wasn't supposed to open any drawers in the office, and I knew Wolfe had some sort of a nutty notion that he was saving the bottle caps for something so I had let them alone. Now, when I entered, he had the drawer half out and was scattering the caps all over the desk, arranging them in piles.

I said, "Mr. E. D. Kimball is in the front room. Do you want him to come in and help you?"

"The devil." Wolfe looked around at his piles, and at me helplessly. He sighed. "Can't he wait a while?"

"Of course, sure. How would next week do?"

He sighed again. "Confound it. Bring him in."

"With that junk scattered all over the desk? Oh, all right, I told him you're eccentric." I had kept my voice lowered; now I lowered it some more to let him know how Kimball had shaped up and what I had said to him. He nodded, and I went to get Kimball.

Kimball had his worried-amused look back on again. I introduced him and pulled a chair around for him, and after they had exchanged a few words I said to Wolfe, "If you won't need me, sir, I'll get on to those reports." He nodded, and I got fixed at my desk with papers all around and half underneath a pad which I used for a notebook on such occasions. I had got my signs so abbreviated that I could get down every word of some pretty fast talk and still give the impression to a careless eye that I was just shuffling around looking for last week's delicatessen bill.

Wolfe was saying, "You are perfectly correct, Mr. Kimball. A man's time is his own only by sufferance. There are many ways in which he may be dispossessed: flood, famine, war, marriage—not to speak of death, which is the most satisfactory of all because it closes the question finally."

"Goodness gracious." Kimball was fidgety. "I do not see why that should make it satisfactory."

"You came very near finding out, a week ago last Sunday." Wolfe wiggled a finger at him. "You are a busy man, Mr. Kimball, and you have just returned to your office after a week's absence. Why, under those circumstances, did you take time this morning to come to see me?"

Kimball stared at him. "That's what I want you to tell me."

"Good. You came because you were confused. That is not a desirable condition for a man in the extreme of danger, as you are. I see no indication in your face of alarm or fear, merely confusion. That is astonishing, knowing as I do what Mr. Goodwin has told you. He has informed you that on June fourth, twelve days ago, it was nothing but inadvertence that killed Peter Oliver Barstow, and the same inadvertence saved your life. You met his statement with incredulity, crudely expressed. Why?"

"Because it's nonsense." Kimball was impatient. "Rubbish."

"Before, you said poppycock. Why?"

"Because it is. I didn't come here to argue about that. If the police get into difficulties trying to explain something they don't happen to understand and want to make up any sort of a fancy tale to cover themselves, that's all right, I believe in letting every man handle his own business his own way, but they don't need to expect me to take any stock in it, and they can leave me out of it. I'm a busy man with something better to do. You're wrong, Mr. Wolfe, I didn't come to see you because I was confused, and I certainly didn't come to give you a chance to try to scare me. I came because the police apparently are trying to mix me up in a fancy tale that might give me a lot of trouble and publicity I don't want, and your man gave me to understand you could show me how to avoid it. If you can, go ahead and I'll pay you for it. If you can't, say so, and I'll find better advice."

"Well." Wolfe leaned back in his chair and let his half-shut eyes study the broker's face. Finally he shook his head. "I'm afraid I can't show you how to escape trouble, Mr. Kimball. I might with good fortune show you how to escape death. Even that is uncertain."

"I have never expected to escape death."

"Do not quibble. I mean of course unpleasant and imminent death. I shall be frank with you, sir. If I do not at once bid you good day and let you depart on your business, it is not because of my certain knowledge that you are confronting death like a fool. I refrain from contributing to certain Christian enterprises because I think that no man should be saved by coercion. But here I am guided by self-interest. Mrs. Barstow has offered a reward of fifty thousand dollars for the discovery of her husband's murderer. I intend to discover him; and to do so I need only learn who it was that tried to kill you on June fourth and will proceed to do so within a reasonable time if means are not found of preventing him. If you will help me, it will be convenient for both of us; if you will not, it may well be that only through some misstep or mischance in his successful second attempt shall I be able to bring him to account for his abortive first one. Naturally it would be all the same to me."

Kimball shook his head. But he didn't get up; instead, he was settling into his chair. Still he showed no sign of alarm, he merely looked interested. He said, "You're a good talker, Mr. Wolfe. I don't think you're going to be of any use to me, since you seem to like fancy tales as well as the police, but you're a good talker."

"Thank you. You like good talking?"

Kimball nodded. "I like everything good. Good talking, and good trading, and good manners, and good living. I don't mean high living, I mean good. I've tried to live a good life myself, and I like to think everyone else does. I know some can't, but I think they try to. I was thinking of that in the car a little while ago, riding up here with your man. I'm not saying that the tale he told me made no impression on me at all; of course it did. When I told him it was poppycock I meant it, and I still mean it, but nevertheless it got me thinking. What if somebody had tried to kill me? Who would it be?"

He paused, and Wolfe murmured at him, "Well, who would it be?"

"Nobody." Kimball was emphatic.

I thought to myself, If this guy turns out like Barstow, so lovable a mosquito wouldn't bite him, I'm through.

Wolfe said, "I once met a man who had killed two other men because he had been bettered in a horse trade."

Kimball laughed. "I'm glad he wasn't in grain. If his method of averaging down was universal I would have been killed not once, but a million times. I'm a good trader, it's the one thing I'm proud of. What I love is wheat. Of course what you love is a fancy tale and a good murder, and that's all right, that's your business. What I love is wheat. Do you know there are seven hundred million bushels of wheat in the world? And I know where every one of them is this minute. Every one."

"You probably own a hundred or so yourself."

"No, not one. I'm out. Tomorrow I'll be back in, or next week. But I was saying, I'm a good trader. I've come out on top in a good many deals, but no one has any kick coming, I've stuck to the rules. That's what I was thinking on the way riding up here. I don't know all the details of this Barstow business, just what I've read in the papers. As I understand it, they haven't found the driver. I don't believe it ever existed. But even if they found it, and even if I did lend mine to Barstow on the first tee, I still would have a hard time believing anyone intended it for me. I've stuck to the rules and played fair, in my business and in my private life."

He paused. Wolfe murmured, "There are many kinds of injuries, Mr. Kimball. Real, fancied, material, spiritual, trivial, fatal—"

"I've never injured anyone."

"Really? Come now. The essence of sainthood is expiation. If you will permit it, take me. Whom have I not injured? I don't know why your presence should stimulate me to confession, but it does. Forget the Barstow murder, since to you it is poppycock; forget the police; we shall find means of preventing their becoming a nuisance to you. I enjoy talking with you; unless your affairs are really pressing. I would not keep you from anything urgent."

"You won't." Kimball looked pleased. "When anything's urgent I attend to it. The office has got along without me for a week; an hour more won't hurt them."

Wolfe nodded approvingly. "Will you have a glass of beer?"

"No, thanks. I don't drink."

"Ah." Wolfe pressed the button. "You're an extraordinary man, sir. You have learned to abstain, and you are at the same time a good businessman and a philosopher. One glass, Fritz. But we were speaking of injuries, and I was hovering on confession. Whom have I not injured? That of course is rhetorical; I would not pose as a ruffian; and I suffer from a romantic conscience. Even so, making all allowances, it is not easy for me to understand why I am still alive. Less than a year ago a man sitting in the chair you now occupy promised to kill me at his earliest convenience. I had pulled the foundations of his existence from under him from purely mercenary motives. There is a woman living not twenty blocks from here, and a remarkably intelligent one, whose appetite and disposition would be vastly improved by news of my death. I could continue these examples almost to infinity. But there are others more difficult to confess and more impossible to condone. Thank you, Fritz."

Wolfe removed the opener from the drawer and opened a bottle and dropped the cap into the drawer before he closed it again. Then he filled a glass and gulped it down. Kimball was saying, "Of course every man has to take the risks of his profession."

Wolfe nodded. "That's the philosopher in you again. It is easy to see, Mr. Kimball, that you are a cultured and an educated man. Perhaps you will understand the obscure psychology which prompts—well, me, for instance, to persist in an action which deserves unqualified condemnation. There is a woman under this roof at this moment, living on the top floor of this building, who cannot wish me dead only because her heart is closed to venom by its own sweetness. I torture her daily, hourly. I know I do and that knowledge tortures me; still I persist. You can guess at the obscurity of the psychology and the depth of the torture when I tell you that the woman is my mother."

I got it all down as he said it, and I almost glanced up at him in surprise, he said it so convincingly, with little emotion in his voice but the impression that the feeling underneath was so overwhelming that it was kept down only by a determined will. For a second he darned near had me feeling sorry for his mother, though it was I who, balancing the bank account each month, checked off the debit item for his remittance to her at her home in Budapest.

"Goodness gracious," Kimball said.

Wolfe downed another glass of beer and slowly shook his head from side to side. "You will understand why I can recite a category of injuries. I can justly claim familiarity."

It seemed to me that Kimball wasn't going to take the hint. He was looking sympathetic and self-satisfied. In fact, he smirked. "I'm wondering why you think I'm an educated man."

Wolfe's eyebrows went up. "Isn't it obvious?"

"It's a compliment if you think so. I quit school—out in Illinois—when I was twelve, and ran away from home. It wasn't much of a home, with an uncle and aunt. My parents were dead. I haven't been in a school since. If I'm educated it's self-education."

"Not the worst kind." Wolfe's voice was low and quiet, not much more than a murmur; the voice that he used to say "Go on" without saying it. "You are another proof of it, sir. And New York is itself an education for a lad of that age if he has spirit and character."

"Probably. It might be, but I didn't come to New York. I went to Texas. After a year on the Panhandle, to Galveston, and from there to Brazil and the Argentine."

"Indeed! You did have spirit; and your education is cosmopolitan."

"Well, I covered a lot of territory. I was in South America twenty years, mostly in the Argentine. When I came back to the States I nearly had to go to school again to learn English. I've lived—well, I've lived a lot of funny ways. I've seen a lot of rough stuff and I've taken part in it, but wherever and whatever it was I always did one thing, I always stuck to the rules. When I came back to the States I was selling beef, but gradually I worked into grain. That was where I found myself; grain takes a man not afraid to guess and ready to ride his guess the way a *gaucho* rides a horse."

"You were a *gaucho*?"

"No, I've always been a trader. It was born in me. Now I wonder if you would believe this. Not that I'm ashamed of it; sitting in my office sometimes, with a dozen markets waiting to see which way I'm going to jump, I remember it and I'm proud of it. For two years I was a rope peddler."

"Not really."

"Yes. Three thousand miles a season in the saddle. I still show it when I walk."

Wolfe was looking at him admiringly. "A real nomad, Mr. Kimball. Of course you weren't married then."

"No. I married later, in Buenos Aires. I had an office then on the Avenida de Mayo—"

He stopped. Wolfe poured another glass of beer. Kimball was looking at him, but his eyes were following the movement without seeing it, for obviously the vision was inside. Something had pulled him up short and transported him to another scene.

Wolfe nodded at him and murmured, "A memory—I know—"

Kimball nodded back. "Yes—a memory. That's a funny thing. Goodness gracious. It might almost seem as if I had thought of that on account of what you said about injuries. The different kinds—fancied injuries, fatal injuries. But this wasn't one at all, the only injury was to me. And it wasn't fancied. But I have a conscience too, as you said you have, only I don't think there's anything romantic about it."

"The injury was to you."

"Yes. One of the worst injuries a man can suffer. It was thirty years ago, and it's still painful. I married a girl, a beautiful Argentine girl, and we had a baby boy. The boy was only two years old when I came home from a trip a day too early and found my best friend in my bed. The boy was on the floor with his toys. I stuck to the rules; I've told myself a thousand times that if I had it to do over I'd do it again. I shot twice—"

Wolfe murmured, "You killed them."

"I did. The blood ran onto the floor and got on one of the toys. I left the boy there—I've often wondered why I didn't shoot him too, since I was sure he wasn't mine—and went to a café and got drunk. That was the last time I drank—"

"You came to the States—"

"A little later, a month later. There was no question of escaping, you don't have to run away from that in the Argentine, but I wound things up and left South America for good, and I've only been back once, four years ago."

"You brought the boy with you?"

"No. That's what I went back for. Naturally I didn't want him, my wife's family took him. They lived out on the Pampa, that's where I got her from. The boy's name was Manuel, and that had been my friend's name; I had suggested naming him after my friend. I came back

alone, and for twenty-six years I lived alone, and I found the market a
better wife than the one I had tried. But I suppose there was a doubt in
me all the time, or maybe as a man gets older he softens up. Maybe I
just got lonely, or maybe I wanted to persuade myself that I really had a
son. Four years ago I got things in shape and went to Buenos Aires. I
found him right away. The family had gone broke when he was young
and they were mostly dead, and he had had a hard time of it, but he
had made good. When I found him he was one of the best aviators in
the Argentine army. I had to persuade him to break away. For a while
he tried my office, but he wasn't cut out for it, and he's going into the
airplane business with my money. I bought a place up in Westchester
and built a new house on it, and I only hope when he gets married he
won't take any trips that end the way mine did."

"Of course he knows—about his mother?"

"I don't think so. I don't know, it's never been mentioned. I hope not.
Not that I've got any remorse about it; if I had it to do over I'd do it
again. I don't pretend, even to him, that Manuel is exactly the son I
would want to get if I could just file a buy order; after all, he's Argentine and I'm Illinois. But his name's Kimball and he's got a head on
him. He'll get an American girl, I hope, and that will even it up."

"Indubitably." Wolfe had left his beer untasted so long that the foam
was gone, leaving it as still as tea. He reached for the glass and gulped
it. "Yes, Mr. Kimball, you proved your point; the injury was to you. But
you—let us say—took care of it. If there was an injury to the boy you are
repairing it handsomely. Your confession is scarcely as damaging as
mine; I perforce admit culpability; as Mr. Goodwin would say, I have
no out. But if the boy feels the injury?"

"No."

"But if by chance he does?"

I saw Kimball's eyes fall. It was sometimes not easy to meet Wolfe's
eyes, but Kimball the trader should have been impervious to any eye.
He wasn't. He didn't try it again. Abruptly he got up and, standing,
said, "He doesn't. I took no such advantage of your confession, Mr.
Wolfe."

"You may, sir." Wolfe didn't stir. "You are welcome to all advantages. Why not be frank? There is no danger in me to the innocent."
He looked at his watch. "In five minutes there will be lunch. Lunch
with me. I do not pretend to be your friend, but certainly for you or
yours I have no ill-will. Thirty years ago, Mr. Kimball, you faced a
bitter disappointment and acted upon it with energy; have you lost your
nerve? Let us see what might be done. Lunch with me."

But Kimball wouldn't. As a matter of fact, it seemed to me that for the first time he looked scared. He wanted to get away from there. I didn't quite get it.

Wolfe tried some more to persuade him to stay, but Kimball wasn't having any. He quit looking scared and got polite. He said goodness gracious, he had no idea it was so late, and that he was sorry Wolfe was able to suggest nothing to prevent the police from making a nuisance of themselves, and that he trusted Wolfe would consider their conversation confidential.

I went to the door with him. I offered to drive him back downtown, but he said no, he could get a taxi at the corner. From the stoop I watched him shoving off, and he was right, you could see he had been in a saddle enough to bend his knees out.

When I got back to the office Wolfe wasn't there, so I went on to the dining room. He was getting himself set in front of his chair, with Fritz behind ready to push it. After he had got fixed I sat down. I had never known him to discuss business during a meal, but I was thinking that day he might. He didn't. However, he did violate a custom; ordinarily he loved to talk as he ate, leisurely and rambling on any subject that might happen to suggest itself, as much to himself as to me, I suspected, though I think I was always a good audience. That day he didn't say a word. In between his bites I could see his lips pushing out and pulling back again. He didn't even remember to commend Fritz for the dishes; so as Fritz cleared away for the coffee I tossed a wink at him and he nodded back with a solemn smile, as much as to say that he understood and would bear no grudge.

In the office after lunch Wolfe got into his chair, still silent. I straightened up the papers on my desk and removed from the pad the sheets that I had used and clipped them together. Then I sat down and waited for the spirit to move him. After a while he pulled a sigh that would have fed a blacksmith's bellows all afternoon, shoved his chair back so he could get the drawer of his desk open, and began raking the piles of bottle caps into the drawer. I watched him. When it was finished and the drawer shut he said, "Mr. Kimball is an unhappy man, Archie."

I said, "He's a slicker."

"Perhaps. Nevertheless, unhappy. He is beset from many sides. His son wants to kill him, and intends to. But if Kimball admits that fact, even to himself, he is done for and he knows it. His son, and through his son the future Kimballs, are now all he has to live for. So he cannot admit it and will not. But if he doesn't admit it, and not only admit it but do something about it, again he is done for, for shortly he will die and probably in a thoroughly disagreeable manner. The dilemma is too much for him, and no wonder, for it has additional complications. He wants help, but he dares not ask for it. The reason he dares not ask for it is that like all mortal fools he hopes against all hope. What if—he does not admit this, but no man is so poor that he cannot afford a *what if*—what if his son did attempt to kill him and by mischance killed Barstow instead? Might the son not take that mischance as an omen? Might he not be persuaded—the father could even discuss it with him, man to man—might he not be persuaded to make a sensible trade with destiny and give his father's life for the one he has inadvertently taken? That way Kimball could live to see a grandchild on his knee. In the meantime, until that trade, which would be the most triumphant one of his career, could be consummated, there would be great and constant danger. It would be enough to frighten a younger and an honester man. But he dares not ask for help, for in doing so he would expose his son to a peril as great as the one that confronts himself. It is an admirable dilemma; I have rarely seen one with so many horns and all of them so sharp. It so confused Kimball that he did something which I suspect has been rare with him; he acted like a fool. He exposed his son without gaining any protection for himself. The facts behind the fear he blurted out; the fear itself he denied."

Wolfe stopped. He leaned back in his chair and let his chin fall and laced his fingers on his belly.

"Okay," I said. "Okay for Kimball. Now Manuel. I told you he made me nervous. But aside from that, shall I take the typewriter and make a list of all the swell proof we have that he killed Barstow?"

"Confound it." Wolfe sighed. "I know, the picture must be varnished. The can is empty, Archie. In fact, the can itself is gone. There is nothing."

I nodded. "If I may make a suggestion? There is a flying field at Armonk, which is only a few miles from Pleasantville. If I may drive up there and get curious?"

"You may. But I doubt if he used a public flying field. He would prefer privacy. So before you go, try this. Take this down."

"Long?"

"Very short."

I got a pad and pencil. Wolfe dictated:

Whoever saw me land in the pasture with my airplane Monday evening, June fifth, please communicate. Am winning a bet and will share.

I said, "Good. Swell. But it might have been a golf links."

Wolfe shook his head. "Still too public, and too much loud objection. Leave it pasture; it will have to be definite. No, do not phone it. Stop at the *Times* office on your way uptown; leave it, and make sure the answers will reach us. Also—yes, the other papers, morning and evening, with similar proper arrangements. Manuel Kimball is ingenious enough to be annoying; should he see the advertisement it might occur to him to acquire the answers."

I got up. "All right, I'm off."

"Just a moment. Does White Plains come before Armonk?"

"Yes."

"Then on your way see Anderson. Tell him everything except Carlo Maffei and the Argentine. Present it to him; a fine gesture. Also tell him that E. D. Kimball is in imminent and constant danger and should have protection. Kimball of course will deny it and the precaution will be futile; nevertheless, when men undertake to meddle in the affairs of violent persons as you and I do, certain duties are assumed and should not be neglected."

I knew it had to be done, but I said, "I'd just as soon give Anderson a piece of information as tip a subway guard."

"Soon, now," Wolfe replied, "we may be in a position to send him a bill."

XIV

WHAT with stopping to put the ads in and the Friday afternoon summer traffic, by the time I got to the District Attorney's office in White Plains it was nearly four o'clock. I hadn't bothered to telephone ahead to see if Anderson or Derwin would be in because I had to go through White Plains anyhow to get to Armonk.

They were both there. The girl at the desk threw me a smile when I went up to her, and I liked that; when the time comes that they stop remembering you it means that your pan is losing its shine. Instead of asking my name or who I wanted to see, she nodded and pressed down a key on the switchboard. I said, "Who do you think I am, the prodigal son?" She said, "They'll kill you instead of the calf." After she had talked into the phone a couple of seconds one of the doors snapped open and Derwin came out.

He came up to me. "What do you want?"

I grinned. "This is hot. Can you get Ben Cook here in a hurry?" Because I didn't like fits I went right on. "I want to tell Mr. Anderson something. Or you, or both of you."

I never did find out, I don't know to this day, what that White Plains bunch thought they had been doing during the six days that had passed since the autopsy. There was a hint or two, of course; that Friday afternoon Anderson told me that Corbett had spent two days at Holland University. Probably they got hold of a rumor that there was a student there whom Barstow had kept in school an extra hour or some such sizzler. I know they hadn't come within a mile of anything warm. Though it was hard to believe, it was a fact that Anderson didn't even know that Barstow had been using a new bag of golf clubs that had been given to him by his wife as a birthday present, until I told him. I only got one piece of news that afternoon: a New York chemist had said definitely that Barstow's blood showed snake venom. It was that report that had got Anderson and Derwin's minds off of golf clubs and dwelling fondly on copperheads; and though I hate like the devil to admit it, it gave me a few bad hours, too. Although it left the needle unexplained, I had seen odder things than a needle in a man's stomach accounted for by coincidence. Copperheads were not unknown in Westchester; what if one had been visiting the Green Meadow Club that Sunday and bit Barstow? On the foot or anywhere. It was about good enough for a headache. The snake-venom report hadn't been given to the newspapers, and it wasn't given to me until after Anderson and Derwin had my tale, so it didn't cramp my style.

And of course even if the Green Meadow fairway had been carpeted with copperheads a foot deep, Anderson and Derwin couldn't get around the fact that Nero Wolfe had told them exactly what the autopsy would show them.

Derwin took me into Anderson's room. Anderson was there with another man, not a dick, he looked like a lawyer. I sat down and hooked my panama on my knee.

Anderson said, "What's on your mind?"

I just simply didn't like that man. I couldn't even have any fun with him, to speak of, because whatever it was disagreeable about him, his face and his manner, was so deep and primitive that the only possible way to get any real satisfaction would have been to haul off and plug him in the nose. Derwin was different; he certainly wasn't my favorite uncle, but he would take a lot of kidding.

I said, "Information from Nero Wolfe. Maybe you'd better call a stenographer."

He had to pass a few remarks first, but I went patient and forbearing on him. What was the use of thinking up a lot of snappy come-backs when I couldn't use the one I wanted to? So pretty soon he saw he wasn't getting anywhere, and called a stenographer, and I spieled it off. I told about the birthday present, and the whereabouts of Barstow's golf bag and who had put it there, and the loan of Kimball's driver on the first tee. I suggested that they find out all about Kimball's bag, where he kept it and who had access to it, though I knew that anyone approaching from that direction would never get anywhere, for Manuel must have had any number of opportunities. Then I gave them Wolfe's message about protection for Kimball. I made that strong. I said that Wolfe felt that the responsibility for the safety of a citizen whose life was in jeopardy was a burden for the authorities to assume, and that he would not be answerable, to himself or anyone else, for anything that might happen to E. D. Kimball at any moment.

When I got through Anderson asked questions, and some I answered and some I didn't. He kept it up quite a while, until finally I had to grin at him.

"Mr. Anderson," I said, "you're trying to lure me on."

He was smooth. "But not succeeding, Goodwin. I'll be frank with you. When the autopsy verified Wolfe's prediction, I thought he knew who did it. When the reward was offered and he didn't grab it, I knew he didn't know. We know everything you do now, and a lot more, except the one detail of how Wolfe came to make the prediction in the first place. I'd like to know that, though I don't believe it can be of much value since Wolfe doesn't get anywhere with it. All the same, you might tell me. I'll tell you anything and everything. For instance, this morning snake venom was identified in Barstow's blood."

"Thanks. That saves me the trouble of reading tonight's papers."

"The papers haven't got it. I can tell you a few other things too."

So he did; he mentioned Corbett's trip to the university and a lot of other junk, and wound it up with a lecture on copperheads. Wanting to get on to Armonk, and to be alone to see if the snake-venom news sounded hollow when you dropped it on the sidewalk, I thanked him and got up and put on my hat, and he got sore. I didn't bother any more; I reminded him about protecting E. D. Kimball and walked out.

Since it was only a few miles out of the way and I didn't know how long it would take me at Armonk, I decided to drop in at the Barstows' first. From a booth on Main Street I telephoned; Sarah Barstow was home. Twenty minutes later I was turning into their drive. The same guard was there, and when I stopped he gave me a look and nodded me on.

Some people were on the front terrace having tea. I went to the side door, and Small took me to the sun room at the back, only since it was afternoon the blinds were all up and the glass was in shadow. Small told me that Miss Barstow would join me shortly, and asked if I would have some tea.

I said, "You didn't think that up all alone."

Of course not a flicker. "Miss Barstow told me to offer you tea, sir."

"Sure. She would. A glass of milk would be nice."

In a minute he was back with the milk, and when it was about half gone Sarah Barstow came in. I had told her on the phone it was just a social call, nothing to worry about, and as I got up and looked at her coming toward me, natural and young and human, I thought to myself that if she ever started a clinic for broken hearts I'd be the first in line if I wasn't too busy.

I said to her, "You've had a nap since I saw you last."

She smiled. "I've slept forever. Sit down."

I took my chair and picked up my glass. "Thank you for the milk, Miss Barstow. It's swell milk, too. I'm sorry to call you away from your friends, but it won't take long. I've just been over at Mr. Anderson's office having a chat. I told him about the birthday present and about your night trip to the Tarrytown ferry. Now wait a minute, you certainly are quick on the trigger. It don't mean a thing, it was just strategy, you know, what generals lose battles with. That junk is all out. There never was any phony driver in your father's bag, when your mother gave it to him or any other time. Nobody ever tried to kill him. He died by an accident."

She was staring at me. I waited to let her digest it. She said, "Then it wasn't murder at all— Nero Wolfe was wrong—but how—"

"I didn't say it wasn't murder. Wolfe wasn't wrong. The accident happened on the first tee. Your father's caddy was off with his bag, and your father borrowed E. D. Kimball's driver. It was that borrowed driver that did it. It was a rotten break, that's all. Nobody wanted to kill him."

She said, "My father—I knew my father—"

I nodded. "Yes, I guess you knew your father all right. That's all I wanted to tell you, Miss Barstow. I didn't like to phone it, because I don't know when Anderson will want to release it. So it's confidential. I didn't want you to find out from him what I had told him and maybe think I had double-crossed you. If he should be so curious that he begins asking you why you go around throwing golf bags in the river, in spite of the fact that that's all washed up, tell him to go to hell. That's why I told you that. The reason I told you about Kimball lending his driver was because I know it can't be any fun lying in bed wondering who murdered your father when you ought to be asleep. Nobody murdered him. But it would be okay to keep that in the family for a while." I got up. "That's all."

She sat still. She looked up at me. "Are you going? I think I'll sit here a little. Thank you, Mr. Goodwin. You didn't finish your milk."

I picked up the glass and emptied it and went on out. I was thinking that even on a busy day I might find time to drop in at that clinic.

By the time I got to Armonk it was after six o'clock, but the sun was still high and a couple of planes were perched on the field and another one was just landing. There were signs all around, FLY $5, and TRY THE SKY, and other come-ons, painted on the fence and the walls of the wooden hangars. It wasn't much of a field as far as equipment was concerned, that is, it wasn't very elaborate, but the field itself was good-sized and well kept and flat as a pancake. I parked the roadster off the highway and went through the gate alongside one of the hangars. There was no one around outside except the pilot and two passengers getting out of the plane that had just landed. I went along, looking in the doors, and in the third hangar found a couple of guys throwing pennies at a crack.

They straightened up and looked at me and I nodded.

"Hello." I grinned. "I hate to interrupt your game, but I'm looking for a map, a bound book of flying maps. Maybe that isn't the technical term for it, but I'm not a flyer."

One of them was just a kid. The other one, a little older, in a mechanic's uniform, shook his head.

"We don't sell maps."

"I don't mean I want to buy one. I'm looking for one, bound in red leather, that my brother left here a week ago Monday. June fifth, it was. You probably remember. He knew I was coming past here today on my way to the Berkshires and asked me to stop and get it. He landed here at your field, in his private plane, around six o'clock that evening, and took off again around ten. He's pretty sure he must have left the map here somewhere."

The mechanic was shaking his head. "He didn't land at this field."

I was surprised. "What? Of course he did. He ought to know what field he landed at."

"Maybe he ought to, but he don't, not if he says he landed here. There's been no machine here except ours for over a month, except a biplane that came down one morning last week."

"That's funny." I couldn't understand it. "Are you sure? Maybe you weren't here."

"I'm always here, mister. I sleep here. If you ask me, I think your brother had better find his map. I think he needs it."

"It sure looks that way. Are there any other fields around here?"

"Not very close. There's one at Danbury, and one up toward Pough-keepsie."

"Well. This is one on him. Sorry I interrupted your game. I'm much obliged."

"Don't mention it."

I went out and sat in the roadster to decide what to do. The mechanic hadn't talked like a man earning the five-spot that someone had given him to keep his mouth shut; he had just been telling what had happened, or rather what hadn't happened. Armonk was out. Poughkeepsie too; for although Manuel might have made it there in twenty minutes in his plane, he had to have time to get to wherever he had left his car and drive to where he was going to meet Carlo Maffei. He had almost certainly met Maffei near some subway station uptown in New York, and the date had been for seven-thirty. He could never have made it from Poughkeepsie. Danbury, I thought, was barely possible, and I headed the roadster north.

I didn't like to do that at all, for it was June 16, the anniversary of the day little Tommie Williamson had been restored to his parents in Wolfe's office, and Mr. and Mrs. Burke Williamson and Tommie—four years older now—were going to celebrate as usual by dining with Wolfe. Each year they tried to get him to go to their place, but they never succeeded. They were all right, and I liked Tommie, but the point I had in mind was the importance that Fritz attached to that occasion. Of course he knew that Williamson owned a chain of hotels, and I suppose he wanted to show him what a pity it was that hotels never had anything fit to eat. As Saul Panzer would say, lovin' babe, what a feed! One-fifth of that cargo was labeled for my hold, and instead of being there to stow it away where it belonged, at eight o'clock that evening I was un-enjoying myself at a fern and palm joint in Danbury with a plate of liver and bacon that had absolutely been fried in differential grease.

Nothing went right in Danbury. After the lubricated liver I went out to the flying field. Nobody knew anything. I waited around, and finally long after dark a man showed up who gave me complete dissatisfaction. He kept records but didn't need to, for he remembered what minute the sun had set every day since Easter. When I left I was certain that Manuel Kimball had never been near the place; and though it was a grand summer night I didn't particularly enjoy the drive back to New York. It was after midnight when I reached Thirty-fifth Street; the Williamsons had departed and Wolfe had gone to bed.

In the top drawer of my desk was a note in his fine slender writing: "Archie, if you learned nothing, in the morning try the metal-worker advertisement; and if your grace and charm can again entice Miss Fiore, have her here at eleven. N. W."

I never like to eat late at night unless it seems unavoidable, but I went to the kitchen anyhow for a glass of milk and to look sadly over the remains, like a man visiting the graveyard where his sweetheart's bones are resting. Then I went on upstairs and turned in.

I slept late. While I was eating breakfast Fritz told me about the dinner I had missed, but I was only politely interested; yesterday's meals never concern me much. Looking through the newspaper, I turned to the classified ads to see the one I had put in the day before; it was there and I thought it read good. Before I went out I went to the office and cleaned around a little, for it wasn't going to be much of a morning.

One of the various little things that were keeping me doubtful about Manuel Kimball was the fact that the metal-worker ad was keyed at the downtown office. Wouldn't he have been more apt—since even a man plotting murder will not ignore convenience—to use Times Square or 125th Street? But of course that wasn't a real objection, just one of the little things you think about when you're looking around for something to hang a chance on. In any event, I was counting on getting nowhere with that ad.

That's where I got to. To walk into the *Times* downtown classified ad office and try to find out what girl took a particular ad two months before, and what kind of a person handed it in and who called for the replies, was about like asking a Coney Island lifeguard if he remembers the fellow with a bald head who went in bathing on the Fourth of July. I had stopped at the D.A.'s office on the way down and got Purley Stebbins to go with me with his badge, but the only one that did any good was him since I had to buy him a drink. By going over the files I did learn that the ad had appeared in the issue of April 16, and while that spoiled nothing since it fitted in all right, I couldn't even figure that it paid for the drink.

I took Purley back to his temple of justice and went on to Sullivan Street.

Mrs. Ricci wasn't going to let me in. She came to the door herself and put on a scowl as soon as she saw me. I grinned at her and told her I had come to take Anna Fiore for a ride, and I behaved like a gentleman in the face of all her observations until she began shoving the door on me so hard that my foot nearly slipped. Then I got businesslike.

"See here, Mrs. Ricci, wait a minute, you might as well listen while you've still got some breath. Now listen! Anna is in bad, not with us but with the police. Cops. She told us something that could get her in a lot of trouble if the police knew it. They don't know it and we don't want them to know it, but they suspect something. My boss wants to put Anna wise. He's got to. Do you want her to go to jail? Come on now, and cut out the injured womanhood."

She glared at me. "You just lie."

"No. Never. Ask Anna. Trot her out."

"You stay here."

"Right."

She shut the door and I sat down on the top step and lit a cigarette. Since it was Saturday the street was a madhouse again. I got hit on the shin with a ball and my eardrums began to stretch out, but otherwise it was a good show. I had just flipped the butt away when I heard the door open behind me and got up.

Anna came out with her hat and jacket on. Mrs. Ricci, standing behind her on the threshold, said, "I phoned Miss Maffei. She says you're all right, anyway I don't believe it. If you get Anna into trouble my husband will kill you, her father and mother are dead and she is a good girl, no matter if her head is full of flies."

"Don't you worry, Mrs. Ricci." I grinned at Anna. "Don't you want to go for a ride?"

She nodded, and I led her out to the roadster.

If I ever kill anybody I'm pretty sure it will be a woman. I've seen a lot of stubborn men, a lot of men who knew something I wanted to know and didn't intend to tell me, and in quite a few cases I couldn't make him tell no matter what I tried; but in spite of how stubborn they were they always stayed human. They always gave me a feeling that if only I hit on the right lever I could pry it out of them. But I've seen women that not only wouldn't turn loose; you knew damn well they wouldn't. They can get a look on their faces that would drive you crazy, and I think some of them do it on purpose. The look on a man's face says that he'll die before he'll tell you, and you think you may bust that up; a woman's look says that she would just about as soon tell you as not, only she isn't going to.

I sat and watched Anna Fiore for an hour that morning while Wolfe tried every trick he knew, and if she got away whole it was only because

I remembered that you mustn't kill the goose that has the golden egg inside of her even if she won't lay it. Of course I didn't know whether she really had the golden egg and Wolfe didn't either, but there was no other goose we could think of that had any eggs at all.

Anna and I got to Thirty-fifth Street before eleven and were waiting for Wolfe when he came down. He started on her easy, as if all he wanted to do was tell her a story, not to get anything out of her, just to keep her informed. He told her that the man who had sent her the hundred dollars was the one who killed Carlo Maffei; that he was wicked and dangerous; that the man knew that she knew something he didn't want known and that he might therefore kill her; that Miss Maffei was a nice woman; that Carlo Maffei had been a nice man and should not have been killed and that the man who had killed him should be caught and punished.

Looking at Anna's face, I saw we were up against it.

Wolfe went into the subtleties of contract. He explained several times, using different kinds of words, that a contract between two parties was valid only when they both voluntarily agreed to it. She was under no contract of silence with the murderer because no contract had been made; he had merely sent her money and told her what to do. He had even given her an alternative; she could have burned the money if she had wanted to. She could burn it now. Wolfe opened the drawer of his desk and took out five new twenty-dollar bills and spread them out in front of her.

"You can burn them now, Miss Fiore. It would be sacrilege, and I would have to leave the room, but Mr. Archie will help you. Burn them, and you may have these to take their place. You understand, I will give you these—here, I lay them on the desk. You still have the money?"

She nodded.

"In your stocking?"

She pulled up her skirt and twisted her leg around and the bump was there.

Wolfe said, "Take it out." She unfastened the top of her stocking and reached inside and pulled out the twenties and unfolded them. Then she looked at me and smiled.

"Here," Wolfe said, "here are matches. Here is a tray. I shall leave the room and Mr. Archie will help you and give you this new money. Mr. Archie would be very pleased."

Wolfe glanced at me, and I said, "Come on, Anna, I know you've got a good heart. You know Mr. Maffei was good to you, and you ought to be good to him. We'll burn it together, huh?"

I made the mistake of reaching out with my hand, just starting to reach out, and the twenties went back into her sock like a streak of lightning. I said, "Don't get scared, and don't be foolish. Nobody will touch your money as long as I'm around. You can burn it yourself; I won't even help you."

She said to me, "I never will."

I nodded. "You said that before, but you see it's different now. Now you have to burn it to get this other money."

She shook her head, and what a look she had on her face! She may not have had much of a mind, but what there was of it was all made up. She said, "I don't have to. I never will. I know, Mr. Archie, you think I'm not very bright. I think that too because everybody says I'm not. But I'm not dumb, I mean I'm not all dumb. This is my money and I never will burn it. I won't spend it until I can get married. That's not very dumb."

"You'll never get married if the man kills you the way he killed Mr. Maffei."

"He won't kill me."

I thought, By heaven, if he doesn't I will.

Wolfe took a new tack. He began trying to trick her. He asked her questions about her parents, her early life, her duties and habits at the Riccis', her opinions of this and that. She seemed relieved and answered pretty well, but she took her time, especially when he got on to the rooming-house. And the first time he started to edge up on her, by asking something about cleaning Carlo Maffei's room, she closed up like a clam. He started somewhere else and came around by another way, but the same stone wall shut him off. It was really beautiful of her; I would have admired it if I had had time. Dumb or not, she had it fixed up inside so that something went click when Carlo Maffei's name or anything associated with him was approached and it worked just as well as Wolfe's sagacity worked. He didn't give up. He had taken a quiet casual tone, and knowing his incredible patience and endurance I was thinking that after all there was a chance he might wear her down in a couple of weeks.

The door of the office opened. Fritz was there. He closed the door behind him and, when Wolfe nodded, came over and presented a card on the tray. Wolfe took it and looked at it and I saw his nostrils open a little.

He said, "A pleasant surprise, Archie," and handed the card across the desk and I reached and took it. The card said:

MANUEL KIMBALL

XV

I stood up.

Wolfe sat a moment silent, his lips pushing out and in, then he said, "Show the gentleman into the front room, Fritz. The hall is so dark I would scarcely recognize his face if I saw him there. Just a moment. Be sure the blinds are up in the front room; and leave the door to the hall open so there will be plenty of air."

Fritz went out. Wolfe said, his voice a little quieter even than usual, "Thank you, Miss Fiore. You have been very patient and have kept within your rights. Would you mind if Mr. Archie does not take you home? He has work to do. Mr. Fritz is an excellent driver. Archie, will you take Miss Fiore to the kitchen and arrange with Fritz? You might then accompany her to the entrance."

I nodded. "I get you. Come on, Anna."

She started, too loud, "Can't Mr. Archie—"

"Don't talk. I'll take you home some other day. Come on."

I got her into the kitchen, and explained to Fritz the pleasure that awaited him. I don't think I had ever really felt sorry for Anna until I saw that Fritz didn't blush when I told him to take her home. That was terrible. But I left the feeling sorry till later; while Fritz was getting his apron off and his coat and hat on I was figuring how to handle it.

I said, "Look here, Anna, let's have some fun. You said something about getting married, and that made me wonder what kind of a man you'd like to marry. There's a man sitting in the front room now, I'll bet he's just the kind. Very good-looking. As we go out we'll stop and look through the door at him, and then I'll go outside with you and you will tell me if he's the kind. Will you do that?"

Anna said, "I know the kind—"

"All right. Don't talk. I don't want him to hear your voice, so he won't know we're looking at him. Ready, Fritz?"

We went out. Fritz had followed instructions and left the door open between the hall and the front room, and I steered Anna to the left of the hall so she wouldn't be too close to the door. Manuel Kimball was in there, a good view, in an armchair, with one knee hanging over the other. Having heard our steps he was looking in our direction, but it was so dark in the hall he couldn't see much. I had a hand on Anna's elbow and my eyes on her face as she looked in at Kimball. I let her look a couple of seconds and then eased her toward the entrance where

Fritz was holding the door open for us. Outside, I closed the door behind me.

"Is that the kind you like, Anna?"

"No. Mr. Archie, if I tell you—"

"Some other day. That's the girl. So long. It won't matter if lunch is late, Fritz, I've an idea we may be late too, and there'll be no guest."

I ducked back in and went past the open front-room door to the office. Wolfe hadn't moved. I said, "She never saw him before. Or if she did, she could give Lynn Fontanne a furlong start and lope in ahead of her." He inclined his head. I asked, "Shall I bring him in?" He inclined his head again.

I went directly through to the front room, by the connecting door. Manuel Kimball got up from his chair and faced around and bowed. I said, "Sorry to keep you waiting. We had a young lady client who thinks we can bring back her husband just by whistling to him, and it's not that easy. Come this way."

Wolfe didn't feel formal enough to get up, but he kept his hands laced on his belly. As I led Manuel toward him he said, "How do you do, Mr. Kimball. You will forgive me for not rising; I am not rude, merely unwieldy. Be seated."

I couldn't see any signs that Manuel Kimball was suffering with agitation, but he did look concentrated. His black eyes seemed smaller than when I had seen him before, and concerned with something too important to permit of darting around everywhere to see what they could see. He was wiry and neat in a lightweight, finely tailored suit, with a yellow bow tie and yellow gloves in his pocket. He wasn't bothering with me. After he got into the chair which was still warm from Anna Fiore, his eyes went to Wolfe and stayed there.

Wolfe asked, "Will you have some beer?"

He nodded his head. "Thank you."

I took the hint. In the kitchen I got a couple of bottles from the icebox and a glass from the shelf and fixed up a tray. I made it snappy because I didn't want to miss anything. I went back with the tray and put it on Wolfe's desk, and then sat down at my desk and pulled some papers out of a drawer and got things fixed up. Manuel Kimball was talking.

". . . told me of his visit to your office yesterday. My father and I are on a completely confidential basis. He told me everything you said to him. Why did you say what you did?"

"Well." Wolfe pulled out his drawer to get the opener, removed the cap from a bottle and dropped it into the drawer, and filled a glass. He watched the foam a moment, then turned back to Manuel. "In the first place, Mr. Kimball, you say that your father repeated everything to you that I told him. You can hardly know that. So let us be properly selective. Your tone is minatory. What specifically do you wish to berate me for? What did I say to your father that you would rather I had left unsaid?"

Manuel smiled, and got colder. "Don't try to twist my words, Mr. Wolfe. I am not expressing my preferences, I am asking you to account for statements that seem to me unwarranted. I have that right, as the son of a man who is getting old. I have never before seen my father frightened, but you have frightened him. You told him that Barstow was killed as a result of borrowing my father's golf driver."

"I did, indeed."

"You admit it. I trust that your man there taking this down will include your confession. What you told my father is criminal nonsense. I have never believed the tale of the poisoned needle as regarded Barstow; I believe it less now. What right have you to invent such absurdities and distress, first the whole Barstow family, now my father, with them? Probably it is actionable, my lawyer will know about that. Certainly it is unjustifiable and it must be stopped."

"I don't know." Wolfe appeared to be considering; as for me, I was handing it to Manuel for being cute enough to get what I was doing in the first five minutes; not many had done that. Wolfe downed a glass of beer and wiped his lips. "I really don't know. If it is actionable at all, I suppose it could only be through a complaint of libel from the murdered. I don't suppose you had that in mind?"

"I have only one thing in mind." Manuel's eyes were even smaller. "That it has got to stop."

"But, Mr. Kimball," Wolfe protested, "give me a chance. You accused me of inventing absurdities. I have invented nothing. The invention, and a most remarkable and original one, even brilliant—and I am careful of words—was another's; only the discovery was mine. If the inventor were to say to me what you have said, I would put him down for a commendably modest man. No, sir, I did not invent that golf driver."

"And no one else did. Where is it?"

"Alas." Wolfe turned a hand palm up. "I have yet to see it."

"What proof is there that it ever existed?"

"The needle that it propelled into Barstow's belly."

"Bah. Why from a golf driver? Why on the first tee?"

"The wasp came from nowhere, and synchronized."

"No good, Mr. Wolfe." Manuel's intent little black eyes were scornful. "It's what I said, criminal nonsense. If you have no better proof than that, I repeat, I have a right to demand that you retract. I do so. I have this morning called on Mr. Anderson, the District Attorney at White Plains. He agrees with me. I demand that you see my father and retract and apologize; likewise the Barstows if you have told them. I have reason to suspect that you have."

Wolfe shook his head slowly from side to side. After a moment he said regretfully, "It's too bad, Mr. Kimball."

"It is. But you caught the crow, now you can eat it."

"No. You misunderstand me. I mean it's too bad that you are dealing with me. I am perhaps the only man on this hemisphere whom your courage and wit cannot defeat, and by incredibly bad luck you find yourself confronted by me. I am sorry; but just as you have assumed a task suitable for your abilities, I have found one congenial for mine. You will forgive me for wheeling onto your flank, since you have made it impossible for me to meet you frontally. I hardly suppose that you expected your direct attack to gain its feigned objective; you could hardly have had so poor an opinion of me as that. Your true objective must have been concealed, and probably it was the discovery of the nature and extent of the evidence I have so far acquired. But surely you know that, for how else could I have foretold the result of the autopsy? I beg you, let me finish. Yes, I know when and where and by whom the golf driver was made, I know where the man who made it is now, and I know what results to expect from the advertisement which I inserted in this morning's newspapers and which you have perhaps seen."

Not a muscle on Manuel's face had stirred, and no change was perceptible in his tone. His eyes kept straight on Wolfe as he said, "If you know all that—I doubt if you do—is that not information for the District Attorney?"

"Yes. Do you want me to give it to him?"

"I? I want? Of course, if you have it."

"Good." Wolfe wiggled a finger at him. "I'll tell you what you do, Mr. Kimball. Do me a favor. On your way home this afternoon stop at Mr. Anderson's office; tell him what information I have and suggest that he send for it. Now—I am sorry—it is past my lunch hour. May I offer you a compliment? If almost anyone else I have known were in your position I would try to detain him longer on the chance of learning something. With you, I feel that eating my lunch will be more profitable."

Manuel was on his feet. "I should tell you, I am going from here to my lawyer. You will hear from him."

Wolfe nodded. "Certainly your best move. Obvious, but still the best. Your father would wonder if you did not."

Manuel Kimball turned and went. I got up and started after him for the courtesy of the house, but he was out of the front door before I made it.

I went back to Wolfe. He was leaning back with his eyes closed. I asked loud enough to wake him up, "Did that guy come here to find out if he'd have to go ahead and kill his father during the week end?"

He sighed. His eyes opened and he shook his head. "Lunch, Archie."

"It won't be ready for ten minutes. Fritz only got back at one."

"The anchovies and celery will divert us."

So we went to the dining room.

Right there, at that point, the Barstow-Kimball case went dead. At least Wolfe went dead, and that was the case as far as I was concerned. It wasn't a relapse, he just closed up. While plenty went into him during lunch, of course nothing came out; and when the meal was finished he went to the office and sat. I sat at my desk and caught up with a few things, but there wasn't much to do, and I kept glancing at Wolfe, wondering when he would open up. Although his eyes were closed he must have felt my glances, for all of a sudden he looked at me and said, "Confound it, Archie, cannot paper be made not to rattle?"

I got up. "All right, I'll beat it. But damn it, where? Have you lost your tongue?"

"Anywhere. Go for a walk."

"And return?"

"Any time. It doesn't matter. Dinner."

"Are you waiting for Manuel to bump off his old man?"

"Go, Archie."

It seemed to me that he was rubbing it in, since it was already three-thirty and in another half-hour he would himself have left to go up to the plant rooms. But seeing the mood he was in, I got my hat from the hall and went out.

I went to a movie to think, and the more I thought the more uncomfortable I got. Manuel Kimball's visit and his challenge, for that was what it amounted to, darned near succeeded as far as I was concerned. I had been aware that we weren't quite ready to tell Mrs. Barstow what address to mail the check to, but I hadn't fully realized how awfully empty our bag was. We had found out some things to our own satisfaction, but we had no more proof that there had been a murder than we had had when we started. Let alone who had done it. But that wasn't all; the worst was that there was no place to go from there. Granted that it was Manuel Kimball, how could we tie him up? Find the golf driver. Fat chance. I could see him in his plane flying low over the river or a reservoir, dropping the club out with a chunk of lead wired to the shaft. Trace the poison to him. About the same chance. He had been planning this for years maybe, certainly months; he may even have had the poison with him when he came up with his father from the Argentine; anyway, he could have got it from there at any time—and try and find out. Get him to talk on the telephone with Mrs. Ricci and have her recognize his voice. Sure, that was it; any jury would convict on that without leaving the courtroom.

I sat in a movie three hours without seeing anything that happened on the screen, and all I got was a headache.

I never did know what Wolfe was up to that Saturday afternoon and Sunday. Was he just bumping his head against the wall, as I was? Maybe; he wasn't very sociable. Or was he possibly waiting for Manuel to make a move? But the only move Manuel could have made would have been to kill his father, and then where would we have been? Anderson would have left us out in the cold, and while neither Wolfe nor I would have worn any black for E. D. Kimball we certainly would have done so for the fifty grand. As far as E. D. Kimball was concerned, I figured that by rights he had been killed on June fourth anyway and he might be grateful for two weeks of grace. But Wolfe wasn't waiting for that; I was sure he didn't expect it from what he said about Manuel Sunday afternoon. It was then that he opened up and talked a little, but not to much point. He was being philosophic.

It was raining; it rained all that Sunday. I wrote some letters and went through two Sunday papers and spent a couple of hours on the roof chinning with Horstmann and looking over the plants, but no matter what I did I was in a bad humor. The damn rain never let up once. Not that it would have bothered me if I had had anything to do; I don't notice rain or shine if I'm out in it busy; but monkeying around that dry dark quiet house all day long with that constant patter outside and never a let-up didn't help my disposition a bit. I was thankful when something happened around five-thirty that I could get good and sore about.

I was in the office yawning over a magazine when the telephone rang. It took me a few seconds to unwind myself out of the armchair I was in and get across to my desk, and when I got the receiver to my ear I was surprised to hear Wolfe's voice. He was answering from the plant-room phone. He always took calls in the plant room when I was out, but usually when he knew I was in the house he left them to me. But it was his voice.

"This is Wolfe."

Another voice: "This is Durkin, Mr. Wolfe. Everything is okay. She went to church this morning, and a while ago she came out and went to a candy store and bought an ice-cream cone. She's back in now, I expect for the night."

"Thank you, Fred. You'd better stay there until ten o'clock. Saul will be there in the morning at seven, and you resume at two."

"Yes, sir. Anything else?"

"That's all."

I banged the receiver onto the hook, thinking there was a chance it might crack Wolfe's eardrum.

When he came into the office half an hour afterward I didn't look up, and I was careful to be buried in my magazine enough to make sure it wasn't upside down. I held onto that pose another half-hour, turning a page when I thought of it. I was boiling.

Wolfe's voice, finally: "It's raining, Archie."

I didn't look up. "Go to hell. I'm reading."

"Oh no. Surely not, in those fitful gusts. I wish to inquire, would it be a good plan in the morning for you to collect the replies to our advertisement and follow their suggestions?"

I shook my head. "No, sir. The excitement would be too much for me."

Wolfe's cheeks folded up. "I begin to believe, Archie, that a persistent rain distresses you even more acutely than it does me. You are not merely imitating me?"

"No, sir. It's not the rain, you know damn well it isn't." I dropped the magazine on the floor and glared at him. "If the very best way you can think of to catch the cleverest murderer that ever gave me a highball is to start a game of tiddlywinks in Sullivan Street, you might at least have told me so I could remember Durkin in my prayers. Praying is all I'm good for maybe. What's Durkin trying to do, catch Anna hocking the golf stick?"

Wolfe wiggled a finger at me. "Compose yourself, Archie. Why taunt me? Why upbraid me? I am merely a genius, not a god. A genius may discover the hidden secrets and display them; only a god could create new ones. I apologize to you for failing to tell you of Durkin; my mind was occupied; I telephoned him yesterday after you went for a walk. He is not trying to catch Miss Fiore but to protect her. In the house she is probably safe; outside, probably not. I do not think Manuel Kimball will proceed to devise means of completing his enterprise until he is satisfied that there is no danger of his being called to account for his first attempt, which failed through no fault of his. It was perfectly conceived and perfectly executed. As for us, I see no possibility but Miss Fiore; *clever* is too weak a word for Manuel Kimball; he has his own genius. I would not ask for a better means of defeating a rainy

Sunday than contemplation of the beauty of his arrangements. He has left us nothing but Miss Fiore, and Durkin's function is to preserve her."

"*Preserve* is good. Since she might as well be sealed up in a can."

"I think the can may be opened. We shall try. But that must wait until we are completely satisfied as to June fifth. By the way, is Maria Maffei's telephone number in the book? Good. Of course, we do not know what Miss Fiore is guarding so jealously. If it turns out to be trivial and insufficient, then we must abandon the skirmish and plan a siege. No man can commit so complicated a deed as a murder and leave no vulnerable points; the best he can do is render them inaccessible save to a patience longer than his own and an ingenuity more inspired. In Manuel Kimball's case those specifications are—well, considerable. If in fact Miss Fiore is guarding the jewel that we seek, I earnestly hope that he is not aware of it; if he is, she is as good as dead."

"With Durkin protecting her?"

"We cannot protect from lightning, we can only observe it strike. I have explained that to Fred. If Manuel Kimball kills that girl we shall have him. But I think he will not. Remember the circumstances under which he sent her the hundred dollars. At that time he could not have supposed that she knew anything that could connect him with Barstow, or he would not have made so inadequate a gesture. He knew only her first name. Probably Carlo Maffei had mentioned it, and had said enough of her character and of some small discovery she had made to suggest to Manuel Kimball, after he had killed Maffei, to risk a hundred dollars on the chance of additional safety without the possibility of added danger. If that surmise is correct, and if Miss Fiore knows nothing beyond what Kimball was aware that she knew, we are in for a siege. Saul Panzer will go to South America; I warned him yesterday on the telephone to be in readiness. Your program, already in my mind, will be elaborate and tiresome. It would be a pity, but we would have no just grievance against Manuel Kimball. It was only by his ill fortune, and my unwarranted pertinacity in asking Miss Fiore a trivial question a second time, that the first piece of his puzzle was discovered."

Wolfe stopped. I got up and stretched. "All I have to say is, he's a dirty spiggoty."

"No, Archie, Mr. Manuel Kimball is an Argentinian."

"Spiggoty to me. I want a glass of milk. Can I bring you some beer?" He said no, and I went to the kitchen.

I felt better. There were times when Wolfe's awful self-assurance gave me a touch of a dash of a suggestion of a pain in the neck, but there were other times when it was as good as a flock of pure and beautiful maidens smoothing my brow. This was one of the latter. After I had finished with a sufficient quantity of milk and cookies I went out to a movie and didn't miss a scene. When I went home it was still raining.

But Monday morning was beautiful. I got out early. Even in New York the washed air was so fresh and sweet in the sunlight that it somehow dissolved all the motor exhausts and the other million smells sneaking out of windows and doors and alleys and elevator lids, and made it a pleasure to breathe. I stepped on it. By half past eight I was out of Bronx Park and turning into the parkway.

I had collected more than twenty answers to the ad and had gone through them. About half of them were phony, chiselers trying to horn in or poor fish trying to be funny. Some others were honest enough but off of my beat; apparently June fifth had been a good day for landing in pastures with airplanes. Three of them not only looked good but fitted together; it seemed that they had all seen the same plane land in a meadow somewhere a couple of miles east of Hawthorne. That was too good to be true.

But it wasn't. A mile out of Hawthorne, following the directions in the letter, I left the highway and turned into an uphill dirt road with the ruts left washed out and stony by the rain. After a while the road got so narrow and doubtful that it looked as if it might play out any minute, and I stopped at a house and asked where the Carters lived. On up. I went on.

The Carter residence, on top of the hill, was about ready to fall down. It hadn't been painted since the war, and the grass was weeds. But the dog that got up to meet me was friendly and happy, and the wash on the line looked clean in the sunshine. I found Mrs. Carter around back, getting the rest of the wash through. She was skinny and active, with a tooth gone in front.

"Mrs. T. A. Carter?"

"Yes, sir."

"I've come to see you about your reply to an ad I put in Saturday's paper. About my landing with my airplane. Your letter is quite complete. You saw me land?"

She nodded. "I sure did. I didn't see the ad though, Minnie Vawter saw it and I had told her about the airplane and she remembered it and brought the ad up Saturday afternoon. It was lucky I had told her about it. Sure I saw you land."

"I wouldn't have supposed you could see me from here."

"Sure, look. This is a pretty high hill." She led me across the yard and through a clump of sumacs. "See that view? My husband says that view's worth a million dollars. See the reservoir, like a lake?" She pointed. "That field down there's where you landed. I wondered what was up, I thought you'd broke something. I've seen plenty of airplanes in the air, but I never saw one land before."

I nodded. "That's it all right. Thanks to the completeness of your letter, there's not much I need to ask you. You saw me land at ten minutes past six, and saw me get out and walk south across the meadow, toward the road. You came into the house then to look at the dinner on the stove, and saw me no more. At twilight my plane was still there; you went to bed at half past nine, and in the morning it was gone."

"That's right. I thought it would be better to put it all in the letter, because—"

"Correct. I imagine you are usually correct, Mrs. Carter. Your description of my plane is better than I could do myself. And from such a distance; you have good eyes. By the way, could you tell me who lives in that house down there, the white one?"

"Sure. Miss Wellman. She's an artist from New York. It was Art Barrett, the man that works for her, that drove you to Hawthorne."

"Oh. Of course. Yes, that's the place. I'm much obliged to you, Mrs. Carter, you're going to help me win my bet. It was a question of how many people saw me."

I decided to give her a five-spot. The Lord knows she needed it, judging from appearances; and she had sewed Manuel Kimball up tighter than a bag of bran. I don't know how sure Wolfe had been of Manuel up to that point, but I do know that he postponed the works for Anna Fiore until after June fifth was settled. I hadn't been sure at all. I never did like my feelings as well as Wolfe liked his; they often got me talking big, but they always left me uneasy until I got satisfactory facts to tuck them in with. So I figured that Mrs. Carter's hand-out was cheap at five bucks. Manuel Kimball was settled with us. To get enough to settle him with a jury was another matter, but as far as we were concerned he was all set. Mrs. Carter got her hand all around the five-dollar bill and started toward the house, remarking that the wash wouldn't finish itself.

I stood a minute looking down at the meadow far below. That was where Manuel Kimball had landed and left his plane; across that field he had walked to the white house and asked a man there to drive him to Hawthorne; at Hawthorne, which was only a few miles from his home, he had either had his own car waiting or had rented one at a garage; he had driven to New York, stopping probably at White Plains to telephone Carlo Maffei and arrange a meeting. He was already screwed up, and alarmed, because Maffei had abandoned the trip to Europe; and when he met him that evening at seven-thirty and Maffei produced the clipping he had cut from the *Times* that morning and began to talk about how hard it was to keep his mouth shut about golf drivers, that was plenty for Manuel. With Maffei in the car with him, he drove to some secluded nook and found an opportunity to sink a knife five inches into Carlo's back at the point where the heart was waiting for it. Leaving the knife there to hold the blood in, he drove around the countryside until he found the sort of spot he needed, dragged Maffei's body out of the car and carried it into a thicket, returned to the car, and drove to Hawthorne, where he got a taxi to take him back to the white house that was there in the valley below me. If he needed help taking off in the plane, Art Barrett and the taxi-driver were both handy. Around ten o'clock he landed on his own private lighted field and told Skinner that it was really more fun flying at night than in the daytime.

There was nothing wrong with that, except possibly one thing: it was giving Carlo Maffei credit for a lot of activity between his ears to suppose that reading that piece about Barstow's death was enough to put him wise. But I laid that away; there was no knowing what might have happened before to make Maffei suspicious, and the mere oddity of the outlandish contraption he had been paid so well to construct had certainly made him wonder.

I decided not to tackle Art Barrett. I couldn't very well present myself as the aviator as I had with Mrs. Carter, since he had driven Manuel to Hawthorne, and there was nothing he could tell me that would be worth the trouble of doping out an approach. For the present I had enough. There would be time for that later, if we needed him for a case. The other two replies to the ad could wait too. I was itching to get back to Thirty-fifth Street, remembering that Wolfe had promised to use a can opener on Anna Fiore if I succeeded in pulling Manuel Kimball down out of the clouds for the evening of June fifth.

I stopped at the clothesline for a good-by to Mrs. Carter, got the roadster turned around by inching back and forth between the boulders that lined the narrow road, and floated off downhill toward the highway.

I discovered I was singing, and I asked myself, Why all the elation? All I had found was the proof that we were on a spoke and not on the rim; we still had to get to the hub, and we were just as far away from that as we had been before. I went on singing anyhow, rolling along the Parkway; and at Fordham Road I stopped and telephoned Wolfe what I had got. He was already down from the plant rooms, and when I halted at Thirty-sixth Street for a red light Tiffany's whistle was blowing noon.

I left the roadster in front. Wolfe was in the office. He was seated at his desk, and Fritz was bringing in a tray with a glass and two bottles of beer.

Wolfe said, "Good morning, Friend Goodwin."

"What?" I stared. "Oh, I get you." I had left my hat on. I went to the hall and tossed it on a hook and came back. I sat down and grinned. "I wouldn't go sour now even for Emily Post. Didn't I tell you Manuel Kimball was just a dirty spiggoty? Of course it was your ad that did it."

Wolfe didn't look as if he was on my boat; he didn't seem interested. But he nodded and said, "You found the pasture."

"I found everything. A woman that saw him land and knows just which parts of his plane are red and which blue, and a man that drove him to Hawthorne—everything we could ask for."

"Well." He wasn't looking at me.

"Well! What are you trying to do, get me sore again? What's the matter—"

The palm of his hand coming up from the chair arm stopped me. "Easy, Archie. Your discovery is worthy of celebration, but you must humor me by postponing it. Your explosive return chanced unfortunately to interrupt an interesting telephone call I was about to make. I was reaching for the book when you entered; possibly you can save me that effort. Do you happen to know the Barstow number?"

"Sure. Something's up, huh? Do you want it?"

"Get it, please, and listen in. Miss Sarah Barstow."

I went to my desk, glanced at the book to make sure of the number, and called. In a moment Small's voice was in my ear. I asked to speak to Miss Barstow, and after a little wait she was on the wire and I nodded to Wolfe. He took off his receiver. I kept mine at my ear.

He said, "Miss Barstow? . . . This is Nero Wolfe. . . . Good morning. I am taking the liberty of calling to inquire if the orchids reached you safely. . . . No, orchids. . . . I beg your pardon? . . . Oh. It is a mistake apparently. Did you not do me the honor of sending me a note this morning requesting me to send you some orchids? . . . You sent no note? . . . No, no, it is quite all right. . . . A mistake of some sort, I am sorry. . . . Good-by."

We hung up. Wolfe leaned back in his chair. I put on a grin.

"You're getting old, sir. In the younger set we don't send the girls orchids until they ask for them."

Wolfe's cheeks stayed put. His lips were pushing out and in, and I watched him. His hand started for the drawer to get the opener for a bottle, but he pulled his hand back again without touching the drawer.

He said, "Archie, you have heard me say that I am an actor. I am afraid I have a weakness for dramatic statement. It would be foolish not to indulge it when a good opportunity is offered. There is death in this room."

I suppose I must have involuntarily glanced around, for he went on, "Not a corpse; I mean not death accomplished but death waiting. Waiting only for me perhaps, or for all of us; I don't know. It is here. While I was upstairs this morning with the plants Fritz came up with a note —this note."

He reached in his pocket and took out a piece of paper and handed it to me. I read it:

Dear Mr. Wolfe—

Last week, at your house, Mr. Goodwin kindly presented me with two orchids, remarkably beautiful. I am daring to be cheeky enough to ask if you can send me six or eight more of them? They were so lovely. The messenger will wait for them, if you do decide to be generous. I shall be so grateful!

Sarah Barstow

I said, "It don't sound like her."

"Perhaps not. You know her better than I do. I of course remembered the *Brassocattlaelias Truffautianas* in her hand when she came downstairs with you. Theodore and I cut a dozen and boxed them, and Fritz took them down. When I came to the office at eleven o'clock and sat at my desk there was a smell of a stranger in the air. I am too sensitive to strangers, that is why I keep these layers over my nerves. I knew of course of the stranger who had called, but I was uncomfortable. I sent for Fritz. He told me that the young man who had brought the note and waited for the orchids had had with him a fiber box, an oblong box with a handle. On departing he had taken the box with him; Fritz saw it in his hand as he left the house. But for at least ten minutes the young man was alone in the front room; the door between that room and the office was unlocked; the door from the hall to the office was closed."

Wolfe sighed. "Alas, Miss Barstow did not write the note."

I was on my feet and going toward him, saying, "You get out of here." He shook his head. "Come on," I demanded, "I can jump and you can't. Damn it, come on, quick! I'm used to playing with bombs. Fritz! Fritz!" Fritz came running. "Fill up the sink with water. To the top. Mr. Wolfe, for God's sake get out of here, it may go off any second. I'll find it."

I heard Fritz back in the kitchen starting the water. Wolfe wouldn't budge, and the Lord knows I couldn't budge him. He shook his head and wiggled a finger at me.

"Archie, please. Stop that! Don't touch anything. There is no bomb. They tick or they sizzle, and I have good ears and have listened. Besides, Mr. Kimball has not had time since his call to construct a good one, and he would use no other. It is not a bomb. I beg you, no trepidation; drama, but not trepidation. I have reflected, and I have felt. Consider: when Mr. Kimball was in this room he saw me make no movement worthy the name but one. He saw me open the drawer of my desk and put my hand in it. If that suggests nothing to you, I am sure it did to him. We shall see."

I jumped at him, for I thought he was going to open the drawer, but he waved me back; he was merely getting ready to leave his chair. He said, "Get my red-thorn walking stick. Confound it, will you do as I say?"

I ran to the hall and got the stick from the stand and ran back. Wolfe was moving around the desk. He came clear around to the side opposite his chair, and reached over for the tray and pulled it across to him, with the glass and bottles still on it.

"Now," he said, "please do it this way. No, first close the door to the hall." I went and closed the door and returned. "Thank you. Grasp the stick by its other end. Reach across the desk and catch the tip of the handle on the lower edge of the drawer-front. Push, and the drawer will open. Wait. Open it, if you can, quite slowly; and be ready to free the stick quickly should it occur to you to use it for any other purpose. Proceed."

I proceeded. The tip of the handle's curve caught nicely under the edge of the drawer, but on account of the angle I had to keep the drawer wouldn't start. I tried to push so as to open the drawer gradually, but I had to push harder, and suddenly the drawer popped out half a foot and I nearly dropped the stick. I lifted up to get the stick loose, and yelled, "Look out!"

Wolfe had got a beer bottle in each hand, by the neck, and he brought one of them crashing onto the desk but missed the thing that had come out of the drawer. It was coming fast and its head was nearly to the edge of the desk where we were while its tail was still in the drawer. I had got the stick loose and was pounding at its head but it kept slashing around and I couldn't hit it, and the desk was covered with beer and the pieces of the broken bottle. I was ready to jump back and was grabbing Wolfe to pull him back with me when he came down with the second bottle right square on the ugly head and smashed it flat as a piece of tripe. The long brown body writhed all over the desk, but it was done for.

The second bottle had busted too, and we were splattered all over.

Wolfe stepped back and pulled out his handkerchief and began to wipe his face. I held on to the stick.

"*Nom de Dieu!*"

It was Fritz, horrified.

Wolfe nodded. "Yes. Fritz, here's a mess for you. I'm sorry. Get things."

XVI

I TRIED it again. "*Fair-duh-lahnss?*"

Wolfe nodded. "Somewhat better. Still too much *n* and not enough nose. You are not a born linguist, Archie. Your defect is probably not mechanical. To pronounce French properly you must have within you a deep antipathy, not to say scorn, for some of the most sacred of the Anglo-Saxon prejudices. In some manner you manage without that scorn, I do not quite know how. Yes, fer-de-lance. *Bothrops atrox*. Except for the bushmaster, it is the most dreaded of all the vipers."

Fritz had cleaned up the mess, with my help, and served lunch, and we had eaten. When the snake had finished writhing I had stretched it out on the kitchen floor and measured it: six feet, three inches. At the middle it was almost as thick as my wrist. It was a dirty yellowish brown, and even dead it looked damn mean. After measuring it I stood up and, poking at it with the yardstick, wondered what to do with it—observing to Wolfe, standing near, that I couldn't just stuff it in the garbage pail. Should I take it and throw it in the river?

Wolfe's cheeks folded. "No, Archie, that would be a pity. Get a carton and excelsior from the basement, pack it nicely, and address it to Mr. Manuel Kimball. Fritz can take it to the post office. It will relieve Mr. Kimball's mind."

That had been done, and it hadn't spoiled my lunch. Now we were back in the office, waiting for Maria Maffei, whom Wolfe had telephoned after receiving my call from Fordham Road.

I said, "It comes from South America."

Wolfe was leaning back in his chair content, with half-shut eyes. He was not at all displeased that it had been his blow that had killed it, though he had expressed regret for the beer. He murmured, "It does. It is a crotalid, and one of the few snakes that will strike without challenge or warning. Only last week I was looking at a picture of it, in one of the books you procured for me. It is abundant throughout South America."

"They found snake venom in Barstow."

"Yes. That could have been suspected when the analysis was found difficult. The needle must have been well smeared. These considerations, Archie, will become of moment if Anna Fiore fails us and we must have recourse to a siege. Many things will be discoverable with sufficient patience and—well, abandonment of reserve. Is there somewhere on the Kimball estate a pit where Manuel has carried rats to his fer-de-lance? Did he extract the venom himself by teasing its bite into the pulp of a banana? Unlikely. Has he an Argentine friend who sent the poison to him? More likely. The young man—dark and handsome, Fritz says—who brought the note not from Miss Barstow, and who is admirably deft with vipers, will he be found to be on duller days an usher in a Hundred and Sixteenth Street movie theater? Or a seaman on a South American boat, providentially arrived at the port of New York only yesterday? Difficult questions, but each has its answer, if it comes to a siege. It is likely that Manuel Kimball arranged some time ago for the journey of the fer-de-lance, as a second string to his bow; thinking that if the contrivance designed by man should for any reason fail it would be well to give nature's own mechanism a chance. Then, when it arrived, there was a more urgent need for it; vengeance stepped back for safety. And now, to this moment at least, he has neither."

"Maybe. But he just barely missed getting one, and he may get the other any minute."

Wolfe wiggled a finger at me. "Faulty, Archie, inexcusably faulty. Vengeance will continue to wait. Mr. Manuel Kimball is not a creature of impulse. Should circumstances render him suddenly desperate he would act with desperation, but even then not impulsively. But Miss Maffei is due in half an hour, and you should know the arrangements before she arrives. Your notebook."

I got at my desk, and he dictated twenty minutes without stopping. After the first two minutes I put on a grin and kept it on till the end. It was beautiful, it was without a flaw, and it covered every detail. He had even allowed for Maria Maffei's refusal or her inability to persuade Anna; in that case the action was approximately the same, but the characters were shifted around; I was to take it with Anna. He had telephoned Burke Williamson and arranged for a clear stage for us, and Saul Panzer was to call at the office at six o'clock for the sedan and his instructions. When he had finished dictating it was all so clear that there were few questions for me to ask. I asked those few and ran back over the pages. He was leaning back in his chair, full of beer, pretending he wasn't pleased with himself.

I said, "All right, I admit it, you're a genius. This will get it if she's got it."

He nodded without concern.

Maria Maffei arrived on the dot. I was waiting for her on my toes and got to the door before Fritz was out of the kitchen. She was dressed in black, and if I had met her on the street I doubt if I would have known her, she looked so worn out. I was so full of Wolfe's program that I had a grin ready for her, but I killed it in time. She wasn't having any grins. After I saw her I didn't feel like grinning anyway; it sobered me up to see what the death of a brother might do to a woman. She was ten years older and the bright life in her eyes was gone.

I took her to the office and moved a chair in front of Wolfe for her and went to my desk.

She exchanged greetings with Wolfe and said, "I suppose you want money."

"Money for what?" Wolfe asked.

"For finding my brother Carlo. You didn't find him. Neither did the police. Some boys found him. I won't pay you any money."

"You might." Wolfe sighed. "I hadn't thought of that, Miss Maffei. I'm sorry you suggested it. It arouses me to sordid considerations. But for the moment let us forget it; you owe me nothing. Forget it. But let me ask you—I am sorry if it is painful, but it is necessary—you saw your brother's body?"

Her eyes were dull on him, but I saw that I had been wrong: the life in them was not gone, it had merely sunk within, waiting back there as if in ambush. She said quietly, "I saw him."

"You saw perhaps the hole in his back. The hole made by the knife of the man who killed him."

"I saw it."

"Good. And if there was a chance of my discovering the man who used that knife and bringing him to punishment, and I needed your help, would you help me?"

In the dull eyes a gleam came and went. Maria Maffei said, "I would pay you money for that, Mr. Wolfe."

"I suspect you would. But we shall forget that for the present. It is another kind of assistance I require. Since you are intelligent enough to make reasonable assumptions, and therefore to be made uncomfortable when only unreasonable ones are available, I had better explain to you. The man who murdered your brother is sought by me, and by others, for another act he committed. An act more sensational and not less deplorable. I know who he is, but your help is needed—"

"You know? Tell me!" Maria Maffei had jerked forward in her chair, and this time the gleam in her eyes stayed.

Wolfe wiggled a finger at her. "Easy, Miss Maffei. I am afraid you must delegate your vengeance. Remember that those of us who are both civilized and prudent commit our murders only under the complicated rules which permit us to avoid personal responsibility. Let us get on. You can help. You must trust me. Your friend Fanny's husband, Mr. Durkin, will tell you that I am to be trusted; besides, he will also help. I wish to speak of Miss Anna Fiore, the girl who works at the rooming-house where your brother lived. You know her?"

"Of course I know her."

"Does she like you and trust you?"

"I don't know. She is a girl who hides her flowers."

"If any? A tender way of putting it; thank you. Could you go in my automobile this evening, with a driver, and persuade Miss Fiore to take a long ride with you; give her a good excuse, so she would go willingly?"

Maria Maffei looked at him; after a moment she nodded. "She would go. It would be a strange thing, I would have to think—"

"You will have time for that. I prefer to leave it to your wit to invent the excuse; you will use it better if it is your own. But that is all that will be left to you; one of my men will drive the car; in all the rest you must carefully and precisely follow my instructions. Or rather, Mr. Goodwin's instructions. Archie, if you please." Wolfe put his hands on the edge of the desk and shoved his chair back, and got himself up. "You will forgive me for leaving you, Miss Maffei, it is the hour for my plants. Perhaps when you and Mr. Goodwin have finished you would like him to bring you up to see them."

He left us.

I didn't take Maria Maffei upstairs to see the orchids that day; it was nearly five o'clock when I had finished with her, and I had something else to do. She didn't balk at all, but it took a lot of explaining, and then I went over the details three times to make sure she wouldn't get excited and ball it up. We decided it would better for her to make a preliminary call on Anna and get it arranged, so I took her out and put her in a taxi and saw her headed for Sullivan Street.

Then I started on my own details. I had to get the knife and the masks and the guns ready, and arrange with the garage for hiring a car, since we couldn't take a chance on Anna recognizing the roadster, and get hold of Bill Gore and Orrie Cather. I had suggested them, and Wolfe said okay. He had already told Durkin to report at seven o'clock.

I got it all done, but without any time to spare. At six-thirty I ate a hurry-up dinner in the kitchen, while Wolfe was in the office with Saul Panzer. On his way out Saul looked in at the kitchen to make a face at me, as if his ugly mug wasn't good enough without any embroidery. He called in to me, "Enjoy it, Arch, it may be your last meal, you're not dealing with a quitter this night!"

I had my mouth full, so I only said, "Shrivel, shrimp."

Bill Gore and Durkin were there on time, and Orrie wasn't late enough to matter. I gave them the story, and rehearsed Orrie several times because a lot depended on him. We hadn't been together on anything for over two years, and it seemed like old times to see him again twisting his thin lips and looking around for a place to squirt his tobacco juice.

Wolfe was still in at his dinner when we got away a little before eight o'clock. The garage had given me a black Buick sedan, and it had four wheels and an engine but it wasn't the roadster. Orrie got in front with me and Bill Gore and Durkin in the back. I thought to myself that it was too bad it was only a set-up, because with those three birds I would have contracted to stop anything from a Jersey bus to a truck of hooch. Orrie said I should have hung a sign on the radiator, *Highwaymen's Special*. I grinned, but only with my mouth. I knew everything had to go exactly right and it was up to me, and what Wolfe had said about Anna Fiore was true: her mental vision was limited, but within its limits she might see things that a broader vision would miss entirely.

I went up the west side and got onto the Sawmill River Road. The Williamson place was in the back country east of Tarrytown, on a secondary road; I knew the way as well as I knew Thirty-fifth Street on account of my trips there four years before. I had expected to make it by nine-thirty but traffic up to Yonkers had held me up a little, and it was a few minutes later than that and I had the lights on when I turned into the drive where I had once picked Mrs. Williamson up in a faint and carried her to the pond to throw water on her.

I drove on up to the house, about a third of a mile, and left the three in the car and went and rang the doorbell. Tanzer, the butler, remembered me and we shook hands. I told him I wouldn't go in, I just wanted to speak to his boss a minute. Burke Williamson came right away; he shook hands too and said he was sorry they had missed me Friday night. I said I was sorry too.

"I'm a little late, Mr. Williamson, I came on up just to make sure that everything's set. No loose servants out hunting lightning bugs? Can we go ahead?"

"Everything's arranged." He laughed. "No one will disturb your sinister plot. Of course we're all itching with curiosity. I don't suppose we could get behind a bush and watch?"

I shook my head. "You'd better stay in the house, if you don't mind. I won't see you again, I've got to make a quick getaway. Wolfe will phone you tomorrow, I expect, to thank you."

"He needn't bother. I'll never do enough to make Nero Wolfe owe me any thanks."

I went back to the car and turned it around and started back down the drive. I had the spot picked out, about halfway down, a full three hundred yards from the public road, where high shrubbery was on both sides with trees just beyond and it would be good and dark. There the drive was narrow enough so that I could block it with the sedan without bothering to swing it crosswise.

I got the sedan into position and turned off the lights and we all got out. It was nearly ten o'clock and our prey was due at a quarter past. I passed around the guns and gave Orrie the knife, and then handed out the masks and we put them on. We were a hard-looking bunch and I couldn't help grinning at Orrie's wisecracks, though to tell the truth I was pretty much keyed up. The thing had to go absolutely right. I went over it again with them. They had it pat, and we scattered into the bushes. It was plenty dark. They began calling back and forth to one another, and pretty soon I told them to shut up so I could listen.

After a couple of minutes the sound came up from below of Wolfe's sedan going into second on the grade. I couldn't see the lights on account of the bushes, but soon I did. They got brighter, and then I saw the car. It buzzed along, getting close, and when the driver saw my sedan right ahead it slowed down. I left the bushes on a run, jumped to the running-board of Wolfe's sedan just as it came to a stop, and shoved my gun into the face of Saul Panzer on the driver's seat.

The others were with me. Bill Gore was on my side, on the running-board, sticking his gun through the open window; Orrie, with Durkin behind him, was opening the other tonneau door. Maria Maffei was screaming. There was no sound from Anna.

Orrie said, "Get out of there quick. Come on, do you want me to put a hole in you?"

Anna came out and stood on the ground by the running-board. Bill Gore went in and got Maria Maffei and hauled her out. Orrie growled, "Shut your trap, you." He called to me, "If that driver grunts let him have it. Turn out the lights."

Bill Gore said, "I've got her purse, it's fat."

"Which one?"

"This one."

"All right, keep it, and keep her trap shut. If she yells rap her one." Orrie turned to Durkin. "Here, hold this one while I put a light on her."

Durkin moved behind Anna and gripped her arms, and Orrie put a flashlight on her face. She looked pale and her lips were clamped tight; she hadn't let out a chirp. Orrie held his light right against her and his masked face was just behind it. He said, "It's you all right. By God, I've got you. So you will tell people about Carlo Maffei cutting out newspaper clippings and talking on the phone and everything you ought to forget. Will you? You won't any more. The knife that was good enough for Carlo Maffei is good enough for you. Tell him hello for me."

He pulled out the long sticker and waved it and it gleamed in the light of the flash. He was too damn good. Maria Maffei yelled and jumped for him and nearly got away from Bill Gore. Bill, who weighed two hundred and no fat, got all around her. Durkin was pulling Anna Fiore back away from the knife and saying to Orrie, "None of that! Cut it! You said you wouldn't. None of that!" Orrie stopped waving the knife and put the light on Anna again.

"All right." He made it sound bloodthirsty. "Where's your purse? I'll get you later. Come on, don't stand there shaking your head. Where's your purse? Where's that hundred dollars I sent you? No? Hold her, I'll frisk her for it."

He started for her stocking, and Anna was a wildcat. She busted loose from Durkin and let out a squawk that must have reached to White Plains. Orrie grabbed for her and tore her sleeve half off; Durkin was on her again, and when she saw she couldn't get away she put on a kicking and biting exhibition that made me glad I was leaving that to the help. Durkin finally got her snug, with an arm wrapped around her pinning her arms and his other hand holding her head back, but Orrie never did get his hand inside her stocking, he had to tear it right off. I saw the getaway would have to be quick or we'd have to tie her up, so I had Saul back his car along the edge of the drive so I could get by with mine. Durkin came carrying Anna Fiore, still kicking and trying to bite him, and shoved her into the tonneau; Orrie was with him, growling at her, "You kept my money, did you? You wouldn't burn it, huh? Next time you'll keep your mouth shut."

I ran to the Buick and started the engine and rolled alongside. The others piled in. As we started off Maria Maffei was yelling at us, but I didn't hear Anna's voice. I twisted around the curves of the drive as fast as was practicable, and as soon as I had turned into the public road I stepped on it.

Bill Gore in the back seat was laughing about ready to choke. I got to the Sawmill River Road and turned south, and eased down to forty. Orrie, beside me, wasn't saying anything. I asked him, "You got the money?"

"Yeah, I got it." He didn't sound very sweet. "I think I'll keep it until

I find out if Nero Wolfe carries workmen's compensation insurance."

"Why, did she get you?"

"She bit me twice. That lassie didn't think any more of that hundred bucks than I do of my right eye. If you'd told me I had to subdue a tiger with my bare hands I'd have remembered I had a date."

Bill Gore started laughing again.

I thought it had been pretty well staged. Wolfe couldn't ask better than that. The only thing I had been afraid of was that Anna would get such a scare thrown into her that she would fold up for good, but now that didn't seem likely. I was glad Wolfe had thought of using Maria Maffei and she had been ready for the job, for I wouldn't have cared a bit about driving Anna Fiore back to town with her empty sock. The only question now was, what did she have and how soon would we get it? Would Wolfe's program carry through to the end as he had outlined it, and if it did what kind of a climax would she hand us?

Anyhow, my next move was to get back to the office without delay, so I didn't take time to distribute my passengers where they belonged. I dropped Bill Gore off at Ninetieth Street and took Durkin and Orrie on downtown and left them at the Times Square subway station. Since it wouldn't do to leave the Buick out in front, I drove to the garage and delivered it, and walked home.

I hadn't cared much for the notion Manuel Kimball had got about the sort of present that would be appropriate for Nero Wolfe, and on leaving I had told Fritz to put the bolt on as soon as we got out, so now I had to ring him up to let me in. It was nearly midnight, but he came to the first ring.

Wolfe was in the office, eating cookies and marking items in Hoehn's catalogue. I went in and stood, waiting for him to look up. He did so at length and said, "On time."

I nodded. "And not on my shield, but Orrie Cather is, nearly. She bit him. She bit Durkin too. She was a holy terror. Your play went off swell. They ought to be here soon; I'm going up and dress for the next act. Can I have a glass of milk?"

Wolfe said, "Good," and turned back to his catalogue.

I took the milk upstairs with me to my room, and sipped it in between while I was getting undressed and putting on my pajamas. This part of the stunt seemed to me pretty fussy, but I didn't mind because it gave me a chance to doll up in the dressing-gown Wolfe had given me a couple of years before, which I hadn't had on more than about once. I lit a cigarette and finished the milk, then put on the dressing-gown and gave it the once-over in the mirror. While I was doing that I heard a car drive up and stop outside, and I moved closer to the open window and heard Saul Panzer's voice, and then Maria Maffei's. I sat down and lit another cigarette.

I sat there nearly half an hour. I heard Fritz letting them in, and their voices in the hall as they passed on their way to the office, and then all I got was silence. I waited so long that I was beginning to wonder whether it wasn't working right, or Wolfe was finishing his charade without me. Then there were footsteps in the hall, and in a minute on the stairs, and Fritz was at my door saying that Wolfe wanted me in the office. I waited a little, long enough to get awake and into my dressing-gown, as if I had been asleep, and ruffled up my hair, and went down.

Wolfe was seated at his desk. Maria Maffei was in a chair in front of him and Anna in one against the wall. Anna was a sight, with one sleeve nearly off, a leg bare, her face dirty, and her hair all over.

I stared. "Miss Maffei! Anna! Did they set the dogs on you?"

Wolfe wiggled a finger at me. "Archie. I'm sorry to have to disturb you. Miss Maffei and Miss Fiore have been subjected to violence. They were driving into the country, to visit Miss Maffei's sister, when they were set upon by brigands. Their car was stopped; they were treated with discourtesy, and robbed. Miss Maffei's purse was taken, and her rings. Miss Fiore was despoiled of the money which she has shown to us and which she so hardly earned."

"No!" I said. "Anna! They didn't take that money!"

Anna's eyes were on me. I met them all right, but after a second I thought it would do to turn back to Wolfe.

Anna said, "*He* took it."

Wolfe nodded. "Miss Fiore got the impression that the man who took her money was the one who had sent it to her. I have advised her and Miss Maffei to go to the police at once, but they do not fancy that suggestion. Miss Maffei mistrusts the police on principle. Miss Fiore seems to have conceived the idea that we, more especially you, are more likely to be of help. Of course you are not at the moment properly dressed to go out in search of robbers, and the scene is thirty miles off, but Miss Fiore asked for you. Does anything occur to you?"

"Well," I said. "This is awful. It's terrible. And me upstairs sound asleep. I wish you had got me to drive you to the country, Anna; if you had this wouldn't have happened, I don't care who it was that tried to get your money. I don't believe it could have been the man who sent it to you; that man kills people; he would have killed you."

Anna's eyes were going back and forth between Wolfe and me, but I no longer thought there might be suspicion in them; she was only stunned, overwhelmed by her unimaginable loss. She said, "He wanted to kill me. I bit him."

"Good for you. You see, Anna, what happens when you try to act decent with a bad man. If you had burned that money the other day when I wanted you to, and told us what you know about things, now you would have Mr. Wolfe's money. Now you can't burn the money because you haven't got it, and the only way you could get it back would be if I could catch him. Remember, he's the man who killed Carlo Maffei. And look what he did to you! Tore your dress and pulled off your stockings—did he hurt you?"

Anna shook her head. "He didn't hurt me. Could you catch him?"

"I could try. I could if I knew where to look."

"Would you give it back to me?"

"Your money? I sure would."

Anna looked down at her bare leg, and her hand slid slowly under the hem of her skirt and rested on the spot where the twenties had been. Maria Maffei started to speak, but Wolfe wiggled her into silence. Anna was still looking at her leg when she said, "I've got to undress."

I was slow; Wolfe got it at once. He spoke. "Ah. Certainly. Archie: the lights in the front room. Miss Maffei: if you will accompany Miss Fiore?"

I went to the front room and turned the lights on and closed the windows and the curtains. Anna and Miss Maffei had followed me in and stood there waiting for me to leave; as I went out I gave Anna a friendly grin; she looked pale but her eyes were brighter than I had ever seen them. In the office I closed the door behind me. Wolfe was sitting up in his chair, not leaning back; there was nothing to remark on the drowsy patient hemisphere of his face, but his forearms extended along the arms of the chair and the forefinger of his right hand was moving so that its tip described a little circle over and over on the polished wood. For Wolfe that was going pretty far in the way of agitation.

I sat down. Faint sounds of movements and voices came from the front room. They were taking long enough. I said, "This is a swell toga you gave me."

Wolfe looked at me, sighed, and let his eyes go half shut again.

When the door opened I sprang up. Anna came through in front, clutching a piece of paper in her hand; her torn sleeve had been pinned together and her hair fingered back. She came up to me and stuck the paper at me and mumbled, "Mr. Archie." I wanted to pat her on the shoulder but I saw she was sure to cry if I did, so I just nodded and she went back to her chair and Maria Maffei to hers. The paper was a fat little manila envelope. I turned to Wolfe's desk to hand it to him, but he nodded to me to open it. It wasn't sealed. I pulled out the contents and spread them on the desk.

There was quite a collection. Wolfe and I took our time inspecting it. Item, the Barstow death clipping that Carlo Maffei had cut from the *Times* on June fifth. Item, a series of drawings on separate little sheets, exact and fine, with two springs and a trigger and a lot of complications; the shape of one was the head of a golf driver. Item, a clipping from a Sunday Rotogravure, a photograph of Manuel Kimball standing by his airplane, and a caption with his name commenting on the popularity of aviation among the Westchester younger set. At the bottom was written in pencil, "The man I made the golf club for. See drawings. May 26, 1933. Carlo Maffei." Item, a ten-dollar bill. It was a gold note, and there was pencil-writing on it too, the signatures of four people: Sarah Barstow, Peter Oliver Barstow, Lawrence Barstow, and Manuel Kimball. The signatures had been written with a broad-pointed soft pencil and covered half of one side of the bill.

I looked it all over a second time and then murmured at Wolfe, "Lovin' babe."

He said, "I tolerate that from Saul Panzer, Archie, I will not from you. Not even as a tribute to this extraordinary display. Poor Carlo Maffei! To combine the foresight that assembled this with the foolhardiness that took him to his fatal rendezvous! We alone profit by the foresight, he pays for the foolhardiness himself—a contemptible bargain. Miss Maffei, you have lost your purse but gained the means of stilling the ferment of your blood; the murderer of your brother is known and the weapon for his punishment is at hand. Miss Fiore, you will get your money back. Mr. Archie will get it and return it, I promise you. He will do it soon, for I can guess how little promises mean to you; the fierce flame of reality is your only warmth and light; the reality of twenty-dollar bills. Soon, Miss Fiore. Please tell me: when did Mr. Maffei give you all this?"

Anna talked. Not what you could call volubly, but willingly enough to Wolfe's questions. He got every detail and had me take it down. She had actually seen the driver. For many days Carlo Maffei had forbidden her to enter his room when he was there working, and had kept his closet locked; but one day during his absence the closet door had opened to her trial only to disclose nothing to her curiosity more uncommon than a golf club evidently in process of construction. On Maffei's return, finding that the driver was not placed as he had left it, he had been sufficiently disturbed to inform her that if she ever mentioned the golf club he would cut her tongue out. That was all she knew about it. The envelope had been given to her on June fifth, the day Maffei disappeared. Around seven o'clock, just after he had answered the telephone call, she had gone upstairs for something and he had called her into his room and given her the envelope. He had told her that he would ask her to return it in the morning, but that if he did not come back that night and nothing was heard from him Anna was to deliver the envelope to his sister.

When Anna told that Maria Maffei got active. She jumped up and started toward the girl. I went after her, but Wolfe's voice like a whip beat me to it.

"Miss Maffei!" He wiggled his finger. "To your chair. Be seated, I say! Thank you. Your brother was already dead. Save your fury. After pulling Miss Fiore's hair you would, I suppose, inquire why she did not give you the envelope. That appears to me obvious; perhaps I can save her the embarrassment of replying. I do not know whether your brother told her not to look into the envelope; in any event, she looked. She saw the ten-dollar bill; it was in her possession. Miss Fiore, before Carlo Maffei gave you that envelope, what was the largest sum you ever had?"

Anna said, "I don't know."

I asked her, "Did you ever have ten dollars before?"

"No, Mr. Archie."

"Five dollars?"

She shook her head. "Mrs. Ricci gives me a dollar every week."

"Swell. And you buy your shoes and clothes?"

"Of course I do."

I threw up my hands. Wolfe said, "Miss Maffei, you or I might likewise be tempted by a kingdom, only its boundaries would not be so modest. She probably struggled, and by another sunrise might have won and delivered the envelope to you intact; but that morning's mail brought her another envelope, and this time it was not merely a kingdom, it was a glorious world. She lost; or perhaps it is somewhere down as a victory; we cannot know. At any rate her struggle is over. And now, Miss Maffei, do this and make no mistake: take Miss Fiore home with you and keep her there. Your driver is waiting outside for you. You can explain to your employer that your niece has come for a visit. Explain as you please, but keep Miss Fiore safe until I tell you that the danger is past. Under no circumstances is she to go to the street. Miss Fiore, you hear?"

"I will do what Mr. Archie says."

"Good. Archie, you will accompany them and explain the requirements. It will be only a day or so."

I nodded and went upstairs to put the dressing-gown away for another year and get some clothes on.

XVII

WHEN I got back after escorting Anna and Maria Maffei to the apartment on Park Avenue where Maria Maffei was housekeeper, the office was dark and Wolfe had gone upstairs. There was a note for me: "Archie, learn from Miss Barstow her excuse for mutilating United States currency. N. W." I knew that would be it. I went on up to the hay, but out of respect to Manuel Kimball I stepped to the rear of the upper hall to look for a line of light under Wolfe's door. There wasn't any. I called out, "Are you all in one bed?"

Wolfe's voice came. "Confound it, don't badger me!"

"Yes, sir. Is the switch on?"

"It is."

I went to my own room and the bed I was ready for; it was after two o'clock.

In the morning there was a drizzle, but I didn't mind. I took my time at breakfast and told Fritz to keep the bolt on while I was gone, and then with a light raincoat and a rubber hat went whistling along on my way to the garage. One thing that gave me joy was an item in the morning paper which said that the White Plains authorities were on the verge of being satisfied that the death of Peter Oliver Barstow had resulted from an accidental snake bite and that various other details of the tragedy not connected with that theory could all be explained by coincidence. It would have been fun to call up Harry Foster at the *Gazette* and let him know how safe it would be to stick pins in Anderson's chair for him to sit on, but I couldn't risk it because I didn't know what Wolfe's plans were in that direction. Another source of joy was the completeness of the briefcase which Anna Fiore had been carrying around all the time pinned to whatever she wore underneath. When I considered that it must have been there that first day I had called at Sullivan Street with Maria Maffei and I hadn't been keen enough to smell it, I felt like kicking myself. But maybe it was just as well. If the envelope had been delivered to Maria Maffei there was no telling what might have happened.

I telephoned the Barstow place from uptown, and when I got there around nine-thirty Sarah Barstow was expecting me. In the four days since I had last seen her she had made some changes in her color scheme; her cheeks would have made good pinching; her shoulders sat

straight with all the sag gone. I got up from my seat in the sun room, a
drizzle room that day, when she came in, and she came over and shook
hands. She told me her mother was well again, and this time Dr. Bradford said more likely than not she was well for good. Then she asked if
I wanted a glass of milk!

I grinned. "I guess not, thanks. As I told you on the phone, Miss
Barstow, this time it's a business call. Remember, the last time I said it
was social? Today, business." I pulled an envelope from my pocket and
got out the ten-dollar bill and handed it to her. "Nero Wolfe put it this
way: what excuse did you have for mutilating United States currency?"

She looked at it, puzzled, for a second, then smiled, and then a
shadow went over her face, the shadow of her dead father. "Where did
you ever—where did you get it?"

"Oh, a hoarder turned it in. But how did those names get on there?
Did you write yours?"

She nodded. "Yes, we all did. I think I told you—didn't I?—that one
day last summer Larry and Manuel Kimball played a match of tennis
and my father and I acted as umpire and linesman. They had a bet on
it, and Larry paid Mr. Kimball with a ten-dollar bill and Mr. Kimball
wanted us to write our names on it as a souvenir. We were sitting—on
the side terrace—"

"And Manuel Kimball took the bill?"

"Of course. He won it."

"And this is it?"

"Certainly, there are our signatures. Mr. Goodwin, I suppose it's
just vulgar curiosity, but where did you ever get it?"

I took the bill and replaced it carefully in the envelope—not Carlo
Maffei's envelope, a patent one with a clip on it so the signatures
wouldn't rub any more than they had already—and put it in my pocket.

"I'm sorry, Miss Barstow. Since it's just vulgar curiosity you can wait.
Not long, I hope. And may I say without offense, you're looking swell.
I was thinking when you came in, I'd like to pinch your cheeks."

"What!" She stared, then she laughed. "*That's* a compliment."

"It sure is. If you know how many cheeks there are I wouldn't bother
to pinch. Good day, Miss Barstow."

We shook hands while she still laughed.

Headed south again through the drizzle, I considered that the ten-
dollar bill clinched it. The other three items in Carlo Maffei's envelope
were good evidence, but this was something that no one but Manuel
Kimball could have had, and it had got to Carlo Maffei. How? I wondered. Well: Manuel Kimball had kept it in his wallet as a souvenir.
His payments of money, one or more, to Maffei for making the driver,

had been made not in a well-lighted room but in places dark enough to defeat the idle curiosity of observers; and in the darkness the souvenir had been included in a payment. Probably Manuel had later discovered his carelessness and demanded the souvenir back, and Maffei had claimed it had been spent unnoticed. That might have aroused Manuel's early suspicions of Maffei, and certainly it accounted for Maffei's recognition of the significance of the death, and its manner, of Peter Oliver Barstow; for that name, and two other Barstow names, had been signed on the ten-dollar bill he was preserving.

Yes, Manuel Kimball would live long enough to be sorry he had won that tennis match.

At White Plains, on a last-minute decision, I slowed down and turned off the parkway. It looked to me as if it was all over and the only thing left was a brief call at the District Attorney's office to explain the facts of life to him; and in that case there was no point in my driving through the rain all the way down to Thirty-fifth Street and clear back again. So I found a telephone booth and called Wolfe and told him what I had learned from Sarah Barstow, and asked him what next. He told me to come on home. I mentioned that I was right there in White Plains with plenty of time and inclination to do any errands he might have in mind. He said, "Come home. Your errand will be here waiting for you."

I got back onto the parkway.

It was a little after eleven when I arrived. I couldn't park right in front of the house as usual, because another car was there, a big black limousine. After turning off my engine I sat for a minute staring at the limousine, particularly at the official plate hanging alongside the license plate. I allowed myself the pleasure of a beautiful grin, and I got out and just for fun went to the front of the limousine and spoke to the chauffeur.

"Mr. Anderson is in the house?"

He looked at me a couple of seconds before he could make up his mind to nod. I turned and ran up the steps with the grin still on.

Anderson was with Wolfe in the office. When I went in I pretended not to see him; I went across to Wolfe's desk and took the envelope out of my pocket and handed it to him. "Okay," I said, "I've written the date of the match on the envelope." He nodded and told me to put it in the safe. I opened the heavy door and took my time about finding the drawer where the rest of Anna's briefcase was stowed away. Then I turned and let my eyes fall on the visitor and looked surprised.

"Oh," I said. "It's you! Good morning, Mr. Anderson."

He mumbled back at me.

"If you ever get your notebook, Archie, we shall proceed." Wolfe was using his drawly voice, and when I heard it I knew that one lawyer was in for a lot of irritation. "No, not at your desk, pull a chair around and be one of us. Good. I have just been explaining to Mr. Anderson that the ingenious theory of the Barstow case which he is trying to embrace is an offense to truth and an outrage on justice, and since I cherish the one and am on speaking terms with the other, it is my duty to demonstrate to him its inadequacy. I shall be glad of your support. Mr. Anderson is a little put out at the urgency of my invitation to him to call, but as I was just remarking to him, I think we should be grateful that the telephone permits the arrangement on short notice of these little informal conferences. On reflection, Mr. Anderson, I'm sure you will agree."

Anderson's neck was swelling. There was never anything very lovely about him, but now he was trying to keep his meanness down because he knew he had to, and it kept choking him trying to come up. His face was red and his neck bulged. He said to Wolfe, "You can tell your man to put his notebook away. You're a bigger ass than I thought you were, Wolfe, if you imagine you can put over this sort of thing."

"Take it down, Archie." Wolfe's drawl was swell. "It is irrelevant, being merely an opinion, but get it down. Mr. Anderson, I see that you misapprehend the situation; I had not supposed you were so obtuse. I gave you a free choice of alternatives on the telephone, and you chose to come here. Being here, in my house, you will permit me to direct the activity of its inmates; should you become annoyed beyond endurance, you may depart without ceremony or restraint. Should you depart, the procedure will be as I have indicated: within twenty-four hours Mr. Goodwin will drive in my car to your office in White Plains. Behind him, in another car, will be an assortment of newspaper reporters; beside him will be the murderer of Peter Oliver Barstow and Carlo Maffei; in his pocket will be the indubitable proof of the murderer's guilt. I was minded to proceed—"

Anderson broke in. "Carlo Maffei? Who the devil is that?"

"Was, Mr. Anderson. Not is. Carlo Maffei was an Italian craftsman who was murdered in your county on Monday evening, June fifth—stabbed in the back. Surely the case is in your office."

"What if it is? What has that got to do with Barstow?"

"They were murdered by the same man."

Anderson stared. "By God, Wolfe, I think you're crazy."

"I'm afraid not." Wolfe sighed. "There are times when I would welcome such a conclusion as an escape from life's meaner responsibilities —what Mr. Goodwin would call an out—but the contrary evidence is overwhelming. But to our business. Have you your checkbook with you?"

"Ah." Anderson's lips twisted. "What if I have?"

"It will make it more convenient for you to draw a check to my order for ten thousand dollars."

Anderson said nothing. He put his eyes straight into Wolfe's and kept them there, and Wolfe met him. Wolfe sighed. Finally Anderson said, smooth, "It might make it convenient, but not very reasonable. You are not a hijacker, are you?"

"Oh, no." Wolfe's cheeks folded up. "I assure you, no. I have the romantic temperament, but physically I'm not built for it. You do not grasp the situation? Let me explain. In a way, it goes four years back, to the forgetfulness you displayed in the Goldsmith case. I regretted that at the time, and resolved that on some proper occasion you should be reminded of it. I now remind you. Two weeks ago I came into possession of information which presented an opportunity to extend you a favor. I wished to extend it; but with the Goldsmith case in my memory and doubtless, so I thought, in yours also, it seemed likely that delicacy of feeling would prevent you from accepting a favor from me. So I offered to sell you the information for a proper sum; that of course was what the proffer of a wager amounted to; the proof that you understood it so was furnished by your counter-offer to Mr. Goodwin of a sum so paltry that I shall not mention it."

Anderson said, "I offered a substantial fee."

"Mr. Anderson! Please. Don't drag us into absurdities." Wolfe leaned back and laced his fingers on his belly. "Mr. Goodwin and I have discovered the murderer and have acquired proof of his guilt; not plausible proof, jury proof. That brings us to the present. The murderer, of course, is not my property, he belongs to the sovereign State of New York. Even the information I possess is not my property; if I do not communicate it to the State I am liable to penalties. But I can choose my method. First: you will now give me your personal check for ten thousand dollars, this afternoon Mr. Goodwin will go to your bank and have it certified, and tomorrow morning he will conduct you to the murderer, point him out to you, and deliver the proof of his guilt—all in a properly diffident and unostentatious manner. Or, second: we shall proceed to organize the parade to your office as I have described it: the prisoner, the press, and the proof, with a complete absence of diffidence. Take your choice, sir. Though you may find it hard to believe, it is of little concern to me, for while it would give me pleasure to receive your check, I have a great fondness for parades."

Wolfe stopped. Anderson looked at him, silent and smooth, calculating. Wolfe pressed the button on his desk and, when Fritz appeared, ordered beer. Every chance I got to look up from my notebook, I stared at Anderson; I could see it made him sore, and I stared all I could.

Anderson asked, "How do I know your proof is any good?"

"My word, sir. It is as good as my judgment. I pledge both."

"There is no possible doubt?"

"Anything is possible. There is no room for doubt in the minds of a jury."

Anderson twisted his lips around. Fritz brought the beer, and Wolfe opened a bottle and filled a glass.

Anderson said, "Ten thousand dollars is out of the question. Five thousand."

"Pfui! You would dicker? Contemptible. Let it be the parade." Wolfe picked up his glass of beer and gulped it.

"Give me the proof and tell me the murderer and you can have the check the minute I've got him."

Wolfe wiped his lips and sighed. "Mr. Anderson, one of us has to trust the other. Do not compel me to advance reasons for the preference I have indicated."

Anderson began to put up an argument. He was tough, no doubt about that, he was no softy. Of course he didn't have any real reasons or persuasions, but he had plenty of words. When he stopped Wolfe just shook his head. Anderson went on, and then again, but all he got was the same reply. I took it all down, and I had to admit there wasn't any whine in it. He was fighting with damn poor ammunition, but he wasn't whining.

He wrote the check in a fold he took from his pocket, holding it on his knee, with his fountain pen. He wrote it like a good bookkeeper, precisely and carefully, without haste, and then with the same preciseness filled in the spaces on the stub before he tore the check off and laid it on Wolfe's desk. Wolfe gave me a nod and I reached over and picked up the check and looked it over. I was relieved to see it was on a New York bank; that would save me a trip to White Plains before three o'clock.

Anderson got up. "I hope you never regret this, Wolfe. Now, when and where?"

Wolfe said, "I shall telephone."

"When?"

"Within twenty-four hours. Probably within twelve. I can get you at any time, at your office or your home?"

Anderson said, "Yes," turned on the word, and left. I got up and went to the hall and watched him out. Then I went back to the office and leaned the check up against a paperweight and blew a kiss at it.

Wolfe was whistling; that is, his lips were rounded into the proper position and air was going in and out, but there was no sound. I loved seeing him do that; it never happened when anybody was there but me, not even Fritz. He told me once that it meant he was surrendering to his emotions.

I put my notebook away and stuck the check in my pocket and pulled the chairs back where they belonged. After a little Wolfe said, "Archie, four years is a long time."

"Yes, sir. And ten grand is a lot of money. It's nearly an hour till lunch; I'll run down to the bank now and get their scrawl on it."

"It is raining. I thought of you this morning, adventuring beyond the city. Call for a messenger."

"Good Lord, no. I wouldn't miss the fun of having this certified for a gallon of milk."

Wolfe leaned back, murmured, "Intrepid," and closed his eyes.

I got back in time to bust the tape at lunch.

I figured, naturally, that the hour had struck, but to my surprise Wolfe seemed to have notions of leisure. He was in no hurry about anything. He took his time at the table, with two long cups of coffee at the end, and after lunch he went to the office and reposed in his chair without appearing to have anything of importance on his mind. I fussed around. After a while he roused himself enough to give me some directions: first, type out Anna Fiore's statement completely and chronologically; second, have photostatic copies made, rush, of the contents of Carlo Maffei's envelope; third, go to the Park Avenue apartment and return Maria Maffei's purse to her and have Anna Fiore sign the statement in duplicate before witnesses; and fourth, check with Horstmann the shipment of pseudo-bulbs which had arrived the preceding day on the *Cortez.*

I asked him, "Maybe you're forgetting something?" He shook his head, faintly so as not to disturb his comfort, and I let it slide. I was curious but not worried, for I could tell by the look on his face that he was adding something up to the right answer.

For the rest of the afternoon I was busy. I went out first, to a studio down on Sixth Avenue, to get them started on the photostats, and I made sure that they understood that if the originals were lost or injured they had better use the fire escape when they heard me coming. Then back to the office, to type Anna's statement. I fixed it up in swell shape and it took quite a while. When I went out to the roadster again the rain had stopped and it was brightening up, but the pavements were still wet. I had telephoned the apartment where Maria Maffei worked, and when I got there she was expecting me. I would hardly have known her. In a neat well-cut housekeeper's dress, black, with a little black thing across the top of her hair, she looked elegant, and her manner was as Park Avenue as the doorman at the Pierre. Well, I thought, they're all different in the bathtub from what they're like at Schrafft's. I was almost afraid to hand her her purse, it seemed vulgar. But she took it. Then she led me to a room away off, and there was Anna Fiore sitting looking out of a window. I read the statement to her, and she signed it, and Maria Maffei and I signed as witnesses.

Anna said next to nothing with her tongue, but her eyes kept asking me one question all the time, from the minute I entered the room. When I got up to go I answered it. I patted her on the shoulder and said, "Soon, Anna. I'll get your money real soon, and bring it right to you. Don't you worry."

She just nodded and said, "Mr. Archie."

After I got the photostats from the studio I saw no point in leaving the roadster out ready for action if there wasn't going to be any, so I garaged it and walked home. Until dinner time I was busy checking up the *Cortez* shipment and writing letters to the shippers about the casualties. Wolfe was pottering around most of the time while I was upstairs with Horstmann, but at six o'clock he left us and Horstmann and I went on checking.

It was after eight o'clock by the time dinner was over. I was getting the fidgets. Seven years with Nero Wolfe had taught me not to bite my nails waiting for the world to come to an end, but there were times when I was convinced that an eccentric was a man who ought to have his nose pulled. That evening he kept the radio going all through dinner.

As soon as it was over and he nodded to Fritz to pull his chair back, I got up and said, "I guess I won't sit in the office and watch you yawn. I'll try a movie."

Wolfe said, "Good. No man should neglect his cultural side."

"What!" I exploded. "You mean—damn it all, you would let me go and sit in a movie while maybe Manuel Kimball is finishing his packing for a nice little trip to his native land? Then I can go to the Argentine and buy a horse and ride all over the damn Pampa whatever that is looking for him? Do you think all it takes to catch a murderer is to sit in your damn office and let your genius work? That may be most of it, but it also takes a pair of eyes and a pair of legs and sometimes a gun or two. And the best thing you can think of is to tell me to go to a movie, while you—"

He showed me the palm of his hand to stop me. Fritz had pulled his chair back and he was up, a mountain on its feet. "Archie," he said.

"Spare me. A typical man of violence; the placidity of a hummingbird. I did not suggest the movie, you did. Even were Manuel Kimball a man to tremble at shadows, there has been no shadow to disturb him. Why should Manuel Kimball take a trip, to his native land or anywhere else? There is nothing he is less likely to take at this moment, I should say. If it will set your mind at rest, I can tell you that he is at his home, but not packing for a trip. I was speaking to him on the telephone only two hours ago. Fritz, the buzzer, attend the front door, please. He will receive another telephone call from me in the morning at eight o'clock, and I assure you he will wait for it."

"I hope he does." I wasn't satisfied. "I tell you, monkeying around at this stage is dangerous. You've done your part, a part no other living man could do, and now it's simple but it's damn important. I just go there and wrap myself around him, and stay wrapped until you tell Anderson to go and get him. Why not?"

Wolfe shook his head. "No, Archie. I understand your contention: that a point arrives when finesse must retire and leave the coup de grâce for naked force. I understand it, and I deny it vehemently. But come; guests are arriving; will you stop in the office a moment before you proceed to your entertainment?"

He turned and went to the office, and I followed him, wondering what the devil kind of a charade he was getting up. Whatever it was, I didn't like it.

Fritz had gone to the door, and the guests had been shown into the office ahead of us. I had no definite ideas as to who it might be, but certainly I didn't expect that bunch. I stared around at them. It was Fred Durkin and Bill Gore and Orrie Cather. My first thought was that Wolfe had got the funny notion that I needed all that army to subdue the fer-de-lance, as I had decided to call Manuel Kimball instead of the spiggoty, but of course Wolfe knew me too well for that. I tossed a nod around to them and grinned when I saw a gauze bandage on Orrie's left wrist. Anna Fiore had got under his skin all right.

After Wolfe got into his chair he asked me to get a pencil and a large piece of paper and make a rough map of the Kimball estate. With the guests there I asked no questions; I did as he said. I told him that I was acquainted with the ground only immediately around the house and the landing field, and he said that would do. While I made the map, sitting at my desk, Wolfe was telling Orrie how to get the sedan from the garage at six-thirty in the morning, and instructing the other two to meet him there at that hour.

I took the map to Wolfe at his desk. He looked it over a minute and said, "Good. Now tell me, if you were sending three men to that place to make sure that Manuel Kimball did not leave without being seen, and to follow him if seen, how would you dispose of them?"

I asked, "Under cover?"

"No. Exposed would do."

"How long?"

"Three hours."

I considered a minute. "Easy. Durkin on the highway, across from the entrance to the drive, with the sedan backed into a gate so it could start quick either way. Bill Gore in the bushes—about here—where he could cover all approaches to the house except the back. Orrie on top of a hill back here, about a third of a mile off, with field glasses, and a motorcycle down on the road. But they might as well stay home and play pinochle, since they can't fly."

Wolfe's cheeks folded. "Saul Panzer can. The clouds will have eyes. Thank you, Archie. That is all. We will not keep you longer from your entertainment."

I knew from his tone that I was to go, but I didn't want to. If there had to be a charade I wanted to help make it up. I said, "The movies have all been closed. Raided by the Society for the Suppression of Vice."

Wolfe said, "Then try a harlot's den. When gathering eggs you must look in every nest."

Bill Gore snickered. I gave Wolfe as dirty a look as I could manage, and went to the hall for my hat.

XVIII

I WAS awake Wednesday morning before seven o'clock, but I didn't get up. I watched the sun slanting against the windows, and listened to the noises from the street and the boats and ferries on the river, and figured that since Bill and Fred and Orrie had been instructed to meet at the garage at six-thirty they must already be as far as the Grand Concourse. My part hadn't been handed to me. When I had got home the night before Wolfe had gone up to bed, and there had been no note for me.

I finally tumbled out and shaved and dressed, taking my time, and went downstairs. Fritz was in the kitchen, buzzing around contented. I passed him some kind of a cutting remark, but realizing that it wasn't fair to take it out on him I made up for it by eating an extra egg and reading aloud to him a piece from the morning paper about a vampire bat that had had a baby in the zoo. Fritz came from the part of Switzerland where they talk French. He had a paper of his own every morning, but it was in French and it never seemed very likely to me that there was much in it. I was always surprised when I saw a word in it that meant anything up-to-date; for instance, the word Barstow which had been prominent in the headlines for a week.

I was starting the second cup of coffee when the phone rang. I went to the office and got the receiver to my ear, but Wolfe had answered from his room. I listened. It was Orrie Cather reporting that they had arrived and that everything was set. That was all. I went back to my coffee in the kitchen.

After a third cup and a cigarette I moseyed into the office. Sooner or later, I thought, genius will impart its secrets; sooner or later; compose yourself; just straighten things around and dust off the desk and fill the fountain pen and make everything nice for teacher. Sooner or later, honey—you damn fool. I wasn't getting the fidgets, I had them. A couple of times I took off the receiver and listened, but I didn't catch Wolfe making any calls. I got the mail and put it on his desk, and opened the safe. I pulled out the drawer where the Maffei stuff was just to make sure it hadn't walked off. The envelope into which I had put the photostats felt thin, and I took them out. One set was gone. I had had two sets made, and only one was there. That gave me my first hint about Wolfe's charade, but I didn't follow it up very far, because as I was sticking the envelope back into the drawer Fritz came in and said that Wolfe wanted to see me in his room.

I went up. His door was open. He was up and dressed all but his coat; the sleeves of his yellow shirt—he used two fresh shirts every day, always canary yellow—looked like enormous floating sheeps' bladders as he stood at his mirror brushing his hair. I caught his eyes in the mirror, and he winked at me! I was so astonished that I suppose my mouth fell open.

He put the brush down and turned to me. "Good morning, Archie. You have had breakfast? Good. It is pleasant to see the sun again, after yesterday's gray unceasing trickle. Get the Maffei documents from the safe. By all means take a gun. Proceed to White Plains and get Mr. Anderson at his office—he will be awaiting you—and drive him to the Kimball estate. Show him Manuel Kimball; point, if necessary. When Manuel Kimball has been apprehended deliver the documents to Mr. Anderson. Return here, and you will find that Fritz will have prepared one of your favorite dishes for lunch."

I said, "Okay. But why all the mystery—"

"Comments later, Archie. Save them, please. I am due upstairs in ten minutes and I have yet to enjoy my chocolate."

I said, "I hope you choke on it," and turned and left him.

With the Carlo Maffei stuff and Anna's statement on my breast and a thirty-eight, loaded this time, on my hip, I walked to the garage. It was warm and sunny, June twenty-first, the day for the sun to start back south. It was a good day for the finale of the fer-de-lance, I thought, the longest one of the year. I filled up with gas and oil and water, made it crosstown to Park Avenue, and turned north. As I passed the marble front of the Manhattan Trust Company I saluted; that was where I had had Anderson's check certified. Going north on the parkway at that hour of the morning there was plenty of room, but I kept my speedometer at forty or under; Wolfe had told Anderson this would be unostentatious, and besides, I wasn't in the mood for repartee with a motor cop. I was pretty well on edge. I always am like that when I'm really on my way for a man; there never seems to be quite enough air for me; I breathe quicker and everything I touch—the steering wheel, for instance—seems to be alive with blood going in it. I don't like the feeling much but I always have it.

Anderson was waiting for me. In his office the girl at the desk tossed me a nod and got busy on the phone. In a minute Anderson came out. There were two men with him, carrying their hats and looking powerful. One of them was H. R. Corbett; the other was new to me. Anderson stopped to say something to the girl at the desk, then came over to me.

"Well?" he said.

I grinned. "I'm ready if you are. Hello, Corbett. You going along?"

Anderson said, "I'm taking two men. You know what the job is. Is that enough?"

I nodded. "All we'll need 'em for is to hold my hat anyway. Let's go."

The third guy opened the door and we filed out.

Anderson came with me in the roadster; the other two followed us in a closed car, official, but I noticed it wasn't Anderson's limousine. Going down Main Street all the traffic cops saluted my passenger, and I grinned, considering how surprised they would have been if they had known how much the District Attorney was paying for that little taxi ride. I opened her up as soon as I got onto the highway, and rolled over the hills, up and down, so fast that Anderson looked at me. He didn't know but what the speed was part of the program, so I kept going, slowing down only at the points where I had to make a turn and needed to make sure that Corbett, trailing along behind, had caught it. It took just twenty-five minutes from the White Plains courthouse to the entrance to the Kimball drive; the clock on my dash said 10:40 as I slowed up to turn in.

Durkin was there, across the road, sitting on the running-board of the sedan which had been backed in as I had suggested. I waved at him but didn't stop. Anderson asked, "That Wolfe's man?" I nodded and swept into the drive. I had gone about a hundred feet when Anderson said, "Stop!" I pushed the pedals down, shifted into neutral, and pulled the hand brake.

Anderson said, "This is E. D. Kimball's place. You've got to show me right here."

I shook my head. "Nothing doing. You know Nero Wolfe, and that'll do for you. I'm obeying orders. Do I go on?"

Corbett's car had stopped right behind us. Anderson was looking at me, his mouth twisted with uncertainty. I had my ears open, straining, not for Anderson's reply, but for what I was taking for the sound of an airplane. Even if I had been willing to get out and look up I couldn't, on account of trees. But it was an airplane, sure. I shifted and started forward on the jump.

Anderson said, "By God, Goodwin, I hope you know what you're risking. If I had known—"

I stopped him. "Shut up!"

I pulled up at the house and ran over and rang the bell. In a minute the door was opened by the fat butler.

"I'd like to speak to Mr. Manuel Kimball."

"Yes, sir. Mr. Goodwin? He is expecting you. He told me to ask you to go to the hangar and wait for him there."

"Isn't he there?"

The butler hesitated, and he certainly looked worried. "I believe he intended to go aloft in his plane."

I nodded and ran back to the car. Corbett had got out and walked to the roadster and was talking with Anderson. As I got in Anderson turned to me and started, "Look here, Goodwin—"

"Did you hear me say shut up? I'm busy. Look out, Corbett."

I shot forward onto the back drive and headed for the graveled road that led to the hangar. On that, out from under the trees, the sound of the airplane was louder. I made the gravel fly, and whirled to a stop on the concrete platform in front of the hangar. The mechanic, Skinner, was standing there in the wide open door. I jumped out and went over to him.

"Mr. Manuel Kimball?"

Skinner pointed up, and I looked. It was Manuel Kimball's plane, high, but not too high for me to see the red and blue. It seemed to make a lot of noise, and the next second I saw why, when I caught sight of another plane circling in from the west, higher than Manuel's and going faster. It was helping with the noise. Both planes were circling, dark and beautiful in the sun. I brought my head down to sneeze.

Skinner said, "He's got company this morning."

"So I see. Who is it?"

"I don't know. I saw it first a little after eight o'clock and it's been fooling around up there ever since. It's a Burton twin-motor, it's got a swell dip."

I remember Wolfe saying the clouds would have eyes. There weren't any clouds, but no doubt about the eyes.

I asked, "What time did Mr. Kimball go up?"

"A little after ten. They came out around nine-thirty, but the second seat wasn't ready and I had to fix the straps."

I knew what it meant as soon as he said it, but I asked him anyhow. I said, "Oh, is there someone with him?"

"Yes, sir, his father. The old gentleman's having a ride. It's only his third time up. He nearly backed out when the seat wasn't ready, but we got him in."

I looked up at the airplanes again. Manuel Kimball and his father having a ride together, up there in the sun, the wind, and the roar. No conversation probably, just a morning ride.

I started toward the roadster, to speak to Anderson. Corbett had left his car and came to meet me. I stopped to listen to him. "Well, we've come to your party, where's your guest of honor?"

I brushed past him and went on to the roadster. Seeing no point in giving the mechanic an earful, I lowered my voice. "You'll have to wait, Mr. Anderson. Barstow's murderer is taking an airplane ride. I'm sorry you won't get him on time, but you'll get him."

Anderson said, "Get in here. I want a showdown."

I shook my head. Maybe it was just contrariness, but I was set on carrying it out exactly as Wolfe had ordered. "That's not next on the program." Corbett had come up, around on the other side of the roadster, and now he stuck his face in at the window and said to Anderson, "If he's got anything you want I'd be glad to get it for you."

I had my mouth open to invite him formally when I heard my name called. I turned. Skinner had left the hangar and was approaching me; in one hand he had a golf driver and in the other an envelope. I stared at him. He was saying, "I forgot. You're Mr. Goodwin? Mr. Kimball left these for you."

I got to him and grabbed. The driver! I looked at it, but there was nothing to see; in outward appearance it was just a golf club. But of course it was it. Lovin' babe! I tucked it under my arm and looked at the envelope; on the outside was written, "Mr. Nero Wolfe." It was unsealed, and I pulled out the contents, and had in my hand the set of photostats I had missed from the safe. They were fastened with a paper clip, and slipped under the clip was a piece of paper on which I read: "Thank you, Nero Wolfe. In appreciation of your courtesy I am leaving a small gift for you. Manuel Kimball." I looked up at the sky. The red and blue airplane of the leading character in Wolfe's charade was still there, higher, I thought, circling, with the other plane above. I put the photostats back into the envelope.

Corbett was in front of me. "Here, I'll take that."

"Oh no. Thanks, I can manage."

He sprang like a cat and I wasn't expecting it. It was neat. He got the envelope with one hand and the driver with the other. He started for the roadster. Two jumps put me in front of him, and he stopped. I wasn't monkeying. I said, "Look out, here it comes," and plugged him on the jaw with plenty behind it. He wobbled and dropped his loot, and I let him get his hands up, and then feinted with my left and plugged him again. That time he went down. His boy friend came running up, and Skinner from his side. I turned to meet the boy friend, but Anderson's voice, with more snap in it than I knew he had, came from the roadster.

"Curry! Lay off! Cut it!"

Curry stopped. I stepped back. Corbett got up, glaring wild. Anderson again: "Corbett, you too! Lay off!"

I said, "Not on my account, Mr. Anderson. If they want to play snatch and run I'll take them both on. They need to be taught a little respect for private property."

I stooped to pick up the driver and the envelope. It was while I was bent over, reaching down, that I heard Skinner's yell.

"Good God! He's lost it!"

For an instant I imagined he meant I had lost the driver, and I thought he was crazy. Then, as I straightened up and glanced at him and saw where he was looking, I jerked my eyes and my head up. It was Manuel Kimball's plane directly overhead, a thousand feet up. It was twisting and whirling as if it had lost its senses, and coming down. It seemed to be jerking and coiling back and forth, it didn't look as if it was falling straight, but I suppose it was. It was right above us—faster —I stared with my mouth open—

"Look out!" Skinner was shouting. "For God's sake!"

We ran for the hangar door. Anderson was out of the roadster and with us. We got inside the door and turned in time to see the crash. Black lightning split the air. A giant report, not thunderous like a big gun, an instantaneous ear-splitting snap. Pieces flew; splinters lay at our feet. It had landed at the edge of the concrete platform, not ten yards from Corbett's car. We jumped out and ran for the wreckage, Skinner calling, "Look out for an explosion!"

What I saw first wasn't pretty. The only way I knew it had been E. D. Kimball was that it was mixed up with a strap in the position of the back seat and Skinner had said that the old gentleman had gone up for a ride. Apparently it had landed in such a way that the front seat had got a different kind of a blow, for Manuel Kimball could have been recognized by anybody. His face was still together and even pretty well in shape. Skinner and I got him loose while the others worked at the old gentleman. We carried them away from there and inside the hangar and put them on some canvas on the floor.

Skinner said, "You'd better move your cars. An explosion might come yet." I said, "When I move my car I'll keep on moving it. Now's a good time. Mr. Anderson. You may remember that Nero Wolfe promised I would be diffident. That's me." I pulled the documents from my pocket and handed them to him. "Here's your proof. And there's your man on the floor, the one with the face."

I picked up Manuel Kimball's envelope and the golf driver from the floor where I had dropped them, and beat it. It took me maybe four seconds to get the roadster started and out of there and shooting down the road.

At the entrance, turning onto the highway, I stopped long enough to call to Durkin, "Call your playmates and come on home. The show's over."

I got to White Plains in twenty-two minutes. The roadster never did run nicer. I telephoned Wolfe at the same drugstore where two weeks before I had phoned him that Anderson had gone to the Adirondacks and I had only Derwin to bet with. He answered right off, and I gave him the story, brief but complete.

He said, "Good. I hope I haven't offended you, Archie. I thought it best that your mind should not be cluttered with the lesser details. Fritz is preparing to please your palate. By the way, where is White Plains? Would it be convenient for you to stop on your way at Scarsdale? Gluekner has telephoned me that he has succeeded in hybridizing a *Dendrobium Melpomene* with a *Findlayanum* and offers me a seedling."

XIX

It CERTAINLY didn't look like much. It was a sick-looking pale blue and was so small you could get it in an ordinary envelope without folding it. It looked even smaller than it was because the writing in the blank spaces was tall and scrawly; but it was writing with character in it. That, I guessed, was Sarah Barstow. The signature below, Ellen Barstow, was quite different—fine and precise. It was Saturday morning, and the check had come in the first mail; I was giving it a last fond look as I handed it in at the teller's window. I had phoned Wolfe upstairs that a Barstow envelope was there and he had told me to go ahead and open it and deposit the check.

At eleven o'clock Wolfe entered the office and went to his desk and rang for Fritz and beer. I had the Barstow case expense list all typed out for his inspection, and as soon as he had finished glancing through the scanty mail I handed it to him. He took a pencil and went over it slowly, checking each item. I waited. When I saw him hit the third item from the bottom and stop at it, I swallowed.

Wolfe raised his head. "Archie. We must get a new typewriter."

I just cleared my throat. He went on, "This one is too impulsive. Perhaps you didn't notice: it has inserted an extra cipher before the decimal point in the amount opposite Anna Fiore's name. I observe that you carelessly included the error in summing up."

I managed a grin. "Oh! Now I get you. I forgot to mention it before. Anna's nest-egg has hatched babies, it's a thousand dollars now. I'm taking it down to her this afternoon."

Wolfe sighed. The beer came, and he opened a bottle and gulped a glass. He put the expense list under the paperweight with the mail and leaned back in his chair. "Tomorrow I shall cut down to five quarts."

My grin felt better. I said, "You don't have to change the subject. I wouldn't make the mistake of calling you generous even if you said to double it; you'd still be getting a bargain. Do you know what Anna will do with it? Buy herself a husband. Look at all the good you're doing."

"Confound it. Don't give her anything. Tell her the money cannot be found."

"No, sir. I'll give her the money and let her dig her own grave. I'm not violent, the way you are, and I don't put myself up as a substitute for fate."

Wolfe opened his eyes. He had been drowsy for three days, and I thought it was about time something woke him up. He murmured, "Do you think you're saying something, Archie?"

"Yes, sir. I'm asking where you got the breezy notion of killing E. D. Kimball."

"Where his son got the notion, you mean?"

"No, you. Don't quibble. You killed him."

Wolfe shook his head. "Wrong, Archie. I quibble? E. D. Kimball was killed by the infant son whom he deserted sitting on the floor among his toys in a pool of his mother's blood. If you please. Properly speaking, E. D. Kimball was not killed last Wednesday morning, but on Sunday, June fourth. Through one of the unfortunate accidents by which blind chance interferes with the natural processes of life and death, Barstow died instead. It is true that I helped to remedy that error. I had Durkin deliver to Manuel Kimball copies of our evidence against him, and I telephoned Manuel Kimball that he was surrounded, on the earth and above the earth. I left it to nature to proceed, having ascertained that E. D. Kimball was at home and would not leave that morning."

I said, "You told me once that I couldn't conceal truth by building a glass house around it. What are you trying it for? You killed him."

Wolfe's cheeks folded. He poured another glass of beer and leaned back again and watched the foam. When nothing was left of it but a thin white rim he looked at me and sighed.

"The trouble is," he murmured, "that as usual you are so engrossed in the fact that you are oblivious to its environment. You stick to it, Archie, like a leech on an udder. Consider the situation that faced me. Manuel had tried to kill his father. By an accident beyond his control the innocent Barstow had been killed instead. Evidence that would convict Manuel of murder was in my possession. How should I use it? Had I been able to afford the luxury of a philosophic attitude, I should of course not have used it at all, but that attitude was beyond my means, it was an affair of business. Put myself up as a substitute for fate? Certainly; we do it constantly; we could avoid it only by complete inaction. I was forced to act. If I had permitted you to get Manuel Kimball, without warning, and deliver him alive to the vengeance of the people of the State of New York, he would have gone to the chair of judicial murder a bitter and defeated man, his heart empty of the one deep satisfaction life had offered to it; and his father, equally bitter and no less defeated, would have tottered through some few last years with nothing left to trade. If I had brought that about I would have been responsible for it, to myself, and the prospect was not pleasing. Still I had to act. I did so, and incurred a responsibility which is vastly less displeasing.

You would encompass the entire complex phenomenon by stating bluntly that I killed E. D. Kimball. Well, Archie. I will take the responsibility for my own actions; I will not also assume the burden of your simplicity. Somehow you must bear it."

I grinned. "Maybe. I don't mean maybe I can bear it, I mean maybe all you've just said. Also, maybe I'm simple. I'm so simple that a simple thought occurred to me as I was walking back from the bank this morning."

"Indeed." Wolfe gulped his glass of beer.

"Yes, sir. It occurred to me that if Manuel Kimball had been arrested and brought to trial you would have had to put on your hat and gloves, leave the house, walk to an automobile, ride clear to White Plains, and sit around a courtroom waiting for your turn to testify. Whereas now, natural processes being what they are, and you having such a good feeling for phenomena, you can just sit and hold your responsibilities on your lap."

"Indeed," Wolfe murmured.

MURDER BY THE BOOK

I

SOMETHING remarkable happened that cold Tuesday in January. Inspector Cramer, with no appointment, showed up a little before noon at Nero Wolfe's old brownstone on West Thirty-fifth Street and, after I had ushered him into the office and he had exchanged greetings with Wolfe and lowered himself into the red leather chair, he said right out, "I dropped in to ask a little favor."

What was remarkable was his admitting it. From my chair at my desk I made an appropriate noise. He sent me a sharp glance and asked if I had something.

"No, sir," I told him courteously, "I'm right on top. You just jolted that out of me. So many times I've seen you come here for a favor and try to bull it or twist it, it was quite a shock." I waved it away tolerantly. "Skip it."

His face, chronically red, deepened a shade. His broad shoulders stiffened, and the creases spreading from the corners of his gray-blue eyes showed more as the eyelids tightened. Then, deciding I was playing for a blurt, he controlled it. "Do you know," he asked, "whose opinion of you I would like to have? Darwin's. Where were you while evolution was going on?"

"Stop brawling," Wolfe muttered at us from behind his desk. He was testy, not because he would have minded seeing either Cramer or me draw blood, but because he always resented being interrupted in the middle of a London *Times* crossword puzzle. He frowned at Cramer. "What favor, sir?"

"Nothing strenuous." Cramer relaxed. "A little point about a homicide. A man's body fished out of the East River a week ago yesterday, off Ninetieth Street. He had been—"

"Named Leonard Dykes," Wolfe said brusquely, wanting to make it brief so he could finish the puzzle before lunch. "Confidential clerk in a law office, around forty, had been in the water perhaps two days. Evidence of a severe blow on the head, but had died of drowning. No one charged by last evening. I read all the homicide news."

"I bet you do." That having slipped out by force of habit, Cramer de-

cided it wasn't tactful and smiled it off. He could smile when he wanted
to. "Not only is no one charged, we haven't got a smell. We've done
everything, you know what we've done, and we're stopped. He lived
alone in a room-and-bath walk-up on Sullivan Street. By the time we got
there it had been combed—not torn apart, but someone had been
through it good. We didn't find anything that's been any help, but we
found one thing that might possibly help if we could figure it out."

He got papers from his breast pocket, from them selected an envelope,
and from the envelope took a folded sheet of paper. "This was inside a
book, a novel. I can give you the name of the book and the numbers of
the pages it was found between, but I don't think that has a bearing."
He got up to hand the paper to Wolfe. "Take a look at it."

Wolfe ran his eyes over it, and, since I was supposed to be up on
everything that went on in that office so as to be eligible for blame if and
when required, I arose and extended a hand. He passed it over.

"It's in Dykes's handwriting," Cramer said. "The paper is a sheet
from a scratch pad there on a table in his room. There were more pads
like it in a drawer of the table."

I was giving it a look. The paper was white, ordinary, six by nine,
and at the top was the word "Tentative," underscored, written with
pencil in a neat almost perpendicular hand. Below it was a list of
names:

Sinclair Meade
Sinclair Sampson
Barry Bowen
David Yerkes
Ernest Vinson
Dorian Vick
Baird Archer
Oscar Shiff
Oscar Cody
Lawrence McCue
Mark McCue
Mark Flick
Mack Flick
Louis Gill
Lewis Gill

I handed it back to Cramer and returned to my chair.

"Well?" Wolfe asked impatiently.

"I was on my way uptown and dropped in to show it to you." Cramer
folded the sheet and put it in the envelope. "Not so much to get help, it

probably has nothing to do with the homicide, but it's got me irritated and I wondered what you'd say, so I dropped in. A list of fifteen names written by Dykes on a piece of his scratch paper, and not one of them can be found in any phone directory in the metropolitan area! Or anywhere else. We can find no record anywhere of a man with any of those names. None of Dykes's friends or associates ever heard of a man with one of those names, so they say. I mean, taking the first and last names together, as they are on that list. Of course we haven't checked the whole damn country, but Dykes was a born and bred New Yorker, with no particular connections elsewhere that we know of. What the hell kind of a list of names is that?"

Wolfe grunted. "He made them up. He was considering an alias, for himself or someone else."

"We thought of that, naturally. If so, no one ever used it that we can find."

"Keep trying if you think it's worth it."

"Yeah. But we're only human. I just thought I'd show it to a genius and see what happened. With a genius you never know."

Wolfe shrugged. "I'm sorry. Nothing has happened."

"Well, by God, I hope you'll excuse me"—Cramer got up. He was sore, and you couldn't blame him—"for taking up your time and no fee. Don't bother, Goodwin."

He turned and marched out. Wolfe bent over his crossword puzzle, frowned at it, and picked up his pencil.

II

CRAMER's crack about no fee had of course been deserved. Wolfe hated to start his brain going on what he called work, and during the years I had been on his payroll the occasions had been rare when anything but a substantial retainer had jarred him into it. But he is not a loafer. He can't be, since his income as a private detective is what keeps that old house going, with the rooms on the roof full of orchid plants, with Theodore Horstmann as tender, and Fritz Brenner serving up the best meals in New York, and me, Archie Goodwin, asking for a raise every time I buy a new suit, and sometimes getting it. It takes a gross of at least ten thousand a month to get by.

That January and the first half of February business was slow, except for the routine jobs, where all Wolfe and I had to do was supervise Saul Panzer and Fred Durkin and Orrie Cather, and for a little mix-up with a gang of fur hijackers during which Fred and I got shot at. Then, nearly six weeks after the day Cramer dropped in to see what would happen if he showed a piece of paper to a genius, and got a brush-off, a man named John R. Wellman phoned on Monday morning for an appointment, and I told him to come at six that afternoon. When he arrived, a few minutes early, I escorted him to the office and sat him in the red leather chair to wait until Wolfe came down from the plant rooms, sliding the little table near his right elbow, for his convenience if he needed to do any writing, for instance in a checkbook. He was a plump short guy, going bald, without much of a nose to hold up his rimless glasses. His plain gray suit and haberdashery didn't indicate opulence, but he had told me on the phone that he was a wholesale grocer from Peoria, Illinois, and there had been time to get a report from the bank. We would take his check if that was on the program.

When Wolfe entered, Wellman stood up to shake hands. Sometimes Wolfe makes an effort to conceal his dislike of shaking hands with strangers, and sometimes he doesn't. This time he did fairly well, then rounded the corner of his desk and got his seventh of a ton deposited in the only chair on earth that really suits him. He rested his forearms on the arms of the chair and leaned back.

"Yes, Mr. Wellman?"

"I want to hire you," Wellman said.

"For what?"

"I want you to find—" He stopped short, and his jaw muscles began to work. He shook his head violently, took off his glasses, dug at his eyes with his fingertips, put the glasses back on, and had trouble getting them adjusted. "I'm not under very good control," he apologized. "I haven't had enough sleep lately and I'm tired. I want you to find the person who killed my daughter."

Wolfe shot a glance at me, and I got my notebook and pen. Wellman, concentrating on Wolfe, wasn't interested in me. Wolfe asked him, "When and where and how did she die?"

"She was run over by a car in Van Cortlandt Park seventeen days ago. Friday evening, February second." Wellman had himself in hand now. "I ought to tell you about her."

"Go ahead."

"My wife and I live in Peoria, Illinois. I've been in business there over twenty years. We had one child, one daughter, Joan. We were very—" He stopped. He sat completely still, not even his eyes moving, for a long moment, and then went on. "We were very proud of her. She graduated from Smith with honors four years ago and took a job in the editorial department of Scholl and Hanna, the book publishers. She did well there—I have been told that by Scholl himself. She was twenty-six last November." He made a little gesture. "Looking at me, you wouldn't think I'd have a beautiful daughter, but she was. Everybody agreed she was beautiful, and she was extremely intelligent."

He got a large envelope from his side pocket. "I might as well give you these now." He left his chair to hand Wolfe the envelope. "A dozen prints of the best likeness we have of her. I got them for the police to use, but they weren't using them, so you can. You can see for yourself."

Wolfe extended a hand with one of the prints, and I arose to take it. Beautiful is a big word, but there's no point in quibbling, and if that was a good likeness Joan Wellman had been a good-looking girl. There was slightly too much chin for my taste, but the forehead and eyes were all any father had a right to expect.

"She was beautiful," Wellman said, and stopped and was still again.

Wolfe couldn't stand to see people overcome. "I suggest," he muttered, "that you avoid words like 'beautiful' and 'proud.' The colder facts will serve. You want to hire me to learn who drove the car that hit her?"

"I'm a damn fool," Wellman stated.

"Then don't hire me."

"I don't mean I'm a damn fool to hire you. I mean I intend to handle this efficiently and I ought to do it." His jaw muscles moved, but not through loss of control. "It's like this. We got a wire two weeks ago Saturday that Joan was dead. We drove to Chicago and took a plane to New York. We saw her body. The car wheels had run over the middle of her, and there was a big lump on her head over her right ear. I talked to the police and the medical examiner."

Wellman was being efficient now. "I do not believe Joan was walking in that secluded spot in that park, not a main road, on a cold evening in the middle of winter, and neither does my wife. How did she get the lump on her head? The car didn't hit her head. The medical examiner say it's possible she fell on her head, but he's careful how he says it, and I don't believe it. The police claim they're working on it, doing all they can, but I don't believe that either. I think they think it was just a hit-and-run driver, and all they're doing is to try to find the car. I think my daughter was murdered, and I think I know the name of the man that killed her."

"Indeed." Wolfe's brows went up a little. "Have you told them so?"

"I certainly have, and they just nod and say they're working on it. They haven't got anywhere and they're not going to. So I decided to come to you—"

"Have you any evidence?"

"I call it evidence, but I guess they don't." He took an envelope from his breast pocket. "Joan wrote home every week, hardly ever missed." He removed a sheet of paper from the envelope and unfolded it. "This is a copy I had typed, I let the police have the original. It's dated February first, which was a Thursday. I'll read only part of it.

Oh, I must tell you, I have a new kind of date tomorrow evening. As you know, since Mr. Hanna decided that our rejections of manuscripts must have the personal touch, except when it's just tripe, which I must say most of it is, I return quite a lot of stuff with a typed note with my name signed, and so do the other readers. Well, last fall sometime I did that with the manuscript of a novel by a man named Baird Archer, only I had forgotten all about it, until yesterday there was a phone call for me, at the office, and a man's voice said he was Baird Archer, and did I remember the note I had sent him returning his manuscript, and I said I did. He asked if anyone else had read it, and I said no, and then he propositioned me! He said he would pay me twenty dollars an hour to discuss the novel with him and make suggestions to improve it! How do you like that? Even if it's only five hours, that will be an extra hundred dollars for the exchequer, only it won't stay in the exchequer very long, as you know, my darling and doting parents, if you know me, and you ought to. I'm to meet him tomorrow right after office hours.

Wellman waggled the paper. "Now she wrote that on—"

"May I see it, please?" Wolfe was leaning forward with a gleam in his eye. Apparently something about Joan Wellman's letter home had given him a kick, but when Wellman handed it to him he gave it only a brief glance before passing it to me. I read it clear through with my eyes while my ears recorded their talk for the notebook.

"She wrote that," Wellman said, "on Thursday, February first. Her appointment with that man was the next day, Friday, right after office hours. Early Saturday morning her body was found on that out-of-the-way road in Van Cortlandt Park. What's wrong with thinking that that man killed her?"

Wolfe was leaning back again. "Was there any evidence of assault? Assault as a euphemism for rape?"

"No." Wellman's eyes went shut, and his hands closed into fists. After a moment the eyes opened again. "Nothing like that. No sign at all of that."

"What do the police say?"

"They say they're still trying to find that man Archer and can't. No trace of him. I think—"

"Nonsense. Of course there's a trace. Publishers must keep records. He submitted a manuscript of a novel last fall, and it was returned to him with a note from your daughter. Returned how and where?"

"It was returned by mail to the only address he gave, General Delivery, Clinton Station. That's on West Tenth Street." Wellman's fists became hands again, and he turned a palm up. "I'm not saying the police have just lain down on the job. Maybe they've even done the best they can, but the fact remains that it's been seventeen days now and they haven't got anywhere, and I don't like the way they talked yesterday and this morning. It looks to me like they don't want it to be an unsolved murder, and they want to call it manslaughter, and that's all it would be if it was a hit-and-run accident. I don't know about these New York police, but you tell me, they might do a thing like that, mightn't they?"

Wolfe grunted. "It is conceivable. And you want me to prove it was murder and find the murderer, with evidence?"

"Yes." Wellman hesitated, opening his mouth and closing it again. He glanced at me and returned to Wolfe. "I tell you, Mr. Wolfe, I am willing to admit that what I am doing is vindictive and wicked. My wife thinks it is, and so does the pastor of my church. I was home one day last week, and they both said so. It is sinful to be vindictive, but here I am, and I'm going through with it. Even if it was just a hit-and-run accident I don't think the police are going to find him, and whatever it was I'm not going back to Peoria and sell groceries until he's found and made to pay for it. I've got a good paying business, and I own some property, and I never figured on dying a pauper, but I will if I have to, to get the murderous criminal that killed my daughter. Maybe I shouldn't say that. I don't know you too well, I only know you by reputation, and maybe you won't want to work for a man who can say an unchristian thing like that, so maybe it's a mistake to say it, but I want to be honest about it."

Wellman took his glasses off and started wiping them with a handkerchief. That showed his better side. He didn't want to embarrass Wolfe by keeping his eyes on him while Wolfe was deciding whether to take on a job for such an implacable bastard as John R. Wellman of Peoria, Illinois.

"I'll be honest too," Wolfe said dryly. "The morality of vengeance is not a factor in my acceptance or refusal of a case. But it was a mistake for you to say it, because I would have asked for a retainer of two thousand dollars and now I'll make it five thousand. Not merely to gouge you, though. Since the police have turned up nothing in seventeen days, it will probably take a lot of work and money. With a few more facts I'll have enough to start on."

"I wanted to be honest about it," Wellman insisted.

When he left, half an hour later, his check was under a paperweight on my desk, along with the copy of Joan Wellman's last letter home, and there was an assortment of facts in my notebook—plenty, as Wolfe had said, for a start. I went to the hall with him and helped him on with his coat. When I opened the door to let him out he wanted to shake hands, and I was glad to oblige.

"You're sure you won't mind," he asked, "if I ring you fairly often? Just to find out if there's anything new? I'll try not to make a nuisance of myself, but I'm like that. I'm persistent."

"Any time," I assured him. "I can always say 'no progress.'"

"He *is* good, isn't he? Mr. Wolfe?"

"He's the best." I made it positive.

"Well—I hope—all right." He crossed the sill into an icy wind from the west, and I stood there until he had descended from the stoop to the sidewalk. The shape he was in, he might have tumbled down those seven steps.

Returning down the hall, I paused a moment before entering the office, to sniff. Fritz, as I knew, was doing spareribs with the sauce Wolfe and he had concocted and, though the door to the kitchen was closed, enough came through for my nose, and it approved. In the office, Wolfe was leaning back with his eyes closed. I picked up Wellman's check, gave it an admiring glance, went and put it in the safe, and then crossed to Wolfe's desk for another look at one of the prints of Joan Wellman's likeness. As near as you can tell from a picture, it would have been nice to know her.

I spoke. "If you're working, knock off. Dinner in ten minutes."

Wolfe's eyes opened.

I asked, "Have we got a murder or not?"

"Certainly we have." He was supercilious.

"Oh. Good for us. Because she wouldn't go for a walk in the park in February?"

"No." He humphed. "You should have a better reason."

"Me? Thanks. Me have a reason?"

"Yes. Archie. I have been training you for years to observe. You are slacking. Not long ago Mr. Cramer showed us a list of names on a sheet of paper. The seventh name on that list was Baird Archer. The evening she was killed Miss Wellman had an appointment with a man named Baird Archer. Leonard Dykes who wrote that list of names was murdered. It would be silly not to hypothesize that Miss Wellman was also murdered."

I turned on my heel, took the two paces to my swivel chair, turned it so I would face him, and sat. "Oh, that," I said carelessly. "I crossed that off as coincidence."

"Pfui. It never struck you. You're slacking."

"Okay. I am not electronized."

"There is no such word."

"There is now. I've used it." I was getting indignant. "I mean I am not lightning. It was six weeks ago that Cramer showed us that list of names, and I gave it the merest glance. I know you did too, but look who you are. What if it were the other way around? What if I had remembered that name from one short glimpse of that list six weeks ago, and you hadn't? I would be the owner of this house and the bank account, and you would be working for me. Would you like that? Or do you prefer it as it is? Take your pick."

He snorted. "Call Mr. Cramer."

"Right." I swiveled to the phone and dialed.

III

If you like Anglo-Saxon, I belched. If you fancy Latin, I eructed. No matter which, I had known that Wolfe and Inspector Cramer would have to put up with it that evening, because that is always a part of my reaction to sauerkraut. I don't glory in it or go for a record, but neither do I fight it back. I want to be liked just for myself.

If either Cramer or Wolfe noticed it he gave no sign. I was where I belonged during an evening session in the office and, with Wolfe behind his desk and Cramer in the red leather chair, I was to one side of the line of fire. It had started off sociably enough, with Wolfe offering refreshment and Cramer choosing bourbon and water, and Fritz bringing it, and Cramer giving it a go and saying it was good whisky, which was true.

"You said on the phone," he told Wolfe, "you have something I can use."

Wolfe put his beer glass down and nodded. "Yes, sir. Unless you no longer need it. I've seen nothing in the paper recently about the Leonard Dykes case—the body fished out of the river nearly two months ago. Have you got it in hand?"

"No."

"Any progress?"

"Nothing—no."

"Then I would like to consult you about something, because it's a little ticklish." Wolfe leaned back and adjusted himself for comfort. "I have to make a choice. Seventeen days ago the body of a young woman named Joan Wellman was found on a secluded road in Van Cortlandt Park. She had been struck by an automobile. Her father, from Peoria, Illinois, is dissatisfied with the way the police are handling the matter and has hired me to investigate. I saw him just this evening; he left only two hours ago, and I phoned you immediately. I have reason to think that Miss Wellman's death was not an accident and that there was an important connection between the two homicides—hers and Dykes's."

"That's interesting," Cramer conceded. "Something your client told you?"

"Yes. So I'm faced with an alternative. I can make a proposal to your colleague in the Bronx. I can offer to tell him of this link connecting the two deaths, which will surely be of great help to him, on the condition that he collaborates with me, within reason, to satisfy my client —when the case is solved—that I have earned my fee. Or I can make that proposal to you. Since the death of my client's daughter occurred in the Bronx and therefore is in your colleague's jurisdiction, perhaps I should go to him, but on the other hand Dykes was killed in Manhattan. What do you think?"

"I think," Cramer growled, "I expected something like this and here it is. You want me to pay for information about a murder by promising to help you collect a fee, and you threaten to take it to the Bronx if I won't buy. If he won't buy either, then you withhold it? Huh?"

"I have no information to withhold."

"Goddammit, you said you—"

"I said I have reason to think the two deaths are connected. It's based on information, of course, but I have none that the police do not have. The Police Department is a huge organization. If your staff and the Bronx staff get together on this it's likely that sooner or later they'll get where I am. I thought this would save you time and work. I can't be charged with withholding information when I know nothing that the police don't know—collectively."

Cramer snorted. "Some day," he said darkly, and snorted again.

"I offer this," Wolfe said, "because you might as well have it, and because the case looks complex enough to need a lot of work and my resources are limited. I make the offer conditional because if with my hint you solve it in a hurry without further consultation with me, I don't want my client to refuse to pay my bill. I am willing to put it like this: if, when it's finished, you think it likely that the Wellman case would not have been solved if Mr. Wellman had not come to me, you tell him so, not for publication."

Wolfe levered himself forward to reach for his glass and drink.

"I'll take it that way," Cramer stated. "Let's have it."

Wolfe wiped his lips with his handkerchief. "Also Mr. Goodwin is to be permitted to look over the two files—on Dykes and on Miss Wellman."

"I don't have the Wellman file."

"When I explain the connection you'll get it."

"It's against Department regulations."

"Indeed? I beg your pardon. It would be mutually helpful to share information, and it would waste my time and my client's money to collect again the facts you already have, but of course a violation of regulations is unthinkable."

Cramer glared at him. "You know," he said, "one of the many reasons you're hard to take is that when you're being sarcastic you don't sound sarcastic. That's just one of your offensive habits. Okay, I'll see you get facts. What's this connection?"

"With the condition as stated."

"Hell yes. I'd hate to see you starve."

Wolfe turned to me. "Archie. That letter?"

I got it from under the paperweight and handed it to him.

"This," he told Cramer, "is a copy of a letter Miss Wellman wrote to her parents on Thursday, February first. She was killed the evening of the next day, Friday." He held it out, and Cramer got up to take it. "Read it all if you like, but the relevant part is the marked paragraph."

Cramer ran over it. He took his time, and then sat frowning at it. Looking up at Wolfe, he kept the frown. "I've seen that name somewhere. Baird Archer. Isn't that it?"

Wolfe nodded. "Shall we see how long it takes you to dig it up?"

"No. Where?"

"On the list of names written by Leonard Dykes which you came here to show me six weeks ago. It was seventh on the list, I think—possibly eighth. Not sixth."

"When did you first see this letter?"

"This evening. My client gave it to me."

"I'll be damned." Cramer gawked at him and at the relevant paragraph. He folded the letter with slow deliberate fingers and put it in his pocket.

"The original," Wolfe told him, "is in the possession of your colleague in the Bronx. That's my copy."

"Yeah. I'll borrow it." Cramer reached for his glass, took a swallow, and focused his eyes on a corner of Wolfe's arc-wood desk. He took another swallow and went back to studying the desk. So alternating, two more swallows with intervals for desk study emptied the glass. He put it down on the little table.

"What else have you got?"

"Nothing."

"What have you done?"

"Nothing. Since I saw that letter, I have dined."

"I bet you have." Cramer came up out of his chair, still springy in spite of his years. "I'll be going. Damn it, I was going home."

He headed for the hall. I followed.

When I returned to the office after letting the law out, Wolfe was placidly opening a bottle of beer.

"What do you say," I suggested, "I get on the phone and call in Saul and Fred and Orrie, and you lay it out, and we set a deadline, sundown tomorrow would do, for solving *both* cases? Just to make a monkey out of Cramer?"

Wolfe scowled at me. "Confound it, don't bounce like that. This will be no skirmish. Mr. Cramer's men have been looking, more or less, for a Baird Archer for seven weeks. The Bronx men have been looking for one for seventeen days. Now they'll get serious about it. What if there isn't one?"

"We know there was enough of one to date Joan Wellman for February second."

"We do not. We know only that she wrote her parents that a stranger on the telephone had said he was Baird Archer, and that a manuscript of a novel bearing that name had been submitted to her employers, read by her, and returned in the mail to a Baird Archer at General Delivery." Wolfe shook his head. "No, this will be more than a skirmish. Before we're through Mr. Wellman may indeed be a pauper unless his rancor wears thin. Let the police do their part."

Knowing him as I did, I didn't care for that. I sat down. "Sitzlust again?" I demanded offensively.

"No. I said let the police do their part. This will take work. We'll start with the assumption, not risky I think, that Miss Wellman's letter to her parents was straightforward. If so, it had something for us besides the name of Baird Archer. He asked her if anyone else had read his manuscript and she said no. It could have been an innocent question, but in the light of what happened to her it raises a point. Was she killed because she had read the manuscript? As a conjecture that is not inane. How many public stenographers are there in the city? Say in Manhattan?"

"I don't know. Five hundred. Five thousand."

"Not thousands surely. People who make presentable copies of documents or manuscripts from drafts."

"That's typing services, not public stenographers."

"Very well." Wolfe drank beer and leaned back. "I thought of suggesting this to Mr. Cramer, but if we're to spend some of Mr. Wellman's money this is as good a way to start as any. I would like to know what that novel was about. Baird Archer may have typed the manuscript himself, but he may not. We'll put Saul and Fred and Orrie on a round of the typing services. Have them here at eight in the morning and I'll give them instructions. There is a possibility not only of learning about the novel, but also of getting a description of Baird Archer."

"Right." This was more like it. "It wouldn't hurt me to stretch my legs too."

"You will. There's a chance, though this may be slimmer, that the novel had previously been submitted to another publisher. It's worth trying. Start with the better firms, of the class of Scholl and Hanna. But not tomorrow. Tomorrow get all you can from the police files on both Miss Wellman and Dykes, covering everything. For instance, did Dykes have a typewriter in his apartment?"

I lifted a brow. "Do you think Dykes was Baird Archer?"

"I don't know. He wrote that list of names, obviously inventions. He certainly wasn't Baird Archer on February second, since he had been dead five weeks. You will also go to Scholl and Hanna. In spite of what Miss Wellman wrote her parents, it's possible that someone else read that manuscript, or at least glanced through it. Or Miss Wellman may have said something about it to one of her associates. Or, less likely, Baird Archer may have delivered the manuscript in person and be remembered—of course that was last fall, months ago."

Wolfe heaved a sigh and reached for his glass. "I suggest that you extend the deadline beyond sundown tomorrow."

"What the hell," I said generously, "I'll give you till Friday."

It was just as well I didn't say what Friday.

IV

WHAT with getting Saul and Fred and Orrie sicked onto the typing services, and dealing with the morning mail, and going to the bank to deposit Wellman's check, it was well after ten o'clock Tuesday when I got to Cramer's office on Twentieth Street. He wasn't there but had left instructions with Sergeant Purley Stebbins. I am one of the few people Purley knows that he has not completely made up his mind about. Since I'm a private detective, the sooner I die, or at least get lost outside the city limits, the better—of course that's basic, but he can't quite get rid of the suspicion that I might have made a good cop if I had been caught in time.

I not only got a look at the files, I even got to talk with two of the help who had worked on Dykes and one from the Bronx who had worked on Joan Wellman. By the time I left, a little before three, I had a lot in my notebook and more in my head.

For here I'll trim it down. Leonard Dykes, forty-one, found banging up against a pile in the East River on New Year's Day, had for eight years been a clerk, not a member of the bar, in the office of the law firm of Corrigan, Phelps, Kustin and Briggs. Up to a year ago the firm's name had been O'Malley, Corrigan and Phelps, but O'Malley had been disbarred and there had been a reorganization. Dykes had been unmarried, sober, trustworthy, and competent. He had played cards every Tuesday evening with friends, for small stakes. He had twelve thousand dollars in government bonds and a savings account, and thirty shares of United States Steel, which had been inherited by a married sister who lived in California, his only close relative. No one discoverable had hated or feared him or wished him ill. One sentence in one report said, "No women at all." There was a photograph of him after he had been hauled out of the river, not attractive, and one of him alive that had been taken from his apartment. To be objective, I'll put it that he had been less unattractive before drowning than after. He had had pop-eyes, and his chin had started backing up about a quarter of an inch below his mouth.

The other thousand or so facts in the file on Dykes had as little discernible bearing on his murder as those I have given for samples.

On Joan Wellman, the Bronx had not been as much in love with the hit-and-run theory as Wellman suspected, but it was just as well that her father did not have access to the police file. They didn't care much for Joan's version of her Friday date in her letter home, especially since they could find no one among her office associates to whom she had mentioned it. I gave them a low mark on that, knowing how full offices are of petty jealousies and being willing to give our client's daughter credit for enough sense to keep her mouth shut about her private affairs. Aside from the search for the car that had run over her, the Bronx had mostly concentrated on her boy friends. If you want to give the average dick a job he really likes, sit him down with a man who has been seen fairly recently in the company of a pretty girl who has just died a sudden and violent death. Think of the questions he can ask. Look at the

ground he can cover, no matter who the man is, with no risk of a come-
back that will cost him anything.

So the Bronx had done the boy friends up brown, especially an advertising copywriter named Atchison, apparently because his name
began with "A" and had a "c" and an "h" in it, and it had dawned upon
some eagle eye that Archer did too, and what more do you want? Luckily for Atchison, he had taken a four-thirty train Friday afternoon,
February second, to spend the weekend with friends at Westport. Two
dicks had worked like dogs trying to pry that alibi loose, with no success.

As far as I could tell from the file, it looked as if Joan had had not
only beauty and intelligence but also good old-fashioned virtue. The
three boy friends who had been flushed were unanimous on that. They
had admired and respected her. One of them had been after her for a
year to marry him and had had hopes. If any of them had had reason to
prefer her dead, the Bronx had failed to dig up a hint of it.

I went back home and typed it all up for Wolfe, and got reports
on the phone from Saul and Fred and Orrie.

I spent most of Wednesday at the office of Scholl and Hanna on
Forty-fifth Street. What I got out of it was a respectful appreciation of
the book-publishing business as a means of corralling jack. The office
took up two whole floors, with nothing spared anywhere in the way of
rugs and furniture. Scholl was in Florida, I was told, and Hanna never
got in until ten-thirty. I was escorted down a hall to the room of a junior
executive who needed a haircut and was chewing gum, and when I
showed him the note I had from our client he said they would be glad
to cooperate with the bereaved father of their late employee, and I
could ask questions of any of the staff I cared to see, starting with him
if I wanted to. But would I please tell him, had something new turned
up? City detectives, three of them, had been there again yesterday, for
hours, and now here was Nero Wolfe's Archie Goodwin. What was
stirring? I told him something harmless and began on him.

The fact that Wolfe never leaves the office on business, unless there
is an incentive more urgent than the prospect of a fee, such as saving
his own skin, has a lot to do with the way I work. When I'm out on a
case and get something helpful I like to recognize it before I deliver it to
Wolfe, but as I left Scholl and Hanna's I couldn't see a crumb. It was
hard to believe that I had spent nearly five hours in the office where
Joan Wellman had worked, questioning everybody from the office boy
to Hanna himself, without getting a single useful item, but that was
how it looked. The one thing that tied in at all was an entry in the
columns of a big book I had been shown. I give it with the column
headings:

NUMBER: 16237

DATE: Oct. 2

NAME AND ADDRESS: Baird Archer, General Delivery,
                  Clinton Station, N. Y. City

TITLE: Put Not Your Trust

DETAIL: Novel 246 pp.

POSTAGE ENCLOSED: 63¢

READ BY: Joan Wellman

DISPOSITION: Rejected ret'd. mail Oct. 27

That was my haul. The manuscript had been received by mail. No one had ever heard of Baird Archer, except for that entry. No one else had looked at the manuscript or remembered anything about it. If Joan had made any comment on it to anyone they had forgotten it. She had not mentioned the phone call from Baird Archer or her appointment with him. I could go on with negatives for a page.

When I reported to Wolfe that evening I told him, "It looks to me as if we're all set. Two hundred and forty-six sheets of typewriter paper weigh a lot more than twenty-one ounces. Either he wrote on both sides, or he used thin light paper, or he didn't enclose enough postage. All we have to do is find out which and we've got him."

"Harlequin," he growled.

"Have you a better suggestion? From what I've brought in?"

"No."

"Did I get anything at all?"

"No."

"Okay. That's what I mean. Two days of me, nothing. Two days of the boys calling on typing services, nothing. At two hundred bucks a day, four C's of Wellman's money already gone. This would be all right for an agency or the cops, that's how they work, but it's not your way. I'll bet you a week's pay you haven't turned your brain on it once during the forty-eight hours!"

"On what?" he demanded. "I can't grapple with a shadow. Get me something of him—a gesture, an odor, a word, a sound he made. Bring me something."

I had to admit, though of course not to him, that he had a point. You could say that Cramer had a trained army looking for Baird Archer, but it wouldn't mean much. They had no idea what he looked like. They had no evidence that anyone had ever known him, or even met him, by that name. There was no proof that Baird Archer had ever been anything *but* a name. It would be about the same if you just made up a name for a man, say Freetham Choade, and then tried to find him. After you look in the phone book, what do you do next?

I spent the rest of that week collecting some very interesting data about the quality and tone of publishers' offices. I learned that Simon and Schuster, in Rockefeller Center, had fallen hard for modern and didn't give a damn what it cost; that Harper and Brothers liked old desks and didn't care for ashtrays; that The Viking Press had a good eye for contours and comeliness when hiring female help; that The Macmillan Company had got itself confused with a Pullman car; and so on. I covered the whole trade, big and little, and the only concrete result was a dinner date with a young woman at Scribner's who struck me as worth following up on the chance that she might have something I would like to know about. No one anywhere knew anything about a Baird Archer. If he had submitted the manuscript of "Put Not Your Trust" to any other firm than Scholl and Hanna, there was no record or memory of it.

Over the weekend I had a couple of talks with Purley Stebbins. If we were getting nowhere fast, so were the cops. They had uncovered a Baird Archer somewhere down in Virginia, but he was over eighty and couldn't read or write. Their big idea was to find some link between Leonard Dykes and Joan Wellman, and three of Cramer's best men were clawing away at it. When I reported that to Wolfe Sunday evening he snorted.

"Jackassery. I gave them the link."

"Yes, sir," I said sympathetically. "That was what tired you out."

"I am not tired out. I am not even tired."

"Then I lied to our client. The second time he called today I told him that you were exhausted with overwork on his case. I had to tell him something drastic because he's getting impatient. What's wrong with the beer? Too cold?"

"No. I am considering you. Most of these typing services are run by women, aren't they?"

"Not most. All."

"Then you will start on that tomorrow morning. You may be luckier than Saul and Fred and Orrie, but they will continue at it too. We'll finish that job before we try something else. Some of the women are surely young and personable. Don't overwork."

"I won't." I gazed at him admiringly. "It's uncanny, these flashes of inspiration you get. Absolutely brilliant!"

He exploded. "Confound it, what have I got? Get me something! Will you get me something?"

"Certainly." I was composed. "Drink your beer."

So the next day, Monday, after finishing the morning office chores, I took a geographical section of the list Saul and I had compiled, and went at it. The other three had covered downtown Manhattan up to Fourteenth Street, the Grand Central section, and the West Side from Fourteenth to Forty-second. That day Fred was in Brooklyn, Orrie in the Bronx, and Saul on the East Side. I took the West Side from Forty-second Street up.

At ten-thirty I was in bedlam, having entered through a door inscribed BROADWAY STENOGRAPHIC SERVICE. In a room big enough to accommodate comfortably five typewriter desks and typists, double that number were squeezed in, hitting the keys at about twice my normal speed. I was yelling at a dame with a frontage that would have made a good bookshelf.

"A woman like you should have a private room!"

"I have," she said haughtily, and led me through a door in a partition to a cubbyhole. Since the partition was only six feet high, the racket bounced down on us off the ceiling. Two minutes later the woman was telling me, "We don't give out any information about clients. Our business is strictly confidential."

I had given her my business card. "So is ours!" I shouted. "Look, it's quite simple. Our client is a reputable firm of book publishers. They have a manuscript of a novel that was submitted to them, and they're enthusiastic about it and want to publish it, but the page of the script that had the author's name and address got lost somehow and can't be found. They remember the author's name, Baird Archer, but not the address, and they want to get in touch with him. They might not be so anxious if they didn't want to publish the novel, but they do. His name is not in any phone book. The manuscript came in the mail, unsolicited. They've advertised and got no answer. All I want to know, did you type a manuscript of a novel for a man named Baird Archer, probably last September? Sometime around then? The title of the novel was 'Put Not Your Trust.'"

She stayed haughty. "Last September? They've waited long enough to inquire."

"They've been trying to find him."

"If we typed it a page couldn't have got lost. It would have been fastened into one of our folders."

The boys had told me of running into that one. I nodded. "Yes, but editors don't like to read fastened scripts. They take the folders off. If you typed it for him, you can bet he would want you to help us find him. Give the guy a break."

She had remained standing. "All right," she said, "I'll look it up as soon as I get something straightened out." She left me.

I waited for her twenty minutes, and then another ten while she fussed through a card file. The answer was no. They had never done any work for a Baird Archer. I took an elevator up to the eighteenth floor, to the office of the Raphael Typing Service.

Those first two calls took me nearly an hour, and at that rate you can't cover much ground in a day. They were all kinds and sizes, from a big outfit in the Paramount Building called Metropolitan Stenographers, Inc., down to two girls with their office in their room-bath-and-kitchenette in the upper Forties. For lunch I had canneloni at Sardi's, on John R. Wellman, and then resumed.

It was warm for February, but it was trying to make up its mind whether to go in for a steady drizzle, and around three o'clock, as I dodged through the sidewalk traffic to enter a building on Broadway in the Fifties, I was wishing I had worn my raincoat instead of my brown topcoat. My quarry in that building was apparently one of the small ones, since its name on my list was just the name of a woman, Rachel Abrams. The building was an old one, nothing fancy, with Caroline, women's dresses, on the left of the entrance, and the Midtown Eatery on the right. After stopping in the lobby to remove my topcoat and give it a shake, and consulting the building directory, I took the elevator to the seventh floor. The elevator man told me to go left for 728.

I went left, rounded a corner to the right, continued, turned right again, and in ten paces was at Room 728. The door was wide open, and I stuck my head in to verify the number, 728, and to see the inscription:

RACHEL ABRAMS
Stenography
and Typing

I stepped into a room about ten by twelve, not more, with a typewriter desk, a little table, a couple of chairs, a clothes rack, and an old green metal filing cabinet. A woman's hat and cloth coat hung on the rack, and an umbrella, and at the back of the typewriter desk was a vase of yellow daffodils. On the floor were some sheets of paper, scattered around. That was accounted for by the fact that the one window was raised, way up, and a strong draft was whirling through.

Something else was coming through too: voices from down in the street that were shouts. Three steps took me to the window, and I looked out and down. People had stopped in the drizzle and were gawking. Three men, from different directions, were running across the street toward the building, and on this side a group was forming on the sidewalk. In the center of the group two men were bending over a figure of a woman prostrate on the sidewalk, with her skirt up, showing her bare legs, and her head twisted sideways. I have good eyes, but from seven floors up, in the dim light of the drizzle blown by the wind, things were blurred. Most of the group were looking at the huddled figure, but some were gazing straight up at me. Off to the left a hundred feet, a cop was trotting toward the group.

I assert that it took me not more than three seconds to realize what had happened. I assert it not to get a credit mark, since I can't prove it, but to account for what I did. Of course it was only a hunch, but I had never had one that felt like a better bet. Wolfe had told me to get him something, and I had missed getting it by three minutes or maybe only two. I was so sure of it that what I did was automatic. Pulling back from the window and straightening, I darted a glance at the desk and one at the filing cabinet. I started with the desk only because it was nearer.

That was probably the briefest search on record, or close to it. The shallow middle drawer was eliminated with one look. The top left drawer held paper and carbons and envelopes. The one below it had three compartments, with miscellaneous contents, and in the middle one was a notebook bound in brown imitation leather. At the top of the first page was written the word "Receipts," and the first entry was dated Aug. 7, 1944. I flipped the pages to 1950, began with July, ran my eye over the items, and there it was: "Sept. 12, Baird Archer, $60.00 dep." Six lines down another entry said: "Sept. 23, Baird Archer, $38.40 in full."

"Of all the goddam lousy luck," I said with feeling and, slipping the notebook in my pocket, made for the door. There was a bare chance that Rachel Abrams had enough life left in her to talk a little. As I rounded the second turn in the hall an elevator door opened and a flatfoot emerged. I was so engrossed that I didn't even glance at him, which was a mistake because cops can't bear not to be glanced at, especially when they're on something hot. He stopped in my path and demanded, "Who are you?"

"Governor Dewey," I told him. "How do you like me without the mustache?"

"Oh, a wag. Show me some identification."

I raised the brows. "How did I get behind the Iron Curtain without knowing it?"

"I'm in a hurry. What's your name?"

I shook my head. "Honest, officer, I don't like this. Take me to the nearest Kremlin and I'll tell the sergeant." I stepped and pushed the down button.

"Aw, nuts." He tramped down the hall.

An elevator stopped and I entered. The elevator man was telling his passengers about the excitement. The street lobby was deserted. Out on the sidewalk the crowd was thick now, ignoring the drizzle, and I had to get authoritative to elbow my way through to the front. A cop was there, commanding them to stand back. I had a line ready to hand him to get me an approach, but when I got close enough for an unobstructed view I saw I wouldn't need it. She was smashed good, and there would be no more talking from a head that had taken that angle to the shoulders. Nor did I have to ask her name, since I had heard everybody telling everybody else, Rachel Abrams, as I pushed my way through the mob. I pushed my way out again, went to the corner and grabbed a taxi, and gave the driver the number on West Thirty-fifth Street.

When I mounted the stoop and let myself in with my key it was five minutes past four, so Wolfe had gone up for his afternoon conference with the orchids. Hanging my hat and topcoat in the hall, I ascended the three flights to the plant rooms on the roof. For all the thousands of times I have seen that display of show-offs, they still take my eye and slow me down whenever I go through, but that day I didn't even know they were there, not even in the warm room, though the Phalaenopsis were in top bloom and the Cattleyas were splashing color all around.

Wolfe was in the potting room with Theodore, transferring young *Dendrobium chrysotoxums* from fours to fives. As I approached he snapped at me, "Can't it wait?"

"I suppose so," I conceded. "She's dead. I just want permission to phone Cramer. I might as well, since I was seen by the elevator man who let me off at her floor, and a cop, and my fingerprints are on her desk."

"Who is dead?"

"The woman who typed that manuscript for Baird Archer."

"When and how?"

"Just now. She died while I was in the elevator going up to her office on the seventh floor. She was going down faster, out of her window. What killed her was hitting the sidewalk."

"How do you know she typed the manuscript?"

"I found this in her desk." I took the notebook from my pocket and showed him the entries. His hands were too dirty to touch it, and I held it before his eyes. I asked him, "Do you want details now?"

"Confound it. Yes."

As I reported in full he stood with the tips of his dirty fingers resting on the potting bench, his head turned to me, his lips tight, his brow creased with a frown. His yellow smock, some half an acre in area, was exactly the color of the daffodils on Rachel Abrams' desk.

When I had finished the story I inquired grimly, "Shall I expound?" He grunted.

"I should have stuck around, but it wouldn't have done any good because I was too goddam mad to function. If I had been three minutes earlier I would have had her alive. Also, if she was pushed out of the window I would have had the pusher alive, and you told me to get you something, and it would have been a pleasure to get you that. The lucky bastard. He must have entered a down elevator, or passed down the hall on his way to the stairs, not more than thirty seconds before I stepped out on that floor. When I looked out of the window he was probably there on the sidewalk, walking away because he wasn't morbid."

Wolfe's eyes opened and half shut again.

"If you're thinking," I said aggressively, "that she wasn't pushed, one will get you ten. I do not believe that the woman who typed that manuscript picked today to jump out of the window or to fall out by accident."

"Nevertheless, it's possible."

"I deny it. It would be too goddam silly. Okay, you said to get you something, and at least I got you this." I tapped the notebook with a finger.

"It doesn't help much." Wolfe was glum. "It establishes that Miss Wellman was killed because she had read that manuscript, but we were already going on that assumption. I doubt if it would gratify Miss Abrams to know that her death validated an assumption for us. Most people expect more than that of death. Mr. Cramer will want that notebook."

"Yeah. I shouldn't have copped it, but you said to get you something and I wanted to produce it. Shall I take it to him or phone him to send for it?"

"Neither. Put it here on the bench. I'll wash my hands and phone him. You have work to do. It's possible that Miss Abrams told someone something about the contents of that novel she typed. Try it. See her family and friends. Get a list of them. Saul and Fred and Orrie will phone in at five-thirty. You will phone at five-twenty-five, to tell me where I can tell them to join you. Divide the list among you."

"My God," I protested, "we're stretching it thinner and thinner. Next you'll be trying to get it by photo-offset from her typewriter platen."

He ignored it and headed for the sink to wash his hands. I went to

my room, one flight down, for my raincoat. Downstairs I stopped in
the kitchen to tell Fritz I wouldn't be home for dinner.

V

IT WAS more than I had bargained for. Having got the home address of
a Rachel Abrams from the Bronx phone book, having learned by dialing
the number and speaking briefly with a female voice that that was it,
and having hit the subway before the rush hour, I had congratulated
myself on a neat fast start. I entered the old apartment building on
178th Street a block off the Grand Concourse less than an hour after
Wolfe had told me to see her family and friends.

But now I realized that I had been too damn fast. The woman who
opened the door of 4E to me was meeting my eyes straight and inquiring
placidly, "You're the one that phoned? What is with my Rachel?"

"Are you Rachel's mother?" I asked.

She nodded and smiled. "Since some years I am. I have never been
told the opposite. What is?"

I hadn't bargained for this. I had taken it for granted that either a
cop or a journalist would have relayed the news before I got there, and
had been ready to cope with tears and wailing, but obviously I had
beat them to it. Of course the thing to do was spill it to her, but her
quiet self-satisfaction when she said "my Rachel" was too much for me.
Nor could I say excuse it please, wrong number, and fade, because I
had a job to do, and if I muffed it merely because I didn't like it I was
in the wrong line of business. So I tried my damnedest to grin at her,
but I admit that for a couple of seconds I was no help to the conversation.

Her big dark friendly eyes stayed straight at mine.

"I will maybe ask you to come in and sit," she said, "when you tell
me what you want."

"I don't think," I told her, "I need to take much of your time. I told
you my name on the phone, Archie Goodwin. I'm getting some stuff
together for an article on public stenographers. Does your daughter
discuss her work with you?"

She frowned a little. "You could ask her. Couldn't you?"

"Sure I could, if there's some reason why I shouldn't ask you."

"Why should there be a reason?"

"I don't know any. For instance, say she types a story or an article for
a man. Does she tell you about him—what he looked like and how he
talked? Or does she tell you what the story or article was about?"

The frown had not gone. "Would that be not proper?"

"Not at all. It's not a question of being proper, it's just that I want to make it personal, talking with her family and friends."

"Is it there will be an article about her?"

"Yes." That was not a lie. Far from it.

"Is it her name will be printed?"

"Yes."

"My daughter never talks about her work to me or her father or her sisters, only one thing, the money she makes. She tells about that because she gives me a certain part, but not for me, for the family, and one sister is in college. She does not tell me what men look like or about her work. If her name is going to be printed everybody ought to know the truth."

"You're absolutely right, Mrs. Abrams. Do you know—"

"You said you will talk with her family and friends. Her father will be home at twenty minutes to seven. Her sister Deborah is here now, doing her homework, but she is only sixteen—too young? Her sister Nancy will not be here today, she is with a friend, but she will be here tomorrow at half-past four. Then you want friends. There is a young man named William Butterfield who wants to marry her, but he is—"

She stopped short, with a twinkle in her eye. "If you will pardon me, but that is maybe too personal. If you want his address?"

"Please."

She gave me a number on Seventy-sixth Street. "There is Hulda Greenberg, she lives downstairs on the second floor, Two C. There is Cynthia Free, only that is not her real name. You know about her."

"I'm sorry, I'm afraid I don't."

"She acts on the stage."

"Oh, sure. Cynthia Free."

"Yes. She went to high school with Rachel, but she quit. I will not speak against her. If my daughter is once a friend she is always a friend. I will be getting old now, but what will I have? I will have my husband and Deborah and Nancy, and enough friends I have, many friends, but I know I will always have my Rachel. If her name is to be printed that must be part of it. I will tell you more about her, Mr. Goodwin, if you will come in and sit—oy, the phone. Excuse me, please?"

She turned and trotted inside. I stayed put. In a moment I heard her voice, faintly.

"Hello. . . . This is Mrs. Abrams. . . . Yes. . . . Yes, Rachel is my daughter. . . . Who is it you say? . . ."

There was no doubt about its being my move. The only question was whether to leave the door standing open or close it. It seemed better to close it. I reached for the knob, pulled it to quickly but with no bang, and headed for the stairs.

Out on the sidewalk, glancing at my wrist and seeing 5:24, I went to the corner for a look, saw a drugstore down a block, walked there, found a phone booth, and dialed the number. Fritz answered and put me through to the plant rooms.

When Wolfe was on I told him, "I've had a talk with Rachel's mother. She says her daughter never discusses her work at home. We were using the present tense because she hadn't got the news yet. She wants to see her Rachel's name in print, and thanks to that son of a bitch I missed by three minutes, she will. I didn't tell her because it would have wasted time. Tomorrow, when she knows that discussing her daughter's work may help to find the guy that killed her, she might possibly remember something, though I doubt it. I have some names, but they're scattered around town. Tell the boys to call me at this number." I gave it to him.

He spoke. "Mr. Cramer insists on seeing you. I gave him the information, and he sent for the notebook, but he wants to see you. He is sour, of course. You might as well go down there. After all, we are collaborating."

"Yeah. On what? Okay, I'll go. Don't overdo."

I waited in the booth to corner it. When the calls came I gave William Butterfield to Saul, Hulda Greenberg to Fred, and Cynthia Free to Orrie, telling them all to collect additional names and keep going. Then I hiked to the subway.

Down at Homicide on West Twentieth Street I learned how sour Cramer was. Over the years my presence has been requested at that address many times. When it's a case of our having something he would like to get, or he thinks it is, I am taken inside at once to his own room. When it's only some routine matter, I am left to Sergeant Purley Stebbins or one of the bunch. When all that is really wanted or expected is a piece of my hide, I am assigned to Lieutenant Rowcliff. If and when I am offered a choice of going to heaven or hell it will be simple; I'll merely ask, "Where's Rowcliff?" We were fairly even—he set my teeth on edge about the same as I did his—until one day I got the notion of stuttering. When he gets worked up to a certain point he starts to stutter. My idea was to wait till he was about there and then stutter just once. It more than met expectations. It made him so mad he had to stutter, he couldn't help it, and then I complained that he was mimicking me. From that day on I have had the long end and he knows it.

I was with him an hour or so, and it was burlesque all the way, because Wolfe had already given them my story and there was nothing I could add. Rowcliff's line was that I had overstepped when I searched her desk and took the notebook, which was true, and that I had certainly taken something besides the notebook and was holding out. We went all around that, and back and forth, and he had a statement typed for me to sign, and after I signed it he sat and studied it and thought up more questions. Finally I got tired.

"Look," I told him, "this is a lot of bull and you know it. What are you trying to do, b-b-b-break my spirit?"

He clamped his jaw. But he had to say something. "I'd rather b-b-b-break your goddam neck," he stated. "Get the hell out of here."

I went, but not out. I intended to have one word with Cramer. Down the hall I took a left turn, strode to the door at the end, and opened it without knocking. But Cramer wasn't there, only Purley Stebbins, sitting at a table working with papers.

"You lost?" he demanded.

"No. I'm giving myself up. I just c-c-c-cooked Rowcliff and ate him. Aside from that, I thought someone here might want to thank me. If I hadn't been there today, the precinct boys would probably have called it a jump or a fall, and no one would have ever gone through that book and found those entries."

Purley nodded. "So you found the entries."

"So I did."

"And took the book home to Wolfe."

"And then, without delay, turned it over."

"By God, so you did. Thank you. Going?"

"Yes. But I could use a detail without waiting for the morning paper. What's in the lead on how Rachel Abrams got out of the window?"

"Homicide."

"By flipping a coin?"

"No. Finger marks on her throat. Preliminary, the M.E. says she was choked. He thinks not enough to kill her, but we won't know until they're through at the laboratory."

"And I missed him by three minutes."

Purley cocked his head. "Did you?"

I uttered a colorful word. "One Rowcliff on the squad is enough," I told him and beat it. Out in the anteroom I went to a phone booth, dialed, got Wolfe, and reported, "Excuse me for interrupting your dinner, but I need instructions. I'm at Homicide on Twentieth Street, without cuffs, after an hour with Rowcliff and a word with Purley. From marks on her throat the dope is that she was choked and tossed out the window. I told you so. I divided the three names Mrs. Abrams gave me among the help, and told them to get more and carry on. There should be another call on the family either tonight or tomorrow, but not by me. Mrs. Abrams might open up for Saul, but not for me, after today. So I need instructions."

"Have you had dinner?"

"No."

"Come home."

I went to Tenth Avenue and flagged a taxi. It was still drizzling.

VI

WOLFE does not like conferences with clients. Many's the time he has told me not to let a client in. So when, that evening, following instructions, I phoned Wellman at his hotel and asked him to call at the office the next morning at eleven, I knew it looked as bad to Wolfe as it did to me.

Eight days had passed since we had seen our client, though we had had plenty of phone calls from him, some local and some from Peoria. Apparently the eight days hadn't done him any good. Either he was wearing the same gray suit or he had two of them, but at least the tie and shirt were different. His face was pasty. As I hung his coat on the rack I remarked that he had lost some weight. When he didn't reply I thought he hadn't heard me, but after we had entered the office and he and Wolfe had exchanged greetings and he was in the red leather chair, he apologized.

"Excuse me, what did you say about my weight?"

"I said you had lost some."

"I guess so. I haven't been eating much and I don't seem to sleep. I go back home and go to the office or the warehouse, but I'm no darned good, and I take a train back here, and I'm no good here either." He went to Wolfe. "He told me on the phone you didn't have any real news but you wanted to see me."

Wolfe nodded. "I didn't want to, I had to. I must put a question to you. In eight days I have spent—how much, Archie?"

"Around eighteen hundred bucks."

"Nearly two thousand dollars of your money. You said you were going through with this even if it pauperized you. A man should not be held to a position taken under stress. I like my clients to pay my bills without immoderate pangs. How do you feel now?"

Wellman looked uncomfortable. He swallowed. "I just said I don't eat much."

"I heard you. A man should eat." Wolfe gestured. "Perhaps I should first describe the situation. As you know, I regard it as established that your daughter was murdered by the man who, calling himself Baird Archer, phoned for an appointment with her. Also that he killed her because she had read the manuscript she told about in her letter to you. The police agree."

"I know they do." Wellman was concentrating. "That's something. You did that."

"I did more. Most of your money has been spent in an effort to find someone who could tell us something about either the manuscript or Baird Archer, or both. It missed success by a narrow margin. Yesterday afternoon a young woman named Rachel Abrams was murdered by being pushed from a window of her office. Mr. Goodwin entered her office three minutes later. This next detail is being withheld by the police and is not for publication. In a notebook in her desk Mr. Goodwin found entries showing that last September a Baird Archer paid her ninety-eight dollars and forty cents for typing a manuscript. Of course that clinches it that your daughter was killed because of her knowledge of the manuscript, but I was already acting on that assumption, so it doesn't help any. We are—"

"It proves that Baird Archer did it!" Wellman was excited. "It proves that he's still in New York! Surely the police can find him!" He came up out of the chair. "I'm going—"

"Please, Mr. Wellman." Wolfe patted the air with a palm. "It proves that the murderer was in that building yesterday afternoon, and that's all. Baird Archer is still nothing but a name, a will-o'-the-wisp. Having missed Rachel Abrams by the merest tick, we still have no one alive who has ever seen or heard him. As for finding his trail from yesterday, that's for the police and they do it well; we may be sure that the building employees and tenants and passers-by are being efficiently badgered. Sit down, sir."

"I'm going up there. To that building."

"When I have finished. Sit down, please?"

Wellman lowered himself, and nearly kept going to the floor when his fanny barely caught the edge of the leather. He recovered and slid back a few inches.

"I must make it plain," Wolfe said, "that the chance of success is now minute. I have three men interviewing Miss Abrams' family and friends, to learn if she spoke to any of them about Baird Archer or his manuscript, but they have already talked with the most likely ones and have got nothing. Mr. Goodwin has seen everyone at the office of Scholl and Hanna who could possibly have what we're after, and he has also called on other publishers. For a week the police, with far greater re-

sources than mine, have been doing their best to find a trace of either
Baird Archer or the manuscript. The outlook has never been rosy; now
it is forlorn."

Wellman's glasses had slipped down on his nose, and he pushed
them back. "I asked about you before I came here," he protested. "I
thought you never gave up."

"I'm not giving up."

"Excuse me. I thought you sounded like it."

"I'm merely describing the situation. Forlorn is not too strong a word.
It would indeed be desperate but for one possibility. The name Baird
Archer was first seen on a sheet of paper in the handwriting of Leonard
Dykes. It would not be poopery to assume that when he wrote that list
of names, obviously invented, he was choosing a pseudonym for a
manuscript of a novel, whether written by him or another. But it is a
fact, not an assumption, that he included that name in a list he compiled, and that that was the name of Miss Abrams' client, and it was
also the name on the manuscript read by your daughter, and the name
given by the man who phoned her for an appointment. If I make this
too elaborate it is because I must make sure that it is completely clear."

"I like it clear."

"Good." Wolfe sighed. He was not enjoying himself. "I undertook to
learn about that manuscript through your daughter's associates or the
person who typed it, and I have met defeat. I've been licked. The only
connection with Baird Archer that has not been explored is that of
Leonard Dykes, and it is certainly flimsy, the bare fact that he wrote
that name down; but to explore it is our only hope."

"Then go ahead."

Wolfe nodded. "That's why I needed to see you. This is February
twenty-seventh. Dykes was fished out of the water on New Year's Day.
He had been murdered. The police rarely skimp on a murder, and the
law office where Dykes worked assuredly saw a great deal of them. Mr.
Goodwin has been permitted to see the file. People there were even
asked then about Baird Archer, along with the other names on that
list Dykes had written. Dykes had few intimacies or interests outside
the office where he worked. Then, eight days ago, I showed the police
that the name of Baird Archer connected Dykes's death with that of
your daughter, and of course they again went after the people in that
law office and are still after them. All possible questions have probably
been asked, not once but over and over, of those people. It would be
useless for me to open an inquiry there in the conventional manner.
They wouldn't even listen to my questions, let alone answer them."

Wellman was concentrating. "You're saying you can't do it."

"No. I'm saying the approach must be oblique. Young women work in law offices. Mr. Goodwin may have his equal in making the acquaintance of a young woman and developing it into intimacy, but I doubt it. We can try that. However, it will be expensive, it will probably be protracted, and it may be futile—for your purpose and mine. If there were only one young woman and we knew she had information for us, it would be simple, but there may be a dozen or more. There's no telling what it will cost, or how long it will take, or whether we'll get anything. That's why I had to ask you, shall we try it or do you want to quit?"

Wellman's reaction was peculiar. He had been concentrating on Wolfe, to be sure he got it clear, but now he had shifted to me, and his look was strange. He wasn't exactly studying me, but you might have thought I had suddenly grown an extra nose or had snakes in my hair. I sent my brows up. He turned to Wolfe.

"Do you mean—" He cleared his throat. "I guess it's a good thing you asked me. After what I said here that day you have a right to think I would stand for anything, but that's a little too—with my money—a dozen young women—first one and then another like that—"

"What the devil are you suggesting?" Wolfe demanded.

I not only kept my face straight, I stepped in, for three good reasons: we needed the business, I wanted to get a look at Baird Archer, and I did not want John R. Wellman to go back and tell Peoria that New York detectives debauched stenographers wholesale on order.

"You misunderstand," I told Wellman. "Much obliged for the compliment, but by intimacy Mr. Wolfe meant holding hands. He's right that sometimes I seem to get along with young women, but it's because I'm shy and they like that. I like what you said about its being your money. You'll have to take my word for it. If things start developing beyond what I think you would approve, I'll either remember it's your money and back off or I'll take off of the expense account all items connected with that subject."

"I'm not a prude," Wellman protested.

"This is farcical!" Wolfe bellowed.

"I'm not a prude," Wellman insisted manfully, "but I don't know those young women. I know this is New York, but some of them may be virgins."

"Absolutely possible," I agreed. I reproved Wolfe. "Mr. Wellman and I understand each other. His money is not to be used beyond a certain point, and he'll take my word for it. That right, Mr. Wellman?"

"I guess that'll do," he conceded. Meeting my eyes, he decided his glasses needed cleaning, removed them, and wiped them with his handkerchief. "Yes, that'll do."

Wolfe snorted. "There is still my question. The expense, the time it will take, the slender prospect of success. Also it will be in effect an investigation of the death of Leonard Dykes, not of your daughter. The approach will be oblique in more ways than one. Well, sir? Do we proceed or quit?"

"We proceed." Our client, still our client, put his glasses back on. "If I might—I would like to be assured that our relations are confidential. I wouldn't want my wife or my pastor to know about this—uh—this development."

Wolfe was looking as if he might bellow again, so I put in fast, "They won't, not from us. No one will."

"That's good. Do you want another check?"

Wolfe said we didn't, not just yet. That seemed to dispose of all the issues, but Wellman wanted to ask some questions, chiefly about Rachel Abrams and the building where her office was. Apparently he intended to go up there and poke around, and I was all for it, anything to get him outside before he got to worrying again about virgins, or Wolfe's resentment at having to confer with a client got out of hand.

After showing Wellman out I returned to the office. Wolfe was leaning back, scowling, running a fingertip around a race track on the arm of his chair.

I stretched and yawned. "Well," I remarked, "I suppose I'd better go up and change my clothes. The light brown, you know. They like a soft material that doesn't scratch when they put their head on your shoulder. Meanwhile you can be thinking up my instructions."

"There will be no instructions," he growled. "Confound it, get me something, that's all." He leaned forward to ring for beer.

VII

MY REMARK about changing my clothes had of course been a feeble gag. Starting contacts with the personnel in the office of Corrigan, Phelps, Kustin and Briggs would require more elaborate outfitting than a light brown suit, though it was a good shade and a nice soft fabric. As Wolfe had told Wellman, everyone there would certainly be fed up with questions about Leonard Dykes and the name of Baird Archer, and if I had merely gone there and opened fire I would have been bounced.

I did go up to my room though, to think it over away from Wolfe and the phone. The approach was simple. What did we have too much of that girls liked, besides me? That was a cinch: orchids, especially at that time of year, when there were thousands of blossoms and practically all of them would be left on the plants till they wilted. In a quarter of an hour I went down again to the office and announced to Wolfe, "I'm going to need a lot of orchids."

"How many?"

"I don't know. Maybe four or five dozen to start with. I want a free hand."

"You won't get it. Consult me. No *Cypripedium Lord Fisher,* no *Dendrobium Cybele,* no—"

"Not gaudy enough anyway. I'll stick to Cattleyas, Brassos, and Laelios."

"You know the rarities."

"Sure. I ought to."

I went out and took a taxi to Homicide on Twentieth Street. There I hit a snag. Purley Stebbins was out to lunch. It would have been useless to try to get what I wanted from any of the riffraff, so I insisted on seeing Cramer and got waved down the hall to his room. He was at his desk, eating pickles and salami and drinking buttermilk. When I told him I wanted to take a look at the Dykes file and make a list of the employees at the law office where he had worked, he said he was busy and had no time to argue and would I please go away.

"Yes, sir," I said politely. "We give you all we have. We connect Dykes and Wellman for you. We tie in Abrams before she's even cold, and hand it over. You still have nowhere to go, but neither have we. Now all I want is a list of names which I could get elsewhere by spending a couple of hours and maybe twenty bucks, but you're too busy. I think it's what you eat. It's your stomach. Good God, look at that lunch."

He swallowed a mixture of pickle and salami he had been chewing, pushed a button, and spoke to the intercom.

"Rossi? I'm sending Goodwin in, Archie Goodwin. Let him take the Leonard Dykes file and make a list of the employees in that law office. That's all he does. Stay with him. Got it?"

A metallic voice crackled, "Right, Inspector."

I got back to Thirty-fifth Street in time for lunch, having stopped at a stationery store for some plain gummed labels. The other things I would need were on hand.

After lunch I went to it. There were sixteen female names on my list. I might have been able to dig out of the file who was what, but it would have been a job, and anyhow I didn't want to discriminate. A filing clerk was just as apt to be my meat as the confidential secretary of James A. Corrigan, the senior partner. As a starter all I needed was the names, and I went to the office and typed a label for each of them. I also typed, on plain pieces of paper, sixteen times so as not to use carbons:

> These orchids are so rare that they
> cannot be bought. I picked them
> for you. If you care to know why,
> phone me at PE 3-1212.
> Archie Goodwin

With the labels and typed notes in an envelope in my pocket, I ascended to the plant rooms, got a basket and knife, went to the warm room, and started cutting. I needed forty-eight, three apiece, but took a few extra because some were not perfect, mostly *Cattleyas Dionysius, Katadin* and *peetersi, Brassocattleyas Calypso, fournierae* and *Nestor,* and *Laeliocattleyas barbarossa, Carmencita* and *St. Gothard.* It was quite a collection. Theodore had offered to help, and I had no objection. The only one he tried to talk me out of was *Calypso,* because they weren't blooming so well, but I was firm.

In the potting room we got out boxes and tissue and ribbon, and Theodore packed them expertly and inserted the typed notes while I pasted on the labels and fought with the ribbon. The damn ribbon was what took time. Wolfe is better at it than either Theodore or me, but this was my party. When the last bow was tied and the sixteen boxes were carefully packed in a large carton, it was twenty minutes to four. Still time. I lugged the carton downstairs, got my hat and coat, went out and found a taxi, and gave the driver the address, on Madison Avenue in the Forties.

The office of Corrigan, Phelps, Kustin and Briggs was on the eighteenth floor of one of those buildings that think there is nothing like marble in big slabs if you want real class, with double doors for an entrance at the end of a wide corridor. The automatic door-closer was strong enough to push a horse out, and my entry was a little clumsy on account of the carton. In the long anteroom a couple of guys were on chairs, another one was pacing up and down, and back of a rail a three-shades-of-blond sourpuss was fighting it out with a switchboard. Near her, inside the rail, was a table. I took the carton there, put it on the floor by the rail, opened it, and began removing the ribboned boxes and putting them on the table.

She sent me a withering glance. "Mother's Day in February?" she inquired wearily. "Or atom bombs, perhaps?"

I finished my unpacking and then stepped to her. "On one of those

boxes," I told her, "you will find your name. On the others there are
other names. They should be delivered today. It may possibly make you
take a brighter view—"

I stopped because I had lost her. She had left the switchboard and
made a beeline for the table. I don't know what it was that she was
hoping life had in store for her, but it must have been something that
could be put in a small box, the way she went for it. As she started her
eye over the labels, I crossed to the door, pulled it open by getting a
firm foothold, and departed.

If that was typical of the reaction of females in that office to ribboned
boxes there was no telling how soon I would be getting a phone call, so
I told the taxi driver it would be okay if he made it to Thirty-fifth Street
in less than an hour, but with the midtown traffic at that time of day
it made no difference.

When we had finally made it and I had mounted the stoop and let
myself in, I went to the kitchen and asked Fritz, "Any calls?"

He said no. There was a gleam in his eye. "If you need any help
with all the ladies, Archie, for my age I am not to be ignored. A Swiss
has a long usefulness."

"Thanks. I may need you. Theodore told you?"

"No. Mr. Wolfe told me."

"The hell he did."

I was supposed to report myself in whenever I returned from an
errand, so I went to the office and buzzed the plant rooms, where Wolfe
spent every afternoon from four to six, on the house phone.

"I'm back," I told him. "Delivered according to plan. By the way,
I'll put them on Wellman's account at three dollars per. A bargain for
him."

"No. I do not sell orchids."

"He's a client. They were a required item."

"I do not sell orchids," he said gruffly and hung up. I got out the work
book and figured the time and expenses of Saul and Fred and Orrie,
who had been called off, and made out their checks.

The first call came a little before six. I usually answer, "Nero Wolfe's
office, Archie Goodwin speaking," but thought it advisable, temporarily,
to make a cut, and said merely, "Archie Goodwin speaking."

A dry clipped voice, but still female, asked, "Is this Mr. Archie Goodwin?"

"Yes."

"My name is Charlotte Adams. I have received a box of orchids with
a note from you inside. Thank you very much."

"You're welcome. They're nice, aren't they?"

"They're beautiful, only I don't wear orchids. Are they from Mr. Nero Wolfe's conservatory?"

"Yes, but he doesn't call it that. Go ahead and wear them, that's what they're for."

"I'm forty-eight years old, Mr. Goodwin, so the possible reasons for your sending me orchids are rather restricted. More so than with some of the other recipients. Why did you send them?"

"I'll be frank with you, Miss Adams. *Miss* Adams?"

"No. Mrs. Adams."

"I'll be frank anyway. Girls keep getting married and moving to Jackson Heights, and my list of phone numbers is getting pretty ragged. I asked myself what would girls like to see that I can offer, and the answer was ten thousand orchids. They're not mine, but I have access. So you're cordially invited to come tomorrow evening at six o'clock, nine-fourteen West Thirty-fifth Street, and look at the orchids, and then we'll all have dinner together, and I see no reason why we shouldn't have a good time. Have you got the address?"

"Am I supposed to swallow this rigmarole, Mr. Goodwin?"

"Don't bother to swallow it. Do your swallowing tomorrow at dinner. I promise it will be fit to swallow. Will you come?"

"I doubt it," she said, and hung up.

Wolfe had entered during the conversation and got established behind his desk. He was frowning at me and pulling at his lower lip with a finger and thumb.

I addressed him. "A bum start. Nearly fifty, married, and a wise guy. She had checked the number somehow and knew it was yours. However, I intended to tell them that anyhow. We've got—"

"Archie."

"Yes, sir."

"What was that flummery about dinner?"

"No flummery. I haven't told you, I've decided to ask them to stay to dinner. It will be much—"

"Stay to dinner *here*?"

"Certainly."

"No." It was his flattest no.

I flared. "That," I said, as flat as him, "is childish. You have a low opinion of women and—now let me finish—anyhow, you don't want them around. But because this case has completely dried up on you, you have dumped this in my lap, and I need all the play I can get, and besides, are you going to send a crowd of your fellow beings, regardless of sex, away from your house hungry at the dinner hour?"

His lips were tight. He parted them to speak. "Very well. You can take them to dinner at Rusterman's. I'll phone Marko and he'll give you a private room. When you know how many—"

The phone rang, and I swiveled and got it and told the transmitter, "Archie Goodwin speaking."

A feminine voice said, "Say something else."

"It's your turn," I stated.

"Was it you that brought the boxes?"

It was the switchboard misanthrope. "Right," I admitted. "Did they all get delivered?"

"Yes, all but one. One was home sick. Brother, did you stir up some hell around there! Is it true that you're the Archie Goodwin that works for Nero Wolfe?"

"I am. This is his number."

"Well, well! The note said to call it and ask why. Why?"

"I'm lonely and I'm giving a party. Tomorrow at six. Here at Nero Wolfe's place. The address is in the book. You will be in no danger if enough of you come. Plenty of orchids, plenty of drinks, a chance to know me better, and a dinner fit for Miss America. May I ask your name?"

"Sure, Blanche Duke. You say tomorrow at six?"

"That's right."

"Would you care to make a note of something?"

"I love to make notes."

"Put down Blanche Duke. Isn't that a hell of a name? Two jiggers of dry gin, one of dry vermouth, two dashes of grenadine, and two dashes of Pernod. Got it?"

"Yeah."

"I may come tomorrow, but if I don't, try that yourself. I never know what I'm going to do tomorrow."

I told her she'd better come, swiveled, and spoke to Wolfe. "That's better than Mrs. Adams, at least. Not so bad for the first hour after the office closed. About taking them to Rusterman's, they'd probably like going to the best restaurant in New York, but—"

"You won't take them to Rusterman's."

"No? You said—"

"I've reconsidered. You will give them dinner here. I'll arrange the menu with Fritz—perhaps Mondor patties, and duckling with cherries and grapes. For women, the Pasti Grey Riesling will be good enough; I'm glad to have a use for it."

"But you don't care for it."

"I won't be here. I shall leave at five minutes to six, dine with Marko, and spend the evening with him."

I have often stated, in these reports of Wolfe's activities, that he never leaves the house on business, but I suppose now I'll have to qualify it. Strictly speaking, I could say that his intention was not to leave the house *on* business, merely on account of business, but that would be quibbling.

I protested. "You ought to be here to look them over. They'll be expecting to see you. Mrs. Adams is forty-eight, about right for you, and she can't have a happy home life or she wouldn't be working. Besides, how do you—"

The phone rang. I got it and said who I was. A high soprano made me hold the receiver away from my ear.

"Mr. Goodwin, I simply had to call you! Of course it isn't proper, since I've never met you, but if I don't tell you my name and never see you I don't think it will be such a terrible misstep, do you? Those are the loveliest orchids I have ever seen! I'm going to a little party this evening, just a few of us at a friend's apartment, and I'm going to wear them, and can you imagine what they'll say? And can you imagine what I'll say when they ask me who gave them to me? I simply can't imagine! Of course I can say they're from an unknown admirer, but really I'm not the kind of girl who would dream of having unknown admirers, and I haven't the faintest idea what I'll say when they ask me, but I simply can't resist wearing them because . . ."

When I hung up, five minutes later, Wolfe muttered at me, "You didn't invite her."

"No," I assented. "She's a virgin. And as far as I'm concerned she always will be."

VIII

THAT was the first time in history that a bunch of outsiders had been let into the plant rooms with Wolfe not there. The awful responsibility damn near got Theodore down. Not only did he regard it as up to him to see that none of them toppled a bench over or snitched a blossom from one of the rare hybrids, but also I had arranged a fancy assortment of liquids on a table in the potting room, which was being freely patronized by some of the guests, and he was afraid one of them would spill a glass of 80-proof into a pot that he had been nursing for ten years. I was sorry to give him that added anxiety, but I wanted them relaxed.

I had done all right. I had got only seven phone calls, but apparently there had been talk at the office during Wednesday, for ten of them showed up, arriving in two groups. Also there had been two calls on

Wednesday while I was out. My journey was necessary, a trip to the Bronx to call on Mrs. Abrams. She was anything but delighted to see me, but I wanted to ask her to do something and I rode it out. I finally talked her into it. I also had to sign up John R. Wellman, but that was comparatively easy and all it took was a phone call to his hotel.

From a purely personal standpoint they were above average as a job lot, and it would have been no ordeal to get acquainted and quench their thirst and tell them about orchids if I hadn't been so busy sorting them out for future reference. I might as well save you the bother of doing likewise if you don't want to take the trouble, for it won't make much difference. I can tell you that now, but there was no one to tell me that then.

But I was working like a dog getting their names and stations filed. By dinnertime I had them pretty well arranged. Charlotte Adams, 48, was the secretary of the senior partner, James A. Corrigan. She was bony and efficient and had not come for fun. The only other one her age was a stenographer, plump and pimply, with a name that made her giggle cheerfully when she told you: Helen Troy. Next, going down by ages, was Blanche Duke, the tri-shaded blonde. I had mixed a shaker of her formula. She had made two trips to the potting room for refills and then had decided to save steps and take the shaker around with her.

One or two of the other seven may have been crowding thirty, but most of them still had some twenties to cover. One was a little more than I had counted on. Her name was Dolly Harriton, and she was a member of the bar. She wasn't yet one of the firm, but judging from the set of her good-looking chin and the smooth quick take of her smart gray eyes, she soon would be or else. She had the air, as she moved along the aisles, of collecting points for cross-questioning an orchid-grower being sued by his wife for non-support.

Nina Perlman, a stenographer, was tall and straight with big slow-moving dark eyes. Mabel Moore, a typist, was a skinny little specimen wearing red-rimmed glasses. Sue Dondero, Emmett Phelps's secretary, with fine temples and no perceptible lipstick, came close from all angles to my idea of a girl to have around. Portia Liss, a filing clerk, should either have had something done to her teeth or quit laughing so much. Claire Burkhardt, a stenographer, was either just out of high school or was cheating. Eleanor Gruber, Louis Kustin's secretary, was probably the one I would have invited if I had invited only one. She was the kind you look at and think she should take off just one or two pounds, and then you ask where from and end by voting for the status quo. Her eyes didn't actually slant; it was the way the lids were drawn.

By the time we went down to dinner I had picked up a few little scraps, mostly from Blanche Duke, Sue Dondero, and Eleanor Gruber. Tuesday at quitting time Corrigan, the senior partner, had called them into his room to tell them that PE 3-1212 was Nero Wolfe's phone number, and Archie Goodwin was Wolfe's confidential assistant, and that Wolfe might have been engaged by an opposing interest in one of the firm's cases. He had suggested that it might be desirable to ignore the notes in the boxes of orchids, and had warned them to guard against any indiscretion. Today, Wednesday, when the idea of making a party of it had caught on (this from Blanche Duke after she had been toting the shaker around a while), Mabel Moore had spilled it to Mrs. Adams, and Mrs. Adams, presumably after consulting with Corrigan, had decided to come along. I got other scattered hints of personalities and quirks and frictions, but not enough to pay for the drinks.

At 7:25 I herded them into the potting room to tell them that wine had been chilled for dinner, but that if any of them preferred to continue as started they were welcome. Blanche Duke raised her shaker on high and said she was a one-drink woman. There was a chorus of approval, and they all loaded themselves with bottles and accessories. I led the way. Going through the intermediate room, Helen Troy caught her heel between the slats of the walk, teetered, waved a bottle, and down came two pots of *Oncidium varicosum*. There were gasps and shrieks.

I said grandly, "Good for her. She showed great presence of mind, she held onto the bottle. Follow me, walking on orchids."

When I had got them downstairs and into the dining room, which looked festive enough for anybody, with the gleaming white cloth and silver and glass and more orchids, and told them to leave the head of the table for me but otherwise sit as they chose, I excused myself, went to the kitchen, and asked Fritz, "Are they here?"

He nodded. "Up in the south room. Quite agreeable and comfortable."

"Good. They know they may have to wait a long while?"

"Yes, it's understood. How are you succeeding?"

"Not bad. Two of them don't drink, but on the whole we are on our way to gaiety. All set?"

"Certainly."

"Shoot."

Rejoining the party, I took the chair at the head, Wolfe's place, the first time I had ever sat there. Most of them lifted their glasses to welcome me back after a long absence. I was touched and thought an acknowledgment was called for. As Fritz entered with the soup tureen,

I pushed my chair back and stood. Portia Liss kept on chattering, and Dolly Harriton, the member of the bar, shushed her.

"Oyez, oyez!" Helen Troy cried.

I spoke. "Ladies and no gentlemen thank God, I have a lot of speeches to make, and I might as well get one done. Thank you for coming to my party. There is only one thing I would rather look at than orchids, and you are it. [Applause.] In the absence of Mr. Wolfe I shall follow his custom and introduce to you the most important member of this household, Mr. Fritz Brenner, now dishing soup. Fritz, a bow, please. [Applause.] I am going to ask you to help me with a little problem. Yesterday I received a phone call from a lady, doubtless fair, who refused to tell me her name. I beg you to supply it. I shall repeat some, by no means all, of what she said to me, hoping it will give you a hint. I am not a good mimic but shall do my best.

"She said: 'Mr. Goodwin, I simply had to call you! Of course it isn't proper, since I've never met you, but if I don't tell you my name and never see you I don't think it will be such a terrible misstep, do you? Those are the loveliest orchids I have ever seen! I'm going to wear them to a little party this evening, and can you imagine what they'll say? And can you imagine what I'll say when they ask who gave them to me? I simply can't imagine! Of course I can say they're from an unknown admirer, but really—'"

There was no use going on because the shrieks and hoots were drowning me out. Even Mrs. Adams loosened up enough to smile. Claire Burkhardt, the high-school girl, choked on a bite of roll. I sat down and started on my soup, flushed with triumph. When it was a little quieter I demanded, "Her name?"

So many shouted it together that I had to get it from Sue Dondero, on my right. It was Cora Barth. I did not file it.

With Fritz having eleven places to serve, I had told him to leave the liquids to me. An advantage of that arrangement was that I knew what each one was drinking and could keep the refills coming without asking any questions, and another was that Sue Dondero offered to help me. Not only was it nice to have her help, but also it gave me a chance to make a suggestion to her, while we were together at the side table, which I had wanted to make to someone upstairs but hadn't got around to. She said yes, and it was agreed that for a signal I would pull at my right ear.

"I am pleased to see," I told her, "that you are sticking to vermouth and soda. A girl with temples like yours has an obligation to society. Keep 'em smooth."

"Not to society," she dissented. "To spelling. Whisky or gin gives me a hangover, and if I have a hangover I can't spell. Once I spelled lien l-e-a-n."

"Good God. No, that's for Nina Perlman."

Having done all right with the soup, they did even better with the Mondor patties. As for talk and associated noises, they kept it going without much help from me, except for filling in a few gaps. But I was glad Wolfe wasn't there to see how they treated the duckling, all but Eleanor Gruber and Helen Troy. The trouble was, they were full. I watched them pecking at it, or not even pecking, with two exceptions, and decided that something drastic was called for if I didn't want a letdown. I raised my voice to get attention.

"Ladies, I need advice. This is—"

"Speech, speech!" Claire Burkhardt squeaked.

"He's making one, you idiot!" somebody told her.

"Oyez, oyeth," said Helen Troy.

"This," I said, "is a democracy. No one can shove anything down people's throats, not even Fritz's salad. As your host and by no means unknown admirer, I want you to have a good time and go away from here saying, 'Archie Goodwin can be trusted. He had us at his mercy, but he gave us a chance to say yes or no.'"

"Yes!" Blanche Duke called.

"Thank you." I inclined my head. "I was about to ask, how many feel like eating salad? If you want it, Fritz will enjoy serving it. But what if you don't? Yes or no?"

There were six or seven noes.

"Do you still say yes, Miss Duke?"

"My God, no. I didn't know you meant salad."

"Then we'll skip it. However, I won't ask for a vote on the almond parfait. You should taste it, at least." I turned to Fritz, at my elbow. "That's how it is, Fritz."

"Yes, sir." He started removing plates still loaded with his duckling, one of his best dishes. I wasted no sympathy on him because I had warned him. I have had much more opportunity than he has to learn the eating habits of American females. At an affair of the Society of Gourmets that duckling would have drawn cheers.

Their reaction to the almond parfait made up for it some. In their relaxed condition they were more or less ignoring the code, and a couple of them took spoonfuls while Fritz was still serving. Portia Liss exclaimed, "Oh! It's absolutely heavenly! Isn't it, Mrs. Adams?"

"I can't say, Portia. I haven't any."

But a few minutes later she conceded grudgingly, "It's remarkable. Quite remarkable."

Others had extravagant comments. Helen Troy finished first. She arose and shoved her chair back and put her palms on the table to lean on. Her pimples were purple now instead of pink.

"Oyeth, oyeth," she said.

"Who's making a speech?" someone demanded.

"I am. This is my maiden effort."

Someone tittered.

"My *maiden* effort," she insisted, "at my age. I've been thinking what we can do for Mr. Goodwin and I'm standing up to put it in the form of a motion. I move that one of us goes and puts her arms around Mr. Goodwin's neck and kisses him and calls him Archie."

"Which one?" Mabel Moore demanded.

"We'll vote on it. I nominate me. I'm already up."

There were cries of dissent. Claire Burkhardt, at Helen Troy's left, got her elbow and pulled her back onto her chair. Nominations were made. Someone suggested they should draw lots. Half an hour earlier I would have let it slide, on the chance that Sue or Eleanor would get elected, which would have been a pleasant experience, but at this stage I didn't want to risk having a tone set that it might be hard to jostle them out of. So I spoke up.

"Don't you think you ought to consult me?"

"Don't butt in," Blanche Duke said rudely.

"I'm sorry, but I have to. This is dangerous. If a certain one of you came close to me right now and put her arms around me and kissed me, I might be able to remember I'm your host and I might not. Whereas—"

"Which one?" voices demanded.

I ignored them. "Whereas if any other one did it, I couldn't keep from showing my disappointment. You can't expect me to tell you her name. We'll forget it. Anyhow, nobody seconded the motion, so it would be illegal."

I pulled at my right ear. "Another thing, the motion was put wrong. Doing it that way, who would it please most? Not me. You. I would much rather kiss than be kissed. But don't misunderstand me, you're my guests, and I would be happy to do something to please you. I'd love to please you. If you have a suggestion?"

Sue Dondero came through fine. "I have two."

"Good. One at a time."

"First, let all of us call you Archie."

"Easy. If I may call you Charlotte and Blanche and Dolly and Mabel and Portia and Eleanor and Claire and Nina and Helen and Sue."

"Of course. Second, you're a detective. Tell us something about being a detective—something exciting."

"Well." I hesitated and looked around, left and right. "Maybe I should treat it like the salad. Yes or no?"

I wasn't sure all of them said yes, but plenty of them did. Fritz had the coffee cups in place and was pouring. I edged my chair back a little, crossed my legs, and worked my lips, considering.

"I'll tell you," I said finally, "what I think I'll do. I could tell you about some old case that was finished long ago, but it might be more interesting if I pick one that we're working on right now. I can skip the parts that we're keeping to ourselves, if any. Do you like that idea?"

They said they did. Except Mrs. Adams, whose lips had suddenly become a thin line, and Dolly Harriton, whose smart gray eyes might have been a little disconcerting if she had been closer.

I made it casual. "I'll have to hit only the high spots or it will take all night. It's a murder case. Three people have been murdered: a man named Leonard Dykes, who worked in the office where you are; a girl named Joan Wellman, an editor in a publishing firm; and a girl named Rachel Abrams, a public stenographer and typist."

There were murmurings, and looks were exchanged. Nina Perlman said emphatically, in a soft satin voice that five or six Manhattans had had no effect on, "I didn't do it."

"Three murders by one person?" Eleanor Gruber asked.

"I'll come to that. Our first connection with it, not much of one, a cop came and showed us a list of fifteen men's names which had been written on a piece of paper by Leonard Dykes. They had found it between the pages of a book in Dykes's room. Mr. Wolfe and I weren't much interested and barely glanced at it. Then—"

"Why did the cop show you the list?" Dolly Harriton put in.

"Because they hadn't found any men to fit any of the names, and he thought we might have a suggestion. We didn't. Then, six weeks later, a man named John R. Wellman called and wanted us to investigate the death of his daughter, whose body had been found in Van Cortlandt Park—run over by a car. He thought she had been murdered, not killed by accident. He told us all about it, and showed us a copy of a letter Joan, his daughter, had written home. In it she said she had had a phone call from a man who gave his name as Baird Archer, author of a novel which he had submitted to Joan's firm some months back."

"Oh, my God," Blanche Duke said morosely. "Baird Archer again."

"I don't want to bore you," I declared.

Most of them said I wasn't.

"Okay. Joan had read Archer's novel and rejected it with a letter signed by her. On the phone he offered to pay her twenty dollars an hour to discuss his novel with him and tell him how to improve it, and she made a date to meet him the next day after office hours. So she said in her letter home. It was the evening of the next day that she was killed."

I reached for my coffee cup, drank some, and leaned back. "Now hold on to your hats. It had been six weeks since the cop had shown us that list of names, and we had just glanced at it. But when Mr. Wolfe and I saw Joan's letter home we immediately recognized the name of Baird Archer as one of those on Dykes's list. That proved there was some kind of connection between Leonard Dykes and Joan Wellman, and since they had both died suddenly and violently, and Joan had a date with Archer the day she died, it made it likely that their deaths were connected too, and connected with Archer. When you asked for something exciting about being a detective, if you meant something like tailing a murderer in Central Park and getting shot at, okay, that has its attractions, but it's not half as exciting as our spotting that name. If we hadn't, there would be one cop working on Dykes's death in his spare time, and another one in the Bronx likewise on Joan Wellman, instead of the way it is, which you know something about. That's what I call exciting."

It didn't seem essential to give the precise circumstances of the recognition of Baird Archer's name. If Wolfe had been there he would have told it his way, but he wasn't, and I was. Glancing around to see that coffee refills were being attended to and that cigarettes and matches were at hand for everyone, I resumed.

"Next I'm going to spill something. If it gets printed the cops won't like it, and they sure won't like me, but they don't anyhow. A girl named Rachel Abrams was a public stenographer and typist with a little one-room office on the seventh floor of a building up on Broadway. Day before yesterday she went out the window and smashed to death on the sidewalk. More excitement for me as a detective, which is what I'm supposed to be talking about. It would probably have been called suicide or an accident if I hadn't happened to walk into her office two or three minutes after she had gone out the window. In a drawer of her desk I found a little brown book in which she had kept a record of her receipts and expenses. Under receipts there were two entries showing that last September she had been paid ninety-eight dollars and forty cents by a man named Baird Archer."

"Ah," Dolly Harriton said. There were other reactions.

"I'll be dreaming about Baird Archer," Nina Perlman muttered.

"I am already," I told her. "As you can see, here's a job for a detective if there ever was one. I won't try to tell you how the cops are going at it, of course one or more of them has talked with all of you the past two

days, but here's how we see it, and how we'll go on seeing it unless
something shows we're wrong. We believe that Dykes's death was somehow connected with the manuscript of that novel. We believe that
Joan Wellman was killed because she had read that manuscript. We
believe that Rachel Abrams was killed because she had typed that
manuscript. So naturally we want Baird Archer, and we want the
manuscript. We've got to find one or both, or we're licked. Any suggestions?"

"Good Lord," Sue Dondero said.

"Get a copy of the novel," Portia Liss offered.

Someone snickered.

"Look," I said impulsively, "unless you object I'm going to do something. There are a couple of people connected with this case upstairs
now, waiting to see Mr. Wolfe. I think it would be interesting if they
came down and told you about it." I pressed the floor button with my
toe. "Unless you've had enough?"

"Who are they?" Mrs. Adams wanted to know.

"The father of Joan Wellman and the mother of Rachel Abrams."

"It won't be very gay," Dolly Harriton commented.

"No, it won't. Things and people mixed up with detectives are seldom gay."

"I want to see 'em," Helen Troy said loudly. "It's human nature."

Fritz had entered, and I spoke to him. "Where are Mrs. Abrams and
Mr. Wellman, Fritz? In the south room?"

"Yes, sir."

"Will you please ask them to be good enough to come down here?"

"Yes, sir."

He went. I inquired about drinks and got three orders.

IX

BLANCHE DUKE darned near ruined it.

When Wellman and Mrs. Abrams were ushered in by Fritz, ten
pairs of eyes were focused on them, though in two or three cases the
focusing required a little effort. I arose, performed the introductions,
and brought them to the two chairs I had placed, one on either side
of me. Mrs. Abrams, in a black silk dress or maybe rayon, was tight-
lipped and scared but dignified. Wellman, in the same gray suit or its
twin, was trying to take in all their faces without seeming to. He sat
straight, not touching the back of the chair. I had my mouth open to
speak when Blanche beat me to it.

"You folks need a drink. What'll you have?"

"No, thanks," Wellman said politely. Mrs. Abrams shook her head.

"Now listen," Blanche insisted, "you're in trouble. I've been in trouble all my life, and I know. Have a drink. Two jiggers of dry gin, one jigger of dry vermouth—"

"Be quiet, Blanche," Mrs. Adams snapped.

"Go to hell," Blanche snapped back. "This is social. You can't get Corrigan to fire me, either, you old papoose."

I would have liked to toss her out a window. I cut in. "Did I mix that right, Blanche, or didn't I?"

"Sure you did."

"Call me Archie."

"Sure you did, Archie."

"Okay, and I'm doing this right too. I do everything right. Would I let Mrs. Abrams and Mr. Wellman go without drinks if they wanted them?"

"Certainly not."

"Then that settles it." I turned to my right, having promised Mrs. Abrams that Wellman would be called on first. "Mr. Wellman, I've been telling these ladies about the case that Mr. Wolfe and I are working on, and they're interested, partly because they work in the office where Leonard Dykes worked. I told them you and Mrs. Abrams were upstairs waiting to see Mr. Wolfe, and I thought you might be willing to tell them something about your daughter Joan. I hope you don't mind?"

"I don't mind."

"How old was Joan?"

"She was twenty-six. Her birthday was November nineteenth."

"Was she your only child?"

"Yes, the only one."

"Was she a good daughter?"

"She was the best daughter a man ever had."

There was an astonishing interruption—at least, astonishing to me. It was Mrs. Abrams' voice, not loud but clear. "She was no better than my Rachel."

Wellman smiled. I hadn't seen him smile before. "Mrs. Abrams and I have had quite a talk. We've been comparing notes. It's all right, we won't fight about it. Her Rachel was a good daughter too."

"No, there's nothing to fight about. What was Joan going to do, get married or go on with her career, or what?"

He was still a moment. "Well, I don't know about that. I told you she graduated from Smith College with honors."

"Yes."

"There was a young fellow from Dartmouth we thought maybe she was going to hitch up with, but she was too young and had sense enough to know it. Here in New York—she was here working for those publishers nearly four years—she wrote us back in Peoria about different—"

"Where's Peoria?" Blanche Duke demanded.

He frowned at her. "Peoria? That's a city out in Illinois. She wrote us about different fellows she met, but it didn't sound to us like she was ready to tie up. We got to thinking it was about time, anyway her mother did, but she thought she had a big future with those publishers. She was getting eighty dollars a week, pretty good for a girl of twenty-six, and Scholl told me just last August when I was here on a trip that they expected a great deal of her. I was thinking of that yesterday afternoon. I was thinking that we expected a great deal of her too, her mother and me, but that we had already had a great deal."

He ducked his head forward to glance at Mrs. Abrams and came back to me. "Mrs. Abrams and I were talking about that upstairs. We feel the same way about it, only with her it's only been two days, and she hasn't had so long to think it over. I was telling her that if you gave me a pad of paper and a pencil and asked me to put down all the different things I can remember about Joan, I'll bet there would be ten thousand different things, more than that—things she did and things she said, times she was like this and times she was like that. You haven't got a daughter."

"No. You have much to remember."

"Yes, I have. What got me to thinking like that, I was wondering if I deserved what happened because I was too proud of her. But I wasn't. I thought about it this way, I thought there had been lots of times she did something wrong, like when she was little and told lies, and even after she grew up she did things I didn't approve of, but I asked myself, can I point to a single thing she ever did and honestly say I wish she hadn't done that? And I couldn't."

His eyes left me and went to my guests. He took his time, apparently looking for something in each face.

"I couldn't do it," he said firmly.

"So she was perfect," Claire Burkhardt remarked. It wasn't really a sneer, but it enraged Blanche Duke. She blazed at Claire.

"Will you kindly get lost, you night-school wonder? The man's in trouble! His daughter's dead! Did you graduate from college with honors?"

"I never went to night school," Claire said indignantly. "I went to Oliphant Business Academy!"

"I didn't say she was perfect," Wellman protested. "She did quite a few things I didn't think were right when she did them. All I was trying to tell you ladies, she's dead now and it's different. I wouldn't change a thing about her if I could, not one single thing. Look at you here now, all this drinking—if your fathers were here or if they knew about it, would they like it? But if you got killed tonight and they had to take you home and have you buried, after they had had time to think it over, do you suppose they'd hold it against you that you'd been drinking? Certainly not! They'd remember how wonderful you'd been, that's all, they'd remember all the things you had done to be proud of!"

He ducked his head. "Wouldn't they, Mrs. Abrams? Isn't that how you feel about your Rachel?"

Mrs. Abrams lifted her chin. She spoke not to Wellman but to the gathering. "How I feel about my Rachel." She shook her head. "It's been only two days. I will be honest with you ladies. While Mr. Wellman was talking I was sitting here thinking. My Rachel never took a drink. If I had ever seen her take a drink I would have called her a bad daughter in strong words. I would have been so angry it would have been terrible. But if it could be that she was here now, sitting at that table with you, and she was drinking more than any of you, so that she was so drunk she would look at me and not know me, I would say to her, 'Drink, Rachel! Drink, drink, drink!'"

She made a little gesture. "I want to be honest, but maybe I'm not saying it right. Maybe you don't know what I mean."

"We know what you mean," Eleanor Gruber muttered.

"I mean only I want my Rachel. I'm not like Mr. Wellman. I have two more daughters. My Deborah is sixteen and she is smart in high school. My Nancy is twenty and she goes to college, like Mr. Wellman's Joan. They are both smarter than Rachel and they are more fashionable. Rachel did not make eighty dollars every week like Joan, with office rent to pay and other things, but she did good all the time and once she made one hundred and twelve dollars in one week, only she worked nights too. But you ladies must not think I put her nose down on it. Some of our friends thought that, but they were wrong. She was glad in her heart that Nancy and Deborah are smart, and she made Nancy go to college. If she got some dollars ahead I would say, 'Buy yourself a pretty dress or take a little trip,' and she would laugh and say, 'I'm a working girl, Mamma.' She called me Mamma, but Nancy and Deborah call me Mom, and that's the whole difference right there."

She gestured again. "You know she is only dead two days?" It sounded rhetorical, but she insisted. "You know that?"

There were murmurings. "Yes, we know."

"So I don't know how it will be when it is longer, like Mr. Wellman. He has thought about it a long time and he is spending money for Mr. Wolfe to find the man that killed his Joan. If I had money like him maybe I would spend it that way too, but I don't know. All I think about now is my Rachel. I try to see why it happened. She was a working girl. She did her work good and got paid for it the regular rates. She never hurt anybody. She never made any trouble. Now Mr. Goodwin tells me a man asked her to do work for him, and she did it good, and he paid her the regular rates, and then after some time goes by he comes back and kills her. I try to see why that happened, and I can't. I don't care how much explaining I get, I don't think I can ever see why any man had to kill my Rachel, because I know so well about her. I know there's not a man or woman anywhere that could stand up and say, 'Rachel Abrams did a bad thing to me.' You ladies know how hard that is, to be the kind of woman so that nobody can say that. I'm not that kind of woman."

She paused. She tightened her lips, and then released them to say, "I did a bad thing to my Rachel once." Her chin started to quiver. "Excuse me, please." She faltered, arose, and made for the door.

John R. Wellman forgot his manners. Without a word, he popped up, circled behind my chair, and followed Mrs. Abrams. His voice came from the hall, and then silence.

The guests were silent too. "There's more coffee," I told them. "Anybody want some?"

No takers. I spoke. "One thing Mrs. Abrams said wasn't strictly accurate. She said I told her that the man who paid Rachel for typing the script came back and killed her. What I told her was that Rachel was killed because she had typed the script, but not that it was the man who had paid her for typing it."

Three of them were dabbing at their eyes with their handkerchiefs. Two others should have been.

"You don't know that," Dolly Harriton challenged.

"To prove it, no. But we like it."

"You're crazy," Helen Troy asserted.

"Yeah? Why?"

"You said the death of Leonard Dykes was connected with these two. Did you mean the same man killed all of them?"

"I didn't say so, but I would for a nickel. That's what I think."

"Then you're crazy. Why should Con O'Malley kill those girls? He didn't—"

"Be quiet, Helen," Mrs. Adams said sharply.

She ignored it. "He didn't kill—"

"Helen, be quiet! You're drunk."

"I am not drunk! I was, but I'm not now. How could anybody be drunk after listening to those two?" To me: "Con O'Malley didn't kill Leonard Dykes on account of any manuscript. He killed him because it was Dykes that got him disbarred. Everybody—"

She was drowned out. Half of them spoke and the other half shouted. It may have been partly to relieve the feelings that had been piled up by Wellman and Mrs. Abrams, but there was more to it than that. Both Mrs. Adams and Dolly Harriton tried to shut them up, but nothing doing. Looking and listening, I caught enough scraps to gather that a long-standing feud had blazed into battle. As near as I could make out, Helen Troy, Nina Perlman, and Blanche Duke were arrayed against Portia Liss, Eleanor Gruber, and Mabel Moore, with Sue Dondero interested but not committed, and Claire Burkhardt, the night-school wonder, not qualified for combat. Mrs. Adams and Dolly Harriton were outside.

In one of those moments of comparative calm that even the hottest fracas will have, Blanche Duke tossed a grenade at Eleanor Gruber. "What were you wearing when O'Malley told you? Pajamas?"

That shocked them into silence, and Mrs. Adams took advantage of it. "This is disgraceful," she declared. "You ought to be ashamed of yourselves. Blanche, apologize to Eleanor."

"For what?" Blanche demanded.

"She won't," Eleanor said. She turned a white face to me. "We should all apologize to you, Mr. Goodwin."

"I don't think so," Dolly Harriton said dryly. "Since Mr. Goodwin staged this, I must admit cleverly and effectively, I hardly believe he has an apology coming. Congratulations, Mr. Goodwin."

"I must decline them, Miss Harriton. I haven't congratulations coming either."

"I don't care," Eleanor insisted to me, "what you have coming. I'm going to say this. After what Blanche said to me. And what you must have heard before. Do you know who Conroy O'Malley is?"

"Sure. I've been allowed to have a look at the police file on Leonard Dykes. A former member of the firm who got disbarred about a year ago."

She nodded. "He was the senior member. The name of the firm was O'Malley, Corrigan and Phelps. I was his secretary. Now I am Louis Kustin's secretary. Must I say that what Blanche said, her insinuation about my relations with Mr. O'Malley, that that was pure malice?"

"There's no must about it, Miss Gruber. Say it if you want to, or just skip it."

"I do say it. It's too bad, because really I like Blanche, and she likes me. This was starting to die down, and then the police came back and stirred it up again, and now you say it was something you told them about these two girls being killed that made them come back. I'm not blaming you, but I wish you hadn't, because—well, you saw what happened here just now. Could you hear what we said?"

"Some."

"Anyway, you heard Helen say that Conroy O'Malley killed Dykes because Dykes got him disbarred. That isn't true. O'Malley was disbarred for bribing a foreman of a jury in a civil suit. I don't know who it was that informed the court, that never came out, but it was certainly someone connected with the other side. Of course it made a lot of talk in the office, all kinds of wild talk—that Louis Kustin had done the informing because O'Malley didn't like him and wouldn't make him a member of the firm, and that—"

"Is this wise, Eleanor?" Dolly Harriton asked coldly.

"I think so," Eleanor said, not fazed. "He ought to understand." She went on to me: "—and that others had done it, Mr. Corrigan and Mr. Briggs among them, for similar reasons, and that Leonard Dykes had done it because O'Malley was going to fire him. I wouldn't even be surprised if there was talk that I had done it, I suppose because he wouldn't buy me some new pajamas. As the months went by there wasn't so much of it, and then Leonard Dykes got killed and it started up again. I don't know who began it that O'Malley had killed Dykes because he found out that Dykes had been the informer to the court, but someone did, and it was worse than ever. Just a lot of wild talk. No one really knew anything. You heard Blanche ask me if I was wearing pajamas when O'Malley told me something."

She seemed to think she had asked a question, so I grunted an affirmative.

"Well, what he told me, just a few weeks ago, was that he had heard that it was the jury foreman's wife who had written the anonymous letter to the judge telling about the bribing. It isn't likely that I was wearing pajamas, because I don't wear them in the office, and it was in the office that he told me—of course he's no longer connected with the firm, but he comes there once in a while. The talk that O'Malley killed Dykes is simply ridiculous."

"Why don't you say what you think?" Helen Troy demanded. "You think Uncle Fred killed Dykes. Why don't you say so?"

"I've never said I think that, Helen."

"But you do."

"*I* do," Blanche Duke stated, still ready to tangle.

"Who is Uncle Fred?" I asked.

Helen answered. "He's my uncle, Frederick Briggs. They don't like him. They think he informed on O'Malley because he wouldn't make him a partner, and Dykes found out about it and threatened to tell O'Malley, and Uncle Fred killed Dykes to keep him from telling. You know perfectly well you think that, Eleanor."

"*I* do," Blanche repeated.

"You girls work in a law office," Dolly Harriton said warningly, "and you should realize that gabbing in the women's room is one thing, and talking like this to Mr. Goodwin is quite another. Didn't you ever hear of slander?"

"I'm not slandering anyone," Eleanor declared, and she wasn't. She looked at me. "The reason I tell you all this, I think you've wasted a lot of orchids and food and drink. Your client is Mr. Wellman, and you're investigating the death of his daughter, and you went to all this trouble and expense because you think there was a connection between her and Leonard Dykes. That list of names he wrote that was found in his room—what if some friend was there one evening and said he was trying to choose a name to use on something he had written, and Dykes and the friend made up some names and Dykes wrote them down? There are a dozen ways it could have happened. And from what you say, that name Baird Archer is absolutely the only thing that connects Dykes with Joan Wellman and Rachel Abrams."

"No." I contradicted her. "There's another. They were all three murdered."

"There are three hundred homicides in New York every year." Eleanor shook her head. "I'm just trying to put you straight. You got us all worked up, or Mrs. Abrams and Mr. Wellman did, and from that row we had you might think you have started something, but you haven't. That's why I told you all that. We all hope you find the man that killed those girls, I know I do, but I don't think you'll ever do it this way."

"Look," Nina Perlman said, "I've got an idea. Let's all chip in and hire him to find out who informed on O'Malley and who killed Dykes. Then we'd know."

"Nonsense!" Mrs. Adams snapped.

Portia Liss objected. "I'd rather hire him to catch the man that killed the girls."

"That's no good," Blanche told her. "Wellman has already hired him for that."

"How much do you charge?" Nina asked.

She got no reply, not that I resented it, but because I was busy. I had left my chair and gone to the side table, where there was a large celadon bowl, and, getting a couple of sheets from my pocket notebook and tearing them into pieces, was writing on the pieces. Blanche, asking what I was doing, got no reply either until I had finished writing, put the pieces of paper in the bowl, and, carrying the bowl, returned to the table and stood behind Mrs. Adams.

"Speech," I announced. Helen Troy did not say oyez.

"I admit," I said, "that I have ruined the party, and I offer my regrets. If you think that I am rudely sending you home I regret that too, but it must be faced that I have doused all hope of continued revelry. I do offer a little consolation, with the permission of Mr. Wolfe. For a period of one year from date each of you will be sent upon request three orchids each month. You may request three at one time or separately, as you prefer. Specifications of color will be met as far as possible."

There were appropriate noises and expressions. Claire Burkhardt wanted to know, "Can we come and pick them out?"

I said that might be arranged, by appointment only. "Earlier," I went on, "it was suggested that one of you be chosen to demonstrate on my person your appreciation for this occasion. Maybe you no longer feel like it, but if you do I have a proposal. In this bowl are ten pieces of paper, and on each piece I have written one of your names. I will ask Mrs. Adams to take one of the pieces from the bowl, and the one whose name is drawn will accompany me forthwith to the Bobolink, where we will dance and dally until one of us gets tired. I don't tire easily."

"If my name is in there you will please remove it," Mrs. Adams ultimatumed.

"If it's drawn," I told her, "you can draw another. Does anyone else wish to be excused?"

Portia Liss said, "I promised to be home by midnight."

"Simple. Get tired at eleven-thirty." I held the bowl above the level of Mrs. Adams' eyes. "Will you draw one, please?"

She didn't like doing it, but it was a quick and easy way of getting the party over and done with, so after a second's hesitation she reached up over the rim of the bowl, withdrew a slip, and put it on the table.

Mabel Moore, at her left, called out, "Sue!"

I removed the other slips and stuck them in a pocket.

Sue Dondero protested, "My Lord, I can't go to the Bobolink in these clothes!"

"It doesn't have to be the Bobolink," I assured her. "I guess you're stuck, unless you want us to draw again."

"What for?" Blanche snorted. "What do you bet they didn't all say Sue?"

I didn't dignify it with a denial. I merely took nine slips from my right-hand pocket and tossed them on the table. Later on in the evening there might be occasion to show Sue the nine in my left-hand pocket, those I had taken from the bowl.

X

ORDINARILY Fritz takes Wolfe's breakfast tray up to him at eight o'clock, but that Thursday he phoned down to say he wanted to see me before he went up to the plant rooms at nine, and I thought I might as well save Fritz a trip. So at 8:05, having catered, I pulled a chair around and sat. Sometimes Wolfe breakfasted in bed and sometimes at the table by the window. That morning the sun was shining in and he was at the table. Looking at the vast expanse of yellow pajamas in the bright sun made me blink. He never says a word if he can help it until his orange juice is down, and he will not gulp orange juice, so I gave a fair imitation of sitting patiently. Finally he put the empty glass down, cleared his throat explosively, and started spreading the half-melted butter on a hot griddle cake.

He spoke. "What time did you get home?"

"Two-twenty-four."

"Where did you go?"

"With a girl to a night club. She's the one. The wedding is set for Sunday. Her folks are in Brazil, and there's no one to give her away, so you'll have to give me away."

"Pfui." He took a bite of buttered griddle cake and ham. "What happened?"

"Outline or blow by blow?"

"Outline. We'll fill in later."

"Ten came, including a female lawyer, young and handsome but tough, and an old warhorse. They drank upstairs and wrecked only two Oncidiums. By the—"

"*Forbesi?*"

"No. *Varicosum.* By the time we descended they were genial. I sat at your place. I had warned Fritz that the soup and patties would fill them up and they would snoot the duckling, and they did. I made speeches, which were well received, but no mention of murder until coffee, when I was asked to tell them about detective work, as arranged, and obliged. I set forth our current problem. At an appropriate moment I sent for our client and Mrs. Abrams, and if you had been there you would have been stirred, though of course you wouldn't admit it. They admitted it by wiping their eyes. By the way, Wellman had a nerve to suspect me of going too far too fast. He never met Mrs. Abrams until last evening, and he took her home. Oh, yes, I told them about finding Baird Archer's name in Rachel Abrams' account book, because I had to tie her in to clear the track for Mrs. Abrams. If it gets printed Cramer will yap, but it was me that found the book, and he admits I talk too much."

"So do I." Wolfe took a sip of steaming black coffee. "You say they were stirred?"

"Yes. Their valves opened. But all they did was start a free-for-all about who informed on O'Malley, the former senior partner, and got him disbarred for bribing a jury foreman, and about who killed Dykes. They have assorted theories, but if they have any evidence worth buying they're saving it. One named Eleanor Gruber, who is a looker but too busy being clever—she was O'Malley's secretary and is now Louis Kustin's—she undertook to straighten me out. She hates to see us waste our time trying to clinch a link between Dykes and Joan and Rachel, because there isn't any. Nobody contradicted her. I decided to adjourn and try one at a time, having been introduced, selected one named Sue Dondero, Emmett Phelps's secretary, and took her to a night club and spent thirty-four of our client's dollars. The immediate objective was to get on a satisfactory personal basis, but I found an opportunity to let her know that we intend, if necessary, to blow the firm of Corrigan, Phelps, Kustin and Briggs into so many little pieces that the Department of Sanitation will have us up for cluttering the streets. As I said, the wedding is Sunday. I hope you'll like her."

I upturned a palm. "It all depends. If one or more of them has really got a finger caught, either a firm member or an employee, I may have made a start at least. If not, Miss Gruber is not only shapely but sensible, and I may ditch Sue for her. Time will tell, unless you want to tell me now."

Wolfe had finished with the ham, and the eggs done with black butter and sherry, and was starting the windup, a griddle cake with no butter but plenty of thyme honey. In the office he would have been scowling, but he would not allow himself to get into a scowling mood while eating.

"I dislike business with breakfast," he stated.

"Yeah, I know you do."

"You can fill in later. Get Saul and put him on the disbarment of Mr. O'Malley."

"That was covered fairly well in the police file on Dykes. I've told you about it."

"Nevertheless, put Saul on it. Put Fred and Orrie on Dykes's associations outside that law office."

"He didn't have any to speak of."

"Put them on it. We've made this assumption and we'll either validate it or void it. Pursue your acquaintance with those women. Take one of them to lunch."

"Lunch isn't a good time. They only have—"

"We'll argue later. I want to read the paper. Have you had breakfast?"

"No. I got up late."

"Go and eat."

"Glad to."

Before I did so, I called Saul and Fred and Orrie and told them to come in for briefing. After breakfast I had that to attend to and also various office chores I had got behind on. There was a phone call from Purley Stebbins, who wanted to know how I had made out with my dinner party, and I asked him which one or ones he was tailing, or, as an alternative, which one he had on a line, but he brushed me off. I made no attempt to arrange to buy a lunch. So fast a follow-up on Sue would have been bad strategy, and a midday fifty minutes with one of the others would have given me no scope. Besides, I had had less than five hours' sleep and hadn't shaved.

When Wolfe came down to the office at eleven he went over the morning mail, dictated a couple of letters, looked through a catalogue, and then requested a full report. To him a full report means every word and gesture and expression, and I have learned to fill the order not only to his satisfaction but to mine. It took more than an hour. When I was through, after asking a few questions, he issued a command.

"Phone Miss Troy and take her to lunch."

I remained calm. "I understand and sympathize," I told him, "but I can't oblige. You're desperate and therefore impulsive. I could present an overwhelming case against it, but will mention only two items: first, it's nearly one o'clock and that's too late, and second, I don't feel like it. There are some things I know more about than you do, and one of them is my extractive ability with women. Take it from me, it would be hard to conceive a lousier idea than for me to invite a middle-aged lawyer's niece with pimples to a quick bite in a crowded midtown beanery, especially since she is probably right now on a stool at a fountain lunch working on a maple-nut sundae."

He shivered.

"I'm sorry to upset you, but maple-nut sundaes are—"

"Shut up," he growled.

All the same, I was quite aware that it was up to me. True, Saul and Fred and Orrie were out collecting, but they were even farther away from Joan Wellman than I was, and that was some distance. If one of those ten females, or one of the other six whom I hadn't met, had just one measly little fact tucked away that would start Wolfe's lips pushing out and in, no one but me was going to dig it out, and if I didn't want it to drag on into the Christmas season, only ten months away, I had better pull something.

Back in the office after lunch, Wolfe was seated at his desk, reading a book of lyrics by Oscar Hammerstein, his mind a million miles from murder, and I was wandering around trying to think of something to pull, when the phone rang and I went to answer it.

A woman's voice told me, "Mr. Corrigan would like to speak to Mr. Wolfe. Put Mr. Wolfe on, please."

I made a face. "Get home all right, Mrs. Adams?"

"Yes."

"Good. Mr. Wolfe is busy reading poetry. Put Corrigan on."

"Really, Mr. Goodwin."

"I'm stubborner than you are, and you made the call, I didn't. Put him on." I covered the transmitter and told Wolfe, "Mr. James A. Corrigan, the senior partner."

Wolfe put the book down and took his instrument. I stayed on, as always when I wasn't signaled to get off.

"This is Nero Wolfe."

"This is Jim Corrigan. I'd like to have a talk with you."

"Go ahead."

"Not on the phone, Mr. Wolfe. It would be better to meet, and some of my associates would like to sit in. Would it be convenient for you to call at our office, say around five-thirty? One of my associates is in court."

"I don't call at people's offices, Mr. Corrigan. I stay in my office. I won't be available at five-thirty, but six would do if you wish to come."

"Six would be all right, but it would be better to make it here. There will be four of us—perhaps five. Six o'clock here?"

"No, sir. If at all, here."

"Hold the wire a minute."

It was more like three minutes. Then he was on again. "Sorry to keep you waiting. All right, we'll be there at six or a little after."

Wolfe cradled his phone, and I did likewise.

"Well," I remarked, "at least we touched a sore spot somewhere. That's the first cheep we've got out of anybody in ten days."

Wolfe picked up his book.

XI

THAT was the biggest array of legal talent ever gathered in the office. Four counselors-at-law in good standing and one disbarred.

James A. Corrigan (secretary, Charlotte Adams) was about the same age as his secretary, or maybe a little younger. He had the jaw of a prizefighter and the frame of a retired jockey and the hungriest pair of eyes I ever saw—not hungry the way a dog looks at a bone you're holding up but the way a cat looks at a bird in a cage.

Emmett Phelps (secretary, Sue Dondero) was a surprise to me. Sue had told me that he was the firm's encyclopedia, the guy who knew all the precedents and references and could turn to them with his eyes shut, but he didn't look it. Something over fifty, and a couple of inches over six feet, broad-shouldered and long-armed, on him a general's or admiral's uniform would have looked fine.

Louis Kustin (secretary, Eleanor Gruber) was the youngster of the bunch, about my age. Instead of hungry eyes he had sleepy ones, very dark, but that must have been a cover because Sue had told me that he was their trial man, and hot, having taken over the tougher courtroom assignments when O'Malley had been disbarred. He looked smaller than he was on account of the way he slumped.

Frederick Briggs, Helen Troy's Uncle Fred, had white hair and a long bony face. If he had a secretary I hadn't met her. From the way he blinked like a half-wit at everyone who spoke, it seemed a wonder he had been made a partner even in his seventh decade—or it could have been his eighth—but it takes all kinds to make a law firm. I wouldn't have hired him to change blotters.

Conroy O'Malley, who had been the senior partner and the courtroom wizard until he got bounced off the bar for bribing a juror, looked as bitter as you would expect, with a sidewise twist to his mouth that seemed to be permanent. With his mouth straightened and the sag out of his cheeks and a flash in his eye, it wouldn't have been hard to imagine him dominating a courtroom, but as he was then he couldn't have dominated a phone booth with him alone in it.

I had allotted the red leather chair to Corrigan, the senior partner, with the others in an irregular arc facing Wolfe's desk. Usually, when there are visitors, I don't get out my notebook and pen until Wolfe says to, but there was no law against my trying an experiment, so I had them ready and when Corrigan opened up I began scribbling. The reaction was instantaneous and unanimous. They all yapped at once, absolutely horrified and outraged. I looked astonished.

Wolfe, who knows me fairly well, thought he was going to slip me a caustic remark, but he had to chuckle. The idea of getting the goats of four lawyers and one ex-lawyer at one crack appealed to him too.

"I don't think," he told me mildly, "we'll need a record of this."

I put the notebook on my desk in easy reach. They didn't like it there so handy. Throughout the conference they took turns darting glances at me to make sure I wasn't sneaking in some symbols.

"This is a confidential private conversation," Corrigan stated.

"Yes, sir," Wolfe conceded. "But not privileged. I am not your client."

"Quite right." Corrigan smiled, but his eyes stayed hungry. "We wouldn't mind if you were. We are not a hijacking firm, Mr. Wolfe, but I don't need to say that if you ever need our services it would be a pleasure and an honor."

Wolfe inclined his head an eighth of an inch. I raised a brow the same distance. So they had brought butter along.

"I'll come straight to the point," Corrigan declared. "Last evening you got more than half of our office staff down here and tried to seduce them."

"Seduction in its statutory sense, Mr. Corrigan?"

"No, no, of course not. Orchids, liquors, exotic foods—not to tempt their chastity but their discretion. Administered by your Mr. Goodwin."

"I take responsibility for Mr. Goodwin's actions on my premises as my agent. Are you charging me with a malum? In se or prohibitum?"

"Not at all. Neither. Perhaps I started badly. I'll describe the situation as we see it, and you correct me if I'm wrong. A man named Wellman has engaged you to investigate the death of his daughter. You have decided that there is a connection between her death and two others, those of Leonard Dykes and Rachel Abrams. In—"

"Not decided. Assumed as a working hypothesis."

"All right. And you're working on it. You have two reasons for the assumption: the appearance of the name Baird Archer in all three cases, and the fact that all three died violently. The second is merely coincidental and would have no significance without the first. Looked at objectively, it doesn't seem like a very good reason. We suspect you're concentrating on this assumption because you can't find anything else to concentrate on, but of course we may be wrong."

"No. You're quite right."

They exchanged glances. Phelps, the six-foot-plus encyclopedia, muttered something I didn't catch. O'Malley, the ex, was the only one who didn't react at all. He was too busy being bitter.

"Naturally," Corrigan said reasonably, "we can't expect you to spread your cards out. We didn't come here to question you, we came to let you question us."

"About what?"

"Any and all relevant matters. We're willing to spread our cards out, Mr. Wolfe; we have to. Frankly, our firm is in a highly vulnerable position. We've had all the scandal we can absorb. Only a little over a year ago our senior partner was disbarred and narrowly escaped a felony conviction. That was a major blow to the firm. We reorganized, months passed, we were regaining lost ground, and then our chief confidential clerk, Leonard Dykes, was murdered, and it was all reopened. There was never a shred of evidence that there was any connection between O'Malley's disbarment and Dykes's death, but it doesn't take evidence to make scandal. It affected us even more seriously than the first blow; the effect was cumulative. Weeks went by, and Dykes's murder was still unsolved, and it was beginning to die down a little, when suddenly it came back on us through the death of someone we had never heard of, a young woman named Joan Wellman. However, that was much less violent and damaging. It was confined mostly to an effort by the police to find some trace, through us or our staff, of a man who was named Baird Archer, or who had used that name, and the effort was completely unsuccessful. After a week of that it was petering out too, and then here they came again, we didn't know why at the time, but now we know it was because of the death of another young woman we had never heard of, named Rachel Abrams. At that point don't you think we had a right to feel a little persecuted?"

Wolfe shrugged. "I doubt if it matters what I think. You did feel persecuted."

"We certainly did. We do. We have had enough. As you know, the Abrams girl died three days ago. Again what the police are after is a trace of a Baird Archer, though God knows if there were any trace of such a man or such a name at our office they should have dug it up long ago. Anyhow, there's nothing we can do except hope they find their damned Baird Archer, and wait for this to begin to die down too. That's how we felt yesterday. Do you know what happened in court this afternoon? Louis Kustin was trying an important case for us, and during a recess opposing counsel came up to him and said—what did he say, Louis?"

Kustin stirred in his chair. "He asked me what I was doing about a new connection when our firm dissolves." His voice had a sharp edge, not at all sleepy like his eyes. "He was trying to get me sore to spoil my style. He didn't succeed."

"You see," Corrigan told Wolfe. "Well, that's how we felt yesterday. Then those boxes of orchids came with notes from your man Goodwin. Then today we learn what happened last night. We learn what happened here, and we also learn that Goodwin told one of our staff that you have an idea that a trail to the murderer of the Wellman girl can be picked up at our office, that he never saw you more bullheaded about an idea, and that your client and you both intend to go the limit. We know enough about you and your methods to know what that means. As long as you've got that idea you'll never let go. The police and the talk may die down and even die out, but you won't, and God knows what you'll do to our staff. You've damn near got them scratching and pulling hair already."

"Nuts," I cut in. "They've been at it for months."

"They were cooling off. You got 'em tight and then brought in a bereaved father and mother to work on their nerves. God only knows what you'll do next." Corrigan returned to Wolfe. "So here we are. Ask us anything you want to. You say that idea is a working hypothesis, go ahead and work on it. You're investigating the murder of Joan Wellman, and you think one of us has something for you, maybe all of us. Here we are. Get it over with."

Corrigan looked at me and asked politely, "Could I have a drink of water?"

I took it for granted that he meant with something in it and asked him what, meanwhile pushing a button for Fritz, since I wasn't supposed to leave a conference unless I had to. Also I broadened the invitation. Two of them liked Scotch, two bourbon, and one rye. They exchanged remarks. Briggs, the blinking half-wit, got up to stretch and crossed the room for a look at the big globe, probably with the notion of trying to find out where he was. I noticed that Wolfe did not order beer, which seemed to be stretching things pretty thin. I had nothing against his habit of using reasonable precaution not to take refreshment with a murderer, but he had never seen any of those birds before and he had absolutely nothing to point at them with. Bullheaded was putting it mildly.

Corrigan put his half-empty glass down and said, "Go ahead."

Wolfe grunted. "As I understand it, sir, you invite me to ask questions and satisfy myself that my assumption is not valid. That could take all night. I'm sorry, but my dinner dish this evening is not elastic."

"We'll go out and come back."

"And I can't commit myself to satisfaction by an hour or even a day."

"We don't expect a commitment. We just want to get you off our necks as soon as possible without having our organization and our reputation hurt worse than they are already."

"Very well. Here's a question. Which one of you first suggested this meeting with me?"

"What difference does that make?"

"I'm asking the questions, Mr. Corrigan."

"So you are. It was—" The senior partner hesitated. "Yes, it was Phelps."

"No," Phelps contradicted him. "You came to my room and asked me what I thought of it."

"Then it was you, Fred?"

Briggs blinked. "I really couldn't say, Jim. I make so many suggestions, I may well have made this one. I know Louis phoned in at his lunch recess to ask for some figures, and we were discussing it."

"That's right," Kustin agreed. "You said it was being considered."

"You're having a hell of a time answering a simple question," a biting voice told them. It was Conroy O'Malley, the ex. "The suggestion came from me. I phoned you around eleven o'clock, Jim, and you told me about Nero Wolfe smashing in, and I said the only thing to do was have a talk with him."

Corrigan screwed up his lips. "That's right. Then I went in to get Emmett's opinion."

Wolfe went at O'Malley. "You phoned Mr. Corrigan around eleven this morning?"

"Yes."

"What about?"

"To get the news. I had been out of town for a week, and the minute I returned the police had got at me again about Baird Archer. I wondered why."

"What were you doing out of town?"

"I was in Atlanta, Georgia, getting facts about the delivery of steel for a bridge."

"On behalf of whom?"

"This firm." O'Malley's mouth twisted until it was distorted almost to a diagonal. "You don't think my old associates would let me starve, do you? No indeed. I eat every day. Not only do I get a share of the income from unfinished business when I left, I am also given work to do outside the office. Do you know what is the outstanding characteristic of my former associates? Love for their fellow man." He tapped his chest with a forefinger. "I am their fellow man."

"Goddammit, Con," Phelps blurted, "where does that get you? What do you want? What do you expect?"

A gleam had come and gone in Kustin's sleepy eyes as O'Malley spoke. He said dryly, "We're here to answer Wolfe's questions. Let's keep the answers responsive."

"No," Wolfe said, "this isn't a courtroom. Sometimes an unresponsive answer is the most revealing, almost as good as a lie. But I hope you will resort to lies as little as possible, since they will be of use to me only when exposed and that's a lot of work. For instance, I am going to ask each of you if you have ever tried your hand at writing fiction or had a marked and sustained desire to write fiction. If you all say no, and if later, through interviews with friends and acquaintances, I find that one of you lied, that will be of some value to me, but it will save trouble if you'll tell the truth short of serious embarrassment. Have you ever tried writing fiction, Mr. O'Malley? Or wanted to, beyond a mere whim?"

"No."

"Mr. Briggs?"

"No."

He got five noes.

Wolfe leaned back and surveyed them. "Of course," he said, "it is clearly essential to my assumption that either Leonard Dykes or someone he knew wrote a piece of fiction long enough to be called a novel—Dykes himself by preference, since he was killed. Doubtless the police have touched on this in questioning you, and you have disclaimed any knowledge of such an activity by Dykes, but I like things firsthand. Mr. Corrigan, have you ever had any information or hint, from any source, that Dykes had written, was writing, or wanted or intended to write, a work of fiction?"

"No."

"Mr. Phelps?"

Five noes again.

Wolfe nodded. "That shows why, even if you put up with this for a solid week, I can't engage not to harass your staff. For that kind of operation Mr. Goodwin is highly qualified. If you admonish those young women not to see him, I doubt if it will work. If they disobey and you fire them, you will merely make them riper for him. If you warn them specifically that any knowledge they may have, however slight, of Dykes's literary performances or ambitions is not to be disclosed, sooner or later Mr. Goodwin will know it, and I shall ask why you don't want me to get facts. And if any of them does innocently have such knowledge, perhaps from some remark once heard, we'll get it."

They didn't care for that. Louis Kustin was displaying a bored smile. "We're not schoolboys, Wolfe. We graduated long ago. Speaking for myself, you're welcome to any fact you can get, no matter what, that's conceivably connected with your case. I don't know any. I'm here—all of us are—to satisfy you on that point."

"Then tell me this, Mr. Kustin." Wolfe was placid. "I gather that although the disbarment of Mr. O'Malley was a blow to the firm's reputation, you personally benefited from it by being made a partner and by replacing Mr. O'Malley as chief trial counsel. Is that correct?"

Kustin's eyes woke up. They gleamed. "I deny that that has any connection with your case."

"We're proceeding on my assumption. Of course you may decline to answer, but if you do, what are you here for?"

"Answer him, Louis," O'Malley said jeeringly. "Just say yes."

They looked at each other. I doubt if either of them had ever regarded opposing counsel with just that kind of hostility. Then Kustin's eyes, anything but sleepy now, returned to Wolfe and he said, "Yes."

"And naturally your share of the firm's profits was increased?"

"Yes."

"Substantially?"

"Yes."

Wolfe's glance went left. "You too benefited, Mr. Corrigan? You became the senior partner with an increased share?"

Corrigan's prizefighter's jaw was jutting. "I became the senior in a firm that was damn near on the rocks. My percentage of the profits went up, but the profits went down. I would have done better to cut loose."

"Was there anything to stop you?" O'Malley inquired. From his tone I would have guessed that he hated Corrigan about one-fifth as much as he did Kustin.

"Yes, Con, there was. I had my associates to think of. My name was on the door with theirs. There was loyalty to stop me."

Suddenly, totally without warning, O'Malley bounded to his feet. I suppose he had done it a thousand times in a courtroom, to object to a question or dramatize a motion to dismiss, but it startled the others as much as it did me. He flung up an arm and called out in a ringing voice, "Loyalty!" Then he dropped back into his chair, picked up his glass and raised it, said, "To loyalty," and drank.

The four firm members glanced at one another. I changed my mind about O'Malley's ability to dominate a phone booth.

Wolfe spoke. "And you, Mr. Briggs? You also moved up when Mr. O'Malley was out?"

Briggs blinked violently. "I resent this," he said stiffly. "I am opposed to this whole procedure. I know something of you, Mr. Wolfe, and I regard your methods as unethical and reprehensible. I am here under protest."

"Frederick," O'Malley said gravely, "should be on the bench. He should have been appointed to the bench as soon as he was out of law school. He would be an ideal judge. He has the kind of daring mind that glories in deciding an issue without understanding it."

Phelps, the encyclopedia, protested, "Everybody can't be brilliant like you, Con. Maybe it's just as well they can't."

O'Malley nodded at him. "You're dead right, Emmett. But you're always right. I've never resented it, you know, your always being right, I don't know why. Not because you're the only one who didn't profit by my downfall; I never resented it."

"I did profit. I moved up one and I get a bigger cut." Phelps went to Wolfe. "We all profited by our partner's misfortune, or we will, if this doesn't ruin us altogether. Even I. Strictly speaking, I am not an attorney-at-law; I am a scholar. To a lawyer the most interesting case is the one he is currently engaged in. To me the most interesting case is one that was tried in Vienna in 1568. I inject this only to explain why this case of yours is to me unutterably dull. It might not be if I had myself killed Dykes and those two young women, but I doubt it. I would be attentive, naturally, but not interested. You will forgive me, I hope."

That, I thought, might be useful in future conversations with Sue Dondero, Phelps's secretary. From her scanty remarks about her boss I hadn't got that slant on him, and surely she would like to know more about him if she didn't already. Girls feel that it's their duty to know all about their bosses.

Wolfe was cocking his head at the encyclopedia. "Murders bore you, Mr. Phelps?"

"I didn't say that. 'Bore' is an active verb. I am merely indifferent."

"But isn't your livelihood involved?"

"Yes. That's why I'm here. I came and I'll talk, but don't expect to arouse me."

"Then I won't try." Wolfe's eyes moved. "By the way, Mr. O'Malley, why are you here?"

"Loyalty." I had refilled O'Malley's glass, and he lifted it. "To loyalty!"

"To whom? Your former associates? I was getting the impression that you are not too well disposed toward them."

"That just shows"—O'Malley put his glass down—"how wrong appearances can be. My old friends Jim and Emmett and Louis and Fred?

I'd go through hell for them—in fact I have. Isn't that acceptable as my motive for coming?"

"I'd prefer something a little less moot."

"Then try this. I was a man of extraordinary talent and not without ambition. My talent had been developed and my faculties trained to one end: to enter a courtroom with a briefcase, confront a judge and jury, and so manipulate their thoughts and emotions that I got the verdict I wanted. I hadn't lost a case for four years when one day I found myself faced by certain defeat; there was no question about it. Under that pressure I did something foolish: I bribed a juror, the first and only time. I got a hung jury, and a few weeks later got a settlement out of court, and I thought I was safely out of it, when suddenly it hit me. Someone informed the court, they got the juror in and worked on him and broke him, and there I was. Insufficient evidence saved me from a felony conviction, the jury was divided six to six, but I was disbarred."

"Who informed the court?"

"I didn't know at the time. Now I have reason to believe it was the juror's wife."

"Were any of your associates privy to your act?"

"No. They wouldn't have stood for it. They were shocked—the shock of righteous men—meaning by 'righteous men' those who have not been caught. They were also loyal, they helped me fight it, but it was hopeless. So here I am, a man with an extraordinary talent that can't be used. I can use it only in one place and I am not allowed to go there. Moreover, I am stigmatized. People who could use my talents outside of courtrooms don't want them. And I'm broke. I'm in no position to postulate that I should go on living; there seems no point in it; but through perversity I'm going to. My only source of income is this firm, payments on account of business that was unfinished when I left, and they give me errands to do. So it is to my interest for the firm to prosper. I offer that as my reason for coming here with them. If you don't like it either, I have still another alternative. Would you like to hear it?"

"If it isn't too fanciful."

"It's not fanciful at all. I am embittered against my former associates because they let me down. I think it quite possible that one of them killed Dykes and the two women, though I have no idea why, and that you're going to hang on until you get it, and I want to see it happen. Do you like that better?"

"It has attractions."

"Or here's another. I myself killed Dykes and the women, though again I have no idea why, and I think you're more dangerous than the police and want to keep an eye on you." O'Malley picked up his glass. "That's four, that should be enough."

"It'll do for the time being," Wolfe concurred. "Of course they're mutually exclusive. In one your associates helped you fight and in another they let you down. Which was it actually?"

"They fought like tigers to save me."

"Goddammit, Con," Phelps exploded, "we did! We let everything else go! We did our damnedest!"

O'Malley was unmoved. "Then you'd better take that one," he told Wolfe. "Number Two. It has corroboration, which is always a help."

"I prefer it anyway." Wolfe glanced up at the clock on the wall. "I want all you can tell me about Dykes, gentlemen, but it's my dinnertime. As I said, I'm sorry we're not prepared for guests."

They left their chairs. Corrigan asked, "What time do you want us back?"

Wolfe made a face. He hated the prospect of work during digestion. "Nine o'clock?" he suggested. "Will that suit?"

They said it would.

XII

WHEN, an hour after midnight, Wolfe finally called it a day and let them go, it looked as if I would be seeing a lot of the girls. Not that they had balked at answering questions. We had at least four thousand facts, an average of a thousand an hour, but if anyone had offered me a dime for the lot it would have been a deal. We were full of information to the gills, but not a glimmer of Baird Archer or fiction writing or anything pertaining thereto. Wolfe had even sunk so low as to ask where and how they had spent the evening of February second and the afternoon of February twenty-sixth, though the cops had of course covered that and double-checked it.

Especially we knew enough about Leonard Dykes to write his biography, either straight or in novel form. Having started in as office boy, by industry, application, loyalty, and a satisfactory amount of intelligence, he had worked up to office manager and confidential clerk. He was not married. He had smoked a pipe, and had once got pickled on two glasses of punch at an office party, proving that he was not a drinker. He had had no known interest in anything outside his work except baseball in summer and professional hockey games in winter. And so forth and so on. None of the five had any notion about who had killed him or why.

They kept getting into squabbles about anything and everything. For instance, when Wolfe was asking about Dykes's reaction to the disbarment of O'Malley, and was told by Corrigan that Dykes had written him a letter of resignation, Wolfe wanted to know when. Sometime in the summer, Corrigan said, he didn't remember exactly, probably in July. Wolfe asked what the letter had said.

"I forget how he put it," Corrigan replied, "but he was just being scrupulous. He said he had heard that there was talk among the staff that he was responsible for O'Malley's trouble, that it was baseless, but that we might feel it would be harmful to the firm for him to continue. He also said that it was under O'Malley as senior that he had been made office manager, and that the new regime might want to make a change, and that therefore he was offering his resignation."

Wolfe grunted. "Was it accepted?"

"Certainly not. I called him in and told him that we were completely satisfied with him, and that he should ignore the office gossip."

"I'd like to see his letter. You have it?"

"I suppose it was filed—" Corrigan stopped. "No, it wasn't. I sent it to Con O'Malley. He may have it."

"I returned it to you," O'Malley asserted.

"If you did I don't remember it."

"He must have," Phelps declared, "because when you showed it to me—no, that was another letter. When you showed me Dykes's resignation you said you were going to send it to Con."

"He did," O'Malley said. "And I returned it—wait a minute, I'm wrong. I returned it to Fred, in person. I stopped in at the office, and Jim wasn't there, and I gave it to Fred."

Briggs was blinking at him. "That," he said stiffly, "is absolutely false. Emmett showed me that letter." He blinked around. "I resent it, but I'm not surprised. We all know that Con is irresponsible and a liar."

"Goddammit, Fred," Phelps objected, "why should he lie about a thing like that? He didn't say he showed it to you, he said he gave it to you."

"It's a lie! It's absolutely false!"

"I don't believe," Wolfe interposed, "that the issue merits such heat. I would like to see not only that letter but also anything else that Dykes wrote—letters, memoranda, reports—or copies of them. I want to know how he used words. I would like that letter to be included if it is available. I don't need a stack of material—half a dozen items will do. May I have them?"

They said he might.

When they had gone I stretched, yawned, and inquired, "Do we discuss it now or wait till morning?"

"What the devil is there to discuss?" Wolfe shoved his chair back and arose. "Go to bed." He marched out to his elevator.

Next day, Friday, I had either bum luck or a double brush-off, I wasn't sure which. Phoning Sue Dondero to propose some kind of joint enterprise, I was told that she was leaving town that afternoon for the weekend and wouldn't return until late Sunday evening. Phoning Eleanor Gruber as the best alternative, I was told that she was already booked. I looked over the list, trying to be objective about it, and settled on Blanche Duke. When I got her I must admit she didn't sound enthusiastic, but probably she never did at the switchboard. She couldn't make it Friday but signed up for Saturday at seven.

We were getting reports by phone from Saul and Fred and Orrie, and Friday a little before six Saul came in person. The only reason I wouldn't vote for Saul Panzer for President of the United States is that he would never dress the part. How he goes around New York, almost anywhere, in that faded brown cap and old brown suit, without attracting attention as not belonging, I will never understand. Wolfe has never given him an assignment that he didn't fill better than anyone else could except me, and my argument is why not elect him President, buy him a suit and hat, and see what happens?

He sat on the edge of one of the yellow chairs and asked, "Anything fresh?"

"No," I told him. "As you know, it is usually impossible to tell just when a case will end, but this time it's a cinch. When our client's last buck is spent we'll quit."

"As bad as that? Is Mr. Wolfe concentrating?"

"You mean is he working or loafing. He's loafing. He has started asking people where they were at three-fifteen Monday afternoon, February twenty-sixth. That's a hell of a way for a genius to perform."

Wolfe entered, greeted Saul, and got behind his desk. Saul reported. Wolfe wanted full details as usual, and got them: the names of the judge, jury foreman, and others, the nature of the case that O'Malley had been losing, including the names of the litigants, and so forth. The information had gone to the court by mail in an unsigned typewritten letter, and had been detailed enough for them to go for the juror after a few hours' checkup. Efforts to trace the informing letter had failed. After an extended session with city employees, the juror had admitted getting three thousand dollars in cash from O'Malley, and more than half of it had been recovered. Louis Kustin had been defense attorney at the trials of both the juror and O'Malley, and by brilliant performances had got hung juries in both cases. Saul had spent a day trying to get to the archives for a look at the unsigned typewritten informing letter, but had failed.

The bribed juror was a shoe salesman named Anderson. Saul had had two sessions with him and his wife. The wife's position stood on four legs: one, she had not written the letter; two, she had not known that her husband had taken a bribe; three, if she had known he had taken a bribe she certainly wouldn't have told on him; and four, she didn't know how to typewrite. Apparently her husband believed her. That didn't prove anything, since the talent of some husbands for believing their wives is unbounded, but when Saul too voted for her that was enough for Wolfe and me. Saul can smell a liar through a concrete wall. He offered to bring the Andersons in for Wolfe to judge for himself, but Wolfe said no. Saul was told to join Fred and Orrie in the check of Dykes's friends and acquaintances outside the office.

Saturday morning a large envelope arrived by messenger. Inside was a note from Emmett Phelps, the six-foot scholar who was indifferent to murder, typed on the firm's letterhead:

Dear Mr. Wolfe:

        I am sending herewith, as you requested, some material written by Leonard Dykes.

        Included is his letter of resignation dated July 19, 1950, which you said you would like to see. Evidently Mr. O'Malley's statement that he had returned the letter to Mr. Briggs was correct, since it was here in our files. Mr. O'Malley was in the office yesterday and I told him the letter had been found.

        Kindly return the material when you have finished with it.

                        Sincerely,
                        Emmett Phelps

Dykes's letter of resignation was a full page, single-spaced, but all it said was what Corrigan had told us—that on account of the staff gossip that he had informed on O'Malley and so damaged the firm's reputation, and, further, because the new regime might want to make a change, he respectfully submitted his resignation. He had used three times as many words as he needed. As for the rest of the material—memoranda, reports, and copies of letters—it may have shown Wolfe how Dykes used words, but aside from that it was as irrelevant as last year's box score. Wolfe waded through it, passing each item to me as he finished, and I read every word, not wanting to leave an opening for another remark about my powers of observation like the time I had muffed the name of Baird Archer. When I had finished I handed the lot back to him, with some casual comment, and got at my typewriter to do some letters he had dictated.

I was banging away when he suddenly demanded, "What does this stand for?"

I got up to go and look. In his hand was Dykes's letter of resignation. He slid it across to me. "That notation in pencil in the corner. What is it?"

I looked at it, a pencil scribble like this:

$$Ps\,146\text{-}3$$

I nodded. "Yeah, I noticed it. Search me. Public School 146, Third Grade?"

"The S is lower case."

"So it is. Am I supposed to pop it out?"

"No. It's probably frivolous, but its oddity stirs curiosity. Does it suggest anything to you?"

I pursed my lips to look thoughtful. "Not offhand. Does it to you?"

He reached for it and frowned at it. "It invites speculation. With a capital P and a small S, it is presumably not initials. I know of only one word or name in the language for which 'Ps' is commonly used as an abbreviation. The figures following the 'Ps' increase the likelihood. Still no suggestion?"

"Well, 'Ps' stands for postscript, and the figures—"

"No. Get the Bible."

I crossed to the bookshelves, got it, and returned.

"Turn to Psalm One-forty-six and read the third verse."

I admit I had to use the index. Having done so, I turned the pages, found it, and gave it a glance.

"I'll be damned," I muttered.

"Read it!" Wolfe bellowed.

I read aloud. " 'Put not your trust in princes, nor in the son of man, in whom there is no help.' "

"Ah," Wolfe said, and sighed clear to his middle.

"Okay," I conceded. " 'Put Not Your Trust' was the title of Baird Archer's novel. At last you've got a man on base, but by a fluke. I hereby enter it for the record in coincidences that the item you specially requested had that notation on it and you spotted it. If that's how—"

"Pfui," Wolfe snorted. "There was nothing coincidental about it, and any lummox could have interpreted that notation."

"I'm a superlummox."

"No." He was so pleased he felt magnanimous. "You got it for us. You got those women here and scared them. You scared them so badly that one or more of them felt it necessary to concede a connection between Baird Archer and someone in that office."

"One of whom? The women?"

"I think not. I prefer a man, and it was the men I asked for material written by Dykes. You scared a man or men. I want to know which one or ones. You have an engagement for this evening?"

"Yes. With a blond switchboard operator. Three shades of blond on one head."

"Very well. Find out who made that notation on Dykes's letter in that square distinctive hand. I hope to heaven it wasn't Dykes himself." Wolfe frowned and shook his head. "I must correct myself. All I expect you to learn is whose hand that notation resembles. It would be better not to show the letter and the notation itself."

"Sure. Make it as tough as you can."

But it wasn't as tough as it sounded because the handwriting was so easy to imitate. During the afternoon I practiced it plenty before I prepared my bait. When I left for my date at 6:40 I had with me, in the breast pocket of my newest lightweight blue suit, one of the items that had been sent us—a typewritten memorandum from Leonard Dykes—with a penciled notation in the margin made by me:

$$CO3-4620$$

XIII

BLANCHE DUKE surprised me that evening. She had two shots of her special formula—gin, vermouth, grenadine, and Pernod—before dinner, and then quit. No more. Also she wore a nice simple blue dress and went easy with cosmetics. Also, most important, she could dance much better than Sue Dondero. On the whole, while she was not something for the Bobolink to stare at, she certainly needed no excuses, and she made the Bobolink band seem even better than it was. By ten o'clock I would have been perfectly willing to split the check with our client. But I was there on business.

When we went back to our table after I had fancied up a samba all I could and she had kept with me as though we had done it a hundred times, and I insisted that with dinner only a memory it was time for a drink, she refused.

"Look," I objected, "this isn't going right. All I'm getting out of it is a good time, when I'm supposed to be working. The idea was to get you lit enough to loosen up, and you're drinking water. How can I get you babbling if you won't drink?"

"I like to dance," she stated.

"No wonder, the way you do it. So do I, but I've got a problem. I've got to quit enjoying myself and drag something out of you."

She shook her head. "I don't drink when I'm dancing because I like to dance. Try me tomorrow afternoon while I'm washing my hair. I hate washing my damn hair. What makes you think there's something in me to drag out?"

Our waiter was hovering, and I appeased him with an order for something.

"Well," I told her, "there ought to be, since you think O'Malley killed Dykes. You must have some reason—"

"I don't think that."

"You said you did Wednesday evening."

She waved a hand. "It gets Eleanor Gruber's goat. She's crazy about O'Malley. I don't think that at all. I think Len Dykes committed suicide."

"Oh. Whose goat does that get?"

"Nobody's. It might get Sue's, but I like her, so I don't say it, I just think it."

"Sue Dondero? Why her?"

"Well—" Blanche frowned. "Of course you didn't know Len Dykes."

"No."

"He was a funny duck. He was a nice guy in a way, but he was funny. He had inhibitions about women, but he carried a picture of one in his wallet, and who do you think it was? His sister, for God's sake! Then one day I saw him—"

She stopped abruptly. The band had struck up a conga. Her shoulders moved to the beat. There was only one thing to do. I stood up and extended a hand, and she came, and we edged through to the floor. A quarter of an hour later we returned to the table, sat, and exchanged glances of unqualified approval.

"Let's get the dragging over with," I suggested, "and then we can do some serious dancing. You were saying that one day you saw Dykes—doing what?"

She looked blank a moment, then nodded. "Oh, yes. Do we really have to go on with this?"

"I do."

"Okay. I saw him looking at Sue. Brother, that was a look! I kidded him about it, which was a mistake, because it made him decide to pick me to tell about it. It was the first time—"

"When was this?"

"A year ago, maybe more. It was the first time he had ever put an eye on a woman, at his age! And he had fallen for her so hard he might as well have had an ulcer. He kept it covered all right, except with me, but I certainly got it. He tried to date her, but nothing doing. He asked me what to do, and I had to tell him something, so I told him Sue was the kind of girl who was looking for glamour, and he ought to get famous somehow, like getting elected senator or pitching for the Yankees or writing a book. So he wrote a book, and the publishers wouldn't take it, and he killed himself."

I showed no excitement. "He told you he wrote a book?"

"No, he never mentioned it. Along about then he stopped talking about her, and I never brought it up because I didn't want to get him started again. But it was one of the things I suggested, and there's all this racket about a book that got rejected, so why can't I put two and two together?"

I could have objected that suicide by Dykes in December wouldn't help to explain the murder of Joan Wellman and Rachel Abrams in February, but I wanted to get to the point before the band started up again. I took a sip of my drink.

I smiled at her to keep it friendly. "Even if you're right about the suicide, what if you're shifting the cast? What if it was you instead of Sue he put his eye on?"

She snorted. "Me? If you mean that for a compliment, try again."

"I don't." My hand went to my breast pocket and came out with a folded paper. "This is a memorandum on office expenses prepared by Dykes, dated last May." I unfolded it. "I was going to ask you why he scribbled your home phone number on it, but now you can just say it was while he was telling you about Sue and asking your advice, so what's the use." I started to refold it.

"*My* phone number?" she demanded.

"Yep. Columbus three, four-six-two-oh."

"Let me see it."

I handed it to her, and she took a look. She held it to her right to get more light and looked again. "Len didn't write that," she declared.

"Why not?"

"It's not his writing."

"Whose is it? Yours?"

"No. It's Corrigan's. He writes square like that." She was frowning at me. "What is this, anyhow? Why should Corrigan be putting my phone number on this old memo?"

"Oh, forget it." I reached and took the paper from her fingers. "I thought maybe Dykes had written it and just thought I'd ask. Corrigan may have wanted to phone you about something after office hours." A rattle came from the drum, and the band slid into a trot. I put the memo in my pocket and stood up. "Skip it. Let's see how we like this."

We liked it fine.

When I got home, around two, Wolfe had gone up to bed. I slid the bolts on the front and back doors, twirled the knob of the safe, and drank a glass of milk before ascending. People are never satisfied. What was on my mind as I pulled the covers up was the contrariness of life. Why couldn't it have been Sue who danced like that instead of Blanche? If a man could figure out some way of combining . . .

The Sunday schedule at Wolfe's house was different since Marko Vukcic, his closest friend and the owner of Rusterman's Restaurant, had talked him into installing a pool table in the basement. It was now routine for Wolfe to spend Sunday morning in the kitchen with Fritz, preparing something special. At one-thirty Marko would arrive to help appreciate it, after which they would go to the basement for a five-hour session with the cues. I rarely took part, even when I was around, because it made Wolfe grumpy when I got lucky and piled up a big run.

That Sunday I fully expected to upset the schedule when Wolfe, having breakfasted in his room, entered the kitchen and I told him, "That notation on that letter is in the handwriting of James A. Corrigan, the senior partner."

He scowled at me a moment, then turned to Fritz. "I have decided," he said aggressively, "not to use the goose fat."

I raised my voice. "That notation on that let—"

"I heard you! Take the letter to Mr. Cramer and tell him about it."

It would have done no good to scream, not when he used that tone, so I controlled myself. "You have trained me," I said stiffly, "to remember conversations verbatim, including yours. Yesterday you said you wanted to know who we had scared and whose hand that notation resembles. I spent a whole evening and a wad of Wellman's dough finding out. To hand it to Cramer, for God's sake? What if it is Sunday? If they're scared they'll come. May I use the phone?"

His lips had tightened. "What else did you get?"

"Nothing. That's what you asked for."

"Very well. Satisfactory. Fritz and I are going to do a guinea hen, and there is barely time. If you get Mr. Corrigan down here, or even all of them, what will happen? I will show him that notation and he will deny all knowledge of it. I will ask where that letter has been, and will be told that it has been easily accessible to all of them. That will take perhaps five minutes. Then what?"

"Nuts. If you insist on playing pool instead of working on Sunday, wait till tomorrow. Why hand it to Cramer?"

"Because for its one purpose he is as good as I am—even better. It validates for them, if not for me, my assumption that someone in that firm has a guilty connection with the murder of three people. We have already scared him into this; with that letter a police inspector may scare him into something else. Take it to Mr. Cramer and don't bother me. You know quite well that for me pool is not play; it is exercise."

He strode to the refrigerator.

I had a notion to spend a couple of hours with the Sunday papers before going downtown, but decided there was no point in my being childish just because Wolfe was. Besides, with him I never knew. It could be that he merely wanted to cook and eat and play pool instead of working, but it could also be that he was pulling something fancy. He often got subtle without letting me in on it, and it wasn't impossible that there was something about that notation, or the way we got it, that made him figure it would be better to turn it over to Cramer than spring it himself. Walking the fifteen blocks to Twentieth Street with a cold March wind whipping at me from the right, I considered the matter and concluded that it might either rain or snow.

Cramer wasn't in, but Sergeant Purley Stebbins was. He gave me the chair at the end of his desk and listened to my tale. I gave it all to him except the detail of how we had learned it was Corrigan's handwriting, seeing no necessity of dragging Blanche into it. I merely told him that we had good reason to believe that it looked like Corrigan's writing. Of course he knew that Baird Archer's novel had been titled "Put Not Your Trust." He looked around for a Bible to check on the third verse of the 146th Psalm, but couldn't find one.

He was skeptical, but not about that. "You say Wolfe got this letter yesterday?" he demanded.

"Right."

"And he's done nothing about it?"

"Right."

"He hasn't asked Corrigan about it, or any of the others?"

"Right."

"Then what the hell's wrong with it?"

"Nothing that I know of. We're cooperating."

Purley snorted. "Nero Wolfe passing us a juicy item like this without first squeezing it for himself? Poop."

"If you don't like it," I said with dignity, "I'll take it back and see if I can get you something better. Would you accept a signed confession with dates and places?"

"I'll accept a signed statement from you, telling how you got this."

"Glad to, if you'll give me a decent typewriter."

What I got was what I expected, an Underwood about my age. I demanded a new ribbon, and they finally dug one up.

Back at home I did a few chores in the office and then got comfortable with the Sunday papers. Wolfe came in now and then for a section to take to the kitchen. Around noon he entered, sat behind his desk, and requested a full report of my evening with Miss Duke. Evidently the guinea hen was under control. I obliged, thinking he might let me in on the strategy if that was what it was, but all I got was a nod.

That was all for Sunday, except that after dinner I got invited to the pool game and made a run of twenty-nine, and after supper I was instructed to tell Saul and Fred and Orrie to report in at eleven in the morning.

They were there when Wolfe came down from the plant rooms: Saul Panzer, small and wiry, in his old brown suit; Fred Durkin, with his round red face and spreading bald spot, in the red leather chair by right of seniority; and Orrie Cather, with his square jaw and crew cut, looking young enough to still be playing pro football. Wolfe took Fred first, then Orrie, and Saul last.

Adding what they told us to what we already knew from the police file and the girls and the firm members, including Blanche's little contribution Saturday evening, we were certainly up on Leonard Dykes. I could give you fifty pages on him, but it would leave you just where we were, so what's the use? If anyone who had known him had any idea who had killed him or why, they weren't saying. Saul and Fred and Orrie were three good men, and they hadn't got the faintest glimmer, though they had covered every possible source except Dykes's sister, who was in California. Wolfe kept them till lunchtime and then cut them loose. Saul, who hated to turn in an empty bag even more than I did, offered to spend another day or two at it on his own, but Wolfe said no.

When they had gone Wolfe sat and stared across the room at nothing a full three minutes before he pushed back his chair, though Fritz had announced lunch. Then he heaved a deep sigh, got himself up, and growled at me to come on.

We had just returned to the office after a silent meal that was anything but convivial when the doorbell rang and I went to answer it. Not many times has it given me pleasure to see a cop on that stoop, but that was one of them. Even a humble dick would have been a sign that something had happened or might be ready to happen, and this was Inspector Cramer himself. I opened up and invited him to cross the sill, took his hat and coat, and escorted him to the office without bothering to announce him.

He grunted at Wolfe, and Wolfe grunted back. He sat, got a cigar from his vest pocket, inspected it, stuck it between his teeth, moved his jaw to try it at various angles, and took it out again.

"I'm deciding how to start this," he muttered.

"Can I help?" Wolfe asked politely.

"Yes. But you won't. One thing, I'm not going to get sore. It wouldn't do any good, because I doubt if I've got anything on you that would stick. Is that deal we made still on?"

"Of course. Why not?"

"Then you will kindly fill me in. When you decided to trick us into taking a jab at someone, why did you pick Corrigan?"

Wolfe shook his head. "You had better start over, Mr. Cramer. That's the worst possible way. There was no trick—"

Cramer cut in rudely and emphatically with a vulgar word. He went on. "I said I'm not going to get sore, and I'm not, but look at it. You get hold of that letter with that notation on it, the first real evidence anyone has seen that links someone in that office with Baird Archer and therefore with the murders. A real hot find. There were several ways you could have used it, but you pass them all up and send the letter down to me. I send Lieutenant Rowcliff up there this morning. Corrigan admits the notation resembles his handwriting, but absolutely denies that he made it or ever saw it or has any idea what it stands for. The others all make the same denials."

Cramer cocked his head. "I've sat here many a time and listened to you making an assumption on poorer ground than what I've made this one on. I don't know how you got hold of a sample of Corrigan's handwriting, but that would have been easy. And I don't know whether it was you or Goodwin who made that notation on that letter, and I don't care. One of you did. All I want to know is, why? You're too smart and too lazy to play a trick like that just for the hell of it. That's why I'm not sore and I'm not going to get sore. You expected it to get you something. What?"

He put the cigar in his mouth and sank his teeth in it.

Wolfe regarded him. "Confound it," he said regretfully, "we're not going to get anywhere."

"Why not? I'm being goddam reasonable."

"You are indeed. But we can't meet. You will listen to me only if I

concede your assumption that Mr. Goodwin or I made the notation on
the letter, imitating Corrigan's hand. You will not listen to me if I deny
that and substitute my own assumption, that the notation was in fact a
trick but not mine. Will you?"

"Try it."

"Very well. Someone wanted to provide me with evidence that would
support the line I was taking, but of such a nature and in such a manner that I would be left exactly where I was. Its pointing at Corrigan
may have been deliberate or merely adventitious; it had to point at
someone, and it may be that Corrigan was selected because he is somehow invulnerable. I preferred not to make an ass of myself by acting on
it. All I would have got was a collection of denials. As it now stands,
Lieutenant Rowcliff got the denials, and I am uncommitted. They
don't know—*he* doesn't know—how I took it. For my part, I don't know
who he is or what is moving him or why he wants to prod me, but I
would like to know. If he acts again I may find out."

Wolfe upturned a palm. "That's all."

"I don't believe it."

"I didn't expect you to."

"Okay. I've listened to it on your assumption, now try mine. You
made the notation on the letter yourself and made me a present of it.
Why?"

"No, Mr. Cramer. I'm sorry, but that's beyond my powers. Unless
you also assume that I've lost my senses, and in that case why waste
time on me?"

"I won't." Cramer left his chair, and as he did so his determination
not to get sore suddenly went up the flue. He hurled his unlit cigar at
my wastebasket, missed by a yard, and hit me on the ankle. "Fat bloated
lousy liar," he rasped, and turned and tramped out.

Thinking that under the circumstances it was just as well to let him
wriggle into his coat unaided, I stayed put. But also thinking that he
might take a notion to try a simple little trick himself, when the front
door slammed I got up and moseyed to the hall for a look through the
one-way glass panel, and saw him cross to the sidewalk and get into his
car, the door of which had been opened for an inspector.

When I returned to the office Wolfe was leaning back with his eyes
closed and his brow creased. I sat. I hoped to God he didn't feel as help-
less and useless as I did, but from the expression on his face I had another hope coming. I looked at my wrist and saw 2:52. When I looked
again it said 3:06. I wanted to yawn but thought I didn't deserve to,
and choked it.

Wolfe's voice blurted, "Where's Mr. Wellman?"

"In Peoria. He went Friday."

He had opened his eyes and straightened up. "How long does it take an airplane to get to Los Angeles?"

"Ten or eleven hours. Some of them more."

"When does the next one go?"

"I don't know."

"Find out. Wait. Have we ever before been driven to extremities as now?"

"No."

"I agree. His gambit of that notation on that letter—what for? Confound him! Nothing but denials. You have the name and address of Dykes's sister in California."

"Yes, sir."

"Phone Mr. Wellman and tell him that I propose to send you to see her. Tell him it is either that or abandon the case. If he approves the expenditure, reserve a seat on the next plane and get packed. By then I shall have instructions ready for you. Is there plenty of cash in the safe?"

"Yes."

"Take enough. You are willing to cross the continent in an airplane?"

"I'll risk it."

He shuddered. He regards a twenty-block taxi ride as a reckless gamble.

XIV

I HADN'T been to the West Coast for several years. I slept most of the night but woke up when the stewardess brought morning coffee and then kept my eyes open for a look down at the country. There is no question that a desert landscape is neater than where things have simply got to grow, and of course they don't have the weed problem, but from up above I saw stretches where even a few good big weeds would have been a help.

My watch said 11:10 as the plane taxied to a stop on the concrete of the Los Angeles airport, and I set it back to ten past eight before I arose and filed out to the gangway and off. It was warm and muggy, with no sign of the sun. By the time I got my suitcase and found a taxi I had to use a handkerchief on my face and neck. Then the breeze through the open window came at me, and, not wanting to get pneumonia in a foreign country, I shut the window. The people didn't look as foreign as some of the architecture and most of the vegetation. Before we got to the hotel it started to rain.

I had a regulation breakfast and then went up and had a regulation bath. My room—it was the Riviera—had too many colors scattered around but was okay. It smelled swampy, but I couldn't open a window on account of the rain. When I was through bathing and shaving and dressing and unpacking it was after eleven, and I got at the phone and asked Information for the number of Clarence O. Potter, 2819 Whitecrest Avenue, Glendale.

I called the number, and after three whirs a female voice told my ear hello.

I was friendly but not sugary. "May I speak to Mrs. Clarence Potter, please?"

"This is Mrs. Potter." Her voice was high but not squeaky.

"Mrs. Potter, my name is Thompson, George Thompson. I'm from New York, and you never heard of me. I'm here on a business trip, and I would like to see you to discuss an important matter. Any time that will suit you will suit me, but the sooner the better. I'm talking from the Riviera Hotel and I can come out now if that will be convenient."

"Did you say Thompson?"

"That's right, George Thompson."

"But why do you—what's it about?"

"It's a personal matter. I'm not selling anything. It's something I need to know about your deceased brother, Leonard Dykes, and it will be to your advantage if it affects you at all. I'd appreciate it if I could see you today."

"What do you want to know about my brother?"

"It's a little too complicated for the telephone. Why not let me come and tell you about it?"

"Well, I suppose—all right. I'll be home until three o'clock."

"Fine. I'll leave right away."

I did so. All I had to do was grab my hat and raincoat and go. But down in the lobby I was delayed. As I was heading for the front a voice called Mr. Thompson, and with my mind on my errand I nearly muffed it. Then I reined and turned and saw the clerk handing a bellboy a yellow envelope.

"Telegram for you, Mr. Thompson."

I crossed and got it and tore it open. It said, "CONFOUND IT DID YOU ARRIVE SAFELY OR NOT." I went out and climbed into a taxi and told the driver we were bound for Glendale but the first stop would be a drugstore. When he pulled up in front of one I went into a phone booth and sent a wire: "Arrived intact am on my way to appointment with subject."

During the thirty-minute drive to Glendale it rained approximately three-quarters of an inch. Whitecrest Avenue was so new it hadn't been paved yet, and Number 2819 was out almost at the end, with some giant sagebrush just beyond, hanging on the edge of a gully, only I suppose it wasn't sagebrush. There were two saggy palms and another sort of a tree in the front yard. The driver stopped at the edge of the road in front, with the right wheels in four inches of rushing water in the gutter, and announced, "Here we are."

"Yeah," I agreed, "but I'm not a Seabee. If you don't mind turning in?"

He muttered something, backed up for an approach, swung into the ruts of what was intended for a driveway, and came to a stop some twenty paces from the front door of the big pink box with maroon piping. Having already told him he wasn't expected to wait, I paid him, got out, and made a dive for the door, which was protected from the elements by an overhang about the size of a card table. As I pushed the button a three-by-six panel a little below the level of my eyes slid aside, leaving an opening through which a voice came.

"Mr. George Thompson?"

"That's me. Mrs. Potter?"

"Yes. I'm sorry, Mr. Thompson, but I phoned my husband what you said, and he said I shouldn't let a stranger in, you see it's so remote here, so if you'll just tell me what you want . . ."

Outside the raincoat the pouring rain was slanting in at me, amused at the card-table cover. Inside the raincoat there was almost as much dampness as outside, from sweat. I wouldn't have called the situation desperate, but it did need attention. I inquired, "Can you see me through that hole?"

"Oh, yes. That's what it's for."

"How do I look?"

There was a noise that could have been a giggle. "You look wet."

"I mean do I look depraved?"

"No. No, you really don't."

Actually I was pleased. I had come three thousand miles to pull a fast one on this Mrs. Potter, and if she had received me with open arms I would have had to swallow scruples. Now, being kept standing out in that cloudburst on a husband's orders, I felt no qualms.

"Look," I offered, "here's a suggestion. I'm a literary agent from New York, and this will take us at least twenty minutes and maybe more. Go to the phone and call up some friend, preferably nearby. Tell her to hold the wire, come and unlock the door, and run back to the phone. Tell the friend to hang on. I'll enter and sit across the room from you. If I make a move you'll have your friend right there on the phone. How will that do?"

"Well—we just moved here a month ago and my nearest friend is miles away."

"Okay. Have you got a kitchen stool?"

"A kitchen stool? Certainly."

"Go get it to sit on and we'll talk through the hole."

The noise that could have been a giggle was repeated. Then came the sound of a turned lock, and the door swung open.

"This is silly," she said defiantly. "Come on in."

I crossed the threshold and was in a small foyer. She stood holding the door, looking brave. I took my raincoat off. She closed the door, opened a closet door and got a hanger, draped the dripping coat on it, and hooked it on the corner of the closet door. I hung my hat on the same corner.

"In that way," she said, nodding to the right, and I turned a corner into a big room that was mostly glass on one side, with glass doors, closed, to the outdoors at the far end. At the other end was a phony fireplace with phony logs glowing. The red and white and yellow rugs were matched by the cushions on the wicker furniture, and a table with books and magazines had a glass top.

She invited me to sit, and I did so. She stood far enough off so that I would have had to make three good bounds to grab her, and it is only fair to say that it might have been worth the effort. She was three inches shorter, some years older, and at least ten pounds plumper than my ideal for grabbing, but with her dark twinkling eyes in her round little face she was by no means homely.

"If you're wet," she said, "move over by the fire."

"Thanks, this is all right. This ought to be a nice room when the sun's shining."

"Yes, we think we'll like it very much." She sat down on the edge of a chair with her feet drawn back, maintaining her distance. "Do you know why I let you in? Your ears. I go by ears. Did you know my brother Len?"

"No, I never met him." I crossed my legs and leaned back, as evidence that I wasn't gathered for a pounce. "I'm much obliged to my ears for getting me in out of the rain. I believe I told you I'm a literary agent, didn't I?"

"Yes."

"The reason I had to see you, I understand you were your brother's only heir. He left everything to you?"

"Yes." She moved back in her chair a little. "That's how we bought this place. It's all paid for, cash, no mortgage."

"That's fine. Or it will be when it stops raining and the sun comes out. The idea is this, Mrs. Potter, since you were the sole legatee under your brother's will everything he had belongs to you. And I'm interested in something that I think he had—no, don't be alarmed, it's nothing that you've already used. Possibly you've never even heard of it. When did you last see your brother?"

"Why, six years ago. I never saw him after nineteen forty-five, when I got married and came to California." She flushed a little. "I didn't go back when he died, to the funeral, because we couldn't afford it. I would have gone if I had known he had left me all that money and bonds, but I didn't know that until afterwards."

"Did you correspond? Did you get letters from him?"

She nodded. "We always wrote once a month, sometimes oftener."

"Did he ever mention that he had written a book, a novel? Or that he was writing one?"

"Why, no." Suddenly she frowned. "Wait a minute, now maybe he did." She hesitated. "You see, Len was always thinking he was going to do something important, but I don't think he ever told anyone but me. After Father and Mother died I was all he had, and I was younger than him. He didn't want me to get married, and for a while he didn't write, he didn't answer my letters, but then he did, and he wrote long letters, pages and pages. Why, did he write a book?"

"Have you kept his letters?"

"Yes, I—I kept them."

"Have you still got them?"

"Yes. But I think you ought to tell me what you want."

"So do I." I folded my arms and regarded her, her round little honest face. In out of the rain, I was feeling a qualm, and this was the moment when I had to decide whether to trick her or let her in on it—a vital point, which Wolfe had left to my own judgment after meeting her. I looked at her face, with the twinkle gone from her eyes, and decided. If it came out wrong I could kick myself back to New York instead of taking a plane.

"Listen, Mrs. Potter. Will you listen carefully, please?"

"Of course I will."

"Okay. This is what I was going to tell you. It's not what I *am* telling you, only what I *intended* to. I'm George Thompson, a literary agent. I have in my possession a copy of a manuscript of a novel entitled 'Put

Not Your Trust,' written by Baird Archer. But I have reason to believe that Baird Archer was a pen name used by your brother, that your brother wrote the novel—but I'm not sure about it. I also have reason to believe that I can sell the novel to one of the big movie companies for a good price, around fifty thousand dollars. You are your brother's sole heir. I want, with you, to go through the letters your brother wrote you, looking for evidence that he wrote or was writing the novel. Whether we find such evidence or not, I want to deposit the manuscript in the vault of a local bank for safekeeping, and I want you to write a letter to a certain law firm in New York, the firm your brother worked for. In the letter I want you to say that you have a copy of the manuscript of a novel written by your brother under the name of Baird Archer, giving the title of the novel, that an agent named Thompson thinks he can sell it to the movies for fifty thousand dollars, and that you want their legal advice in the matter because you don't know how such things should be done. I also want you to say that Thompson has read the manuscript but you have not. Get that?"

"But if you can sell it—" She was wide-eyed. It didn't alter my opinion of her. A prospect of fifty thousand unexpected bucks is enough to open eyes, no matter how honest they are. She added, "If it's my property I can just tell you to sell it, can't I?"

"You see," I reproached her, "you didn't listen."

"I did—too! I lis—"

"No. You did not. I warned you that that was only what I *intended* to tell you. There was some truth in it, but darned little. I do think that your brother wrote a novel of that title under the name of Baird Archer, and I would like to go through his letters to see if he mentioned it, but I have no copy of the manuscript, there is no prospect of selling it to the movies, I am not a literary agent, and my name is not George Thompson. Now, having—"

"Then it was all lies!"

"No. It would have—"

She was out of her chair. "Who are you? What's your name?"

"Have my ears changed any?" I demanded.

"What do you want?"

"I want you to listen. It wasn't a lie if I didn't say it, even if I intended to. Now here's what I do say, and it's the truth. You might as well sit down, because this is even longer."

She sat, but on about a third of the chair seat.

"My name," I said, "is Archie Goodwin. I'm a private detective, and I work for Nero Wolfe, also a private detec—"

"Nero Wolfe!"

"Right. It will please him to know that you had heard of him, and I'll be sure to tell him. He has been hired by a man named Wellman to find out who murdered his daughter. And another girl has been murdered, one named Rachel Abrams. Also, before that, your brother was murdered. We have reason to believe that the same person committed all three murders. It's a long and complicated reason, and I'll skip it. If you want the details later you can have them. I'll just say that our theory is that your brother was killed because he wrote that novel, Joan Wellman was killed because she had read it, and Rachel Abrams was killed because she had typed it."

"The novel—Len wrote?"

"Yes. Don't ask me what was in it, because we don't know. If we did, I wouldn't have had to come out here to see you. I came to get you to help us catch a man that murdered three people, and one of them was your brother."

"But I can't—" She gulped. "How can I help?"

"I'm telling you. I could have tricked you into helping. I've just proved it. You would have come along for a chance at fifty thousand dollars, you know darned well you would. You'd have let me go through your brother's letters for evidence, and whether we found it or not you'd have written the letter to the law firm. That's all I'm asking you to do, only now I'm giving it to you straight and asking you to do it not for a pile of dough but to help catch the man that killed your brother. If you would have done it for money, and you would, don't you think you ought to do it to bring a murderer to justice?"

She was frowning, concentrating. "But I don't see— You only want me to write a letter?"

"That's right. It's like this. We think your brother wrote that novel, and it was a vital element in the murders. We think that someone in that law office is involved and either committed the murders or knows who did. We think that someone is desperately determined that the contents of that manuscript shall not be known to any living person. If we're right, and you send the kind of letter I described, he'll have to move and move quick, and that's all we need, to start him moving. If we're wrong, your sending the letter will do nobody any harm."

She was keeping the frown. "What did you say you wanted me to say in the letter?"

I repeated it, with fuller detail. Toward the end she began slowly shaking her head. When I stopped she spoke.

"But that would be a lie—saying you have a copy of the manuscript when you haven't. I couldn't tell them a deliberate lie!"

"Maybe not," I said regretfully. "If you're the kind of person who

has never told a lie in all your life, I can't expect you to tell one just to
help find the man who killed your brother—and who also killed two
young women, ran a car over one of them and pushed the other one
out of a window. Even if it couldn't possibly hurt any innocent person,
I wouldn't want to urge you to tell your very first lie."

"You don't have to be sarcastic." Her face had turned a mild pink. "I
didn't say I never told a lie. I'm no angel. You're perfectly right, I would
have done it for the money, only then I wouldn't have known it was a
lie." Suddenly her eyes twinkled. "Why don't we start over and do it the
other way?"

I would have liked to give her a good hug. "Listen," I suggested,
"let's take things in order. We've got to go through his letters first anyhow, there's no objection to that, then we can decide on the next step.
You get the letters, huh?"

"I guess so." She arose. "They're in a box in the garage."

"Can I help?"

She said no, thanks, and left me. I got up and crossed to a window to
look out at the California climate. I would have thought it was beautiful if I had been a seal. It would be beautiful anyway if one of Dykes's
letters had what I was after. I wasn't asking for anything elaborate like
an outline of the plot; just one little sentence would do.

When she came back, sooner than I expected, she had two bundles
of white envelopes in her hands, tied with string. She put them down
on the glass-topped table, sat, and pulled the end of a bowknot.

I approached. "Start about a year ago. Say March of last year." I
pulled a chair up. "Here, give me some."

She shook her head. "I'll do it."

"You might miss it. It might be just a vague reference."

"I won't miss it. I couldn't let you read my brother's letters, Mr.
Thompson."

"Goodwin. Archie Goodwin."

"Excuse me. Mr. Goodwin." She was looking at postmarks.

Evidently she meant it, and I decided to table my motion, at least
temporarily. Meanwhile I could do a job. I got out my notebook and pen
and started writing at the top of a sheet:

Corrigan, Phelps, Kustin & Briggs
522 Madison Avenue
New York, N. Y.
Gentlemen:

      I am writing to ask your advice because my brother
worked for you for many years up to the time of his death. His

name was Leonard Dykes. I am his sister and in his will he left everything to me, but I suppose you know that.

A man named Walter Finch has just been to see me. He says he is a literary agent. He says that last year my brother wrote a novel.

I stopped to consider. Mrs. Potter was reading a letter, with her teeth clamped on her lower lip. Well, I thought, I can put it in, and it will be easy enough to take it out if we have to. I resumed with my pen:

I already knew that because my brother mentioned it once in a letter, but that was all I knew about it. Mr. Finch says he has a copy of the manuscript and its title is "Put Not Your Trust," and my brother put the name of Baird Archer on it as the author, but my brother really wrote it. He says he thinks that he can sell it to the movies for $50,000.00, and he says since my brother left everything to me I am the legal owner of it and he wants me to sign a paper that he is my agent and I will pay him 10 per cent of what he gets for it from the movies.

I am writing to you air mail because it is a big sum of money and I know you will give me good advice. I don't know any lawyer here that I know I can trust. I want to know if the 10 per cent is all right and should I sign the paper. Another thing I want to know is that I haven't seen the manuscript except just the envelope he has it in and he won't leave it with me, and it seems to me I ought to see it and read it if I am going to sell it because I ought to know what I am selling.

Please answer by air mail because Mr. Finch says it is urgent and we must act quick. Thanking you very much.

Sincerely yours,

It didn't come out that way all at once. I did a lot of crossing out and changing, and the preceding was the final result, of which I made a clear copy. I read it over and passed it. There was the one sentence that might have to come out, but I hoped to God it wouldn't.

My accomplice was reading steadily, and I had kept an eye on her progress. There were four envelopes in a little stack at her right, finished, and if she had started with March and he had written one a month, she was up to July. My fingers itched to reach for the next one. I sat and controlled them until she finished another one and began folding it for return to the envelope, and then got up to take a walk. She was reading so damn slow. I crossed to the glass doors at the far end of the room and looked out. In the rain a newly planted tree about twice my height was slanting to one side, and I decided to worry about that but couldn't get my mind on it. I got stubborn and determined that I damn well was going to worry about that tree, and was fighting it out when suddenly her voice came.

"I knew there was something! Here it is. Listen!"

I wheeled and strode. She read it out.

"Here is something just for you, Peggy dear. So many things have been just for you all my life. I wasn't going to tell even you about this, but now it's finished and I have to. I have written a novel! Its title is 'Put Not Your Trust.' For a certain reason it can't be published under my name and I have to use a nom de plume, but that won't matter much if you know, so I'm telling you. I have every confidence that it will be published, since I am by no means a duffer when it comes to using the English language. But this is strictly for you alone. You mustn't even tell your husband about it."

Mrs. Potter looked up at me, at her elbow. "There! I had forgotten that he mentioned the title, but I knew—no! What are you—"

She made a quick grab, but not quick enough. I had finally pounced. With my left hand I had snatched the letter from her fingers, and with my right the envelope from the table, and then backed off out of reach.

"Take it easy," I told her. "I'd go through fire for you and I've already gone through water, but this letter goes home with me. It's the only evidence on earth that your brother wrote that novel. I'd rather have this letter than one from Elizabeth Taylor begging me to let her hold my hand. If there's anything in it that you don't want read in a court-room that part won't be read, but I need it all, including the envelope. If I had to I would knock you down and walk on you to get out of here with it. You'd better take another look at my ears."

She was indignant. "You didn't have to grab it like that."

"Okay, I was impulsive and I apologize. I'll give it back, and you can hand it to me, with the understanding that if you refuse I'll take it by force."

Her eyes twinkled, and she knew it, and flushed a little. She extended a hand. I folded the letter, put it in the envelope, and handed it to her. She looked at it, glanced at me, held it out, and I took it.

"I'm doing this," she said gravely, "because I think my brother would want me to. Poor Len. You think he was killed because he wrote that novel?"

"Yes. Now I know it. It's up to you whether we get the guy that killed him." I got out my notebook, tore out a sheet, and handed it to her. "All you have to do is write that letter on your own paper. Maybe not quite all. I'll tell you the rest."

She started to read it. I sat down. She looked beautiful. The phony logs in the phony fireplace looked beautiful. Even the pouring rain—but no, I won't overdo it.

XV

I PHONED Wolfe at 3:23 from a booth in a drugstore somewhere in Glendale. It is always a pleasure to hear him say "Satisfactory" when I have reported on an errand. This time he did better. When I had given him all of it that he needed, including the letter written by Dykes that I had in my pocket and the one written by Mrs. Potter that I had just put an air-mail stamp on and dropped in the slot at the Glendale Post Office, there was a five-second silence and then an emphatic "Very satisfactory." After another five bucks' worth of discussion of plans for the future, covering contingencies as well as possible, I dove through the rain to my waiting taxi and gave the driver an address in downtown Los Angeles. It rained all the way. At an intersection we missed colliding with a truck by an eighth of an inch, and the driver apologized, saying he wasn't used to driving in the rain. I said he soon would be, and he resented it.

The office of the Southwest Agency was on the ninth floor of a dingy old building with elevators that groaned and creaked. It occupied half the floor. I had been there once before, years back, and, having phoned that morning from the hotel that I would probably be dropping in, I was more or less expected. In a corner room a guy named Ferdinand Dolman, with two chins, and fourteen long brown hairs deployed across a bald top, arose to shake hands and exclaim heartily, "Well, well! Nice to see you again! How's the old fatty?"

Few people know Nero Wolfe well enough to call him the old fatty, and this Dolman was not one of them, but it wasn't worth the trouble to try to teach him manners, so I skipped it. I exchanged words with him enough to make it sociable and then told him what I wanted.

"I've got just the man for you," he declared. "He happens to be here right now, just finished a very difficult job. This is a break for you, it really is." He picked up a phone and told it, "Send Gibson in."

In a minute the door opened and a man entered and approached. I gave him one look, and one was enough. He had a cauliflower ear, and his eyes were trying to penetrate a haze that was too thick for them.

Dolman started to speak, but I beat him to it. "No," I said emphatically, "not the type. Not a chance."

Gibson grinned. Dolman told him he could go, and he did so. When the door had closed behind him I got candid. "You've got a nerve, trotting in that self-made ape. If he just did a difficult job I'd hate to see who does your easy ones. I want a man who is educated or can talk like it, not too young and not too old, sharp and quick, able to take on a bushel of new facts and have them ready for use."

"Jesus." Dolman clasped his hands behind his head. "J. Edgar Hoover maybe?"

"I don't care what his name is, but if you haven't got one like that, say so, and I'll go shopping."

"Certainly we've got one. With over fifty men on the payroll? Certainly we've got one."

"Show him to me."

He finally did, I admit that, but not until after I had hung around for more than five hours and had interviewed a dozen prospects. I also admit I was being finicky, especially since there was a good chance that all he would ever do was collect his twenty a day and expenses, but after getting it set up as I had I didn't want to run a risk of having it bitched up by some little stumble. The one I picked was about my age, named Nathan Harris. His face was all bones and his fingers were all knuckles, and if I knew anything about eyes he would do. I didn't go by ears, like Peggy Potter.

I took him to my room at the Riviera. We ate in the room, and I kept him there, briefing him, until two in the morning. He was to go home and get some luggage and register at the South Seas Hotel under the name of Walter Finch, and get a room that met the specifications I gave him. I let him make notes all he wanted, with the understanding that he was to have it all in his head by the time it might be needed, which could be never. One decision I made was to tell him only what Walter Finch, the literary agent, might be expected to know, not to hold out on him but to keep from cluttering his mind, so when he left he had never heard the names of Joan Wellman or Rachel Abrams, or Corrigan, Phelps, Kustin and Briggs.

Going to bed, I opened the window three inches at the bottom, and in the morning there was a pool that reached to the edge of the rug. I got my wristwatch from the bed-stand and saw 9:20, which meant 12:20 in New York. At the Glendale Post Office they had told me that the letter would make a plane which would land at La Guardia at eight in the morning New York time, so it should be delivered at Madison

Avenue any time now, possibly right this minute as I stretched and yawned.

One of my worries was Mr. Clarence Potter. Mrs. Potter had assured me that her husband wouldn't try to interfere, whether he approved or not, but it tied a knot in me, especially with an empty stomach, to think of the damage he could do with a telegram to Corrigan, Phelps, Kustin and Briggs. It was too much for me. Before I even shut the window or went to the bathroom I called the Glendale number. Her voice answered.

"Good morning, Mrs. Potter. This is Archie Goodwin. I was just wondering—did you tell your husband about it?"

"Yes, of course. I told you I was going to."

"I know you did. How did he take it? Should I see him?"

"No, I don't think so. He doesn't quite understand it. I explained that you have no copy of the manuscript and there doesn't seem to be one anywhere, but he thinks we should try to find one and perhaps it can be sold to a movie studio. I told him we should wait for an answer to my letter, and he agreed. I'm sure he'll understand when he thinks it over."

"Of course he will. Now about Walter Finch. I've got him, and he's in his room at the South Seas. He's a little taller than average, and you'd probably guess him at thirty-five. He has a bony face, and bony hands with long fingers, and dark brown eyes that you might call black. He looks straight at you when he talks, and his voice is a medium baritone, you'd like it. Do you want to write that down?"

"I don't need to."

"Sure you've got it?"

"Yes."

"I believe you. I'll be in my room at the Riviera all day. Call me any time if anything happens."

"All right, I will."

There's a loyal little woman with twinkles, I thought, hanging up. She knows damn well she's married to a dumbbell, but by gum she'll never say so. I phoned down for breakfast and newspapers, washed and brushed my teeth, and ate in my pajamas. Then I called the South Seas Hotel and asked for Walter Finch. He was there in his room, 1216, and said he was getting along fine with his homework. I told him to stay put until further notice.

When I had showered and shaved and dressed, and finished with the newspapers and looked out at the rain some, I phoned down for magazines. I refused to let myself start listening for the phone to ring because it might be all day and night and into another day before there was a peep, and it wouldn't help to wear my nerves out. However, I did look at my watch fairly often, translating it into New York time, as I gave the magazines a play. Eleven-fifty meant two-fifty. Twelve-twenty-five meant three-twenty-five. Four minutes after one meant four minutes after four. One-forty-five meant a quarter to five, nearing the end of the office day. I tossed a magazine aside and went to a window to admire the rain again, then called room service and ordered lunch.

I was chewing a bite of albacore steak when the phone rang. To show how composed I was, I finished chewing and swallowing before I picked it up. It was Mrs. Potter.

"Mr. Goodwin! I just had a phone call! From Mr. Corrigan!"

I was glad I had finished swallowing. "Fine! What did he say?"

"He wanted to know all about Mr. Finch. I said just what you told me to." She was talking too fast, but I didn't interrupt. "He asked where the manuscript is, and I told him Mr. Finch has it. He asked if I had seen it or read it, and I said no. He told me not to sign any paper or agree to anything until he has seen me. He's taking a plane in New York and he'll get to Los Angeles at eight in the morning and he's coming right here to see me."

It was a funny thing. I was swallowing albacore, although I would have sworn that it was already down. It tasted good.

"Did he sound as if he suspected anything?"

"He did not! I did it perfectly!"

"I'm sure you did. If I was there I'd pat you on the head. I might even go further than that, so it's just as well I'm not there. Do you want me to come out and go over it again? What you'll say to him?"

"I don't think it's necessary. I remember everything."

"Okay. He'll want to get to Finch as soon as possible, but he may ask you a lot of questions. What do you say if he asks to see the letter from your brother in which he mentioned writing a novel?"

"I say I haven't got it. That I didn't keep it."

"Right. He'll probably get to your place around nine o'clock. What time does your husband leave?"

"Twenty minutes past seven."

"Well. It's a million to one that you'll be in no danger, even if he's a killer, since he knows you have never seen the manuscript, but we can't take a chance. I can't be there myself because I have to be in Finch's room before he gets there. Now listen. At eight in the morning a man will come and show you his credentials from the Southwest Agency, a detective agency. Hide him where he can hear what goes on, but be darned sure he's well hid. Keep him—"

"No, that's silly! Nothing's going to happen to me!"

"You bet it isn't. Three murders is enough for one manuscript. He'll be there, and you—"

"My husband can take the morning off and stay home."

"No. I'm sorry, but that's out. Your talk with Corrigan is going to be ticklish to handle, and we don't want anyone joining in, not even your husband. A man will come with credentials, and you'll let him in and hide him and keep him there until an hour after Corrigan has left. Either that or I come myself, and that would ball it up. What hotel is Finch at?"

"The South Seas."

"Describe him."

"He's rather tall, in his thirties, with a bony face and hands and dark eyes, and he looks straight at you when he talks."

"Right. For God's sake don't get careless and describe me. Remember it was Finch who came to see you—"

"Really, Mr. Goodwin! If you have no confidence in me!"

"I have. I sure have."

"Well, you'd better!"

"I had indeed better. I'll be out part of the afternoon. If you need me, leave word. Good luck, Mrs. Potter."

"Good luck to you too."

The albacore had cooled off some, but it was good, and I finished it. I felt wonderful. I called Finch at the South Seas and told him we had had a bite and had a fish on the hook, and it might be the big one, and I would drop in on him at eight in the morning. He said he was all set. I lifted the receiver to put in a call to New York, then replaced it. It was goofy to suppose there could be any risk in George Thompson's calling Nero Wolfe's number, but I'd rather be goofy than sorry. Taking my raincoat and hat, I went down to the lobby, out into the rain, and to a drugstore in the next block. There I made the call from a booth. When I got Wolfe and reported the development, he grunted across the continent, and that was all. He had no additional instructions or suggestions. I got the impression that I had interrupted him at something important like a crossword puzzle.

I only half drowned finding a taxi to take me to the address of the Southwest Agency. With Dolman I didn't have to be as choosy as the day before, since any mug should be able to keep a man from killing a woman right under his nose, but even so I didn't want any part of Gibson or one like him. He produced a fairly good specimen, and I gave him careful and fully detailed instructions and made him repeat them. From there I went to the South Seas Hotel for a surprise call on Finch, thinking it just as well to check him and also to have a look at the room. He was lying on the bed, reading a book entitled *Twilight of the Absolute,* which seemed a deep dive for a dick, but then, as Finch, he was a literary agent, so I refrained from comment. The room was perfect, of medium size, with the door to the bathroom in the far corner and one to a good big closet off to one side. I didn't stay long because my nerves were jumpy away from the phone in my room at the Riviera. If anything happened I wanted to know it quick. For instance, Clarence Potter would soon be home from work, or was already. What if he didn't understand it some more and decided to take a hand?

But at bedtime the phone hadn't let out a tinkle.

XVI

AT 8:02 Thursday morning I entered Finch's room at the South Seas. He was up and dressed but hadn't had breakfast, and I had only had orange juice before leaving the Riviera. Hanging my hat and raincoat, which had been sprinkled again, in the rear of the big closet, I gave him my order: griddle cakes, ham and eggs, a jar of honey, and coffee. He relayed it to room service, his own requirements being prunes and toast and coffee, which made me dart a glance at him, but he looked okay. When he was through I went to the phone and called the Glendale number and got an answer after four whirs.

"Archie Goodwin, Mrs. Potter. Good morning. Did the man come?"

"Yes, he got here ten minutes ago. He'll hide in the kitchen. You know I'm all excited?"

"Sure, that's all right. It won't matter if it shows; Corrigan will think it's the prospect of fifty thousand bucks. Just take it easy. Do you want to ask anything?"

"No, not a thing."

"Good for you. I'm in Finch's room at the South Seas. Ring me if you need to, and of course when he leaves."

She said she would. I hung up and called the airport. The plane from New York, due at eight o'clock, had landed at 7:50, ten minutes early.

The cuisine at the South Seas wasn't as good as the Riviera, but I cleaned up my share. When we had finished we wheeled the breakfast table into the hall and then had a discussion whether to make the bed. Harris, Finch to you, wanted to make it, but my point was that it would be unrealistic because no literary agent would have got up early enough to leave the room free for the chambermaid at that hour, and he had to concede it. He raised the question of whether I would stand in the closet or sit, and I said I would stand because no chair can be trusted not to squeak with a shift of weight. We had just got that settled when the phone rang. I was seated by it, but told Finch to take it and moved. He went and got it.

"Hello. . . . This is Walter Finch speaking. . . . Yes, I talked with Mrs. Potter. . . . That's right. . . . No, I didn't know she had written you, Mr. Corrigan, I only knew she had written for advice. . . . Yes, but may I speak to her, please?"

Pause.

"Yes, this is Finch, Mrs. Potter. Mr. Corrigan says he wants to see me, representing you about that manuscript. . . . Oh, I see. . . . Yes, I understand. . . . Certainly, I'll consult you before any agreement is made. . . . Please put him on."

Pause.

"Yes, I understand, Mr. Corrigan. . . . No, that's all right, I'm perfectly willing to discuss it. . . . Yes, if you come right away. I have an appointment at eleven. . . . Room Twelve-sixteen, the South Seas. . . . All right, I'll be here."

He hung up and turned to me with a grin. "Got a landing net?"

"No, a gaff. What was the hitch?"

"Nothing serious. He seemed to think he had a client, but she didn't agree. He's coming on his own, to protect the lowly, without prejudice to her."

"If you want me to," I offered, "I'll tell you what's wrong with our civilization."

"I want you to. What?"

"We've quit drinking champagne from ladies' slippers. I would like to drink some from hers."

I sat, bent and untied my laces and took off my shoes, took them to the closet, and put them on the floor out of the way. In my socks I hopped around on the spot where I would be standing, and heard no squeaks.

As I rejoined Finch the phone rang. He got it, spoke, covered the transmitter, and told me, "Mrs. Potter. She wants to know what color slippers you prefer."

I went and took it. "Yes, Mrs. Potter? Archie Goodwin."

"Why, he wasn't here more than ten minutes! He hardly asked me anything! He asked about Mr. Finch, and the letter from my brother, and then he wanted me to say he could represent me as my attorney, and I said what you told me to, but when he spoke to Mr. Finch he tried to make it that he was representing me. I was hoping he would ask more things, the things you said he might ask, but he didn't. There's really nothing to tell you, but I'm calling because I said I would."

"He's gone?"

"Yes, he had his taxi wait for him."

"Well, your part is probably finished, and you can let your bodyguard go if you want to. I was just telling Mr. Finch that I would like to drink champagne from your slipper."

"You what? What did you say?"

"You heard me. Too late. I'll let you know what happens, and you let me know if you hear from him again—immediately."

"I will."

I hung up and turned to Finch. "We've got about twenty minutes. What do you want refreshed?"

"Nothing. I've got it."

"I hope to God you have." I sat. "I could fill you in on Corrigan now, but I still think it's better not to. I'll say this, I am now offering three to one that he's a killer, and if so he's in a damn tight corner with his teeth showing. I don't see how he can possibly jump you under the circumstances, but if he does don't count on me. I won't leave that closet for anything short of murder. If he actually kills you, yell."

"Thanks." He grinned at me. But he slipped his hand inside his coat to his armpit, came out with a gun, and dropped it into his side pocket.

Finch had given Corrigan the room number, and he might phone up from the lobby and might not. Also there was no telling how fast his driver was, and it would be too bad if Corrigan arrived sooner than expected, came straight up to the room, paused at the door, and heard voices. So we stopped talking well ahead of time. I was leaning back, studying the ceiling, when the knock came, and it didn't sound like a chambermaid. I straightened up and left the chair in one motion, and Finch started for the door. Before he reached it I was in the closet, with the door pulled to enough to leave no crack, but unlatched.

The sound of the voice answered one question: it wasn't a ringer, it was the senior partner himself. I heard the door closing and the footsteps passing the closet door, and Finch inviting the visitor to take the armchair. Then Corrigan's voice.

"You understand why I'm here, Mr. Finch. My firm received a letter from Mrs. Potter requesting professional advice."

Finch: "Yes, I understand that."

Corrigan: "According to her, you state that you have in your possession a manuscript of a novel entitled 'Put Not Your Trust,' by Baird Archer, and that the author of it was her deceased brother, Leonard Dykes, who used 'Baird Archer' as a pen name."

I held my breath. Here, right off the bat, was one of the tricky little points I had briefed him on.

Finch: "That's not quite right. I didn't say that I know Dykes was the author. I said I have reason to think he was."

I breathed, not noisily.

Corrigan: "May I ask what reason?"

Finch: "A pretty good one. But frankly, Mr. Corrigan, I don't see why I should let you cross-examine me. You're not representing Mrs. Potter. You heard what she told me on the phone. Naturally I'll tell her anything she wants to know, but why you?"

Corrigan: "Well." A pause. "Other interests than Mrs. Potter's may be involved. I suppose you know that Dykes was an employee of my law firm?"

Finch: "Yes, I know that."

That was a fumble. He did not know that. I bit my lip.

Corrigan: "Just as you have reason to think that Dykes was the author, I have reason to think that other interests are involved. Perhaps we can take a short cut and save time. Let me see the manuscript. Let me go over it now, in your presence. That will settle it."

Finch: "I'm afraid I can't do that. I don't own it, you know."

Corrigan: "But you have it. How did you get it?"

Finch: "Properly and legitimately, in the course of my business as a literary agent."

Corrigan: "You're not listed in the New York phone book. Two agents who were asked have never heard of you."

Finch: "Then you shouldn't be wasting time on me. Really, Mr. Corrigan, this isn't Russia and you're not the MVD. Are you?"

Corrigan: "No. What harm could it possibly do anyone for you to let me look over that manuscript?"

Finch: "It's not a question of harm. It's ordinary business ethics. An agent doesn't show his clients' manuscripts to just anybody who would like to see them. Of course I'd gladly show it to you, in fact I'd be obliged to, if you were representing Mrs. Potter, whom I believe to be the owner of it. But as it is, nothing doing. That's final."

Corrigan: "In effect I *am* representing Mrs. Potter. She wrote my firm for advice. She has complete confidence in me. She refuses to engage me as her attorney only because she fears that a New York law firm would charge her a big fee. We wouldn't. We would charge her nothing."

Finch: "You should tell her that."

Corrigan: "I tried to. People here on the Coast, especially women of her class, have an ingrained suspicion of New Yorkers, you know that. It's a stupid prejudice, and Mrs. Potter is a stupid woman."

I thought to myself, Brother, you couldn't be wronger. He was going on. "You may wonder why I'm making so much of this little matter, flying out here, and I'll tell you. I said other interests may be involved, and I have good reason to think they are—important interests. I warn you now, for the record, that you may dangerously compromise both yourself and Mrs. Potter. On reliable information I believe that that manuscript is libelous. I believe that even in submitting it for sale you are risking severe penalties. I strongly advise you to get competent legal advice on it, and I assure you that I am qualified to give it. I offer it without charge, not through an impulse of benevolence, but to protect the interests I mentioned. Let me see that manuscript!"

Finch: "If I decide I need legal advice I know where to get it. I never saw you before. I've never heard of you. How do I know what or who you are?"

Corrigan: "You don't. Naturally." Sounds indicated that he was leaving his chair. "Here. This may satisfy you. Here are— What's the matter?"

More sounds. Finch: "I'm polite, that's all. When a visitor stands, I stand. Keep your credentials, Mr. Corrigan. I don't care how good they are. As far as I'm concerned you're a stranger trying to stick his nose into my business, and I'm not having any. Flying out here because you think a manuscript may be libelous—that sounds pretty damn fishy. You'll see no manuscript that's in my care. You'll have to—uuhie!"

That's the best I can do at spelling the sound he made. Other immediate sounds were not spellable at all, though fairly interpretable. One was surely a chair toppling. Another was feet moving heavily and swiftly. Others were grunts. Then came three in a row that were unmistakable: a fist or fists landing, and, right after, something that was heavier than a chair hitting the floor.

Finch: "Get up and try again."

A pause with sound effects.

Corrigan: "I lost my head."

Finch: "Not yet. You may next time. Going?"

That ended the dialogue. Corrigan had no exit line that he cared to use. The only sounds that came were footsteps and the opening and closing of the door, then more footsteps and another opening of the door, and, after a wait, its closing and the lock being turned. I stayed put until the closet door swung open without my touching it.

Finch stood grinning. "Well?" he demanded.

"You're on the honors list," I told him. "This is my lucky week, first Mrs. Potter and now you. Where did you plug him?"

"Two body jabs and one on the side of the neck."

"How did he invite it?"

"He swung first and then tried to lock me. That wasn't much, but the strain of that talk, with you listening— I'm hungry. I want some lunch."

"You won't get any, not now, unless it's a sandwich in a taxi. It's your move. He'll see that manuscript or bust, and one will get you ten he's on his way to Mrs. Potter, who he thinks is stupid. You will get there first, if you step on it, and stay there. The address is twenty-eight-nineteen Whitecrest Avenue, Glendale. I'll phone her. Get going!"

"But what—"

"Scoot, damn it! Write me a letter."

He moved. He got hat and raincoat from the closet and was gone. I uprighted the chair that had toppled, straightened a rug, went to the closet for my shoes, and put them on. Then I sat in the armchair by the phone and called the Glendale number.

"Mrs. Potter? Archie Goo—"

"Did he come?"

"He did. I hid in the closet while Finch talked with him. He would give his diploma from law school to see that manuscript. When he saw there was nothing doing he tried to lay Finch out and got knocked down. He left in a hurry, and I'm giving ten to one that he's on his way to you, so I sent Finch and I'm hoping he'll get there before Corrigan does. What—"

"Really, Mr. Goodwin, I'm not afraid!"

"Don't I know it. But Corrigan will bear down hard for you to name him your counsel, and it will take most of the pressure off if Finch is there. Anyway, I think you'll like Finch, he's not coarse and crude like me. You may have to give him some lunch. If you make Corrigan your attorney, no matter what he says, I'll come and throw rocks through your windows."

"That would be coarse and crude, wouldn't it? I honestly think you have no confidence in me at all."

"Little you know. If Corrigan gets there first, stall him until Finch comes, and don't forget Finch has been there before."

"I won't."

We hung up.

Going to a window and seeing with pleasure that it was raining only about half as hard as it had been, I opened it a good four inches to get some air. I raised the question whether to phone Wolfe and decided to await further developments. Having had no opportunity for a look at the morning papers, I phoned down for some, and, when they came, got comfortable. The papers were no damn good, except the sports pages, but I gave them enough of a play to make sure that nothing had happened which required my immediate attention and then picked up Finch's book, *Twilight of the Absolute,* and gave it a try. I got the impression that it probably made sense, but I ran across nothing that convinced me that I had been wrong in trying to get along without it.

The phone rang. It was Finch. He was calling from Mrs. Potter's. He began by reminding me that he had not accepted my offer of ten to one. I agreed. "I know you didn't. He came, did he?"

"Yes. I was in ahead by five minutes. He was surprised to see me and not delighted. He insisted on talking with Mrs. Potter alone, but I listened in from the kitchen with her knowledge and consent. He poured it on about the danger of libel and how it wouldn't cost her anything for him to read the manuscript and give her his professional advice, and the way he put it, it was hard for her to handle. She couldn't brush him off as a stranger, as I had. You should have heard her."

"I would have liked to. What was her line?"

"Simple. She said if there was libel in the manuscript she didn't want to know it and didn't want me to, because then it wouldn't be right to sell it to the movies, but if we just go ahead and sell it, it will be up to the movie people and surely they have good lawyers. He couldn't get it into her head that even so she would be responsible."

"I'll bet he couldn't. Kiss her for me."

"I wouldn't mind a bit. She is sitting here. Frankly, it was a waste of taxi fare to send me out here."

"No. Of course Corrigan has left?"

"Yes. He kept his taxi."

"He may be back. He came to get his hands on that manuscript and he intends to. If he does go back there's no telling what he'll try. Stick around. Stay until you hear from me."

"I think Mrs. Potter feels that her husband doesn't like the idea of men in the house while he's away, especially one at a time."

"He wouldn't, the bubblehead. You stay and do the housework for her. While you're at it, straighten up that tree that's just been planted in the back. It's crooked. I'll see that you get away before Bubblehead gets home."

He said I'd better.

I stretched out my legs, clasped my hands behind my head, and frowned at my toes. It seemed that a call to Wolfe was in order. As far as I could see it was Corrigan's move, but Wolfe might have something to suggest besides sitting on my prat waiting for it. On the other hand, I still had room within the framework of my instructions, and if I could think up one that would be worthy of Mrs. Potter I ought to do it. So I sat and invented bright ideas, but none that really shone, and was working away at the fourth or fifth when I became aware of a noise at the door. A key had been inserted and was being turned. As I was shaping the thought that chambermaids should be trained always to knock before entering a room, the door swung open, and there, facing me, was James A. Corrigan.

He saw me, of course, but I wasn't quick-witted enough to realize instantly that with the light from the window at my back he hadn't recognized me, so when he said something like, "Oh, I beg your pardon, the wrong room," I thought he was showing enough presence of mind for both of us, with some left over. But then he did recognize me and he goggled. Also he gaped.

I arose and spoke. "No, this is it. Come on in."

He stood, frozen.

"Shut the door and come on in," I insisted. "You might as well. I was expecting you. Did you think Finch would be fool enough to run off to Glendale and leave the manuscript here in a drawer unguarded?" He moved, and I added quickly, "If you dash off I won't chase you. I'll call downstairs, and if necessary I'll call the cops, and we'll not only find you but also find out how you got that key. I don't think it's breaking and entering, but by God it's something, and I'll hang it on you."

He hooked his elbow on the edge of the door and swung it. It didn't quite close, and he backed against it until it did. Then he walked on in and stopped at arm's length.

"So you followed me here," he stated. He was a little hoarse. With his jockey's physique and prizefighter's jaw and hungry eyes, he was certainly not imposing. The top of his head was a good inch below my eye level.

He repeated it, this time as a question. "You followed me here?"

I shook my head. "I can't think of a single question you could ask that I would feel like answering. Nor do I want to ask any, except maybe one: why don't you call Nero Wolfe and talk it over with him? Reverse the charge. There's a phone."

He sat down, not to be sociable. It was probably his knees.

"This is persecution," he said.

"Not in the statutes," I objected. "But what you just did is, getting a key to another man's hotel room, whether by bribery or just asking for it. Have you anything to say?"

"No."

"Absolutely nothing?"

"No."

"Are you going to call Mr. Wolfe?"

"No."

"Then I'll use the phone myself. Excuse me." I got the phone book, looked up a number, lifted the receiver, and asked for it. A female voice answered, and I gave my name and asked to speak to Mr. Dolman. In a moment he was on.

"Dolman? Archie Goodwin. I'm in Room Twelve-sixteen at the South Seas Hotel. A man named James A. Corrigan is here with me, but will soon be leaving, and I want him tailed right. Send me three good men at once, and have three more ready to take over as required. He'll prob—"

"What the hell, is he there hearing you?"

"Yes, so don't send Gibson. He'll probably be moving around, so they should have a car. Step on it, will you?"

I hung up, because I was through and also because Corrigan had already started to move around. He was heading for the door. I got to him, gripped a shoulder and hauled him back, and faced him.

He didn't lose his head. "This is assault," he stated.

"Persecution *and* assault," I agreed. "How can I prove you entered this room illegally if I let you leave it? Shall I get the house dick up here?"

He stood, breathing, his hungry eyes on me. I was between him and the door. He turned, went to a chair, and sat. I stayed on my feet.

"They can't get here in less than a quarter of an hour," I told him. "Why not say something?"

Not a word. His big jaw was clamped. I leaned against the closet door and contemplated him.

It was nearer half an hour than a quarter before there was a knock on the door. I went and opened it and invited them to enter, and they filed in past me, and I'll be damned if the third of the trio wasn't Gibson. He grinned at me as he went by. Leaving the door open, I detoured around them and took a look. One of them, a wiry little guy with a crooked nose, spoke.

"I'm Phil Buratti. I'm in charge."

"Good," I told him. "It's a straight tailing job." I jerked a thumb. "This is James A. Corrigan, a lawyer from New York. He'll be leaving any minute. Since he knows you, keep as close as you like. Report direct to me, here."

Buratti stared at me. "He's the subject?"

"Right. Don't lose him."

Gibson let out a guffaw that rattled the windows. Corrigan got up and marched. His direct route to the door was between the trio and me, and he took it. He went on out. The trio didn't move.

"Are you," I demanded, "waiting for the hounds?"

"Loony," Buratti said. "Come on, boys."

He led the way, and they followed.

I shut the door and went to the armchair and sat. Before I phoned Wolfe I wanted to make up my mind how thick I had been to sit there and let Corrigan walk in on me. I looked at my watch and saw 12:20, which meant 3:20 in New York. I decided that I had probably not been brilliant but there was no point in advertising it, and put in a call. The circuits were busy. Of course it was the worst time of day for it, with Los Angeles and Hollywood wanting to get New York before lunch and New York wanting to get the coast on returning from lunch. I sat, walked back and forth, and sat some more. Every ten or fifteen minutes the operator called to say the circuits were still busy. One o'clock came, and a quarter after. Finally my call got through, and I had Wolfe's voice.

I reported with details. I told him about Corrigan's visit with Mrs. Potter, his call on Finch at the hotel ending in a little mild violence, his second trip to Glendale, finding Finch there ahead of him, and Finch's phone call to me. I continued, "When Finch phoned me that Corrigan had left, licked, naturally I figured him to come back to the hotel to get into Finch's room to look for the manuscript. Covering the door of the room from the outside wasn't feasible, since he knew me. I decided to sit tight and welcome him if he came. He did so, with a key. His seeing me here jolted him, as expected. I invited him to talk, but he wanted to be alone, and nothing was said that would help you any. I phoned Dolman, and he sent two men and an ape with a sense of humor, and when Corrigan left, an hour and ten minutes ago, the three were on his tail. That's the status quo."

"There's a man with Mrs. Potter?"

"Yes, I thought I said so. Finch."

"Then there are no new instructions. Stay there."

"I would like to stick another pin in him."

"You have none to stick. How is the albacore?"

"Marvelous."

"It should be. Call me as necessary."

"Yes, sir."

He hung up. That shows that everything is relative. If I had admitted that Corrigan's walking in on me had been a surprise he might have made remarks. Going to the window for a look at the rain, I was reflecting on that point when the phone rang.

It was Buratti. "We're at the airport," he reported. "He came straight here. You said we could keep close, so I was standing right by him when he asked for a seat on the first plane to New York. The best he could do was the TWA that leaves at five o'clock, and he bought a ticket. He's in a phone booth now, making a call. Do we go to New York with him?"

"No, I guess not. I'd like to take Gibson along, but he's probably needed here. Get me a seat on the same plane and wait there for me. I have some errands to do, so don't get impatient. There's a faint chance he's pulling something, so keep an eye on him."

I hung up and then called the Glendale number. Apparently I wouldn't get to see Mrs. Potter again, but at least I could chat with her on the phone.

XVII

SOMEWHERE over New Mexico, or maybe Oklahoma, I decided it hadn't been too brainy to take the same plane as Corrigan. A later one would have done just as well. As it was, with me in Seat Five and him back of me in Fourteen, I would get no sleep. In such a situation logic is not enough. It certainly wouldn't have been logical for him to wander by in that crowded plane and jab a knife in me, especially as I had no briefcase or other receptacle big enough to hold the manuscript of a novel, but I wasn't going to sleep, and I didn't like his being at my rear. I had a notion to ask him to trade seats but voted it down.

It was a long and weary night.

At La Guardia Airport, where we landed in the morning on schedule, he was in a bigger hurry than me. He grabbed his bag and trotted out to a taxi. Before getting my suitcase I went to a booth and phoned Fritz to expect me for breakfast in thirty minutes and mix plenty of batter. As my taxi crossed Queensboro Bridge I saw the sun for the first time in four days.

Wolfe never came downstairs in the morning until after he finished in the plant rooms at eleven o'clock, but Fritz welcomed me home as if I had been gone a year. He met me at the front door, took my suitcase, hung up my hat and coat, escorted me to the kitchen, and put the griddle on. I was perched on a stool drinking orange juice when I heard the elevator, and a moment later Wolfe entered. He was actually breaking a rule. I thought it deserved some recognition and accepted his offer of a handshake. We made appropriate remarks. He sat. The kitchen is the only place on earth where he doesn't mind a chair that lets his fanny lap over the sides. I went to my seat at my breakfast table as Fritz flapped the first cake onto my hot plate.

"He looks skinny," Fritz told Wolfe. Fritz is convinced that without him we would both starve to death in a week.

Wolfe nodded in agreement and told me, "Two flowers are open on a *Cypripedium Minos*."

"Wonderful," I said with my mouth full. When the bite was down, "I assume you want a report. There's—"

"Eat your breakfast."

"I am. Unlike you, I don't mind business with meals. There's nothing but fill-in to add to what you already know, except that I came on the same plane as Corrigan, as arranged. At the airport he took his bag and scooted. I presume that with what you've collected here we're about ready to jump?"

He snorted. "Where? On whom?"

"I don't know."

"Neither do I. When Mr. Wellman first came to see me, eighteen days ago, I assumed that Dykes had written that novel, that he and the two women were killed on account of their knowledge of it, and that someone in that law office was involved. We have validated that assumption, and that's all. We know nothing new."

I swallowed food. "Then my trip to rainy California was a washout."

"By no means. All we could do was force him or them to become visible by movement. All we can do now is continue the process. We'll contrive it."

"Right after breakfast? I've had no sleep."

"We'll see. Movement once started is hard to stop." He glanced at the wall clock. "I'm late. We'll see. It is satisfactory to have you back." He got up and went.

I finished breakfast and looked through the morning paper and went to the office. I wouldn't have been surprised to see a stack of unopened mail, but apparently he had worked his head off during my absence. Bills and other items, out of their envelopes, were neatly arranged on my desk, and the exposed sheet of my desk calendar said March ninth, today. I was touched. I looked over things a little and then took my suitcase and mounted to my room. It was glad to see me back. When I'm up there I always turn the phone extension on, but that time I forgot to. I had unpacked and stripped and showered, and was using my electric shaver, when Fritz appeared at the bathroom door, panting.

"The phone," he said. "Mr. Corrigan wants to speak to Mr. Wolfe."

"Okay. I forgot to turn it on. I'll get it."

I went and flipped the switch and lifted the receiver. "This is Archie Goodwin."

I expected Mrs. Adams, but it was Corrigan himself. He said curtly that he wished to speak to Wolfe, and I told him Wolfe wouldn't be available until eleven. He said they wanted an appointment with him, and I asked who wanted it.

"I and my associates."

"Would eleven o'clock suit you? Or it could be eleven-thirty."

"We would prefer eleven o'clock. We'll be there."

Before I went to finish shaving I buzzed Wolfe on the house phone and told him, "Right you were. Movement once started is hard to stop. The law firm will be here at eleven."

"Ah," he said. "Contrivance may not be needed."

It was only ten-thirty, and I took my time completing my personal chores. I can dress fast, but I don't like to have to. When I went downstairs I was ready for anything, including a two-hour nap, but that would have to wait.

They were ten minutes late, so Wolfe was in the office when they arrived. Before any conversation got started I noticed an interesting little item. Off the end of Wolfe's desk, facing it, the big red leather chair is the most convenient spot for a visitor, and when there are two or more visitors that is obviously the seat for whoever has priority. When that group had been there before, Corrigan, the senior partner, had occupied it, but this time who should pop into it but the white-haired blinking Briggs, Helen Troy's Uncle Fred. Apparently no one remarked it but me, and that was equally interesting. As they sat, Emmett Phelps, the long-armed six-foot encyclopedia, was nearest me; Corrigan was next; then the sleepy-eyed slumpy Louis Kustin, successor to Conroy O'Malley as the firm's trial man; and then the disbarred O'Malley with a bitter twist to his mouth.

Wolfe's eyes went from left to right and back again. "Well, gentlemen?"

Three of them spoke at once.

"I can't converse with bedlam," Wolfe said testily.

Frederick Briggs, in the red leather chair, blinking, took the ball. "At our previous visit," he said slowly and distinctly, "I came with my associates under protest. On that occasion you were invited to question us. This time we have questions to ask you. You may remember that I characterized your methods as unethical and reprehensible, and you justified that criticism when you fabricated a notation on Dykes's letter of resignation, imitating the handwriting of one of us, and gave it to the police. What defense do you offer for that action?"

Wolfe's brows were up. "None, Mr. Briggs."

Briggs blinked furiously. "That is not acceptable. I insist—we insist —on an answer."

"Then I'll give you one." Wolfe was not aroused. "As you say, the notation was in Mr. Corrigan's hand. There are three possible explanations of how it was made. One, by Mr. Corrigan himself some time ago. Two, by me recently. Three, by any one of you, including Mr. Corrigan, either before or after I asked to see the letter. The letter was easily accessible, there in your office files. You, sir, can't possibly know which explanation is correct, unless you made the notation yourself. Questioned by the police, all of you have denied making it. I deny making it." Wolfe flipped a hand. "Surely you don't credit me with a monopoly in mendacity?"

"That's evasive. I insist—"

"Forget it, Fred," Kustin cut in irritably. His sleepy eyes were awake. "I told you, you won't get anywhere with that, and there's no jury to work on even if you knew how to do it. Get to the point."

"He won't." Phelps, the indifferent scholar, was irritated too. "Let Con do it."

O'Malley shook his head. His mouth kept its twist even when he spoke. "Thanks, Emmett, but I'm disbarred. You forget?"

"Go on, Fred," Corrigan told his junior—not in years.

"In my opinion," Briggs maintained, "we should demand an answer on that, but I defer under protest." He blinked at Wolfe. "To proceed. All five of us, including Mr. O'Malley, have a mutual and common interest, to protect the reputation and welfare of our firm. In that interest we are indissolubly joined. Your position, openly stated, has been that a major factor in the death of Leonard Dykes was the manuscript of a novel, presumably written by him under an assumed name; that the manuscript was also a major factor in the deaths of two women; and that one or more members of this firm have guilty knowledge of the manuscript and therefore, inferentially, of the deaths. Is that correct?"

Wolfe nodded. "It's badly put, but I'll pass it."

"Tell your man to take his notebook, and I'll restate it."

"Damn it, Fred," Kustin objected, "he accepted it. What more do you want? Get on."

Briggs blinked at him. "I want to proceed as agreed, without unnecessary interruptions." He went to Wolfe. "Very well, you accept it. Then the contents of that manuscript are a vital element in your investigation. Is that true?"

"Yes."

"And therefore the contents of the manuscript are of vital importance to us, the members of the firm, and Mr. O'Malley. Is that true?"

"Yes."

"And therefore, if we were presented with an opportunity to learn the contents of the manuscript it would be natural and proper for us to make every effort to take advantage of it. Is that true?"

Wolfe rubbed his nose. "I don't want to quibble, but though it would indeed be natural, its propriety might be questioned. If to protect legitimate interests, yes. If to shield a criminal, no."

"There is no question of shielding a criminal."

Wolfe shrugged. "If that is stipulated, what you said is true."

"Very well. It was in furtherance of that effort that Mr. Corrigan went to California. It is in furtherance of that effort that we are here now. We don't know how you managed to anticipate Mr. Corrigan's effort, but you did. Your man not only got there but got inside of him. Since he succeeded in preventing Mr. Corrigan from seeing the manuscript, it may fairly be assumed that he himself did see it, and that therefore you and he are now acquainted with its contents. It was you who involved our firm in this affair. It was you who persuaded the police that we were involved. It was you who forged a notation on a letter we sent you—"

"Withdraw that," Wolfe snapped.

"That won't help, Fred," O'Malley advised him. "Don't drag it in."

Briggs blinked at him and then at Wolfe. "On consideration I withdraw that remark pro tempore, without prejudice. But that doesn't affect my conclusion, that our demand is justified, to be told the substance of that manuscript. You involved us. We demand that you warrant that involvement."

Briggs blinked around. "Well?" he challenged. "Is that clear and cogent?"

They agreed that it was.

Wolfe grunted. "Clear enough," he assented, "but it took you long enough to say it. You gentlemen are making an extraordinary pother, coming here in a body like this. Why the devil didn't one of you merely phone me and ask me to tell you what's in that manuscript? It would have taken you five seconds to ask it and me two seconds to answer it."

"What would you have answered?" Kustin demanded.

"That I'm not quite ready."

"Not quite ready for what?"

"To act."

To appreciate the full effect of those two little words you would have had to hear Wolfe pronounce them. He didn't snarl them or snap them, his voice kept its normal pitch, but if anyone present had anything to fear the full menace of it was in those two calm, precise syllables. They looked at one another.

Briggs asked indignantly, "Do you mean you refuse to tell us anything about it?"

Wolfe nodded. "At the moment, yes. I'm not quite ready. As practicing attorneys, you gentlemen know that the potency of knowledge depends on how and when it is used. I went to some trouble to get this and I intend to get full value from it."

Emmett Phelps stood up. "I told you fellows, didn't I? We're wasting time on him."

"Mr. Phelps is bored," Wolfe said dryly.

"Buy it from him," O'Malley suggested. "Make him an offer. It can be deducted as a legitimate expense, can't it, Emmett?" He left his chair. "Only don't expect me to contribute. I'm broke."

Wolfe spoke up. "I would like to anticipate any future charge of willful malevolence. I take no pleasure in prolonging suspense, either my own or another's. I'm being completely candid when I say that I still need a fact or two before I can act. To move not fully prepared, to disclose myself prematurely, would be folly, and I'm not a fool."

Kustin got to his feet, stepped to the desk, put his hands on it, and leaned forward at Wolfe. "I'll tell you what I think: I think it's a ten-cent bluff. I don't think you know any more about that manuscript than we do. I think you're exactly where you were when we came here a week ago yesterday." He straightened up. "Come on, fellows. He's a goddam fourflusher." He whirled to me. "You too, Goodwin. I wish I'd gone to California instead of Jim Corrigan. You'd have been called."

He marched out. Phelps and O'Malley were at his heels. Corrigan, who had said practically nothing, thought he would speak now, took a step toward the desk, but changed his mind and, with a glance at me, headed for the door. Briggs lifted himself out of the red leather chair, blinked at Wolfe, said, "My appraisal of your methods and tactics has certainly been reinforced here today," and turned and went.

I moseyed to the door to the hall, stood on the sill, and watched them wriggling into their coats. I was perfectly willing to go and let them out, but Phelps got the door open before I moved, and held it for them, so I was saved the trouble. He banged it hard enough to leave no doubt of its closing, and I wheeled, returned to my desk, and permitted myself an all-out yawn. Wolfe was leaning back with his eyes shut.

"Will there be more movement?" I inquired. "Or is it time for a contrivance?"

No reply. I yawned again. "Once in a while," I observed, "you go right to the heart of things and tell a plain unvarnished truth. Like when you said that you still need a fact or two before you can act. It might be objected that you need more than one or two, but that isn't so. The one fact that Phelps, the scholar, is a lover of literature and bumped them off because it was a lousy novel and he couldn't bear it, would do the trick."

No word or sign. Suddenly I blew up. I sprang to my feet and roared, "Goddammit, go to work! Think of something! Do something!"

Without opening his eyes, he muttered, "And I said it was satisfactory to have you back."

XVIII

THAT was an afternoon I wouldn't care to live through again, not even if I knew what the evening was going to bring. To begin with, Wolfe was totally unbearable. After lunch he got behind his desk with a book, and after a dozen assorted attempts to get a conversation started I quit. Then Saul Panzer phoned in, and he growled at me to get off the line. I had already suspected that he had Saul on a trail, since a check of the cash box and book had informed me that he had given Saul three hundred bucks, and that confirmed it. I always resent it when he sees fit to give one of the boys a chore that he thinks I don't need to know about, and that time it was more offensive than usual, since I couldn't very well blab anything, sitting there on my tail, yawning.

Worse than him, though, was me. He had told me twice to take a nap, so naturally I wasn't going to. I wanted to be there if the phone rang. I wanted to be there if Mrs. Adams came to confess to the three murders. But I did not want to make out checks or work on the germination records or go through catalogues. My problem was to stay awake without having anything to keep my eyes open, and it was even tougher after Wolfe went up to the plant rooms at four o'clock. For two solid hours only one notion occurred to me that had any attraction at all, to phone Mrs. Potter in Glendale and tell her I had got home safely, and I vetoed that because it might prove to be habit-forming. But by gum I stayed awake, if you can call it that.

There was another call from Saul just before dinner, and again I was told to get off the line. Wolfe's end of the chat was nothing but grunts. After dinner he told me to go to bed, and God knows I would have liked to, but I got stubborn and went for a walk instead. I dropped in at a movie, found myself getting fascinated with the idea of resting my head on the soft fat female shoulder next to me, jerked away, and got up and went home. It was a little after ten.

Wolfe was at his desk, going through the stack of germination slips that had accumulated while I was away. I asked him, "Any more movement?"

"No."

I gave up. "I might as well go up and lie down a while." I went and twirled the knob of the safe. "I put the bolt on in front and I'll check the back. Good night."

"Good night."

The phone rang. I stepped to my desk and got it.

"Nero Wolfe's residence, Archie Goodwin speaking."

"I want to speak to Wolfe."

"Who is it please?"

"James A. Corrigan."

I covered the transmitter and told Wolfe, "Corrigan. He sounds hoarse and harassed. Do you care to speak to him?"

Wolfe took his instrument, and I put mine back at my ear.

"This is Nero Wolfe. Mr. Corrigan?"

"Yes. I've mailed you a letter, but you're responsible for this, so I think you ought to hear it. I hope you'll hear it in your dreams the rest of your life. This is it. Are you listening?"

"Yes, but—"

"Here it goes."

It busted my eardrum, or felt like it. It was a combination of a roar and a smack. By reflex my wrist moved the receiver away, then I moved it back. There was a confused clatter and a sort of thump, then nothing. I told the transmitter, "Hello, hello!"

Nothing. I cradled it and turned. Wolfe was sitting with the instrument dangling from his hand, scowling at me.

"Well?" he demanded.

"Well yourself. How do I know? I suppose he shot himself."

"Where was he?"

I sneered. "Do you think I staged it?"

"There was a radio going."

"I heard it. 'The Life of Riley.' WNBC."

He replaced the phone, slow motion, and regarded me. "This is preposterous. I don't believe it. Get Mr. Cramer."

I swiveled and dialed and got a voice. I asked for Cramer, and he wasn't there. Neither was Stebbins. I got a sergeant named Auerbach, informed Wolfe, and he took it.

"Mr. Auerbach? This is Nero Wolfe. Are you familiar with the Dykes-Wellman-Abrams case?"

"Yes."

"And with the name James A. Corrigan?"

"Yes, I know the name."

"I just had a phone call. The voice said it was James A. Corrigan, but it was husky and agitated and I can't vouch for it. It said—I think you should put this down. Have you pencil and paper?"

"In a second—okay, shoot."

"He said it was Corrigan, and then, quote, 'You're responsible for this, so I think you ought to hear it. I hope you'll hear it in your dreams the rest of your life. This is it. Are you listening? Here it goes.' Unquote. There came immediately the sound of an explosion, resembling a gunshot, and other confused noises, followed by silence except for the sound of a radio, which had been audible throughout. That's all."

"Did he say where he was phoning from?"

"I've told you all I know. As I said, that's all."

"Where are you now?"

"At my home."

"You'll be there if we want you?"

"Yes."

"Okay." He hung up. So did Wolfe. So did I.

"So your memory's failing," I observed. "You forgot that he said he had mailed you a letter."

"I like to see my mail first, without interference. Where does Mr. Corrigan live?"

I got the Manhattan phone book, turned the pages, and found it. Then, to check, I went and unlocked the filing cabinet, got out the Wellman folder, and fingered through the papers. I announced, "Corrigan lives at one-forty-five East Thirty-sixth Street. Phelps lives at three-seventeen Central Park West. Kustin lives at nine-sixty-six Park Avenue. Briggs lives at Larchmont. O'Malley lives at two-oh-two East Eighty-eighth."

I put the folder back and locked the cabinet. "Am I going to bed now?"

"No."

"I thought not. What, sit here and wait? Even if they find a corpse they might not get around to us until morning. It would take a taxi five minutes to go crosstown to Thirty-sixth and Lexington. The fare would be fifty cents including tip. If it's a blank I can walk home. Do I go?"

"Yes."

I went to the hall for my hat and coat, let myself out, and walked a block north. At Tenth Avenue I flagged a passing taxi, got in, and gave the driver the address.

A radio car was double-parked in front of 145 East Thirty-sixth, with no one in it. I entered the building. On the list of names on the wall of the vestibule, Corrigan was at the top, fifth. I went on in. It was an old private dwelling done over into apartments, with a self-service elevator. The elevator was there at that floor. From somewhere below came a faint sound of voices, but there was no one in sight. I opened the elevator door, entered, pushed the 5 button, and was lifted. When it stopped I emerged. There was only one door, at the right of the small hall, and standing at it was a cop.

"Who are you?" he asked, not sociably.

"Archie Goodwin. I work for Nero Wolfe."

"What do you want?"

"I want to go to bed. Before I can do so I have to find out if we got imposed on. We reported this. The guy that lives here, so he said, phoned us and told us to listen, and then a gun went off or a good imitation of one. He didn't hang up but he was gone, and we phoned Homicide. We don't know if the phone call was from here, and I came to see."

"Why Homicide?"

"This might be connected with a case they're on. We have friends there—sometimes friends, sometimes enemies, you know how it is. Is your colleague inside?"

"No. The door's locked. He went down for the superintendent. What did the guy say on the phone?"

"He just said we ought to hear something and told us to listen, and bang. May I put my ear to the door?"

"What for?"

"To listen to the radio."

"Yeah, I've heard of you. Full of gags. Should I laugh?"

"No gags tonight, I'm too sleepy. We heard the radio on the phone, and I thought I'd check. If you don't mind?"

"Don't touch the door or the knob."

"I won't."

He stepped aside, and I got my ear close to the angle of the door and the jamb. Ten seconds was enough. As I listened there was another sound in the hall, the elevator starting down.

I moved away. "Right. Bill Stern. WNBC."

"It was Bill Stern on the phone?"

"No, but it was WNBC. 'The Life of Riley.' Bill Stern goes on at ten-thirty."

"The Yankees look good, don't they?"

I'm a Giant fan, but I wanted to get inside and had to be tactful. So I said, "They sure do. I hope Mantle comes through."

He did too, but he was skeptical. He thought these wonder boys seldom live up to their billing. He thought various other things, and was telling about them when the elevator returned and its door opened, and we had company. One was his colleague and the other was a little runt with very few teeth and a limp, wearing an old overcoat for a dressing gown. The cop, surprised at sight of me, asked his brother, "Who's this, not precinct?"

"No. Nero Wolfe's Archie Goodwin."

"Oh, him. How come?"

"Save it. Hey, get away from that door! Gimme that key!"

The runt surrendered it and backed off. The cop in command inserted the key and turned it, used his handkerchief to turn the knob, which made me suppress a snicker, pushed the door, and entered, with his colleague at his heels. I was right behind. We were in a narrow hall with a door at either end and one in the middle. The one at the right was open, and the cop headed for that and on through. Two steps inside he stopped, so I just made the sill.

It was a fairly big living room, furnished comfortably by a man for a man. That was merely the verdict of one sweeping glance, for any real survey of the furniture, if required, would have to wait. On a table at the far side, between two windows, was the phone, with the receiver off, lying on the floor. Also on the floor, six inches from the receiver, was the head of James A. Corrigan, with the rest of him stretched out toward a window. A third item on the floor, a couple of feet from Corrigan's hip, was a gun—from where I stood I would have said a Marley .32. The lights were on. Also on was a radio at the end of the table, with Bill Stern telling what he thought of the basketball stink. There was a big dark spot, nearly black at that distance, on Corrigan's right temple.

The cop crossed to him and squatted. In ten seconds, which wasn't long enough, he got upright and spoke. "DOA." There seemed to be a little shake in his voice, and he raised it. "We can't use this phone. Go down and call in. Don't break your neck."

The colleague went. The cop kept his voice up. "Can you see him from there, Goodwin? Come closer, but keep your hands off."

I approached. "That's him. The guy that phoned. James A. Corrigan."

"Then you heard him shoot himself."

"I guess I did." I put one hand on my belly and the other on my throat. "I didn't get any sleep last night and I'm feeling sick. I'm going to the bathroom."

"Don't touch anything."

"I won't."

I wouldn't have been able to get away with it if the radio hadn't been going. It was plenty loud enough to cover my toe steps through the outer door, which was standing open, and in the hall to the door to the stairs. Descending the four flights, I listened a moment behind the door to the ground-floor hall, heard nothing, opened it, and passed through. The runt was standing by the elevator door, looking scared. He said nothing, and neither did I, as I crossed to the entrance. Outside I turned right, walked the half a short block to Lexington Avenue and stopped a taxi, and in seven minutes was climbing out in front of Wolfe's house.

When I entered the office I had to grin. Wolfe's current book was lying on his desk, and he was fussing with the germination slips. It was comical. He had been reading the book, and, when the sound came of me opening the front door, he had hastily ditched the book and got busy with the germination slips, just to show me how difficult things were for him because I hadn't made the entries from the slips on the permanent record cards. It was so childish I couldn't help grinning.

"May I interrupt?" I asked politely.

He looked up. "Since you're back so soon I assume you found nothing of interest."

"Sometimes you assume wrong. I'm back so soon because a flock of scientists would be coming and I might have been kept all night. I saw Corrigan. Dead. Bullet through his temple."

He let the slips in his hand drop to the desk. "Please report."

I did so, in full, including even the cop's thoughts about the Yankees. Wolfe was scowling some when I started and a lot more by the time I finished. He asked a few questions, sat a while tapping with a forefinger on the arm of his chair, and suddenly blurted at me, "Was the man a nincompoop?"

"Who, the cop?"

"No. Mr. Corrigan."

I lifted my shoulders and dropped them. "In California he wasn't exactly brilliant, but I wouldn't say a nincompoop. Why?"

"It's absurd. Totally. If you had stayed there you might have got something that would give some light."

"If I had stayed there I would have been corralled in a corner for an hour or so until someone decided to start in on me."

He nodded grudgingly. "I suppose so." He looked up at the clock and put his thumbs at the edge of his desk to shove his chair back. "Confound it. An exasperating piece of nonsense to go to bed on."

"Yeah. Especially knowing that around midnight or later we'll get either a ring or a personal appearance."

But we didn't. I slept like a log for nine hours.

XIX

SATURDAY morning I never did finish the newspaper accounts of the violent death of James A. Corrigan, the prominent attorney. Phone calls interrupted my breakfast four times. One was from Lon Cohen of the *Gazette,* wanting an interview with Wolfe about the call he had got from Corrigan, and two were from other journalists, wanting the same. I stalled them. The fourth was from Mrs. Abrams. She had read the morning paper and wanted to know if the Mr. Corrigan who had shot himself was the man who had killed her Rachel, though she didn't put it as direct as that. I stalled her too.

My prolonged breakfast was ruining Fritz's schedule, so when the morning mail came I took my second cup of coffee to the office. I flipped through the envelopes, tossed all but one on my desk, glanced at the clock and saw 8:55. Wolfe invariably started for the plant rooms at nine sharp. I went and ran up the flight of stairs to his room and knocked, entered without waiting for an invitation, and announced, "Here it is. The firm's envelope. Postmarked Grand Central Station yesterday, twelve midnight. It's fat."

"Open it." He was standing, dressed, ready to leave.

I did so and removed the contents. "Typewritten, single-spaced, dated yesterday, headed at the top 'To Nero Wolfe.' Nine pages. Unsigned."

"Read it."

"Aloud?"

"No. It's nine o'clock. You can ring me or come up if necessary."

"Nuts. This is just swagger."

"It is not. A schedule broken at will becomes a mere procession of vagaries." He strode from the room.

My eye went to the opening sentence.

I have decided to write this but not sign it. I think I want to write it mainly for its cathartic value, but my motives are confused. The events of the past year have made me unsure about everything. It may be that deep in me much is left of the deep regard for truth and justice that I acquired in my youth, through both religious and secular teaching, and that accounts for my feeling that I must write this. Whatever the motive—

The phone rang downstairs. Wolfe's extension wasn't on, so I had to go down to get it. It was Sergeant Purley Stebbins. Purley would always just as soon talk to me as Wolfe, and maybe rather. He's not dumb by any means, and he has never forgotten the prize boner that Wolfe bluffed him into on the Longren case.

He was brusque but not thorny. He said they wanted to know first-hand about two things, Corrigan's phone call the night before, and my performance in California, especially my contacts with Corrigan. When I told him I would be glad to oblige and come down, he said that wouldn't be necessary because Inspector Cramer wanted to see Wolfe and would drop in at eleven or shortly after. I said that as far as I knew we would let him in, and Purley hung up without saying good-by.

I sat at my desk and read:

Whatever the motive may be, I am going to write it and then decide whether to mail it or destroy it.

Even if I mail it I will not sign it because I do not want to give it legal validity. You will of course show it to the police, but without my signature it will certainly not be released for publication as coming from me. Since the context will clearly identify me by inference, this may seem pointless, but it will serve all desired purposes, whatever my motive may be, without my signature, and those purposes are moral and not legal.

I will try not to dwell at length on my motives. To me they are of more concern than the events themselves, but to you and others it is the events that matter. All you will care about is the factual statement that I wrote the anonymous letter to the court giving information about O'Malley's bribery of a juror, but I want to add that my motive was mixed. I will not deny that moving up to the position of senior partner, with increased power and authority and income, was a factor, but so was my concern for the future of the firm. To have as our senior partner a man who was capable of jury-bribing was not only undesirable but extremely dangerous. You will ask why I didn't merely confront O'Malley with it and demand that he get out. On account of the source and nature of my information, which I won't go into, I did not have conclusive proof, and the relations among the members of the firm would have made the outcome doubtful. Anyway, I did write the informing letter to the court.

Starting a habit, I said to myself, of not signing things. I resumed.

O'Malley was disbarred. That was of course a blow to the firm, but not a fatal one. I became senior partner, and Kustin and Briggs were admitted to membership. As the months passed we recovered lost ground. In the late summer and fall of last year our income was higher than it had ever been, partly on account of Kustin's remarkable performances as a trial lawyer, but I think my leadership was equally responsible. Then, on Monday, December 4, a date I would never forget if I were going to be alive to remember and forget, I returned to the office in the evening to do some work and had occasion to go to Dykes's desk to get a document. It wasn't where I expected to find it and I went through the drawers. In one of them was a brown fiber portfolio and I looked inside. The document wasn't there. It contained a stack of neatly assembled sheets of paper. The top sheet, typed like a title page, said "Put Not Your Trust, A Modern Novel of a Lawyer's Frailty, by Baird Archer." Through curiosity I looked at the next sheet. It began the text, and the first sentence read "It is not true that all lawyers are cutthroats." I read on a little and then sat in Dykes's chair and read more.

It is still almost incredible to me that Dykes could have been such a fool. Through his connection with our office he knew something of the libel law, and yet he wrote that and offered it for publication. Of course it is true that lawyers themselves will do incredible things when their vanity is involved, as O'Malley did when he bribed a juror, and Dykes probably thought that the use of an assumed name would somehow protect him.

The novel was substantially an account of the activities and relationships of our firm. The names were different and most of the scenes and circumstances were invented, but it was unmistakably our firm. It was so badly written that I suppose it would have bored a casual reader, but it did not bore me. It told of O'Malley's bribery of a juror (I use our names instead of those Dykes used) and of my learning of it and sending an anonymous letter to the court, and of O'Malley's disbarment. He had invented an ending. In the novel O'Malley took to drink and died in the alcoholic ward at Bellevue, and I went to see him on his deathbed, and he pointed at me and screamed, "Put not your trust!" In one way the novel was ludicrous. Its ending assumed that O'Malley knew I had informed on him, but there was no adequate explanation of how he had found out.

I took the manuscript home with me. If I had found it by accident and read it, someone else might, and I couldn't risk it. After I got home I realized that I would be unable to sleep, and I went out again and took a taxi to Sullivan Street, where Dykes lived. I got him out of bed and told him I had found the manuscript and read it. In my agitation I did something incredible too. I took it for granted that he knew I had informed on O'Malley and asked how he had found out. I should have assumed that he had invented that.

But it didn't matter. He really had found out. I had not written the informing letter to the court on my typewriter here at my apartment, on which I am writing this. I had taken the precaution of writing it on a machine at the Travelers Club. There wasn't more than one chance in a billion of any risk in that, but that one had been enough. In connection with our defense of O'Malley on the bribery charge, we had photostats of all the exhibits, including the anonymous letter to the court. Dykes had made himself a fairly good expert on documents, and as a matter of routine he inspected the photostat of the anonymous letter. He noticed that the "t" was out of line, crowding the letter to its right, and slanted a little, and he remembered that he had observed that same defect in some other document. And he found it. He found it in a typed memorandum to him which I had typed two months previously on that same machine at the Travelers Club. I had forgotten about it, and even if I had remembered it I would probably have considered the risk negligible. But with that hint to start him, Dykes had compared the photostat with the memorandum under a glass and established that the two had been typed on the same machine. Of course that was not conclusive proof that I had typed and sent the letter to the court, but it convinced Dykes.

It bowled him over that I had found and read the manuscript. He swore that he had had no intention or desire to expose me, and when I insisted that he must have told someone, possibly O'Malley himself, he swore that he hadn't, and I believed him. He had the carbon of the manuscript there in his room. The original had been returned to him by a firm of publishers, Scholl & Hanna, to whom he had submitted it, and he had put it temporarily in his desk at the office, with the intention of putting it in the hands of a literary agent. The longhand manuscript, written by him in longhand, from which the typist had worked, was also there in his room. He turned both the carbon copy and the longhand script over to me, and I took them home when I went and destroyed them. I also destroyed the original of the typed script two days later, after I had reread it.

I felt that I was fairly safe from exposure. I had of course done nothing actionable, but if it became known that I had informed on my partner in an anonymous letter the effect on my career and reputation would have been disastrous. It was not so much anything O'Malley himself could or might do as the attitude of others, particularly two of my present partners and certain other associates. Actually I would have been a ruined man. But I felt fairly safe. If Dykes was telling the truth, and I believed he was, all copies of the manuscript had been destroyed. He gave me the most solemn assurances that he would never speak of the matter to anyone, but my chief reliance was in the fact that it was to his own self-interest to keep silent. His own future depended on the future welfare of the firm, and if he spoke the firm would certainly be disrupted.

I saw Dykes several times at his room in the evening, and on one of those occasions I did a foolish and thoughtless thing, though at the time it seemed of no consequence. No, that's wrong—this occasion was not at his room but at the office after hours. I had taken from the file the letter of resignation which he had written months previously, and it was on my desk. I asked him, for no special reason that I remember, if the title "Put Not Your Trust" was from Shakespeare, and he said no, that it was in the 3rd verse of the 146th Psalm, and I scribbled it in a corner of his letter of resignation, "Ps 146-3."

The phone was ringing, but I finished the paragraph before I answered it. It was Louis Kustin. He didn't sound as if his eyes were looking sleepy. He wanted to speak to Wolfe, and I told him he wouldn't be available until eleven o'clock.

"I suppose he's available to you?" he asked curtly.

"Sure, I live here."

"My associates and I are conferring, and I am speaking on their behalf as well as my own. I'm at my office. Tell Wolfe I want to speak to him as soon as possible. Tell him that the suicide of our senior partner is an irreparable blow to us, and if it can be established that Wolfe willfully and maliciously drove him to it he will be held accountable. Tell him that?"

"It'll ruin the day for him."

"I hope to ruin all his days."

The connection went. I wanted to resume my reading but thought

I'd better pass it on and buzzed the plant rooms on the house phone. Wolfe answered. I reported the conversation.

"Pfui," he said shortly and hung up. I went back to Corrigan.

I felt that I was fairly safe, though I was not completely easy. Toward the end of December I was shocked into a realization of my true position. Dykes came into my office, during office hours, and asked for a raise in pay of 50 per cent. He said that he had expected to make a considerable sum from the sale of his novel, and now that he had surrendered that source of income he would have to have a substantial raise. I saw at once what I should have seen clearly before, that I would be at his mercy for years if not for life, and that his demands would be limited only by his desires. I was literally in a panic but concealed it successfully. I told him that I had to consider the problem of justifying so large a raise to my associates, and asked him to come to my apartment the following evening, Saturday, December 30, to discuss the matter.

By the time he arrived for the appointment I had decided that I would have to kill him. It proved to be an absurdly easy thing to do, as he did not suspect my intention and was not on guard. As he sat I went to his rear on some trivial excuse, picked up a heavy paperweight, and hit him on the head. He crumpled without a sound, and I hit him again. During the four hours that I waited for the deserted streets of late night, or early morning, I had to hit him three more times. During those hours I also went for my car and parked it directly in front. When the time came I got him downstairs and into the car without being observed. I drove uptown to an unused East River pier in the Nineties and rolled the body into the water. I must have been less calm and cool than I thought I was, for I thought he was dead. Two days later, in the newspaper account of the recovery of the body, I learned that he had died of drowning, so when I rolled him in he was only stunned.

It was then two in the morning, and I was not through. I drove downtown to Sullivan Street and let myself into Dykes's apartment with the key I had taken from his pocket. With my bare hands an hour there would have been enough, but with gloves on it took three hours to make a thorough search. I found only three items, but they were well worth it. Two of them were receipts signed by Rachel Abrams for payments for typing made by Baird Archer, and the third was a letter addressed to Baird Archer at General Delivery, Clinton Station, on the letterhead of Scholl & Hanna,

signed by Joan Wellman. I said I made a thorough search, but
there were many books on the shelves, and there wasn't time to
turn through every page of them even if I had thought it necessary.
If I had done so I would have found the sheet of paper on which
Dykes made that list of names with Baird Archer among them,
and you would never have seen it, and I wouldn't be writing you
this now.

For a while, a week or so, I had no intention of doing anything
about Joan Wellman or Rachel Abrams, but then I began to worry.
One of them had typed the script and the other had read it. The
trial of O'Malley and the juror and the disbarment proceedings
had of course been fully reported in the papers, only a year ago.
What if one of those women or both of them had noticed the
similarity, or rather the sameness, between the actual happening
and Dykes's novel? What if they had mentioned it or an occasion
arose for them to mention it in the future? They were less dangerous than Dykes, but they were dangerous, or might be.

That was more and more on my mind, and finally I did something about it. The last day of January, a Wednesday, I phoned
Joan Wellman at her office. I told her I was Baird Archer, and
offered to pay her for advice about my novel, and made an appointment with her for the next day but one, Friday, at five-thirty. We
met in the Ruby Room at the Churchill and had drinks and talked.
She was attractive and intelligent, and I was thinking that it
would be impossible to do her any serious harm, when she asked
me point blank about the remarkable resemblance between the
plot of my novel and an occurrence in real life here in New York
a year ago. She said she wasn't sure she remembered the name of
the disbarred lawyer, she thought it was O'Mara, but probably I
remembered it.

I said I didn't. I said I hadn't consciously used any happening
in real life when I was plotting the novel, but of course it might
have been in my subconscious. She said that as far as she remembered it hadn't come out that O'Mara had been betrayed by one
of his partners, and it would be interesting to look into it and see
if my subconscious had not only copied what had been published
but had also, by insight or intuition, divined what had not been
published. That was enough for me, more than enough.

I guided the talk, while we were having dinner, to a point where
it was appropriate for me to suggest that we drive to my apartment in the Bronx so I could get the manuscript. She gave me a
bad moment when she asked, if I lived in the Bronx, why had I

given my address as General Delivery, Clinton Station, but I gave her an answer that satisfied her. She said she would go with me to get the manuscript but let me know that she wouldn't go up to my apartment. I was sorry I had met her in so public a place as the Ruby Room, but neither of us had seen anyone we knew and I resolved to go ahead.

I went alone to get my car and picked her up in front of the Churchill and drove to Washington Heights. There, in a side street, it was as simple as it had been with Dykes. I remarked that the windshield was misted on the inside and reached behind me as if for my handkerchief, got a heavy wrench I had placed there when I went for my car, and hit her with it. She didn't even groan. I tried to prop her up but couldn't, and lifted her over into the back onto the floor. On the way to Van Cortlandt Park I stopped several times to take a look at her. Once she seemed to be stirring, and I had to hit her again.

I drove to a secluded road in the park. There was no one in sight, but it was only ten o'clock and there was a chance that a car might come along at the worst moment, even in February, so I left the park, drove around for two hours, and then returned to the park and the secluded road. The risk was then at a minimum, and anyhow I had to take it. I took her out of the car, put her on the road near the edge, and ran the car over her. Then I drove away fast. When I was miles away I stopped under a light and inspected the car for signs of blood or other evidence, but I had been careful to go slowly when passing over her and I could find nothing.

I put the thing down on my desk, looked at my watch, and saw 9:35. In Peoria, Illinois, it was 8:35, and John R. Wellman, according to the schedule he had given me, would be at his place of business. I reached for the phone and put in a call and soon had him.

"Mr. Wellman? Archie Goodwin. I promised to let you know immediately if anything broke. Corrigan, senior partner in that law firm, was found dead on the floor of his apartment last night with a hole in his head and a gun lying nearby. I would—"

"Did he shoot himself?"

"I don't know. As a purely personal opinion, it looks like it. I would call that a break, but whether good or bad is for Mr. Wolfe to decide, not me. I'm just keeping my promise and telling you. As it stands this minute, that's all I can say. Mr. Wolfe is busy upstairs."

"Thank you, Mr. Goodwin. Thank you very much. I'll go to Chicago and take a plane. I'll call you when I reach New York."

I told him that would be fine, hung up, and returned to my reading.

There was only one other living person who knew the contents of that manuscript, Rachel Abrams, who had typed it. There was only one logical and sensible thing to do.

Until three months ago I had never been conscious of anything in my mind or heart to justify any concept of myself as a potential murderer. I believed that I understood myself at least as well as most people. I was aware that there was an element of casuistry in my self-justification for what I had done to O'Malley, but without that intellectual resource no man could preserve his self-esteem. At any rate, I was an altogether different being from the moment I rolled Dykes's body from the pier into the water. I didn't know it at the time, but I do now. The change was not so much in my conscious mind as in the depths. If the processes of the subconscious can be put into rational terms at all, I think mine were something like this: (a) I have murdered a man in cold blood; (b) I am a decent and humane person, as men go, certainly not vicious or depraved; therefore (c) the conventional attitude toward the act of murder is invalid and immoral.

My inner being could not permit me to feel any moral repulsion at the thought of killing Joan Wellman, certainly not enough to restrain me, for if killing her was morally unacceptable how could I justify the killing of Dykes? By killing Joan Wellman the process was completed. After that, given adequate motive, I could have killed any number of people without any sign of compunction.

So in contemplating the murder of Rachel Abrams my only concerns were whether it was necessary and whether it could be performed without undue risk. I decided it was necessary. As for the risk, I left that to circumstances. With her I could not use the same kind of subterfuge I had used with Joan Wellman, since she had known Dykes as Baird Archer. My plan was so simple that it was really no plan at all. I merely went to her office one rainy afternoon, unannounced. If she had had an associate there with her, or if any one of a dozen other possible obstacles had arisen, I would have gone away and devised a procedure. But she had only one room and was there alone. I told her I wanted a typing job done, approached her to show her what it was, grasped her throat, had her unconscious in half a minute, opened the window, and lifted her and pushed her out. Unfortunately I had no time to search for records; of course I had no time at all. I left, ran down the stairs to the next floor, and took the elevator there, having got off there on my way up. When I left the building her body was on the sidewalk and a crowd was already collecting. Three days later, when my associates and I came to see you, I learned that I had been ahead of your man Goodwin by not more than two minutes. I took that as conclusive evidence that luck was on my side, even though he found entries in her records that connected her with Baird Archer. If he had got to her alive he would have learned the contents of the manuscript.

By that time, the day we called on you, nine days ago, I knew I was in danger but was confident that I could ward it off. You knew of Baird Archer and the manuscript and had connected them with Dykes and therefore with our office, but that was all. Your noticing that scribbled "Ps 146-3" on Dykes's letter of resignation in my handwriting, and correctly interpreting it, increased the danger only slightly if at all, since my plain square hand can be easily imitated by almost anyone and my associates unanimously supported me in convincing the police that you must have made the notation yourself in an effort to trick us.

Wednesday, when the letter from Mrs. Potter arrived, I did not suspect that you had anything to do with it. I thought it was a deadly blow that fate had dealt me at the worst possible moment. It was brought to me, but since it had been addressed not to an individual but to the firm our mail clerk had read it, and therefore I had to show it to my associates. We discussed it and agreed with no dissent that it was essential for us to learn what was in the manuscript, and that one of us must go immediately to California. There was a division of opinion as to who should go, and of course I had to insist that it must be me. Since I was the senior partner my view prevailed and I left by the first available plane.

You know what happened in California. I was in great peril, but I was not desperate until I went to Finch's room in his absence and found Goodwin there. From that moment my position was manifestly hopeless, but I refused to give up. Since, through Goodwin, you had certainly learned the content of the manuscript, my betrayal of O'Malley was sure to be disclosed, but it might yet be possible to avoid a charge of murder. All night, on the plane, with Goodwin seated there only a few feet from me, I considered possible courses and plans.

I had phoned one of my partners from Los Angeles, and they were all at the office when I arrived this morning, going directly from the airport. Their unanimous opinion was that we should call on you and demand to be told the substance of the manuscript. I argued strongly for an alternative course but could not sway them. When we went to your office I was prepared to face the disclosure of my betrayal of O'Malley, supposing that you would tell us about the manuscript, but instead of that you dealt me another blow. You told us nothing, saying that you were not quite ready to act and that you still needed a fact or two. For me that could have only one meaning. You did not intend to expose my betrayal of O'Malley until you were fully prepared to use it as evidence on a charge of murder, and you would not have said that to us unless you expected soon to be prepared. I didn't know which fact or two you still needed, but it didn't matter. Obviously you had me or you would soon get me.

My associates wanted a luncheon conference, but I pleaded fatigue from my night on the plane and came here to my apartment. Again my subconscious had taken command, for it came to me in a rush of sudden surprise that I had irrevocably determined to kill myself. I did not dispute the decision. I calmly accepted it. The further decision, whether to leave behind me an account of my disaster and what led to it, has not yet been made. I have spent hours writing this. I shall now read it over and decide. If I send it at all it will go to you, since it is you who have destroyed me. Again here at the end, as at the beginning, what interests me most is my motive. What is it in me that wants to send this to you, or to anyone? But if I start on that I will never end. If I do send it I will not attempt to tell you what to do with it, since in any case you will do as you see fit. That is what I am doing; I am doing as I see fit.

That was all. I jiggled the sheets together, refolded them, slipped them into the envelope, and went and mounted the three flights to the plant rooms. Wolfe, wearing one of his new yellow smocks, was in the potting room inspecting the roots of some Dendrobiums he had knocked out of the pots. I handed him the envelope and told him, "You'll have to read this."

"When I come down."

"Cramer is coming at eleven. If you read it with him sitting there he'll get impatient. If you talk with him without reading it I would prefer not to be present."

"What does it say?"

"A full confession. Betrayal of his partner O'Malley, three murders
—the works."

"Very well. I'll wash my hands."

He went to the sink and turned the faucet on.

XX

"This," Wolfe told Inspector Cramer, "is correct not only in substance
but also in text."

He held in his hand a typed copy, brought by Cramer, of what Corrigan had said to us on the phone just before the bang, as reported by
Wolfe to Sergeant Auerbach.

Cramer looked at me. "You were on the line too, Goodwin? You
heard it?"

I nodded, arose, got the paper from Wolfe, read it, and handed it
back. "Right. That's what he said."

"I want a statement to that effect signed by both of you."

"Certainly," Wolfe acceded.

Cramer was in the red leather chair, leaning back comfortably, like
a man intending to stay a while. "Also," he said, not belligerently, "I
want a statement from Goodwin giving all details of his trip to California. But first I would like to hear him tell it."

"No," Wolfe said firmly.

"Why not?"

"On principle. Through habit you put it as a demand, and it's a bad
habit. I don't like it."

"What he did in California led to a violent death in my jurisdiction."

"Establish that."

"Nuts," Cramer growled. "I ask it as a favor. Not to me, to the People
of the State of New York."

"Very well. Having had an authentic discovery of mine, the notation
in Corrigan's handwriting on Dykes's letter, denounced by them and
you as a trick, I thought it only fair to even up by contriving a trick. I
needed—"

"So you still claim that notation was made by Corrigan?"

"No. I never made that claim. I only denied that it was made by Mr.
Goodwin or me. I needed to demonstrate that someone in that office
was involved in Baird Archer's manuscript and therefore in the murders,
and I proceeded to do so. Tell him about it, Archie."

"Yes, sir. Leaving out what?"

"Nothing."

If I had been alone with Cramer and he had told me to leave out nothing I would have had some fun, but under the circumstances I refrained. I gave it to him straight, accurate and complete, from my checking in at the Riviera to my last view of Corrigan's rear at La Guardia Airport as he trotted out to a taxi. When I finished he had a few questions, and I answered them straight too.

He was chewing an unlit cigar. He took it from his mouth and turned to Wolfe. "What it amounts to, you tricked—"

"If you please," Wolfe interposed. "Since you have part you should have all. Yesterday morning, less than three hours after Corrigan's return, they came here—all five of them. They demanded that I tell them what was in the manuscript, and I refused. I would have had to refuse in any case, since I didn't know, but I told them that I wasn't quite ready to act, that I needed one or two more facts. I permitted them to assume that my preparations were all but complete."

Cramer nodded. "You tricked him into killing himself."

"Did I? Did he kill himself?"

"Goddammit, didn't he?"

"I don't know. You have investigated, I haven't. What have you concluded?"

Cramer scratched his ear. "There's nothing against suicide. It was his gun, fired at contact. Smudges on it, no clear prints. His prints on the phone. He had been dead less than an hour when the examiner arrived. No evidence so far of anyone else being there. He had been struck a hard blow on the side of the head but could have got it from the corner of the table when he fell, and probably did. There was—"

Wolfe waved it away. "From you, 'nothing against suicide' is enough. On that sort of thing you are not to be impugned. But it is still open?"

"It's not closed. That's why I'm here. I just said you tricked him into killing himself, and you may or may not hear more about that, but right now I want a lot more than you've given me. If it was suicide, why? Because he thought you knew what was in that damn manuscript? Because he thought you had him? For what? Murder? I want a lot more, a hell of a lot, and I'm here to get it."

Wolfe pursed his lips. "Well." He opened a desk drawer. "This came in my morning mail." He took a fat envelope from the drawer. "See if that answers your questions." He held it out.

Cramer got up to take the envelope and sat down again. He inspected the outside of the envelope before he removed the contents. He unfolded the sheets, read a little, looked at Wolfe, made a growling noise, and read some more. As he finished the first page and transferred it to the back, he inquired, "You say this came this morning?"

"Yes, sir."

He had no more to say or to ask until he got to the end. Wolfe leaned back, shut his eyes, and relaxed. I kept my eyes open. I kept them on Cramer's face, but all I saw was a man so intent and absorbed that he had no expression at all. When he finished he went back to a place on the third or fourth page and read it over. Then he looked at Wolfe, with his lips tightened to a thin line.

"You got this three hours ago," he muttered.

Wolfe opened his eyes. "I beg your pardon?"

"You got this three hours ago. You know how to phone my office. Sergeant Stebbins talked to Goodwin at nine o'clock. Goodwin didn't mention it."

"I hadn't read it yet," I stated. "It had just come."

"You know my number."

"Bosh," Wolfe said testily. "This is ridiculous. Have I concealed it or destroyed it?"

"No, you haven't." Cramer wiggled the sheets. "What evidence is there that Corrigan wrote this?"

"None."

"What evidence is there that you didn't dictate it to Goodwin and he wrote it?"

"None." Wolfe straightened up. "Mr. Cramer. You might as well leave. If you are in a frame of mind to think me capable of so extravagant an imbecility, all communication is blocked." He wiggled a finger. "You have that thing. Take it and go."

Cramer ignored it. "You maintain that Corrigan wrote this."

"I do not. I maintain only that I received it in today's mail, and that I have no knowledge of who wrote it beyond the thing itself. I suppose other evidence is procurable. If there is a typewriter in Corrigan's apartment, and if investigation shows it was written on that machine, that would be pertinent."

"You have no knowledge of it whatever beyond what you've told me?"

"I have not."

"Do you know of any evidence other than this that Corrigan committed the murders?"

"No."

"Or that he betrayed his partner O'Malley?"

"No."

"Do you believe this to be an authentic confession by Corrigan?"

"I'm not prepared to say. I've read it only once, rather hurriedly. I was going to ask you to let Mr. Goodwin make a copy for me, but I'll get along without it."

"You won't have to. I'll see that you get a copy, with the understanding that there is to be no publication of it without my consent." Cramer folded the sheets and put them in the envelope. "It's covered with your and Goodwin's prints now, and mine. But we'll try it."

"If it's a fake," Wolfe said dryly, "I should think that a man capable of contriving it would know about fingerprints."

"Yeah, everybody knows about fingerprints."

Cramer rubbed his kneecaps with his palms, regarding Wolfe with his head cocked. The chewed cigar, which had previously taken no part in the conversation, slipped from his fingers and fell to the floor, but he made no move to retrieve it.

He spoke. "I admit this is damn neat. It will stand a lot of checking, but I admit it's neat. What are you going to do now, send your client a bill?"

"No."

"Why not?"

"My client, Mr. Wellman, has his share of gumption. Before I bill him both he and I must be satisfied that I have earned my fee." Wolfe's eyes moved. "Archie. Trained as you are, can I rely on you for an accurate copy of that communication from—ostensibly—Mr. Corrigan?"

"It's pretty long," I objected, "and I read it once."

"I said I'll send you a copy," Cramer stated.

"I know you did. I would like to have it as soon as possible. It would be gratifying to have it validated, both by your investigation and my scrutiny, since that would mean that I have exposed a murderer and forced him to a reckoning without a scrap of evidence against him. We still have none, not a tittle, except that unsigned communication."

"I know we haven't."

"Then by all means check it, every detail, every word. Do you want a comment?"

"Yes."

"A focus of interest is the anonymous letter informing on O'Malley. Suppose it was sent not by Corrigan, but by one of the others. In that case that confession may be factually correct in every important detail but one, the identity of the culprit; and the real culprit, finding me too close for comfort, may have decided to shift the burden onto Corrigan, not concerned that the shift required one more murder. So of first importance is the question, was it Corrigan who betrayed O'Malley? You will of course need the informing letter to the court or a photostat of it, and something authentically typed on the machine at the Travelers

Club. You will need to know whether any of the others frequented that club or otherwise had access to that machine. With your authority, that kind of inquiry is vastly easier for you than for me."

Cramer nodded. "What else?"

"At present, nothing."

"What are you going to do?"

"Sit here."

"Some day you'll get chair sores." Cramer got up. He saw the cigar on the floor, stooped to pick it up, crossed to my wastebasket, and dropped it in. His manners were improving. He started for the door, halted, and turned. "Don't forget those statements, what Corrigan said —by the way, what about that? Was it him on the phone or wasn't it?"

"I don't know. As I said, the voice was husky and agitated. It could have been, but if not no great talent for mimicry would have been needed."

"That's a help. Don't forget the statements, what Corrigan or somebody said on the phone, what Goodwin did in California, and now getting this thing in the mail. Today."

Wolfe told him certainly, and he turned and went.

I looked at my watch. I addressed my employer. "Kustin phoned nearly three hours ago, as I reported. He wanted you to phone him quick so he can warn you that they're going to hold you accountable. Shall I get him?"

"No."

"Shall I call Sue or Eleanor or Blanche and make a date for tonight?"

"No."

"Shall I think of things to suggest?"

"No."

"Then it's all over? Then Corrigan wrote that thing and shot himself?"

"No. Confound it. He didn't. Take your notebook. We might as well get those statements done."

XXI

FORTY-EIGHT hours later, Monday morning at eleven, Inspector Cramer was back again.

At our end much had been accomplished. I had got a haircut and a shampoo. I had spent some pleasant hours with Lily Rowan. I had spent half an hour with Wellman, our client, who had called at the office after taking a plane from Chicago and was staying over to await developments. I had had two good nights' sleep and had taken a walk to the Battery and back, with a stopover at Homicide on Twentieth Street to deliver the statements Cramer had requested. I had made five copies of Corrigan's confession, from the copy Cramer had sent us as agreed. I had answered three phone calls from Saul Panzer, switched him to Wolfe, and got off the line by command. I had answered thirty or forty other phone calls, none of which would interest you. I had done some office chores, and had eaten six meals.

Wolfe had by no means been idle. He had eaten six meals too.

One thing neither of us had done, we had read no newspaper account of Corrigan's unsigned confession. There hadn't been any, though of course the death of a prominent attorney by a gunshot had been adequately covered, including pointed reference to previous regrettable occurrences connected with his firm. Evidently Cramer was saving the confession for his scrapbook, though it wasn't autographed.

Monday morning he sat in the red leather chair and announced, "The DA's office is ready to call it suicide."

Wolfe, at his desk, was pouring beer. He put the bottle down, waited for the foam to subside to the right level so that the tilt would get him beer and would also moisten his lips with foam, lifted the glass, and drank. He liked to let the foam dry on his lips, but not when there was company, so he used his handkerchief before he spoke.

"And you?"

"I don't see why not." Cramer, having accepted the invitation to help with the beer, which he rarely did, had his glass in his hand. "I could tell you how it stands."

"Please do."

"It's like this. The confession was typed on the machine in his apartment. He's had it there for years. He has always done quite a little typing—kept a supply of the firm's paper and envelopes there. His secretary, Mrs. Adams, admits that there is nothing about the typing or the text to cause a reasonable doubt that he typed it."

"Admits?"

"Yes. She defends him. She won't believe he betrayed O'Malley or committed murder." Cramer emptied his glass and put it down. "I can give you more on the confession, plenty more, but the DA isn't prepared to impeach it, and neither am I. We can't challenge any of its facts. As for the dates of the murders, December thirtieth, February second, and February twenty-sixth, of course Corrigan had already been checked on that along with all the others. The file had him alibied for the twenty-sixth, the afternoon Rachel Abrams was killed, but digging into it we find that it's loose. We'd want to dig more on it if he was alive to take to a jury and we had to face a defense, but he's dead and there'll be no jury. We can't get a check on December fourth, the day he says he was at his office in the evening and found Dykes's manuscript and read it. There are no other dates to check."

Wolfe grunted. "How are the others on the dates? Did you go over that?"

"Some. They're all about the same as Corrigan; there's nothing too tight to rip open. As I think I told you once, none of them is completely eliminated by an alibi—except O'Malley the day Rachel Abrams was killed. He was in Atlanta, but now that we know what was in the manuscript he's out anyway. All it spilled about him was that he had been disbarred for bribing a juror, and God knows that was no secret. Unless you think the confession lies about the manuscript?"

"No. On that point I credit it unreservedly."

"Then it doesn't matter where O'Malley was." Cramer reached to empty his bottle into his glass and settled back. "Now about the typewriter at the Travelers Club. It's still there, in an alcove off of the writing room, but it was overhauled about two months ago. That doesn't stop us, because in the firm's files we found two items Corrigan had typed on it, memoranda to Mrs. Adams. We got the original of the anonymous letter to the court informing on O'Malley and it was typed on that machine, absolutely no question about it. Corrigan used it occasionally. He ate dinner there two or three times a week and played bridge there Thursday evenings. None of the others is a member. Two of them, Kustin and Briggs, have been brought there once or twice by Corrigan for dinner, but that's all. So it looks—"

"This," Wolfe cut in, "is important. Extremely. How closely was it examined? A dinner guest might conceivably have used a typewriter, especially if he needed one that couldn't be traced to him."

"Yeah, I know. Saturday you called it a focus of interest. I had Stebbins handle it himself, with instructions to make it good, and he did. Besides, look at it. Say you're Kustin or Briggs, going there as a guest to eat with Corrigan. Say you use that typewriter for that particular purpose. You can't do it, you can't even get in that room, without either Corrigan or an attendant knowing about it, probably both of them, and that would be pretty damn dumb. Wouldn't it?"

"Yes."

"So it looks as if Corrigan did inform on his partner. That alone makes the confession a lot easier to buy, signed or unsigned, and the DA's office feels the same way about it. Isn't that practically what you said Saturday? Is there anything wrong with that argument?"

"No." Wolfe made a noise that could have been a chuckle. "I will accept an apology."

"The hell you will. For what?"

"You accused me, or Mr. Goodwin, of making that cryptic notation on Dykes's letter of resignation. Well?"

Cramer picked up his glass and drank, in no hurry. He set the glass down. "Uh-huh," he conceded. "I still say it looked like a typical Wolfe stunt, and I'm not apologizing. That's the one detail in that confession that it's hard to dope. The confession says he made the notation in December, so of course it wasn't there when they all saw the letter last summer, that's all right, but it must have been there a week ago Saturday when the letter was sent to you. Yet three of them say it wasn't. Phelps asked his secretary, a girl named Dondero, to see if it was in the files, and she dug it out and took it to him. O'Malley had come to the office that morning, for a conference at Corrigan's request, and was with Phelps in his room when the girl brought the letter in, and they both looked at it. They won't swear the notation wasn't on it, but they both think they would have noticed it if it had been, and they didn't notice it. Not only that, the girl says she would testify under oath that there was no such notation on the letter. She says she would positively have noticed it if it had been. Phelps dictated his letter to you, and she typed it, and Phelps signed it, and she put it and Dykes's letter of resignation, and the other material written by Dykes, into an envelope addressed to you, and sent for a messenger and took the envelope to the anteroom and left it with the switchboard girl to be given to the messenger when he came. So how do I dope it?"

Wolfe upturned a palm. "Phelps and O'Malley leave it open. The girl is lying."

"What the hell for?"

"Force of habit. The etiquette of the sex."

"Nuts. We couldn't brush it off with a gag if we had to take it to a jury. As it is, I suppose we can let it slide. We have to if we're going to buy the confession."

Wolfe turned his head. "Archie. We gave Mr. Cramer the letter from Dykes bearing the notation?"

"Yes, sir."

"The envelope too? The envelope it came to us in?"

"No, sir."

"We have the envelope?"

"Yes, sir. As you know, we keep everything until a case is closed—except what we hand to the cops."

Wolfe nodded. "It may possibly be needed to save us from a charge as accessories." He returned to Cramer. "What about the District Attorney's office? Are they willing to let it slide?"

"They think it's minor. If the rest of the confession stands up, yes."

"Has the confession been shown to Corrigan's associates?"

"Certainly."

"Do they credit it?"

"Yes and no. It's hard to tell because they're half batty. A year ago their senior partner disbarred, and now their new senior partner confessing to three murders and killing himself—they're in a hell of a fix. Briggs thinks they ought to denounce the confession as a fake and hold you liable, but he's just babbling. He doesn't say you or Goodwin shot Corrigan, but he might as well. Phelps and Kustin say that even if the confession is true it's invalid because it isn't signed, and any publication of it would be libelous. They think we ought to bury it. But they also think we should accept it as true. Why not? Corrigan's dead, and that would make the three murders finished business and they could start gathering up the pieces. Their feeling about you is approximately the same as Briggs', but they're realistic about it. None of them will look O'Malley in the eye, though he gives them plenty of chances to. He sticks it in them and twists it. He sent some flowers to the wife of the juror he bribed, with a letter of apology for thinking she informed on him, and before he sent the letter he read it aloud to them with Lieutenant Rowcliff present and asked their opinion of it."

There was only an inch of beer left in Cramer's glass. He got it and drained it and then settled back, not through yet. He rubbed the side of his nose with a fingertip. "I guess that covers it. It looks like a wrap-up. The DA will be ready to give the press a statement as soon as they decide whether to release the confession. Thank God they decide that and not me. But on the main question, do we cross off the murders or don't we, I'll have to go along and maybe I'm ready to, only there's you to think of. That's why I'm here. Once or twice I have kicked a hat that you had hid a brick in, and I don't want a sore toe. You connected Joan Wellman with Dykes by spotting that name, Baird Archer. You tied in Rachel Abrams by having Goodwin there two minutes late. You pulled the stunt that got Corrigan a bullet in his head. So I repeat a question I asked you day before yesterday: are you ready to send your client a bill?"

"No," Wolfe said flatly.

"I thought not," Cramer growled. "What are you waiting for?"

"I'm through waiting." Wolfe struck the arm of his chair with his palm, a gesture so violent that with him it was the next thing to hysterics. "I have to be. This can't go on forever. I'll have to do it with what I've got or not at all."

"What have you got?"

"Nothing that you haven't. Absolutely nothing. It may not be enough, but I see no chance of getting more. If I—"

The phone rang, and I swiveled and got it. It was Saul Panzer. He wanted Wolfe. Wolfe took it and gave me the sign to get off, and I did so. The part of the conversation that Cramer and I listened to was not exciting. Mostly it was grunts, at intervals. Apparently Saul had plenty to say. At the end Wolfe told him, "Satisfactory. Report here at six o'clock," and hung up.

He turned to Cramer. "I'll have to amend that statement. I now have something that you do not have, but it was easily available to you if you had gone after it. I'm better off than I was, but not much. I never will be, and I'm going to act. You're welcome to participate if you care to."

"In what?"

"A risky but resolute effort to expose a murderer. That's the best I can offer."

"You can offer some information. What did you just get, and who is it?"

Wolfe shook his head. "You would insist on further inquiry and let the moment slip, and further inquiry would be fruitless. He has been too smart for you and almost too smart for me. I'm going to close with him and I may get him. You may participate or not, as you please."

"Participate how?"

"By getting them here, all of them. This evening at nine o'clock. Including the ten women that Mr. Goodwin entertained at dinner two weeks ago. I need them all, or I may. And of course come yourself."

"If I get them here I take a hand."

Wolfe sighed. "Mr. Cramer. Three weeks ago we agreed to cooperate. I have done so faithfully. I have given you everything I got, without reciprocation. Where do we stand? You, utterly routed, are ready to join with the District Attorney in unconditional surrender. You have been bamboozled. I have not. I know him, his motive, and his strategy. I intend to rush him. You say you should take a hand?"

Cramer was not overwhelmed. "I say if I get them here I am officially responsible and I'm in charge."

"Very well, then you decline. Mr. Goodwin will get them here. If you come you will not get in. I hope to be ready to communicate with you before midnight."

Cramer sat and scowled. His lips tightened. He opened his mouth, said nothing, and pressed his lips tight again. I was pretty well acquainted with him, and I knew by his eyes that he was going to take it. But he couldn't just knuckle under, he had to keep his independence and show his spirit and prove that he was by no means cowed. So he said, "I'll bring Sergeant Stebbins along."

XXII

WE NEEDED seventeen chairs if they all came, and a phone call from Stebbins around four o'clock informed me that they would. With four from the front room, one from the hall, two from my room, and two from Fritz's room, Fritz and I got them collected and arranged in the office. We had an argument. Fritz insisted there should be a table of liquid refreshments, that Wolfe regarded that as a minimum of hospitality for invited guests, and I fought it. Not so much on account of the basic situation, since more than one murderer had been served a highball or other mixture in that room. The trouble was the females, particularly Helen Troy and Blanche Duke. I did not want the former, at some ticklish spot where everything might hang on a word and a tone, to jump up and call out, "Oyez, oyeth!" And if the latter, whose inhibitions were totally unreliable, got a shaker full of her formula mixed and worked on it, she might do or say anything. So I was firm.

Fritz couldn't appeal to Wolfe because he wasn't accessible. He was there at his desk, but not for us. Five minutes after Cramer left he had leaned back, closed his eyes, and started pushing his lips in and out, which meant he was working, and hard. He kept at it until lunch, took only half of his customary hour for the meal, returned to the office, and started in again. He left for the plant rooms at four o'clock as usual, but when I went up there on an errand he was standing in a corner of the intermediate room frowning at a Cochlioda hybrid that had nothing whatever wrong with it, and he wasn't even aware that I was passing through. A little later he phoned down to tell me to send Saul up to him when he came. So I wasn't present at their conference. Nor did I get any kind of an instruction for the evening. If he was planning a charade, apparently it was going to be a solo.

Wolfe did speak to me once, shortly after lunch; he asked me to bring him the letter from Phelps enclosing the material from Dykes, and the envelope it had come in. I did so, and, after he had inspected them with a magnifying glass, he kept them. And I took one step on my own. Wellman was still in town, and I phoned and invited him to attend because I thought he had certainly paid for a ticket. I didn't phone

Mrs. Abrams because I knew she wouldn't care for it no matter what happened.

At dinnertime I took another step. As Wolfe sat behind his desk staring at nothing, pulling at his lip with a thumb and forefinger, I saw that he was in no shape to entertain a guest and went and told Fritz that Saul and I would eat in the kitchen with him. Then I returned to the office and announced it to Wolfe. He put his eyes on me without seeing me, let out a low growl, and muttered, "All right, but it won't help any."

"Can I do anything?" I asked.

"Yes. Shut up."

I had spoken not more than twenty words to him since Cramer had left, seven hours ago.

At ten after nine they had all arrived, but Wolfe was still in the dining room, with the door closed. Leaving the front door and the hall to Saul, I had stayed in the office to supervise the seating. I kept the red leather chair for Cramer and put the lawyers in the front row, including O'Malley. Wellman was off in the corner near the globe. Sergeant Purley Stebbins was against the wall, back of Cramer. For Saul Panzer I had put a chair at the end of my desk. My intention had been to group the ten females at the rear of their employers, and I had so placed the chairs, but they had ideas of their own, at least some of them. For about half a minute I stood talking to Cramer with my back to them, and, when I turned, four of them had moved to the couch. From my chair at my desk I couldn't take in the couch without swiveling or twisting my neck ninety degrees, but I decided to skip it. If Wolfe wanted his audience more compact he could say so.

At twelve after nine I sent Saul to tell Wolfe they were all present, and a moment later Wolfe entered. He went straight to his desk, with no halt for a greeting, not even for Cramer, and sat. The murmurs and mutterings stopped. Wolfe got himself settled, taking his time, moved his head slowly over the arc from left to right, and back again. Then his eyes darted left, and he spoke.

"Do you want to say anything, Mr. Cramer?"

Cramer cleared his throat. "No. They understand that there's nothing official about this and I'm here as an observer."

"You told us to come," Louis Kustin said aggressively.

"I invited you. You all know the way out."

"May I make a statement?" O'Malley asked.

"What about?"

"I want to congratulate Mr. Wolfe, and thank him. He has found the answer to a question I've been trying to find for a year and couldn't. We're all in his debt and we ought to say so."

"We are not!" It was Briggs, blinking furiously. "I would like to make a statement! In my opinion, what Wolfe has done is actionable. I say this after full consideration. I came here because I am convinced—"

"Shut up!" Wolfe roared.

They gazed at him, astonished.

He gazed back, moving his head to include the lot. "I do not intend," he said coldly, "to let you degrade this to gibberish. We are concerned with death and a dealer of death. I do this work to earn a living, but I am conscious of its dignities and obligations. I hope and believe that in the next two or three hours, here together, we are going to learn the truth about the deaths of four people, and, in doing so, get a start on preparations for the death of one of you. That's what we're here for. I can't do it alone, but I'll have to guide it."

He closed his eyes, tight, and opened them again. "All of you knew Mr. Corrigan, who died Friday evening. You know of a document, ostensibly written by him, in which he confessed that he had betrayed his former partner and had murdered three people." He opened a drawer and took out papers. "This is a copy of that confession. It was shrewdly conceived and brilliantly executed, but it wasn't good enough for me. It has one fatal defect. The writer couldn't possibly avoid including it, because in that detail the facts were known to others, and the incident was an essential part of the story. When Corrigan—"

"Are you impeaching it?" Kustin demanded. "Are you saying that Corrigan didn't write it?"

"I am."

There were noises, including audible words. Wolfe ignored them, waited, and continued.

"When Corrigan was in California his every move was known and reported, so this confession had to accept that record. But that is the fatal defect. According to this confession, Corrigan knew what was in the manuscript written by Leonard Dykes—he had read it through twice. But in Los Angeles all his efforts were focused on one objective: to get a look at the manuscript. That is emphasized by the fact that he left Mrs. Potter's house, with Finch there, to hurry to Finch's hotel room to search for the manuscript. If he already knew what was in it that was senseless. What good would it do him to find it? If you say that he wanted to destroy it, that too would have been senseless, since Finch had read it. According to this confession, he had already killed two women for the sole reason that they had read the manuscript. If he found and destroyed Finch's copy, Finch would be on guard and after him."

Wolfe shook his head. "No. Corrigan's objective, plainly and unmistakably, was to see the manuscript. He wanted to know what it contained. Mr. Goodwin was there and saw him and heard him. Do you agree, Archie?"

I nodded. "I do."

"Then he had never seen the manuscript, certainly he hadn't read it, and this confession is spurious. There is a corroborative point." Wolfe tapped the paper. "It says here that Dykes told him that all copies of the manuscript had been destroyed, there were no others, and that he believed it. Indeed he must have believed it fully, for otherwise he would hardly have undertaken the murders of the two women; but certainly, when the letter came from Mrs. Potter, saying that a literary agent had a copy of the manuscript, he would have suspected a snare and would have proceeded quite differently."

Wolfe turned a palm up. "Well?"

"I would have understood this this morning," Cramer rasped.

"Are you challenging the whole confession?" Phelps inquired.

"Are you saying," O'Malley demanded, "that Corrigan didn't squeal on me?"

"No. To both of you. But a purported confession shown to be clearly false in so important a detail loses all claim to validity, both as to content and as to authorship. It can be credited only in those parts that are corroborated. For instance, Mr. Cramer has verified it that the anonymous letter to the court was typed on a machine at the Travelers Club, that Corrigan had access to it and used it, and that none of the others did. Therefore I accept that detail as established, and also the account of Corrigan's visit to California, but nothing else, and certainly not the authorship. Of course Corrigan didn't write it."

"Why not?" It came from two of the women in unison. It was the first cheep out of them.

"If he didn't know what was in the manuscript, and he didn't, why did he kill people? There is no discernible reason. If he didn't kill people, why does he confess to it? No, he didn't write this."

"Did he kill himself?" Mrs. Adams blurted. She looked ten years older, and she was already old enough.

"I shouldn't think so. If he did, it was he who got me on the phone to hear the shot and told me he had mailed me a letter, meaning this—"

"What's that?" Cramer demanded. "He said he had mailed you a letter?"

"Yes. I left that out of my report to you because I don't want my mail intercepted. He said that. Mr. Goodwin heard it. Archie?"

"Yes, sir."

"And since he didn't write this thing he would hardly tell me he had mailed it to me. No, madam, he didn't kill himself. We might as well deal with that next—unless someone wants to maintain that Corrigan wrote the confession?"

No one did.

Wolfe took them in. "For this a new character is required, and we'll call him X. This will have to be a hodgepodge, partly what he must have done and partly what he could have done. Certainly he spent some hours yesterday between noon and ten in the evening at Corrigan's apartment, composing and typing this document. Certainly Corrigan was there too. He had been hit on the head, and was either unconscious from the blow or had been tied and gagged. I prefer it that he was conscious, knowing something of X as I do, and that X, as he typed the confession—which may have been composed beforehand and merely had to be copied—read it aloud to Corrigan. He wore gloves, and, when he was through, he pressed Corrigan's fingertips to the paper and envelope here and there, certainly on the postage stamp.

"I don't know whether his schedule was left to exigency or was designed, but I would guess the latter, for X is fond of alibis, and we'll probably find that he has one ready for last evening from nine-thirty to ten-thirty. Anyway, at ten o'clock he turned on the radio, if he hadn't already done so, hit Corrigan on the head again, at the same spot as before, with something heavy and hard enough to stun but not kill, put him on the floor near the telephone, and dialed my number. While talking to me, making the voice unrecognizable with huskiness and agitation, he pressed the muzzle of Corrigan's own revolver against his head and, at the proper moment, pulled the trigger and dropped the gun and the phone on the floor. He may also have fallen heavily to the floor himself; I think he would have. If he did he didn't stay there long. I said he was wearing gloves. He made Corrigan's dead hand grip the gun, put the gun on the floor, and left, perhaps twenty seconds after the shot had been fired. I haven't even inquired if the door had to be locked from the outside with a key; if it did, X had had ample opportunity to procure one. He dropped the letter to me, this confession, into the nearest mailbox. I lose him at the mailbox. We'll hear of his next move when we are confronted with his alibi."

Wolfe's eyes moved. "I invite comment."

Three lawyers spoke at once. Cramer outspoke them. "How much of it can you prove?"

"Nothing. Not a word."

"Then what does it get us?"

"It clears away the rubbish. The rubbish was the assumptions that Corrigan wrote that confession and killed himself. I have shown that one is false and the other is not invulnerable. Depriving you of a suicide was simple. Giving you a murder, and a murderer, is harder. May I proceed?"

"If you've got something better than guesses, yes."

"I've got a question," Kustin put in. "Is this a buildup for charging someone in this room with murder?"

"Yes."

"Then I want to speak with you privately."

"The devil you do." Wolfe was indignant. To control his emotions, he closed his eyes and waggled his head. Then he told Kustin dryly, "So you're beginning to see something, now that I've cleared away some of the rubbish? And you'd like to point at it? I'll do the pointing, Mr. Kustin." His eyes moved. "Before I go on to particulars, another comment. At my first reading of this"—he tapped the paper—"I saw the flaw that told me that Corrigan hadn't written it: his performance in Los Angeles made it obvious that he had never read the manuscript. But it could have been written by you, Mr. Kustin, or you, Mr. Phelps, or you, Mr. Briggs. It could have been any one of you, instead of Corrigan, who had done the deeds which this document attributes to Corrigan. That was why it was of first importance to learn if any of you had had access to the typewriter at the Travelers Club. Learning that you hadn't, and therefore had not exposed O'Malley, it was clear that if one of you had committed three murders it must have been for some other motive than concealment of a betrayal of your former partner."

"Get down to it," Cramer growled.

Wolfe ignored him. He looked over the heads of the lawyers and inquired abruptly, "Is one of you ladies named Dondero?"

I twisted my neck. Sue was one of the four on the couch. Startled, she stared at him. "Yes, I am." She was a little flushed and pretty as a picture.

"You are Mr. Phelps's secretary?"

"Yes."

"A week ago Saturday, nine days ago, Mr. Phelps dictated a brief letter to me, to be sent by messenger. There were enclosures for it—items of material written by Leonard Dykes, from the files, including a letter of resignation he wrote last July. Do you remember that incident?"

"Yes. Certainly."

"I understand that you have recently been questioned about it by the police; that you have been shown the Dykes letter and your attention has been called to a certain notation, 'Ps one-forty-six, three,' in a corner of it, in pencil, in a handwriting resembling Corrigan's; and that you state flatly that the notation was not on the letter that Saturday morning when it was sent to me. Is that correct?"

"Yes, it is," Sue said firmly.

"Are you positive the notation was not on the letter at the time you enclosed it in the envelope with the other material?"

"I am."

"You're a positive person, aren't you, Miss Dondero?"

"Well—I know what I saw and what I didn't see."

"Admirable and remarkable." Wolfe was terse but not hostile. "Few of us can say that and support it. How many typewriters did you use that morning?"

"I don't know what you mean. I used one. Mine."

"Mr. Phelps dictated the letter to me, and you typed it on your machine. Is that right?"

"Yes."

"And you addressed an envelope to me on the same machine?"

"Yes."

"How positive are you of that?"

"I'm absolutely positive."

"How much chance is there that for some trivial reason, no matter what, you used a different machine for addressing the envelope?"

"Absolutely none. I was there at my desk, and I did the envelope right after I typed the letter. I always do."

"Then we have a problem." Wolfe opened a drawer of his desk and took out a sheet of paper and an envelope, handling the envelope gingerly, holding it by a corner. "This is the letter and the envelope; Mr. Goodwin will attest that and so will I. The variation is apparent to the naked eye, and I have examined them with a glass. They were not typed on the same machine."

"I don't believe it!" Sue exclaimed.

"Come here and look at them. No, please, only Miss Dondero. The envelope must not be touched."

I made room for her to get by. She went to his desk and leaned over for a close-up. She straightened. "That's a different envelope. I didn't type that. I always put 'By Messenger' in caps and lower case and underline it. That's all in caps and it's not underlined. Where did you get it?"

"If you please, Miss Dondero, take your seat." Wolfe returned the sheet and envelope to the drawer, touching only the tip of the envelope. He waited until Sue was back on the couch and he had her face before he told her, "Thank you for being positive. That's a help. But you're sure you put the letter and enclosures into the envelope you had typed?"

"Yes, I am."

"And sealed it?"

"Yes."

"And left it lying on your desk, perhaps, or in a basket?"

"No, I didn't. It was to go by messenger, and I had sent for one. I went immediately to the anteroom and put it on Blanche's desk and asked her to give it to the messenger when he came."

"Who is Blanche?"

"The receptionist. Miss Duke."

Wolfe's eyes moved. "Which of you is Miss Duke?"

Blanche raised a hand, high. "I am. And I get the idea, I'm quick. You're going to ask me if I put the stuff in another envelope, and I'm going to say I didn't. And I don't know who did. But Mr. O'Malley came and said something about something left out and took the envelope away with him."

"Mr. O'Malley?"

"Yes."

"Did he bring it back?"

"Yes."

"How soon? How long was he gone with it?"

"I don't know, I guess three or four minutes. Anyway he brought it back, and when the messenger came I gave it to him."

"Did you notice whether it was the same envelope?"

"My God, no!"

"This is important, Miss Duke. Will you testify that Mr. O'Malley took the envelope from your desk, left the room with it, and shortly returned with it or with a similar one?"

"What do you mean, will I? I am!"

Wolfe's eyes left her to move right and back again, still above the heads of the lawyers. "We seem to be solving our problem," he remarked. "One more detail would help. Clearly we must assume that Mr. O'Malley addressed another envelope and transferred the material to it. If so, it seems likely that one of you ladies saw him do it, though I don't know how the typewriters are placed in that office. What about it? That Saturday morning, nine days ago, did any of you see Mr. O'Malley address an envelope on a typewriter?"

No reply. He had their eyes all right, but not their tongues.

He nodded understandingly. "It may be, of course, that he used a machine that wasn't under observation. Or he may have been seen by one of the staff who is not present, and that will bear inquiry. But I should make sure that all of you understand the situation. This envelope is vital evidence. If Mr. O'Malley handled it and typed an address on it, it will probably show his prints, for I don't suppose he wore gloves in the office that morning. Not only that, it will be a simple matter to learn which machine it was written on. If it was a machine that is on the desk of one of you ladies, and you were there that morning, and Mr. O'Malley denies that he used it, you may find yourself in an uncomfortable spot. The police may properly ask—"

"It was my machine." It was a sullen mutter, so low that it barely got through, and it came from the beautiful Eleanor, of all people.

"Ah. May I have your name?"

"Eleanor Gruber." She muttered it.

"You will please tell us about it, Miss Gruber."

"I was at the filing cabinet and he asked if—"

"Mr. O'Malley?"

"Yes. He asked if he could use my machine, and I said yes. That was all."

"Did he address an envelope on it?"

"I don't know. I was at the cabinet with my back turned. I said it was my machine, but I should have said it may have been."

"There was a supply of the firm's envelopes in your desk?"

"Certainly. In the top drawer."

"How long was he at it?"

"I don't—very briefly."

"Not more than a minute or so?"

"I said very briefly. I didn't time it."

"But long enough to address an envelope?"

"Of course, that only takes seconds."

"Did you see an envelope in his hand?"

"No. I wasn't looking. I was busy."

"Thank you, Miss Gruber. I'm sorry your memory needed jogging, and I'm glad it's refreshed." Wolfe focused on Conroy O'Malley. "Mr. O'Malley, you ought to have a word. I won't frame a tedious detailed question, but merely ask, did you do the things these people say you did that Saturday morning?"

O'Malley was a different man. The bitter twist to his mouth was gone, and so was the sag of his cheeks. He was ten years younger, and his eyes gleamed almost like eyes in the dark with a light on them. His voice had a sharp edge.

"I'd rather listen to you. Until you're through."

"Very well. I'm not through. Is it plain that I'm accusing you of murder?"

"Yes. Go on."

Purley Stebbins got up, detoured around Cramer and Briggs, got an empty chair, put it just behind O'Malley's right elbow, and sat. O'Malley didn't glance at him. Wolfe was speaking.

"Manifestly, establishing that O'Malley got at that letter in order to make that notation on it in Corrigan's hand before it came to me will not convict him of murder. By then all of you had heard the title of Baird Archer's novel, 'Put Not Your Trust,' and anyone could have known or learned that it came from the third verse of the Hundred and Forty-sixth Psalm. But it shows that he wanted to present me with evidence that someone in your office was connected with the manuscript and therefore with the crimes, and that that someone was Corrigan. I am going—"

"Why Corrigan?" Kustin demanded.

"That's what I'm coming to. I'm going to have to tell you things I can't prove, as I did with X. It is still X, only now I call him O'Malley. An odd thing about this confession is that nearly every detail of it is true and strictly accurate. The man who wrote it did find the manuscript in Dykes's desk and read it; he found that its contents were as described; he went to see Dykes and talked with him as related; he killed Dykes essentially for the reason given, fear of what might result from his knowledge of the contents of the manuscript; he killed Miss Wellman and Miss Abrams for a like reason. But it was O'Malley who wrote the confession. He—"

"You're crazy," Kustin blurted. "The manuscript revealed that Corrigan had informed on O'Malley. Is that right?"

"Yes."

"And O'Malley learned that fact by finding and reading the manuscript?"

"Yes."

"So he killed three people to keep it from being known that Corrigan had informed on him? For God's sake!"

"No. He killed three people so he could safely kill a fourth." Wolfe was on his way now. "When he learned that it was Corrigan who had ruined his career, destroyed him, he determined to kill Corrigan. But no matter how cleverly he managed it, Dykes would be an intolerable menace. Dykes knew that O'Malley knew of Corrigan's treachery, and if Corrigan met a sudden and violent death, no matter how, Dykes might speak. So first Dykes had to go, and he did. Then Joan Wellman —was she also a menace? O'Malley had to find out, and he arranged **to** meet her. He may have thought he intended her no harm—the confession says so—but when she spoke of the resemblance of the novel's plot to an event in real life, and even came close to remembering his name, that, as the confession says, was more than enough for him. Five hours later she was dead."

There was a noise from the rear of the room, the sound of a chair scraping. John R. Wellman was on his feet and moving. Eyes went to him. Wolfe stopped speaking, but Wellman came on tiptoe, off to one side, around the corner and along the wall to the chair which Purley Stebbins had vacated. It had an unobstructed view of the lawyers.

"Excuse me," he said, apparently to everyone, and sat.

There were murmurs from the women. Cramer shot a glance at Wellman, evidently decided that he was not getting set as a nemesis, and looked at Wolfe.

"There remained," Wolfe resumed, "only one source of possible danger, Rachel Abrams. O'Malley had probably been told about her by Dykes, but whether he had or not, he had found the receipts she had given Baird Archer when he searched Dykes's apartment. I'll read a few lines from the confession." He fingered the sheets, found the place, and read:

"My inner being could not permit me to feel any moral repulsion at the thought of killing Joan Wellman, certainly not enough to restrain me, for if killing her was morally unacceptable how could I justify the killing of Dykes? By killing Joan Wellman the process was completed. After that, given adequate motive, I could have killed any number of people without any sign of compunction. So in contemplating the murder of Rachel Abrams my only concerns were whether it was necessary and whether it could be performed without undue risk. I decided it was necessary."

Wolfe looked up. "This is indeed a remarkable document. There we have a man relieving his mind, perhaps even soothing his soul, by coolly expounding the stages of his transformation into a cold-blooded killer, but avoiding the consequent penalty by ascribing the deeds and the onus to another person. It was an adroit and witty stratagem, and it would have triumphed if Mr. Wellman had not engaged my services and remained resolute in spite of repeated checks and disappointments.

"But I'm ahead of myself. This confession is all right as far as it goes, but it leaves gaps. By the day he went for Rachel Abrams, the twenty-sixth of February, two weeks ago today, she was more than a remote threat. He knew—"

"You still mean O'Malley?" Kustin cut in.

"Yes."

"Then you're talking too fast. O'Malley was in Atlanta two weeks ago today."

Wolfe nodded. "I'll get to that. By that day he knew that I was on the case and was concentrating on Baird Archer and the manuscript, and the possibility that I might find Rachel Abrams certainly did not escape him. He had to deal with her first, and he did—a scant two minutes before Mr. Goodwin reached her. And there he was. The preliminaries were completed. He was ready for what had always been his real objective: the murder of Corrigan. To abandon it was unthinkable, but now it was not so simple. Needing to learn how much I knew, he phoned Corrigan to suggest that all of you should come here and invite my questions, and you came. It may be that my asking to see Dykes's letter of resignation first gave him the idea of putting it all onto Corrigan; that's of no moment; in any case, he contrived to put that notation in Corrigan's hand on the letter before it reached me, as the first step."

Wolfe paused to glance at Wellman, but our client was merely gazing at O'Malley, with no apparent intention of taking part. He went on. "When the police confronted you with the notation, of course O'Malley had to join you in your claim of ignorance and your charge that I must have made the notation myself. Then came the letter from Mrs. Potter, and naturally that suited him admirably. He knew it was a decoy, either mine or Mr. Cramer's, for he was confident that all copies of the manuscript had been destroyed. I have had no report of your conference that day, but I would give odds that he maneuvered with all his dexterity to arrange that Corrigan should be the one to go to California. The result met his highest expectations. On Corrigan's return you came together to see me again and, as it seemed to O'Malley, I played directly into his hand by refusing to say anything except that I was about ready to act. That made the threat, to whoever was its object, ominous and imminent; that made it most plausible that Corrigan, granting he was the object, would prefer self-destruction and would choose that moment for it; and O'Malley moved swiftly and ruthlessly. It was only ten hours after he left here with you that he dialed my number to let me hear the shot that killed Corrigan."

"You foresaw that?" Kustin demanded.

"Certainly not. At the time you left here I had added only one presumption to my scanty collection: that Corrigan had never seen the manuscript and didn't know what was in it. Regarding the rest of you I was still at sea. I was still merely trying to prod you into movement, and it can't be denied that I succeeded. Are you ready to say something, Mr. O'Malley?"

"No. I'm still listening."

"As you please. I'm about through." Wolfe looked at Kustin. "You said that O'Malley was in Atlanta the day Rachel Abrams was killed. Can you certify that, or do you only mean that he was supposed to be?"

"He was there on business for the firm."

"I know. In fact it is not true that my eye on you gentlemen has been totally impartial until two days ago. The first time you came here O'Malley managed to get it on the record with me that he had returned to New York only that morning after a week in Georgia, and I noted it. I don't suppose you know Saul Panzer?"

"Saul Panzer? No."

"That is Mr. Panzer, there at the end of Mr. Goodwin's desk. If he ever wants to know anything about you, tell him; you might as well. Four days ago I asked him to investigate O'Malley's movements during the week in question, and he has done so. Saul, tell us about it."

Saul got his mouth open but no words out, because Cramer suddenly came to life. He snapped, "Hold it, Panzer!" To Wolfe: "Is this what you got on the phone this morning?"

"Yes."

"And you're going to hand it to him like this? Just dump the bag for him? You are not!"

Wolfe shrugged. "Either I go on or you do. This morning you said you would take a hand and I said no. Now you're welcome. Take it if you want it."

"I want it." Cramer was on his feet. "I want that letter and envelope. I want Panzer. I want statements from the three women. Mr. O'Malley, you'll go downtown with Sergeant Stebbins for questioning."

O'Malley was not impressed. "On what charge, Inspector?"

"I said for questioning. If you insist on a charge you'll get one."

"I would want my counsel present."

"You can phone him from the District Attorney's office."

"Luckily I don't have to phone him. He's here." O'Malley turned his head. "Louis?"

Kustin, meeting his former associate's eye, didn't hesitate. "No," he said flatly. "I'm out, Con. I can't do it."

It put O'Malley off balance, but it didn't floor him. He didn't try to press, Kustin's tone having settled it. He turned back to Cramer, but his view was obstructed. John R. Wellman had left his chair and was standing there facing him, and spoke.

"I'm Joan Wellman's father, Mr. O'Malley. I don't know, because it's pretty complicated, but I'd like to see something. I'd like to see if you feel like shaking hands with me." He extended his hand. "There it is. Do you feel like it or don't you?"

Into the heavy silence came a smothered gasp from one of the females. O'Malley nearly made it. He tried. Looking up at Wellman, he started to lift a hand, then his neck muscles gave, his head dropped, and he used both hands to cover his face.

"I guess you don't," Wellman said, and turned and headed for the door.

XXIII

ONE day last week I made a station-to-station call to a number in Glendale, California. When I got it I began, "Peggy? This is Archie. Calling from New York."

"Hello, Archie. I was thinking you might call."

I made a face. I had been familiar deliberately, with a specific purpose, to find a flaw. There was just a chance she might fake indignation, or she might be coy, or she might even pretend not to know who it was. Nothing doing. She was still her—too short, too plump, and too old, but the one and only Mrs. Potter.

"It's all over," I told her. "I knew you'd want to know. The jury was out nine hours, but they finally came through with it, first degree murder. As you know, he was tried for Rachel Abrams, not your brother, but that doesn't make any difference. Convicting him for one was convicting him for all four."

"Yes, of course. I'm glad it's over. Thank you for calling. You sound so close, as if you were right here."

"Yeah, so do you. What's it doing out there, raining?"

"Oh, no, bright sunshine, warm and bright. Why, is it raining in New York?"

"It sure is. I guess I bring it on. Do you remember how I looked that day through the peephole?"

"I certainly do! I'll never forget it!"

"Neither will I. Good-by, Peggy."

"Good-by, Archie."

I hung up and made another face. What the hell, I thought, in another twenty years Bubblehead may be dead, and age and contours won't matter much, and I'll grab her.

THREE WITNESSES

THE NEXT WITNESS

I

I HAD had previous contacts with Assistant District Attorney Irving Mandelbaum, but had never seen him perform in a courtroom. That morning, watching him at the chore of trying to persuade a jury to clamp it on Leonard Ashe for the murder of Marie Willis, I thought he was pretty good and might be better when he had warmed up. A little plump and a little short, bald in front and big-eared, he wasn't impressive to look at, but he was businesslike and self-assured without being cocky, and he had a neat trick of pausing for a moment to look at the jury as if he half expected one of them to offer a helpful suggestion. When he pulled it, not too often, his back was turned to the judge and the defense counsel, so they couldn't see his face, but I could, from where I sat in the audience.

It was the third day of the trial, and he had called his fifth witness, a scared-looking little guy with a pushed-in nose who gave his name, Clyde Bagby, took the oath, sat down, and fixed his scared brown eyes on Mandelbaum as if he had abandoned hope.

Mandelbaum's tone was reassuring. "What is your business, Mr. Bagby?"

The witness swallowed. "I'm the president of Bagby Answers Ink."

"By 'Ink' you mean 'Incorporated'?"

"Yes, sir."

"Do you own the business?"

"I own half the stock that's been issued, and my wife owns the other half."

"How long have you been operating that business?"

"Five years now—nearly five and a half."

"And what is the business? Please tell the jury about it."

Bagby's eyes went left for a quick, nervous glance at the jury box but came right back to the prosecutor. "It's a telephone-answering business, that's all. You know what that is."

"Yes, but some members of the jury may not be familiar with the operation. Please describe it."

The witness licked his lips. "Well, you're a person or a firm or an organization and you have a phone, but you're not always there and you want to know about calls that come in your absence. So you go to a telephone-answering service. There are several dozen of them in New York, some of them spread all over town with neighborhood offices, big operations. My own operation, Bagby Answers Ink, it's not so big because I specialize in serving individuals, houses and apartments, instead of firms or organizations. I've got offices in four different exchange districts—Gramercy, Plaza, Trafalgar, and Rhinelander. I can't work it from one central office because—"

"Excuse me, Mr. Bagby, but we won't go into technical problems. Is one of your offices at six-eighteen East Sixty-ninth Street, Manhattan?"

"Yes, sir."

"Describe the operation at that address."

"Well, that's my newest place, opened only a year ago, and my smallest, so it's not in an office building, it's an apartment—on account of the labor law. You can't have women working in an office building after two a.m. unless it's a public service, but I have to give my clients all-night service, so there on Sixty-ninth Street I've got four operators for the three switchboards, and they all live right there in the apartment. That way I can have one at the boards from eight till two at night, and another one from two o'clock on. After nine in the morning three are on, one for each board, for the daytime load."

"Are the switchboards installed in one of the rooms of the apartment?"

"Yes, sir."

"Tell the jury what one of them is like and how it works."

Bagby darted another nervous glance at the jury box and went back to the prosecutor. "It's a good deal like any board in a big office, with rows of holes for the plugs. Of course it's installed by the telephone company, with the special wiring for connections with my clients' phones. Each board has room for sixty clients. For each client there's a little light and a hole and a card strip with the client's name. When someone dials a client's number his light goes on and a buzz synchronizes with the ringing of the client's phone. How many buzzes the girl counts before she plugs in depends on what client it is. Some of them want her to plug in after three buzzes, some want her to wait longer. I've got one client that has her count fifteen buzzes. That's the kind of specialized individualized service I give my clients. The big outfits, the

ones with tens of thousands of clients, they won't do that. They've com-
mercialized it. With me every client is a special case and a sacred trust."

"Thank you, Mr. Bagby." Mandelbaum swiveled his head for a swift
sympathetic smile at the jury and swiveled it back again. "But I wasn't
buzzing for a plug for your business. When a client's light shows on
the board, and the girl has heard the prescribed number of buzzes, she
plugs in on the line, is that it?"

I thought Mandelbaum's crack was a little out of place for that set-
ting, where a man was on trial for his life, and turned my head right
for a glance at Nero Wolfe to see if he agreed, but one glimpse of his
profile told me that he was sticking to his role of a morose martyr and
so was in no humor to agree with anyone or anything.

That was to be expected. At that hour of the morning, following his
hard-and-fast schedule, he would have been up in the plant rooms on
the roof of his old brownstone house on West Thirty-fifth Street, bossing
Theodore for the glory of his celebrated collection of orchids, even
possibly getting his hands dirty. At eleven o'clock, after washing his
hands, he would have taken the elevator down to his office on the
ground floor, arranged his oversized corpus in his oversized chair behind his desk, rung for Fritz to bring beer, and started bossing Archie
Goodwin, me. He would have given me any instructions he thought
timely and desirable, for anything from typing a letter to tailing the
mayor, which seemed likely to boost his income and add to his reputation as the best private detective east of San Francisco. And he would
have been looking forward to lunch by Fritz.

And all that was "would-have-been" because he had been subpoenaed
by the State of New York to appear in court and testify at the trial of
Leonard Ashe. He hated to leave his house at all, and particularly he
hated to leave it for a trip to a witness-box. Being a private detective,
he had to concede that a summons to testify was an occupational hazard
he must accept if he hoped to collect fees from clients, but this cloud
didn't even have that silver lining. Leonard Ashe had come to the office
one day about two months ago to hire him, but had been turned down.
So neither fee nor glory was in prospect. As for me, I had been subpoenaed too, but only for insurance, since I wouldn't be called unless
Mandelbaum decided Wolfe's testimony needed corroboration, which
wasn't likely.

It was no pleasure to look at Wolfe's gloomy phiz, so I looked back at
the performers. Bagby was answering. "Yes, sir, she plugs in and says,
'Mrs. Smith's residence,' or, 'Mr. Jones's apartment,' or whatever she has
been told to say for that client. Then she says Mrs. Smith is out and is

there any message, and so on, whatever the situation calls for. Sometimes the client has called and given her a message for some particular caller." Bagby flipped a hand. "Just anything. We give specialized service."

Mandelbaum nodded. "I think that gives us a clear picture of the operation. Now, Mr. Bagby, please look at that gentleman in the dark blue suit sitting next to the officer. He is the defendant in this trial. Do you know him?"

"Yes, sir. That's Mr. Leonard Ashe."

"When and where did you meet him?"

"In July he came to my office on Forty-seventh Street. First he phoned, and then he came."

"Can you give the day in July?"

"The twelfth. A Monday."

"What did he say?"

"He asked how my answering service worked, and I told him, and he said he wanted it for his home telephone at his apartment on East Seventy-third Street. He paid cash for a month in advance. He wanted twenty-four-hour service."

"Did he want any special service?"

"He didn't ask me for any, but two days later he contacted Marie Willis and offered her five hundred dollars if she—"

The witness was interrupted from two directions at once. The defense attorney, a champion named Jimmy Donovan whose batting average on big criminal cases had topped the list of the New York bar for ten years, left his chair with his mouth open to object; and Mandelbaum showed the witness a palm to stop him.

"Just a minute, Mr. Bagby. Just answer my questions. Did you accept Leonard Ashe as a client?"

"Sure, there was no reason not to."

"What was the number of his telephone at his home?"

"Rhinelander two-three-eight-three-eight."

"Did you give his name and that number a place on one of your switchboards?"

"Yes, sir, one of the three boards at the apartment on East Sixty-ninth Street. That's the Rhinelander district."

"What was the name of the employee who attended that board—the one with Leonard Ashe's number on it?"

"Marie Willis."

A shadow of stir and murmur rippled across the packed audience, and Judge Corbett on the bench turned his head to give it a frown and then went back to his knitting.

Bagby was going on. "Of course at night there's only one girl on the three boards—they rotate on that—but for daytime I keep a girl at her own board at least five days a week, and six if I can. That way she gets to know her clients."

"And Leonard Ashe's number was on Marie Willis's board?"

"Yes, sir."

"After the routine arrangements for serving Leonard Ashe as a client had been completed, did anything happen to bring him or his number to your personal attention?"

"Yes, sir."

"What and when? First, when?"

Bagby took a second to make sure he had it right before swearing to it. "It was Thursday, three days after Ashe had ordered the service. That was July fifteenth. Marie phoned me at my office and said she wanted to see me privately about something important. I asked if it could wait till she was off the board at six o'clock, and she said yes, and a little after six I went up to Sixty-ninth Street and we went into her room at the apartment. She told me Ashe had phoned her the day before and asked her to meet him somewhere to discuss some details about servicing his number. She told him such a discussion should be with me, but he insisted—"

A pleasant but firm baritone cut in. "If Your Honor pleases." Jimmy Donovan was on his feet. "I submit that the witness may not testify to what Marie Willis and Mr. Ashe said to each other when he was not present."

"Certainly not," Mandelbaum agreed shortly. "He is reporting what Marie Willis told *him* had been said."

Judge Corbett nodded. "That should be kept clear. You understand that, Mr. Bagby?"

"Yes, sir." Bagby bit his lip. "I mean Your Honor."

"Then go ahead. What Miss Willis said to you and you to her."

"Well, she said she had agreed to meet Ashe because he was a theatrical producer and she wanted to be an actress. I hadn't known she was stage-struck but I know it now. So she had gone to his office on Forty-fifth Street as soon as she was off the board, and after he talked some and asked some questions he told her—this is what she told me—he told her he wanted her to listen in on calls to his home number during the daytime. All she would have to do, when his light on her board went on and the buzzes started, if the buzzes stopped and the light went off—that would mean someone had answered the phone at his home—she would plug in and listen to the conversation. Then each evening she would phone him and report. That's what she said Ashe had asked her to do. She said he counted out five hundred dollars in bills and offered them to her and told her he'd give her another thousand if she went along."

Bagby stopped for wind. Mandelbaum prodded him. "Did she say anything else?"

"Yes, sir. She said she knew she should have turned him down flat, but she didn't want to make him sore, so she told him she wanted to think it over for a day or two. Then she said she had slept on it and decided what to do. She said of course she knew that what Ashe was after was phone calls to his wife, and aside from anything else she wouldn't spy on his wife, because his wife was Robina Keane, who had given up her career as an actress two years ago to marry Ashe, and Marie worshiped Robina Keane as her ideal. That's what Marie told me. She said she had decided she must do three things. She must tell me about it because Ashe was my client and she was working for me. She must tell Robina Keane about it, to warn her, because Ashe would probably get someone else to do the spying for him. It occurred to me that her real reason for wanting to tell Robina Keane might be that she hoped—"

Mandelbaum stopped him. "What occurred to you isn't material, Mr. Bagby. Did Marie tell you the third thing she had decided she must do?"

"Yes, sir. That she must tell Ashe that she was going to tell his wife. She said she had to because at the start of her talk with him she had promised Ashe she would keep it confidential, so she had to warn him she was withdrawing her promise."

"Did she say when she intended to do those three things?"

The witness nodded. "She had already done one of them, telling me. She said she had phoned Ashe and told him she would be at his office at seven o'clock. That was crowding it a little, because she had the evening shift that day and would have to be back at the boards at eight o'clock. It crowded me too because it gave me no time to talk her out of it. I went downtown with her in a taxi, to Forty-fifth Street, where Ashe's office was, and did my best but couldn't move her."

"What did you say to her?"

"I tried to get her to lay off. If she went through with her program it might not do any harm to my business, but again it might. I tried to persuade her to let me handle it by going to Ashe and telling him she had told me of his offer and I didn't want him for a client, and then drop it and forget it, but she was dead set on warning Robina Keane, and to do that she had to withdraw her promise to Ashe. I hung on until she entered the elevator to go up to Ashe's office, but I couldn't budge her."

"Did you go up with her?"

"No, that wouldn't have helped any. She was going through with it, and what could I do?"

So, I was thinking to myself, that's how it is. It looked pretty tough to me, and I glanced at Wolfe, but his eyes were closed, so I turned my head the other way to see how the gentleman in the dark blue suit seated next to the officer was taking it. Apparently it looked pretty tough to Leonard Ashe too. With deep creases slanting along the jowls of his dark bony face from the corners of his wide full mouth, and his sunken dark eyes, he was certainly a prime subject for the artists who sketch candidates for the hot seat for the tabloids, and for three days they had been making the most of it. He was no treat for the eyes, and I took mine away from him, to the left, where his wife sat in the front row of the audience.

I had never worshiped Robina Keane as my ideal, but I had liked her fine in a couple of shows, and she was giving a good performance for her first and only courtroom appearance—either being steadfastly loyal to her husband or putting on an act, but good in either case. She was dressed quietly and she sat quietly, but she wasn't trying to pretend she wasn't young and beautiful. Exactly how she and her older and un-beautiful husband stood with each other was anybody's guess, and everybody was guessing. One extreme said he was her whole world and he had been absolutely batty to suspect her of any hoop-rolling; the other extreme said she had quit the stage only to have more time for certain promiscuous activities, and Ashe had been a sap not to know it sooner; and anywhere in between. I wasn't ready to vote. Looking at her, she might have been an angel. Looking at him, it must have taken something drastic to get him that miserable, though I granted that being locked up two months on a charge of murder would have some effect.

Mandelbaum was making sure the jury had got it. "Then you didn't go up to Ashe's office with Marie Willis?"

"No, sir."

"Did you go up later, at any time, after she had gone up?"

"No, sir."

"Did you see Ashe at all that evening?"

"No, sir."

"Did you speak to him on the telephone that evening?"

"No, sir."

Looking at Bagby, and I have looked at a lot of specimens under fire, I decided that either he was telling it straight or he was an expert liar, and he didn't sound like an expert. Mandelbaum went on. "What did you do that evening, after you saw Marie Willis enter the elevator to go up to Ashe's office?"

"I went to keep a dinner date with a friend at a restaurant—Hornby's on Fifty-second Street—and after that, around half-past eight, I went up to my Trafalgar office at Eighty-sixth Street and Broadway. I have six boards there, and a new night girl was on, and I stayed there with her a while and then took a taxi home, across the park to my apartment on East Seventieth Street. Not long after I got home a phone call came from the police to tell me Marie Willis had been found murdered in my Rhinelander office, and I went there as fast as I could go, and there was a crowd out in front, and an officer took me upstairs."

He stopped to swallow, and stuck his chin out a little. "They hadn't moved her. They had taken the plug cord from around her throat, but they hadn't moved her, and there she was, slumped over on the ledge in front of the board. They wanted me to identify her, and I had—"

The witness wasn't interrupted, but I was. There was a tug at my sleeve, and a whisper in my ear—"We're leaving, come on." And Nero Wolfe arose, sidled past two pairs of knees to the aisle, and headed for the rear of the courtroom. For his bulk he could move quicker and smoother than you would expect, and as I followed him to the door and on out to the corridor we got no attention at all. I was assuming that some vital need had stirred him, like phoning Theodore to tell him or ask him something about an orchid, but he went on past the phone booths to the elevator and pushed the down button. With people all around I asked no questions. He got out at the main floor and made for Centre Street. Out on the sidewalk he backed up against the granite of the courthouse and spoke.

"We want a taxi, but first a word with you."

"No, sir," I said firmly. "First a word *from* me. Mandelbaum may finish with that witness any minute, and the cross-examination may not take long, or Donovan might even reserve it, and you were told you would follow Bagby. If you want a taxi, of course you're going home, and that will just—"

"I'm not going home. I can't."

"Right. If you do you'll merely get hauled back here and also a fat fine for contempt of court. Not to mention me. I'm under subpoena too. I'm going back to the courtroom. Where are you going?"

"To six-eighteen East Sixty-ninth Street."

I goggled at him. "I've always been afraid of this. Does it hurt?"

"Yes. I'll explain on the way."

"I'm going back to the courtroom."

"No. I'll need you."

Like everyone else, I love to feel needed, so I wheeled, crossed the sidewalk, flagged a taxi to the curb, and opened the door. Wolfe came and climbed in, and I followed. After he had got himself braced against the hazards of a carrier on wheels and I had given the driver the address, and we were rolling, I said, "Shoot. I've heard you do a lot of explaining, but this will have to be good."

"It's preposterous," he declared.

"It sure is. Let's go back."

"I mean Mr. Mandelbaum's thesis. I will concede that Mr. Ashe might have murdered that girl. I will concede that his state of mind about his wife might have approached mania, and therefore the motive suggested by that witness might have been adequate provocation. But he's not an imbecile. Under the circumstances as given, and I doubt if Mr. Bagby can be discredited, I refuse to believe he was ass enough to go to that place at that time and kill her. You were present when he called on me that day to hire me. Do you believe it?"

I shook my head. "I pass. You're explaining. However, I read the papers too, and also I've chatted with Lon Cohen of the *Gazette* about it. It doesn't have to be that Ashe went there for the purpose of killing her. His story is that a man phoned him—a voice he didn't recognize— and said if Ashe would meet him at the Bagby place on Sixty-ninth Street he thought they could talk Marie out of it, and Ashe went on the hop, and the door to the office was standing open, and he went in and there she was with a plug cord tight around her throat, and he opened a window and yelled for the police. Of course if you like it that Bagby was lying just now when he said it wasn't him that phoned Ashe, and that Bagby is such a good businessman that he would rather kill an employee than lose a customer—"

"Pfui. It isn't what I like, it's what I don't like. Another thing I didn't like was sitting there on that confounded wooden bench with a smelly woman against me. Soon I was going to be called as a witness, and my testimony would have been effective corroboration of Mr. Bagby's testimony, as you know. It was intolerable. I believe that if Mr. Ashe is convicted of murder on the thesis Mr. Mandelbaum is presenting it will be a justicial transgression, and I will not be a party to it. It wasn't easy to get up and go because I can't go home. If I go home they'll come and drag me out, and into that witness-box."

I eyed him. "Let's see if I get you. You can't bear to help convict Ashe of murder because you doubt if he's guilty, so you're scooting. Right?"

The hackie twisted his head around to inform us through the side of his mouth, "Sure he's guilty."

We ignored it. "That's close enough," Wolfe said.

"Not close enough for me. If you expect me to scoot with you and invite a stiff fine for running out on a subpoena, which you will pay, don't try to guff me. Say we doubt if Ashe is guilty, but we think he may get tagged because we know Mandelbaum wouldn't go to trial without a good case. Say also our bank account needs a shot in the arm, which is true. So we decide to see if we can find something that will push Mandelbaum's nose in, thinking that if Ashe is properly grateful a measly little fine will be nothing. The way to proceed would be for you to think up a batch of errands for me, and you go on home and read a book and have a good lunch, but that's out because they'd come and get you. Therefore we must both do errands. If that's how it stands, it's a fine day and I admit that woman was smelly, but I have a good nose and I think it was Tissot's Passion Flower, which is eighty bucks an ounce. What are we going to do at Sixty-ninth Street?"

"I don't know."

"Good. Neither do I."

II

It was a dump, an old five-story walk-up, brick that had been painted yellow about the time I had started working for Nero Wolfe. In the vestibule I pushed the button that was labeled *Bagby Answers, Inc.*, and when the click came I opened the door and led the way across the crummy little hall to the stairs and up one flight. Mr. Bagby wasn't wasting it on rent. At the front end of the hall a door stood open. As we approached it I stepped aside to let Wolfe go first, since I didn't know whether we were disguised as brush peddlers or as plumbers.

As Wolfe went to speak to a girl at a desk I sent my eyes on a quick survey. It was the scene of the murder. In the front wall of the room three windows overlooked the street. Against the opposite wall were ranged the three switchboards, with three females with headphones seated at them. They had turned their heads for a look at the company.

The girl at the desk, which was near the end window, had only an ordinary desk phone, in addition to a typewriter and other accessories. Wolfe was telling her, "My name is Wolfe and I've just come from the courtroom where Leonard Ashe is being tried." He indicated me with a jerk of his head. "This is my assistant, Mr. Goodwin. We're checking on subpoenas that have been served on witnesses, for both the prosecution and the defense. Have you been served?"

With his air and presence and tone, only one woman in a hundred would have called him, and she wasn't it. Her long, narrow face tilted up to him, she shook her head. "No, I haven't."

"Your name, please?"

"Pearl Fleming."

"Then you weren't working here on July fifteenth."

"No, I was at another office. There was no office desk here then. One of the boards took office calls."

"I see." His tone implied that it was damned lucky for her that he saw. "Are Miss Hart and Miss Velardi and Miss Weltz here?"

My brows wanted to lift, but I kept them down, and anyway there was nothing startling about it. True, it had been weeks since those names had appeared in the papers, but Wolfe never missed a word of an account of a murder, and his skull's filing system was even better than Saul Panzer's.

Pearl Fleming pointed to the switchboards. "That's Miss Hart at the end. Miss Velardi is next to her. Next to Miss Verlardi is Miss Yerkes. She came after—she replaced Miss Willis. Miss Weltz isn't here; it's her day off. They've had subpoenas, but—"

She stopped and turned her head. The woman at the end board had removed her headphone, left her seat, and was marching over to us. She was about my age, with sharp brown eyes and flat cheeks and a chin she could have used for an icebreaker if she had been a walrus.

"Aren't you Nero Wolfe, the detective?" she demanded.

"Yes," he assented. "You are Alice Hart?"

She skipped it. "What do you want?"

Wolfe backed up a step. He doesn't like anyone so close to him, especially a woman. "I want information, madam. I want you and Bella Velardi and Helen Weltz to answer some questions."

"We have no information."

"Then I won't get any, but I'm going to try."

"Who sent you here?"

"Autokinesis. There's a cardinal flaw in the assumption that Leonard Ashe killed Marie Willis, and I don't like flaws. It has made me curious, and when I'm curious there is only one cure—the whole truth, and I intend to find it. If I am in time to save Mr. Ashe's life, so much the better; but in any case I have started and will not be stopped. If you and the others refuse to oblige me today there will be other days—and other ways."

From her face it was a toss-up. Her chin stiffened, and for a second she was going to tell him to go soak his head; then her eyes left him for me, and she was going to take it. She turned to the girl at the desk. "Take my board, will you, Pearl? I won't be long." To Wolfe, snapping it: "We'll go to my room. This way." She whirled and started.

"One moment, Miss Hart." Wolfe moved. "A point not covered in the newspaper accounts." He stopped at the boards, behind Bella Velardi at the middle one. "Marie Willis's body was found slumped over on the ledge in front of the switchboard. Presumably she was seated at the switchboard when the murderer arrived. But you live here—you and the others?"

"Yes."

"Then if the murderer was Mr. Ashe, how did he know she was alone on the premises?"

"I don't know. Perhaps she told him she was. Is that the flaw?"

"Good heavens, no. It's conceivable that she did, and they talked, and he waited until a light and buzzes had her busy at the board, with her back to him. It's a minor point, but I prefer someone with surer knowledge that she was alone. Since she was small and slight, even you are not excluded"—he wiggled a finger—"or these others. Not that I am now prepared to charge you with murder."

"I hope not," she snorted, turning. She led the way to a door at the end of the room, on through, and down a narrow hall. As I followed, behind Wolfe, I was thinking that the reaction we were getting seemed a little exaggerated. It would have been natural, under the circumstances, for Miss Velardi and Miss Yerkes to turn in their seats for a good look at us, but they hadn't. They had sat, rigid, staring at their boards. As for Alice Hart, either there had been a pinch of relief in her voice when she asked Wolfe if that was the flaw, or I was in the wrong business.

Her room was a surprise. First, it was big, much bigger than the one in front with the switchboards. Second, I am not Bernard Berenson, but I have noticed things here and there, and the framed splash of red and yellow and blue above the mantel was not only a real Van Gogh, it was bigger and better than the one Lily Rowan had. I saw Wolfe spotting it as he lowered himself onto a chair actually big enough for him, and I pulled one around to make a group, facing the couch Miss Hart dropped onto.

As she sat she spoke. "What's the flaw?"

He shook his head. "I'm the inquisitor, Miss Hart, not you." He aimed a thumb at the Van Gogh. "Where did you get that picture?"

She looked at it, and back at him. "That's none of your business."

"It certainly isn't. But here is the situation. You have of course been questioned by the police and the District Attorney's office, but they were restrained by their assumption that Leonard Ashe was the culprit. Since I reject that assumption and must find another in its stead, there can be no limit to my impertinence with you and others who may be involved. Take you and that picture. If you refuse to say where you got it, or if your answer doesn't satisfy me, I'll put a man on it, a competent man, and he'll find out. You can't escape being badgered, madam; the question is whether you suffer it here and now, by me, or face a prolonged inquiry among your friends and associates by meddlesome men. If you prefer the latter don't waste time with me; I'll go and tackle one of the others."

She was tossing up again. From her look at him it seemed just as well that he had his bodyguard along. She tried stalling. "What does it matter where I got that picture?"

"Probably it doesn't. Possibly nothing about you matters. But the picture is a treasure, and this is an odd address for it. Do you own it?"

"Yes. I bought it."

"When?"

"About a year ago. From a dealer."

"The contents of this room are yours?"

"Yes. I like things that—well, this is my extravagance, my only one."

"How long have you been with this firm?"

"Five years."

"What is your salary?"

She was on a tight rein. "Eighty dollars a week."

"Not enough for your extravagance. An inheritance? Alimony? Other income?"

"I have never married. I had some savings, and I wanted—I wanted these things. If you save for fifteen years you have a right to something."

"You have indeed. Where were you the evening that Marie Willis was killed?"

"I was out in Jersey, in a car with a friend—Bella Velardi. To get cooled off—it was a hot night. We got back after midnight."

"In your car?"

"No, Helen Weltz had let us take hers. She has a Jaguar."

My brows went up, and I spoke. "A Jaguar," I told Wolfe, "is quite a machine. You couldn't squeeze into one. Counting taxes and extras, four thousand bucks isn't enough."

His eyes darted to me and back to her. "Of course the police have asked if you know of anyone who might have had a motive for killing Marie Willis. Do you?"

"No." Her rein wasn't so tight.

"Were you friendly with her?"

"Yes, friendly enough."

"Has any client ever asked you to listen in on calls to his number?"

"Certainly not!"

"Did you know Miss Willis wanted to be an actress?"

"Yes, we all knew that."

"Mr. Bagby says he didn't."

Her chin had relaxed a little. "He was her employer. I don't suppose he knew. When did you talk with Mr. Bagby?"

"I didn't. I heard him on the witness stand. Did you know of Miss Willis's regard for Robina Keane?"

"Yes, we all knew that too. Marie did imitations of Robina Keane in her parts."

"When did she tell you of her decision to tell Robina Keane that her husband was going to monitor her telephone?"

Miss Hart frowned. "I didn't say she told me."

"Did she?"

"No."

"Did anyone?"

"Yes, Miss Velardi. Marie had told her. You can ask her."

"I shall. Do you know Guy Unger?"

"Yes, I know him. Not very well."

Wolfe was playing a game I had often watched him at, tossing balls at random to see how they bounced. It's a good way to try to find a lead if you haven't got one, but it may take all day, and he didn't have it. If one of the females in the front room took a notion to phone the cops or the DA's office about us we might have visitors any minute. As for Guy Unger, that was another name from the newspaper accounts. He had been Marie Willis's boy friend, or had he? There had been a difference of opinion among the journalists.

Miss Hart's opinion was that Guy Unger and Marie had enjoyed each other's company, but that was as far as it went—I mean her opinion. She knew nothing of any crisis that might have made Unger want to end the friendship with a plug cord. For another five minutes Wolfe went on with the game, tossing different balls from different angles, and then abruptly arose.

"Very well," he said. "For now. I'll try Miss Velardi."

"I'll send her in." Alice Hart was on her feet, eager to cooperate. "Her room is next door." She moved. "This way."

Obviously she didn't want to leave us with her Van Gogh. There was a lock on a bureau drawer that I could probably have manipulated in twenty seconds, and I would have liked to try my hand on it, but Wolfe was following her out, so I went along—to the right, down the hall to another door, standing open. Leaving us there, she strode on flat heels toward the front. Wolfe passed through the open door with me behind.

This room was different—somewhat smaller, with no Van Gogh and the kind of furniture you might expect. The bed hadn't been made, and Wolfe stood and scowled at it a moment, lowered himself gingerly onto a chair too small for him with worn upholstery, and told me curtly, "Look around."

I did so. Bella Velardi was a crack-lover. A closet door and a majority of the drawers in a dressing table and two chests were open to cracks of various widths. One of the reasons I am still shy a wife is the risk of getting a crack-lover. I went and pulled the closet door open, and, having no machete to hack my way into the jungle of duds, swung it back to its crack and stepped across to the library. It was a stack of paperbacks on a little table, the one on top being entitled *One Mistake Too Many*, with a picture of a double-breasted floozie shrinking in terror from a musclebound baboon. There was also a pile of recent editions of *Racing Form* and *Track Dope*.

"She's a philanthropist," I told Wolfe. "She donates dough to the cause of equine genetics."

"Meaning?"

"She bets on horse races."

"Does she lose much?"

"She loses. How much depends on what she bets. Probably tidy sums, since she takes two house journals."

He grunted. "Open drawers. Have one open when she enters. I want to see how much impudence these creatures will tolerate."

I obeyed. The six drawers in the bigger chest all held clothes, and I did no pawing. A good job might have uncovered some giveaway under a pile of nylons, but there wasn't time for it. I closed all the drawers to show her what I thought of cracks. Those in the dressing table were also uninteresting. In the second drawer of the smaller chest, among other items, was a collection of photographs, mostly unmounted snaps, and, running through them, with no expectations, I stopped at one for a second look. It was Bella Velardi and another girl, with a man standing between them, in bathing outfits with the ocean for background. I went and handed it to Wolfe.

"The man?" I asked. "I read newspapers too, and look at the pictures, but it was two months ago, and I could be wrong."

He slanted it to get the best light from a window. He nodded. "Guy Unger." He slipped it into a pocket. "Find more of him."

"If any." I went back to the collection. "But you may not get a chance at her. It's been a good four minutes. Either she's getting a full briefing from Miss Hart, or they've phoned for help, and in that case—"

The sound came of high heels clicking on the uncarpeted hall. I closed the second drawer and pulled the third one open, and was inspecting its contents when the clicks got to the door and were in the room. Shutting it in no hurry and turning to Bella Velardi, I was ready to meet a yelp of indignation, but didn't have to. With her snappy black eyes and sassy little face she must have been perfectly capable of indignation, but her nerves were too busy with something else. She decided to pretend she hadn't caught me with a drawer open, and that was screwy. Added to other things, it made it a cinch that these phone answerers had something on their minds.

Bella Velardi said in a scratchy little voice, "Miss Hart says you want to ask me something," and went and sat on the edge of the unmade bed, with her fingers twisted together.

Wolfe regarded her with his eyes half closed. "Do you know what a hypothetical question is, Miss Velardi?"

"Of course I do."

"I have one for you. If I put three expert investigators on the job of finding out approximately how much you have lost betting on horse races in the past year, how long do you think it would take them?"

"Why, I—" She blinked at him with a fine set of long lashes. "I don't know."

"I do. With luck, five hours. Without it, five days. It would be simpler for you to tell me. How much have you lost?"

She blinked again. "How do you know I've lost anything?"

"I don't. But Mr. Goodwin, who is himself an expert investigator, concluded from publications he found on that table that you are a chronic bettor. If so, there's a fair chance that you keep a record of your gains and losses." He turned to me. "Archie, your search was interrupted. Resume. See if you can find it." Back to her. "At his elbow if you like, Miss Velardi. There is no question of pilfering."

I went to the smaller chest. He was certainly crowding his luck. If she took this without calling a cop she might not be a murderess, but she sure had a tender spot she didn't want touched.

Actually she didn't just sit and take it. As I got a drawer handle to pull it open she loosened her tongue. "Look, Mr. Wolfe, I'm perfectly willing to tell you anything you want to know. Perfectly!" She was leaning toward him, her fingers still twisted. "Miss Hart said I mustn't be surprised at anything you asked, but I was, so I guess I was flustered. There's no secret about my liking to bet on the races, but the amounts

I bet—that's different. You see, I have friends who—well, they don't want people to know they bet, so they give me money to bet for them. So it's about a hundred dollars a week, sometimes more, maybe up to two hundred."

If she liked to bet on any animals other than horses, one would have got her ten that she was a damn liar. Evidently Wolfe would have split it with me, since he didn't even bother to ask her the names of the friends.

He merely nodded. "What is your salary?"

"It's only sixty-five, so of course I can't bet much myself."

"Of course. About the windows in that front room. In summer weather, when one of you is on duty there at night, are the windows open?"

She was concentrating. "When it's hot, yes. Usually the one in the middle. If it's very hot, maybe all of them."

"With the shades up?"

"Yes."

"It was hot July fifteenth. Were the windows open that night?"

"I don't know. I wasn't here."

"Where were you?"

"I was out in Jersey, in a car with a friend—Alice Hart. To get cooled off. We got back after midnight."

Wonderful, I thought. That settled that. One woman might conceivably lie, but surely not two.

Wolfe was eying her. "If the windows were open and the shades up the evening of July fifteenth, as they almost certainly were, would anyone in her senses have proceeded to kill Marie Willis so exposed to view? What do you think?"

She didn't call him on the pronoun. "Why, no," she conceded. "That would have been—no, I don't think so."

"Then she—or he—must have closed the windows and drawn the shades before proceeding. How could Leonard Ashe, in the circumstances as given, have managed that without alarming Miss Willis?"

"I don't know. He might have—no, I don't know."

"He might have what?"

"Nothing. I don't know."

"How well do you know Guy Unger?"

"I know him fairly well."

She had been briefed all right. She was expecting that one.

"Have you seen much of him in the past two months?"

"No, very little."

Wolfe reached in his pocket and got the snapshot and held it out. "When was this taken?"

She left the bed and was going to take it, but he held on to it. After a look she said, "Oh, that," and sat down again. All of a sudden she exploded, indignation finally breaking through. "You took that from my drawer! What else did you take?" She sprang up, trembling all over. "Get out of here! Get out and stay out!"

Wolfe returned the snap to his pocket, arose, said, "Come, Archie, there seems to be a limit after all," and started for the door. I followed.

He was at the sill when she darted past me, grabbed his arm, and took it back. "Wait a minute, I didn't mean that. I flare up like that. I just—I don't care about the damn picture."

Wolfe pulled loose and got a yard of space. "When was it taken?"

"About two weeks ago—two weeks ago Sunday."

"Who is the other woman?"

"Helen Weltz."

"Who took it?"

"A man that was with us."

"His name?"

"His name is Ralph Ingalls."

"Was Guy Unger Miss Weltz's companion, or yours?"

"Why, we—we were just together."

"Nonsense. Two men and two women are never just together. How were you paired?"

"Well—Guy and Helen, and Ralph and me."

Wolfe sent a glance at the chair he had vacated and apparently decided it wasn't worth the trouble of walking back to it. "Then since Miss Willis died Mr. Unger's interest has centered on Miss Weltz?"

"I don't know about 'centered.' They seem to like each other, as far as I know."

"How long have you been working here?"

"At this office, since it opened a year ago. Before that I was at the Trafalgar office for two years."

"When did Miss Willis tell you she was going to tell Robina Keane of her husband's proposal?"

She had expected that one too. "That morning. That Thursday, the fifteenth of July."

"Did you approve?"

"No, I didn't. I thought she ought to just tell him no and forget it. I told her she was asking for trouble and she might get it. But she was so daddled on Robina Keane—" Bella shrugged. "Do you want to sit down?"

"No, thank you. Where is Miss Weltz?"

"This is her day off."

"I know. Where can I find her?"

She opened her mouth and closed it. She opened it again. "I'm not sure. Wait a minute," she said, and went clicking down the hall to the front. It was more like two minutes when she came clicking back and reported, "Miss Hart thinks she's at a little place she rented for the summer up in Westchester. Do you want me to phone and find out?"

"Yes, if you would."

Off she went, and we followed. In the front room the other three were at the boards. While Bella Velardi spoke to Miss Hart, and Miss Hart went to the phone at the desk and got a number and talked, Wolfe stood and frowned around, at the windows, the boards, the phone answerers, and me. When Miss Hart told him Helen Weltz was on the wire he went to the desk and took it.

"Miss Weltz? This is Nero Wolfe. As Miss Hart told you, I'm looking into certain matters connected with the murder of Marie Willis, and would like to see you. I have some other appointments but can adjust them. How long will it take you to get to the city? . . . You can't? . . . I'm afraid I can't wait until tomorrow. . . . No, that's out of the question. . . . I see. You'll be there all afternoon? . . . Very well, I'll do that."

He hung up and asked Miss Hart to tell me how to get to the place in Westchester. She obliged, and beyond Katonah it got so complicated that I got out my notebook. Also I jotted down the phone number. Wolfe had marched out with no amenities, so I thanked her politely and caught up with him halfway down the stairs. When we were out on the sidewalk I inquired, "A taxi to Katonah?"

"No." He was cold with rage. "To the garage for the car."

We headed west.

III

As we stood inside the garage, on Thirty-sixth Street near Tenth Avenue, waiting for Pete to bring the car down, Wolfe came out with something I had been expecting.

"We could walk home," he said, "in four minutes."

I gave him a grin. "Yes, sir. I knew it was coming—while you were on the phone. To go to Katonah we would have to drive. To drive we would have to get the car. To get the car we would have to come to the garage. The garage is so close to home that we might as well go and

have lunch first. Once in the house, with the door bolted and not answering the phone, we could reconsider the matter of driving to Westchester. So you told her we would go to Katonah."

"No. It occurred to me in the cab."

"I can't prove it didn't. But I have a suggestion." I nodded at the
door to the garage office. "There's a phone in there. Call Fritz first. Or
shall I?"

"I suppose so," he muttered, and went to the office door and entered,
sat at the desk, and dialed. In a moment he was telling Fritz who and
where he was, asking some questions, and getting answers he didn't
like. After instructing Fritz to tell callers that he hadn't heard from us
and had no idea where we were, and telling him not to expect us home
until we got there, he hung up, glared at the phone, and then glared
at me.

"There have been four phone calls. One from an officer of the court,
one from the District Attorney's office, and two from Inspector Cramer."

"Ouch." I made a face. "The court and the DA, sure, but not Cramer.
When you're within a mile of a homicide of his he itches from head to
foot. You can imagine what kind of suspicions your walking out under
a subpoena would give him. Let's go home. It will be interesting to see
whether he has one dick posted out in front, or two or three. Of course
he'll collar you and you may get no lunch at all, but what the hell."

"Shut up."

"Yes, sir. Here comes the car."

As we emerged from the office the brown sedan rolled to a stop before us and Pete got out and opened the rear door for Wolfe, who refuses to ride in front because when the crash comes the broken glass
will carve him up. I climbed in behind the wheel, released the brake
and fingered the lever, and fed gas.

At that time of day the West Side Highway wasn't too crowded, and
north of Henry Hudson Bridge, and then on the Sawmill River Parkway, there was nothing to it. I could have let my mind roam if it had
had anywhere to roam, but where? I was all for earning a little token
of gratitude by jerking Leonard Ashe out from under, but how? It was
so damn childish. In his own comfortable chair in his office, Wolfe
could usually manage to keep his genius under control, but on the hard
courtroom bench, with a perfumed woman crowded against him, knowing he couldn't get up and go home, he had dropped the reins, and now
he was stuck. He couldn't call it off and go back to court and apologize
because he was too darned pigheaded. He couldn't go home. There
was even a chance he couldn't go to Katonah for a wild goose. When I
saw in the rear-view mirror a parkway police car closing in on us from

behind, I tightened my lips, and when he passed on by and shot ahead I relaxed and took a deep breath. It would have been pretty extreme to broadcast a general alarm for a mere witness AWOL, but the way Cramer felt about Wolfe it wouldn't have been fantastic.

As I slowed down for Hawthorne Circle I told Wolfe it was a quarter to two and I was hungry and what about him, and was instructed to stop somewhere and get cheese and crackers and beer, and a little farther on I obeyed. Parked off a side road, he ate the crackers and drank the beer, but rejected the cheese after one taste. I was too hungry to taste.

The dash clock said 2:38 when, having followed Alice Hart's directions, I turned off a dirt road into a narrow rutted driveway, crawled between thick bushes on both sides, and, reaching an open space, stepped on the brake to keep from rubbing a bright yellow Jaguar. To the left was a gravel walk across some grass that needed mowing, leading to a door in the side of a little white house with blue trim. As I climbed out two people appeared around the corner of the house. The one in front was the right age, the right size, and the right shape, with blue eyes and hair that matched the Jaguar, held back smooth with a yellow ribbon.

She came on. "You're Archie Goodwin? I'm Helen Weltz. Mr. Wolfe? It's a pleasure. This is Guy Unger. Come this way. We'll sit in the shade of the old apple tree."

In my dim memory of his picture in the paper two months back, and in the snap I had found in Bella Velardi's drawer, Guy Unger hadn't looked particularly like a murderer, and in the flesh he didn't fill the bill any better. He looked too mean, with mean little eyes in a big round face. His gray suit had been cut by someone who knew how, to fit his bulgy shoulders, one a little lower than the other. His mouth, if he had opened it wide, would have been just about big enough to poke his thumb in.

The apple tree was from colonial times, with windfalls of its produce scattered around. Wolfe glowered at the chairs with wooden slats which had been painted white the year before, but it was either that or squat, so he engineered himself into one. Helen Weltz asked what we would like to drink, naming four choices, and Wolfe said no, thank you, with cold courtesy. It didn't seem to faze her. She took a chair facing him, gave him a bright, friendly smile, and included me with a glance from her lively blue eyes.

"You didn't give me a chance on the phone," she said, not complaining. "I didn't want you to have a trip for nothing. I can't tell you anything about that awful business, what happened to Marie. I really can't, because I don't know anything. I was out on the Sound on a boat. Didn't she tell you?"

Wolfe grunted. "That's not the kind of thing I'm after, Miss Weltz. Such routine matters as checking alibis have certainly been handled competently by the police, to the limit of their interest. My own interest has been engaged late—I hope not too late—and my attack must be eccentric. For instance, when did Mr. Unger get here?"

"Why, he just—"

"Now, wait a minute." Unger had picked up an unfinished highball from a table next to him and was holding it with the fingertips of both hands. His voice wasn't squeaky, as you would expect, but a thick baritone. "Just forget me. I'm looking on, that's all. I can't say I'm an impartial observer, because I'm partial to Miss Weltz, if that's all right with her."

Wolfe didn't even glance at him. "I'll explain, Miss Weltz, why I ask when Mr. Unger got here. I'll explain fully. When I went to that place on Sixty-ninth Street and spoke with Miss Hart and Miss Velardi I was insufferable, both in manner and in matter, and they should have flouted me and ordered me out, but they didn't. Manifestly they were afraid to, and I intend to learn why. I assume that you know why. I assume that, after I left, Miss Hart phoned you again, described the situation, and discussed with you how best to handle me. I surmise that she also phoned Mr. Unger, or you did, and he was enough concerned about me to hurry to get here before I arrived. Naturally I would consider that significant. It would reinforce my suspicion that—"

"Forget it," Unger cut in. "I heard about you being on your way about ten minutes ago, when I got here. Miss Weltz invited me yesterday to come out this afternoon. I took a train to Katonah, and a taxi."

Wolfe looked at him. "I can't challenge that, Mr. Unger, but it doesn't smother my surmise. On the contrary. I'll probably finish sooner with Miss Weltz if you'll withdraw. For twenty minutes, say?"

"I think I'd better stay."

"Then please don't prolong it with interruptions."

"You behave yourself, Guy," Helen scolded him. She smiled at Wolfe. "I'll tell you what I think, I think he just wants to show you how smart he is. When I told him Nero Wolfe was coming you should have heard him! He said maybe you're famous for brains and he isn't, but he'd like to hear you prove it, something like that. I don't pretend to have brains. I was just scared!"

"Scared of what, Miss Weltz?"

"Scared of you! Wouldn't anybody be scared if they knew you were coming to pump them?" She was appealing to him.

"Not enough to send for help." Wolfe wouldn't enter into the spirit of it. "Certainly not if they had the alternative of snubbing me, as you have. Why don't you choose it? Why do you suffer me?"

"Now *that's* a question." She laughed. "I'll show you why." She got up and took a step, and reached to pat him on the shoulder and then on top of the head. "I didn't want to miss a chance to touch the great Nero Wolfe!" She laughed again, moved to the table and poured herself a healthy dose of bourbon, returned to her chair, and swallowed a good half of it. She shook herself and said, "Brrrrr. That's why!"

Unger was frowning at her. It didn't need the brains of a Nero Wolfe, or even a Guy Unger, to see that her nerves were teetering on an edge as sharp as a knife blade.

"But," Wolfe said dryly, "having touched me, you still suffer me. Of course Miss Hart told you that I reject the thesis that Leonard Ashe killed Marie Willis and propose to discredit it. I'm too late to try any of the conventional lines of inquiry, and anyway they have all been fully and competently explored by the police and the District Attorney on one side and Mr. Ashe's lawyer on the other. Since I can't expect to prove Mr. Ashe's innocence, the best I can hope to establish is a reasonable doubt of his guilt. Can you give it to me?"

"Of course not. How could I?"

"One way would be to suggest someone else with motive and opportunity. Means is no problem, since the plug cord was there at hand. Can you?"

She giggled, and then was shocked, presumably at herself for giggling about murder. "Sorry," she apologized, "but you're funny. The way they had us down there at the District Attorney's office, and the way they kept after us, asking all about Marie and everybody she knew, and of course what they wanted was to find out if there was anybody besides that man Ashe that might have killed her. But now they're trying Ashe for it, and they wouldn't be trying him if they didn't think they could prove it, and here you come and expect to drag it out of me in twenty minutes. Don't you think that's funny for a famous detective like you? I do."

She picked up her glass and drained it, stiffened to control a shudder, and got up and started for the table. Guy Unger reached and beat her to the bottle. "You've had enough, Helen," he told her gruffly. "Take it easy." She stared down at him a moment, dropped the glass on his lap, and went back to her chair.

Wolfe eyed her. "No, Miss Weltz," he said. "No, I didn't expect to drag a disclosure from you in twenty minutes. The most I expected was support for my belief that you people have common knowledge of something that you don't want revealed, and you have given me that. Now I'll go to work, and I confess I'm not too sanguine. It's quite possible that after I've squandered my resources on it, time and thought and money and energy, and enlisted the help of half a dozen able investigators, I'll find that the matter you people are so nervous about has no bearing on the murder of Marie Willis and so is of no use to me, and of no concern. But I can't know that until I know what it is, so I'm going to know. If you think my process of finding out will cause inconvenience to you and the others, or worse, I suggest that you tell me now. It will—"

"I have nothing to tell you!"

"Nonsense. You're at the edge of hysteria."

"I am not!"

"Take it easy, Helen." Guy Unger focused his mean little eyes on Wolfe. "Look, I don't get this. As I understand it, what you're after is an out for Leonard Ashe on the murder. Is that right?"

"Yes."

"And that's all?"

"Yes."

"Would you mind telling me, did Ashe's lawyer hire you?"

"No."

"Who did?"

"Nobody. I developed a distaste for my function as a witness for the prosecution, along with a doubt of Mr. Ashe's guilt."

"Why doubt his guilt?"

Wolfe's shoulders went up a fraction of an inch, and down again. "Divination. Contrariety."

"I see." Unger pursed his midget mouth, which didn't need pursing. "You're shooting at it on spec." He leaned forward. "Understand me, I don't say that's not your privilege. Of course you have no standing at all, since you admit nobody hired you, but if Miss Weltz tells you to go to hell that won't take you off her neck if you've decided to go to town. She'll answer anything you want to ask her that's connected with the murder, and so will I. We've told the police and the District Attorney, why not you? Do you regard me as a suspect?"

"Yes."

"Okay." He leaned back. "I first met Marie Willis about a year ago, a little more. I took her out a few times, maybe once a month, and then later a little oftener, to dinner and a show. We weren't engaged to be married, nothing like that. The last week in June, just two weeks before her death, she was on vacation, and four of us went for a cruise on my boat, up the Hudson and Lake Champlain. The other two were friends of mine, a man and a woman—do you want their names?"

"No."

"Well, that was what got me in the murder picture, that week's cruise she had taken on my boat so recently. There was nothing to it, we had just gone to have a good time, but when she was murdered the cops naturally thought I was a good prospect. There was absolutely nothing in my relations with Marie that could possibly have made me want to kill her. Any questions?"

"No."

"And if they had dug up a motive they would have been stuck with it, because I certainly didn't kill her the evening of July fifteenth. That was a Thursday, and at five o'clock that afternoon I was taking my boat through the Harlem River and into the sound, and at ten o'clock that night I was asleep on her at an anchorage near New Haven. My friend Ralph Ingalls was with me, and his wife, and Miss Helen Weltz. Of course the police have checked it, but maybe you don't like the way they check alibis. You're welcome to check it yourself if you care to. Any questions?"

"One or two." Wolfe shifted his fanny on the board slats. "What is your occupation?"

"For God's sake. You haven't even read the papers."

"Yes, I have, but that was weeks ago, and as I remember it they were vague. 'Broker,' I believe. Stockbroker?"

"No, I'm a freewheeler. I'll handle almost anything."

"Have you an office?"

"I don't need one."

"Have you handled any transactions for anyone connected with that business, Bagby Answers, Incorporated? Any kind of transaction?"

Unger cocked his head. "Now that's a funny question. Why do you ask that?"

"Because I suspect the answer is yes."

"Why? Just for curiosity."

"Now, Mr. Unger." Wolfe turned a palm up. "Since apparently you had heard of me, you may know that I dislike riding in cars, even when Mr. Goodwin is driving. Do you suppose I would have made this excursion completely at random? If you find the question embarrassing, don't answer it."

"It's not embarrassing." Unger turned to the table, poured an inch of bourbon in his glass, added two inches of water from a pitcher, gave it a couple of swirls, took a sip, and another one, and finally put the glass down and turned back to Wolfe.

"I'll tell you," he said in a new tone. "This whole business is pretty damn silly. I think you've got hold of some crazy idea somewhere, God knows what, and I want to speak with you privately." He arose. "Let's take a little walk."

Wolfe shook his head. "I don't like conversing on my feet. If you want to say something without a witness, Miss Weltz and Mr. Goodwin can leave us. Archie?"

I stood up. Helen Weltz looked up at Unger, and at me, and then slowly lifted herself from her chair. "Let's go and pick flowers," I suggested. "Mr. Unger will want me in sight and out of hearing."

She moved. We picked our way through the windfalls of the apple tree, and of two more trees, and went on into a meadow where the grass and other stuff was up to our knees. She was in the lead. "Goldenrod I know," I told her back, "but what are the blue ones?"

No answer. In another hundred yards I tried again. "This is far enough unless he uses a megaphone."

She kept going. "Last call!" I told her. "I admit he would be a maniac to jump Mr. Wolfe under the circumstances, but maybe he is one. I learned long ago that with people involved in a murder case nothing is impossible."

She wheeled on me. "He's not involved in a murder case!"

"He will be before Mr. Wolfe gets through with him."

She plumped down in the grass, crossed her legs, buried her face in her hands, and started to shake. I stood and looked down at her, expecting the appropriate sound effect, but it didn't come. She just went on shaking, which wasn't wholesome. After half a minute of it I squatted in front of her, made contact by taking a firm grip on her bare ankle, and spoke with authority.

"That's no way to do it. Open a valve and let it out. Stretch out and kick and scream. If Unger thinks it's me and flies to the rescue that will give me an excuse to plug him."

She mumbled something. Her hands muffled it, but it sounded like "God help me." The shakes turned into shivers and were tapering off. When she spoke again it came through much better. "You're hurting me," she said, and I loosened my grip on her ankle and in a moment took my hand away, when her hands dropped and she lifted her head.

Her face was flushed, but her eyes were dry. "My God," she said, "it would be wonderful if you put your arms around me tight and told me, 'All right, my darling, I'll take care of everything, just leave it to me.' Oh, that would be wonderful!"

"I may try it," I offered, "if you'll brief me on what I'd have to take care of. The arms around you tight are no problem. Then what?"

She skipped over it. "God," she said bitterly, "am I a fool! You saw my car. My Jaguar."

"Yeah, I saw it. Very fine."

"I'm going to burn it. How do you set fire to a car?"

"Pour gasoline on it, all over inside, toss a match in, and jump back fast. Be careful what you tell the insurance company or you'll end up in the can."

She skipped again. "It wasn't only the car, it was other things too. I had to have them. Why didn't I get me a man? I could have had a dozen, but no, not me. I was going to do it all myself. It was going to be *my* Jaguar. And now here I am, and you, a man I never saw before—it would be heaven if you'd just take me over. I'm telling you, you'd be getting a bargain!"

"I might, at that." I was sympathetic but not mealy. "Don't be too sure you're a bad buy. What are the liabilities?"

She twisted her neck to look across the meadow toward the house. Wolfe and Unger were in their chairs under the apple tree, evidently keeping their voices down, since no sound came, and my ears are good. She turned back to me. "Is it a bluff? Is he just trying to scare something out of us?"

"No, not just. If he scares something out, fine. If not, he'll get it the hard way. If there's anything to get he'll get it. If you're sitting on a lid you don't want opened, my advice is to move, the sooner the better, or you may get hurt."

"I'm already hurt!"

"Then hurt worse."

"I guess I can be." She reached for one of the blue flowers and pulled it off with no stem. "You asked what these are. They're wild asters, just the color of my eyes." She crushed it with her fingers and dropped it. "I already know what I'm going to do. I decided walking over here with you. What time is it?"

I looked at my wrist. "Quarter past three."

"Let's see, four hours—five. Where can I see Nero Wolfe around nine o'clock in town?"

From long habit I started to say at his office, but remembered it was out of bounds. "His address and number are in the phone book," I told her, "but he may not be there this evening. Phone and ask for Fritz. Tell him you are the Queen of Hearts, and he'll tell you where Mr. Wolfe is. If you don't say you're the Queen of Hearts he won't tell you anything because Mr. Wolfe hates to be disturbed when he's out. But why not save time and trouble? Evidently you've decided to tell him something, and there he is. Come on and tell him now."

She shook her head. "I can't. I don't dare."

"On account of Unger?"

"Yes."

"If he can ask to speak privately with Mr. Wolfe, why can't you?"

"I tell you I don't dare!"

"We'll go and come back as soon as Unger leaves."

"He's not going to leave. He's going to ride to town with me."

"Then record it on tape and use me for tape. You can trust my memory. I guarantee to repeat it to Mr. Wolfe word for word. Then when you phone this evening he will have had time—"

"Helen! *Helen!*" Unger was calling her.

She started to scramble up, and I got upright and gave her a hand. As we headed across the meadow she spoke, barely above a whisper. "If you tell him I'll deny it. Are you going to tell him?"

"Wolfe, yes. Unger, no."

"If you do I'll deny it."

"Then I won't."

As we approached they left their chairs. Their expressions indicated that they had not signed a mutual nonaggression pact, but there were no scars of battle. Wolfe said, "We're through here, Archie," and was going. Nobody else said anything, which made it rather stiff. Following Wolfe around the house to the open space, I saw that it would take a lot of maneuvering to turn around without scraping the Jaguar, so I had to back out through the bushes to the dirt road, where I swung the rear around to head the way we had come.

When we had gone half a mile I called back to my rear-seat passenger, "I have a little item for you!"

"Stop somewhere," he ordered, louder than necessary. "I can't talk like this."

A little farther on there was roadside room under a tree, and I pulled over and parked.

I twisted around in the seat to face him. "We got a nibble," I said, and reported on Helen Weltz. He started frowning, and when I finished he was frowning more.

"Confound it," he growled, "she was in a panic, and it'll wear off."

"It may," I conceded. "And so? I'll go back and do it over if you'll write me a script."

"Pfui. I don't say I could better it. You are a connoisseur of comely young women. Is she a murderess in a funk trying to wriggle out? Or what is she?"

I shook my head. "I pass. She's trying to wriggle all right, but for out of what I would need six guesses. What did Unger want privately? Is he trying to wriggle too?"

"Yes. He offered me money—five thousand dollars, and then ten thousand."

"For what?"

"Not clearly defined. A retaining fee for investigative services. He was crude about it for a man with brains."

"I'll be damned." I grinned at him. "I've often thought you ought to get around more. Only five hours ago you marched out of that courtroom in the interest of justice, and already you've scared up an offer of ten grand. Of course it may have nothing to do with the murder. What did you tell him?"

"That I resented and scorned his attempt to suborn me."

My brows went up. "He was in a panic, and it'll wear off. Why not string him along?"

"It would take time, and I haven't any. I told him I intend to appear in court tomorrow morning."

"Tomorrow?" I stared. "With what, for God's sake?"

"At the least, with a diversion. If Miss Weltz's panic endures, possibly with something better, though I didn't know that when I was talking with Mr. Unger."

I looked it over. "Uh-huh," I said finally. "You've had a hard day, and soon it will be dark and dinnertime, and then bedtime, and deciding to go back to court tomorrow makes it possible for you to go home. Okay, I'll get you there by five o'clock."

I turned and reached for the ignition key, but had barely touched it when his voice stopped me. "We're not going home. Mr. Cramer will have a man posted there all night, probably with a warrant, and I'm not going to risk it. I had thought of a hotel, but that might be risky too, and now that Miss Weltz may want to see me it's out of the question. Isn't Saul's apartment conveniently located?"

"Yes, but he has only one bed. Lily Rowan has plenty of room in her penthouse, and we'd be welcome, especially you. You remember the time she squirted perfume on you."

"I do," he said coldly. "We'll manage somehow at Saul's. Besides, we have errands to do and may need him. We must of course phone him first. Go ahead. To the city."

He gripped the strap. I started the engine.

IV

For more years than I have fingers Inspector Cramer of Homicide had been dreaming of locking Wolfe up, at least overnight, and that day he darned near made it. He probably would have if I hadn't spent an extra dime. Having phoned Saul Panzer, and also Fritz, from a booth in a drugstore in Washington Heights, I called the *Gazette* office and got Lon Cohen. When he heard my voice he said, "Well, well. Are you calling from your cell?"

"No. If I told you where I am you'd be an accomplice. Has our absence been noticed?"

"Certainly, the town's in an uproar. A raging mob has torn the courthouse down. We're running a fairly good picture of Wolfe, but we need a new one of you. Could you drop in at the studio, say in five minutes?"

"Sure, glad to. But I'm calling to settle a bet. Is there a warrant for us?"

"You're damn right there is. Judge Corbett signed it first thing after lunch. Look, Archie, let me send a man—"

I told him much obliged and hung up. If I hadn't spent that dime and learned there was a warrant, we wouldn't have taken any special precaution as we approached Saul's address on East Thirty-eighth Street and would have run smack into Sergeant Purley Stebbins, and the question of where to spend the night would have been taken off our hands.

It was nearly eight o'clock. Wolfe and I had each disposed of three orders of chili con carne at a little dump on 170th Street where a guy named Dixie knows how to make it, and I had made at least a dozen phone calls trying to get hold of Jimmy Donovan, Leonard Ashe's attorney. That might not have been difficult if I could have left word that Nero Wolfe had something urgent for him, and given a number for him to call, but that wouldn't have been practical, since an attorney is a sworn officer of the law, and he knew there was a warrant out for Wolfe, not to mention me. So I hadn't got him, and as we crawled with the traffic through East Thirty-eighth Street the sight of Wolfe's scowl in the rear-view mirror didn't make the scene any gayer.

My program was to let him out at Saul's address between Lexington and Third, find a place to park the car, and join him at Saul's. But just as I swung over and was braking I saw a familiar broad-shouldered figure on the sidewalk, switched from the brake to the gas pedal, and kept going. Luckily a gap had opened, and the light was green at Third Avenue, so I rolled on through, found a place to stop without blocking traffic, and turned in the seat to tell Wolfe, "I came on by because I decided we don't want to see Saul."

"You did." He was grim. "What flummery is this?"

"No flummery. Sergeant Purley Stebbins was just turning in at the entrance. Thank God it's dark or he would have seen us. Now where?"

"At the entrance of Saul's address?"

"Yes."

A short silence. "You're enjoying this," he said bitterly.

"I am like hell. I'm a fugitive from justice, and I was going to spend the evening at the Polo Grounds watching a ball game. Where now?"

"Confound it. You told Saul about Miss Weltz."

"Yes, sir. I told Fritz that if the Queen of Hearts phones she is to call Saul's number, and I told Saul that you'd rather have an hour alone with her than a blue orchid. You know Saul."

Another silence. He broke it. "You have Mr. Donovan's home address."

"Right. East Seventy-seventh Street."

"How long will it take to drive there?"

"Ten minutes."

"Go ahead."

"Yes, sir. Sit back and relax." I fed gas.

It took only nine minutes at that time of evening, and I found space to park right in the block, between Madison and Park. As we walked to the number a cop gave us a second glance, but Wolfe's size and carriage rated that much notice without any special stimulation. It was just my nerves. There were a canopy and a doorman, and rugs in the lobby. I told the doorman casually, "Donovan. We're expected," but he hung on.

"Yes, sir, but I have orders— Your name, please?"

"Judge Wolfe," Wolfe told him.

"One moment, please."

He disappeared through a door. It was more like five moments before he came back, looking questions but not asking them, and directed us to the elevator. "Twelve B," he said.

Getting off at the twelfth floor, we didn't have to look for B because a door at the end of the foyer was standing open, and on the sill was Jimmy Donovan himself. In his shirt sleeves, with no necktie, he looked more like a janitor than a champion of the bar, and he sounded more like one when he blurted, "It's you, huh? What kind of a trick is this? *Judge* Wolfe!"

"No trick." Wolfe was courteous but curt. "I merely evaded vulgar curiosity. I had to see you."

"You can't see me. It's highly improper. You're a witness for the prosecution. Also a warrant has been issued for you, and I'll have to report this."

He was absolutely right. The only thing for him to do was shut the door on us and go to his phone and call the DA's office. My one guess why he didn't, which was all I needed, was that he would have given his shirt, and thrown in a necktie, to know what Wolfe was up to. He didn't shut the door.

"I'm not here," Wolfe said, "as a witness for the prosecution. I don't intend to discuss my testimony with you. As you know, your client, Leonard Ashe, came to me one day in July and wanted to hire me, and I refused. I have become aware of certain facts connected with what he told me that day which I think he should know about, and I want to tell him. I suppose it would be improper for me to tell you more than that, but it wouldn't be improper to tell him. He is on trial for first-degree murder."

I had the feeling I could see Donovan's brain working at it behind his eyes. "It's preposterous," he declared. "You know damn well you can't see him."

"I can if you'll arrange it. That's what I'm here for. You're his counsel. Early tomorrow morning will do, before the court sits. You may of course be present if you wish, but I suppose you would prefer not to. Twenty minutes with him will be enough."

Donovan was chewing his lip. "I can't ask you what you want to tell him."

"I understand that. I won't be on the witness stand, where you can cross-examine me, until tomorrow."

"No." The lawyer's eyes narrowed. "No, you won't. I can't arrange for you to see him; it's out of the question. I shouldn't be talking to you. It will be my duty to report this to Judge Corbett in the morning. Good evening, gentlemen."

He backed up and swung the door shut, but didn't bang it, which was gracious of him. We rang for the elevator, were taken down, and went out and back to the car.

"You'll phone Saul," Wolfe said.

"Yes, sir. His saying he'll report to the judge in the morning meant he didn't intend to phone the DA now, but he might change his mind. I'd rather move a few blocks before phoning."

"Very well. Do you know the address of Mrs. Leonard Ashe's apartment?"

"Yes, Seventy-third Street."

"Go in that direction. I have to see her, and you'd better phone and arrange it."

"You mean now."

"Yes."

"That should be a cinch. She's probably sitting there hoping a couple of strange detectives will drop in. Do I have to be Judge Goodwin?"

"No. We are ourselves."

As I drove downtown on Park, and east on Seventy-fourth to Third Avenue, and down a block, and west on Seventy-third, I considered the approach to Robina Keane. By not specifying it Wolfe had left it to me, so it was my problem. I thought of a couple of fancy strategies, but by the time I got the car maneuvered to the curb in the only vacant spot between Lexington and Madison I had decided that the simplest was the best. After asking Wolfe if he had any suggestions and getting a no, I walked to Lexington and found a booth in a drugstore.

First I called Saul Panzer. There had been no word from the Queen of Hearts, but she had said around nine o'clock and it was only eight-forty. Sergeant Stebbins had been and gone. What he had said was that the police were concerned about the disappearance of Nero Wolfe because he was an important witness in a murder case, and they were afraid something might have happened to him, especially since Archie Goodwin was also gone. What he had not said was that Inspector Cramer suspected that Wolfe had tramped out of the courtroom hellbent on messing the case up, and he wanted to get his hands on him quick. Had Wolfe communicated with Saul, and did Saul know where he was? There was a warrant out for both Wolfe and Goodwin. Saul had said no, naturally, and Purley had made some cutting remarks and left.

I dialed another number, and when a female voice answered I told it I would like to speak to Mrs. Ashe. It said Mrs. Ashe was resting and couldn't come to the phone. I said I was speaking for Nero Wolfe and it was urgent and vital. It said Mrs. Ashe absolutely would not come to the phone. I asked it if it had ever heard of Nero Wolfe, and it said of course. All right, I said, tell Mrs. Ashe that he must see her immediately and he can be there in five minutes. That's all I can tell you on the phone, I said, except that if she doesn't see him she'll never stop regretting it. The voice told me to hold the wire, and was gone so long I began to wish I had tried a fancy one, but just as I was reaching for the handle of the booth door to let in some air it came back and said Mrs. Ashe would see Mr. Wolfe. I asked it to instruct the lobby guardians to admit us, hung up, went out and back to the car, and told Wolfe, "Okay. You'd better make it good after what I told her. No word from Helen Weltz. Stebbins only asked some foolish questions and got the answers he deserved."

He climbed out, and we walked to the number. This one was smaller and more elegant, too elegant for rugs. The doorman was practically Laurence Olivier, and the elevator man was his older brother. They were chilly but nothing personal. When we were let out at the sixth floor the elevator man stayed at his open door until we had pushed a button and the apartment door had opened and we had been told to enter.

The woman admitting us wasn't practically Phyllis Jay, she *was* Phyllis Jay. Having paid $4.40 or $5.50 several times to see her from an orchestra seat, I would have appreciated this free close-up of her on a better occasion, but my mind was occupied. So was hers. Of course she was acting, since actresses always are, but the glamour was turned off because the part didn't call for it. She was playing a support for a friend in need, and kept strictly in character as she relieved Wolfe of his hat and cane and then escorted us into a big living room, across it, and through an arch into a smaller room.

Robina Keane was sitting on a couch, patting at her hair. Wolfe stopped three paces off and bowed. She looked up at him, shook her head as if to dislodge a fly, pressed her fingertips to her eyes, and looked at him again. Phyllis Jay said, "I'll be in the study, Robbie," waited precisely the right interval for a request to stay, didn't get it, and turned and went. Mrs. Ashe invited us to sit, and, after moving a chair around for Wolfe, I took one off at the side.

"I'm dead tired," she said. "I'm so empty, completely empty. I don't think I ever— But what is it? Of course it's something about my husband?"

Either the celebrated lilt of her voice was born in, or she had used it so much and so long that it might as well have been. She looked all in, no doubt of that, but the lilt was there.

"I'll make it as brief as I can," Wolfe told her. "Do you know that I have met your husband? That he called on me one day in July?"

"Yes, I know. I know all about it—now."

"It was to testify about our conversation that day that I was summoned to appear at his trial, by the State. In court this morning, waiting to be called, an idea came to me which I thought merited exploration, and if it was to bring any advantage to your husband the exploration could not wait. So I walked out, with Mr. Goodwin, my assistant, and we have spent the day on that idea."

"What idea?" Her hands were fists, on the couch for props.

"Later for that. We have made some progress, and we may make more tonight. Whether we do or not, I have information that will be of considerable value to your husband. It may not exculpate him, but at least it should raise sufficient doubt in the minds of the jury to get him acquitted. The problem is to get the information to the jury. It would take intricate and prolonged investigation to get it in the form of admissible evidence, and I have in mind a short cut. To take it I must have a talk with your husband."

"But he— How can you?"

"I must. I have just called on Mr. Donovan, his attorney, and asked him to arrange it, but I knew he wouldn't; that was merely to antici- pate you. I knew that if I came to you, you would insist on consulting him, and I have already demonstrated the futility of that. I am in con- tempt of the court, and a warrant has been issued for my arrest. Also I am under subpoena as a witness for the prosecution, and it is improper for the defense counsel even to talk with me, let alone arrange an in- terview for me with his client. You, as the wife of a man on trial for his life, are under no such prescription. You have wide acquaintance and great personal charm. It would not be too difficult, certainly not im- possible, for you to get permission to talk with your husband tomorrow morning before the court convenes; and you can take me with you. Twenty minutes would be ample, and even ten would do. Don't men- tion me in getting the permission; that's important; simply take me with you and we'll see. If it doesn't work there's another possible expedient. Will you do it?"

She was frowning. "I don't see— You just want to talk with him?"

"Yes."

"What do you want to tell him?"

"You'll hear it tomorrow morning when he does. It's complicated and conjectural. To tell you now might compromise my plan to get it to the jury, and I won't risk it."

"But tell me what it's about. Is it about me?"

Wolfe lifted his shoulders to take in a deep breath, and let them sag again. "You say you're dead tired, madam. So am I. I would be inter- ested in you only if I thought you were implicated in the murder of Marie Willis, and I don't. At considerable risk to my reputation, my self- esteem, and possibly even my bodily freedom, I am undertaking a step which should be useful to your husband and am asking your help; but I am not asking you to risk anything. You have nothing to lose, but I have. Of course I have made an assumption that may not be valid: that, whether you are sincerely devoted to your husband or not, you don't want him convicted of murder. I can't guarantee that I have the key that will free him, but I'm not a novice in these matters."

Her jaw was working. "You didn't have to say that." The lilt was gone. "Whether I'm devoted to my husband. My husband's not a fool, but he acted like one. I love him very dearly, and I want—" Her jaw worked. "I love him very much. No, I don't want him convicted of murder. You're right, I have nothing to lose, nothing more to lose. But if I do this I'll have to tell Mr. Donovan."

"No. You must not. Not only would he forbid it, he would prevent it. This is for you alone."

She abandoned the prop of her fists and straightened her back. "I thought I was too tired to live," she said, lilting again, "and I am, but it's going to be a relief to do something." She left the couch and was on her feet. "I'm going to do it. As you say, I have a wide acquaintance, and I'll do it all right. You go on and make some more progress and leave this to me. Where can I reach you?"

Wolfe turned. "Saul's number, Archie."

I wrote it on a leaf of my notebook and went and handed it to her. Wolfe arose. "I'll be there all night, Mrs. Ashe, up to nine in the morning, but I hope it will be before that."

I doubted if she heard him. Her mind was so glad to have a job that it had left us entirely. She did go with us to the foyer to see us out, but she wasn't there. I was barely across the threshold when she shut the door.

We went back to the car and headed downtown on Park Avenue. It seemed unlikely that Purley Stebbins had taken it into his head to pay Saul a second call, but a couple of blocks away I stopped to phone, and Saul said no, he was alone. It seemed even more unlikely that Stebbins had posted a man out front, but I stopped twenty yards short of the number and took a good long look. There was a curb space a little further down, and I squeezed the car into it and looked some more before opening the door for Wolfe to climb out. We crossed the street and entered the vestibule, and I pushed the button.

When we left the self-service elevator at the fifth floor Saul was there to greet us. I suppose to some people Saul Panzer is just a little guy with a big nose who always seems to need a shave, but to others, including Wolfe and me, he's the best free-for-all operative that ever tailed a subject. Wolfe had never been at his place before, but I had, many times over the years, mostly on Saturday nights with three or four others for some friendly and ferocious poker. Inside, Wolfe stood and looked around. It was a big room, lighted with two floor lamps and two table lamps. One wall had windows, another was solid with books, and the other two had pictures and shelves that were cluttered with everything from chunks of minerals to walrus tusks. In the far corner was a grand piano.

"A good room," Wolfe said. "Satisfactory. I congratulate you." He crossed to a chair, the nearest thing to his idea of a chair he had seen all day, and sat. "What time is it?"

"Twenty minutes to ten."

"Have you heard from that woman?"

"No, sir. Will you have some beer?"

"I will indeed. If you please."

In the next three hours he accounted for seven bottles. He also handled his share of liver pâté, herring, sturgeon, pickled mushrooms, Tunisian melon, and three kinds of cheese. Saul was certainly prancing as a host, though he is not a prancer. Naturally, the first time Wolfe ate under his roof, and possibly the last, he wanted to give him good grub, that was okay, but I thought the three kinds of cheese was piling it on a little. He sure would be sick of cheese by Saturday. He wasn't equipped to be so fancy about sleeping. Since he was the host it was his problem, and his arrangement was Wolfe in the bedroom, me on the couch in the big room, and him on the floor, which seemed reasonable.

However, at a quarter to one in the morning we were still up. Though time hadn't dragged too heavily, what with talking and eating and drinking and three hot games of checkers between Wolfe and Saul, all draws, we were all yawning. We hadn't turned in because we hadn't heard from Helen Weltz, and there was still a dim hope. The other thing was all set. Just after midnight Robina Keane had phoned and told Wolfe she had it fixed. He was to meet her in Room 917 at 100 Centre Street at half-past eight. He asked me if I knew what Room 917 was, and I didn't. After that came he leaned back in his chair and sat with his eyes closed for a while, then straightened up and told Saul he was ready for the third game of checkers.

At a quarter to one he left his chair, yawned and stretched, and announced, "Her panic wore off. I'm going to bed."

"I'm afraid," Saul apologized, "I have no pajamas you could get into, but I've got—"

The phone rang. I was nearest, and turned and got it. "This is Jackson four-three-one-oh-nine."

"I want— This is the Queen of Hearts."

"It sure is. I recognize your voice. This is Archie Goodwin. Where are you?"

"In a booth at Grand Central. I couldn't get rid of him, and then— but that doesn't matter now. Where are you?"

"In an apartment on Thirty-eighth Street with Mr. Wolfe, waiting for you. It's a short walk. I'll meet you at the information booth, upper level, in five minutes. Will you be there?"

"Yes."

"Sure?"

"Of course I will!"

I hung up, turned, and said loftily, "If it wore off it wore on again. Make some coffee, will you, Saul? She'll need either that or bourbon. And maybe she likes cheese."

I departed.

V

AT SIX minutes past ten in the morning Assistant District Attorney Mandelbaum was standing at the end of his table in the courtroom to address Judge Corbett. The room was packed. The jury was in the box. Jimmy Donovan, defense attorney, looking not at all like a janitor, was fingering through some papers his assistant had handed him.

"Your Honor," Mandelbaum said, "I wish to call a witness whom I called yesterday, but he was not available. I learned only a few minutes ago that he is present. You will remember that on my application you issued a warrant for Mr. Nero Wolfe."

"Yes, I do." The judge cleared his throat. "Is he here?"

"He is." Mandelbaum turned and called, "Nero Wolfe!"

Having arrived at one minute to ten, we wouldn't have been able to get in if we hadn't pushed through to the officer at the door and told him who we were and that we were wanted. He had stared at Wolfe and admitted he recognized him, and let us in, and the attendant had managed to make room for us on a bench just as Judge Corbett entered. When Wolfe was called by Mandelbaum and got up to go forward I had enough space.

He walked down the aisle, through the gate, mounted the stand, turned to face the judge, and stood.

"I have some questions for you, Mr. Wolfe," the judge said, "after you are sworn."

The attendant extended the Book and administered the oath, and Wolfe sat. A witness chair is supposed to take any size, but that one just barely made it.

The judge spoke. "You knew you were to be called yesterday. You were present, but you left and could not be found, and a warrant was issued for you. Are you represented by counsel?"

"No, sir."

"Why did you leave? You are under oath."

"I was impelled to leave by a motive which I thought imperative. I will of course expound it now if you so order, but I respectfully ask your indulgence. I understand that if my reason for leaving is unsatisfactory I will be in contempt of court and will suffer a penalty. But I ask, Your Honor, does it matter whether I am adjudged in contempt now, or later, after I have testified? Because my reason for leaving is inherent in my testimony, and therefore I would rather plead on the charge of contempt afterwards, if the court will permit. I'll still be here."

"Indeed you will. You're under arrest."

"No, I'm not."

"You're not under arrest?"

"No, sir. I came here voluntarily."

"Well, you are now." The judge turned his head. "Officer, this man is under arrest." He turned back. "Very well. You will answer to the contempt charge later. Proceed, Mr. Mandelbaum."

Mandelbaum approached the chair. "Please tell the jury your name, occupation, and address."

Wolfe turned to the jury box. "I am Nero Wolfe, a licensed private detective, with my office in my house at nine-fourteen West Thirty-fifth Street, Manhattan, New York City."

"Have you ever met the defendant in this case?" Mandelbaum pointed. "That gentleman."

"Yes, sir. Mr. Leonard Ashe."

"Where and under what circumstances did you meet him?"

"He called on me at my office, by appointment, at eleven o'clock in the morning of Tuesday, July thirteenth, this year."

"What did he say to you on that occasion?"

"That he wished to engage my professional services. That he had, the preceding day, arranged for an answering service for the telephone at his residence on Seventy-third Street in New York. That he had learned, upon inquiry, that one of the employees of the answering service would be assigned to his number and would serve it five or six days a week. That he wanted to hire me to learn the identity of that employee, and to propose to her that she eavesdrop on calls made during the daytime to his number, and report on them either to him or to me—I can't say definitely which, because he wasn't clear on that point."

"Did he say why he wanted to make that arrangement?"

"No. He didn't get that far."

Donovan was up. "Objection, Your Honor. Conclusion of the witness as to the intention of the defendant."

"Strike it," Mandelbaum said amiably. "Strike all of his answer except the word 'No.' Your answer is 'No,' Mr. Wolfe?"

"Yes, sir."

"Did the defendant suggest any inducement to be offered to the employee to get her to do the eavesdropping?"

"He didn't name a sum, but he indicated that—"

"Not what he indicated. What he said."

I allowed myself a grin. Wolfe, who always insisted on precision, who loved to ride others, especially me, for loose talk, and who certainly knew the rules of evidence, had been caught twice. I promised myself to find occasion later to comment on it.

He was unruffled. "He said that he would make it worth her while, meaning the employee, but stated no amount."

"What else did he say?"

"That was about all. The entire conversation was only a few minutes. As soon as I understood clearly what he wanted to hire me to do, I refused to do it."

"Did you tell him why you refused?"

"Yes, sir."

"What did you say?"

"I said that while it is the function of a detective to pry into people's affairs, I excluded from my field anything connected with marital difficulties and therefore declined his job."

"Had he told you that what he wanted was to spy on his wife?"

"No, sir."

"Then why did you mention marital difficulties to him?"

"Because I had concluded that that was the nature of his concern."

"What else did you say to him?"

Wolfe shifted in the chair. "I would like to be sure I understand the question. Do you mean what I said to him that day, or on a later occasion?"

"I mean that day. There was no later occasion, was there?"

"Yes, sir."

"Are you saying that you had another meeting with the defendant, on another day?"

"Yes, sir."

Mandelbaum held a pose. Since his back was to me I couldn't see his look of surprise, but I didn't have to. In his file was Wolfe's signed statement, saying among other things that he had not seen Leonard Ashe before or since July 13. His voice went up a notch. "When and where did this meeting take place?"

"Shortly after nine o'clock this morning, in this building."

"You met and spoke with the defendant in this building today?"

"Yes, sir."

"Under what circumstances?"

"His wife had arranged to see and speak with him, and she allowed me to accompany her."

"How did she arrange it? With whom?"

"I don't know."

"Was Mr. Donovan, the defense counsel, present?"

"No, sir."

"Who was?"

"Mrs. Ashe, Mr. Ashe, myself, and two armed guards, one at the door and one at the end of the room."

"What room was it?"

"I don't know. There was no number on the door. I think I could lead you to it."

Mandelbaum whirled around and looked at Robina Keane, seated on the front bench. Not being a lawyer, I didn't know whether he could get her to the stand or not. Of course a wife couldn't be summoned to testify against her husband, but I didn't know if this would have come under that ban. Anyway, he either skipped it or postponed it. He asked the judge to allow him a moment and went to the table to speak in an undertone to a colleague. I looked around. I had already spotted Guy Unger, in the middle of the audience on the left. Bella Velardi and Alice Hart were on the other side, next to the aisle. Apparently the Sixty-ninth Street office of Bagby Answers, Inc., was being womaned for the day from other offices. Clyde Bagby, the boss, was a couple of rows in front of Unger. Helen Weltz, the Queen of Hearts, whom I had driven from Saul's address to a hotel seven hours ago, was in the back, not far from me.

The colleague got up and left, in a hurry, and Mandelbaum went back to Wolfe.

"Don't you know," he demanded, "that it is a misdemeanor for a witness for the State to talk with the defendant charged with a felony?"

"No, sir, I don't. I understand it would depend on what was said. I didn't discuss my testimony with Mr. Ashe."

"What did you discuss?"

"Certain matters which I thought would be of interest to him."

"What matters? Exactly what did you say?"

I took a deep breath, spread and stretched my fingers, and relaxed. The fat son-of-a-gun had put it over. Having asked that question, Mandelbaum couldn't possibly keep it from the jury unless Jimmy Donovan was a sap, and he wasn't.

Wolfe testified. "I said that yesterday, seated in this room awaiting your convenience, I had formed a surmise that certain questions raised by the murder of Marie Willis had not been sufficiently considered and investigated, and that therefore my role as a witness for the prosecution was an uncomfortable one. I said that I had determined to satisfy myself on certain points; that I knew that in leaving the courtroom I would become liable to a penalty for contempt of court, but that the integrity of justice was more important than my personal ease; that I had been confident that Judge Corbett would—"

"If you please, Mr. Wolfe. You are not now pleading to a charge of contempt."

"No, sir. You asked what I said to Mr. Ashe. He asked what surmise I had formed, and I told him—that it was a double surmise. First, that as one with long experience in the investigation of crime and culprits, I had an appreciable doubt of his guilt. Second, that the police had been so taken by the circumstances pointing to Mr. Ashe—his obvious motive and his discovery of the body—that their attention in other directions had possibly been somewhat dulled. For example, an experienced investigator always has a special eye and ear for any person occupying a privileged position. Such persons are doctors, lawyers, trusted servants, intimate friends, and, of course, close relatives. If one in those categories is a rogue he has peculiar opportunities for his scoundrelism. It occurred to me that—"

"You said all this to Mr. Ashe?"

"Yes, sir. It occurred to me that a telephone-answering service was in the same kind of category as those I have mentioned, as I sat in this room yesterday and heard Mr. Bagby describe the operation of the switchboards. An unscrupulous operator might, by listening in on conversations, obtain various kinds of information that could be turned to account—for instance, about the stock market, about business or professional plans, about a multitude of things. The possibilities would be limitless. Certainly one, and perhaps the most promising, would be the discovery of personal secrets. Most people are wary about discussing or disclosing vital secrets on the telephone, but many are not, and in emergencies caution is often forgotten. It struck me that for getting the kind of information, or at least hints of it, that is most useful and profitable for a blackmailer, a telephone-answering service has potentialities equal to those of a doctor or lawyer or trusted servant. Any operator at the switchboard could simply—"

"This is mere idle speculation, Mr. Wolfe. Did you say all that to the defendant?"

"Yes, sir."

"How long were you with him?"

"Nearly half an hour. I can say a great deal in half an hour."

"No doubt. But the time of the court and jury should not be spent on irrelevancies." Mandelbaum treated the jury to one of his under-

standing glances, and went back to Wolfe. "You didn't discuss your
testimony with the defendant?"

"No, sir."

"Did you make any suggestions to him regarding the conduct of his
defense?"

"No, sir. I made no suggestions to him of any kind."

"Did you offer to make any kind of investigation for him as a contribution to his defense?"

"No, sir."

"Then why did you seek this interview with him?"

"One moment." Donovan was on his feet. "I submit, Your Honor,
that this is the State's witness, and this is not proper direct examination.
Surely it is cross-examination, and I object to it."

Judge Corbett nodded. "The objection is sustained. Mr. Mandelbaum, you know the rules of evidence."

"But I am confronted by an unforeseen contingency."

"He is still your witness. Examine him upon the merits."

"Also, Your Honor, he is in contempt."

"Not yet. That is in abeyance. Proceed."

Mandelbaum looked at Wolfe, glanced at the jury, went to the table
and stood a moment gazing down at it, lifted his head, said, "No more
questions," and sat down.

Jimmy Donovan arose and stepped forward, but addressed the bench
instead of the witness stand. "Your Honor, I wish to state that I knew
nothing of the meeting this morning, of the witness with my client,
either before or after it took place. I only learned of it here and now. If
you think it desirable, I will take the stand to be questioned about it
under oath."

Judge Corbett shook his head. "I don't think so, Mr. Donovan. Not
unless developments suggest it."

"At any time, of course." Donovan turned. "Mr. Wolfe, why did you
seek an interview this morning with Mr. Ashe?"

Wolfe was relaxed but not smug. "Because I had acquired information which cast a reasonable doubt on his guilt, and I wanted to get it
before the court and the jury without delay. As a witness for the prosecution, with a warrant out for my arrest, I was in a difficult situation.
It occurred to me that if I saw and talked with Mr. Ashe the fact would
probably be disclosed in the course of my examination by Mr. Mandelbaum; and if so, he would almost certainly ask me what had been said.
Therefore I wanted to tell Mr. Ashe what I had surmised and what I
had discovered. If Mr. Mandelbaum allowed me to tell all I had said to

Mr. Ashe, that would do it. If he dismissed me before I finished, I thought it likely that on cross-examination the defense attorney would give me an opportunity to go on." He turned a palm up. "So I sought an interview with Mr. Ashe."

The judge was frowning. One of the jurors made a noise, and the others looked at him. The audience stirred, and someone tittered. I was thinking Wolfe had one hell of a nerve, but he hadn't violated any law I had ever heard of, and Donovan had asked him a plain question and got a plain answer. I would have given a ream of foolscap to see Donovan's face.

If his face showed any reaction to the suggestion given him, his voice didn't. "Did you say more to Mr. Ashe than you have already testified to?"

"Yes, sir."

"Please tell the jury what you said to him."

"I said that I left this room yesterday morning, deliberately risking a penalty for contempt of court, to explore my surmises. I said that, taking my assistant, Mr. Archie Goodwin, with me, I went to the office of Bagby Answers, Incorporated, on Sixty-ninth Street, where Marie Willis was murdered. I said that from a look at the switchboards I concluded that it would be impossible for any one operator—"

Mandelbaum was up. "Objection, Your Honor. Conclusions of the witness are not admissible."

"He is merely relating," Donovan submitted, "what he said to Mr. Ashe. The Assistant District Attorney asked him to."

"The objection is overruled," Judge Corbett said dryly.

Wolfe resumed. "I said I had concluded that it would be impossible for any one operator to eavesdrop frequently on her lines without the others becoming aware of it, and therefore it must be done collusively if at all. I said that I had spoken at some length with two of the operators, Alice Hart and Bella Velardi, who had been working and living there along with Marie Willis, and had received two encouragements for my surmise: one, that they were visibly disturbed at my declared intention of investigating them fully and ruthlessly, and tolerated my rudeness beyond reason; and two, that it was evident that their personal expenditures greatly exceeded their salaries. I said—may I ask, sir, is it necessary for me to go on repeating that phrase, 'I said'?"

"I think not," Donovan told him. "Not if you confine yourself strictly to what you said to Mr. Ashe this morning."

"I shall do so. The extravagance in personal expenditures was true also of the third operator who had lived and worked there with Marie

Willis, Helen Weltz. It was her day off, and Mr. Goodwin and I drove
to her place in the country, near Katonah in Westchester County. She
was more disturbed even than the other two; she was almost hysterical.
With her was a man named Guy Unger, and he too was disturbed.
After I had stated my intention to investigate everyone connected with
Bagby Answers, Incorporated, he asked to speak with me privately and
offered me ten thousand dollars for services which he did not specify.
I gathered that he was trying to bribe me to keep my hands off, and I
declined the offer."

"You said all that to Mr. Ashe?"

"Yes, sir. Meanwhile Helen Weltz had spoken privately with Mr.
Goodwin, and had told him she wanted to speak with me, but must
first get rid of Mr. Unger. She said she would phone my office later.
Back in the city, I dared not go to my home, since I was subject to arrest and detention, so Mr. Goodwin and I went to the home of a friend,
and Helen Weltz came to us there some time after midnight. My attack
had broken her completely, and she was in terror. She confessed that
for years the operation had been used precisely as I had surmised. All
of the switchboard operators had been parties to it, including Marie
Willis. Their dean, Alice Hart, collected information—"

There was an interruption. Alice Hart, on the aisle, with Bella Velardi next to her, got up and headed for the door, and Bella followed
her. Eyes went to them from all directions, including Judge Corbett's,
but nobody said or did anything, and when they were five steps from
the door I sang out to the guard, "That's Alice Hart in front!"

He blocked them off. Judge Corbett called, "Officer, no one is to
leave the room!"

The audience stirred and muttered, and some stood up. The judge
banged his gavel and demanded order, but he couldn't very well
threaten to have the room cleared. Miss Hart and Miss Velardi gave it
up and went back to their seats.

When the room was still the judge spoke to Wolfe. "Go ahead."

He did so. "Alice Hart collected information from them and gave
them cash from time to time, in addition to their salaries. Guy Unger
and Clyde Bagby also gave them cash occasionally. The largest single
amount ever received by Helen Weltz was fifteen hundred dollars,
given her about a year ago by Guy Unger. In three years she received a
total of approximately fifteen thousand dollars, not counting her salary.
She didn't know what use was made of the information she passed on to
Alice Hart. She wouldn't admit that she had knowledge that any of it
had been used for blackmailing, but she did admit that some of it could
have been so used."

"Do you know," Judge Corbett asked him, "where Helen Weltz is now?"

"Yes, sir. She is present. I told her that if she came and faced it the District Attorney might show appreciation for her help."

"Have you anything to add that you told Mr. Ashe this morning?"

"I have, Your Honor. Do you wish me to differentiate clearly between what Helen Weltz told me and my own exposition?"

"No. Anything whatever that you said to Mr. Ashe."

"I told him that the fact that he had tried to hire me to learn the identity of the Bagby operator who would service his number, and to bribe her to eavesdrop on his line, was one of the points that had caused me to doubt his guilt; that I had questioned whether a man who was reluctant to undertake such a chore for himself would be likely to strangle the life out of a woman and then open a window and yell for the police. Also I asked him about the man who telephoned him to say that if Ashe would meet him at the Bagby office on Sixty-ninth Street he thought they could talk Miss Willis out of it. I asked if it was possible that the voice was Bagby's, and Ashe said it was quite possible, but if so he had disguised his voice."

"Had you any evidence that Mr. Bagby made that phone call?"

"No, Your Honor. All I had, besides my assumptions from known facts and my own observations, was what Miss Weltz had told me. One thing she had told me was that Marie Willis had become an imminent threat to the whole conspiracy. She had been ordered by both Unger and Bagby to accept Ashe's proposal to eavesdrop on his line, and not to tell Mrs. Ashe, whom Miss Willis idolized; and she had refused and announced that she was going to quit. Of course that made her an intolerable peril to everyone concerned. The success and security of the operation hinged on the fact that no victim ever had any reason to suspect that Bagby Answers, Incorporated, was responsible for his distress. It was Bagby who got the information, but it was Unger who used it, and the tormented under the screw could not know where the tormentor had got the screw. So Miss Willis's rebellion and decision to quit—combined, according to Miss Weltz, with an implied threat to expose the whole business—were a mortal menace to any and all of them, ample provocation for murder to one willing to risk that extreme. I told Mr. Ashe that all this certainly established a reasonable doubt of his guilt, but I also went beyond that and considered briefly the most likely candidate to replace him. Do you wish that too?"

The judge was intent on him. "Yes. Proceed."

"I told Mr. Ashe that I greatly preferred Mr. Bagby. The mutual alibi of Miss Hart and Miss Velardi might be successfully impeached, but they have it, and besides I have seen and talked with them and was not impressed. I exclude Miss Weltz because when she came to me last evening she had been jolted by consternation into utter candor, or I am a witless gull; and that excludes Mr. Unger too, because Miss Weltz claims certain knowledge that he was on his boat in the Sound all of that evening. As for Mr. Bagby, he had most at stake. He admits that he went to his apartment around the time of the murder, and his apartment is on Seventieth Street, not far from where the murder occurred. I leave the timetable to the police; they are extremely efficient with timetables. Regarding the telephone call, Mr. Ashe said it could have been his voice."

Wolfe pursed his lips. "I think that's all—no, I also told Mr. Ashe that this morning I sent a man, Saul Panzer, to keep an eye on Mr. Bagby's office in Forty-seventh Street, to see that no records are removed or destroyed. I believe that covers it adequately, Your Honor. I would now like to plead to the charge of contempt, both on behalf of Mr. Goodwin and of myself. If I may—"

"No." Judge Corbett was curt. "You know quite well you have made that charge frivolous by the situation you have created. The charge is dismissed. Are you through with the witness, Mr. Donovan?"

"Yes, Your Honor. No more questions."

"Mr. Mandelbaum?"

The Assistant District Attorney got up and approached the bench. "Your Honor will appreciate that I find myself in an extraordinary predicament." He sounded like a man with a major grievance. "I feel that I am entitled to ask for a recess until the afternoon session, to consider the situation and consult with my colleagues. If my request is granted, I also ask that I be given time, before the recess is called, to arrange for five persons in the room to be taken into custody as material witnesses—Alice Hart, Bella Velardi, Helen Weltz, Guy Unger, and Clyde Bagby."

"Very well." The judge raised his eyes and his voice. "The five persons just named will come forward. The rest of you will keep your seats and preserve order."

All of them obeyed but two. Nero Wolfe left the witness chair and stepped down to the floor, and as he did so Robina Keane sprang up from her place on the front bench, ran to him, threw her arms around his neck, and pressed her cheek against his. As I said before, actresses always act, but I admit that was unrehearsed and may have been artless. In any case, I thoroughly approved, since it indicated that the Ashe family would prove to be properly grateful, which after all was the main point.

VI

THE thought may have occurred to you, that's all very nice, and no doubt Ashe sent a handsome check, but after all one reason Wolfe walked out was because he hated to sit against a perfumed woman on a wooden bench waiting for his turn to testify, and he had to do it all over again when the state was ready with its case against the real murderer. It did look for a while as if he might have to face up to that, but a week before the trial opened he was informed that he wouldn't be needed, and he wasn't. They had plenty without him to persuade a jury to bring in a verdict of guilty against Clyde Bagby.

WHEN A MAN MURDERS...

I

"THAT'S just it," she declared, trying to keep her voice steady. "We're not actually married."

My brows went up. Many a time, seated there at my desk in Nero Wolfe's office, I have put the eye on a female visitor to estimate how many sound reasons she might offer why a wedding ring would be a good buy, but usually I don't bother with those who are already hitched, so my survey of this specimen had been purely professional, especially since her husband was along. Now, however, I changed focus. She would unquestionably grade high, after allowing for the crease in her forehead, the redness around her eyes, and the tension of her jaw muscles, tightening her lips. Making such allowances was nothing new for me, since most of the callers at that office are in trouble, seldom trivial.

Wolfe, who had just come down from the plant rooms on the roof and got his impressive bulk settled in his oversized chair behind his desk, glared at her. "But you told Mr. Goodwin—" he began, stopped, and turned to me. "Archie?"

I nodded. "Yes, sir. A man on the phone said his name was Paul Aubry, and he and his wife wanted to come to see you as soon as possible, and I told him six o'clock. I didn't tell him to bring their marriage certificate."

"We have one," she said, "but it's no good." She twisted her head around and up. "Tell him, Paul."

She was in the red leather chair near the end of Wolfe's desk. It is roomy, with big arms, and Paul Aubry was perched on one of them, with an arm extended along the top of the back. I had offered him one of the yellow chairs, which are perfectly adequate, but apparently he preferred to stick closer to his wife, if any.

"It's one hell of a mess!" he blurted.

He wasn't red-eyed, but there was evidence that he was sharing the trouble. His hand on top of the chair-back was tightened into a fist, his fairly well-arranged face was grim, and his broad shoulders seemed to be hunched in readiness to meet an attack. He bent his head to meet her upward look.

"Don't you want to tell him?" he asked.

She shook her head. "No, you." She put out a hand to touch his knee and then jerked it away.

His eyes went to Wolfe. "We were married six months ago—six months and four days—but now we're not married, according to the law. We're not married because my wife, Caroline—" He paused to look down at her, and, his train of thought interrupted, reached to take her hand, but it moved, and he didn't get it.

He stood up, squared his shoulders, faced Wolfe, and spoke faster and louder. "Four years ago she married a man named Sidney Karnow. A year later he enlisted in the Army and was sent to Korea. A few months later she was officially informed that he was dead—killed in action. A year after that I met her and fell in love with her and asked her to marry me, but she wouldn't until two years had passed since Karnow died, and then she did. Three weeks ago Karnow turned up alive—he phoned his lawyer here from San Francisco—and last week he got his Army discharge, and Sunday, day before yesterday, he came to New York."

Aubry hunched his shoulders like Jack Dempsey ready to move in. "I'm not giving her up," he told the world. "I—will—not—give—her—up!"

Wolfe grunted. "It's fifteen million to one, Mr. Aubry."

"What do you mean, fifteen million?"

"The People of the State of New York. They're lined up against you, officially at least. I'm one of them. Why in heaven's name did you come to me? You should have cleared out with her days ago—Turkey, Australia, Burma, anywhere—if she was willing. It may not be too late if you hurry. Bon voyage."

Aubry stood a moment, took a deep breath, turned and went to the yellow chair I had placed, and sat. Becoming aware that his fists were clenched, he opened them, cupped his hands on his knees, and looked at Caroline. He lifted a hand and let it fall back to his knee. "I can't touch you," he said.

"No," she said. "Not while—no."

"Okay, you tell him. He might think I was bulling it. You tell him."

She shook her head. "He can ask me. I'm right here. Go ahead."

He went to Wolfe. "It's like this. Karnow was an only child, and his parents are both dead, and he inherited a pile, nearly two million dollars. He left a will giving half of it to my—to Caroline, and the other half to some relatives, an aunt and a couple of cousins. His lawyer had the will. After notice of his death came it took several months to get the will probated and the estate distributed, on account of special formalities in a case like that. Caroline's share was a little over nine hundred thousand dollars, and she had it when I met her, and was living on the income. All I had was a job selling automobiles, making around a hundred and fifty a week, but it was her I fell in love with, not the million, just for your information. When we got married it was her idea that I ought to buy an agency, but I'm not saying I fought it. I shopped around and we bought a good one at a bargain, and—"

"What kind of agency?"

"Automobile." Aubry's tone implied that that was the only kind of agency worth mentioning. "Brandon and Hiawatha. It took nearly half of Caroline's capital to swing it, but in the past three months we've cleared over twenty thousand after taxes, and the future was looking rosy—when this happened. I was figuring—but to hell with that, that's sunk. This proposition we want to offer Karnow, it's not my idea and it's not Caroline's, it's ours. It just came out of all our talking and talking after we heard Karnow was alive. Last week we went to Karnow's lawyer, Jim Beebe, to get him to propose it to Karnow, but we couldn't persuade him. He said he knew Karnow too well—he was in college with him—and he knew Karnow wouldn't even listen to it. So we decided—"

"What was the proposal?"

"We thought it was a fair offer. We offered to turn it all over to him, the half-million Caroline has left, and the agency, the whole works, if he would consent to a divorce. Also I would continue to run the agency if he wanted to hire me. Also Caroline would ask for no settlement and no alimony."

"It was my idea," she said.

"It was ours," he insisted.

Wolfe was frowning at them. My brows were up again. Evidently he really was in love with her and not the dough, and I'm all for true love up to a point. As for her, my attitude flopped back to the purely professional. Granting that she was set to ditch her lawful husband, if she felt that her Paul was worth a million bucks to her it would have taken too much time and energy to try to talk her out of it. Cocking an eye at his earnest phiz, which was passable but no pin-up, I would have said that she was overpricing him.

He was going on. "So when Beebe wouldn't do it and we learned that Karnow had come to New York, we decided I would see him myself and put it up to him. We only decided that last night. I had some business appointments this morning, and this afternoon I went to his hotel—he's at the Churchill—and went up to his room. I didn't phone ahead because I've never seen him, and I wanted to see him before I spoke with him. I wanted a look at him."

Aubry stopped to rub a palm across his forehead, pressing hard. When his hand dropped to his thigh it became a fist again. "One trouble," he said, "was that I wasn't absolutely sure what I was going to say. The main proposition, that was all right, but there were two other things in my mind. The agency is incorporated, and half of the stock is in Caroline's name and half in mine. Well, I could tell him that if he didn't take the offer I would hang on to my half and fight for it, but I hadn't decided whether to or not. The other thing, I could tell him that Caroline is pregnant. It wouldn't have been true, and I guess I wouldn't have said it, but it was in my mind. Anyhow it doesn't matter because I didn't see him."

He clamped his jaw and then relaxed it. "This is where I didn't shine, I admit that, but it wasn't just cold feet. I went up to the door of his room, twenty-three-eighteen, without phoning, and I lifted my hand to knock, but I didn't. Because I realized I was trembling, I was trembling all over. I stood there a while to calm down, but I didn't calm. I realized that if I went in there and put it to him and he said nothing doing, there was no telling what might happen. The way I was feeling I was a lot more apt to queer it than help it. So I just ducked it. I'm not proud of it, but I'm telling you, I gave it a miss and came away. Caroline was waiting for me in a bar down the street, and I went and told her, and that wasn't easy either, telling her I had muffed it. Up to then she had thought I could handle about anything that came along. She thought I was good."

"I still do, Paul," she told him.

"Yeah? I can't touch you."

"Not now. Not until—" Her hand fluttered. "Don't keep saying that."

"Okay, we'll skip it." He went back to Wolfe. "So I told her the man-to-man approach was a bum idea, and we sat and chewed at it. We decided that none of our friends was up to it. The lawyer I use for the agency wouldn't be worth a damn. When one of us thought of you —I forget which—it clicked with both of us, and I went to a booth to phone for an appointment. Maybe you can get him down here and you make him the proposition yourself, or if he won't come you can send

Archie Goodwin to see him. Caroline has the idea it might be better to send Goodwin because Karnow's thin-skinned and you might irritate him. We'll leave that to you. I wish I could say if you get him to take our offer you can write your own ticket, any amount you want to make it, but in that case we won't be any too flush so I have to mention it. Five thousand dollars, something like that, we could manage that all right. But for God's sake go to it—now, today, tonight!"

Wolfe cleared his throat. "I'm not a lawyer, Mr. Aubry, I'm a detective."

"I know that, but what's the difference? You have a reputation for getting things out of people. We want you to detect a way of getting Karnow to accept our proposition."

Wolfe grunted. "I could challenge your diction, but you're in no mood to debate semantics. And my fees are based on the kind and amount of work done. Your job seems fairly simple. In describing it to me, how candid have you been?"

"Completely. Absolutely."

"Nonsense. Complete candor is beyond the reach of man or woman. If Mr. Karnow accepts your proposal, can I rely on you to adhere to its terms as you have stated them?"

"Yes. You're damn right you can."

Wolfe's head turned. "Mrs. Karnow, are you—"

"She's not Mrs. Karnow!" Aubry barked. "She's my wife!"

Wolfe's shoulders went up half an inch and dropped back. "Madam, are you sure you understand the proposal and will faithfully adhere to it?"

"Yes," she said firmly.

"You know that you will be relinquishing a dower right, a legal right, in a large property?"

"Yes."

"Then I must ask a few questions about Mr. Karnow—of you, since Mr. Aubry has never met him. You had no child by him?"

"No."

"You were in love when you married, presumably?"

"We thought—I guess we were. Yes, say we were."

"Did it cool off?"

"Not exactly." She hesitated, deciding how to put it. "Sidney was sensitive and high-strung—you see, I still say 'was' because for so long I thought he was dead. I was only nineteen when we were married, and I suppose I didn't know how to take him. He enlisted in the Army because he thought he ought to, because he hadn't been in the World

War and he thought he should do his share of peeling potatoes—that was how he put it—but I didn't agree with him. I had found out by then that what I thought wasn't very important, nor what I felt either. If you're going to try to get him to agree to this of course you want to know what he's like, but I don't really know myself, not after all this time. Maybe it would help for you to read the letters I got from him after he enlisted. He only sent me three, one from Camp Givens and two from Korea—he didn't like writing letters. My husb—Paul said I should bring them along to show you."

She opened her bag, fished in it, and produced some sheets of paper clipped together. I went to get them and hand them to Wolfe, and, since I would probably be elected to deliver the proposal, I planted myself at his elbow and read along with him. All three letters are still in the archives in our office, but I'll present only one, the last one, to give you a sample of the tone and style:

Dear Carrie my true and loving mate I hope:

Pardon me, but my weakness is showing. I would like to be where you are this minute and tell you why I didn't like your new dress, and you would go and put on another one, and we would go to Chambord and eat snails and drink Richebourg and then go to the Velvet Yoke and eat lady fingers and drink tomato soup, and then we would go home and take hot baths and go to sleep on fine linen sheets spread over mattresses three feet thick, covered with an electric blanket. After several days of that I would begin to recognize myself and would put my arms around you and we would drown in delight.

Now I suppose I should tell you enough about this place to make you understand why I would rather be somewhere else, but that would be too easy to bother with, and anyway, as you well know, I hate to write, and especially I hate to try to write what I feel. Since the time is getting closer and closer when I'll try to kill somebody and probably succeed, I've been going through my memory for things about death. Herodotus said, "Death is a delightful hiding-place for weary men." Epictetus said, "What is death but a bugbear?" Montaigne said, "The deadest deaths are the best." I'll quote those to the man I'm going to kill and then he won't mind so much.

Speaking of death, if he should get me instead of me getting him, something I did before I left New York will give you quite a shock. I wish I could be around to see how you take it. You claim you have never worried about money, that it's not worth it. Also you've told me that I always talk sardonic but haven't got it in me to act sardonic. This will show you. I'll admit I have to die to get the last laugh, but that will be sardonic too. I wonder do I love you or hate you? They're hard to tell apart. Remember me in thy dreams.

Your sardonic
Kavalier Karnow

As I went to my desk to put the letters under a paperweight Caroline was speaking. "I wrote him two long letters every week. I must have sent him over fifty letters, and he never mentioned them the few times he wrote. I want to try to be fair to him, but he always said he was egocentric, and I guess he was."

"Not *was*," Aubry said grimly. "*Is*. He *is*." He asked Wolfe, "Doesn't that letter prove he's a nut?"

"He is—uh—picturesque," Wolfe conceded. He turned to Caroline. "What had he done before he left New York that—upon his death—gave you quite a shock?"

She shook her head. "I don't know. Naturally I thought he had changed his will and left me out. After word came that he was dead I showed that letter to the lawyer, Jim Beebe, and told him what I thought, and he said it did sound like it, but there had been no change made in the will as far as he knew, and Sidney must have been stringing me."

"Not too adroitly," Wolfe objected. "It isn't so simple to disinherit a wife. However, since he didn't try— What do you know about the false report of his death?"

"Only a little from an item in the paper," she said, "but Jim Beebe told me some more. He was left for dead in the field in a retreat, but actually he was only stunned, and he was taken prisoner. He was a prisoner for nearly two years, and then he escaped across the Yalu River, and then he was in Manchuria. By that time he could talk their language—he was wonderful with languages—and he made friends in a village and wore their clothes, and it seems—I'm not sure about this, but apparently he was converted to communism."

"Then he's a jackass," Wolfe asserted.

"Oh, no, he's not a jackass." She was positive. "Maybe he was just being picturesque. Anyhow, a few months after the truce was signed and the fighting stopped he finally decided he had had enough of it and went back across the Yalu and made his way to South Korea and reported to an army post, and they sent him home. And now he's here." She stretched her hands out, at arm's length. "Please, Mr. Wolfe? Please?"

Though of course she didn't know it, that was bad tactics. Wolfe's reaction to an emotional appeal from a man is rarely favorable, and from a woman, never. He turned away from the painful sight, to me. "Archie. You're in my hire, and I can dispatch you on errands within the scope of my métier, but this one isn't. Are you willing to tackle it?"

He was being polite. What he really meant was: Five grand will pay a lot of salaries, including yours, and you will please proceed to earn it for me. So, wishing to be polite too, I suggested a compromise. "I'm willing to go get him and bring him here, and you can tackle it."

"No," he said flatly. "Regarding the proposal as quixotic, as I do, I would be a feeble advocate. I abandon it to your decision."

"I deeply appreciate it," I assured him. "Nuts. If I say no I won't hear the last of it for months, so I'll meet you all the way and say yes. I'll take a shot at it."

"Very well. We'll discuss it after dinner, and in the morning you can—"

They drowned him out, both of them cutting in to protest. They couldn't wait until tomorrow, they had to know. They protested to him and then appealed to me. Why put it off? Why not now? I do not react to emotional appeals the way Wolfe does, and I calmed them down by agreeing with them.

"Very well," Wolfe acquiesced, which was noble of him. "But you must have with you the proposal in writing, in duplicate, signed by Mr. Aubry and—uh—you, madam. You must sign it as Caroline Karnow. Archie. At the bottom, on the left, type the word 'accepted' and a colon. Under the circumstances he would be a nincompoop not to sign it, but it would probably be imprudent to tell him so. Your notebook, please?"

I swiveled and got it from the drawer.

II

I RAPPED with my knuckles, smartly but not aggressively, on the door of Room 2318 on the twenty-third floor of the Hotel Churchill.

The clients had wanted to camp in Wolfe's office to await word from me, but I had insisted they should be as handy as possible in case developments called for their personal appearance, and they were downstairs in the Tulip Bar, not, I hoped, proceeding to get lit. People in serious trouble have a tendency to eat too little or drink too much, or both.

I knocked again, louder and longer.

On the way in the taxi I had collected a little more information about Sidney Karnow, at least as he had been three years back. His attitude toward money had been somewhat superior, but he had shown no inclination to scatter his pile around regardless. So far as Caroline knew, he hadn't scattered it at all. He had been more than decent about meeting her modest requirements, and even anticipating them. That gave me no lead, but other details did. The key words were "egocentric," which was bad, and "proud," which was good. If he really had pride and wasn't just using it as a cover for something that wouldn't stand daylight, fine. No proud man would want to eat his breakfasts with a woman who was eager to cough up nearly a million bucks for the privilege of eating them with another guy. That, I had decided, was the line to take, but I would have to go easy on the wording until I had sized him up.

Evidently the sizing up would be delayed, since my knocking got no response. Not wanting to risk a picturesque refusal to make an appointment, I hadn't phoned ahead. I decided to go down and tell the clients that patience would be required for ten minutes or ten hours, and take on a sandwich and a glass of milk and then come up for another try, but before I turned away my hand went automatically to the knob for a twist and a push, and the door opened. I stood a second, then pushed it a foot farther, stuck my head in, and called, "Mr. Karnow! Karnow!"

No answer. I swung the door open and crossed the sill. Beyond the light I was letting in was darkness, and I would probably have backed out and shut the door and beat it if I hadn't had such a good nose. When it told me there was a faint odor that I should recognize, and a couple of sniffs confirmed it, I found the wall switch and flipped it, and moved on in. A man was there, spread-eagled on the floor near an open door, flat on his back.

I took a step toward him—that was involuntary—then wheeled and went and closed the door to the hall, and returned. At a glance, from the description Caroline had given me, it was Sidney Karnow. He was dressed, but without a jacket or tie. I squatted and slipped a hand inside his shirt and held my breath; nothing doing. I picked a few fibers from the rug and put them over his nostrils; they didn't move. I got the lashes of his right eye between finger and thumb and pulled the lid partly down; it came stiffly and didn't want to go back. I lifted his hand and pressed hard on a fingernail, and then removed the pressure; it stayed white. Actually I was overdoing it, because the temperature of the skin of his chest had been enough.

I stood up and looked down at him. It was unquestionably Karnow. I looked at my wristwatch and saw 7:22. Through the open door beyond him I could see the glitter of bathroom tiles and fittings, and, detouring around his outstretched arm, I went and squatted again for a close-up of two objects on the floor. One was a GI sidearm, a .45. I didn't touch it. The other was a big wad of bathtowels, and I touched it enough to learn, from a scorched hole and powder black, that it had been used to muffle the gun. I had seen no sign on the body of a bullet's entrance or exit, and to find it I would have had to turn him over, and what did it matter? I got erect and shut my eyes to think. It is my habit, long established, when I open doors where I haven't been invited, to avoid touching the knob with my fingertips. Had I followed it this time? I decided yes. Also, had I flipped the light switch with my knuckle? Again yes. Had I made prints anywhere else? No.

I crossed to the switch and used my knuckle again, got out my handkerchief to open the door and pull it shut after me, took an elevator down to the lobby floor, found a phone booth, and dialed a number. The voice that answered belonged to Fritz. I told him I wanted Wolfe.

He was shocked. "But Archie, he's at dinner!"

"Yeah, I know. Tell him I've been trapped by cannibals and they're slicing me, and step on it."

It was a full two minutes before Wolfe's outraged voice came. "Well, Archie?"

"No, sir. Not well. I'm calling from a booth in the Churchill lobby. I left the clients in the bar, went up to Karnow's room, found the door unlocked, and entered. Karnow was on the floor, dead, shot with an army gun. The gun's there, but it wasn't suicide, the gun was muffled with a wad of towels. How do I earn the five grand now?"

"Confound it, in the middle of a meal."

If you think that was put on, you're wrong. I know that damn fat genius. That was how he felt, and he said it, that's all.

I ignored it. "I left nothing in the room," I told him, "and I had no audience, so we're fancy free. I know it's hard to talk with your mouth full, but—"

"Shut up." Silence for four seconds, then: "Did he die within the past ninety minutes?"

"No. The skin on his chest has started to cool off."

"Did you see anything suggestive?"

"No. I was in there maybe three minutes. I wanted to interrupt your dinner. I can go back and give it a whirl."

"Don't." He was curt. "There's nothing to be gained by deferring the discovery. I'll have Fritz notify the police anonymously. Bring Mr. Aubry and Mrs. Karnow—have they eaten?"

"They may be eating now. I told them to."

"See that they eat, and then bring them here on a pretext. Devise one."

"Don't tell them?"

"No. I'll tell them. Have them here in an hour and ten minutes, not sooner. I've barely started my dinner—and now this."

He hung up.

After crossing the lobby and proceeding along one of the long, wide, and luxurious corridors, near the entrance to the Tulip Bar I was stopped by an old acquaintance, Tim Evarts, the first assistant house dick, only they don't call him that, of the Churchill. He wanted to chin, but I eased him off. If he had known that I had just found a corpse in one of his rooms and forgot to mention it, he wouldn't have been so chummy.

The big room was only half filled with customers at that hour. The clients were at a table over in a corner, and as I approached and Aubry got up to move a chair for me I gave them both a mark for good conduct. Presumably they were on the sharpest edge of anxiety to hear what I was bringing, but they didn't yap or claw at me.

When I was seated I spoke to their waiting faces. "No answer to my knock. I'll have to try again. Meanwhile let's eat."

I couldn't see that their disappointment was anything but plain, wholesome disappointment.

"I can't eat now," Caroline said wearily.

"I strongly advise it," I told her. "I don't mean a major meal, but something like a piece of melon and a sturgeon sandwich? We can get that here. Then I'll try again, and if there's still no answer we'll see. You can't stick around here all night."

"He might show up any minute," Aubry suggested. "Or he might come in and leave again. Wouldn't it be better if you stayed up there?"

"Not on an empty stomach." I was firm. "And I'll bet Mrs.— What do I call you?"

"Oh, call me Caroline."

"I'll bet you haven't eaten for a week. You may need some energy, so you'd better refuel."

That was a tough half-hour. She did eat a little, and Aubry cleaned up a turkey sandwich and a hunk of cheese, but she was having a hard time to keep from showing that she thought I was a cold-blooded pig, and Aubry, as the minutes went by, left no doubt of his attitude. It was pretty gloomy. When my coffee cup was empty I told them to sit tight, got up and went out and down the corridor to the men's room, locked myself in a cubicle against the chance that Aubry might appear, and stayed there a quarter of an hour. Then I returned to the bar and went to their table and told them, "No answer. I phoned Mr. Wolfe, and he has an idea and wants to see us right away. Let's go."

"No," Caroline said.

"What for?" Aubry demanded.

"Look," I said, "when Mr. Wolfe has an idea and wants me to hear it, I oblige him. So I'm going. You can stay here and soak in the agony, or you can come along. Take your pick."

From their expressions it was a good guess that they were beginning to think that Wolfe was a phony and I was a slob, but since their only alternative was to call the deal off and start hunting another salesman for their line, they had to string along. After Aubry paid the check we left, and in the corridor I steered them to the left and around to an exit on a side street, to avoid the main lobby, because by that time some city employees had certainly responded to Fritz's anonymous phone call to headquarters, and from remarks they had made I had learned that the Aubrys were known at the Churchill. The doorman who waved up a taxi for us called them by name.

At the house I let us in with my key, and, closing the door, shot the chain bolt. As I escorted them down the hall to the office a glance at my wrist told me it was 8:35, so I hadn't quite stretched it to the hour and ten minutes Wolfe had specified, but pretty close. He emerged from the door to the dining room, which is across the hall from the office, stood there while we filed in, and then followed, the look on his face as black as the coffee he had just been sipping. After crossing to his desk and lowering his overwhelming bulk into his chair, he growled at them, "Sit down, please."

They stayed on their feet. Aubry demanded, "What's the big idea? Goodwin says you have one."

"You will please sit down," Wolfe said coldly. "I look at people I'm talking to, especially when I suspect them of trying to flummox me, and my neck is not elastic."

His tone made it evident that what was biting him was nothing trivial. Caroline sidled to the red leather chair and sat on its edge. Aubry plopped on the yellow one and met Wolfe's level gaze.

"You suspect?" he asked quietly. "Who? Of what?"

"I think one of you has seen and talked with Mr. Karnow—today. Perhaps both of you."

"What makes you think so?"

"I reserve that. Whether and when I disclose it depends on you. While complete candor is too much to expect, it should at least be approximated when you're briefing a man for a job you want done. When and where did you see Mr. Karnow, and what was said?"

"I didn't. I have never seen him. I told you that. What's the idea of this?"

Wolfe's head moved. "Then it was you, madam?"

Caroline was staring at him, her brow creased. "Are you suggesting that I saw my—that I saw Sidney Karnow today?"

"Precisely."

"Well, I didn't! I haven't seen him at all! And I want to know why you're suggesting that!"

"You will." Wolfe rested his elbows on the chair arms, leaned forward, and gave her his straightest and hardest look. She met it. He turned his head to the right and aimed the look at Aubry, and had it met again.

The doorbell rang.

Fritz was in the kitchen doing the dishes, so I got up and went to the hall and flipped the switch of the light out on the stoop and took a look through the one-way glass panel of the front door. What I saw deserved admiration. Sergeant Purley Stebbins of Manhattan Homicide West knew that that panel was one-way glass and he was visible, but he wasn't striking a pose; he just stood there, his big broad pan a foot away from the glass, to him opaque, a dick doing his duty.

I went and opened the door and spoke through the two-inch crack which was all the chain bolt would allow. "Hello there. It wasn't me, honest."

"Okay, comic." His deep bass was a little hoarse, as usual. "Then I won't take you. Let me in."

"For what?"

"I'll tell you. Do you expect me to talk through this damn crack?"

"Yes. If I let you in you'll tramp right over me to bust in on Mr. Wolfe, and he's in a bad humor. So am I. I can spare you ten seconds to loosen up. One, two, three, four—"

He cut me off. "You were just up at the Hotel Churchill. You left there about a half an hour ago with a man named Paul Aubry and his wife, and got into a taxi with them. Where are they? Did you bring them here?"

"May I call you Purley?" I asked.

"You goddam clown."

"All right, then, I won't. After all these years you should know better. Eighty-seven and four-tenths per cent of the people, including licensed detectives, who are asked impertinent questions by cops, answer quick because they are either scared or ignorant of their rights or anxious to cooperate. That lets me out. Give me one reason why I should tell you anything about my movements or any companions I may have had, and make it good."

Silence. After a moment I added, "And don't try to avoid giving me a shock. Since you're Homicide, someone is dead. Who?"

"Who do you think?"

"Huh-uh. I won't try to guess because I might guess the right one and I'd be in the soup."

"I want to be around when you are. Sidney Karnow was killed in his room at the Churchill this afternoon. He had been reported dead in Korea and had just turned up alive, and had learned that his wife had married Paul Aubry. As if I was telling you anything you don't know."

He couldn't see my face through the crack, so I didn't have to bother about managing it. I asked, "Karnow was murdered?"

"That's the idea. He was shot in the back of the head."

"Are you saying I knew about it?"

"Not so far. But you knew about the situation, since you were there with Aubry and the woman. I want 'em, and I want 'em now, and are they here? If not, where are they?"

"I see," I said judiciously. "I admit you have given me a reason. Be seated while I go take a look." I pushed the door shut, went back to the office and crossed to my desk, took a pencil and my memo pad, and wrote:

> Stebbins. Says K. murdered. We were seen leaving hotel. Asks are they here and if not where.

I got up to hand it to Wolfe, and he took it in with a glance and slipped it into the top drawer of his desk. He looked at Caroline and then at Aubry. "You don't need me," he told them. "Your problem has been solved for you. Mr. Karnow is dead."

They gawked at him.

"Of course," he added, "you now have another problem, which may be even thornier."

Caroline was stiff, frozen. "I don't believe it," Aubry said harshly.

"It seems authentic," Wolfe declared. "Archie?"

"Yes, sir. Sergeant Stebbins of Homicide is out on the stoop. He says that Karnow was murdered, shot in the back of the head, this afternoon in his room at the Churchill. Mr. Aubry and Mrs. Karnow were seen leaving the hotel with me, and he wants to know if they're here, and if not, where? He says he wants them."

"Good God," Aubry said. Caroline had let out a gasp, but no word. She was still rigid.

Her lips moved, and I thought she asked, "He's dead?" but it was too low to be sure.

Wolfe spoke. "So you have another problem. The police will give you a night of it, and possibly a week or a month. Mr. Stebbins cannot enter this house without a search warrant, and if you were my clients I wouldn't mind letting him wait on the stoop while we considered the matter, but since the job you gave me is now not feasible I am no longer in your hire. I have on occasion welcomed an opportunity to plague the police, but never merely for pastime, so I must bid you good evening."

Caroline had left her chair and gone to Aubry with her hands out, and he had taken them and pulled her to him. Evidently the ban was off.

"However," Wolfe continued, "I have a deep repugnance to letting the police take from my house people who have been moved to consult me and who have not been formally charged with a crime. There is a back way out, leading to Thirty-fourth Street, and Mr. Goodwin will take you by it if you feel that you would like a little time to discuss matters."

"No," Aubry said. "We have nothing to run from. Tell him we're here. Let him in."

Wolfe shook his head. "Not in my house, to drag you out. You're sure you don't want to delay it?"

"Yes."

"Then Archie, will you please handle it?"

I arose, told them, "This way, please," and headed for the door, but stopped and turned when I heard Caroline find her voice behind me.

"Wait a minute," she said, barely loud enough for me to get it. She was standing facing Aubry, gripping his lapels. "Paul, don't you think —shouldn't we ask Mr. Wolfe—"

"There's nothing to ask him." Aubry was up, with an arm across her shoulders. "I've had enough of Wolfe. Come on, Caro mia. We don't have to ask anybody anything."

They came and followed me into the hall. As Aubry was getting his hat from the rack I opened the door, leaving the chain bolt on, and spoke to Purley. "What do you know, they were right here in the office. That's a break for you. Now if—"

"Open the door!"

"In a moment. Mr. Wolfe is peevish and might irritate you, so if you'll remove yourself, on down to the sidewalk, I'll let them out, and they are yours."

"I'm coming in."

"No. Don't even think of it."

"I want you too."

"Yeah, I thought so. I'll be along shortly. Twentieth Street?"

"Now. With me."

"Again no. I have to ask Mr. Wolfe if there's anything we wouldn't want to bother you with, and if so what. Where do I go, Twentieth Street?"

"Yes, and not tomorrow."

"Right. Glad to oblige. The subjects are here at my elbow, so if you'll just descend the steps—and be careful, don't fall."

He muttered something I didn't catch, turned, and started down. When he was at the bottom of the seven steps I removed the bolt, swung the door open, and told our former clients, "Okay. In return for the sandwiches and coffee, here's a suggestion. Don't answer a single damn question until you have got a lawyer and talked with him. Even if—"

I stopped because my audience was going. Aubry had her arm as they crossed the stoop and started down. Not wishing to give Purley the pleasure of having me watch him take them, I shut the door, replaced the bolt, and returned to the office. Wolfe was leaning back with his eyes closed.

"I'm wanted," I told him. "Do I go?"

"Of course," he growled.

"Are we saving anything?"

"No. There's nothing to save."

"The letters from Karnow to his wife are in my desk. Do I take them and turn them over?"

"No. They are her property, and doubtless she will claim them."

"Did I discover the body?"

"Certainly not. To what purpose?"

"None. Don't worry if I'm late."

I went to the hall for my hat and beat it.

III

SINCE I wasn't itching to oblige Homicide, and it was a pleasant evening for a walk, I decided to hoof it the fifteen blocks to Twentieth Street, and also to do a little chore on the way. If I had done it in the office Wolfe would have pulled his dignity on me and pretended to be outraged, though he knew as well as I did that it's always desirable to get your name in the paper, provided it's not in the obituary column. So I went to a phone booth in a drugstore on Tenth Avenue, dialed the *Gazette* number, asked for Lon Cohen, and got him.

"Scrap the front page," I told him, "and start over. If you don't want it I'll sell it to the *Times*. Did you happen to know that Paul Aubry and his wife, Mrs. Sidney Karnow to you, called on Nero Wolfe this afternoon, and I went somewhere with them, and brought them back to Mr. Wolfe's office, and fifteen minutes ago Sergeant Purley Stebbins came and got them? Or maybe you don't even know that Karnow was murd—"

"Yeah, I know that. What's the rest of it? Molasses you licked off your fingers?"

"Nope. Guaranteed straight as delivered. I just want to get my employer's name in the paper. Mine is spelled, A-R-C-H—"

"I know that too. Who else has got this?"

"From me, nobody. Only you, son."

"What did they want Wolfe to do?"

Of course that was to be expected. Give a newspaperman an inch and he wants a column. I finally convinced him that that was all for now and resumed my way downtown.

At Manhattan Homicide West on Twentieth Street I was hoping to be assigned to Lieutenant Rowcliff so I could try once more to make him mad enough to stutter, but I got a college graduate named Eisenstadt who presented no challenge. All he wanted was facts, and I dished them out, withholding, naturally, that I had entered the room. It took less than an hour, including having my statement typed and signed, and I declined his pressing invitation to stick around until Inspector Cramer got in. I told him another fact, that I was a citizen in good standing, or fair at least, with a known address, and could be found if and when needed.

Back at the office Wolfe was yawning at a book. The yawn was an act. He wanted to make it clear to me that losing a fee of five grand was nothing to get riled about. I had a choice: either proceed to rile him or go up to bed. They were equally attractive, and I flipped a quarter and caught it. He didn't ask me what I was deciding because he thought I wanted him to. It was heads, and I told him my session at Homicide wasn't worth reporting, said good night, and mounted the two flights to my room.

In the morning, at breakfast in the kitchen, with Fritz supplying me with hot griddle cakes and the paper propped in front of me, I saw that I had given Lon not one inch but two. He had stretched it because it was exclusive. Aside from that, there was a pile of miscellaneous information, such as that Karnow had an Aunt Margaret named Mrs. Raymond Savage, and she had a son Richard, and a daughter Ann, now married to one Norman Horne. There was a picture of Ann, and also one of Caroline, not very good.

I seldom see Wolfe in the morning until eleven, when he comes down from the plant rooms, and that morning I didn't see him at all. A little after ten a call came from Sergeant Stebbins to invite me to drop in at the District Attorney's office at my earliest inconvenience. I don't apologize for taking only four minutes to put weights on papers on my desk, phone up to Wolfe, and get my hat and go, because there was a chance of running into our former clients, and they might possibly be coming to the conclusion that they hadn't had enough of Wolfe after all.

I needn't have been in such a hurry. In a large anteroom on an upper floor at 155 Leonard Street I sat for nearly half an hour on a hard wooden chair, waiting. I was about ready to go over to the window and tell the veteran female that another three minutes was all I could spare when another female appeared, coming from a corridor that led within. That one was not veteran at all, and I postponed my ultimatum. The way she moved was worthy of study, her face invited a full analysis, her clothes deserved a complete inventory, and either her name was Ann Savage Horne or the *Gazette* had run the wrong picture.

She saw me taking her in, and reciprocated frankly, her head tilted a little to one side, came and sat on a chair near mine, and gave me the kind of straight look that you expect only from a queen or a trollop.

I spoke. "What's that stole?" I asked her. "Rabbit?"

She smiled to dazzle me and darned near made it. "Where did you get the idea," she asked back, "that vulgarity is the best policy?"

"It's not policy; I was born vulgar. When I saw your picture in the paper I wondered what your voice was like, and I wanted to hear it. Talk some more."

"Oh. You're one up on me."

"I don't mind squaring it. I am called Goodwin, Archie Goodwin."

"Goodwin?" She frowned a little. She brightened. "Of course! You're in the paper too—if you're that one. You work for Nero Wolfe?"

"I practically *am* Nero Wolfe, when it comes to work. Where were you yesterday afternoon from eleven minutes past two until eighteen minutes to six?"

"Let's see. I was walking in the park with my pet flamingo. If you think that's no alibi, you're wrong. My flamingo can talk. Ask me some more."

"Can your flamingo tell time?"

"Certainly. It wears a wristwatch on its neck."

"How can it see it?"

She nodded. "I knew you'd ask that. It has been trained to tie its neck in a knot, just a plain single knot, and when it does that the watch is on a bend so that—well, Mother?" She was suddenly out of her chair and moving. "What, no handcuffs on anybody?"

Mother, Sidney Karnow's Aunt Margaret, leading a procession emerging from the corridor, would have made two of her daughter Ann and more than half of Nero Wolfe. She was large not only in bulk but also in facial detail, each and all of her features being so big that space above her chin was at a premium. Beside her was a thin young man, runty by comparison, wearing black-rimmed glasses, and behind them were two other males, one, obviously, from his resemblance to Mother, Ann's brother Richard, and the other a tall loose-jointed specimen who would have been called distinguished-looking by any woman between sixteen and sixty.

As I made my swift survey the flamingo trainer was going on. "Mother, this is Mr. Goodwin—the Archie Goodwin who was at the Churchill yesterday with Caroline and Paul. He's grilling me. Mr. Goodwin, my mother, my brother Dick, my husband, Norman Horne —no, not the one with the cheaters, that's Jim Beebe, the lawyer to end all laws. *This* is my husband." The distinguished-looking one had pushed by and was beside her. She was flowing on. "You know how disappointed I was at the District Attorney being so god-awful polite to us, but Mr. Goodwin is different. He's going to give me the third degree—physically, I mean; he's built for it, and I expect I'll go to pieces and confess—"

Her husband's palm pressed over her mouth, firm but not rough, stopped her. "You talk too much, darling," he said tolerantly.

"It's her sense of humor," Aunt Margaret explained. "All the same, Ann dear, it *is* out of place, with poor Sidney just cruelly murdered. *Cruelly.*"

"Nuts," Dick Savage snapped.

"It *was* cruel," his mother insisted. "Murder *is* cruel."

"Sure it was," he agreed, "but for us Sid has been dead more than two years, and he's been alive again only two weeks, and we never even saw him, so what do you expect?"

"I suggest," Beebe the lawyer put in, in a high thin voice that fitted his stature perfectly, "that this is rather a public spot for a private discussion. Shall we go?"

"I can't," Ann declared. "Mr. Goodwin is going to wear me down and finally break me. Look at his hard gray eyes. Look at his jaw."

"Now, darling," Norman Horne said affectionately, and took her elbow and started her toward the door. The others filed after them, with Beebe in the rear. Not one mentioned the pleasure it had given them to meet me, though the lawyer did let me have a nod of farewell as he went by.

As I stood and watched the door closing behind them the veteran female's voice came. "Mr. Mandelbaum will see you, Mr. Goodwin."

Only two assistant district attorneys rate corner rooms, and Mandelbaum wasn't one of them. Halfway down the corridor, his door was standing open, and, entering, I had a surprise. Mandelbaum was at his desk, and across from him, on one of the two spare chairs that the little room sported, was a big husky guy with graying hair, a broad red face, and gray eyes that had been found hard to meet by tougher babies than Mrs. Norman Horne. If she called mine hard she should have seen those of Inspector Cramer of Homicide.

"I'm honored," I said appreciatively and accepted Mandelbaum's invitation to use the third chair.

"Look at me," Cramer commanded.

I did so with my brows up, which always annoys him.

"I'm late for an appointment," he said, "so I'll cut it short. I've just been up to see Wolfe. Of course he corroborates you, and he says he has no client. I've read your statement. I tell you frankly that we have no proof that you entered that hotel room."

"Now I can breathe again," I said with feeling.

"Yeah. The day you stop I'll eat as usual. I admit we have no proof, as yet, that you went in that room, but I know damn well you did. Information that the body was there came to us over the phone in a voice that was obviously disguised. You won't deny that I know pretty well by now how you react to situations."

"Sure. Boldly, bravely, and brilliantly."

"I only say I know. Leaving Aubry and Mrs. Karnow down in the bar, you go up and knock on the door of Karnow's room, and get no answer. In that situation there's not one chance in a thousand that you would leave without trying the knob."

"Then I must have."

"So you did?"

I stayed patient and reasonable. "Either I didn't try the knob—"

"Can it. Of course you did, and you found the door wasn't locked. So you opened it and called Karnow's name and got no answer, and you went in and saw the body. That I know, because I know you, and also because of what followed. You went back down to the bar and sat with them a while, and then took them back to Wolfe. Why? Because you knew Karnow had been murdered. If you had merely gone away when your knock wasn't answered, you would have stuck there until Karnow showed, if it took all night. And that's not half of it. When

Stebbins went to Wolfe's place after them, with no warrant and no charge entered, Wolfe meekly handed them over! He says they were no longer his clients, since Stebbins had brought the news that Karnow was dead, but why weren't they? Because he won't take a murderer for a client knowingly, and he thought Aubry had killed Karnow. That's why."

I shook my head. "Gee, if you already know everything, I don't see why you bother with me."

"I want to know exactly what you did in that room, and whether you changed anything or took anything." Cramer leaned to me. "Look, Goodwin, I advise you to unload. The way it's going, I fully expect Aubry to break before the day's out, and when he does we'll have it all, including what you told them you had seen in Karnow's room when you rejoined them in the bar, and why the three of you went back to Wolfe's place. If you let me have it now I won't hold it against you that— What are you grinning for?"

"I'm thinking of Mr. Wolfe's face when I tell him this. When Stebbins came with the news that Karnow was dead, and therefore the job was up the flue, Mr. Wolfe hinted as far as his dignity would let him that he would consider another job if they had one, but they sidestepped it. So this will upset him. He keeps telling me we mustn't get discouraged, that some day you will be right about something, but this will be a blow—"

Cramer got up and tramped from the room.

I let Mandelbaum have the tail end of the grin. "Is he getting more sensitive?"

"Someday," the Assistant DA declared, "certain people are going to decide that Wolfe and you are doing more harm than good, and you won't have so much fun without a license. I'm too busy to play games. Please beat it."

When I got back to Thirty-fifth Street, a little after noon, Wolfe was at his desk, fiddling with stacks of cards from the files, plant germination records. I asked if he wanted a report of my visit with Mandelbaum and Cramer, and he said none was needed because he had talked with Cramer and knew the nature of his current befuddlement. I said I had met Karnow's relatives and also his lawyer, and would he care for my impressions, and got no reply but a rude grunt, so I passed it and went to my desk to finish some chores that had been interrupted by Stebbins' phone call. I had just started in when the doorbell rang, and I went to the hall to answer it.

Caroline Karnow was there on the stoop. I went and opened the door, and she stepped in.

"I want to see Mr. Wolfe," she blurted, and proved it by going right on, to the office door and in. I am supposed to block visitors until I learn if Wolfe will see them, but it would have taken a flying tackle, and I let her go and merely followed. By the time I got there she was in the red leather chair as if she owned it.

Wolfe, a germination card in each hand, was scowling at her.

"They've arrested him," she said. "For murder."

"Naturally," Wolfe growled.

"But he didn't do it!"

"Also naturally. I mean naturally you would say that."

"But it's true! I want you to prove it."

Wolfe shook his head. "Not required. They must prove he did. You're all tight, madam. Too tight. Have you eaten today?"

"Good Lord," she said, "all you two think about is eating. Last night him, and now—" She started to laugh, at first a sort of gurgle, and then really out with it. I got up and went to her, took her head between my hands to turn her face up, and kissed her on the lips unmistakably. With some customers that is more satisfactory than a slap, and just as effective. I paid no attention to her first convulsive jerks, and released her head only when she quit shaking and got hold of my hair. I pulled loose and backed up a step.

"What on earth—" She gasped.

I decided she had snapped out of it, went to the kitchen and asked Fritz to bring crackers and milk and hot coffee, and returned. As I sat at my desk she demanded, "Did you have to do that?"

"Look," I said, "evidently you came to get Mr. Wolfe to help you. He can't stand hysterical women, and in another four seconds he would have been out of the room and would have refused to see you again. That's one angle of it. I am going on talking to give both you and Mr. Wolfe a chance to calm down. Another angle is that if you think it's undesirable to be kissed by me I am willing to submit it to a vote by people who ought to know."

She was passing her hands over her hair. "I suppose I should thank you?"

"You're welcome."

"Are you recovered," Wolfe rasped, "or not?"

"I'm all right." She swallowed. "I haven't slept, and it's quite true I haven't eaten anything, but I'm all right. They've arrested Paul for murder. He wants me to get a lawyer, and of course I have to, but I don't know who. The one he uses in business is no good for this, and certainly Jim Beebe won't do, and two other lawyers I know—I don't think they're much good. I told Paul I was coming to you, and he said all right."

"You want me to recommend a lawyer?"

"Yes, but we want you too. We want you to do—well, whatever you do." Suddenly she was flushing, and the color was good for her face. "Paul says you charge very high, but I suppose I have lots of money again, now that Sidney is dead." The flush deepened. "I've got to tell you something. Last night when you told us about it, that Sidney had been murdered, for just one second I thought Paul had done it—one awful second."

"I know you did. Only I would say ten seconds. Then you went to him."

"Yes. I went and touched him and let him touch me, and then it was over, but it was horrible. And that's partly why I must ask you, do you believe Paul killed him?"

"No," Wolfe said flatly.

"You're not just saying that?"

"I never just say anything." Wolfe suddenly realized that he had swiveled his chair away from her when she started to erupt, and now swung it back. "Mr. Cramer, a policeman, came this morning and twitted me for having let a murderer hoodwink me. When he had gone I considered the matter. It would have to be that Mr. Aubry, having killed Mr. Karnow, and having discussed it with you, decided to come and engage me to deal with Karnow in order to establish the fact that he didn't know Karnow was dead. That is Mr. Cramer's position, and I reject it. I sat here for an hour yesterday, listening to Mr. Aubry and looking at him, and if he had just come from killing the man he was asking me to deal with, I am a dolt. Since I am not a dolt, Mr. Aubry is not a murderer. Therefore— Yes, Fritz. Here's something for you, madam."

I would like to think it was my kiss that gave her an appetite, but I suppose it was the assurance from Wolfe that he didn't think her Paul was guilty of murder. She disposed not only of the crackers and milk but also of a healthy portion of toast spread with Fritz's liver pâté and chives, while Wolfe busied himself with the cards and I found something to do on my desk.

"I do thank you," she said. "This is wonderful coffee. I feel better."

It is so agreeable to Wolfe to have someone enjoy food that he had almost forgiven her for losing control. He nearly smiled at her.

"You must understand," he said gruffly, "that if you hire me to investigate there are no reservations. I think Mr. Aubry is innocent, but if I find he isn't I am committed to no evasion or concealment. You understand that?"

"Yes. I don't— All right."

"For counsel I suggest Nathaniel Parker. Inquire about him if you wish; if you settle on him we'll arrange an appointment. Now, if Mr. Aubry didn't kill Karnow, who did?"

No reply.

"Well?" Wolfe demanded.

She put the coffee cup down. "Are you asking me?"

"Yes."

"I don't know."

"Then we'll return to that. You said Mr. Aubry has been arrested for murder. Has that charge been entered, or is he being held as a material witness?"

"No, murder. They said I couldn't get bail for him."

"Then they must have cogent evidence, surely something other than the manifest motive. He has talked, of course?"

"He certainly has."

"He has told of his going to the door of Karnow's room yesterday afternoon?"

"Yes."

"Do you know what time that was?"

"Half past three. Very close to that."

"Then opportunity is established, and motive. As for the weapon, the published account says it was Karnow's. Has that been challenged?"

"Not that I know of."

"Then the formula is complete; but a man cannot be convicted by a formula and should not be charged by one. Have they got evidence? Do you know?"

"I know one thing." She was frowning at him, concentrated, intent. "They told Paul that one of his business cards was found in Sidney's pocket—the agency name and address, with his name in the corner— and asked him to account for it. He said he and his salesmen hand out dozens of cards every day, and Sidney could have got one many different places. Then they told him this card had his fingerprints on it— clear, fresh ones—and asked him to account for that."

"Could he?"

"He didn't to them, but he did to me later, when they let me see him."

"How did he account for it?"

She hesitated. "I don't like to, but I have to. He had remembered that last Friday afternoon, when he went to a conference at Jim Beebe's office, he had left one of his cards there on Jim's desk."

"Who was at the conference?"

"Besides Paul—and Jim, of course—there were Sidney's Aunt Margaret—Mrs. Savage—and Dick Savage, and Ann and her husband, Norman Horne."

"Were you there?"

"No. I—I didn't want to go. I had had enough of all the talk."

"You say he left one of his cards on Mr. Beebe's desk. Do you mean he remembers that the card was on the desk when he left the conference?"

"Yes, he's pretty sure it was, but anyway, he left first. All the others were still there."

"Has Mr. Aubry now told the police of this?"

"I don't think so. He thought he wouldn't, because he thought it would look as if he were trying to accuse one of Sidney's relatives, and that would hurt more than it would help. That was why I didn't like to tell you about it, but I knew I had to."

Wolfe grunted. "You did indeed, madam. You are in no position to afford the niceties of decent reticence. Since your husband was almost certainly killed by someone who was mortally inconvenienced by his resurrection, and we are excluding you and Mr. Aubry, his other heirs invite scrutiny and will get it. According to what Mr. Aubry told me yesterday, there are three of them: Mrs. Savage, her son, and her daughter. Where is Mr. Savage?"

"He died years ago. Mrs. Savage is Sidney's mother's sister."

"She got, as did her son and her daughter, nearly a third of a million. What did that sum mean to her? What were her circumstances?"

"I guess it meant a great deal. She wasn't well off."

"What was she living on?"

"Well—Sidney had been helping her."

Wolfe tightened his lips and turned a palm up. "My dear madam. Be as delicate as you please about judgments, but I merely want facts. Must I drag them out of you? A plain question: was Mrs. Savage living on Mr. Karnow's bounty?"

She swallowed. "Yes."

"What has she done with her legacy? Has she conserved it? The fact as you know it."

"No, she hasn't." Caroline's chin lifted a little. "You're quite right, I'm being silly—and anyway, lots of people know all about it. Mrs. Savage bought a house in New York, and last winter she bought a villa in southern France, and she wears expensive clothes and gives big parties. I don't know how much she has left. Dick had a job with a downtown broker, but he quit when he got the inheritance from Sidney, and he is still looking for something to do. He is—well, he likes to be with women. It's hard to be fair to Ann because she has wasted herself.

She is beautiful and clever, and she's only twenty-six, but there she is, married to Norman Horne, just throwing herself away."

"What does Mr. Horne do?"

"He tells people about the time twelve years ago when he scored four touchdowns for Yale against Princeton."

"Is that lucrative?"

"No. He says he isn't fitted for a commercial society. I can't stand him, and I don't understand how Ann can. They live in an apartment on Park Avenue, and she pays the rent, and as far as I know she pays everything. She must."

"Well." Wolfe sighed. "So that's the job. While Mr. Aubry's motive was admittedly more powerful than theirs, since he stood to lose not only his fortune but also his wife, they were by no means immune to temptation. How much have you been associating with them the past two years?"

"Not much. With Aunt Margaret and Dick almost not at all. I used to see Ann fairly often, but very little since she married Norman Horne."

"When was that marriage?"

"Two years ago. Soon after the estate was distributed." She stopped, and then decided to go on. "That was one of Ann's unpredictable somersaults. She was engaged to Jim Beebe—announced publicly, and the date set—and then, without even bothering to break it off, she married Norman Horne."

"Was Mr. Horne a friend of your husband's?"

"No, they never met. Ann found Norman—I don't know where. They wouldn't have been friends even if they had met, because Sidney wouldn't have liked him. There weren't many people Sidney did like."

"Did he like his relatives?"

"No—if you want facts. He didn't. He saw very little of them."

"I see." Wolfe leaned back and closed his eyes, and his lips began to work, pushing out and then pulling in, out and in, out and in. He only does that when he has something substantial to churn around in his skull. But that time I thought he was being a little premature, since he hadn't even seen them yet, not one. Caroline started to say something, but I shook my head at her, and she subsided.

Finally Wolfe opened his eyes and spoke. "You understand, madam, that the circumstances—particularly the finding of Mr. Aubry's card, bearing his fingerprints, on the body—warrant an explicit assumption: that your husband was killed by one of the six persons present at the conference in Mr. Beebe's office Friday afternoon; and, eliminating Mr. Aubry, five are left. You know them all, if not intimately at least familiarly, and I ask you: is one of them more likely than another? For any reason at all?"

She shook her head. "I don't know. Do we have to—is this the only way?"

"It is. That's our assumption until it's discredited. I want your best answer."

"I don't know," she insisted.

I decided to contribute. "I doubt," I put in, "if this would be a good buy at a nickel, but this morning at the DA's office I met the whole bunch. I had a little chat with Mrs. Horne, who seems to like gags, and when the others appeared she introduced me to them. She told them I was going to give her the third degree, and she added, I quote, 'I expect I'll go to pieces and confess—' Unquote. At that point Horne put his hand on her mouth and told her she talked too much. Mrs. Savage said it was her sense of humor."

"That's like Ann," Caroline said. "Exactly like her, at her worst."

Wolfe grunted. "Mr. Goodwin has a knack for putting women at their worst. He's no help, and neither are you. You seem not to realize that unless I can expose one of those five as the murderer of your husband, Mr. Aubry is almost certainly doomed."

"I do realize it. It's awful, but I do." Her lips tightened. In a moment she spoke. "And I want to help! All night I was trying to think, and one thing I thought of—what Sidney said in his letter about something that would shock me. You said yesterday it's not simple to disinherit a wife, but couldn't he have done it some other way? Couldn't he have signed something that would give someone a claim on the estate, perhaps the whole thing? Isn't there some way he could have arranged for the—shock?"

"Conceivably," Wolfe admitted. "But there would have had to be an authentic transfer of ownership and possession, and there wasn't. Or if he established a trust it would have had to be legally recorded, and the estate would never have been distributed. You'll have to do better than that." He cleared his throat explosively and straightened up. "Very well. I must tackle them. Will you please have them here at six o'clock, madam? All of them?"

Her eyes widened at him. "Me? Bring them here?"

"Certainly."

"But I can't! How? What could I say? I can't tell them that you think one of them killed Sidney, and you want— No! I can't!" She came forward in the chair. "Don't you see it's just impossible? Anyhow, they wouldn't come!"

Wolfe turned. "Archie. You'll have to get them. I prefer six o'clock, but if that isn't feasible after dinner will do." He glanced up at the wall clock. "Phone Mr. Parker and make an appointment for Mrs. Karnow. Phone Saul and tell him I want him here as soon as possible. Then lunch. After lunch, proceed." He turned to the client. "Will you join us, madam? Fritz's rice-and-mushroom fritters are, if I may say so, palatable."

IV

SINCE this is a democracy, thank God, please prepare to vote. All those in favor of my describing in full detail my efforts to the utmost, lasting a good five hours, to fill Wolfe's order for three males and two females, say aye. I hear none. Since my eardrums are sensitive I won't ask for the noes.

Then I'll sketch it. James M. Beebe, I found, was not one of the machines in one of the huge legal factories that occupy so many floors in so many of New York's skyscrapers. He was soloing it in a modest space on the tenth floor of a midtown building. The woman in the little anteroom, the only visible or audible employee, with a typewriter on her left and a telephone on her right, said Mr. Beebe would be back soon, and, if you call thirty-five minutes soon, he was.

The inner room he led me to must have been a little cramped with a conference of six people. Its furniture was adequate but by no means ornate. Beebe, who had looked runty alongside Mrs. Savage, could not be called impressive seated at his desk, with a large percentage of the area of his thin face taken up by the black-rimmed glasses. When I showed him my credentials, a note signed by Caroline Karnow saying that Nero Wolfe was acting for her, and told him that Wolfe would like to discuss the situation with those chiefly concerned at his office that afternoon or evening, he said that he understood that the police investigation was making progress, and that he questioned the wisdom of an investigation of a murder by a private detective.

Wise or not, I said, Mrs. Karnow surely had the right to hire Wolfe if she wanted to. He conceded that. Also surely the widow of his former friend and client might reasonably expect him to cooperate in her effort to discover the truth. Wasn't that so?

He looked uncomfortable. He saw that a pencil on his desk was not in its proper place, and moved it, and studied it a while to decide if that was the best spot after all. At length he came back to me.

"It's like this, Mr. Goodwin," he piped. "I sympathize deeply with Mrs. Karnow, of course. But any obligation I am under is not to her, but to my late friend and client, Sidney Karnow. I certainly will do anything I can to help discover the truth, but it is justifiable to suppose that in employing Nero Wolfe Mrs. Karnow's primary purpose, if not her sole purpose, is to save Paul Aubry. As an officer of the law I cannot conscientiously participate in that. I am not Aubry's attorney. I beg you to understand."

I kept after him. He stood pat. Finally, following instructions from Wolfe, I put a question to him.

"I suppose," I said, "you won't mind helping to clear up a detail. At a conference in this room last Friday afternoon Aubry left one of his business cards on your desk. It was there when he left. What happened to it?"

He cocked his head and frowned. "Here on my desk?"

"Right."

The frown deepened. "I'm trying to remember—yes, I do remember. He suggested I might phone him later, and he put it there."

"What happened to it?"

"I don't know."

"Did you phone him?"

"No. As it turned out, there was no occasion to."

"Would you mind seeing if the card is around? It's fairly important."

"Why is it important?"

"That's a long story. But I would like very much to see that card. Will you take a look?"

He wasn't enthusiastic about it, but he obliged. He looked among and under things on top of his desk, including the blotter, in the desk drawers, and around the room some—as, for instance, on top of a filing cabinet. I got down on my knees to see under the desk. No card.

I scrambled to my feet. "May I ask your secretary?"

"What's this all about?" he demanded.

"Nothing you would care to participate in. But the easiest way to get rid of me is to humor me on this one little detail."

He lifted the phone and spoke to it, and in a moment the door opened and the employee entered. He told her I wanted to ask her something, and I did so. She said she knew nothing about any card of Paul Aubry's. She had never seen one, on Beebe's desk or anywhere else, last Friday or any other day. That settled, she backed out, pulling the door with her.

"It's a little discouraging," I told Beebe. "I was counting on collecting that card. Are you sure you don't remember seeing one of the others pick it up?"

"I've told you all I remember—that Aubry put a card on my desk."

"Was there an opportunity for one of them to pick it up without your noticing?"

"There might have been. I don't know what you're trying to establish, Mr. Goodwin, but I will not be led by you to a commitment, even here privately. Probably during the meeting here on Friday I had occasion to leave this chair to get something from my files. I won't say that gave someone an opportunity to remove something from my desk, but I can't prohibit you from saying so." He got to his feet. "I'm sorry I can't be more helpful."

"So am I," I said emphatically.

I arose and turned to go, but halfway to the door his voice came. "Mr. Goodwin."

I turned. He had left his chair and was standing at the end of the desk, stiff and straight. "I'm a lawyer," he said in a different tone, "but I am also a man. Speaking as a man, I ask you to consider my position. My friend and client has been murdered, and the police are apparently convinced that they have the murderer in custody. Nero Wolfe, acting for Mrs. Karnow, wants to prove them wrong. His only hope of success is to fasten the guilt elsewhere. Isn't that the situation?"

"Roughly, yes."

"And you ask me to cooperate. You mentioned a conference in this office last Friday. Besides myself, there were five people here—you know who they were. None of them was, or is, my client. They were all dismayed by the return of Sidney Karnow alive. They were all in dread of personal financial calamity. They all asked me, one way or another, to intercede for them. I have of course given this information to the police, and I see no impropriety in my giving it also to Nero Wolfe. Beyond that I have absolutely no information or evidence that could possibly help him. I tell you frankly, if Paul Aubry is guilty I hope he is convicted and punished; but if one of the others is guilty I hope he—or she —is punished, and if I knew anything operant to that end I certainly would not withhold it."

He lifted a hand and dropped it. "All I'm trying to say—as a lawyer I'm not supposed to be vindictive, but as a man perhaps I am a little. Whoever killed Sidney Karnow should be punished." He turned and went back to his chair.

"A damn fine sentiment," I agreed, and left him.

On the way to the next customer I found a booth and phoned Wolfe a report. All I got in return was a series of grunts.

The house Mrs. Savage had bought was in the Sixties, over east of Lexington Avenue. I am not an expert on Manhattan real estate, but after a look at the narrow gray brick three-layer item my guess was that it had set her back not more than a tenth of her three hundred thousand, not counting the mortgage. When there was no answer to my rings I felt cheated. I hadn't expected anything as lavish as a dolled-up butler, but not even a maid to receive detectives?

It was only a ten-minute walk to the Park Avenue address of Mr. and Mrs. Norman Horne. My luck stayed stubborn. The hallman said they were both out, phoned up at my request, and got no answer.

I like to walk around Manhattan, catching glimpses of its wild life, the pigeons and cats and girls, but that day I overdid it, back and forth between my two objectives. Finally, from an ambush in a hamburger hell on Sixty-eighth Street, where I was sipping a glass of milk, I saw Aunt Margaret navigate the sidewalk across the street and enter the gray brick. I finished the milk, crossed over, and pushed the button.

She opened the door a few inches, thought she saw a journalist, said, "I have nothing to say," and would have closed the door if it hadn't been for my foot.

"Wait a minute," I objected. "We've been introduced—by your daughter, this morning. The name is Archie Goodwin."

She let the door come another inch for a better view of me, and the pressure of my foot kept it going. I crossed the threshold.

"Of course," she said. "We were rude to you, weren't we? The reason I said I have nothing to say, they tell me that's what I must say to everybody, but it's quite true that my daughter introduced you, and we *were* rude. What do you want?"

She sounded to me like a godsend. If I could kidnap her and get her down to the office, and phone the rest of them that we had her and she was being very helpful, it was a good bet that they would all come on the run to yank her out of our clutches.

I gave her a friendly eye and a warm smile. "I'll tell you, Mrs. Savage. As your daughter told you, I work for Nero Wolfe. He thinks there are some aspects of this situation that haven't been sufficiently considered. To mention only one, there's the legal principle that a criminal may not profit by his crime. If it should be proved that Aubry killed your nephew, and that Mrs. Karnow was an accessory, what happens to her half of the estate? Does it go to you and your son and daughter, or what? That's the sort of thing Mr. Wolfe wants to discuss with you. If you'll come on down to his office with me, he's waiting there for you. He wants to know how you feel about it, and he wants your advice. It will only take us—"

A roar came from above. "What's going on, Mumsy?"

Heavy feet were descending stairs behind Mrs. Savage, in a hurry. She turned. "Oh, Dickie? I supposed you were asleep."

He was in a silk dressing gown that must have accounted for at least two Cs of Cousin Sidney's dough. I could have choked him. He had been there all the time. After ignoring all my bell-ringing for the past two hours, here he was horning in just when I was getting a good start on a snatch.

"You remember Mr. Goodwin," his mother was telling him. "Down at that place this morning? He wants to take me to see Nero Wolfe. Mr. Wolfe wants to ask my advice about a very interesting point. I think I should go, I really do."

"I don't," Dick said bluntly.

"But Dickie," she appealed, "I'm sure you agree that we should do all we can to get this awful business over and done with!"

"Sure I do," he conceded. "God knows I do. But how it could help for you to go and discuss it with a private detective— No, I don't see it."

They looked at each other. The mutual resemblance was so remarkable that you might say they had the same face, allowing for the difference in age; and also they were built alike. Her bulk was more bone and meat than fat, and so was his.

When she spoke I got a suspicion that I had misjudged her. Her tone was new, dry and cool and meaningful. "I think I ought to go," she said.

He appealed now. "Please, Mumsy. At least we can talk it over. You can go later, after dinner." He turned to me. "Could she see Wolfe this evening?"

"She could," I admitted. "Now would be better."

"I really am tired," she told me. Her tone was back to what might have been normal. "All this awful business. After dinner would be better. What is the address?"

I got my wallet, took out a card, and handed it to her. "By the way," I observed, "that reminds me. At that meeting last Friday at Mr. Beebe's office, Aubry put one of his cards on Beebe's desk and left it there. Do you happen to remember what became of it?"

Mrs. Savage said promptly, "I remember he took out a card, but I don't—"

"Hold it," Dick barked at her, gripping her arm so hard that she winced. "Go upstairs."

She tried to twist loose, found it wouldn't work, and leveled her eyes at him to stare him off. That didn't work either. His eyes were as level as hers, and harder and meaner. Four seconds of it was enough for her. When he turned her around she didn't resist, and without a word she walked to the stairs and started up. He faced me and demanded, "What's this about a card?"

"What I said. Aubry put one on Beebe's desk—"

"Who says he did?"

"Aubry."

"Yeah? A guy in for murder? Come again."

"Glad to. Beebe says so too."

Dick snorted. "That little louse? That punk?" He lifted a hand to tap my chest with a finger, but a short backward step took me out of range. "Listen, brother. If you and your boss think you can frame an out for Aubry don't let me stop you, but don't come trying to work my mother in, or me either. Is that plain?"

"I merely want to know—"

"The way out," he said rudely, and strode to the door and opened it. Since I stay where I'm not wanted only when there is a chance of gaining something, I took advantage of his courtesy and passed on through to the sidewalk.

I was getting low on prospects. Back at the Park Avenue address, where the hallman and I were by now on intimate terms, he informed me that Mrs. Horne had come in, and he had told her that Mr. Goodwin had called several times and would return, and she had said to send me up.

At Apartment D on the twelfth floor I was admitted by a maid, properly outfitted, who showed me to a living room where a slice of Karnow's money had been used with no great taste but a keen eye to comfort. I sat down, and almost at once got up again when Ann Horne entered. She met me and let me have a hand.

"We'll have to hurry," she said. "My husband may be home any minute. What do you do first, rubber hose?"

She was wearing a nice simple blue dress that either was silk or wanted to be, and had renovated her make-up since coming in from the street.

"Not here," I told her. "Get the stole. I'm taking you to a dungeon."

She flowed onto a couch. "Sit down and describe it to me. Rats, I hope?"

"No, we can't get rats to stay. Bad air." I sat. "As a matter of fact, I've decided the physical approach wouldn't work with you, and we're going after you mentally. That's Mr. Wolfe's department, and he never leaves the house, so I've come to take you down there. You can leave word for your husband, and he can join us."

"That doesn't appeal to me at all. Mentally I'm a wreck already. What's the matter, are you afraid I can't take it?"

"On the contrary, I'm afraid I can't give it. Nature went to a lot of trouble with you, and I'd hate to spoil it. You'd enjoy a session with Nero Wolfe. He's afraid of women anyhow, and you'd scare him stiff."

She pulled a routine that I approved of. Knowing that if she took a cigarette I'd have to get up to light it, she first picked up a lighter and flicked it on, and then reached to a box for the cigarette. A darned good idea.

"What's the score?" she asked, after inhaling and letting it out.

I told her. "Paul Aubry is charged with murder. Mr. Wolfe can earn a big fee only by clearing him. Mr. Wolfe has never let a big fee get away. So Aubry will be cleared. We'll be glad to let you share the glory, though not the fee. Get the stole, and let's go."

"You're irresistible," she said admiringly. "It's too bad about Paul."

"Not at all. When he gets out he can marry his wife."

"*If* he gets out. Do you remember nursery rhymes?"

"I wrote them."

"Then of course you remember this one:

"Needles and pins,
Needles and pins,
When a man murders
His trouble begins."

"Sure, that's one of my favorites. Only Aubry didn't murder."

She nodded. "That's your line, of course, and you're stuck with it." She reached to crush her cigarette in a tray, then suddenly turned to me with her eyes flashing. "All this poppycock! All this twaddle about life being sacred! For everybody there's just one life that's sacred, and everybody knows it! Mine!" She spread her hand on her breast. "Mine! And Sidney's was sacred to him, but he's dead. So it's too bad about Paul."

"If you feel that way about it you ought to be ready to give him a lift."

"I might be if I had anything to lift with."

"Maybe I can furnish something. Last Friday you were at a conference at Jim Beebe's office. Aubry put one of his business cards on Beebe's desk. Why did you pick up that card, and what did you do with it?"

She stared at me a moment. Then she shook her head. "You'll have to get out the rubber hose, or pliers to pull out my nails. Even then I may hold out."

"Didn't you pick up the card?"

"I did not."

"Then who did?"

"I have no idea—if there was a card."

"You don't remember Aubry putting it on the desk? Or seeing it there?"

"No. But this begins to sound like something. You sound as if you're really detecting. Are you?"

I nodded. "This is called the double sly squeeze. First I get you to deny you touched the card, which I have done. Then I display one of Aubry's cards in a cellophane envelope, tell you it has fingerprints on it which I suspect are yours, and dare you to let me take your prints so I can check. You're afraid to refuse—"

"Come and show me how you take my prints. I've never had it done."

I was, I admit it, curious. Was she inviting physical contact because she was like that, or was she expecting to voodoo me, or was she merely passing the time? To find out I got up and went to her, took her offered hand and got it snugly in mine, palm up, and bent over it for a close-up. The hand seemed to be telling me that it didn't mind the operation at all, and with the fingertips of my other hand I spread her fingers apart, bending lower.

Of course I was concentrated on the job. Whether the door from the outside hall to the foyer was opened so quietly that no sound came, or whether my ears caught a sound but I ignored it, what interrupted my investigation was her sudden tight grip on my hand as she straightened up and cried, "Don't! You're hurting me! Norman—thank God!"

My whirl around was checked for a second by her hold on my hand. For her size and sex she had muscle. I suppose to Norman Horne, approaching from behind me, it could have looked as if I were holding her, instead of her me, but even so it must have been obvious that I was turning, and he might have held his fire until I could at least see it coming. As it was, I was off balance when he plugged me on the side of the jaw, and I went clear down, sprawling. Added to the four touchdowns he had scored for Yale against Princeton, that made five.

"He was trying to force me—" Ann was saying with her sense of humor.

Probably I would have scrambled to my feet and departed, since Wolfe wouldn't have appreciated my letting my personal feelings take charge when I was on a job, if it hadn't been for Horne's attitude. He was glaring down at me, with his fists ready, and it was doubtful if he would wait till I got farther up than on my knees. So I did a quick double roll, sprang all the way up, and faced him. He came at me wide open, as if I had been a dummy, and swung. There wouldn't have been the slightest excuse for my missing the exact spot for a dead kidney punch, and I didn't. Air exploded out of him, and he crumpled, not sprawling, but in a compact heap. Then he sort of settled to get comfortable.

His attractive wife took a couple of steps toward him, stopped to look at me, and said, "I'll be damned."

"You will if they consult me," I told her emphatically, turned, went to the foyer and got my hat, and let myself out. On the way down in the elevator I felt my jaw and took a look at it in the mirror, and decided I would live.

I got home just at the dinner hour, seven-thirty, and since it takes an earthquake to postpone a meal in that house, and no mention of business is permitted at the table, my full report of the afternoon had to wait. If the main dish had been something like goulash or calves' brains probably nothing unusual in my technique would have been apparent, but it was squabs, which of course have to be gnawed off the bones, and while I was working on the second one Wolfe demanded, "What the deuce is the matter with you?"

"Nothing. What?"

"You're not eating, you're nibbling."

"Yeah. Broken jaw. With the compliments of Ann Horne."

He stared. "A *woman* broke your jaw?"

"Sorry, no shoptalk at meals. I'll tell you later."

I did so, in the office, after dinner, and after I had looked into a little matter I was wondering about. I had obeyed the instruction, given me before lunch, to phone Saul Panzer, and Saul had said he would be at the office at two-thirty. By that time I had left. When, on the way from the dining room to the office, I asked Wolfe if Saul had come, he replied in one word, "Yes," indicating that that was all I needed to know about it. Thinking it wouldn't hurt me any to know more, I went and opened the safe and got out the little book from the cash drawer. Sometimes, in addition to the name and date and amount, Wolfe scribbles something about the purpose, but that time he hadn't. The latest entry was merely the date and "SP $1000." All that did was make me wonder further what Saul was expected to buy that might cost as much as a grand.

As I reported on my afternoon rounds, giving all conversations verbatim, which isn't so hard when you've had plenty of practice and have learned that nothing less will be acceptable, Wolfe leaned back in his chair with his eyes closed. He was too damn placid. Ordinarily, when he sends me out for bacon and I return empty-handed, he makes some pointed cracks, no matter how hopeless he knows my errand was; but that time, not a one. That meant either that he didn't like the job and

to hell with it, or that I was just a sideshow, including my sore jaw, and
the main attraction was elsewhere. When I was through he didn't open
his eyes or ask a single question.

I groaned with pain. "Since it's obvious that I wasted five hours of
your time, and since if I stay here I may say something that will rile you,
I guess I'll go see Doc Vollmer and have him set my jaw. He'll probably
have to wire it."

"No."

"No what?"

He opened his eyes. "I'm expecting a phone call. Probably not until
tomorrow, but it could come this evening. If it does I'll need you."

"Okay, I'll be upstairs."

I mounted the two flights to my room, turned on the lights, went to
the bathroom mirror to see if there was enough swelling for a compress,
decided there wasn't, and settled myself in my easy chair with a collection of magazines.

Nearly two hours had gone by, and I was yawning, when a sound
came faintly through the open door—the sound of Wolfe's voice. I went
and lifted the phone on my bedside table and put it to my ear. It was
dead. I had neglected to plug it in when I left the office. It would have
been undignified to go to the hall, to the stair landing, and listen, so I
did; but though Wolfe's voice came up at intervals I couldn't get the
words. After enough of that I returned to the room and the easy chair,
but had barely lowered myself into it when a bellow from below came.

"Archie! *Archie!*"

I did not descend the stairs three steps at a time, but I admit I didn't
mosey. Wolfe, at his desk, spoke as I entered the office. "Get Mr.
Cramer."

Getting Inspector Cramer of Homicide, day or night, may be very
simple or it may be impossible. That time it was in between. He was at
his office on Twentieth Street, but in conference and not available, so
I had to bear down and make it plain that if he didn't speak with Nero
Wolfe immediately God only knew what tomorrow's papers would say.

In a couple of minutes his familiar growl was growling at me. "Goodwin? Is Wolfe on?"

I nodded at Wolfe, and he took up his phone. "Mr. Cramer? I don't
know if you know that I'm investigating the Karnow murder. For a
client. Mrs. Karnow engaged me at noon today."

"Go ahead and investigate. What do you want?"

"I understand that Mr. Aubry is being held on a murder charge,
without bail. That's regrettable, because he's innocent. If you are sup-

porting that charge I advise you to reconsider. On the soundness of that advice I stake my professional reputation."

I would have paid admission to see Cramer's face. He knew Wolfe would rather go without eating a whole day than be caught wrong in a flat statement like that.

"That's all I wanted, your advice." The growl was still a growl, but not the same. "Is it all right if I wait till morning to turn him loose?"

"Formalities may require it. May I ask a question? How many of the others—Mrs. Savage, her son, Mr. and Mrs. Horne, Mr. Beebe—have been eliminated by alibis?"

"Crossed off, no one. But Aubry not only has no alibi, he admits he was there."

"Yes, I know. However, it was one of the others. I must now choose between alternatives. Either I proceed independently to disclose and hand over the culprit, or I invite you to partake. Which would you prefer?"

It was nearly silence, but I thought I could hear Cramer breathe. "Are you saying you've got it?"

"I'm saying I am prepared to expose the murderer. It would be a little simpler if you can spare the time, for I must have them here at my office, and for you that will be no problem. If you care to take part could you get them here in half an hour?"

Cramer cussed. Since it's a misdemeanor to use profanity over the phone, and since I don't want to hang a misdemeanor rap on an inspector, I won't quote it. He added, "I'm coming up there. I'll be there in five minutes."

"You won't get in." Wolfe wasn't nasty, but he was firm. "If you come without those people, or without first assuring me that they will be brought, Mr. Goodwin won't even open the door to the crack the chain bolt will permit. He's in a touchy mood because a man hit him on the jaw and knocked him down. Nor am I in any humor to wrangle with you. I gave you your chance. Do you remember that when you were here this morning I told you that I had the last letter Mrs. Karnow received from her husband, and offered to show it to you?"

"Yes."

"And you said you weren't interested in a letter Karnow wrote nearly three years ago. You were wrong. I now offer again to show it to you before I send it to the District Attorney, but only on the condition as stated. Well?"

I'll say one thing for Cramer, he knew when he was out of choices, and he didn't try to prolong it. He cussed again and then got it out. "They'll be there, and so will I."

Wolfe hung up. I asked him, "What about our client? Hadn't she better be present?"

He made a face. "I suppose so. See if you can get her."

V

IT WAS half past eleven when I ushered Norman Horne and his attractive wife to the office and to the two vacant seats in the cluster of chairs that had been placed facing Wolfe's desk. At their left was Mrs. Savage; behind them were Dick Savage, James M. Beebe, and Sergeant Purley Stebbins—only not in that order, because Purley was in the middle, behind Ann Horne. There had been another chair in the cluster, for Caroline Karnow, but she had moved it away, over to the side of the room where the bookshelves were, while I was in the hall admitting Mrs. Savage and Dick. That had put her where Purley couldn't see her without turning his head a full quarter-circle, and he hadn't liked it, but I had let him know that it was none of his damn business where our client sat.

The red leather chair was for Cramer, who was in the dining room with Wolfe. After the Hornes had greeted their relatives, including Caroline, and got seated, I crossed to the dining room and told Wolfe we were ready, and he marched to the office and to his desk, and stood.

"Archie?"

"Yes, sir." I was there. "Front row, from the left, Mr. Horne, Mrs. Horne, Mrs. Savage. Rear, from the left, Mr. Savage, Mr. Stebbins you know, and Mr. Beebe."

Wolfe nodded almost perceptibly, sat, and turned his head. "Mr. Cramer?"

Cramer, standing, was surveying them. "I can't say this is unofficial," he conceded, "since I asked you to come here, and I'm here. But anything Mr. Wolfe says to you is solely on his own responsibility, and you're under no obligation to answer any questions he asks if you don't want to. I want that clearly understood."

"Even so," Beebe piped up, "isn't this rather irregular?"

"If you mean unusual, yes. If you mean improper, I don't think so. You weren't ordered to come, you were asked, and you're here. Do you want to leave?"

Apparently they didn't, at least not enough to make an issue of it. They exchanged glances, and someone muttered something. Beebe said, "We certainly reserve the right to leave."

"Nobody will stop you," Cramer assured him, and sat. He looked at Wolfe. "Go ahead."

Wolfe adjusted himself in his chair to achieve the maximum of comfort, and then moved his eyes, left and right, to take them in. He spoke. "Mr. Cramer assured you that you are not obliged to answer my questions. I can relieve your minds of that concern. I doubt if I'll have a single question to put to any of you, though of course an occasion for one may arise. I merely want to describe the situation as it now stands and invite your comment. You may have none."

He interlaced his fingers at the crest of his central bulge. "The news that Mr. Karnow had been murdered was brought here by Mr. Stebbins early last evening, but my interest in it was only casual until Mrs. Karnow came at noon today and aroused it by hiring me. Then I gave it my attention, and it seemed to me that your obvious motive for murder—Mrs. Savage and her son and daughter, and Mr. Horne as the daughter's husband—was not very compelling. From what my client told me of Mr. Karnow's character and temperament, it seemed unlikely that any of you would so fear harsh and exigent demands from him that you would be driven to the dangerous and desperate act of murder. You had received your legacies legally and properly, in good faith, and surely you would at least have first tried an appeal to his reason and his grace. So one of you must have had a stronger motive."

Wolfe cleared his throat. "That derogation of your obvious motives put me up a stump. There were two people with overpowering motives: Mr. Aubry and Mrs. Karnow. Not only did they stand to forfeit a much larger sum than any of you, but also they faced a deprivation even more intolerable. He would lose her, and she would lose him. It is not surprising that Mr. Cramer and his colleagues were dazzled by the glitter of that powerful motive. I might have been similarly bemused but for two circumstances. The first was that I had concluded that neither Mrs. Karnow nor Mr. Aubry had committed murder. If they had, they had come fresh from that ferocious deed to engage me to negotiate for them with the man one of them had just killed, for the devious purpose of raising the presumption that they didn't know he was dead, and I had sat here and conversed with them for an hour without feeling any twinge of suspicion that they were diddling me. I was compelled either to reject that notion or abandon certain pretensions that feed my ego. The choice wasn't difficult."

"Also Mrs. Karnow was your client," Cramer said pointedly.

Wolfe ignored it, which was just as well. He went on. "The second circumstance was that the possibility of another motive had been suggested to me. It was suggested in a letter which Mrs. Karnow had shown me yesterday—the last letter she had received from her husband, nearly three years ago." He opened a drawer and took out sheets of paper. "Here it is. I'll read only the pertinent excerpt:

"Speaking of death, if he should get me instead of me getting him, something I did before I left New York will give you quite a shock. I wish I could be around to see how you take it. You claim you have never worried about money, that it's not worth it. Also you've told me that I always talk sardonic but haven't got it in me to act sardonic. This will show you. I'll admit I have to die to get the last laugh, but that will be sardonic too. I wonder do I love you or hate you? They're hard to tell apart. Remember me in thy dreams."

He returned the papers to the drawer and closed it. "Mrs. Karnow had the notion that what her husband had done was to make a new will, leaving her out, but that theory was open to two objections. First, a wife cannot be so brusquely disinherited by a man of means; and second, such an act would have been merely malicious, not sardonic. But the phrase 'speaking of death' did imply some connection with his will, and raised the question, how might such a man have so remade his will as to cause such a woman to worry about money? That intention was clearly implied."

Wolfe turned a hand over. "Under the circumstances as I knew them, a plausible conjecture offered itself: that Karnow had made a new will, leaving everything to his wife. That would certainly give her an inescapable worry about money, the same worry he had had—how much should his relatives be pampered? And since it was his money and they were his relatives, for her the worry would be even more bothersome than for him. I would call that sardonic. Also he might have been moved by another consideration, a reluctance to bestow large amounts on them. I had gathered, though Mrs. Karnow didn't make it explicit, that in matters of personal finance and economy Karnow did not regard his relatives as paragons—a judgment that has been verified by their management of their bequests."

Ann Horne's head jerked around, and she told Caroline, "Thank you so much, Lina darling." Caroline made no reply. Judging from her intent face and rigid posture, if she replied to anything it would be an explosion.

"Therefore," Wolfe resumed, "it appeared that the hypothesis that Karnow had made a new will deserved a little exploration. To ask any of you about it would of course have been jackassery. It was reasonable to suppose that for such a chore he would have called upon his friend and attorney, Mr. Beebe, but it seemed impolitic to approach Mr. Beebe on the matter. I don't know whether any of you has ever heard the name Saul Panzer?"

No reply. No shake of a head. They might all have been in a trance.

"I employ Mr. Panzer," Wolfe said, "on important missions for which Mr. Goodwin cannot be spared. He has extraordinary qualities and abilities. I told him that if Mr. Beebe had drafted a new will for Mr. Karnow it had probably been typed by his secretary, and Mr. Panzer undertook to see Mr. Beebe's secretary and try to get on terms with her without arousing her suspicion. I would entrust so ticklish an errand to no other man except Mr. Goodwin. Early this afternoon he called on her in the guise of an investigator from the Federal Security Agency, wanting to clear up some confusion about her Social Security number."

"Impersonating an officer of the law," Beebe protested.

"Possibly," Wolfe conceded. "If such an investigator is an officer of the law, he is a federal officer, and Mr. Panzer can await his doom. In ten minutes he collected an arsenal of data. Mr. Beebe's secretary, whose name is Vera O'Brien, has been with him two and one-half years. Her predecessor, whose name was Helen Martin, left Mr. Beebe's employ in November nineteen-fifty-one to marry a man named Arthur Rabson, and went to live with her husband in Florence, South Carolina, where he owns a garage. So if Karnow made a new will before he left New York, and if Mr. Beebe drafted it, and if Mr. Beebe's secretary typed it, it was typed by the now Mrs. Arthur Rabson."

"Three ifs," Cramer muttered.

"Yes," Wolfe agreed, "but open for test. I was tempted to get Mrs. Rabson on the phone in South Carolina, but it was too risky, so Mr. Panzer took a plane to Columbia, and I phoned there and chartered a smaller one to take him on to Florence. An hour ago, or a little more, I got a phone call from him. He has talked with Mrs. Rabson, she has signed a statement, and she is willing to come to New York if necessary. She says that Mr. Beebe dictated to her a new will for Mr. Karnow in the fall of nineteen-fifty-one, that she typed it, and that she was one of the witnesses to Karnow's signature. The other witness was a woman named Nora Wayne, from a nearby office. She supposes that Miss Wayne did not know the contents of the will. By it Karnow left everything to his wife, and it contained a request that she use discretion in making provision for Karnow's relatives, who were named. Mrs. Rabson didn't know that—"

"Sidney wouldn't do that!" Aunt Margaret cried. "I don't believe it! Jim, are you going to just sit there and blink?"

All eyes were at Beebe except Wolfe's. His were on the move. "I should explain," he said, "that meanwhile Mr. Goodwin was making himself useful. He learned, for instance, that the only item of tangible evidence against Mr. Aubry, a card of his that was found in Mr. Karnow's pocket, had been accessible to all of you last Friday in Mr. Beebe's office."

"How's that?" Cramer demanded.

"You'll get it," Wolfe assured him, "and you'll like it." He focused on Beebe. "The occasion has arisen, I think, Mr. Beebe, for a question. As Mr. Cramer told you, you're not obliged to answer it. What happened to Mr. Karnow's last will?"

Thinking it over later, I decided that Beebe probably took his best bet. Him being a lawyer, you might suppose that he would simply have clammed up, but, knowing as he did that he was absolutely hooked on the will, he undoubtedly figured, in the short time he had for figuring, that the best way was to go ahead and take the little one so as to dodge the big one.

He addressed Cramer. "I would like to speak to you privately, Inspector—you and Mr. Wolfe, if you want him present."

Cramer glanced at Wolfe. Wolfe said, "No. You may refuse to answer, or you may answer here and now."

"Very well." Beebe straightened his shoulders and lifted his chin. At the angle I had on him I couldn't see his eyes behind the black-rimmed glasses. "This will ruin me professionally, and I bitterly regret the part I have played. It was a month or so before the notice came that Sidney had been killed in action that I told Ann about the new will he had made. That was my first mistake. I did it because I—of the way I felt about her. At that time I would have done just about anything she wanted. When word came that Sidney had been killed she came to my office and insisted on my showing her the will. I was even—"

"Watch it, Jim!" Ann, turned in her chair, called to him. "You dirty little liar! Ad libbing it, you'll get all twisted—"

"Mrs. Horne!" Wolfe said sharply. "Would you rather hear him or be taken from the room?"

She stayed turned to Beebe. "Go on, Jim, but watch it."

Beebe resumed, "I was then even more infatuated with her than before. I got the will from the safe and showed it to her, and she took it and stuffed it inside her dress. She insisted on taking it to show to her mother. It's easy to say I should have gone to any length to prevent that—it's easy now, but then I was incapable of opposing her. She took the will with her, and I never saw it again. Two weeks later our engagement was publicly announced. I presented Sidney's former will for probate, and that was completely insane, since I only had Ann's word for it that the new will had been destroyed—even though the girl who had typed the new will had got married and gone away."

Beebe lifted a hand to adjust his cheaters. "I won't say what it was that cured me of my infatuation for Ann Savage. It was—a personal thing, and it was enough to cure me good. I only wish to God it had happened sooner. Of course I couldn't stop the probate of the will without ruining myself. In May the estate was distributed, and later that month Ann married Norman Horne. That ended that business, I thought. I had had my lesson, and it had been a tough one."

He pulled his narrow shoulders back. "Then, two years later, this jolt came. Sidney was alive and would soon be in New York. You can imagine how it hit me, or maybe you can't. I finally got it in focus enough to see that I had only two choices: either fall out of my office window or tell Sidney exactly how it had happened. Meanwhile I had to go through all the motions of talking it over with them and listening to all their crazy suggestions. It wasn't until Monday, day before yesterday, that I decided, and I phoned Ann the next morning, yesterday, that I was going to see Sidney that evening and tell him the whole story. Then came the news that Sidney had been murdered. I don't know who killed him. All I know is what I'm telling you, and of course for me that's enough." He stopped for his mouth to do little spasms. He tagged it. "As a counselor-at-law, I'm through."

I was a little disappointed at Norman Horne. Surely he might have been expected to react manfully and promptly to such an indictment of his attractive wife, but he wasn't even looking at Beebe. He was looking at her, there beside him, and it was not a gaze of loyal and trusting faith. It was just as well that she didn't see it.

She didn't see it because her eyes were on Wolfe. "Is he through?" she asked.

"Apparently, madam, yes. At least for the moment. Would you like to comment?"

"I don't want to make a speech. I don't think I need to. Just that he's a liar. Just lies."

Wolfe shook his head. "I doubt if that's adequate. It wasn't all lies, you know. Mr. Karnow did make a new will; you and Mr. Beebe were engaged to marry but didn't; the estate was distributed under the terms of a previous will, with you as a legatee; and Mr. Karnow did return alive and was murdered. I strongly advise you either to keep silent, even though that would expose you to an adverse presumption, or to tell the truth without reservation. You warned Mr. Beebe of the hazard of an improvised complex lie. I urge you to heed your own warning. Now?"

She glanced aside at her husband, but he had focused on Wolfe. Her head swiveled for a glance to her left, at her mother, but that wasn't met either. She looked at Wolfe. "You're quite a performer, aren't you?"

"Yes," he said.

"I believe you already know the truth."

"If so, for you to try to withhold it would be pointless."

"Well, I'd hate to be pointless. You're right, some of what Jim said was true. He did tell me about the new will, but after the news came that Sidney had been killed in action, not before. He did take it from his safe and let me read it. It did leave everything to Caroline. He said that no one knew its contents except his former secretary, and she had got married and gone to some little town in the South, so she was out of the way. He said there was no other copy of it, and that he was sure Caroline didn't know about it because of a letter she had shown him from Sidney. He said he would destroy it, and I and my mother and brother would inherit under the previous will, if I would marry him. Do you want to know everything we said?"

"I think just the essential points."

"Then I don't need to tell how I really felt about marrying him. I didn't tell him. I agreed to it. I suppose you don't care what I thought, but Sidney was dead, and I thought it was only fair for us to get a share. So I agreed, but I never had any intention of marrying Jim Beebe. He wanted an immediate wedding, before he presented the will for probate, but I talked him out of that, and our engagement was announced. When the will had gone through and the estate had been distributed and we had our share, I married Norman Horne. I didn't know whether Jim had destroyed the new will or not, but that didn't matter because he wouldn't dare to produce it then." She fluttered a hand. "That's all."

"Not quite," Wolfe objected. "The sequel. Mr. Karnow's return."

"Oh, yes." Her tone implied that it was careless of her to overlook that little detail. "Of course Jim killed him. If you mean how I felt about Sidney's turning up alive, you may not believe it, but in a way I was glad of it, because I always liked him. I was sorry for Caroline and Paul, because I liked them too, but I knew Sidney wouldn't try to get our share back from us. There was just one person who didn't dare to face him. Of course Jim did face him when he went to his hotel room, but he wasn't facing him when he killed him—he shot him in the back of the head." She turned to Beebe. "Did you tell him about the will, Jim? I'll bet you didn't. I'll bet he never knew." She turned back to Wolfe. "Will that do for the truth?"

"It'll do for a malicious lie," Beebe squeaked.

Wolfe addressed the law. "I would prefer, Mr. Cramer, to turn the issue of veracity over to you. In my opinion, Mr. Beebe fumbled it, and Mrs. Horne didn't."

At a later date, in a courtroom, a jury concurred. Justice is a fine thing, but that night in Wolfe's office it slipped up on one detail. After Cramer and Stebbins had escorted Beebe out, and the others had gone, Caroline Karnow decided that the occasion called for her returning the kiss she had received in that room twelve hours earlier. But she went right past me, around to Wolfe behind his desk, put her arms around his neck, and gave it to him on both cheeks.

"Wrong address," I said bitterly.

DIE LIKE A DOG

I

I DO sometimes treat myself to a walk in the rain, though I prefer sunshine when there's not enough wind to give the dust a whirl. That rainy Wednesday, however, there was a special inducement: I wanted his raincoat to be good and wet when I delivered it. So with it on my back and my old brown felt on my head, I left the house and set out for Arbor Street, some two miles south in the Village.

Halfway there the rain stopped and my blood had pumped me warm, so I took the coat off, folded it wet side in, hung it on my arm, and proceeded. Arbor Street, narrow and only three blocks long, had on either side an assortment of old brick houses, mostly of four stories, which were neither spick nor span. Number 29 would be about the middle of the first block.

I reached it, but I didn't enter it. There was a party going on in the middle of the block. A police car was double-parked in front of the entrance to one of the houses, and a uniformed cop was on the sidewalk in an attitude of authority toward a small gathering of citizens confronting him. As I approached I heard him demanding, "Whose dog is this?"—referring, evidently, to an animal with a wet black coat standing behind him. I heard no one claim the dog, but I wouldn't have anyway, because my attention was diverted. Another police car rolled up and stopped behind the first one, and a man got out, pushed through the crowd to the sidewalk, nodded to the cop without halting, and went in the entrance, above which appeared the number 29.

The trouble was, I knew the man, which is an understatement. I do not begin to tremble at the sight of Sergeant Purley Stebbins of Manhattan Homicide West, which is also an understatement, but his presence and manner made it a cinch that there was a corpse in that house, and if I demanded entry on the ground that I wanted to swap raincoats with a guy who had walked off with mine, there was no question what would happen. My prompt appearance at the scene of a homicide would arouse all of Purley's worst instincts, backed up by reference to various precedents, and I might not get home in time for dinner, which was going to be featured by grilled squab with a brown sauce which Fritz calls *Vénitienne* and is one of his best.

Purley had disappeared within without spotting me. The cop was a complete stranger. As I slowed down to detour past him on the narrow sidewalk he gave me an eye and demanded, "That your dog?"

The dog was nuzzling my knee, and I stooped to give him a pat on his wet black head. Then, telling the cop he wasn't mine, I went on by. At the next corner I turned right, heading back uptown. I kept my eye peeled for a taxi the first couple of blocks, saw none, and decided to finish the walk. A wind had started in from the west, but everything was still damp from the rain.

Marching along, I was well on my way before I saw the dog. Stopping for a light on Ninth Avenue in the Twenties, I felt something at my knee, and there he was. My hand started for his head in reflex, but I pulled it back. I was in a fix. Apparently he had picked me for a pal, and if I just went on he would follow, and you can't chase a dog on Ninth Avenue by throwing rocks. I could have ditched him by taking a taxi the rest of the way, but that would have been pretty rude after the appreciation he had shown of my charm. He had a collar on with a tag, and could be identified, and the station house was only a few blocks away, so the simplest and cheapest way was to convoy him there. I moved to the curb to look for a taxi coming downtown, and as I did so a cyclone sailed around the corner and took my hat with it into the middle of the avenue.

I didn't dash out into the traffic, but you should have seen that dog. He sprang across the bow of a big truck, wiping its left front fender with his tail, braked landing to let a car by, sprang again, and was under another car—or I thought he was—and then I saw him on the opposite sidewalk. He snatched the hat from under the feet of a pedestrian, turned on a dime, and started back. This time his crossing wasn't so spectacular, but he didn't dally. He came to me and stood, lifting his head and wagging his tail. I took the hat. It had skimmed a puddle of water on its trip, but I thought he would be disappointed if I didn't put it on, so I did. Naturally that settled it. I flagged a cab, took the dog in with me, and gave the driver the address of Wolfe's house.

My idea was to take my hat hound upstairs to my room, give him some refreshment, and phone the ASPCA to send for him. But there was no sense in passing up such an opportunity for a little buzz at Wolfe, so after letting us in and leaving my hat and the raincoat on the rack in the hall, I proceeded to the door to the office and entered.

"Where the devil have you been?" Wolfe asked grumpily. "We were going over some lists at six o'clock, and it's a quarter to seven."

He was in his oversized chair behind his desk with a book, and his eyes hadn't left the page to spare me a glance. I answered him. "Taking that damn raincoat. Only I didn't deliver it, because—"

"What's that?" he snapped. He was glaring at my companion.

"A dog."

"I see it is. I'm in no temper for buffoonery. Get it out of here."

"Yes, sir, right away. I can keep him in my room most of the time, but of course he'll have to come downstairs and through the hall when I take him out. He's a hat hound. There is a sort of a problem. His name is Nero, which, as you know, means 'black,' and of course I'll have to change it. Ebony would do, or Jet, or Inky, or—"

"Bah. Flummery!"

"No, sir. I get pretty darned lonesome around here, especially during the four hours a day you're up in the plant rooms. You have your orchids, and Fritz has his turtle, and Theodore has his parakeets up in the potting room, and why shouldn't I have a dog? I admit I'll have to change his name, though he is registered as Champion Nero Charcoal of Bantyscoot. I have suggested . . ."

I went on talking only because I had to. It was a fizzle. I had expected to induce a major outburst, even possibly something as frantic as Wolfe leaving his chair to evict the beast himself, and there he was gazing at Nero with an expression I had never seen him aim at any human, including me. I went on talking, forcing it.

He broke in. "It's not a hound. It's a Labrador retriever."

That didn't faze me. I'm never surprised at a display of knowledge by a bird who reads as many books as Wolfe does. "Yes, sir," I agreed. "I only said hound because it would be natural for a private detective to have a hound."

"Labradors," he said, "have a wider skull than any other dog, for brain room. A dog I had when I was a boy, in Montenegro, a small brown mongrel, had a rather narrow skull, but I did not regard it as a defect. I do not remember that I considered that dog to have a defect. Today I suppose I would be more critical. When you smuggled that creature in here did you take into account the disruption it would cause in this household?"

It had backfired on me. I had learned something new about the big fat genius: he would enjoy having a dog around, provided he could blame it on me and so be free to beef when he felt like it. As for me, when I retire to the country I'll have a dog, and maybe two, but not in town.

I snapped into reverse. "I guess I didn't," I confessed. "I do feel the need for a personal pet, but what the hell, I can try a canary or a chameleon. Okay, I'll get rid of him. After all, it's your house."

"I do not want to feel responsible," he said stiffly, "for your privation. I would almost rather put up with its presence than with your reproaches."

"Forget it." I waved a hand. "I'll try to. I promise not to rub it in."

"Another thing," he persisted. "I refuse to interfere with any commitment you have made."

"I have made no commitment."

"Then where did you get it?"

"Well, I'll tell you."

I went and sat at my desk and did so. Nero, the four-legged one, came and lay at my feet with his nose just not touching the toe of my shoe. I reported the whole event, with as much detail as if I had been reporting a vital operation in a major case, and, when I had finished, Wolfe was of course quite aware that my presentation of Nero as a permanent addition to the staff had been a plant. Ordinarily he would have made his opinion of my performance clear, but this time he skipped it, and it was easy to see why. The idea of having a dog that he could blame on me had got in and stuck.

When I came to the end and stopped there was a moment's silence, and then he said, "Jet would be an acceptable name for that dog."

"Yeah." I swiveled and reached for the phone. "I'll call the ASPCA to come for him."

"No." He was emphatic.

"Why not?"

"Because there is a better alternative. Call someone you know in the Police Department—anyone. Give him the number on the dog's tag, and ask him to find out who the owner is. Then you can inform the owner directly."

He was playing for time. It could happen that the owner was dead or in jail or didn't want the dog back, and if so Wolfe could take the position that I had committed myself by bringing the dog home in a taxi and that it would be dishonorable to renege. However, I didn't want to argue, so I phoned a precinct sergeant who I knew was disposed to do me small favors. He took Nero's number and said it might take a while at that time of day, and he would call me back. As I hung up, Fritz entered to announce dinner.

The squabs with that sauce were absolutely edible, as they always are, but other phenomena in the next couple of hours were not so pleasing. The table talk in the dining room was mostly one-sided and mostly about dogs. Wolfe kept it on a high level—no maudlin sentiment. He maintained that the basenji was the oldest breed on earth, having originated in Central Africa around 5000 B.C., whereas there was no trace of the Afghan hound earlier than around 4000 B.C. To me all it proved was that he had read a book I hadn't noticed him with.

Nero ate in the kitchen with Fritz and made a hit. Wolfe had told Fritz to call him Jet. When Fritz brought in the salad he announced that Jet had wonderful manners and was very smart.

"Nevertheless," Wolfe asked, "wouldn't you think him an insufferable nuisance as a cohabitant?"

On the contrary, Fritz declared, he would be most welcome.

After dinner, feeling that the newly formed Canine Canonizing League needed slowing down, I first took Nero out for a brief tour and, returning, escorted him up the two flights to my room and left him there. I had to admit he was well behaved. If I had wanted to take on a dog in town it could have been him. In my room I told him to lie down, and he did, and when I went to the door to leave, his eyes, which were the color of caramel, made it plain that he would love to come along, but he didn't get up.

Down in the office Wolfe and I got at the lists. They were special offerings from orchid growers and collectors from all over the world, and it was quite a job to check the thousands of items and pick the few that Wolfe might want to give a try. I sat at his desk, across from him, with trays of cards from our files, and we were in the middle of it, around ten-thirty, when the doorbell rang. I went to the hall and flipped a light switch and saw out on the stoop, through the one-way glass panel in the door, a familiar figure—Inspector Cramer of Homicide.

I went to the door, opened it six inches, and asked politely, "Now what?"

"I want to see Wolfe."

"It's pretty late. What about?"

"About a dog."

It is understood that no visitor, and especially no officer of the law, is to be conducted to the office until Wolfe has been consulted, but this seemed to rate an exception. Wolfe had been known to refuse an audience to people who topped inspectors, and, told that Cramer had come to see him about a dog, there was no telling how he might react in the situation as it had developed.

I considered the matter for about two seconds and then swung the door open and invited cordially, "Step right in."

II

"PROPERLY speaking," Cramer declared as one who wanted above all to be perfectly fair and square, "it's Goodwin I want information from."

He was in the red leather chair at the end of Wolfe's desk, just about filling it. His big round face was no redder than usual, his gray eyes no colder, his voice no gruffer. Merely normal.

Wolfe came at me. "Then why did you bring him in here without even asking?"

Cramer interfered for me. "I asked for you. Of course you're in it. I want to know where the dog fits in. Where is it, Goodwin?"

That set the tone—again normal. He does sometimes call me Archie, after all the years, but it's exceptional. I inquired, "Dog?"

His lips tightened. "All right, I'll spell it. You phoned the precinct and gave them a tag number and wanted to know who owns the dog. When the sergeant learned that the owner was a man named Philip Kampf, who was murdered this afternoon in a house at twenty-nine Arbor Street, he notified Homicide. The officer who had been on post in front of that house had told us that the dog had gone off with a man who had said it wasn't his dog. After we learned of your inquiry about the owner, the officer was shown a picture of you and said it was you who enticed the dog. He's outside in my car. Do you want to bring him in?"

"No, thanks. I didn't entice."

"The dog followed you."

I gestured modestly. "Girls follow me, dogs follow me, sometimes even your own dicks follow me. I can't help—"

"Skip the comedy. The dog belonged to a murder victim, and you removed it from the scene of the murder. Where is it?"

Wolfe butted in. "You persist," he objected, "in imputing an action to Mr. Goodwin without warrant. He did not 'remove' the dog. I advise you to shift your ground if you expect us to listen."

His tone was firm but not hostile. I cocked an eye at him. He was probably being indulgent because he had learned that Jet's owner was dead.

"I've got another ground," Cramer asserted. "A man who lives in that house, named Richard Meegan, and who was in it at the time Kampf was murdered, has stated that he came here to see you this morning and asked you to do a job for him. He says you refused the job. That's what he says." Cramer jutted his chin. "Now. A man at the scene of a murder admits he consulted you this morning. Goodwin shows up at the scene half an hour after the murder was committed, and he entices—okay, put it that the dog goes away with him, the dog that belonged to the victim and had gone to that house with him. How does that look?" He pulled his chin in. "You know damn well the last thing I want in a homicide is to find you or Goodwin anywhere within ten miles of it, because I know from experience what to expect. But when you're there, there you are, and I want to know how and why and what, and by God I intend to. Where's the dog?"

Wolfe sighed and shook his head. "In this instance," he said, almost genial, "you're wasting your time. As for Mr. Meegan, he phoned this morning to make an appointment and came at eleven. Our conversation was brief. He wanted a man shadowed, but divulged no name or any other specific detail because in his first breath he mentioned his wife —he was overwrought—and I gathered that his difficulty was marital. As you know, I don't touch that kind of work, and I stopped him. My vanity bristles even at an offer of that sort of job. My bluntness enraged him, and he dashed out. On his way he took his hat from the rack in the hall, and he took Mr. Goodwin's raincoat instead of his own. Archie. Proceed."

Cramer's eyes came to me, and I obeyed. "I didn't find out about the switch in coats until the middle of the afternoon. His was the same color as mine, but mine's newer. When he phoned for an appointment this morning he gave me his name and address, and I wanted to phone him to tell him to bring my coat back, but he wasn't listed, and Information said she didn't have him, so I decided to go get it. I walked, wearing Meegan's coat. There was a cop and a crowd and a PD car in front of twenty-nine Arbor Street, and, as I approached, another PD car came, and Purley Stebbins got out and went in, so I decided to skip it, not wanting to go through the torture. There was a dog present, and he nuzzled me, and I patted him. I will admit, if pressed, that I should not have patted him. The cop asked me if the dog was mine, and I said no and went on, and headed for home. I was—"

"Did you call the dog or signal it?"

"No. I was at Twenty-eighth and Ninth Avenue before I knew he was tailing me. I did not entice or remove. If I did, if there's some kind of a dodge about the dog, please tell me why I phoned the precinct to get the name of his owner."

"I don't know. With Wolfe and you I never know. Where is it?"

I blurted it out before Wolfe could stop me. "Upstairs in my room."

"Bring it down here."

"Right."

I was up and going, but Wolfe called me sharply. "Archie!"

I turned. "Yes, sir."

"There's no frantic urgency." He went to Cramer. "The animal seems intelligent, but I doubt if it's up to answering questions. I don't want it capering around my office."

"Neither do I."

"Then why bring it down?"

"I'm taking it downtown. We want to try something with it."

Wolfe pursed his lips. "I doubt if that's feasible. Sit down, Archie. Mr. Goodwin has assumed an obligation and will have to honor it. The creature has no master, and so, presumably, no home. It will have to be tolerated here until Mr. Goodwin gets satisfactory assurance of its future welfare. Archie?"

If we had been alone I would have made my position clear, but with Cramer there I was stuck. "Absolutely," I agreed.

"You see," he told Cramer. "I'm afraid we can't permit the dog's removal."

"Nuts. I'm taking it."

"Indeed? What writ have you? Replevin? Warrant for arrest as a material witness?"

Cramer opened his mouth and shut it again. He put his elbows on the chair arms, interlaced his fingers, and leaned forward. "Look. You and Meegan check, either because you're both telling it straight, or because you've framed it, I don't know which, and we'll see. But I'm taking the dog. Kampf, the man who was killed, lived on Perry Street, a few blocks away from Arbor Street. He arrived at twenty-nine Arbor Street, with the dog on a leash, about five-twenty this afternoon. The janitor of the house, named Olsen, lives in the basement, and he was sitting at his front window, and he saw Kampf arrive with the dog and turn in at the entrance. About ten minutes later he saw the dog come out, with no leash, and right after the dog a man came out. The man was Victor Talento, a lawyer, the tenant of the ground-floor apartment. Talento says he left his apartment to go to an appointment, saw the dog in the hall, thought it was a stray, and chased it out, and that's all he knows. Anyhow, Olsen says Talento walked off, and the dog stayed there on the sidewalk."

Cramer unlaced his fingers and sat back. "About twenty minutes later, around ten minutes to six, Olsen heard someone yelling his name and went to the rear and up one flight to the ground-floor hall. Two men were there, a live one and a dead one. The live one was Ross Chaffee, a painter, the tenant of the top-floor studio—that's the fourth floor. The dead one was the man that had arrived with the dog. He had been strangled with the dog's leash, and the body was at the bottom of the stairs leading up. Chaffee says he found it when he came down to go to an appointment, and that's all he knows. He stayed there while Olsen went downstairs to phone. A squad car arrived at five-fifty-eight. Sergeant Stebbins arrived at six-ten. Goodwin arrived at six-ten. Excellent timing."

Wolfe merely grunted. Cramer continued, "You can have it all. The dog's leash was in the pocket of Kampf's raincoat, which was on him. The laboratory says it was used to strangle him. The routine is still in process. I'll answer questions within reason. The four tenants of the house were all there when Kampf arrived: Victor Talento, the lawyer, on the gound floor; Richard Meegan, whose job you say you wouldn't take, second floor; Jerome Aland, a night-club performer, third floor; and Ross Chaffee, the painter with the studio. Aland says he was sound asleep until we banged on his door and took him down to look at the corpse. Meegan says he heard nothing and knows nothing."

Cramer sat forward again. "Okay, what happened? Kampf went there to see one of those four men, and had his dog with him. It's possible he took the leash off in the lower hall to leave the dog there, but I doubt it. At least it's just as possible that he took the dog along to the door of one of the apartments, and the dog was wet and the tenant wouldn't let it enter, so Kampf left it outside. Another possibility is that the dog was actually present when Kampf was killed, but we'll know more about that after we see and handle the dog. The particular thing we want—we're going to take the dog in that house and see which door it goes to. We're going to do that now. There's a man out in my car who knows dogs." Cramer stood up.

Wolfe shook his head. "You must be hard put. You say Mr. Kampf lived on Perry Street. With a family?"

"No. Bachelor. Some kind of a writer. He didn't have to make a living; he had means."

"Then the beast is orphaned. He's in your room, Archie?"

"Yes, sir." I got up and started for the door.

Wolfe halted me. "One moment. Go up and in, lock your door, and stay there till I notify you. Go!"

I went. It was either that or quit my job on the spot, and I resign only when we haven't got company. Also, assuming that there was a valid reason for refusing to surrender the dog to the cops, Wolfe was justified. Cramer, needing no warrant to enter the house because he was already in, wouldn't hesitate to mount to my room to do his own fetching, and stopping him physically would have raised some delicate points. Whereas breaking through a locked door would be another matter.

I didn't lock it, because it hadn't been locked for years and I didn't remember which drawer of my chest the key was in, and while I was searching Cramer might conceivably have made it up the carpeted stairs and come right in, so I left it open and stood on the sill to listen. If I heard him coming I would shut it and brace it with my foot. Nero, or Jet, depending on where you stand, came over to me, but I ordered him back, and he went without a murmur. From below came voices, not cordial, but not raised enough for me to get words. Before long there was the sound of Cramer's heavy steps leaving the office and tramping along the hall, and then the slam of the front door.

I called down, "All clear?"

"No!" It was a bellow. "Wait till I bolt it!" And after a moment: "All right!"

I shut my door and went to the stairs and descended. Wolfe was back in his chair behind his desk, sitting straight. As I entered he snapped at me, "A pretty mess! You sneak a dog in here to badger me, and what now?"

I crossed to my desk, sat, and spoke calmly. "We're way beyond that. You will never admit you bollixed it up yourself, so forget it. When you ask me what now, that's easy. I could say I'll take the dog down and deliver him at Homicide, but we're beyond that too. Not only have you learned that he is orphaned, as you put it, which sounds terrible, and therefore adopting him will probably be simple, but also you have taken a stand with Cramer, and of course you won't back up. If we sit tight with the door bolted I suppose I can take the dog out back for his outings, but what if the law shows up tomorrow with a writ?"

He leaned back and shut his eyes. I looked up at the wall clock: two minutes past eleven. I looked at my wristwatch: also two minutes past eleven. They both said six minutes past when Wolfe opened his eyes.

"From Mr. Cramer's information," he said, "I doubt if that case holds any formidable difficulties."

I had no comment.

"If it were speedily solved," he went on, "your commitment to the dog could be honored at leisure. I had thought until now that my disinclination to permit a policeman to storm in here and commandeer any person or object in this house that struck his fancy was shared by you."

"It is. Within reason."

"That's an ambiguous phrase, and I must be allowed my own interpretation short of absurdity. Clearly the simplest way to settle this matter is to find out who killed Mr. Kampf. It may not be much of a job; if it proves otherwise we can reconsider. An immediate exploration is the thing, and luckily we have a pretext for it. You can go there to get your raincoat, taking Mr. Meegan's with you, and proceed as the occasion offers. The best course would be to bring him here, but, as you know, I wholly rely on your discretion and enterprise in such a juncture."

"Thank you very much," I said bitterly. "You mean now."

"Yes."

"They may still have Meegan downtown."

"I doubt if they'll keep him overnight. In the morning they'll probably have him again."

"I'll have to take the dog out first."

"Fritz will take him out back in the court."

"I'll be damned." I arose. "No client, no fee, no nothing except a dog with a wide skull for brain room." I crossed to the door, turned, said distinctly, "I will be damned," went to the rack for my hat and Meegan's coat, and beat it.

III

THE rain had ended, and the wind was down. After dismissing the taxi at the end of Arbor Street, I walked to Number 29, with the raincoat hung over my arm. There was light behind the curtains of the windows on the ground floor, but none anywhere above, and none in the basement. Entering the vestibule, I inspected the labels in the slots between the mailboxes and the buttons. From the bottom up they read: Talento, Meegan, Aland, and Chaffee. I pushed the button above Meegan, put my hand on the doorknob, and waited. No click. I twisted the knob, and it wouldn't turn. Another long push on the button, and a longer wait. I varied it by trying four short pushes. Nothing doing.

I left the vestibule and was confronted by two couples standing on the sidewalk staring at me, or at the entrance. They exchanged words, decided they didn't care for my returning stare, and passed on. I considered pushing the button of Victor Talento, the lawyer who lived on the ground floor, where light was showing, voted to wait a while for Meegan, with whom I had an in, moved down ten paces to a fire hydrant, and propped myself against it.

I hadn't been there long enough to shift position more than a couple of times when the light disappeared on the ground floor of Number 29, and a little later the vestibule door opened and a man came out. He turned toward me, gave me a glance as he passed, and kept going. Thinking it unlikely that any occupant of that house was being extended the freedom of the city that night, I cast my eyes around, and sure enough, when the subject had gone some thirty paces a figure emerged from an areaway across the street and started strolling. I shook my head in disapproval. I would have waited until the guy was ten paces farther. Saul Panzer would have made it ten more than that, but Saul is the best tailer alive.

As I stood deploring that faulty performance, an idea hit me. They might keep Meegan downtown another two hours, or all night, or he might even be up in his bed asleep. This was at least a chance to take a stab at something. I shoved off, in the direction taken by the subject, who was now a block away. Stepping along, I gained on him. A little beyond the corner I was abreast of the city employee, who was keeping to the other side of the street; but I wasn't interested in him. It seemed to me that the subject was upping the stroke a little, so I did too, really marching, and as he reached the next intersection I was beside him. He had looked over his shoulder when he heard me coming up behind, but hadn't slowed. As I reached him I spoke.

"Victor Talento?"

"No comment," he said and kept going. So did I.

"Thanks for the compliment," I said, "but I'm not a reporter. My name's Archie Goodwin, and I work for Nero Wolfe. If you'll stop a second I'll show you my credentials."

"I'm not interested in your credentials."

"Okay. If you just came out for a breath of air you won't be interested in this either. Otherwise you may be. Please don't scream or look around, but you've got a Homicide dick on your tail. Don't look or he'll know I'm telling you. He's across the street, ninety feet back."

"Yes," he conceded, without changing pace, "that's interesting. Is this your good deed for the day?"

"No. I'm out dowsing for Mr. Wolfe. He's investigating a murder just for practice, and I'm looking for a seam. I thought if I gave you a break you might feel like reciprocating. If you're just out for a walk, forget it, and sorry I interrupted. If you're headed for something you'd like to keep private maybe you could use some expert advice. In this part of town at this time of night there are only two approved methods for shaking a tail, and I'd be glad to oblige."

He looked it over for half a block, with me keeping step, and then spoke. "You mentioned credentials."

"Right. We might as well stop under that light. The dick will keep his distance."

We stopped. I got out my wallet and let him have a look at my licenses, detective and driver's. He didn't skimp it, being a lawyer. I put my wallet back.

"Of course," he said, "I was aware that I might be followed."

"Sure."

"I intended to take precautions. But it may not be—I suppose it's not as simple as it seems. I have had no experience at this kind of maneuver. Who hired Wolfe to investigate?"

"I don't know. He says he needs practice."

"All right, if it's qualified." He stood sizing me up by the street light. He was an inch shorter than me, and some older, with his weight starting to collect around the middle. He was dark-skinned, with eyes to match, and his nose hooked to point down. I didn't prod him. My lucky stab had snagged him, and it was his problem. He was working on it.

"I have an appointment," he said.

I waited.

He went on. "A woman phoned me, and I arranged to meet her. My wire could have been tapped."

"I doubt it. They're not that fast."

"I suppose not. The woman had nothing to do with the murder, and neither had I, but of course anything I do and anyone I see is suspect. I have no right to expose her to possible embarrassment, and I can't be sure of shaking that man off."

I grinned at him. "And me too."

"You mean you would follow me?"

"Certainly, for practice. And I'd like to see how you handle it."

He wasn't returning my grin. "I see you've earned your reputation, Goodwin. You'd be wasting your time, because this woman has no connection with this business, but I should have known better than to make this appointment. I won't keep it. It's only three blocks from here. You might be willing to go and tell her I'm not coming, and I'll get in touch with her tomorrow. Yes?"

"Sure, if it's only three blocks. If you'll return the favor by calling on Nero Wolfe for a little talk. That's what I meant by reciprocating."

He considered it. "Not tonight."

"Tonight would be best."

"No. I'm all in."

"Tomorrow morning at eleven?"

"Yes, I can make it then."

"Okay." I gave him the address. "If you forget it, it's in the book. Now brief me."

He took a respectable roll of bills from his pocket and peeled off a twenty. "Since you're acting as my agent, you have a right to a fee."

I grinned again. "That's a neat idea, you being a lawyer, but I'm not acting as your agent. I'm doing you a favor on request and expecting one in return. Where's the appointment?"

He put the roll back. "Have it your way. The woman's name is Jewel Jones, and she's at the southeast corner of Christopher and Grove Streets, or will be." He looked at his wrist. "We were to meet there at midnight. She's medium height, slender, dark hair and eyes, very good-looking. Tell her why I'm not coming, and say she'll hear from me tomorrow."

"Right. You'd better take a walk in the other direction to keep the dick occupied, and don't look back."

He wanted to shake hands to show his appreciation, but that would have been just as bad as taking the twenty, since before another midnight Wolfe might be tagging him for murder, so I pretended not to notice. He headed east, and I headed west, moving right along without turning my head for a glimpse of the dick. I had to make sure that he didn't see a vision and switch subjects, but I let that wait until I got to Christopher Street. Reaching it, I turned the corner, went twenty feet to a stoop, slid behind it with only my head out, and counted a slow hundred. There were passers-by, a couple and a guy in a hurry, but no dick. I went on a block to Grove Street, passed the intersection, saw no loitering female, continued for a distance, and turned and back-tracked. I was on the fifth lap, and it was eight minutes past twelve, when a taxi stopped at the corner, a woman got out, and the taxi rolled off.

I approached. The light could have been better, but she seemed to meet the specifications. I stopped and asked, "Jones?" She drew herself up. I said, "From Victor."

She tilted her head back to get my face. "Who are you?" She seemed a little out of breath.

"Victor sent me with a message, but naturally I have to be sure it reaches the right party. I've ante'd half of your name and half of his, so it's your turn."

"Who are you?"

I shook my head. "You go first, or no message from Victor."

"Where is he?"

"No. I'll count ten and go. One, two, three, four—"

"My name is Jewel Jones. His is Victor Talento."

"That's the girl. I'll tell you." I did so. Since it was desirable for her to grasp the situation fully, I started with my propping myself on the fire hydrant in front of 29 Arbor Street and went on from there, as it happened, including, of course, my name and status. By the time I finished she had developed a healthy frown.

"Damn it," she said with feeling. She moved and put a hand on my arm. "Come and put me in a taxi."

I stayed planted. "I'll be glad to, and it will be on me. We're going to Nero Wolfe's place."

"We?" She removed the hand. "You're crazy."

"One will get you ten I'm not. Look at it. You and Talento made an appointment at a street corner, so you had some good reason for not wanting to be seen together tonight. It must have been something fairly urgent. I admit the urgency didn't have to be connected with the murder of Philip Kampf, but it could be, and it certainly has to be discussed. I don't want to be arbitrary. I can take you to a Homicide sergeant named Stebbins, and you can discuss it with him; or I'll take you to Mr. Wolfe. I should think you'd prefer Mr. Wolfe, but suit yourself."

She had well-oiled gears. For a second, as I spoke, her eyes flashed like daggers, but then they went soft and appealing. She took my arm again, this time with both hands. "I'll discuss it with you," she said, in a voice she could have used to defrost her refrigerator. "I wouldn't mind that. We'll go somewhere."

I said come on, and we moved, with her maintaining contact with a hand hooked cozily on my arm. We hadn't gone far, toward Seventh Avenue, when a taxi came along and I flagged it and we got in. I told the driver, "Nine-eighteen West Thirty-fifth," and he started.

"What's that?" Miss Jones demanded.

I told her, Nero Wolfe's house. The poor girl didn't know what to do. If she called me a rat that wouldn't help her any. If she kicked and screamed I would merely give the hackie another address. Her best bet was to try to thaw me, and if she had had time for a real campaign, say four or five hours, she might conceivably have made some progress, because she had a knack for it. She didn't coax or argue; she just told me how she knew I was the kind of man she could tell anything to and I would believe her and understand her, and after she had done that she would be willing to go anywhere or do anything I advised, but she was sure I wouldn't want to take advantage . . .

There just wasn't time enough. The taxi rolled to the curb, and I had a bill ready for the driver. I got out, gave her a hand, and escorted her up the seven steps of the stoop, applauding her economy in not wasting breath on protests. My key wouldn't let us in, since the chain bolt would be on, so I pushed the button, and in a moment the stoop light shone on us, and in another the door opened. I motioned her in and followed. Fritz was there.

"Mr. Wolfe up?" I asked.

"In the office." He was giving Miss Jones a look, the look he gives any strange female who enters that house. There is always in his mind the possibility, however remote, that she will bewitch Wolfe into a mania for a mate. After asking him to conduct her to the front room, and putting my hat and the raincoat on the rack, I went on down the hall and entered the office.

Wolfe was at his desk, reading, and curled up in the middle of the room, on the best rug in the house, which was given to Wolfe years ago as a token of gratitude by an Armenian merchant who had got himself in a bad hole, was the dog. The dog greeted me by lifting his head and tapping the rug with his tail. Wolfe greeted me by raising his eyes from the book and grunting.

"I brought company," I told him. "Before I introduce her I should—"

"Her? The tenants of that house are all men! I might have known you'd dig up a woman!"

"I can chase her if you don't want her. This is how I got her." I proceeded, not dragging it out, but including all the essentials. I ended up, "I could have taken her to a spot I know of and grilled her myself, but it would have been risky. Just in a six-minute taxi ride she had me feeling—uh, brotherly. Do you want her or not?"

"Confound it." His eyes went to his book and stayed there long enough to finish a paragraph. He dog-eared it and put it down. "Very well, bring her."

I crossed to the connecting door to the front room, opened it, and requested, "Please come in, Miss Jones." She came, and as she passed through gave me a wistful smile that might have gone straight to my heart if there hadn't been a diversion. As she entered, the dog suddenly sprang to his feet, whirling, and made for her with sounds of unmistakable pleasure. He stopped in front of her, raising his head so she wouldn't have to reach far to pat it, and wagged his tail so fast it was only a blur.

"Indeed," Wolfe said. "How do you do, Miss Jones. I am Nero Wolfe. What's the dog's name?"

I claim she was good. The presence of the dog was a complete surprise to her. But without the slightest sign of fluster she put out a hand to give it a gentle pat, looked around, spotted the red leather chair, went to it, and sat.

"That's a funny question right off," she said, not complaining. "Asking me your dog's name."

"Pfui." Wolfe was disgusted. "I don't know what position you were going to take, but from what Mr. Goodwin tells me I would guess you were going to say that the purpose of your appointment with Mr. Talento was a personal matter that had nothing to do with Mr. Kampf or his death, and that you knew Mr. Kampf either slightly and casually or not at all. Now the dog has made that untenable. Obviously he knows you well, and he belonged to Mr. Kampf. So you knew Mr. Kampf well. If you try to deny that you'll have Mr. Goodwin and other trained men digging all around you, your past and your present, and that will be extremely disagreeable, no matter how innocent you may be of murder or any other wrongdoing. You won't like that. What's the dog's name?"

She looked at me, and I met it. In good light I would have qualified Talento's specification of "very good-looking." Not that she was unsightly, but she caught the eye more by what she looked than how she looked. It wasn't just something she turned on as needed; it was there even now, when she must have been pretty busy deciding how to handle it.

It took her only a few seconds to decide. "His name is Bootsy," she said. The dog, at her feet, lifted his head and wagged his tail.

"Good heavens," Wolfe muttered. "No other name?"

"Not that I know of."

"Your name is Jewel Jones?"

"Yes. I sing in a night club, the Flamingo, but I'm not working right now." She made a little gesture, very appealing, but it was Wolfe who had to resist it, not me. "Believe me, Mr. Wolfe, I don't know anything about that murder. If I knew anything that could help I'd be perfectly willing to tell you, because I'm sure you're the kind of man that understands and you wouldn't want to hurt me if you didn't have to."

That wasn't what she had fed me verbatim. Not verbatim.

"I try to understand," Wolfe said dryly. "You knew Mr. Kampf intimately?"

"Yes, I guess so." She smiled as one understander to another. "For a while I did. Not lately, not for the past two months."

"You met the dog at his apartment on Perry Street?"

"That's right. For nearly a year I was there quite often."

"You and Mr. Kampf quarreled?"

"Oh no, we didn't quarrel. I just didn't see him any more. I had other —I was very busy."

"When did you see him last?"

"Well—you mean intimately?"

"No. At all."

"About two weeks ago, at the club. He came to the club once or twice and spoke to me there."

"But no quarrel?"

"No, there was nothing to quarrel about."

"You have no idea who killed him, or why?"

"I certainly haven't."

Wolfe leaned back. "Do you know Mr. Talento intimately?"

"No, not if you mean—of course we're friends. I used to live there."

"With Mr. Talento?"

"Not *with* him." She was mildly shocked. "I never live with a man. I had the second-floor apartment."

"At twenty-nine Arbor Street?"

"Yes."

"For how long? When?"

"For nearly a year. I left there—let's see—about three months ago. I have a little apartment on East Forty-ninth Street."

"Then you know the others too? Mr. Meegan and Mr. Chaffee and Mr. Aland?"

"I know Ross Chaffee and Jerry Aland, but no Meegan. Who's he?"

"A tenant at twenty-nine Arbor Street. Second floor."

She nodded. "Well, sure, that's the floor I had." She smiled. "I hope they fixed that damn table for him. That was one reason I left. I hate furnished apartments, don't you?"

Wolfe made a face. "In principle, yes. I take it you now have your own furniture. Supplied by Mr. Kampf?"

She laughed—more of a chuckle—and her eyes danced. "I see you didn't know Phil Kampf."

"Not supplied by him, then?"

"A great big no."

"By Mr. Chaffee? Or Mr. Aland?"

"No and no." She went very earnest. "Look, Mr. Wolfe. A friend of mine was mighty nice about that furniture, and we'll just leave it. Archie told me what you're interested in is the murder, and I'm sure you wouldn't want to drag in a lot of stuff just to hurt me and a friend of mine, so we'll forget the furniture."

Wolfe didn't press it. He took a hop. "Your appointment on a street corner with Mr. Talento—what was that about?"

She nodded. "I've been wondering about that. I mean what I would say when you asked me, because I'd hate to have you think I'm a sap, and I guess it sounds like it. I phoned him when I heard on the radio about Phil and where he was killed, there on Arbor Street, and I knew Vic still lived there and I simply wanted to ask him about it."

"You had him on the phone?"

"He didn't seem to want to talk about it on the phone."

"But why a street corner?"

This time it was more like a laugh. "Now, Mr. Wolfe, you're not a sap. You asked about the furniture, didn't you? Well, a girl with furniture shouldn't be seen places with a man like Vic Talento."

"What is he like?"

She fluttered a hand. "Oh, he wants to get close."

Wolfe kept at her until after one o'clock, and I could report it all, but it wouldn't get you any further than it did him. He couldn't trip her or back her into a corner. She hadn't been to Arbor Street for two months. She hadn't seen Chaffee or Aland or Talento for weeks, and of course not Meegan, since she had never heard of him before. She couldn't even try to guess who had killed Kampf. The only thing remotely to be regarded as a return on Wolfe's investment of a full hour was her statement that as far as she knew there was no one who had both an attachment and a claim to Bootsy. If there were heirs she had no idea who they were. When she left the chair to go the dog got up too, and she patted him, and he went with us to the door. I took her to Tenth Avenue and put her in a taxi, and returned.

I got a glass of milk from the kitchen and took it to the office. Wolfe, who was drinking beer, didn't scowl at me. He seldom scowls when he is drinking beer.

"Where's Bootsy?" I inquired.

"No," he said emphatically.

"Okay." I surrendered. "Where's Jet?"

"Down in Fritz's room. He'll sleep there. You don't like him."

"That's not true, but you can have it. It means you can't blame him on me, and that suits me fine." I sipped milk. "Anyhow, that will no longer be an issue after Homicide comes in the morning with a document and takes him away."

"They won't come."

"I offer twenty to one. Before noon."

He nodded. "That was roughly my own estimate of the probability, so while you were out I phoned Mr. Cramer. I suggested an arrangement, and I suppose he inferred that if he declined the arrangement the dog might be beyond his jurisdiction before tomorrow, though I didn't say so. I may have given that impression."

"Yeah. You should be more careful."

"So the arrangement has been made. You are to be at twenty-nine Arbor Street, with the dog, at nine o'clock in the morning. You are to be present throughout the fatuous performance the police have in mind, and keep the dog in view. The dog is to leave the premises with you, before noon, and you are to bring him back here. The police are to make no further effort to constrain the dog for twenty-four hours. While in that house you may find an opportunity to flush something or someone more contributive than that volatile demirep. If you will come to my room before you go in the morning I may have a suggestion."

"I resent that," I said manfully. "When you call her that, smile."

IV

It was a fine bright morning. I didn't take Meegan's raincoat, because I didn't need any pretext and I doubted if the program would offer a likely occasion for the exchange.

The law was there in front, waiting for me. The one who knew dogs was a stocky middle-aged guy who wore rimless glasses. Before he touched the dog he asked me the name, and I told him Bootsy.

"A hell of a name," he observed. "Also that's a hell of a leash you've got."

"I agree. His was on the corpse, so I suppose it's in the lab." I handed him my end of the heavy cord. "If he bites you it's not on me."

"He won't bite me. Would you, Bootsy?" He squatted before the dog and started to get acquainted. Sergeant Purley Stebbins growled, a foot from my ear, "He should have bit you when you kidnaped him."

I turned. Purley was half an inch taller than me and two inches broader. "You've got it twisted," I told him. "It's women that bite me. I've often wondered what would bite you."

We continued exchanging pleasantries while the dog man, whose name was Loftus, made friends with Bootsy. It wasn't long before he announced that he was ready to proceed. He was frowning. "In a way," he said, "it would be better to keep him on leash after I go in, because Kampf probably did. Or did he? Maybe you ought to brief me a little more. How much do we know?"

"To swear to," Purley told him, "damn little. But putting it all together from what we've collected, this is how it looks, and I'll have to be shown different. When Kampf and the dog entered it was raining and the dog was wet. Kampf left the dog in the ground-floor hall. He removed the leash and had it in his hand when he went to the door of one of the apartments. The tenant of the apartment let him in, and they talked. The tenant socked him, probably from behind without warning, and used the leash to finish him. He stuffed the leash in the pocket of the raincoat. It took nerve and muscle both to carry the body

out and down the stairs to the lower hall, but he damn well had to get
it out of his place and away from his door, and any of those four could
have done it in a pinch, and it sure was a pinch. Of course the dog
was already outside, out on the sidewalk. While Kampf was in one of
the apartments getting killed, Talento had come into the lower hall and
seen the dog and chased it out."

"Then," Loftus objected, "Talento's clean."

"No. Nobody's clean. If it was Talento, after he killed Kampf he
went out to the hall and put the dog out in the vestibule, went back in
his apartment and carried the body out and dumped it at the foot of
the stairs, and then left the house, chasing the dog on out to the sidewalk. You're the dog expert. Is there anything wrong with that?"

"Not necessarily. It depends on the dog and how close he was to
Kampf. There wasn't any blood."

"Then that's how I'm buying it. If you want it filled in you can spend
the rest of the day with the reports of the other experts and the statements of the tenants."

"Some other day. That'll do for now. You're going in first?"

"Yeah. Come on, Goodwin."

Purley started for the door, but I objected. "I'm staying with the
dog."

"For God's sake. Then keep behind Loftus."

I changed my mind. It would be interesting to watch the experiment, and from behind Loftus the view wouldn't be good. So I went
into the vestibule with Purley. The inner door was opened by a Homicide colleague, and we crossed the threshold and moved to the far side
of the small lobby, which was fairly clean but not ornate. The colleague
closed the door and stayed there. In a minute he pulled it open again,
and Loftus and the dog entered. Two steps in, Loftus stopped, and so
did the dog. No one spoke. The leash hung limp. Bootsy looked around
at Loftus. Loftus bent over and untied the cord from the collar, and
held it up to show Bootsy he was free. Bootsy came over to me and stood,
his head up, wagging his tail.

"Nuts," Purley said, disgusted.

"You know what I really expected," Loftus said. "I never thought
he'd show us where Kampf took him when they entered yesterday, but
I did think he'd go to the foot of the stairs, where the body was found,
and I thought he might go on to where the body came from—Talento's
door, or upstairs. Take him by the collar, Goodwin, and ease him over
to the foot of the stairs."

I obliged. He came without urging, but gave no sign that the spot held any special interest for him. We all stood and watched him. He opened his mouth wide to yawn.

"Fine," Purley rumbled. "Just fine. You might as well go on with it."

Loftus came and fastened the leash to the collar, led Bootsy across the lobby to a door, and knocked. In a moment the door opened, and there was Victor Talento in a fancy rainbow dressing gown.

"Hello, Bootsy," he said, and reached down to pat.

"Goddammit!" Purley barked. "I told you not to speak!"

Talento straightened up. "So you did." He was apologetic. "I'm sorry, I forgot. Do you want to try it again?"

"No. That's all."

Talento backed in and closed the door.

"You must realize," Loftus told Purley, "that a Labrador can't be expected to go for a man's throat. They're not that kind of dog. The most you could expect would be an attitude, or possibly a growl."

"You can have 'em," Purley growled. "Is it worth going on?"

"By all means. You'd better go first."

Purley headed for me, and I gave him room and then followed him up the stairs. The upper hall was narrow and not very light, with a door at the rear end and another toward the front. We backed up against the wall opposite the front door to leave enough space for Loftus and Bootsy. They came, Bootsy tagging, and Loftus knocked. Ten seconds passed before footsteps sounded, and then the door was opened by the specimen who had dashed out of Wolfe's place the day before and taken my coat with him. He was in his shirt sleeves, and he hadn't combed his hair.

"This is Sergeant Loftus, Mr. Meegan," Purley said. "Take a look at the dog. Have you ever seen it before? Pat it."

Meegan snorted. "Pat it yourself. Go to hell."

"Have you ever seen it before?"

"No."

"Okay, thanks. Come on, Loftus."

As we started up the next flight the door slammed behind us, good and loud. Purley asked over his shoulder, "Well?"

"He didn't like him," Loftus replied from the rear, "but there are lots of people lots of dogs don't like."

The third-floor hall was a duplicate of the one below. Again Purley and I posted ourselves opposite the door, and Loftus came with Bootsy and knocked. Nothing happened. He knocked again, louder, and pretty soon the door opened to a two-inch crack, and a squeaky voice came through.

"You've got the dog."

"Right here," Loftus told him.

"Are you there, Sergeant?"

"Right here," Purley answered.

"I told you that dog don't like me. Once at a party at Phil Kampf's —I told you. I didn't mean to hurt it, but it thought I did. What are you trying to do, frame me?"

"Open the door. The dog's on a leash."

"I won't! I told you I wouldn't!"

Purley moved. His arm, out stiff, went over Loftus's shoulder, and his palm met the door and kept going. The door hesitated an instant and then swung open. Standing there, holding to its edge, was a skinny individual in red-and-green-striped pajamas. The dog let out a low growl and backed up a little.

"We're making the rounds, Mr. Aland," Purley said, "and we couldn't leave you out. Now you can go back to sleep. As for trying to frame you—"

He stopped because the door shut.

"You didn't tell me," Loftus complained, "that Aland had already fixed it for a reaction."

"No, I thought I'd wait and see. One to go." He headed for the stairs.

The top-floor hall had had someone's personal attention. It was no bigger than the others, but it had a nice clean tan-colored runner, and the walls were painted the same shade and sported a few small pictures. Purley went to the rear door instead of the front, and we made room for Loftus and Bootsy by flattening against the wall. When Loftus knocked footsteps responded at once, approaching the door, and it swung wide open. This was the painter, Ross Chaffee, and he was dressed for it, in an old brown smock. He was by far the handsomest of the tenants, tall, erect, with artistic wavy dark hair and features he must have enjoyed looking at.

I had ample time to enjoy them too as he stood smiling at us, completely at ease, obeying Purley's prior instructions not to speak. Bootsy was also at ease. When it became quite clear that no blood was going to be shed, Purley asked, "You know the dog, don't you, Mr. Chaffee?"

"Certainly. He's a beautiful animal."

"Pat him."

"With pleasure." He bent gracefully. "Bootsy, do you know your master's gone?" He scratched behind the black ears. "Gone forever, Bootsy, and that's too bad." He straightened. "Anything else? I'm working. I like the morning light."

"That's all, thanks." Purley turned to go, and I let Loftus and Bootsy by before following. On the way down the three flights no one had any remarks.

As we hit the level of the lower hall Victor Talento's door opened, and he emerged and spoke. "The District Attorney's office phoned. Are you through with me? They want me down there."

"We're through," Purley rumbled. "We can run you down."

Talento said that would be fine and he would be ready in a minute. Purley told Loftus to give me Bootsy, and he handed me the leash.

"I am willing," I said helpfully, "to give you a detailed analysis of the dog's conduct. It will take about a week."

"Go to hell," Purley growled, "and take the goddam dog along."

I departed. Outside the morning was still fine. The presence of two PD cars in front of the scene of a murder had attracted a small gathering, and Bootsy and I were objects of interest as we appeared and started off. We both ignored the stares. We moseyed along, in no hurry, stopping now and then to give Bootsy a chance to inspect something if he felt inclined. At the fourth or fifth stop, more than a block away, I saw the quartet leaving Number 29. Stebbins and Talento took one car and Loftus and the colleague the other, and they rolled off.

I shortened up on Bootsy a little, walked him west until an empty taxi appeared, stopped it and got in, took a five-dollar bill from my wallet, and handed it to the hackie.

"Thanks," he said with feeling. "For what, down payment on the cab?"

"You'll earn it, brother," I assured him. "Is there somewhere within a block or so of Arbor and Court where you can park for anywhere from thirty minutes to three hours?"

"Not three hours for a finif."

"Of course not." I got another five and gave it to him. "I doubt if it will be that long."

"There's a parking lot not too far. On the street without a passenger I'll be solicited."

"You'll have a passenger—the dog. I prefer the street. He's a nice dog. When I return I'll be reasonable. Let's see what we can find."

He pulled the lever and we moved. There are darned few legal parking spaces in all Manhattan at that time of day, and we cruised around several corners before we found one, on Court Street two blocks from Arbor. He backed into it and I got out, leaving the windows down three inches. I told him I'd be back when he saw me, and headed south, turning right at the second corner.

There was no police car at 29 Arbor, and no gathering. That was satisfactory. Entering the vestibule, I pushed the button under Meegan and put my hand on the knob. No click. Pushing twice more and still getting no response, I tried Aland's button, and that worked. After a short wait the click came, and I shoved the door open, entered, mounted two flights, went to the door, and knocked with authority.

The squeaky voice came through. "Who is it?"

"Goodwin. I was just here with the others. I haven't got the dog. Open up."

The door swung slowly to a crack, and then wider. Jerome Aland was still in his gaudy pajamas. "For God's sake," he squeaked, "what do you want now? I need some sleep!"

I didn't apologize. "I was going to ask you some questions when I was here before," I told him, "but the dog complicated it. It won't take long." Since he wasn't polite enough to move aside, I had to brush him, skinny as he was, as I went in. "Which way?"

He slid past me, and I followed him across to chairs. They were the kind of chairs that made Jewel Jones hate furnished apartments, and the rest of the furniture didn't help any. He sat on the edge of one and demanded, "All right, what?"

It was a little tricky. Since he was assuming I was one of the Homicide personnel, it wouldn't do for me to know either too much or too little. It would be risky to mention Jewel Jones, because the cops might not have got around to her at all.

"I'm checking some points," I told him. "How long has Richard Meegan occupied the apartment below you?"

"Hell, I've told you that a dozen times."

"Not me. I said I'm checking. How long?"

"Nine days. He took it a week ago Tuesday."

"Who was the previous tenant? Just before him."

"There wasn't any. It was empty."

"Empty ever since you've been here?"

"No, I've told you, a girl had it, but she moved out about three months ago. Her name is Jewel Jones, and she's a fine artist, and she got me my job at the night club where I work now." His mouth worked. "I know what you're doing, you're trying to make it nasty, and you're trying to catch me getting my facts twisted. Bringing that dog here to growl at me—can I help it if I don't like dogs?"

He ran his fingers, both hands, through his hair. When the hair was messed good he gestured like a night-club performer. "Die like a dog," he said. "That's what Phil did, died like a dog. Poor Phil. I wouldn't want to see that again."

"You said," I ventured, "that you and he were good friends."

His head jerked up. "I did not. Did I say that?"

"More or less. Maybe not in those words. Why, weren't you?"

"We were not. I haven't got any good friends."

"You just said that the girl that used to live here got you a job. That sounds like a good friend. Or did she owe you something?"

"Not a damn thing. Why do you keep bringing her up?"

"I didn't bring her up, you did. I only asked who was the former tenant in the apartment below you. Why, would you rather keep her out of it?"

"I don't have to keep her out. She's not in it."

"Perhaps not. Did she know Philip Kampf?"

"I guess so. Sure she did."

"How well did she know him?"

He shook his head. "Now you're getting personal, and I'm the wrong person. If Phil was alive you could ask him, and he might tell you. Me, I don't know."

I smiled at him. "All that does, Mr. Aland, is make me curious. Somebody in this house murdered Kampf. So we ask you questions, and when we come to one you shy at, naturally we wonder why. If you don't like talking about Kampf and that girl, think what it could mean. For instance, it could mean that the girl was yours, and Kampf took her away from you, and that was why you killed him when he came here yesterday. Or it could—"

"She wasn't mine!"

"Uh-huh. Or it could mean that although she wasn't yours, you were under a deep obligation to her, and Kampf had given her a dirty deal, or he was threatening her with something, and she wanted him disposed of, and you obliged. Or of course it could be merely that Kampf had something on you."

He had his head tilted back so he could look down on me. "You're in the wrong racket," he asserted. "You ought to be writing TV scripts."

I stuck with him only a few more minutes, having got all I could hope for under the circumstances. Since I was letting him assume that I was a city employee, I couldn't very well try to pry him loose for a trip to Wolfe's place. Also I had two more calls to make, and there was no telling when I might be interrupted by a phone call or a courier to one of them from downtown. The only further item I gathered from Jerome Aland was that he wasn't trying to get from under by slipping in any insinuations about his cotenants. He had no opinions or ideas about who had killed poor Phil. When I left he stood up, but he let me go and open the door for myself.

I went down a flight, to Meegan's door, and knocked and waited. Just as I was raising a fist to make it louder and better there were footsteps inside, and the door opened. Meegan was still in his shirt sleeves and still uncombed.

"Well?" he demanded.

"Back again," I said firmly but not offensively. "With a few questions. If you don't mind?"

"You know damn well I mind."

"Naturally. Mr. Talento has been called down to the District Attorney's office. This might possibly save you another trip there."

He sidestepped, and I went in. The room was the same size and shape as Aland's, above, and the furniture, though different, was no more desirable. The table against a wall was lopsided—probably the one that Jewel Jones hoped they had fixed for him. I took a chair at its end, and he took another and sat frowning at me.

"Haven't I seen you before?" he wanted to know.

"Sure, we were here with the dog."

"I mean before that. Wasn't it you in Nero Wolfe's office yesterday?"

"That's right."

"How come?"

I raised my brows. "Haven't you got the lines crossed, Mr. Meegan? I'm here to ask questions, not to answer them. I was in Wolfe's office on business. I often am. Now—"

"He's a fat, arrogant halfwit!"

"You may be right. He's certainly arrogant. Now, I'm here on business." I got out my notebook and pencil. "You moved into this place nine days ago. Please tell me exactly how you came to take this apartment."

He glared. "I've told it at least three times."

"I know. This is the way it's done. I'm not trying to catch you in some little discrepancy, but you could have omitted something important. Just assume I haven't heard it before. Go ahead."

"Oh, my God." His head dropped and his lips tightened. Normally he might not have been a bad-looking guy, with blond hair and gray eyes and a long bony face, but now, having spent the night, or most of it, with Homicide and the DA, he looked it, especially his eyes, which were red and puffy.

He lifted his head. "I'm a commercial photographer—in Pittsburgh. Two years ago I married a girl named Margaret Ryan. Seven months later she left me. I didn't know whether she went alone or with somebody. She just left. She left Pittsburgh too, or anyway I couldn't find her there, and her family never saw her or heard from her. About five months later, about a year ago, a man I know, a businessman I do **work**

for, came back from a trip to New York and said he'd seen her in a theater here with a man. He went and spoke to her, but she claimed he was
mistaken. He was sure it was her. I came to New York and spent a week
looking around but didn't find her. I didn't go to the police because I
didn't want to. You want a better reason, but that's mine."

"I'll skip that." I was writing in the notebook. "Go ahead."

"Two weeks ago I went to look at a show of pictures at the Institute
in Pittsburgh. There was a painting there, an oil, a big one. It was called
'Three Young Mares at Pasture,' and it was an interior, a room, with
three women in it. One of them was on a couch, and two of them were
on a rug on the floor. They were eating apples. The one on the couch
was my wife. I was sure of it the minute I saw her, and after I stood and
studied it I was even surer. There was absolutely no doubt of it."

"We're not challenging that," I assured him. "What did you do?"

"The artist's signature looked like Chapple, but of course the catalogue settled that. It was Ross Chaffee. I went to the Institute office and
asked about him. They thought he lived in New York but weren't sure.
I had some work on hand I had to finish, and it took a couple of days,
and then I came to New York. I had no trouble finding Ross Chaffee;
he was in the phone book. I went to see him at his studio—here in this
house. First I told him I was interested in that figure in his painting,
that I thought she would be just right to model for some photographs I
wanted to do, but he said that his opinion of photography as a medium
was such that he wouldn't care to supply models for it, and he was bowing me out, so I told him how it was. I told him the whole thing. Then
he was different. He sympathized with me and said he would be glad to
help me if he could, but he had painted that picture more than a year
ago, and he used so many different models for his pictures that it was
impossible to remember which was which."

Meegan stopped, and I looked up from the notebook. He said aggressively, "I'm repeating that that sounded phony to me."

"Go right ahead. You're telling it."

"I say it was phony. A photographer might use hundreds of models in
a year, and he might forget, but not a painter. Not a picture like that.
I got a little tactless with him, and then I apologized. He said he might
be able to refresh his memory and asked me to phone him the next day.
Instead of phoning I went back the next day to see him, but he said he
simply couldn't remember and doubted if he ever could. I didn't get tactless again. Coming in the house, I had noticed a sign that there was a
furnished apartment to let, and when I left Chaffee I found the janitor
and rented it, and went to my hotel for my bags and moved in. I knew

damn well my wife had modeled for that picture, and I knew I could find her. I wanted to be as close as I could to Chaffee and the people who came to see him."

I wanted something too. I wanted to say that he must have had a photograph of his wife along and that I would like to see it, but of course I didn't dare, since it was a cinch that he had already either given it to the cops, or refused to, or claimed he didn't have one. So I merely asked, "What progress did you make?"

"Not much. I tried to get friendly with Chaffee but didn't get very far. I met the other two tenants, Talento and Aland, but that didn't get me anywhere. Finally I decided I would have to get some expert help, and that was why I went to see Nero Wolfe. You were there, you know how that came out—that big blob."

I nodded. "He has dropsy of the ego. What did you want him to do?"

"I've told you."

"Tell it again."

"I was going to have him tap Chaffee's phone."

"That's illegal," I said severely.

"All right, I didn't do it."

I flipped a page of the notebook. "Go back a little. During that week, besides the tenants here, how many of Chaffee's friends and acquaintances did you meet?"

"Just two, as I've told you. A young woman, a model, in his studio one day, and I don't remember her name, and a man that was there another day, a man that Chaffee said buys his pictures. His name was Braunstein."

"You're leaving out Philip Kampf."

Meegan leaned forward and put a fist on the table. "Yes, and I'm going on leaving him out. I never saw him or heard of him."

"What would you say if I said you were seen with him?"

"I'd say you were a dirty liar!" The red eyes looked redder. "As if I wasn't already having enough trouble, now you set on me about a murder of a man I never heard of! You bring a dog here and tell me to pat it, for God's sake!"

I nodded. "That's your hard luck, Mr. Meegan. You're not the first man that's had a murder for company without inviting it." I closed the notebook and put it in my pocket. "You'd better find some way of handling your troubles without having people's phones tapped." I arose. "Stick around, please. You may be wanted downtown anyhow."

He went to open the door for me. I would have liked to get more details of his progress with Ross Chaffee, or lack of it, and his contacts with the other two tenants, but it seemed more important to have some words with Chaffee before I got interrupted. As I mounted the two flights to the top floor my wristwatch said twenty-eight minutes past ten.

V

"I KNOW there's no use complaining," Ross Chaffee said, "about these interruptions to my work. Under the circumstances." He was being very gracious about it.

The top floor was quite different from the others. I don't know what his living quarters in front were like, but the studio, in the rear, was big and high and anything but crummy. There were sculptures around, big and little, and canvases of all sizes were stacked and propped against racks. The walls were covered with drapes, solid gray, with nothing on them. Each of two easels—one much larger than the other—held a canvas that had been worked on. There were several plain chairs and two upholstered ones, and an oversized divan, nearly square. I had been steered to one of the upholstered numbers, and Chaffee, still in his smock, had moved a plain one to sit facing me.

"Only don't prolong it unnecessarily," he requested.

I said I wouldn't. "There are a couple of points," I told him, "that we wonder about a little. Of course it could be merely a coincidence that Richard Meegan came to town looking for his wife, and came to see you, and rented an apartment here just nine days before Kampf was murdered, but a coincidence like that will have to stand some going over. Frankly, Mr. Chaffee, there are those, and I happen to be one of them, who find it hard to believe that you couldn't remember who modeled for an important figure in a picture you painted. I know what you say, but it's still hard to believe."

"My dear sir." Chaffee was smiling. "Then you must think I'm lying."

"I didn't say so."

"But you do, of course." He shrugged. "To what end? What deep design am I cherishing?"

"I wouldn't know. You say you wanted to help Meegan find his wife."

"No, not that I wanted to. I was willing to. He was a horrible nuisance."

"He must have been a first-class pest."

"He was. He is."

"It should have been worth some effort to get rid of him. Did you make any?"

"I have explained what I did—in a statement, and signed it. I have nothing to add. I tried to refresh my memory. One of your colleagues suggested that I might have gone to Pittsburgh to look at the picture. I suppose he was being funny."

A flicker of annoyance in his fine dark eyes, which were as clear and bright as if he had had a good eight hours of innocent slumber, warned me that I was supposed to have read his statement, and if I aroused a suspicion that I hadn't he might get personal.

I gave him an earnest eye. "Look, Mr. Chaffee. This thing is bad for all concerned. It will get worse instead of better until we find out who killed Kampf. You men in this house must know things about one another, and maybe some things connected with Kampf, that you're not telling. I don't expect a man like you to pass out dirt just for the hell of it, but any dirt that's connected with this murder is going to come out, and if you know of any and are keeping it to yourself you're a bigger fool than you look."

"Quite a speech." He was smiling again.

"Thanks. You make one."

"I'm not as eloquent as you are." He shook his head. "No, I don't believe I can help you any. I can't say I'm a total stranger to dirt; that would be smug; but what you're after—no. You have my opinion of Kampf, whom I knew quite well; he was in some respects admirable but had his full share of faults. I would say approximately the same of Talento. I have known Aland only casually—certainly not intimately. I know no more of Meegan than you do. I haven't the slightest notion why any of them might have wanted to kill Philip Kampf. If you expect—"

A phone rang. Chaffee crossed to a table at the end of the divan and answered it. He told it yes a couple of times, and then a few words, and then, "But one of your men is here now. . . . I don't know his name, I didn't ask him. . . . He may be, I don't know. . . . Very well, one-fifty-five Leonard Street. . . . Yes, I can leave in a few minutes."

He hung up and turned to me. I spoke first, on my feet. "So they want you at the DA's office. Don't tell them I said so, but they'd rather keep a murder in the file till hell freezes over than have the squad crack it. If they want my name they know where to ask."

I marched to the door, opened it, and was gone.

There were still no PD cars out in front. After turning left on Court Street and continuing two blocks, I was relieved to find the cab still there, with its passenger perched on the seat looking out at the scenery. If the hackie had gone off with him to sell him, or if Stebbins had happened by and hijacked him, I wouldn't have dared to go home at all. He seemed pleased to see me, as he damned well should have been. Dur-

ing the drive to Thirty-fifth Street he sat with his rump braced against
me for a buttress. The meter said only six dollars and something, but I
didn't request any change. If Wolfe wanted to put me to work on a
murder merely because he had got infatuated with a dog, let it cost him
something.

I noticed that when we entered the office Jet went over to Wolfe, in
place behind his desk, without any sign of bashfulness or uncertainty,
proving that the evening before, during my absence, Wolfe had made
approaches, probably had fed him something, and possibly had even
patted him. Remarks occurred to me, but I saved them. I might be called
on before long to spend some valuable time demonstrating that I had
not been guilty of impersonating an officer, and that it wasn't my fault if
murder suspects mistook me for one.

Wolfe put down his empty beer glass and inquired, "Well?"

I reported. The situation called for a full and detailed account, and I
supplied it, with Wolfe leaning back with his eyes closed. When I came
to the end he asked no questions. Instead, he opened his eyes, straightened up, and began, "Call the—"

I cut him off. "Wait a minute. After a hard morning's work I claim
the satisfaction of suggesting it myself. I thought of it long ago. What's
the name of the Institute in Pittsburgh where they have shows of
pictures?"

"Indeed. It's a shot at random."

"I know it is, but it's only a buck. I just spent ten on a taxi. What's
the name?"

"Pittsburgh Art Institute."

I swiveled for the phone on my desk, got the operator, and put in the
call. I got through to the Institute in no time, but it took a quarter of an
hour, with relays to three different people, to get what I was after.

I hung up and turned to Wolfe. "The show ended a week ago yesterday. Thank God I won't have to go to Pittsburgh. The picture was
lent by Mr. Herman Braunstein of New York, who owns it. It was
shipped back to him by express four days ago. He wouldn't give me
Braunstein's address."

"The phone book."

I had it and was flipping the pages. "Here we are. Business on Broad
Street, residence on Park Avenue. There's only one Herman."

"Get him."

"I don't think so. He may be a poop. It might take all day. Why don't
I go to the residence without phoning? It's probably there, and if I can't
get in you can fire me. I'm thinking of resigning anyhow."

He had his doubts, since it was my idea, but he bought it. After considering the problem a little, I went to the cabinet beneath the book-shelves, got out the Veblex camera, with accessories, slung the strap of the case over my shoulder, told Wolfe I wouldn't be back until I saw the picture, wherever it was, and beat it. Before going I dialed Talento's number to tell him not to bother to keep his appointment, but there was no answer. Either he was still engaged at the DA's office or he was on his way to Thirty-fifth Street, and if he came during my absence that was all right, since Jet was there to protect Wolfe.

A taxi took me to the end of a sidewalk canopy in front of one of the palace hives on Park Avenue in the Seventies, and I undertook to walk past the doorman without giving him a glance, but he stopped me. I said professionally, "Braunstein, taking pictures, I'm late," and kept go-ing, and got away with it. After crossing the luxurious lobby to the elevator, which luckily was there with the door open, I entered, saying, "Braunstein, please," and the chauffeur shut the door and pulled the lever. We stopped at the twelfth floor, and I stepped out. There was a door to the right and another to the left, and I turned right without asking, on a fifty-fifty chance, listening for a possible correction from the elevator man, who was standing by with his door open.

It was one of the simplest chores I have ever performed. In answer to my ring the door was opened by a middle-aged female husky, in uni-form with apron, and when I told her I had come to take a picture she let me in, asked me to wait, and disappeared. In a couple of minutes a tall and dignified dame with white hair came through an arch and asked what I wanted. I apologized for disturbing her and said I would deeply appreciate it if she would let me take a picture of a painting which had recently been shown at the Pittsburgh Institute, on loan by Mr. Braunstein. It was called "Three Young Mares at Pasture." A Pittsburgh client of mine had admired it, and had intended to go back and photograph it for his collection, but the picture had gone before he got around to it.

She wanted some information, such as my name and address and the name of my Pittsburgh client, which I supplied gladly without a script, and then led me through the arch into a room not quite as big as Madi-son Square Garden. It would have been a pleasure, and also instructive, to do a little glomming at the rugs and furniture and other miscellane-ous objects, especially the dozen or more pictures on the walls, but that would have to wait. She went across to a picture near the far end, said, "That's it," and lowered herself onto a chair.

It was a nice picture. I had half expected the mares to be without clothes, but they were fully dressed. Remarking that I didn't wonder that my client wanted a photograph of it, I got busy with my equipment, including flash bulbs. She sat and watched. I took four shots from slightly different angles, acting and looking professional, I hoped; got my stuff back in the case; thanked her warmly on behalf of my client; promised to send her some prints; and left. That was all there was to it.

Out on the sidewalk again, I walked west to Madison, turned downtown and found a drugstore, went in to the phone booth, and dialed a number.

Wolfe's voice came. "Yes? Whom do you want?"

I've told him a hundred times that's a hell of a way to answer the phone, but he's too damn pigheaded.

I spoke. "I want you. I've seen the picture, and I wouldn't have thought that stallion had it in him. It glows with color and life, and the blood seems to pulsate under the warm skin. The shadows are transparent, with a harmonious blending—"

"Shut up! Yes or no?"

"Yes. You have met Mrs. Meegan. Would you like to meet her again?"

"I would. Get her."

I didn't have to look in the phone book for her address, having already done so. I left the drugstore and flagged a taxi.

There was no doorman problem at the number on East Forty-ninth Street. It was an old brick house that had been painted a bright yellow and modernized, notably with a self-service elevator, though I didn't know that until I got in. Getting in was a little complicated. Pressing the button marked "Jewel Jones" in the vestibule was easy enough, and also unhooking the receiver and putting it to my ear, and placing my mouth close to the grille, but then it got more difficult.

A voice crackled. "Yes?"

"Miss Jones?"

"Yes. Who is it?"

"Archie Goodwin. I want to see you. Not a message from Victor Talento."

"What do you want?"

"Let me in and I'll tell you."

"No. What is it?"

"It's very personal. If you don't want to hear it from me I'll go and bring Richard Meegan, and maybe you'll tell him."

I heard the gasp. She should have known those house phones are sensitive. After a pause. "Why do you say that? I told you I don't know any Meegan."

"You're way behind. I just saw a picture called 'Three Young Mares at Pasture.' Let me in."

Another pause, and the line went dead. I put the receiver on the hook, and turned and placed my hand on the knob. There was a click, and I pushed the door and entered, crossed the little lobby to the elevator, pushed the button and, when the door opened, slid in, pushed the button marked 5, and was ascending. When the elevator stopped I opened the door and emerged into a tiny foyer. A door was standing open, and on the sill was Miss Jones in a blue negligee. She started to say something, but I rudely ignored it.

"Listen," I said, "there's no sense in prolonging this. Last night I gave you your pick between Mr. Wolfe and Sergeant Stebbins; now it's either Mr. Wolfe or Meegan. I should think you'd prefer Mr. Wolfe because he's the kind of man that understands; you said so yourself. I'll wait here while you change, but don't try phoning anybody, because you won't know where you are until you've talked with Mr. Wolfe, and also because their wires are probably tapped. Don't put on anything red. Mr. Wolfe dislikes red. He likes yellow."

She stepped to me and had a hand on my arm. "Archie. Where did you see the picture?"

"I'll tell you on the way down. Let's go."

She gave the arm a gentle tug. "You don't have to wait out here. Come in and sit down." Another tug, just as gentle. "Come on."

I patted her fingers, not wishing to be boorish. "Sorry," I told her, "but I'm afraid of young mares. One kicked me once."

She turned and disappeared into the apartment, leaving the door standing open.

VI

"DON'T call me Mrs. Meegan!" Jewel Jones cried.

Wolfe was in as bad a humor as she was. True, she had been hopelessly cornered, with no weapons within reach, but he had been compelled to tell Fritz to postpone lunch until further notice.

"I was only," he said crustily, "stressing the fact that your identity is not a matter for discussion. Legally you are Mrs. Richard Meegan. That understood, I'll call you anything you say. Miss Jones?"

"Yes." She was on the red leather chair, but not in it. Just on its edge, she looked as if she were set to spring up and scoot any second.

"Very well." Wolfe regarded her. "You realize, madam, that everything you say will be received skeptically. You are a competent liar. Your offhand denial of acquaintance with Mr. Meegan last night was better than competent. Now. When did Mr. Chaffee tell you that your husband was in town looking for you?"

"I didn't say Mr. Chaffee told me."

"Someone did. Who and when?"

She was hanging on. "How do you know someone did?"

He wiggled a finger at her. "I beg you, Miss Jones, to realize the pickle you're in. It is not credible that Mr. Chaffee couldn't remember the name of the model for that figure in his picture. The police don't believe it, and they haven't the advantage of knowing, as I do, that it was you and that you lived in that house for a year, and that you still see Mr. Chaffee occasionally. When your husband came and asked Mr. Chaffee for the name, and Mr. Chaffee pleaded a faulty memory, and your husband rented an apartment there and made it plain that he intended to persevere, it is preposterous to suppose that Mr. Chaffee didn't tell you. I don't envy you your tussles with the police after they learn about you."

"They don't have to learn about me, do they?"

"Pfui. I'm surprised they haven't got to you already, though it's been only eighteen hours. They soon will, even if not through me. I know this is no frolic for you, here with me, but they will almost make it seem so."

She was thinking. Her brow was wrinkled and her eyes straight at Wolfe. "Do you know," she asked, "what I think would be the best thing? I don't know why I didn't think of it before. You're a detective, you're an expert at helping people in trouble, and I'm certainly in trouble. I'll pay you to help me. I could pay you a little now."

"Not now or ever, Miss Jones." Wolfe was blunt. "When did Mr. Chaffee tell you that your husband was here looking for you?"

"You won't even listen to me," she complained.

"Talk sense and I will. When?"

She edged back on the chair an inch. "You don't know my husband. He was jealous about me even before we married, and then he was worse. It got so bad I couldn't stand it, and that was why I left him. I knew if I stayed in Pittsburgh he would find me and kill me, so I came to New York. A friend of mine had come here—I mean, just a friend. I got a job at a modeling agency and made enough to live on, and I met a lot of people. Ross Chaffee was one of them, and he wanted to use me in a picture, and I let him. Of course he paid me, but that wasn't so important, because soon after that I met Phil Kampf, and he got me a tryout at a night club, and I made it. About then I had a scare, though. A man from Pittsburgh saw me at a theater and came and spoke to me, but I told him he was wrong, that I had never been in Pittsburgh."

"That was a year ago," Wolfe muttered.

"Yes. I was a little leery about the night club, in public like that, but months went by and nothing happened, and then all of a sudden this happened. Ross Chaffee phoned me that my husband had come and asked about the picture, and I asked him for God's sake not to tell him who it was, and he promised he wouldn't. You see, you don't know my husband. I knew he was trying to find me so he could kill me."

"You've said that twice. Has he ever killed anybody?"

"I didn't say anybody; I said me. I seem to have an effect on men." She gestured for understanding. "They just go for me. And Dick— Well, I know him, that's all. I left him a year and a half ago, and he's still looking for me, and that's what he's like. When Ross told me he was here I was scared stiff. I quit working at the club because he might happen to go there and see me, and I didn't hardly leave my apartment until last night."

Wolfe nodded. "To meet Mr. Talento. What for?"

"I told you."

"Yes, but then you were merely Miss Jones. Now you are also Mrs. Meegan. What for?"

"That doesn't change it any. I had heard on the radio about Phil being killed, and I wanted to know about it. I rang Ross Chaffee and I rang Jerry Aland, but neither of them answered, so I rang Vic Talento. He wouldn't tell me anything on the phone, but he said he would meet me."

"Did Mr. Aland and Mr. Talento know you had sat for that picture?"

"Sure they did."

"And that Mr. Meegan had seen it and recognized you, and was here looking for you?"

"Yes, they knew all about it. Ross had to tell them, because he thought Dick might ask them if they knew who had modeled for the picture, and he had to warn them not to tell. They said they wouldn't, and they didn't. They're all good friends of mine."

She stopped to do something. She opened her black leather bag on her lap, took out a purse, and fingered its contents, peering into it. She raised her eyes to Wolfe. "I can pay you forty dollars now, to start. I'm not just in trouble, I'm in danger of my life, really I am. I don't see how you can refuse— You're not listening!"

Apparently he wasn't. With his lips pursed, he was watching the tip of his forefinger make little circles on his desk blotter. Her reproach didn't stop him, but after a moment he moved his eyes to me and said abruptly, "Get Mr. Chaffee."

"No!" she cried. "I don't want him to know—"

"Nonsense," he snapped at her. "Everybody will have to know everything, and why drag it out? Get him, Archie. I'll speak to him."

I got at the phone and dialed. I doubted if he would be back from his session with the DA, but he was. His "hello" was enough to recognize his voice by. I pitched mine low so he wouldn't know it, not caring to start a debate as to whether I had or had not impersonated an officer, and merely told him that Nero Wolfe wished to speak to him.

Wolfe took it at his desk. "Mr. Chaffee? This is Nero Wolfe. . . . I've assumed an interest in the murder of Philip Kampf and have done some investigating. . . . Just one moment, please, don't ring off. . . . Sitting here in my office is Mrs. Richard Meegan, alias Miss Jewel Jones. . . . Please let me finish. . . . I shall of course have to detain her and communicate with the police, since they will want her as a material witness in a murder case, but before I do that I would like to discuss the matter with you and the others who live in that house. Will you undertake to bring them here as soon as possible? . . . No, I'll say nothing further on the phone, I want you here, all of you. If Mr. Meegan is balky, you might as well tell him his wife is here. I'll expect—"

She was across to him in a leap that any young mare might have envied, grabbing for the phone and shrieking at it, "Don't tell him, Ross! Don't bring him! Don't—"

My own leap and dash around the end of the desk was fairly good too. Getting her shoulders, I yanked her back, with enough enthusiasm so that I landed in the red leather chair with her on my lap, and since she was by no means through I wrapped my arms around her, pinning her arms to her sides, whereupon she started kicking my shins with her heels. She kept on kicking until Wolfe finished with Chaffee. When he hung up she suddenly relaxed and was limp, and I realized how warm she felt tight against me.

Wolfe scowled at us. "An affecting sight," he snorted.

VII

THERE were various aspects of the situation. One was lunch. For Wolfe it was unthinkable to have company in the house at mealtime, no matter what his or her status was, without feeding him or her, but he certainly wasn't going to sit at table with a female who had just pounced on him and clawed at him. That problem was simple. She and I were served in the dining room, and Wolfe ate in the kitchen with Fritz. We were served, but she didn't eat much. She kept listening and looking toward the hall, though I assured her that care would be taken to see that her husband didn't kill her on those premises.

A second aspect was the reaction of three of the tenants to their discovery of my identity. I handled that myself. When the doorbell rang and I admitted them, at a quarter past two, I told them I would be glad to discuss my split personality with any or all of them later, if they still wanted to, but they would have to file it until Wolfe was through. Victor Talento had another beef that he wouldn't file, that I had double-crossed him on the message he had asked me to take to Jewel Jones. He wanted to get nasty about it and demanded a private talk with Wolfe, but I told him to go climb a rope.

I also had to handle the third aspect, which had two angles. There was Miss Jones's theory that her husband would kill her on sight, which might or might not be well founded, and there was the fact that one of them had killed Kampf and might go to extremes if pushed. On that I took three precautions: I showed them the Carley .38 I had put in my pocket and told them it was loaded; I insisted on patting them from shoulders to ankles; and I kept Miss Jones in the dining room until I had them seated in the office, on a row of chairs facing Wolfe's desk, and until Wolfe had come in from the kitchen and been told their names. When he was in his chair behind his desk I went across the hall for her and brought her in.

Meegan jumped up and started for us. I stiff-armed him and made it good. She got behind me. Talento and Aland left their chairs, presumably to help protect the mare. Meegan was talking, and so were they. I detoured with her around back of them and got her to a chair at the end of my desk, and when I sat I was in an ideal spot to trip anyone headed for her. Talento and Aland had pulled Meegan down onto a chair between them, and he sat staring at her.

"With that hubbub over," Wolfe said, "I want to be sure I have the names right." His eyes went from left to right. "Talento, Meegan, Aland, Chaffee. Is that correct?"

I told him yes.

"Then I'll proceed." He glanced up at the wall clock. "Twenty hours ago Philip Kampf was killed in the house where you gentlemen live. The circumstances indicate that one of you killed him. But I won't re-hash the multifarious details which you have already discussed at length with the police; you are familiar with them. I have not been hired to work on this case; the only client I have is a dog, and he came to my office by inadvertence. However, it is—"

The doorbell rang. I asked myself if I had put the chain bolt on, and decided I had. Through the open door to the hall I saw Fritz passing to answer it. Wolfe started to go on, but was annoyed by the sound of voices, Fritz's and another's, coming through, and stopped. The voices continued. Wolfe shut his eyes and compressed his lips. The audience sat and looked at him.

Then Fritz appeared in the doorway and announced, "Inspector Cramer, sir."

Wolfe's eyes opened. "What does he want?"

"I told him you are engaged. He says he knows you are, that the four men were followed to your house and he was notified. He says he expected you to be trying some trick with the dog, and he knows that's what you are doing, and he intends to come in and see what it is. Sergeant Stebbins is with him."

Wolfe grunted. "Archie, tell— No. You'd better stay where you are. Fritz, tell him he may see and hear what I'm doing, provided he gives me thirty minutes without interruptions or demands. If he agrees to that, bring them in."

"Wait!" Ross Chaffee was on his feet. "You said you would discuss it with us before you communicated with the police."

"I haven't communicated with them, they're here."

"You told them to come!"

"No. I would have preferred to deal with you men first and then call them, but here they are and they might as well join us. Bring them, Fritz, on that condition."

"Yes, sir."

Fritz went. Chaffee thought he had something more to say, decided he hadn't, and sat down. Talento said something to him, and he shook his head. Jerry Aland, much more presentable now that he was combed and dressed, kept his eyes fastened on Wolfe. For Meegan, apparently, there was no one in the room but him and his wife.

Cramer and Stebbins marched in, halted three paces from the door, and took a survey.

"Be seated," Wolfe invited them. "Luckily, Mr. Cramer, your usual chair is unoccupied."

"Where's the dog?" Cramer barked.

"In the kitchen. You had better suspend that prepossession. It's understood that you will be merely a spectator for thirty minutes?"

"That's what I said."

"Then sit down. But you should have one piece of information. You know the gentlemen, of course, but not the lady. Her current name is Miss Jewel Jones. Her legal name is Mrs. Richard Meegan."

"Meegan?" Cramer stared. "The one in the picture Chaffee painted? Meegan's wife?"

"That's right. Please be seated."

"Where did you get her?"

"That can wait. No interruptions and no demands. Confound it, sit down!"

Cramer went and lowered himself onto the red leather chair. Purley Stebbins got one of the yellow ones and planted it behind the row, between Chaffee and Aland.

Wolfe regarded the quartet. "I was about to say, gentlemen, that it was something the dog did that pointed to the murderer for me. But before—"

"What did it do?" Cramer barked.

"You know all about it," Wolfe told him coldly. "Mr. Goodwin related it to you exactly as it happened. If you interrupt again, by heaven, you can take them all down to your quarters, not including the dog, and stew it out yourself."

He went back to the four. "But before I come to that, another thing or two. I offer no comment on your guile with Mr. Meegan. You were all friends of Miss Jones's, having, I suppose, enjoyed various degrees of intimacy with her, and you refused to disclose her to a husband whom she had abandoned and professed to fear. I will even concede that there was a flavor of gallantry in your conduct. But when Mr. Kampf was murdered and the police swarmed in, it was idiotic to try to keep her out of it. They were sure to get to her. I got to her first only because of Mr. Goodwin's admirable enterprise and characteristic luck."

He shook his head at them. "It was also idiotic of you to assume that Mr. Goodwin was a police officer, and admit him and answer his questions, merely because he had been present during the abortive experiment with the dog. You should have asked to see his credentials. None of you had any idea who he was. Even Mr. Meegan, who had seen him in this office in the morning, was bamboozled. I mention this to anticipate any possible official complaint that Mr. Goodwin impersonated an officer. You know he didn't. He merely took advantage of your unwarranted assumption."

He shifted in his chair. "Another thing. Yesterday morning Mr. Meegan called here by appointment to ask me to do a job for him. With his first words I gathered that it was something about his wife, and I don't take that kind of work, and I was brusque with him. He was offended. He rushed out in a temper, getting his hat and raincoat from the rack in the hall, and he took Mr. Goodwin's coat instead of his own. Late in the afternoon Mr. Goodwin went to Arbor Street, with the coat that had been left in error, to exchange it. He saw that in front of Number twenty-nine there were collected two police cars, a policeman on post, some people, and a dog. He decided to postpone his errand and went on by, after a brief halt during which he patted the dog. He walked home, and had gone nearly two miles when he discovered that the dog was following him. He brought the dog in a cab the rest of the way, to this house and this room."

He flattened a palm on his desk. "Now. Why did the dog follow Mr. Goodwin through the turmoil of the city? Mr. Cramer's notion that the dog was enticed is poppycock. Mr. Goodwin is willing to believe, as many men are, that he is irresistible to both dogs and women, and doubtless his vanity impeded his intellect or he would have reached the same conclusion that I did. The dog didn't follow him; it followed the coat. You ask, as I did, how to account for Mr. Kampf's dog following Mr. Meegan's coat. I couldn't. I can't. Then, since it was unquestionably Mr. Kampf's dog, it couldn't have been Mr. Meegan's coat. It is better than a conjecture, it is next thing to a certainty, that it was Mr. Kampf's coat."

His gaze leveled at the husband. "Mr. Meegan. Some two hours ago I learned from Mr. Goodwin that you maintain that you had never seen or heard of Mr. Kampf. That was fairly conclusive, but before sending for you I had to verify my conjecture that the model who had sat for Mr. Chaffee's picture was your wife. I would like to hear it straight from you. Did you ever meet with Philip Kampf alive?"

Meegan was meeting the gaze. "No."

"Don't you want to qualify that?"

"No."

"Then where did you get his raincoat?"

No answer. Meegan's jaw worked. He spoke. "I didn't have his raincoat, or if I did I didn't know it."

"That won't do. I warn you, you are in deadly peril. The raincoat that you brought into this house and left here is in the hall now, there on the rack. It can easily be established that it belonged to Mr. Kampf and was worn by him. Where did you get it?"

Meegan's jaw worked some more. "I never had it, if it belonged to Kampf. This is a dirty frame. You can't prove that's the coat I left here."

Wolfe's voice sharpened. "One more chance. Have you any explanation of how Kampf's coat came into your possession?"

"No, and I don't need any."

He may not have been pure boob. If he hadn't noticed that he wore the wrong coat home, and he probably didn't, in his state of mind, this had hit him from a clear sky and he had no time to study it.

"Then you're done for," Wolfe told him. "For your own coat must be somewhere, and I think I know where. In the police laboratory. Mr. Kampf was wearing one when you killed him and pushed his body down the stairs—and that explains why, when they were making that experiment this morning, the dog showed no interest in the spot where the body had lain. It had been enveloped, not in his coat but in yours. That can be established too. If you won't explain how you got Mr. Kampf's coat, then explain how he got yours. Is that also a frame?"

Wolfe pointed a finger at him. "I note that flash in your eye, and I think I know what it means. But your brain is lagging. If, after killing him, you took your raincoat off of him and put on him the one that you thought was his, that won't help you any. For in that case the coat that was on the body is Mr. Goodwin's, and certainly that can be established, and how would you explain that? It looks hopeless, and—"

Meegan was springing up, but before he even got well started Purley's big hands were on his shoulders, pulling him back and down. And a new voice sounded.

"I told you he would kill me! I knew he would! He killed Phil!"

Jewel Jones was looking not at her husband, who was under control, but at Wolfe. He snapped at her, "How do you know he did?"

Judging by her eyes and the way she was shaking, she would be hysterical in another two minutes, and maybe she knew it, for she poured it out. "Because Phil told me—he told me he knew Dick was here looking for me, and he knew how afraid I was of him, and he said if I wouldn't come and be with him again he would tell Dick where I was. I didn't think he really would—I didn't think Phil could be as mean as that, and I wouldn't promise, but yesterday morning he phoned me and told me he had seen Dick and told him he thought he knew who had posed for that picture, and he was going to see him again in the afternoon and tell him about me if I didn't promise, and so I promised. I thought if I promised it would give me time to decide what to do. But Phil must have gone to see Dick again anyway—"

"Where had they met in the morning?"

"At Phil's apartment, he said. And he said—that's why I know Dick killed him—he said Dick had gone off with his raincoat, and he laughed about it and said he was willing for Dick to have his raincoat if he could have Dick's wife." She was shaking harder now. "And I'll bet that's what he told Dick! That was like Phil! I'll bet he told Dick I was coming back to him and he thought that was a good trade, a raincoat for a wife! That was like Phil! You don't—"

She giggled. It started with a giggle, and then the valves busted open and here it came. When something happens in that office to smash a woman's nerves, as it has more than once, it usually falls to me to deal with it, but that time three other guys, led by Ross Chaffee, came to her, and I was glad to leave it to them. As for Wolfe, he skedaddled. If there is one thing on earth he absolutely will not be in a room with it's a woman in eruption. He got up and marched out. As for Meegan, Purley and Cramer had him.

When they left with him, they didn't take the dog. To relieve the minds of any of you who have the notion, which I understand is widespread, that it makes a dog neurotic to change its name, I might add that he responds to Jet now as if his mother had started calling him that before he had his eyes open.

As for the raincoat, Wolfe had been right about the flash in Meegan's eye. Kampf had been wearing Meegan's raincoat when he was killed, and of course that wouldn't do, so after strangling him Meegan had taken it off and put on the one he thought was Kampf's. Only it was mine. As a part of the DA's case I went down to headquarters and identified it. At the trial it helped the jury to decide that Meegan deserved the big one. After that was over I suppose I could have claimed it, but the idea didn't appeal to me. My new one is a different color.